QUEEN
OF
SHADOWS

ALSO BY SARAH J. MAAS

The Throne of Glass series

Throne of Glass
Crown of Midnight
Heir of Fire

•

The Assassin's Blade

A Court of Thorns and Roses

QUEEN
OF
SHADOWS

A *Throne of Glass* NOVEL

SARAH J. MAAS

BLOOMSBURY
NEW YORK LONDON OXFORD NEW DELHI SYDNEY

First published in the United States of America in September 2015
by Bloomsbury Children's Books
www.bloomsbury.com

Bloomsbury is a registered trademark of Bloomsbury Publishing Plc

For information about permission to reproduce selections from this book, write to
Permissions, Bloomsbury Children's Books, 1385 Broadway, New York, New York 10018
Bloomsbury books may be purchased for business or promotional use. For information on
bulk purchases please contact Macmillan Corporate and Premium Sales Department at
specialmarkets@macmillan.com

Library of Congress Cataloging-in-Publication Data
Maas, Sarah J.
Queen of shadows : a Throne of glass novel / by Sarah J. Maas.
pages   cm
Sequel to: Heir of fire.
Summary: Everyone Celaena Sardothien loves has been taken from her. Embracing her identity as
Aelin Galathynius, Queen of Terrasen, Celaena returns to the empire—for vengeance, to rescue
her once-glorious kingdom, and to confront the shadows of her past.
ISBN 978-1-61963-604-0 (hardcover) • ISBN 978-1-61963-605-7 (e-book)
[1. Fantasy. 2. Assassins—Fiction. 3. Identity—Fiction.] I. Title.
PZ7.M111575Qu 2015   [Fic]—dc23   2015007763

ISBN 978-1-68119-049-5 (special edition)

Series design by Regina Flath
Typeset by RefineCatch Limited, Bungay, Suffolk
Printed and bound in the U.S.A. by Thomson-Shore Inc., Dexter, Michigan
2 4 6 8 10 9 7 5 3

All papers used by Bloomsbury Publishing, Inc., are natural, recyclable products
made from wood grown in well-managed forests. The manufacturing processes
conform to the environmental regulations of the country of origin.

For Alex Bracken—

For the six years of e-mails,
For the thousands of pages critiqued,
For your tiger heart and your Jedi wisdom,
And for just being you.

I'm so glad I e-mailed you that day.
And so grateful you wrote back.

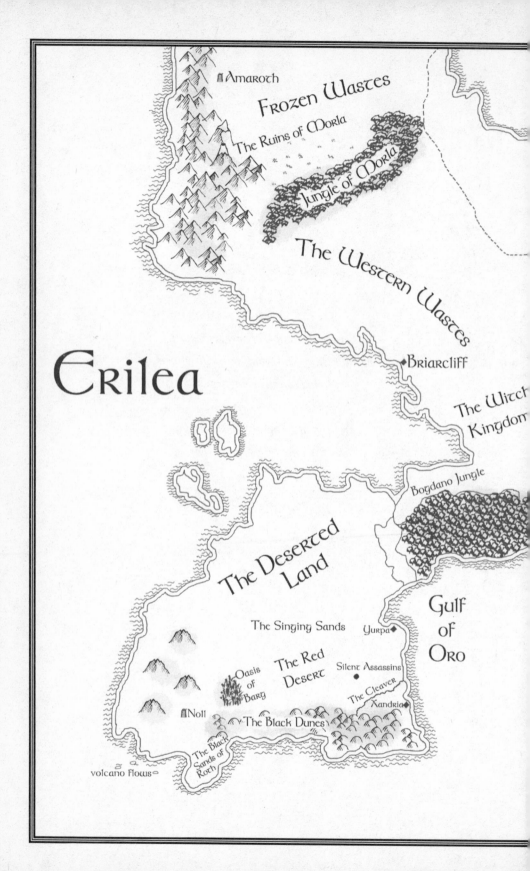

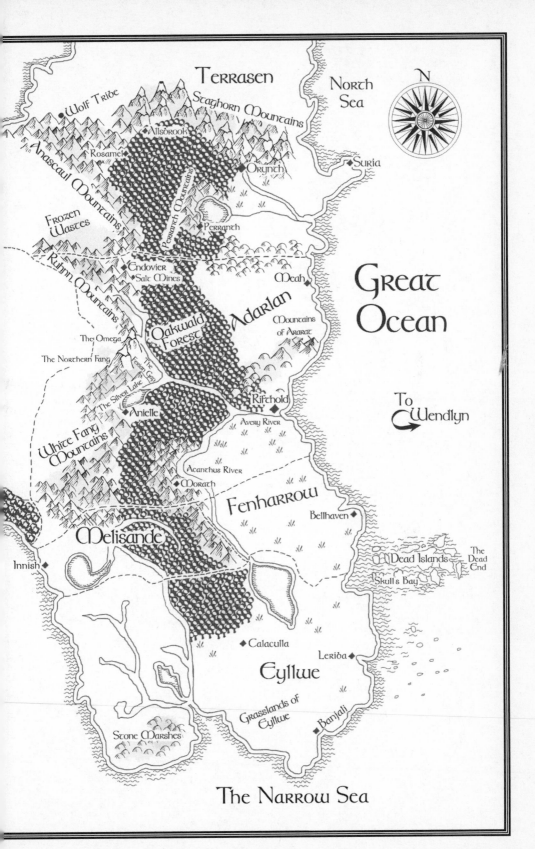

PART ONE

Lady of Shadows

CHAPTER 1

There was a thing waiting in the darkness.

It was ancient, and cruel, and paced in the shadows leashing his mind. It was not of his world, and had been brought here to fill him with its primordial cold. Some invisible barrier still separated them, but the wall crumbled a little more every time the thing stalked along its length, testing its strength.

He could not remember his name.

That was the first thing he'd forgotten when the darkness enveloped him weeks or months or eons ago. Then he'd forgotten the names of the others who had meant so much to him. He could recall horror and despair—only because of the solitary moment that kept interrupting the blackness like the steady beat of a drum: a few minutes of screaming and blood and frozen wind. There had been people he loved in that room of red marble and glass; the woman had lost her head—

Lost, as if the beheading were her fault.

A lovely woman with delicate hands like golden doves. It was not her fault, even if he could not remember her name. It was the fault of the man on the glass throne, who had ordered that guard's sword to sever flesh and bone.

There was nothing in the darkness beyond the moment when that woman's head thudded to the ground. There was nothing *but* that moment, again and again and again—and that thing pacing nearby, waiting for him to break, to yield, to let it in. A prince.

He could not remember if the thing was the prince, or if he himself had once been a prince. Not likely. A prince would not have allowed that woman's head to be cut off. A prince would have stopped the blade. A prince would have saved her.

Yet he had not saved her, and he knew there was no one coming to save him.

There was still a real world beyond the shadows. He was forced to participate in it by the man who had ordered the slaughter of that lovely woman. And when he did, no one noticed that he had become hardly more than a marionette, struggling to speak, to act past the shackles on his mind. He hated them for not noticing. That was one of the emotions he still knew.

I was not supposed to love you. The woman had said that—and then she died. She should not have loved him, and he should not have dared to love her. He deserved this darkness, and once the invisible boundary shattered and the waiting thing pounced, infiltrating and filling him . . . he'd have earned it.

So he remained bound in night, witnessing the scream and the blood and the impact of flesh on stone. He knew he should struggle, knew he *had* struggled in those final seconds before the collar of black stone had clamped around his neck.

But there was a thing waiting in the darkness, and he could not bring himself to fight it for much longer.

CHAPTER 2

Aelin Ashryver Galathynius, heir of fire, beloved of Mala Light-Bringer, and rightful Queen of Terrasen, leaned against the worn oak bar and listened carefully to the sounds of the pleasure hall, sorting through the cheers and moans and bawdy singing. Though it had chewed up and spat out several owners over the past few years, the subterranean warren of sin known as the Vaults remained the same: uncomfortably hot, reeking of stale ale and unwashed bodies, and packed to the rafters with lowlifes and career criminals.

More than a few young lords and merchants' sons had swaggered down the steps into the Vaults and never seen daylight again. Sometimes it was because they flashed their gold and silver in front of the wrong person; sometimes it was because they were vain or drunk enough to think that they could jump into the fighting pits and walk out alive. Sometimes they mishandled one of the women for hire in the alcoves flanking the cavernous space and learned the hard way about which people the owners of the Vaults really valued.

Aelin sipped from the mug of ale the sweating barkeep had slid her moments before. Watery and cheap, but at least it was cold. Above the tang of filthy bodies, the scent of roasting meat and garlic floated to her. Her stomach grumbled, but she wasn't stupid enough to order food. One, the meat was usually courtesy of rats in the alley a level above; two, wealthier patrons usually found it laced with something that left them awakening in the aforementioned alley, purse empty. If they woke up at all.

Her clothes were dirty, but fine enough to mark her as a thief's target. So she'd carefully examined her ale, sniffing and then sipping it before deeming it safe. She'd still have to find food at some point soon, but not until she learned what she needed to from the Vaults: what the hell had happened in Rifthold in the months she'd been gone.

And what client Arobynn Hamel wanted to see so badly that he was risking a meeting here—especially when brutal, black-uniformed guards were roaming the city like packs of wolves.

She'd managed to slip past one such patrol during the chaos of docking, but not before noting the onyx wyvern embroidered on their uniforms. Black on black—perhaps the King of Adarlan had grown tired of pretending he was anything but a menace and had issued a royal decree to abandon the traditional crimson and gold of his empire. Black for death; black for his two Wyrdkeys; black for the Valg demons he was now using to build himself an unstoppable army.

A shudder crawled along her spine, and she drained the rest of her ale. As she set down the mug, her auburn hair shifted and caught the light of the wrought-iron chandeliers.

She'd hurried from the docks to the riverside Shadow Market—where anyone could find anything they wanted, rare or contraband or common-place—and purchased a brick of dye. She'd paid the merchant an extra piece of silver to use the small room in the back of the shop to dye her hair, still short enough to brush just below her collarbones. If those guards had been monitoring the docks and had somehow seen her, they would be looking for a golden-haired young woman. *Everyone* would be looking for a golden-haired young woman, once word arrived in a few weeks that the King's Champion had failed in her task to assassinate Wendlyn's royal family and steal its naval defense plans.

She'd sent a warning to the King and Queen of Eyllwe months ago, and knew they'd take the proper precautions. But that still left one person at risk before she could fulfill the first steps of her plan—the same person who might be able to explain the new guards by the docks. And why the city was noticeably quieter, tenser. Hushed.

If she were to overhear anything regarding the Captain of the Guard and whether he was safe, it would be here. It was only a matter of listening to the right conversation or sitting with the right card partners. What a fortunate coincidence, then, that she'd spotted Tern—one of Arobynn's favored assassins—buying the latest dose of his preferred poison at the Shadow Market.

She'd followed him here in time to spy several more of Arobynn's assassins converging on the pleasure hall. They never did that—not unless their master was present. Usually only when Arobynn was taking a meeting with someone very, very important. Or dangerous.

After Tern and the others had slipped inside the Vaults, she'd waited on the street for a few minutes, lingering in the shadows to see whether Arobynn arrived, but no such luck. He must have already been within.

So she'd come in on the heels of a group of drunken merchants' sons, spotted where Arobynn was holding court, and done her best to remain unnoticed and unremarkable while she lurked at the bar—and observed.

With her hood and dark clothes, she blended in well enough not to garner much attention. She supposed that if anyone was foolish enough to attempt to rob her, it made them fair game to be robbed right back. She *was* running low on money.

She sighed through her nose. If her people could only see her: Aelin of the Wildfire, assassin and pickpocket. Her parents and uncle were probably thrashing in their graves.

Still. Some things were worth it. Aelin crooked a gloved finger at the bald barkeep, signaling for another ale.

"I'd mind how much you drink, girl," sneered a voice beside her.

She glanced sidelong at the average-sized man who had slipped up beside her at the bar. She would have known him for his ancient cutlass if she hadn't recognized the disarmingly common face. The ruddy skin, the beady eyes and thick brows—all a bland mask to hide the hungry killer beneath.

Aelin braced her forearms on the bar, crossing one ankle over the other. "Hello, Tern." Arobynn's second in command—or he had been two years ago. A vicious, calculating little prick who had always been more than eager to do Arobynn's dirty work. "I figured it was only a matter of time before one of Arobynn's dogs sniffed me out."

Tern leaned against the bar, flashing her a too-bright smile. "If memory serves, you were always his favorite bitch."

She chuckled, facing him fully. They were nearly equal in height—and with his slim build, Tern had been unnervingly good at getting into even the most well-guarded places. The barkeep, spotting Tern, kept well away.

Tern inclined his head over a shoulder, gesturing to the shadowy back of the cavernous space. "Last banquette against the wall. He's finishing up with a client."

She flicked her gaze in the direction Tern indicated. Both sides of the Vaults were lined with alcoves teeming with whores, barely curtained off from the crowds. She skipped over the writhing bodies, over the gaunt-faced, hollow-eyed women waiting to earn their keep in this festering shit-hole, over the people who monitored the proceedings from the nearest tables—guards and voyeurs and fleshmongers. But there, tucked into the wall adjacent to the alcoves, were several wooden booths.

Exactly the ones she'd been discreetly monitoring since her arrival.

And in the one farthest from the lights . . . a gleam of polished leather boots stretched out beneath the table. A second pair of boots, worn and muddy, were braced on the floor across from the first, as if the client were ready to bolt. Or, if he were truly stupid, to fight.

He was certainly stupid enough to have let his personal guard stay visible, a beacon alerting anyone who cared to notice that something rather important was happening in that last booth.

The client's guard—a slender, hooded young woman armed to the teeth—was leaning against a wooden pillar nearby, her silky, shoulder-length dark hair shining in the light as she carefully monitored the pleasure hall. Too stiff to be a casual patron. No uniform, no house colors or sigils. Not surprising, given the client's need for secrecy.

The client probably thought it was safer to meet here, when these sorts of meetings were usually held at the Assassins' Keep or one of the shadowy inns owned by Arobynn himself. He had no idea that Arobynn was also a major investor in the Vaults, and it would take only a nod from Aelin's former master for the metal doors to lock—and the client and his guard to never walk out again.

It still left the question of why Arobynn had agreed to meet here.

And still left Aelin looking across the hall toward the man who had shattered her life in so many ways.

Her stomach tightened, but she smiled at Tern. "I knew the leash wouldn't stretch far."

Aelin pushed off the bar, slipping through the crowd before the assassin could say anything else. She could feel Tern's stare fixed right between her shoulder blades, and knew he was aching to plunge his cutlass there.

Without bothering to glance back, she gave him an obscene gesture over her shoulder.

His barked string of curses was far better than the bawdy music being played across the room.

She noted each face she passed, each table of revelers and criminals and workers. The client's personal guard now watched her, a gloved hand slipping to the ordinary sword at her side.

Not your concern, but nice try.

Aelin was half tempted to smirk at the woman. Might have done so, actually, if she wasn't focused on the King of the Assassins. On what waited for her in that booth.

But she was ready—or as ready as she could ever be. She'd spent long enough planning.

Aelin had given herself a day at sea to rest and to miss Rowan. With the blood oath now eternally binding her to the Fae Prince—and him to her—his absence was like a phantom limb. She still felt that way, even when she had so much to do, even though missing her *carranam* was useless and he'd no doubt kick her ass for it.

The second day they'd been apart, she'd offered the ship's captain a silver coin for a pen and a stack of paper. And after locking herself in her cramped stateroom, she'd begun writing.

There were two men in this city responsible for destroying her life and the people she'd loved. She would not leave Rifthold until she'd buried them both.

So she'd written page after page of notes and ideas, until she had a list of names and places and targets. She'd memorized every step and calculation, and then she'd burned the pages with the power smoldering in her veins, making sure every last scrap was nothing more than ash floating out the porthole window and across the vast, night-darkened ocean.

Though she had braced herself, it had still been a shock weeks later when the ship had passed some unseen marker just off the coast and her magic vanished. All that fire she'd spent so many months carefully mastering . . . gone as if it had never existed, not even an ember left flickering in her veins. A new sort of emptiness—different from the hole Rowan's absence left in her.

Stranded in her human skin, she'd curled up on her cot and recalled how to breathe, how to think, how to move her damn body without the immortal grace she'd become so dependent on. She was a useless fool for letting those gifts become a crutch, for being caught unguarded when they were again ripped from her. Rowan definitely would have kicked her ass for *that*—once he'd recovered himself. It was enough to make her glad she'd asked him to stay behind.

So she had breathed in the brine and the wood, and reminded herself that she'd been trained to kill with her bare hands long before she'd ever learned to melt bones with her fire. She did not need the extra strength, speed, and agility of her Fae form to bring down her enemies.

The man responsible for that initial brutal training—the man who had been savior and tormentor, but never declared himself father or brother or lover—was now steps away, still speaking with his oh-so-important client.

Aelin pushed against the tension threatening to lock up her limbs and kept her movements feline-smooth as she closed the final twenty feet between them.

Until Arobynn's client rose to his feet, snapping something at the King of the Assassins, and stormed toward his guard.

Even with the hood, she knew the way he moved. She knew the shape of the chin poking from the shadows of the cowl, the way his left hand tended to brush against his scabbard.

But the sword with the eagle-shaped pommel was not hanging at his side.

And there was no black uniform—only brown, nondescript clothes, spotted with dirt and blood.

She grabbed an empty chair and pulled it up to a table of card players before the client had taken two steps. She slid into the seat and focused on breathing, on listening, even as the three people at the table frowned at her.

She didn't care.

From the corner of her eye, she saw the guard jerk her chin toward her.

"Deal me in," Aelin muttered to the man beside her. "Right now."

"We're in the middle of a game."

"Next round, then," she said, relaxing her posture and slumping her shoulders as Chaol Westfall cast his gaze in her direction.

CHAPTER 3

Chaol was Arobynn's client.

Or he wanted something from her former master badly enough to risk meeting here.

What the *hell* had happened while she was away?

She watched the cards being slapped down on the ale-damp table, even as the captain's attention fixed on her back. She wished she could see his face, see anything in the gloom underneath that hood. Despite the splattering of blood on his clothes, he moved as though no injuries plagued him.

Something that had been coiled tightly in her chest for months slowly loosened.

Alive—but where had the blood come from?

He must have deemed her nonthreatening, because he merely motioned to his companion to go, and they both strolled toward the bar— no, toward the stairs beyond. He moved at a steady, casual pace, though the woman at his side was too tense to pass for unconcerned. Fortunately for them all, no one looked his way as he left, and the captain didn't glance in her direction again.

She'd moved fast enough that he likely hadn't been able to detect that it was her. Good. Good, even if she would have known him moving or still, cloaked or bare.

There he went, up the stairs, not even glancing down, though his companion continued watching her. Who the hell was *that*? There hadn't been any female guards at the palace when she'd left, and she had been fairly certain the king had an absurd no-women rule.

Seeing Chaol changed nothing—not right now.

She curled her hand into a fist, keenly aware of the bare finger on her right hand. It hadn't felt naked until now.

A card landed before her. "Three silvers to join," the bald, tattooed man beside her said as he dealt the cards, inclining his head toward the tidy pile of coins in the center.

Meeting with Arobynn—she'd never thought Chaol was stupid, but *this* . . . Aelin rose from the chair, cooling the wrath that had started to boil in her veins. "I'm dead broke," she said. "Enjoy the game."

The door atop the stone stairs was already shut, Chaol and his companion gone.

She gave herself a second to wipe any expression beyond mild amusement off her face.

Odds were, Arobynn had planned the whole thing to coincide with her arrival. He'd probably sent Tern to the Shadow Market just to catch her eye, to draw her here. Maybe he knew what the captain was up to, whose side the young lord was now on; maybe he'd just lured her here to worm his way into her mind, to shake her up a bit.

Getting answers from Arobynn would come at a price, but it was smarter than running after Chaol into the night, though the urge had her muscles locking up. Months—months and months since she'd seen him, since she'd left Adarlan, broken and hollow.

But no more.

Aelin swaggered the last few steps to the banquette and paused in front of it, crossing her arms as she beheld Arobynn Hamel, the King of the Assassins and her former master, smiling up at her.

Lounging in the shadows of the wooden banquette, a glass of wine before him, Arobynn looked exactly as he had the last time she'd seen him: a fine-boned aristo face, silky auburn hair that grazed his shoulders, and a deep-blue tunic of exquisite make, unbuttoned with an assumed casualness at the top to reveal the toned chest beneath. No sign at all of a necklace or chain. His long, muscled arm was draped across the back of the bench, and his tanned, scar-flecked fingers drummed a beat in time with the hall music.

"Hello, darling," he purred, his silver eyes bright even in the dimness.

No weapons save for a beautiful rapier at his side, its ornate, twisting guards like a swirling wind bound in gold. The only overt sign of the wealth that rivaled the riches of kings and empresses.

Aelin slid onto the bench across from him, too aware of the wood still warm from Chaol. Her own daggers pressed against her with every movement. Goldryn was a heavy weight at her side, the massive ruby in its hilt hidden by her dark cloak—the legendary blade utterly useless in such tight quarters. No doubt why he'd picked the booth for this meeting.

"You look more or less the same," she said, leaning against the hard bench and tugging back her hood. "Rifthold continues to treat you well."

It was true. In his late thirties, Arobynn remained handsome, and as calm and collected as he'd been at the Assassins' Keep during the dark blur of days after Sam had died.

There were many, many debts to be paid for what happened back then.

Arobynn looked her up and down—a slow, deliberate examination. "I think I preferred your natural hair color."

"Precautions," she said, crossing her legs and surveying him just as slowly. No indication that he was wearing the Amulet of Orynth, the royal heirloom he'd stolen from her when he found her half-dead on the banks of the Florine. He'd allowed her to believe the amulet that secretly contained the third and final Wyrdkey had been lost to the river. For a thousand years, her ancestors had unwittingly worn the amulet, and it had made their kingdom—*her* kingdom—a powerhouse: prosperous and safe, the ideal to which all courts in all lands were held. Still, she'd never seen Arobynn wear any sort of chain around his neck. He probably had it squirreled away somewhere at the Keep. "I wouldn't want to wind up back in Endovier."

Those silver eyes sparkled. It was an effort to keep from reaching for a dagger and throwing it hard.

But too much was dependent on him to kill him right away. She'd had a long, long while to think this over—what she wanted to do, how she wanted to do it. Ending it here and now would be a waste. Especially when he and Chaol were somehow tangled up.

Perhaps *that* was why he'd lured her here—so she would spy Chaol with him . . . and hesitate.

"Indeed," Arobynn said, "I'd hate to see you back in Endovier, too. Though I will say these past two years have made you even more striking. Womanhood suits you." He cocked his head, and she knew it was coming before he amended, "Or should I say queen-hood?"

It had been a decade since they'd spoken baldly of her heritage, or of the title he had helped her walk away from, had taught her to hate and fear. Sometimes he'd mentioned it in veiled terms, usually as a threat to keep her bound to him. But he had never once said her true name—not even when he'd found her on that icy riverbank and carried her into his house of killers.

"What makes you think I have any interest in that?" she said casually.

Arobynn shrugged his broad shoulders. "One can't put much faith in gossip, but word arrived about a month ago from Wendlyn. It claimed that a certain lost queen put on a rather spectacular show for an invading legion from Adarlan. Actually, I believe the title our esteemed friends in the empire now like to use is 'fire-breathing bitch-queen.'"

Honestly, she almost found it funny—flattering, even. She'd known word would spread about what she had done to General Narrok and the three other Valg princes squatting like toads inside human bodies. She just hadn't realized everyone would learn of it so quickly. "People will believe anything they hear these days."

"True," Arobynn said. At the other end of the Vaults, a frenzied crowd roared at the fighters slugging it out in the pits. The King of the Assassins looked toward it, smiling faintly.

It had been almost two years since she'd stood in that crowd, watching Sam take on vastly inferior fighters, hustling to raise enough money to get them out of Rifthold and away from Arobynn. A few days later, she'd wound up in a prison wagon bound for Endovier, but Sam . . .

She'd never discovered where they'd buried Sam after Rourke Farran—second in command to Ioan Jayne, the Crime Lord of Rifthold—had tortured and killed him. She'd killed Jayne herself, with a dagger hurled into his meaty face. And Farran . . . She'd later learned that Farran had been murdered by Arobynn's own bodyguard, Wesley, as retribution for what had been done to Sam. But that wasn't her concern, even if Arobynn had killed Wesley to mend the bond between the Assassins' Guild and the new Crime Lord. Another debt.

She could wait; she could be patient. She merely said, "So you're doing business here now? What happened to the Keep?"

"Some clients," Arobynn drawled, "prefer public meetings. The Keep can make people edgy."

"Your client must be new to the game, if he didn't insist on a private room."

"He didn't trust me that much, either. He thought the main floor would be safer."

"He must not know the Vaults, then." No, Chaol had never been here, as far as she knew. She'd usually avoided telling him about the time she'd spent in this festering place. Like she'd avoided telling him a good many things.

"Why don't you just ask me about him?"

She kept her face neutral, disinterested. "I don't particularly care about your clients. Tell me or don't."

Arobynn shrugged again, a beautiful, casual gesture. A game, then. A bit of information to hold against her, to keep from her until it was useful. It didn't matter if it was valuable information or not; it was the withholding, the power of it, that he loved.

Arobynn sighed. "There is so much I want to ask you—to know."

"I'm surprised you're admitting that you don't already know everything."

He rested his head against the back of the booth, his red hair gleaming like fresh blood. As an investor in the Vaults, she supposed he didn't need to bother hiding his face here. No one—not even the King of Adarlan—would be stupid enough to go after him.

"Things have been wretched since you left," Arobynn said quietly.

Left. As if she'd willingly gone to Endovier; as if he hadn't been responsible for it; as if she had just been away on holiday. But she knew him too well. He was still feeling her out, despite having lured her here. Perfect.

He glanced at the thick scar across her palm—proof of the vow she'd made to Nehemia to free Eyllwe. Arobynn clicked his tongue. "It hurts my heart to see so many new scars on you."

"I rather like them." It was the truth.

Arobynn shifted in his seat—a deliberate movement, as all his movements were—and the light fell on a wicked scar stretching from his ear to his collarbone.

"I rather like that scar, too," she said with a midnight smile. That explained why he'd left the tunic unbuttoned, then.

Arobynn waved a hand with fluid grace. "Courtesy of Wesley."

A casual reminder of what he was capable of doing, what he could endure. Wesley had been one of the finest warriors she'd ever encountered. If he hadn't survived the fight with Arobynn, few existed who would. "First Sam," she said, "then me, then Wesley—what a tyrant you've become. Is there anyone at all left in the Keep besides darling Tern, or have you put down every person who displeased you?" She glanced at Tern, loitering at the bar, and then at the other two assassins seated at separate tables halfway across the room, trying to pretend they weren't monitoring every movement she made. "At least Harding and Mullin are alive, too. But they've always been so good at kissing your ass that I have a hard time imagining you ever bringing yourself to kill them."

A low laugh. "And here I was, thinking my men were doing a good job of keeping hidden in the crowd." He sipped from his wine. "Perhaps you'll come home and teach them a few things."

Home. Another test, another game. "You know I'm always happy to teach your sycophants a lesson—but I have other lodgings prepared while I'm here."

"And how long will your visit be, exactly?"

"As long as necessary." To destroy him and get what she needed.

"Well, I'm glad to hear it," he said, drinking again. No doubt from a bottle brought in just for him, as there was no way in the dark god's burning realm that Arobynn would drink the watered-down rat's blood they served at the bar. "You'll have to be here for a few weeks at least, given what happened."

Ice coated her veins. She gave Arobynn a lazy grin, even as she began praying to Mala, to Deanna, the sister-goddesses who had watched over her for so many years.

"You *do* know what happened, don't you?" he said, swirling the wine in his glass.

Bastard—bastard for making her confirm she didn't know. "Does it explain why the royal guard has such spectacular new uniforms?" *Not Chaol or Dorian, not Chaol or Dorian, not Chaol or—*

"Oh, no. Those men are merely a delightful new addition to our city. My acolytes have such fun tormenting them." He drained his glass. "Though I'd bet good money that the king's new guard was present the day it happened."

She kept her hands from shaking, despite the panic devouring every last shred of common sense.

"No one knows what, exactly, went on that day in the glass castle," Arobynn began.

After all that she had endured, after what she had overcome in Wendlyn, to return to this . . . She wished Rowan were beside her, wished she could smell his pine-and-snow scent and know that no matter what news Arobynn bore, no matter how it shattered her, the Fae warrior would be there to help put the pieces back together.

But Rowan was across an ocean—and she prayed he'd never get within a hundred miles of Arobynn.

"Why don't you get to the point," she said. "I want to have a few hours of sleep tonight." Not a lie. With every breath, exhaustion wrapped tighter around her bones.

"I would have thought," Arobynn said, "given how close you two were, and your *abilities*, that you'd somehow be able to sense it. Or at least hear of it, considering what he was accused of."

The prick was enjoying every second of this. If Dorian was dead or hurt—

"Your cousin Aedion has been imprisoned for treason—for conspiring with the rebels here in Rifthold to depose the king and put you back on the throne."

The world stopped.

Stopped, and started, then stopped again.

"But," Arobynn went on, "it seems you had no idea about that little plot of his, which makes me wonder whether the king was merely looking for an excuse to lure a certain fire-breathing bitch-queen back to these shores. Aedion is to be executed in three days at the prince's birthday party as the main entertainment. Practically screams *trap*, doesn't it? I'd be a little more subtle if I'd planned it, but you can't blame the king for sending a loud message."

Aedion. She mastered the swarm of thoughts that clouded her

mind—batted it aside and focused on the assassin in front of her. He wouldn't tell her about Aedion without a damn good reason.

"Why warn me at all?" she said. Aedion was captured by the king; Aedion was destined for the gallows—as a trap for her. Every plan she had was ruined.

No—she could still see those plans through to the end, still do what she had to. But Aedion . . . Aedion had to come first. Even if he later hated her, even if he spat in her face and called her a traitor and a whore and a lying murderer. Even if he resented what she had done and become, she would save him.

"Consider the tip a favor," Arobynn said, rising from the bench. "A token of good faith."

She'd bet there was more—perhaps tied to a certain captain whose warmth lingered in the wooden bench beneath her.

She stood as well, sliding out of the booth. She knew that more spies than Arobynn's lackeys monitored them—had seen her arrive, wait at the bar, and then head to this banquette. She wondered if her old master knew, too.

Arobynn only smiled at her, taller by a head. And when he reached out, she allowed him to brush his knuckles down her cheek. The calluses on his fingers said enough about how often he still practiced. "I do not expect you to trust me; I do not expect you to love me."

Only once, during those days of hell and heartbreak, had Arobynn ever said that he loved her in any capacity. She'd been about to leave with Sam, and he had come to her warehouse apartment, begging her to stay, claiming that he was angry with her for leaving and that everything he'd done, every twisted scheme, had been enacted out of spite for her moving out of the Keep. She'd never known in what way he'd meant those three words—*I love you*—but she'd been inclined to consider them another lie in the days that followed, after Rourke Farran had drugged her and put his filthy hands all over her. After she'd rotted away in that dungeon.

Arobynn's eyes softened. "I missed you."

She stepped out of his reach. "Funny—I was in Rifthold this fall and winter, and you never tried to see me."

"How could I dare? I thought you'd kill me on sight. But then I got word this evening that you had returned at last—and I hoped you might have changed your mind. You'll forgive me if my methods of getting you here were . . . roundabout."

Another move and countermove, to admit to the how but not the real why. She said, "I have better things to do than care about whether you live or die."

"Indeed. But you would care a great deal if your beloved Aedion died." Her heartbeat thundered through her, and she braced herself. Arobynn continued, "My resources are yours. Aedion is in the royal dungeon, guarded day and night. Any help you need, any support—you know where to find me."

"At what cost?"

Arobynn looked her over once more, and something low in her abdomen twisted at the gaze that was anything but that of a brother or father. "A favor—just one favor." Warning bells pealed in her head. She'd be better off making a bargain with one of the Valg princes. "There are creatures lurking in my city," he said. "Creatures who wear the bodies of men like clothing. I want to know what they are."

Too many threads were now poised to tangle.

She said carefully, "What do you mean?"

"The king's new guard has a few of them among its commanders. They're rounding up people suspected of being sympathetic to magic—or those who once possessed it. Executions every day, at sunrise and sunset. These *things* seem to thrive on them. I'm surprised you didn't notice them lurking about the docks."

"They're all monsters to me." But Chaol hadn't looked or felt like them. A small mercy.

He waited.

So did she.

She let herself break first. "Is this my favor, then? Telling you what I know?" There was little use in denying she was aware of the truth—or asking how he'd become aware that she knew it.

"Part of it."

She snorted. "Two favors for the price of one? How typical."

"Two sides of the same coin."

She stared flatly at him, and then said, "Through years of stealing knowledge and some strange, archaic power, the king has been able to stifle magic, while also summoning ancient demons to infiltrate human bodies for his growing army. He uses rings or collars of black stone to allow the demons to invade their hosts, and he's been targeting former magic-wielders, as their gifts make it easier for the demons to latch on." Truth, truth, truth—but not the whole truth. Not about the Wyrdmarks or Wyrdkeys—never to Arobynn. "When I was in the castle, I encountered some of the men he'd corrupted, men who fed off that power and became stronger. And when I was in Wendlyn, I faced one of his generals, who had been seized by a demon prince of unimaginable power."

"Narrok," Arobynn mused. If he was horrified, if he was shocked, his face revealed none of it.

She nodded. "They devour life. A prince like that can suck the soul right out of you, feed on you." She swallowed, and real fear coated her tongue. "Do the men you've seen—these commanders—have collars or rings?" Chaol's hands had been bare.

"Just rings," Arobynn said. "Is there a difference?"

"I think only a collar can hold a prince; the rings are for lesser demons."

"How do you kill them?"

"Fire," she said. "I killed the princes with fire."

"Ah. Not the usual sort, I take it." She nodded. "And if they wear a ring?"

"I've seen one of them killed with a sword through the heart." Chaol had killed Cain that easily. A small relief, but . . . "Beheading might work for the ones with collars."

"And the people who used to own those bodies—they're gone?"

Narrok's pleading, relieved face flashed before her. "It would seem so."

"I want you to capture one and bring it to the Keep."

She started. "Absolutely not. And why?"

"Perhaps it will be able to tell me something useful."

"Go capture it yourself," she snapped. "Find me another favor to fulfill."

"You're the only one who has faced these things and lived." There was nothing merciful in his gaze. "Capture one for me at your earliest convenience—and I'll assist you with your cousin."

To face one of the Valg, even a lesser Valg . . .

"Aedion comes first," she said. "We rescue Aedion, and then I'll risk my neck getting one of the demons for you."

Gods help them all if Arobynn ever realized that he might control that demon with the amulet he had hidden away.

"Of course," he said.

She knew it was foolish, but she couldn't help the next question. "To what end?"

"This is my city," he purred. "And I don't particularly care for the direction in which it's headed. It's bad for my investments, and I'm sick of hearing the crows feasting day and night."

Well, at least they agreed on something. "A businessman through and through, aren't you?"

Arobynn continued to pin her with that lover's gaze. "Nothing is without a price." He brushed a kiss against her cheekbone, his lips soft and warm. She fought the shudder that trembled through her, and made herself lean into him as he brought his mouth against her ear and whispered, "Tell me what I must do to atone; tell me to crawl over hot coals, to sleep on a bed of nails, to carve up my flesh. Say the word, and it is done. But let me care for you as I once did, before . . . before that madness poisoned my heart. Punish me, torture me, wreck me, but let me help you. Do this small thing for me—and let me lay the world at your feet."

Her throat went dry, and she pulled back far enough to look into that handsome, aristocratic face, the eyes shining with a grief and a predatory intent she could almost taste. If Arobynn knew about her history with Chaol, and had summoned the captain here . . . Had it been for information, to test her, or some grotesque way to assure himself of his dominance? "There is nothing—"

"No—not yet," he said, stepping away. "Don't say it yet. Sleep on it. Though, before you do—perhaps pay a visit to the southeastern section of the tunnels tonight. You might find the person you're looking for." She kept her face still—bored, even—as she tucked away the information. Arobynn moved toward the crowded room, where his three assassins were alert and ready, and then looked back at her. "If you are allowed to change so greatly in two years, may I not be permitted to have changed as well?"

With that, he sauntered off between the tables. Tern, Harding, and Mullin fell into step behind him—and Tern glanced in her direction just once, to give her the exact same obscene gesture she'd given him earlier.

But Aelin stared only at the King of the Assassins, at his elegant, powerful steps, at the warrior's body disguised in nobleman's clothes.

Liar. Trained, cunning liar.

There were too many eyes in the Vaults for her to scrub at her cheek, where the phantom imprint of Arobynn's lips still whispered, or at her ear, where his warm breath lingered.

Bastard. She glanced at the fighting pits across the hall, at the prostitutes clawing out a living, at the men who ran this place, who had profited for too long from so much blood and sorrow and pain. She could almost see Sam there—almost picture him fighting, young and strong and glorious.

She tugged on her gloves. There were many, many debts to be paid before she left Rifthold and took back her throne. Starting now. Fortunate that she was in a killing sort of mood.

It was only a matter of time before either Arobynn showed his hand or the King of Adarlan's men found the trail she'd carefully laid from the docks. Someone would be coming for her—within moments, actually, if the shouts followed by utter silence behind the metal door atop the stairs were any indication. At least that much of her plan remained on course. She'd deal with Chaol later.

With a gloved hand, she plucked up one of the coppers Arobynn had left on the table. She stuck out her tongue at the brutish, unforgiving profile of the king stamped on one side—then at the roaring wyvern gracing the other. Heads, Arobynn had betrayed her again. Tails, the king's men. The iron door at the top of the stairs groaned open, cool night air pouring in.

With a half smile, she flipped the coin with her thumb.

The coin was still rotating when four men in black uniforms appeared atop the stone stairs, an assortment of vicious weapons strapped to their bodies. By the time the copper thudded on the table, the wyvern glinting in the dim light, Aelin Galathynius was ready for bloodshed.

CHAPTER 4

Aedion Ashryver knew he was going to die—and soon.

He didn't bother trying to bargain with the gods. They'd never answered his pleas, anyway.

In the years he'd been a warrior and a general, he'd always known that he would die some way or another—preferably on a battlefield, in a way that would be worthy of a song or a tale around a fire.

This would not be that sort of death.

He would either be executed at whatever grand event the king had planned to make the most of his demise, or he would die down here in this rotting, damp cell, from the infection that was slowly and surely destroying his body.

It had started off as a small wound in his side, courtesy of the fight he'd put up three weeks ago when that butchering monster had murdered Sorscha. He'd hidden the slice along his ribs from the guards who looked him over, hoping that he'd either bleed out or that it'd fester and kill him before the king could use him against Aelin.

Aelin. His execution was to be a trap for her, a way to lure her into risking an attempt to save him. He'd die before he would allow it.

He just hadn't expected it to hurt so damn much.

He concealed the fever from the sneering guards who fed and watered him twice a day, pretending to slowly fall into sullen silence, feigning that the prowling, cursing animal had broken. The cowards wouldn't get close enough for him to reach, and they hadn't noticed that he'd given up trying to snap the chains that allowed him to stand and walk a few paces, but not much else. They hadn't noticed that he was no longer standing very much at all, except to see to his body's needs. The degradation of that was nothing new.

At least he hadn't been forced into one of those collars, though he'd seen one beside the king's throne that night everything went to shit. He would bet good money that the Wyrdstone collar was for the king's own son—and he prayed that the prince had died before he'd allowed his father to leash him like a dog.

Aedion shifted on his pallet of moldy hay and bit back his bark of agony at the pain exploding along his ribs. Worse—worse by the day. His diluted Fae blood was the only thing that had kept him alive this long, trying desperately to heal him, but soon even the immortal grace in his veins would bow to the infection.

It would be such a relief—such a blessed relief to know he couldn't be used against her, and that he would soon see those he had secretly harbored in his shredded heart all these years.

So he bore down on every spike of fever, every roiling fit of nausea and pain. Soon—soon Death would come to greet him.

Aedion just hoped Death arrived before Aelin did.

CHAPTER 5

The night might very well end in *her* blood being shed, Aelin realized as she hurtled down the crooked streets of the slums, sheathing her bloodied fighting knives to keep from dripping a trail behind her.

Thanks to months of running through the Cambrian Mountains with Rowan, her breathing remained steady, her head clear. She supposed that after facing skinwalkers, after escaping ancient creatures the size of small cottages, and after incinerating four demon princes, twenty men in pursuit wasn't all that horrific.

But still a giant, raging pain in her ass. And one that would not likely end pleasantly for her. No sign of Chaol—no whisper of his name on the lips of the men who had surged into the Vaults. She hadn't recognized any of them, but she'd felt the *offness* that marked most of those who had been in contact with Wyrdstone, or been corrupted by it. They wore no collars or rings, but something inside these men had rotted nonetheless.

At least Arobynn hadn't betrayed her—though how *convenient* that he'd left only minutes before the king's new guards had finally found the winding trail she'd left from the docks. Perhaps it was a test, to see whether her abilities remained up to Arobynn's standards, should she accept their little bargain. As she'd hacked her way through body after body, she wondered if he'd even realized that this entire evening had been a test for *him* as well, and that she'd brought those men right to the Vaults. She wondered how furious he would be when he discovered what was left of the pleasure hall that had brought him so much money.

It had also filled the coffers of the people who had slaughtered Sam—and who had enjoyed every moment of it. What a shame that the current owner of the Vaults, a former underling of Rourke Farran and a dealer of flesh and opiates, had accidentally run into her knives. Repeatedly.

She'd left the Vaults in bloody splinters, which she supposed was merciful. If she'd had her magic, she probably would have burned it to ash. But she didn't have magic, and her mortal body, despite months of hard training, was starting to feel heavy and cumbersome as she continued her sprint down the alley. The broad street at its other end was too bright, too open.

She veered toward a stack of broken crates and rubbish heaped against the wall of a brick building, high enough that if she timed it right, she could jump for the windowsill a few feet above.

Behind her, closer now, rushing footsteps and shouts sounded. They had to be fast as hell to have kept up with her all this way.

Well, damn.

She leaped onto the crates, the pile shaking and swaying as she scaled it, each movement concise, swift, balanced. One wrong step and she would go shooting through the rotten wood, or topple the whole thing to the ground. The crates groaned, but she kept moving up and up and up, until she reached the pinnacle and jumped for the overhanging windowsill.

Her fingers barked in pain, digging into the brick so hard that her nails broke inside her gloves. She gritted her teeth and pulled, hauling herself onto the ledge and then through the open window.

She allowed herself two heartbeats to take in the cramped kitchen:

dark and clean, a candle burning from the narrow hall beyond. Palming her knives, the shouting coming closer from the alley below, she raced for the hall.

Someone's home—this was someone's home, and she was leading those men through it. She charged down the hall, the wooden floors shuddering under her boots, scanning. There were two bedrooms, both occupied. Shit. *Shit.*

Three adults were sprawled on dirty mattresses in the first room. And two more adults slept in the other bedroom, one of them shooting upright as she thundered past. "*Stay down,*" she hissed, the only warning she could give before reaching the remaining door in the hall, barricaded with a chair wedged beneath the knob. It was about as much protection as they could find in the slums.

She hurled the chair aside, sending it clattering against the walls of the narrow hallway, where it would slow her pursuers for a few seconds at least. She yanked the apartment door open, the feeble lock splintering with a snap. Half a movement had her hurling a silver coin behind her to pay for the damage—and a better lock.

A communal stairwell lay beyond, the wooden steps stained and rotted. Completely dark.

Male voices echoed too close behind, and banging began at the bottom of the stairwell.

Aelin raced for the ascending stairs. Around and around, her breath now shards of glass in her lungs, until she passed the third level—until the stairs narrowed, and—

Aelin didn't bother being quiet as she slammed into the roof door. The men already knew where she was. Balmy night air smothered her, and she gulped it down as she scanned the roof and the streets below. The alley behind was too wide; the broad street to her left wasn't an option, but— there. Down the alley. That sewer grate.

Perhaps pay a visit to the southeastern section of the tunnels tonight. You might find the person you're looking for.

She knew who he meant. Another little present of his, then—a piece in their game.

With feline ease, she shimmied down the drainpipe anchored to the side of the building. Far above, the shouts grew. They'd reached the roof. She dropped into a puddle of what smelled undoubtedly like piss, and was running before the impact had fully shuddered through her bones.

She hurtled toward the grate, dropping onto her knees and sliding the last few feet until her fingers latched onto the lid, and she hauled it open. Silent, swift, efficient.

The sewers below were mercifully empty. She bit back a gag against the reek already rising up to meet her.

By the time the guards peered over the roof edge, she was gone.

Aelin loathed the sewers.

Not because they were filthy, reeking, and full of vermin. They were actually a convenient way to get around Rifthold unseen and undisturbed, if you knew the way.

She'd hated them ever since she'd been bound up and left to die, courtesy of a bodyguard who hadn't taken so well to her plans to kill his master. The sewers had flooded, and after freeing herself from her bonds, she had swum—actually *swum*—through the festering water. But the exit had been sealed. Sam, by pure luck, had saved her, but not before she'd nearly drowned, swallowing half the sewer along the way.

It had taken her days and countless baths to feel clean. And endless vomiting.

So climbing into that sewer, then sealing the grate above her . . . For the first time that night, her hands shook. But she forced herself past the echo of fear and began creeping through the dim, moonlit tunnels.

Listening.

Heading southeast, she took a large, ancient tunnel, one of the main arteries of the system. It had probably been here from the moment Gavin

Havilliard decided to establish his capital along the Avery. She paused every so often to listen, but there were no signs of her pursuers behind her.

An intersection of four different tunnels loomed ahead, and she slowed her steps, palming her fighting knives. The first two were clear; the third—the one that would take her right into the path of the captain if he was headed to the castle—darker, but wide. And the fourth . . . Southeast.

She didn't need her Fae senses to know that the darkness leaking from the southeastern tunnel wasn't of the usual sort. The moonlight from the grates above didn't pierce it. No noise issued, not even the scampering of rats.

Another trick of Arobynn's—or a gift? The faint sounds she'd been following had come from this direction. But any trail died here.

She paced with feline quiet in front of the line where the murky light faded into impenetrable blackness. Silently, she plucked up a bit of fallen stone and chucked it into the gloom ahead.

There was no answering sound when it should have landed.

"I wouldn't do that if I were you."

Aelin turned toward the cool female voice, casually angling her knives.

The hooded guard from the Vaults was leaning against the tunnel wall not twenty paces behind her.

Well, at least one of them was here. As for Chaol . . .

Aelin held up a knife as she stalked toward the guard, gobbling down every detail. "Sneaking up on strangers in the sewers is also something I'd advise against."

When Aelin got within a few feet, the woman lifted her hands—delicate but scarred, her skin tan even in the pale glow from the streetlights in the avenue above. If she'd managed to sneak up this close, she had to be trained—in combat or stealth or both. Of course she was skilled, if Chaol had her watching his back at the Vaults. But where had he gone now?

"Disreputable pleasure halls and sewers," Aelin said, keeping her knives out. "You certainly live the good life, don't you?"

The young woman pushed off the wall, her curtain of inky hair swaying in the shadows of her hood. "Not all of us are blessed enough to be on the king's payroll, Champion."

She recognized her, then. The real question was whether she'd told Chaol—and where he now was. "Dare I ask why I shouldn't throw stones down that tunnel?"

The guard pointed toward the tunnel closest behind her—bright, open air. "Come with me."

Aelin chuckled. "You'll have to do better than that."

The slender woman stepped nearer, the moonlight illuminating her hooded face. Pretty, if grave, and perhaps two or three years older.

The stranger said a bit flatly, "You've got twenty guards on your ass, and they're cunning enough to start looking down here very soon. I'd suggest you come along."

Aelin was half tempted to suggest she go to hell, but smiled instead. "How'd you find me?" She didn't care; she just needed to feel her out a bit more.

"Luck. I'm on scouting duty, and popped onto the street to discover that you'd made new friends. Usually, we have a strike-first, ask-questions-later policy about people wandering the sewers."

"And who is this 'we'?" Aelin said sweetly.

The woman just began walking down the bright tunnel, completely unconcerned with the knives Aelin still held. Arrogant and stupid, then. "You can come with me, Champion, and learn some things you probably want to know, or you can stay here and wait to see what answers that rock you threw."

Aelin weighed the words—and what she'd heard and seen so far that night. Despite the shiver down her spine, she fell into step beside the guard, sheathing her knives at her thighs.

With each block they trudged through the sewer muck, Aelin used the quiet to gather her strength.

The woman strode swiftly but smoothly down another tunnel, and then another. Aelin marked each turn, each unique feature, each grate, forming a mental map as they moved.

"How did you recognize me?" Aelin said at last.

"I've seen you around the city—months ago. The red hair was why I didn't immediately identify you at the Vaults."

Aelin watched her from the corner of her eye. The stranger might not know who Chaol really was. He could have used a different name, despite what the woman claimed to know about whatever it was she thought Aelin was seeking.

The woman said in that cool, calm voice, "Are the guards chasing you because they recognized you, or because you picked the fight you were so desperate to have at the Vaults?"

Point for the stranger. "Why don't you tell me? Do the guards work for Captain Westfall?"

The woman laughed under her breath. "No—those guards don't answer to him." Aelin bit back her sigh of relief, even as a thousand more questions rattled in her skull.

Her boots squished something too soft for comfort, and she repressed a shudder as the woman stopped before the entrance to another long tunnel, the first half illuminated by moonlight streaming in through the scattered grates. Unnatural darkness drifted out from the far end. A predatory still-ness crept over Aelin as she peered into the gloom. Silence. Utter silence.

"Here," the stranger said, approaching an elevated stone walkway built into the side of the tunnel. Fool—fool for exposing her back like that. She didn't even see Aelin slide free a knife.

They'd gone far enough.

The woman stepped onto the small, slick staircase leading to the walkway, her movements long-limbed and graceful. Aelin calculated the distance to the nearest exits, the depth of the little stream of filth running through the tunnel's center. Deep enough to dump a body, if need be.

Aelin angled her knife and slipped up behind the woman, as close as a lover, and pressed the blade against her throat.

CHAPTER
6

"You get one sentence," Aelin breathed in the woman's ear as she pressed the dagger harder against her neck. "One sentence to convince me not to spill your throat on the ground."

The woman stepped off the stairs and, to her credit, wasn't stupid enough to go for the concealed weapons at her side. With her back against Aelin's chest, her weapons were beyond reach, anyway. She swallowed, her throat bobbing against the dagger Aelin held along her smooth skin. "I'm taking you to the captain."

Aelin dug the knife in a bit more. "Not all that compelling to someone with a blade at your throat."

"Three weeks ago, he abandoned his position at the castle and fled. To join our cause. The *rebel* cause."

Aelin's knees threatened to buckle.

She supposed she should have included three parties in her plans: the king, Arobynn, and the rebels—who might very well have a score to settle with her after she'd gutted Archer Finn last winter. Even if Chaol was working with them.

She shut the thought down before its full impact hit her. "And the prince?"

"Alive, but still at the castle," the rebel hissed. "Is that enough for you to put the knife down?"

Yes. No. If Chaol was now working with the rebels . . . Aelin lowered her knife and stepped back into a pool of moonlight trickling in from an overhead grate.

The rebel whirled and reached for one of her knives. Aelin clicked her tongue. The woman's fingers paused on the well-polished hilt.

"I decide to spare you, and that's how you repay me?" Aelin said, tugging back her hood. "I don't particularly know why I'm surprised."

The rebel let go of her knife and pulled off her own hood, revealing her pretty, tanned face—solemn and wholly unafraid. Her dark eyes fixed on Aelin, scanning. Ally or enemy?

"Tell me why you came here," the rebel said quietly. "The captain says you're on our side. Yet you hid from him at the Vaults tonight."

Aelin crossed her arms and leaned against the damp stone wall behind her. "Let's start with you telling me your name."

"My name is not your concern."

Aelin lifted a brow. "You demand answers but refuse to give me any in return. No wonder the captain had you sit out the meeting. Hard to play the game when you don't know the rules."

"I heard what happened this winter. That you went to the warehouse and killed so many of us. You slaughtered rebels—my friends." That cool, calm mask didn't so much as flinch. "And yet I'm now supposed to believe you were on our side all along. Forgive me if I'm not forthright with you."

"Should I not kill the people who kidnap and beat my friends?" Aelin said softly. "Am I not supposed to react with violence when I receive notes threatening to *kill* my friends? Am I not supposed to gut the self-serving prick who had my beloved friend assassinated?" She pushed off the wall, stalking toward the woman. "Would you like me to apologize? Should I grovel on my knees for any of that?" The rebel's face showed nothing—either from training or genuine iciness. Aelin snorted. "I thought so. So why don't you take me to the captain and save the self-righteous bullshit for later?"

The woman glanced toward the darkness again and shook her head slightly. "If you hadn't put a blade to my throat, I would have told you that we'd arrived." She pointed to the tunnel ahead. "You're welcome."

Aelin debated slamming the woman into the filthy, wet wall just to remind her who, exactly, the King's Champion was, but then ragged breathing scraped past her ears, coming from that darkness. Human breathing—and whispers.

Boots sliding and thumping against stone, more whispers—hushed demands from voices she didn't recognize to *hurry*, and *quiet now*, and—

Aelin's muscles locked up as one male voice hissed, "We've got twenty minutes until that ship leaves. *Move.*"

She knew that voice.

But she still couldn't brace herself for the full impact of Chaol Westfall staggering out of the darkness at the end of the tunnel, holding a limp, too-thin man between himself and a companion, another armed man guarding their backs.

Even from the distance, the captain's eyes locked onto Aelin's.

He didn't smile.

CHAPTER 7

There were two injured people in total, one held between Chaol and his companion, the other sagging between two men she didn't recognize. Three others—two men and another woman—guarded the rear.

The rebel they dismissed with a glance. A friend.

Aelin held each of their gazes as they hurried toward her, their weapons out. Blood was splattered on them all—red blood and black blood that she knew too well. And the two nearly unconscious people . . .

She also knew that emaciated, dried-out look. The hollowness on their faces. She'd been too late with the ones in Wendlyn. But somehow Chaol and his allies had gotten these two out. Her stomach flipped. Scouting— the young woman beside her had been scouting the path ahead, to make sure it was safe for this rescue.

The guards in this city weren't corrupted just by ordinary Valg, as Arobynn had suggested.

No, there was at least one Valg prince here. In these tunnels, if the darkness was any indicator. *Shit.* And Chaol had been—

Chaol paused long enough for a companion to step in to help carry the injured man away. Then he was striding ahead. Twenty feet away now. Fifteen. Ten. Blood leaked from the corner of his mouth, and his bottom lip was split open. They'd *fought* their way out—

"Explain," she breathed to the woman at her side.

"It's not my place," was the woman's response.

She didn't bother to push it. Not with Chaol now in front of her, his bronze eyes wide as he took in the blood on Aelin herself.

"Are you hurt?" His voice was hoarse.

Aelin silently shook her head. Gods. *Gods.* Without that hood, now that she could see his features . . . He was exactly as she remembered— that ruggedly handsome, tan face perhaps a bit more gaunt and stubbly, but still Chaol. Still the man she'd come to love, before . . . before everything had changed.

There were so many things she had thought she'd say, or do, or feel.

A slender white scar slashed down his cheek. She'd given him that. The night Nehemia had died, she'd given him that, and tried to kill him.

Would have killed him. If Dorian hadn't stopped her.

Even then, she'd understood that what Chaol had done, whom he had chosen, had forever cleaved what was between them. It was the one thing she could not forget, could not forgive.

Her silent answer seemed enough for the captain. He looked to the woman beside Aelin—to his scout. *His* scout—who reported to him. As though he were leading them all.

"The path ahead is clear. Stick to the eastern tunnels," she said.

Chaol nodded. "Keep moving," he said to the others, who had now reached his side. "I'll catch up in a moment." No hesitation—and no soft- ness, either. As if he'd done this a hundred times.

They wordlessly continued on through the tunnels, casting glances Aelin's way as they swept past. Only the young woman lingered. Watching.

"Nesryn," Chaol said, the name an order in itself.

Nesryn stared at Aelin—analyzing, calculating.

Aelin gave her a lazy grin.

"*Faliq*," Chaol growled, and the woman slid her midnight eyes toward him. If Nesryn's family name didn't give away her heritage, it was those eyes, slightly uptilted at the corners and lightly lined with kohl, that revealed at least one of her parents was from the Southern Continent. Interesting that the woman didn't try to hide it, that she chose to wear the kohl even while on a mission, despite Rifthold's less-than-pleasant policies toward immigrants. Chaol jerked his chin toward their vanishing companions. "Get to the docks."

"It's safer to have one of us remain here." Again that cool voice—steady.

"Help them get to the docks, then get the hell back to the craftsman district. Your garrison commander will notice if you're late."

Nesryn looked Aelin up and down, those grave features never shifting. "How do we know she didn't come here on his orders?"

Aelin knew very well who she meant. She winked at the young woman. "If I'd come here on the king's orders, Nesryn Faliq, you'd have been dead minutes ago."

No flicker of amusement, no hint of fear. The woman could give Rowan a run for his money for sheer iciness.

"Sunset tomorrow," Chaol said sharply to Nesryn. The young woman stared him down, her shoulders tight, before she headed into the tunnel. She moved like water, Aelin thought.

"Go," Aelin said to Chaol, her voice a thin rasp. "You should go—help them." Or whatever he was doing.

Chaol's bloodied mouth formed a thin line. "I will. In a moment."

No invitation for her to join. Maybe she should have offered.

"You came back," he said. His hair was longer, shaggier than it'd been months ago. "It—Aedion—it's a trap—"

"I know about Aedion." Gods, what could she even *say*?

Chaol nodded distantly, blinking. "You . . . You look different."

She fingered her red hair. "Obviously."

"No," he said, taking one step closer, but only one. "Your face. The way you stand. You . . ." He shook his head, glancing toward the darkness they'd just fled. "Walk with me."

She did. Well, it was more like walking-as-fast-as-they-could-without-running. Ahead, she could just make out the sounds of his companions hurrying through the tunnels.

All the words she'd wanted to say rushed around in her head, fighting to get out, but she pushed back against them for a moment longer.

I love you—that's what he'd said to her the day she left. She hadn't given him an answer other than *I'm sorry.*

"A rescue mission?" she said, glancing behind them. No whisper of pursuit.

Chaol grunted in confirmation. "Former magic-wielders are being hunted and executed again. The king's new guards bring them into the tunnels to hold until it's time for the butchering block. They like the darkness—seem to thrive on it."

"Why not the prisons?" They were plenty dark enough, even for the Valg.

"Too public. At least for what they do to them before they're executed."

A chill snaked down her spine. "Do they wear black rings?" A nod. Her heart nearly stopped. "I don't care how many people they take into the tunnels. Don't go in again."

Chaol gave a short laugh. "Not an option. We go in because we're the only ones who can."

The sewers began to reek of brine. They had to be nearing the Avery, if she'd correctly counted the turns. "Explain."

"They don't notice or really care about the presence of ordinary humans—only people with magic in their bloodline. Even dormant carriers." He glanced sidelong at her. "It's why I sent Ren to the North—to get out of the city."

She almost tripped over a loose stone. "Ren . . . Allsbrook?"

Chaol nodded slowly.

The ground rocked beneath her. Ren Allsbrook. Another child of Terrasen. Still alive. *Alive.*

"Ren's the reason we learned about it in the first place," Chaol said. "We went into one of their nests. They looked right at him. Ignored Nesryn and me entirely. We barely got out. I sent him to Terrasen—to rally the rebels there—the day after. He wasn't too happy about it, believe me."

Interesting. Interesting, and utterly insane. "Those things are demons. The Valg. And they—"

"Drain the life out of you, feed on you, until they make a show of executing you?"

"It's not a joke," she snapped. Her dreams were haunted by the roaming hands of those Valg princes as they fed on her. And every time she would awaken with a scream on her lips, reaching for a Fae warrior who wasn't there to remind her that they'd made it, they'd survived.

"I know it's not," Chaol said. His eyes flicked to where Goldryn peeked over her shoulder. "New sword?"

She nodded. There were perhaps only three feet between them now—three feet and months and months of missing and hating him. Months of crawling out of that abyss he'd shoved her into. But now that she was here . . . Everything was an effort not to say she was sorry. Sorry not for what she'd done to his face, but for the fact that her heart was healed—still fractured in spots, but healed—and he . . . he was not in it. Not as he'd once been.

"You figured out who I am," she said, mindful of how far ahead his companions were.

"The day you left."

She monitored the darkness behind them for a moment. All clear.

He didn't move closer—didn't seem at all inclined to hold her or kiss her or even touch her. Ahead, the rebels veered into a smaller tunnel, one she knew led directly toward the ramshackle docks in the slums.

"I grabbed Fleetfoot," he said after a moment of silence.

She tried not to exhale too loudly. "Where is she?"

"Safe. Nesryn's father owns a few popular bakeries in Rifthold, and has done well enough that he's got a country house in the foothills outside the city. He said his staff there would care for her in secret. She seemed more than happy to torture the sheep, so—I'm sorry I couldn't keep her here, but with the barking—"

"I understand," she breathed. "Thank you." She cocked her head. "A land-owning man's daughter is a rebel?"

"Nesryn is in the city guard, despite her father's wishes. I've known her for years."

That didn't answer her question. "She can be trusted?"

"As you said, we'd all be dead already if she was here on the king's orders."

"Right." She swallowed hard, sheathing her knives and tugging off her gloves, if only because it gave her something to do with her hands. But then Chaol looked—to the empty finger where his amethyst ring had once been. The skin was soaked with the blood that had seeped in through the fabric, some red, some black and reeking.

Chaol gazed at that empty spot—and when his eyes rose to hers again, it became hard to breathe. He stopped at the entrance to the narrow tunnel. Far enough, she realized. He'd taken her as far as he was willing to allow her to follow.

"I have a lot to tell you," she said before he could speak. "But I think I'd rather hear your story first. How you got here; what happened to Dorian. And Aedion. All of it." *Why you were meeting with Arobynn tonight.*

That tentative tenderness in his face hardened into a cold, grim resolve—and her heart cracked a bit at the sight of it. Whatever he had to say wasn't going to be pleasant.

But he just said, "Meet me in forty minutes," and named an address in the slums. "I have to deal with this first."

He didn't wait for a response before jogging down the tunnel after his companions.

Aelin followed anyway.

~

Aelin watched from a rooftop, monitoring the docks of the slums as Chaol and his companions approached the small boat. The crew didn't dare lay anchor—only tying the boat to the rotted posts long enough for the rebels to pass the sagging victims into the arms of the waiting sailors. Then they were rowing hard, out into the dark curve of the Avery and hopefully to a larger ship at its mouth.

She observed Chaol speak quickly to the rebels, Nesryn lingering when he'd finished. A short, clipped fight about something she couldn't hear, and then the captain was walking alone, Nesryn and the others headed off in the opposite direction without so much as a backward glance.

Chaol made it a block before Aelin silently dropped down beside him. He didn't flinch. "I should have known better."

"You really should have."

Chaol's jaw tightened, but he kept walking farther into the slums.

Aelin examined the night-dark, sleeping streets. A few feral urchins darted past, and she eyed them from beneath her hood, wondering which were on Arobynn's payroll and might report to him that she'd been spotted blocks away from her old home. There was no point in trying to hide her movements—she hadn't wanted to, anyway.

The houses here were ramshackle but not wrecked. Whatever working-class families dwelled within tried their best to keep them in shape. Given their proximity to the river, they were likely occupied by fishermen, dock-workers, and maybe the occasional slave on loan from his or her master. But no sign of trouble, no vagrants or pimps or would-be thieves lurking about.

Almost charming, for the slums.

"The story isn't a pleasant one," the captain began at last.

Aelin let Chaol talk as they strode through the slums, and it broke her heart.

She kept her mouth shut as he told her how he'd met Aedion and worked with him, and then how the king had captured Aedion and interrogated Dorian. It took considerable effort to keep from shaking the captain to demand how he could have been so reckless and stupid and taken so long to act.

Then Chaol got to the part where Sorscha was beheaded, each word quieter and more clipped than the last.

She had never learned the healer's name, not in all the times the woman had patched and sewn her up. For Dorian to lose her . . . Aelin swallowed hard.

It got worse.

So much worse, as Chaol explained what Dorian had done to get him out of the castle. He'd sacrificed himself, revealing his power to the king. She was shaking so badly that she tucked her hands into her pockets and clamped her lips together to lock up the words.

But they danced in her skull anyway, around and around.

You should have gotten Dorian and Sorscha out the day the king butchered those slaves. Did you learn nothing *from Nehemia's death? Did you somehow think you could win with your honor intact, without sacrificing something? You shouldn't have left him; how could you let him face the king alone? How could you, how could you, how could you?*

The grief in Chaol's eyes kept her from speaking.

She took a breath as he fell silent, mastering the anger and the disappointment and the shock. It took three blocks before she could think straight.

Her wrath and tears would do no good. Her plans would change again—but not by much. Free Aedion, retrieve the Wyrdkey . . . she could still do it. She squared her shoulders. They were mere blocks away from her old apartment.

At least she could have a place to lie low, if Arobynn hadn't sold the property. He probably would have taunted her about it if he had—or perhaps left her to find it had a new owner. He loved surprises like that.

"So now you're working with the rebels," she said to Chaol. "Or leading them, from the look of it."

"There are a few of us in charge. My territory covers the slums and docks—there are others responsible for different sections of the city. We meet as often as we dare. Nesryn and some of the city guards have been able to get in contact with a few of my men. Ress and Brullo, mostly. They've been looking for ways to get Dorian out. And Aedion. But that dungeon is impenetrable, and they're watching the secret tunnels. We only went into their nest in the sewer tonight because we'd received word from Ress that there was some big meeting at the palace. Turns out they'd left more sentries behind than we'd anticipated."

The castle was impossible to get into—unless she accepted Arobynn's help. Another decision. For tomorrow. "What have you heard about Dorian since you fled?"

A flicker of shame shone in his bronze eyes. He *had* fled, though. He'd left Dorian in his father's hands.

She clenched her fingers into fists to keep from slamming his head into the side of a brick building. How could he have served that monster? How could he not have seen it, not have tried to kill the king anytime he got within striking range?

She hoped that whatever Dorian's father had done to him, however he'd been punished, the prince knew he was not the only one grieving. And after she retrieved Dorian, she would let him know, when he was ready to listen, that she understood—and that it would be hard and long and painful, but he might come back from it, the loss. When he did, with that raw magic of his, free when hers was not . . . It could be critical in defeating the Valg.

"The king hasn't publicly punished Dorian," Chaol said. "Hasn't even locked him up. As far as we can tell, he's still attending events, and will be at this execution–birthday party of his."

Aedion—oh, Aedion. He knew who she was, what she had become, but Chaol hadn't suggested whether her cousin might spit in her face the moment he laid eyes on her. She wouldn't care about it until Aedion was safe, until he was free.

"So, we've got Ress and Brullo inside, and eyes on the castle walls," Chaol went on. "They say that Dorian seems to be behaving normally, but his demeanor is off. Colder, more distant—but that's to be expected after Sorscha was—"

"Did they report him wearing a black ring?"

Chaol shuddered. "No—not a ring." There was something about his tone that made her look at him and wish she didn't have to hear his next words. Chaol said, "But one of the spies claimed that Dorian has a torque of black stone around his neck."

A Wyrdstone collar.

For a moment, all Aelin could manage to do was stare at Chaol. The surrounding buildings pressed on her, a giant pit opening beneath the cobblestones she walked upon, threatening to swallow her whole.

"You're pale," Chaol said, but he made no move to touch her.

Good. She wasn't entirely certain she could handle being touched without ripping his face off.

But she took a breath, refusing to let the enormity of what had happened to Dorian hit her—for now at least. "Chaol, I don't know what to say—about Dorian, and Sorscha, and Aedion. About you being *here*." She gestured to the slums around them.

"Just tell me what happened to you all these months."

She told him. She told him what had happened in Terrasen ten years ago, and what had happened to her in Wendlyn. When she got to the Valg princes, she did not tell him about those collars, because—because he already looked sick. And she did not tell him of the third Wyrdkey—only that Arobynn had stolen the Amulet of Orynth, and she wanted it back. "So now you know why I'm here, and what I did, and what I plan to do."

Chaol didn't reply for an entire block. He'd been silent throughout. He had not smiled.

There was so little left of the guard she'd come to care for as he at last met her gaze, his lips a thin line. He said, "So you're here alone."

"I told Rowan it would be safer for him to remain in Wendlyn."

"No," he said a bit sharply, facing the street ahead. "I mean—you came back, but without an army. Without allies. You came back empty-handed."

Empty-handed. "I don't know what you expected. You—*you* sent me to Wendlyn. If you'd wanted me to bring back an army, you should have been a little more specific."

"I sent you there for your safety, so you could get away from the king. And as soon as I realized who you were, how could I not assume you'd run to your cousins, to Maeve—"

"Have you not been listening to anything I said? About what Maeve is like? The Ashryvers are at her beck and call, and if Maeve does not send aid, *they* will not send aid."

"You didn't even try." He paused on a deserted corner. "If your cousin Galan is a blockade runner—"

"My cousin Galan is none of your concern. Do you even understand what I faced?"

"Do you understand what it was like for us here? While you were off playing with magic, off gallivanting with your faerie prince, do you understand what happened to me—to Dorian? Do you understand what's happening every day in this city? Because your antics in Wendlyn might very well have been the cause of all this."

Each word was like a stone to the head. Yes—yes, maybe, but . . . "My *antics?*"

"If you hadn't been so dramatic about it, hadn't flaunted your defeat of Narrok and practically *shouted* at the king that you were back, he would never have called us to that room—"

"You do not get to blame me for that. For *his* actions." She clenched her fists as she looked at him—really *looked* at him, at the scar that would forever remind her of what he'd done, what she could not forgive.

"So what *do* I get to blame you for?" he demanded as she started walking again, her steps swift and precise. "Anything?"

He couldn't mean that—couldn't possibly mean it. "Are you *looking* for things to blame me for? How about the fall of the kingdoms? The loss of magic?"

"The second one," he said through his teeth, "at least I know without a doubt is not your doing."

She paused again. "What did you say?"

His shoulders tightened. That was all she needed to see to know he'd planned to keep it from her. Not from Celaena, his former friend and lover, but from Aelin—Queen of Terrasen. A threat. Whatever this information about magic was, he hadn't planned to tell her.

"What, exactly, did you learn about magic, Chaol?" she said too quietly.

He didn't reply.

"Tell me."

He shook his head, a gap in the streetlights shadowing his face. "No. Not a chance. Not with you so unpredictable."

Unpredictable. It was a mercy, she supposed, that magic was indeed stifled here, or else she might have turned the street to cinders around them, just to show him how very predictable she was.

"You found a way to free it, didn't you. You know how."

He didn't try to pretend otherwise. "Having magic free would result only in chaos—it would make things worse. Perhaps make it easier for those demons to find and feed on magic-wielders."

"You might very well regret those words when you hear the rest of what I have to say," she hissed, raging and roaring inside. She kept her voice low enough that no one nearby might overhear as she continued. "That collar Dorian is wearing—let me tell you what it does, and let's see if you refuse to tell me then, if you dismiss what I've been doing these past months." With every word, his face further drained of color. A small, wicked part of her reveled in it. "They target magic-wielders, feeding off the power in their blood. They drain the life from those that aren't compatible to take in a Valg demon. Or, considering Rifthold's new favorite pastime, just execute them to drum up fear. They feed on it—fear, misery, despair. It's like wine to them. The lesser Valg, they can seize a mortal's body through those black rings. But their civilization—a whole damn *civilization*," she said, "is split into hierarchies like our own. And their princes want to come to our world very, *very* badly. So the king uses collars. Black Wyrdstone collars." She didn't think Chaol was breathing. "The collars are stronger, capable of helping the demons stay inside human bodies while they devour the person and power inside. Narrok had one inside him. He *begged* me at the end to kill him. Nothing else could. I witnessed monsters you cannot begin to imagine take on one of them and fail. Only flame, or beheading, ends it.

"So you see," she finished, "considering the gifts I have, you'll find that you *want* to tell me what you know. I might be the only person capable of freeing Dorian, or at least giving him the mercy of killing him. If he's even in there." The last words tasted as horrible as they sounded.

Chaol shook his head. Once. Twice. And she might have felt bad for the panic, for the grief and despair on his face. Until he said, "Did it even occur to you to send us a warning? To let *any* of us know about the king's collars?"

It was like a bucket of water had been dumped on her. She blinked. She *could* have warned them—could have tried. Later—she'd think about that later.

"That doesn't matter," she said. "Right now, we need to help Aedion and Dorian."

"There is no *we*." He unfastened the Eye of Elena from around his neck and chucked it at her. It glimmered in the streetlights as it flew between them. She caught it with one hand, the metal warm against her skin. She didn't look at it before sliding it into her pocket. He went on. "There hasn't been a *we* for a while, Celaena—"

"It's Aelin now," she snapped as loudly as she dared. "Celaena Sardothien doesn't exist anymore."

"You're still the same assassin who walked away. You came back only when it was useful for *you*."

It was an effort to keep from sending her fist into his nose. Instead she pulled the silver amethyst ring out of her pocket and grabbed his hand, slamming it into his gloved palm. "Why were you meeting with Arobynn Hamel tonight?"

"How—"

"It doesn't matter. Tell me why."

"I wanted his help to kill the king."

Aelin started. "Are you insane? Did you *tell* him that?"

"No, but he guessed it. I'd been trying to meet with him for a week now, and tonight he summoned me."

"You're a fool for going." She began walking again. Staying in one spot, however deserted, wasn't wise.

Chaol fell into step beside her. "I didn't see any *other* assassins offering their services."

She opened her mouth, then shut it. She curled her fingers, then straightened them one by one. "The price won't be gold or favors. The price will be the last thing you see coming. Likely the death or suffering of the people you care about."

"You think I didn't know that?"

"So you want to have Arobynn kill the king, and what? Put Dorian on the throne? With a Valg demon inside him?"

"I didn't know that until now. But it changes nothing."

"It changes everything. Even if you get that collar off, there's no guarantee the Valg hasn't taken root inside him. You might replace one monster with another."

"Why don't you say whatever it is you're getting at, *Aelin*?" He hissed her name barely loud enough for her to hear.

"Can you kill the king? When it comes down to it, could you kill your king?"

"*Dorian* is my king."

It was an effort not to flinch. "Semantics."

"He killed Sorscha."

"He killed millions before her." Perhaps a challenge, perhaps another question.

His eyes flared. "I need to go. I'm meeting Brullo in an hour."

"I'll come with you," she said, glancing toward the glass castle towering over the northeastern quarter of the city. Perhaps she'd learn a bit more about what the Weapons Master knew about Dorian. And how she might be able to put down her friend. Her blood turned icy, sluggish.

"No, you won't," Chaol said. Her head snapped toward him. "If you're there, I have to answer too many questions. I won't jeopardize Dorian to satisfy your curiosity."

He kept walking straight, but she turned the corner with a tight shrug. "Do what you want."

Noticing she was heading away, he halted. "And what are *you* going to be doing?"

Too much suspicion in that voice. She paused her steps and arched an eyebrow. "Many things. Wicked things."

"If you give us away, Dorian will—"

She cut him off with a snort. "You refused to share your information, Captain. I don't think it's unreasonable for me to withhold mine." She made to walk down the street, toward her old apartment.

"Not captain," he said.

She looked over her shoulder and studied him again. "What happened to your sword?"

His eyes were hollow. "I lost it."

Ah. "So is it Lord Chaol, then?"

"Just Chaol."

For a heartbeat, she pitied him, and part of her wished she could say it more kindly, more compassionately. "There's no getting Dorian out. There's no saving him."

"Like hell there isn't."

"You'd be better off considering other contenders to put on the throne—"

"Do *not* finish that sentence." His eyes were wide, his breathing uneven.

She'd said enough. She rolled her shoulders, leashing her temper. "With my magic, I could help him—I could try to find a way to free him."

But most likely kill him. She wouldn't admit that aloud. Not until she could see him for herself.

"And what then?" Chaol asked. "Will you hold all of Rifthold hostage the way you did Doranelle? Burn anyone who doesn't agree with you? Or will you just incinerate our kingdom from spite? And what of others like you, who feel that they have a score to settle with Adarlan?" He huffed a bitter laugh. "Perhaps we're better off without magic. Perhaps magic doesn't exactly make things fair amongst us mere mortals."

"Fair? You think that any part of this is *fair*?"

"Magic makes people dangerous."

"Magic has saved your life a few times now, if I recall correctly."

"Yes," he breathed, "you and Dorian both—and I'm grateful, I am. But where are the checks against your kind? Iron? Not much of a deterrent, is it? Once magic is free, who is to stop the monsters from coming out again? Who is to stop *you*?"

A spear of ice shot through her heart.

Monster.

It truly had been horror and revulsion that she'd seen on his face that day she revealed her Fae form in the other world—the day she'd cleaved the earth and called down fire to save him, to save Fleetfoot. Yes, there would always need to be checks against any sort of power, but . . . *Monster.*

She wished he'd struck her instead. "So Dorian is allowed to have magic. You can come to terms with his power, and yet my power is an abomination to you?"

"Dorian has never killed anyone. Dorian didn't gut Archer Finn in the tunnels or torture and kill Grave and then chop him up into pieces. Dorian didn't go on a killing spree at Endovier that left dozens dead."

It was an effort to put up that old, familiar wall of ice and steel. Everything behind it was crumbling and shaking. "I've made my peace with that." She sucked on her teeth, trying so damn hard not to go for her weapons as she might once have done, as she still ached to do, and said, "I'll be at my old apartment, should you decide to take your head out of your ass. Good night."

She didn't give him a chance to reply before she stalked down the street.

Chaol stood in the small bedroom of the ramshackle house that had been his squadron's primary headquarters for the past three weeks, staring at a desk littered with maps and plans and notes regarding the palace, the guards' rotations, and Dorian's habits. Brullo had nothing to offer during their meeting an hour earlier—just grim reassurance that Chaol had done the right thing in leaving the king's service and walking away from everything he'd ever worked for. The older man still insisted on calling him captain, despite Chaol's protests.

Brullo had been the one who'd found Chaol and offered to be his eyes inside the castle, not three days after he'd run. *Fled*, Aelin had said. She'd known exactly what word she wielded.

A queen—raging and fiery and perhaps more than a little cruel—had found him tonight. He'd seen it from the moment he'd staggered out of the Valg's darkness to find her standing with a predator's stillness beside Nesryn. Despite the dirt and blood on her, Aelin's face was tan and flushed with color, and—different. Older, as if the stillness and power she radiated had honed not just her soul but also the very shape of her. And when he had seen her bare finger . . .

Chaol took out the ring he'd tucked into his pocket and glanced at the unlit hearth. It would be a matter of minutes to light a blaze and chuck the ring into it.

He turned the ring over between his fingers. The silver was dull and marred with countless scratches.

No, Celaena Sardothien certainly did not exist anymore. That woman—the woman he had loved . . . Perhaps she'd drowned in the vast, ruthless sea between here and Wendlyn. Perhaps she'd died at the hands of the Valg princes. Or maybe he'd been a fool all this time, a fool to look at the lives she'd taken and blood she'd so irreverently spilled, and not be disgusted.

There had been *blood* on her tonight—she'd killed many men before finding him. She hadn't even bothered to wash it off, hadn't even seemed to notice she was wearing the blood of her enemies.

A city—she'd encircled a *city* with her flames, and made a Fae Queen tremble. No one should possess that sort of power. If she could make an entire city burn as retribution for a Fae Queen whipping her friend . . . What would she do to the empire that had enslaved and butchered her people?

He would not tell her how to free magic—not until he knew for certain that she wouldn't turn Rifthold into cinders on the wind.

There was a knock on his door—two efficient beats. "You should be on your shift, Nesryn," he said by way of greeting.

She slipped in, smooth as a cat. In the three years he'd known her, she'd always had that quiet, sleek way of moving. A year ago, a bit shattered and reckless from Lithaen's betrayal, it had intrigued him enough that he'd spent the summer sharing her bed.

"My commander's drunk with his hand up the shirt of whatever new barmaid was in his lap. He won't notice my absence for a while yet." A faint sort of amusement shone in her dark eyes. The same sort of amusement that had been there last year whenever they would meet, at inns or in rooms above taverns or sometimes even up against the wall of an alley.

He'd needed it—the distraction and release—after Lithaen had left him for the charms of Roland Havilliard. Nesryn had just been bored, apparently. She'd never sought him out, never asked when she would see him again, so their encounters had always been initiated by him. A few months later, he hadn't felt particularly bad when he'd gone to Endovier and stopped seeing her. He'd never told Dorian—or Aelin. And when he'd run into Nesryn three weeks ago at one of the rebel gatherings, she hadn't seemed to be holding a grudge.

"You look like a man who got punched in the balls," she said at last.

He cut a glare in her direction. And because he did indeed feel that way, because maybe he was again feeling a bit shattered and reckless, he told her what had happened. Who it had happened with.

He trusted her, though. In the three weeks they'd been fighting and plotting and surviving together, he'd had no choice *but* to trust her. Ren had trusted her. Yet Chaol still hadn't told Ren who Celaena truly was before he'd left. Perhaps he should have. If he'd known that she would come back like this, act this way, he supposed Ren should have learned who he was risking his life for. He supposed Nesryn deserved to know, too.

Nesryn cocked her head, her hair shimmering like black silk. "The King's Champion—and Aelin Galathynius. Impressive." He didn't need to bother to ask her to keep it to herself. She knew exactly how precious that information was. He hadn't asked her to be his second in command for nothing. "I should be flattered she held a knife to my throat."

Chaol glanced again at the ring. He should melt it, but money was scarce. He'd already used up much of what he'd snatched from the tomb.

And he would need it now more than ever. Now that Dorian was . . .

Was . . .

Dorian was gone.

Celaena—*Aelin* had lied about many things, but she wouldn't have lied about Dorian. And she might be the only person able to save him. But if she tried to kill him instead . . .

He sank into the desk chair, staring blankly at the maps and plans he'd been cultivating. Everything—everything was for Dorian, for his friend. For himself, he had nothing left to lose. He was nothing more than a nameless oath-breaker, a liar, a traitor.

Nesryn took a step toward him. There was little concern in her face, but he'd never expected coddling from her. Never wanted it. Perhaps because she alone understood it—what it was like to face a father's disapproval to follow the path that called. But while Nesryn's father had eventually accepted her choice, Chaol's own father . . . He didn't want to think about his father right now, not as Nesryn said, "What she claimed about the prince—"

"It changes nothing."

"It sounds like it changes everything. Including the future of this kingdom."

"Just drop it."

Nesryn crossed her thin arms. She was slender enough that most opponents underestimated her—to their own misfortune. Tonight, he'd seen her rip into one of those Valg soldiers like she was filleting a fish. "I think you're letting your personal history get in the way of considering every route."

He opened his mouth to object. Nesryn lifted a groomed brow and waited.

Maybe he'd been hotheaded just now.

Maybe it had been a mistake to refuse to tell Aelin how to free magic.

And if it cost him Dorian in the process—

He swore softly, the rush of breath guttering the candle on the desk.

The captain he'd once been would have refused to tell her. Aelin was an enemy of his kingdom.

But that captain was no more. That captain had died alongside Sorscha in that tower room. "You fought well tonight," he said, as if that were an answer.

Nesryn clicked her tongue. "I came back because I received a report that three of the city garrisons were called to the Vaults not thirty minutes after we left. Her Majesty," Nesryn said drily, "killed a great number of the king's men, the owners and investors of the hall, and took it upon herself to wreck the place. They won't be open again anytime soon."

Gods above. "Do they know it was the King's Champion?"

"No. But I thought I should warn you. I bet she had a reason for doing it."

Maybe. Maybe not. "You'll find that she tends to do what she wants, when she wants, and doesn't ask for permission first." Aelin probably had just been in a pissy mood and decided to unleash her temper on the pleasure hall.

Nesryn said, "You should have known better than to get tangled up with a woman like that."

"And I suppose you would know everything about getting tangled up with people, given how many suitors are lined up outside your father's bakeries." A cheap shot, maybe, but they'd always been blunt with each other. She hadn't ever seemed bothered by it, anyway.

That faint gleam of amusement returned to her eyes as Nesryn put her hands in her pockets and turned away. "This is why I never get too involved. Too messy."

Why she didn't let anyone in. Ever. He debated asking why—pushing about it. But limiting the questions about their pasts was part of their deal, and had been from the start.

Honestly, he didn't know what he'd expected when the queen returned. Not this.

You do not get to pick and choose which parts of her to love, Dorian had once said to him. He'd been right. So painfully right.

Nesryn let herself out.

At first light, Chaol went to the nearest jeweler and pawned the ring for a handful of silver.

Exhausted and miserable, Aelin trudged back to her old apartment above the unremarkable warehouse. She didn't dare linger outside the large, two-level wooden building that she'd purchased when she'd at last paid off her debts to Arobynn—purchased for herself, to get out of the Keep.

But it had only started to feel like a home once she'd paid off Sam's debts as well, and he'd come to live here with her. A few weeks—that was all she'd been able to share with him.

Then he was dead.

The lock on the large, rolling door was new, and inside the warehouse, the towering stacks of crates full of ink remained in prime condition. No dust coated the stairs in the back. Either Arobynn or another face from her past would be inside.

Good. She was ready for another fight.

When she opened the green door, a knife angled behind her, the apartment was dark. Empty.

But it smelled fresh.

It was a matter of a few moments to check the apartment—the great room, the kitchen (a few old apples, but no other signs of an occupant), her bedroom (untouched), and the guest room. It was there that someone's scent lingered; the bed was not quite perfectly made, and a note lay on the high dresser beside the door.

The captain said I could stay here for a while. Sorry for trying to kill you this winter. I was the one with the twin swords. Nothing personal. —Ren

She swore. *Ren* had been staying here? And—and he still thought she was the King's Champion. The night the rebels had kept Chaol hostage in a warehouse, she had tried to kill him, and had been surprised when he'd held his ground. Oh, she remembered him.

At least he was safe in the North.

She knew herself well enough to admit that the relief was partially that of a coward—that she didn't have to face Ren and see how he might react to who she was, what she'd done with Marion's sacrifice. Given Chaol's own reaction, "not well" seemed like a fair guess.

She walked back into the darkened great room, lighting candles as she went. The large dining table occupying one half of the space was still set with her elegant plates. The couch and two red velvet armchairs before the ornate mantel were a bit rumpled, but clean.

For a few moments, she just stared at the mantel. A beautiful clock had once sat there—until the day she'd learned Sam had been tortured and killed by Rourke Farran. That the torture had gone on for *hours* while she'd sat on her ass in this apartment, packing trunks that were now nowhere to be seen. And when Arobynn had come to deliver the news, she'd taken that beautiful clock and hurled it across the room, where it had shattered against the wall.

She hadn't been back here since then, though someone had cleaned up the glass. Either Ren or Arobynn.

A look at one of the many bookshelves gave her the answer.

Every book she'd packed for that one-way trip to the Southern Continent, for that new life with Sam, had been put back in place. *Exactly* where she'd once kept them.

And there was only one person who would know those details—who would use the unpacked trunks as a taunt and a gift and a quiet reminder of what leaving him would cost her. Which meant Arobynn had no doubt known she would return here. At some point.

She padded into her bedroom. She didn't dare to check whether Sam's clothes had been unpacked into the drawers—or thrown out.

A bath—that's what she needed. A long, hot bath.

She hardly noticed the room that had once been her sanctuary. She lit the candles in the white-tiled bathroom, casting the chamber in flickering gold.

After turning the brass knobs on the oversized porcelain bathtub to start the water flowing, she unstrapped each of her weapons. She peeled off her filthy, bloody clothes layer by layer, until she stood in her own scarred skin and gazed at her tattooed back in the mirror above the sink.

A month ago, Rowan had covered her scars from Endovier with a stunning, scrolling tattoo, written in the Old Language of the Fae—the stories of her loved ones and how they'd died.

She would not have Rowan ink another name on her flesh.

She climbed into the tub, moaning at the delicious heat, and thought of the empty place on the mantel where the clock should have been. The place that had never quite been filled again since that day she'd shattered the clock. Maybe—maybe she'd also stopped in that moment.

Stopped living and started just . . . surviving. Raging.

And maybe it had taken until this spring, when she had been sprawled on the ground while three Valg princes fed on her, when she had at last burned through that pain and darkness, for the clock to start again.

No, she would not add another name of her beloved dead to her flesh.

She yanked a washcloth from beside the tub and scrubbed at her face, bits of mud and blood clouding the water.

Unpredictable. The arrogance, the sheer single-minded selfishness . . .

Chaol had run. He'd *run*, and Dorian had been left to be enslaved by the collar.

Dorian. She'd come back—but too late. Too late.

She dunked the washcloth again and covered her face with it, hoping it would somehow ease the stinging in her eyes. Maybe she'd sent too strong a message from Wendlyn by destroying Narrok; maybe it *was* her fault that Aedion had been captured, Sorscha killed, and Dorian enslaved.

Monster.

And yet . . .

For her friends, for her family, she would gladly be a monster. For Rowan, for Dorian, for Nehemia, she would debase and degrade and ruin herself. She knew they would have done the same for her. She slung the washcloth into the water and sat up.

Monster or no, never in ten thousand years would she have let Dorian face his father alone. Even if Dorian had told her to go. A month ago, she and Rowan had chosen to face the Valg princes *together*—to die together, if need be, rather than do so alone.

You remind me of what the world ought to be; what the world can be, she'd once said to Chaol.

Her face burned. A girl had said those things; a girl so desperate to

SARAH J. MAAS

survive, to make it through each day, that she hadn't questioned why he served the true monster of their world.

Aelin slipped back under the water, scrubbing at her hair, her face, her bloody body.

She could forgive the girl who had needed a captain of the guard to offer stability after a year in hell; forgive the girl who had needed a captain to be her champion.

But she was her own champion now. And she would not add another name of her beloved dead to her flesh.

So when she awoke the next morning, Aelin wrote a letter to Arobynn, accepting his offer.

One Valg demon, owed to the King of the Assassins.

In exchange for his assistance in the rescue *and* safe return of Aedion Ashryver, the Wolf of the North.

CHAPTER 8

Manon Blackbeak, heir of the Blackbeak Witch-Clan, bearer of the blade Wind-Cleaver, rider of the wyvern Abraxos, and Wing Leader of the King of Adarlan's aerial host, stared at the portly man sitting across the black glass table and kept her temper on a tight leash.

In the weeks that Manon and half the Ironteeth legion had been stationed in Morath, the mountain stronghold of Duke Perrington, she had not warmed to him. Neither had any of her Thirteen. Which was why Asterin's hands were within easy reach of her twin blades as she leaned against the dark stone wall, why Sorrel was posted near the doors, and why Vesta and Lin stood guard outside them.

The duke either didn't notice or didn't care. He showed interest in Manon only when giving orders about *her* host's training. Other than that, he appeared relentlessly focused on the army of strange-smelling men that waited in the camp at the foot of the mountain. Or on whatever dwelled under the surrounding mountains—whatever screamed and roared and moaned within the labyrinth of catacombs carved into the heart of the ancient rock. Manon had never asked what was kept or done inside those mountains, though her Shadows had reported whispers of stone altars stained with blood and dungeons blacker than the Darkness itself. If it didn't interfere with the Ironteeth legion, Manon didn't particularly care. Let these men play at being gods.

Usually though, especially in these wretched meetings, the duke's attention was fixed upon the beautiful, raven-haired woman who was never far from his side, as though tethered to him by an invisible chain.

It was to her that Manon now looked while the duke pointed out the areas on the map he wanted Ironteeth scouts to survey. Kaltain—that was her name.

She never said anything, never looked at anyone. A dark collar was clasped around her moon-white throat, a collar that made Manon keep her distance. Such a *wrong* scent around all these people. Human, but also not human. And on this woman, the scent was strongest and strangest. Like the dark, forgotten places of the world. Like tilled soil in a graveyard.

"By next week I want reports on what the wild men of the Fangs are up to," the duke said. His well-groomed rust-colored mustache seemed so at odds with his dark, brutal armor. A man equally comfortable battling in council rooms or on killing fields.

"Anything in particular to look for?" Manon said flatly, already bored. It was an honor to be Wing Leader, she reminded herself; an honor to lead the Ironteeth host. Even if being here felt like a punishment, and even if she hadn't yet received word from her grandmother, the High Witch of the Blackbeak Clan, about what their next move was to be. They were allies with Adarlan—not lackeys at the king's beck and call.

The duke stroked an idle hand down Kaltain's thin arm, its white flesh marred with too many bruises to be accidental.

And then there was the thick red scar just before the dip of her elbow, two inches long, slightly raised. It had to be recent.

But the woman didn't flinch at the duke's intimate touch, didn't show a flicker of pain as his thick fingers caressed the violent scar. "I want an up-to-date list of their settlements," the duke said. "Their numbers, the major paths they use to cross the mountains. Stay invisible, and do not engage."

Manon might have tolerated everything about being stuck in Morath—except for that last order. *Do not engage.* No killing, no fighting, no bleeding men.

The council chamber had only one tall, narrow window, its view cut off by one of the many stone towers of Morath. Not enough open space in this room, not with the duke and his broken woman beside him. Manon lifted her chin and stood. "As you will it."

"Your Grace," the duke said.

Manon paused, half turning.

The duke's dark eyes weren't wholly human. "You will address me as 'Your Grace,' Wing Leader."

It was an effort to keep her iron teeth from snapping down from the slits in her gums. "You're not my duke," she said. "Nor are you *my grace.*"

Asterin had gone still.

Duke Perrington boomed out a laugh. Kaltain showed no indication that she'd heard any of it. "The White Demon," the duke mused, looking Manon over with eyes that roved too freely. Had he been anyone else, she would have gouged those eyes out with her iron nails—and let him scream for a bit before she ripped out his throat with her iron teeth. "I wonder if you won't seize the host for yourself and snatch up my empire."

"I have no use for human lands." It was the truth.

Only the Western Wastes, home of the once-glorious Witch Kingdom. But until they fought in the King of Adarlan's war, until his enemies were defeated, they would not be allowed to reclaim it. Besides, the Crochan curse that denied them true possession of the land held firm—and they were no closer to breaking it than Manon's elders had been five hundred years ago, when the last Crochan Queen damned them with her dying breath.

"And for that, I thank the gods every day." He waved a hand. "Dismissed."

Manon stared him down, again debating the merits of slaughtering him right at the table, if only to see how Kaltain would react to *that*, but Asterin shifted her foot against the stone—as good as a pointed cough.

So Manon turned from the duke and his silent bride and walked out.

Manon stalked down the narrow halls of Morath Keep, Asterin flanking her, Sorrel a step behind, Vesta and Lin bringing up the rear.

Through every slitted window they passed, roars and wings and shouts burst in along with the final rays of the setting sun—and beyond them, the relentless striking of hammers on steel and iron.

They passed a cluster of guards outside the entrance to the duke's private tower—one of the few places where they weren't allowed. The smells that leaked from behind the door of dark, glittering stone raked claws down Manon's spine, and she and her Second and Third kept a wary distance. Asterin even went so far as to bare her teeth at the guards posted in front of that door, her golden hair and the rough leather band she wore across her brow glinting in the torchlight.

The men didn't so much as blink, and their breathing didn't hitch. She knew their training had nothing to do with it—they had a reek to them, too.

Manon glanced over her shoulder at Vesta, who was smirking at every guard and trembling servant they passed. Her red hair, creamy skin, and black-and-gold eyes were enough to stop most men in their tracks—to keep them distracted while she used them for pleasure, and then let them bleed out for amusement. But these guards yielded no reaction to her, either.

Vesta noticed Manon's attention and lifted her auburn brows.

"Get the others," Manon ordered her. "It's time for a hunt." Vesta nodded and peeled away down a darkened hallway. She jerked her chin at Lin, who gave Manon a wicked little grin and faded into the shadows on Vesta's heels.

Manon and her Second and Third were silent as they ascended the half-crumbling tower that housed the Thirteen's private aerie. By day, their wyverns perched on the massive posts jutting out from the tower's side to get some fresh air and to watch the war camp far, far below; by night, they hauled themselves into the aerie to sleep, chained in their assigned areas.

It was far easier than locking them in the reeking cells in the belly of the mountain with the rest of the host's wyverns, where they would only rip each other to shreds and get cramps in their wings. They'd tried housing them there—just once, upon arriving. Abraxos had gone berserk and taken out half his pen, rousing the other mounts until they, too, were bucking and roaring and threatening to bring the Keep down around them. An hour later, Manon had commandeered this tower for the Thirteen. It seemed that the strange scent riled Abraxos, too.

But in the aerie, the reek of the animals was familiar, welcoming. Blood and shit and hay and leather. Hardly a whiff of that *off* smell— perhaps because they were so high up that the wind blew it away.

The straw-coated floor crunched beneath their boots, a cool breeze sweeping in from where the roof had been ripped half off thanks to Sorrel's bull. To keep the wyverns from feeling less caged—and so Abraxos could watch the stars, as he liked to do.

Manon ran an eye over the feeding troughs in the center of the chamber. None of the mounts touched the meat and grain provided by the mortal men who maintained the aerie. One of those men was laying down fresh hay, and a flash of Manon's iron teeth had him scurrying down the stairs, the tang of his fear lingering in the air like a smear of oil.

"Four weeks," Asterin said, glancing at her pale-blue wyvern, visible on her perch through one of the many open archways. "Four weeks, and no action. What are we even doing here? When will we *move?*"

Indeed, the restrictions were grating on them all. Limiting flying to nighttime to keep the host mostly undetected, the stench of these men, the stone, the forges, the winding passages of the endless Keep—they took little bites out of Manon's patience every day. Even the small mountain range in which the Keep was nestled was dense, made only of bare rock, with few signs of the spring that had now blanketed most of the land. A dead, festering place.

"We move when we're told to move," Manon said to Asterin, gazing toward the setting sun. Soon—as soon as that sun vanished over those jagged black peaks—they could take to the skies. Her stomach grumbled. "And if you're going to question orders, Asterin, then I'll be happy to replace you."

"I'm not questioning," Asterin said, holding Manon's gaze for longer than most witches dared. "But it's a waste of our skills to be sitting here like hens in a coop, at the duke's bidding. I'd like to rip open that worm's belly."

Sorrel murmured, "I would advise you, Asterin, to resist the urge." Manon's tan-skinned Third, built like a battering ram, kept her attention solely on the quick, lethal movements of her Second. The stone to Asterin's flame, ever since they'd been witchlings.

"The King of Adarlan can't steal our mounts from us. Not now," Asterin said. "Perhaps we should move deeper into the mountains and camp there, where at least the air is clean. There's no point squatting here."

Sorrel let out a warning growl, but Manon jerked her chin, a silent order to stand down as she herself stepped closer to her Second. "The last thing I need," Manon breathed in Asterin's face, "is to have that mortal swine question the suitability of my Thirteen. Keep yourself in line. And if I hear you telling your scouts any of this—"

"You think I would speak ill of you to inferiors?" A snap of iron teeth.

"I think you—and all of us—are sick of being confined to this shithole, and you have a tendency to say what you think and consider the consequences later."

Asterin had always been that way—and that wildness was exactly why Manon had chosen her as her Second a century ago. The flame to Sorrel's stone . . . and to Manon's ice.

The rest of the Thirteen began filing in as the sun vanished. They took one glance at Manon and Asterin and wisely kept away, their eyes averted. Vesta even muttered a prayer to the Three-Faced Goddess.

"I want only for the Thirteen—for all the Blackbeaks—to win glory on the battlefield," Asterin said, refusing to break Manon's stare.

"We will," Manon promised, loud enough for the others to hear. "But until then, keep yourself in check, or I'll ground you until you're worthy of riding with us again."

Asterin lowered her eyes. "Your will is mine, Wing Leader."

Coming from anyone else, even Sorrel, the honorific would have been normal, expected. Because none of them would ever have dared to cast that *tone* to it.

Manon lashed out, so fast that even Asterin couldn't retreat. Manon's hand closed around her cousin's throat, her iron nails digging into the soft skin beneath her ears. "You step one foot out of line, Asterin, and these"—Manon dug her nails in deeper as blue blood began sliding down Asterin's golden-tan neck—"find their mark."

Manon didn't care that they'd been fighting at each other's sides for a century, that Asterin was her closest relative, or that Asterin had gone to the mat again and again to defend Manon's position as heir. She'd put Asterin down the moment she became a useless nuisance. Manon let Asterin see all of that in her eyes.

Asterin's gaze flicked to the bloodred cloak Manon wore—the cloak Manon's grandmother had ordered her to take from that Crochan after Manon slit her throat, after the witch bled out on the floor of the Omega. Asterin's beautiful, wild face went cold as she said, "Understood."

Manon released her throat, flicking Asterin's blood off her nails as she turned to the Thirteen, now standing by their mounts, stiff-backed and silent. "We ride. Now."

Abraxos shifted and bobbed beneath Manon as she climbed into the saddle, well aware that one misstep off the wooden beam on which he was perched would lead to a very long, very permanent drop.

Below and to the south, countless army campfires flickered, and the smoke of the forges among them rose high in plumes that marred the starry, moonlit sky. Abraxos growled.

"I know, I know, I'm hungry, too," Manon said, blinking the lid above her eye into place as she secured the harnesses that kept her firmly in the saddle. To her left and right, Asterin and Sorrel mounted their wyverns and turned to her. Her cousin's wounds had already clotted.

Manon gazed at the unforgiving plunge straight down the side of the tower, past the jagged rocks of the mountain, and into the open air beyond. Perhaps that was why these mortal fools had insisted that every wyvern and rider make the Crossing at the Omega—so they could come to Morath and not balk at the sheer drop, even from the lowest levels of the Keep.

A chill, reeking wind brushed her face, clogging her nose. A pleading, hoarse scream broke from inside one of those hollowed-out mountains—then went silent. Time to go—if not to fill her belly, then to get away from the rot of this place for a few hours.

Manon dug her legs into Abraxos's scarred, leathery side, and his Spidersilk-reinforced wings glittered like gold in the light of the fires far below. "Fly, Abraxos," she breathed.

Abraxos sucked in a great breath, tucked his wings in tight, and *fell* off the side of the post.

He liked to do that—just tumble off as though he'd been struck dead.

Her wyvern, it seemed, had a wicked sense of humor.

The first time he'd done it, she'd roared at him. Now he did it just to show off, as the wyverns of the rest of the Thirteen had to jump up and out and then plunge, their bodies too big to nimbly navigate the narrow drop.

Manon kept her eyes open as they tumbled down, the wind battering them, Abraxos a warm mass beneath her. She liked to watch every stunned and terrified mortal face, liked to see how close Abraxos got to the stones of the tower, to the jagged, black mountain rock before—

Abraxos flung out his wings and banked hard, the world tilting and then shooting behind. He let out a fierce cry that reverberated over every stone of Morath, echoed by the shrieks of the Thirteen's mounts. On a tower's exterior stairs, a servant hauling a basket of apples cried out and dropped his burden. The apples tumbled one by one by one down the steps winding around the tower, a cascade of red and green in time to the pounding of the forges.

Then Abraxos was flapping up and away over the dark army, over the sharp peaks, the Thirteen falling smoothly into rank behind him.

It was a strange sort of thrill, to ride like this, with just her coven—a unit capable of sacking whole cities by themselves. Abraxos flew hard and fast, he and Manon both scanning the earth as they broke free from the mountains and cruised over the flat farmland before the Acanthus River.

Most humans had fled this region, or had been butchered for war or sport. But there were still a few, if you knew where to look.

On and on they flew, the sliver of a crescent moon rising higher: the Crone's Sickle. A good night for hunting, if the unkind face of the Goddess now watched over them, even though the dark of the new moon—the Crone's Shadow—was always preferred.

At least the Sickle gave off enough light to see by as Manon scanned the earth. Water—mortals liked to live near water, so she headed toward a lake she'd spotted weeks ago but hadn't yet explored.

Fast and sleek as shadows, the Thirteen soared over the night-shrouded land.

At last, moonlight dimly glinted over a small body of water, and Abraxos glided for it, down and down, until Manon could see their reflection on the flat surface, see her red cape fluttering behind her like a trail of blood.

Behind, Asterin whooped, and Manon turned to watch her Second fling her arms out and lean back in her saddle until she was lying flat on her mount's spine, her golden hair unbound and streaming. Such wild ecstasy—there was always a fierce, untamed joy when Asterin flew.

Manon occasionally wondered if her Second sometimes snuck out at night to ride in nothing but her skin, forgoing even a saddle.

Manon faced forward, frowning. Thank the Darkness that the Blackbeak Matron wasn't here to see this, or more than Asterin would be threatened. It would be Manon's own neck, too, for allowing such wildness to bloom. And being unwilling to stomp it out entirely.

Manon spied a small cottage with a fenced field. A light flickered in the window—perfect. Beyond the house, tufts of solid white gleamed, bright as snow. Even better.

Manon steered Abraxos toward the farm, toward the family that—if they were smart—had heard the booming wings and taken cover.

No children. It was an unspoken rule among the Thirteen, even if some of the other Clans had no qualms about it, especially the Yellowlegs. But men and women were fair game, if there was fun to be had.

And after her earlier encounters with the duke, with Asterin, Manon was truly in the mood for some amusement.

CHAPTER
9

After Aelin wrote the damning letter to Arobynn and sent it via one of his feral street urchins, hunger dragged her from the apartment into the gray morning. Bone-tired, she hunted down breakfast, also buying enough for lunch and dinner, and returned to the warehouse an hour later to find a large, flat box waiting on the dining table.

No sign of the lock having been tampered with, none of the windows open any farther than they'd been when she cracked them to let in the river breeze that morning.

But she expected no less from Arobynn—no less than a reminder that he might be King of the Assassins, but he'd clawed and slaughtered his way onto that self-made throne.

It seemed fitting, somehow, that the skies opened up just then, the patter and clink of the downpour washing away the too-heavy silence of the room.

Aelin tugged at the emerald silk ribbon around the cream-colored box until it dropped away. Setting aside the lid, she stared at the folded cloth within for a long moment. The note placed atop it read, *I took the liberty of having some improvements made since the last time. Go play.*

Her throat tightened, but she pulled out the full-body suit of black cloth—tight, thick, and flexible like leather, but without the sheen and suffocation. Beneath the folded suit lay a pair of boots. They'd been cleaned since the last time she'd worn them years ago, the black leather still supple and pliable, the special grooves and hidden blades as precise as ever.

She lifted the heavy sleeve of the suit to reveal the built-in gauntlets that concealed thin, vicious swords as long as her forearm.

She hadn't seen this suit, hadn't worn it, since . . . She glanced at the empty spot on the mantel. Another test—a quiet one, to see just how much she would forgive and forget, how much she would stomach to work with him.

Arobynn had paid for the suit years ago, an exorbitant fee demanded by a master tinkerer from Melisande who had crafted it by hand, built exactly to her measurements. He'd insisted his two best assassins be outfitted in the stealthy, lethal suits, so hers had been a gift, one of many he'd heaped on her as reparation for beating her to hell and then packing her off to the Red Desert to train. She and Sam had *both* taken brutal beatings for their disobedience—and yet Arobynn had made Sam pay for his suit. And then given him second-rate jobs to keep him from swiftly paying off the debt.

She set the suit back in the box and began undressing, breathing in the scent of rain on stone that wafted in through the open windows.

Oh, she could play the devoted protégée again. She could go along with the plan she'd let him create—the plan she'd modify slightly, just enough. She'd kill whoever was needed, whore herself, wreck herself, if it meant getting Aedion to safety.

Two days—just two days—until she could see him again, until she could see with her own eyes that he'd made it, that he'd survived all these years they'd been apart. And even if Aedion hated her, spat on her as Chaol had practically done . . . it would be worth it.

Naked, she stepped into the suit, the smooth, slick material whispering against her skin. Typical of Arobynn not to mention what modifications he'd made—to make it a lethal puzzle for her to sort out, if she was clever enough to survive.

She shimmied into it, careful to avoid triggering the mechanism that brought forth those hidden blades, feeling for any other concealed weapons or tricks. It was the work of another moment before the suit enveloped her completely, and she buckled her feet into the boots.

As she headed for the bedroom, she could already sense the reinforcement added to every weak spot she possessed. The specifications must have been sent months before the suit arrived, by the man who did indeed know about the knee that sometimes twanged, the body parts she favored in combat, the speed with which she moved. All of Arobynn's knowledge of her, wrapped around her in cloth and steel and darkness. She paused before the standing mirror against the far wall of the bedroom.

A second skin. Perhaps made less scandalous by the exquisite detailing, the extra padding, the pockets, the bits of armored decoration—but there was not one inch left to the imagination. She let out a low whistle. Very well, then.

She could be Celaena Sardothien again—for a little longer, until this game was finished.

She might have brooded over it more had splashing hooves and wheels halting outside the warehouse not echoed through the open windows.

She doubted Arobynn would show up so soon to gloat—no, he'd wait until he learned whether she actually went to play with the suit.

That left one other person who'd bother to come by, though she doubted Chaol would waste money on a carriage, even in the rain. Keeping away from sight, she peered out the window through the downpour, taking in the details of the nondescript carriage. No one on the rainy street to observe it—and no sign of who might be within.

Heading for the door, Aelin flicked her wrist, releasing the blade on her left arm. It made no sound as it shot free from the hidden slot in the gauntlet, the metal gleaming in the rain-dim light.

Gods, the suit was as wondrous as it'd been that first day she tried it on; the blade cutting as smoothly through the air as it had when she'd plunged it into her targets.

Her footsteps and the drumming of the rain on the warehouse roof were the only sounds as she descended the stairs, then padded between the crates piled high on the main floor.

Left arm angled to hide the blade within the folds of her cloak, she hauled open the giant rolling warehouse door to reveal the veils of rain billowing past.

A cloaked woman waited under the narrow awning, an unmarked hansom cab for hire loitering behind her on the curb. The driver was watching carefully, rain dripping off the broad rim of his hat. Not a trained eye—just looking out for the woman who'd hired him. Even in the rain, her cloak was a deep, rich gray, the fabric clean and heavy enough to suggest lots of money, despite the carriage.

The heavy hood concealed the stranger's face in shadow, but Aelin glimpsed ivory skin, dark hair, and fine velvet gloves reaching into her cloak—for a weapon?

"Start explaining," Aelin said, leaning against the door frame, "or you're rat meat."

The woman stepped back into the rain—not back, exactly, but toward the carriage, where Aelin noted the small form of a child waiting inside. Cowering.

The woman said, "I came to warn you," and pulled back her hood just enough to reveal her face.

Large, slightly uptilted green eyes, sensuous lips, sharp cheekbones, and a pert nose combined to create a rare, staggering beauty that caused men to lose all common sense.

Aelin stepped under the narrow awning and drawled, "As far as memory serves me, Lysandra, I warned *you* that if I ever saw you again, I'd kill you."

"Please," Lysandra begged.

That word—and the desperation behind it—made Aelin slide her blade back into its sheath.

In the nine years that she'd known the courtesan, never once had she heard Lysandra say please—or sound desperate for anything at all. Phrases like "thank you," "may I," or even "lovely to see you" had never been uttered by Lysandra within Aelin's hearing.

They could have been friends as easily as enemies—both of them orphaned, both found by Arobynn as children. But Arobynn had handed Lysandra over to Clarisse, his good friend and a successful brothel madam. And though Aelin had been trained for killing fields and Lysandra for bedrooms, they'd somehow grown up rivals, clawing for Arobynn's favor.

When Lysandra turned seventeen and had her Bidding, it was Arobynn who had won, using the money Aelin had given him to pay off her own debts. The courtesan had then thrown what Arobynn had done with Aelin's blood money in her face.

So Aelin had thrown something back at her: a dagger. They hadn't seen each other since.

Aelin figured she was perfectly justified in tugging back her hood to reveal her own face and saying, "It would take me less than a minute to kill you and your driver, and to make sure your little protégée in the carriage doesn't say a peep about it. She'd probably be happy to see you dead."

Lysandra stiffened. "She is not my protégée, and she is not in training."

"So she's to be used as a shield against me?" Aelin's smile was razor-sharp.

"Please—please," Lysandra said over the rain, "I need to talk to you, just for a few minutes, where it's safe."

Aelin took in the fine clothes, the hired cab, the rain splashing on the cobblestones. So typical of Arobynn to throw this at her. But she'd let him play this hand; see where it got her.

Aelin squeezed the bridge of her nose with two fingers, then lifted her head. "You know I have to kill your driver."

"No, you don't!" the man cried, scrambling to grab the reins. "I swear—swear I won't breathe a word about this place."

Aelin stalked to the hansom cab, the rain instantly soaking her cloak. The driver could report the location of the warehouse, could endanger everything, but—

Aelin peered at the rain-flecked cab permit framed by the door, illuminated by the little lantern hanging above. "Well, Kellan Oppel of sixty-three Baker Street, apartment two, I suppose you *won't* tell anyone."

White as death, the driver nodded.

Aelin yanked open the carriage door, saying to the child within, "Get out. Both of you inside, now."

"Evangeline can wait here," Lysandra whispered.

Aelin looked over her shoulder, rain splattering her face as her lips pulled back from her teeth. "If you think for one moment that I'm leaving a child alone in a hired carriage in the slums, you can go right back to the cesspit you came from." She peered into the carriage again and said to the cowering girl, "Come on, you. I won't bite."

That seemed to be enough assurance for Evangeline, who scooted closer, the lantern light gilding her tiny porcelain hand before she gripped Aelin's arm to hop from the cab. No more than eleven, she was delicately built, her red-gold hair braided back to reveal citrine eyes that gobbled up the drenched street and women before her. As stunning as her mistress— or would have been, were it not for the deep, jagged scars on both cheeks. Scars that explained the hideous, branded-out tattoo on the inside of the girl's wrist. She'd been one of Clarisse's acolytes—until she'd been marred and lost all value.

Aelin winked at Evangeline and said with a conspirator's grin as she led her through the rain, "You look like my sort of person."

Aelin propped open the rest of the windows to let the rain-cooled river breeze into the stuffy apartment. Thankfully, no one had been on the street in the minutes they'd been outside, but if Lysandra was here, she had no doubt it would get back to Arobynn.

Aelin patted the armchair before the window, smiling at the brutally scarred little girl. "This is my favorite place to sit in the whole apartment when there's a nice breeze coming through. If you want, I have a book or two that I think you'd like. Or"—she gestured to the kitchen to her right—"you might be able to find something delicious on the kitchen table—blueberry tart, I think." Lysandra was stiff, but Aelin didn't particularly give a damn as she added to Evangeline, "Your choice."

As a child in a high-end brothel, Evangeline had probably had too few choices in her short life. Lysandra's green eyes seemed to soften a bit, and Evangeline said, her voice barely audible above the patter of the rain on the roof and windows, "I would like a tart, please." A moment later, she was gone. Smart girl—to know to stay out of her mistress's way.

With Evangeline occupied, Aelin slung off her soaked cloak and used the small remaining dry section to wipe her wet face. Keeping her wrist angled in case she needed to draw the hidden blade, Aelin pointed to the couch before the unlit fire and told Lysandra, "Sit."

To her surprise, the woman obeyed—but then said, "Or you'll threaten to kill me again?"

"I don't make threats. Only promises."

The courtesan slumped against the couch cushions. "Please. How can I ever take anything that comes out of that big mouth seriously?"

"You took it seriously when I threw a dagger at your head."

Lysandra gave her a little smile. "You missed."

True—but she'd still grazed the courtesan's ear. As far as she'd been concerned, it had been deserved.

But it was a woman sitting before her—they were both women now, not the girls they'd been at seventeen. Lysandra looked her up and down. "I prefer you as a blonde."

"I'd prefer you get the hell out of my house, but that doesn't seem likely to happen anytime soon." She glanced at the street below; the cab lingered, as ordered. "Arobynn couldn't send you in one of his carriages? I thought he was paying you handsomely."

Lysandra waved her hand, the candlelight catching on a golden bracelet that barely covered a snakelike tattoo stamped on her slender wrist. "I refused his carriage. I thought it'd set the wrong tone."

Too late for that. "So he did send you, then. To warn me about what, exactly?"

"He sent me to tell you his plan. He doesn't trust messengers these days. But the warning comes from me."

An utter lie, no doubt. But that tattoo—the sigil of Clarisse's brothel, etched on the flesh of all her courtesans from the moment they were sold into her house . . . The girl in the kitchen, the driver below—they could make everything very, very difficult if she gutted Lysandra. But the dagger was tempting as she beheld that tattoo.

Not the sword—no, she wanted the intimacy of a knife, wanted to share breath with the courtesan as she ended her. Aelin asked too quietly, "Why do you still have Clarisse's sigil tattooed on you?"

Do not trust Archer, Nehemia had tried to warn her, drawing a perfect rendering of the snake in her coded message. But what about anyone else with that sigil? The Lysandra that Aelin had known years ago . . . Two-faced, lying, and conniving were among the nicer words Aelin had used to describe her.

Lysandra frowned down at it. "We don't get it stamped out until we've paid off our debts."

"The last time I saw your whoring carcass, you were weeks away from paying them off." Indeed, Arobynn had paid so much at the Bidding two years ago that Lysandra should have been free almost immediately.

The courtesan's eyes flickered. "Do you have a problem with the tattoo?"

"That piece of shit Archer Finn had one." They'd belonged to the same house, the same madam. Maybe they'd worked together in other regards, too.

Lysandra held her gaze. "Archer's dead."

"Because I gutted him," Aelin said sweetly.

Lysandra braced a hand on the back of the couch. "You—" she breathed. But then she shook her head and said softly, "Good. Good that you killed him. He was a self-serving pig."

It could be a lie to win her over. "Say your piece, and then get out."

Lysandra's sensuous mouth tightened. But she laid out Arobynn's plan to free Aedion.

It was brilliant, if Aelin felt like being honest—clever and dramatic and bold. If the King of Adarlan wanted to make a spectacle of Aedion's execution, then they would make a spectacle of his rescue. But to tell her through Lysandra, to draw in another person who might betray her or stand witness against her . . . One more reminder of how easily Aedion's fate could be sealed, should Arobynn decide to make Aelin's life a living hell.

"I know, I know," the courtesan said, taking in the cold gleam in Aelin's eyes. "You needn't remind me that you'll skin me alive if I betray you."

Aelin felt a muscle flicker in her cheek. "And the warning you came to give me?"

Lysandra shifted on the couch. "Arobynn wanted me to tell you the plans so that I might check up on you—test you, see how much you're on his side, see if you're going to betray him."

"I'd be disappointed if he didn't."

"I think . . . I think he also sent me here as an offering."

Aelin knew what she meant, but she said, "Unfortunately for you, I don't have any interest in women. Even when they're paid for."

Lysandra's nostrils flared delicately. "I think he sent me here so you could *kill me*. As a present."

"And you came to beg me to reconsider?" No wonder she'd brought the child, then. The selfish, spineless coward, to use Evangeline as a shield. To bring a child into this world of theirs.

Lysandra glanced at the knife strapped to Aelin's thigh. "Kill me if you want. Evangeline already knows what I suspect, and won't say a word."

Aelin willed her face into a mask of icy calm.

"But I did come to warn you," Lysandra went on. "He might offer you presents, might help you with this rescue, but he is having you watched—and he has his own agenda. That favor you offered him—he didn't tell me what it is, but it's likely to be a trap, in one way or another. I'd consider whether his help is worth it, and see if you can get out of it."

She wouldn't—couldn't. Not for about a dozen different reasons.

When Aelin didn't respond, Lysandra took a sharp breath. "I also came to give you this." She reached a hand into the folds of her rich indigo gown, and Aelin subtly shifted into a defensive position.

Lysandra merely pulled out a worn, faded envelope and gingerly set it on the low table before the couch. It shook the whole way down.

"This is for you. Please read it."

"So you're Arobynn's whore *and* courier now?"

The courtesan took the verbal slap. "This isn't from Arobynn. It's from Wesley." Lysandra seemed to sink into the couch, and there was such an unspeakable grief in her eyes that for a moment, Aelin believed it.

"Wesley," Aelin said. "Arobynn's bodyguard. The one who spent most of his time hating me, and the rest of it contemplating ways to kill me." The courtesan nodded. "Arobynn murdered Wesley for killing Rourke Farran."

Lysandra flinched.

Aelin glanced at the old envelope. Lysandra dropped her gaze to her hands, clutched together so tightly that her knuckles were bone-white.

Worn lines marred the envelope, but the chipped seal had yet to be broken. "Why have you been carrying a letter to me from Wesley for almost two years?"

Lysandra wouldn't look up, and her voice broke as she said, "Because I loved him very much."

Well, of all the things she'd expected Lysandra to say.

"It started off as a mistake. Arobynn would send me back to Clarisse's with him in the carriage as an escort, and at first we were just—just friends. We talked, and he expected nothing. But then . . . then Sam died, and you—" Lysandra jerked her chin at the letter, still lying unopened between them. "It's all in there. Everything Arobynn did, everything he planned. What he asked Farran to do to Sam, and what he ordered done to you. All of it. Wesley wanted you to know, because he wanted you to understand—he needed you to understand, Celaena, that he didn't know until it was too late. He tried to stop it, and did the best he could to avenge Sam. If Arobynn hadn't killed him . . . Wesley was planning to go to Endovier to get you out. He even went to the Shadow Market to find someone who knew the layout of the mines, and got a map of them. I still have it. As proof. I—I can go get it . . ."

The words slammed into her like a barrage of arrows, but she shut out the sorrow for a man she had never taken the time to consider as anything but one of Arobynn's dogs. She wouldn't put it past Arobynn to use Lysandra, to make up this entire story to get her to trust the woman. The Lysandra she'd known would have been more than happy to do it. And Aelin could have played along just to learn where it would take her, what Arobynn was up to and whether he'd trip up enough to reveal his hand, but . . .

What he asked Farran to do to Sam.

She'd always assumed Farran had just tortured Sam in the way he so loved to hurt and break people. But for Arobynn to request specific things be done to Sam . . . It was good she didn't have her magic. Good it was stifled.

Because she might have erupted into flames and burned and burned for days, cocooned in her fire.

"So you came here," Aelin said, as Lysandra discreetly wiped at her eyes with a handkerchief, "to warn me that Arobynn *might* be manipulating me, because you finally realized what a monster Arobynn truly is after he killed your lover?"

"I promised Wesley I would personally give you that letter—"

"Well, you gave it to me, so get out."

Light footsteps sounded, and Evangeline burst from the kitchen, rushing to her mistress with a quiet, nimble grace. With surprising tenderness, Lysandra slipped a reassuring arm around Evangeline as she rose to her feet. "I understand, Celaena, I do. But I am begging you: read that letter. For him."

Aelin bared her teeth. "*Get out.*"

Lysandra walked to the door, keeping herself and Evangeline a healthy distance from Aelin. She paused in the doorway. "Sam was my friend, too. He and Wesley were my only friends. And Arobynn took them both away."

Aelin just raised her brows.

Lysandra didn't bother with a good-bye as she vanished down the stairs.

But Evangeline lingered on the threshold, glancing between her disappearing mistress and Aelin, her lovely hair glimmering like liquid copper.

Then the girl gestured to her scarred face and said, "She did this to me."

It was an effort to keep seated, to keep from leaping down the stairs to slit Lysandra's throat.

But Evangeline went on, "I cried when my mother sold me to Clarisse. Cried and cried. And I think Lysandra had annoyed the mistress that day, because they gave me to her as an acolyte, even though she was weeks away from paying her debts. That night, I was supposed to begin training, and I cried so hard I made myself sick. But Lysandra—she cleaned me up. She told me that there was a way out, but it would hurt, and I would not be the same. I couldn't run, because she had tried running a few times when she was my age, and they had found her and beat her where no one could see."

She had never known—never wondered. All those times she had sneered at and mocked Lysandra while they'd grown up . . .

Evangeline continued, "I said I'd do anything to get out of what the other girls had told me about. So she told me to trust her—and then gave me these. She started shouting loud enough for the others to come running. They thought she cut me out of anger, and said she'd done it to keep me from being a threat. And she let them believe it. Clarisse was so mad that she beat Lysandra in the courtyard, but Lysandra didn't cry—not once. And when the healer said my face couldn't be fixed, Clarisse made Lysandra buy me for the amount I would have cost if I had been a full courtesan, like her."

Aelin had no words.

Evangeline said, "That's why she's still working for Clarisse, why she's still not free and won't be for a while. I thought you should know."

Aelin wanted to tell herself not to trust the girl, that this could be part of Lysandra and Arobynn's plan, but . . . but there was a voice in her head, in her bones, that whispered to her, over and over and over, each time clearer and louder:

Nehemia would have done the same.

Evangeline curtsied and went down the stairs, leaving Aelin staring at the worn envelope.

If she herself could change so much in two years, perhaps so could Lysandra.

And for a moment, she wondered how another young woman's life would have been different if she had stopped to talk to her—really *talk* to Kaltain Rompier, instead of dismissing her as a vapid courtier. What would have happened if Nehemia had tried to see past Kaltain's mask, too.

Evangeline was climbing into the rain-gleaming carriage beside Lysandra when Aelin appeared at the warehouse door and said, "Wait."

CHAPTER 10

Aedion's vision was swimming, his every breath gloriously difficult.

Soon. He could feel Death squatting in the corner of his cell, counting down the last of his breaths, a lion waiting to pounce. Every so often, Aedion would smile toward those gathered shadows.

The infection had spread, and with two days until the spectacle at which he was to be executed, his death was coming none too soon. The guards assumed he was sleeping to pass the time.

Aedion was waiting for his food, watching the small barred window in the top of the cell door for any sign of the guards' arrival. But he was fairly sure he was hallucinating when the door opened and the Crown Prince strolled in.

There were no guards behind him, no sign of any escort as the prince stared from the doorway.

The prince's unmoving face told him immediately what he needed to know: this was not a rescue attempt. And the black stone collar around the prince's throat told him everything else: things had not gone well the day Sorscha had been murdered.

He managed to grin. "Good to see you, princeling."

The prince ran an eye over Aedion's dirty hair, the beard that had grown during the past few weeks, and then over to the pile of vomit in the corner from when he hadn't been able to make it to the bucket an hour ago.

Aedion drawled as best he could, "The least you could do is take me to dinner before looking at me like that."

The prince's sapphire eyes flicked to his, and Aedion blinked past the haze covering his vision. What studied him was cold, predatory, and not quite human.

Quietly, Aedion said, "Dorian."

The thing that was now the prince smiled a little. The captain had said those rings of Wyrdstone enslaved the mind—the soul. He'd seen the collar waiting beside the king's throne, and had wondered if it was the same. Worse.

"Tell me what happened in the throne room, Dorian," Aedion wheezed, his head pounding.

The prince blinked slowly. "Nothing happened."

"Why are you here, Dorian?" Aedion had never addressed the prince by his given name, but using it, reminding him, somehow seemed important. Even if it only provoked the prince into killing him.

"I came to look at the infamous general before they execute you like an animal."

No chance of being killed today, then.

"The same way they executed your Sorscha?"

Though the prince didn't move, Aedion could have sworn he recoiled, as if someone yanked on a leash, as if there was still someone in *need* of leashing.

"I don't know what you're talking about," the thing inside the prince said. But its nostrils flared.

"Sorscha," Aedion breathed, his lungs aching. "Sorscha—your woman, the healer. I was standing beside you when they cut off her head. I heard you screaming as you dove for her body." The thing went a bit rigid, and Aedion pressed, "Where did they bury her, Dorian? What did they do with her body, the body of the woman you loved?"

"I don't know what you're talking about," it said again.

"Sorscha," Aedion panted, his breathing uneven. "Her name was Sorscha, and she loved you—and they killed her. The man who put that collar around your neck killed her."

The thing was quiet. Then it tilted its head. The smile it gave him was horrifying in its beauty. "I shall enjoy watching you die, General."

Aedion coughed out a laugh. The prince—the thing he'd become—turned smoothly and strode out. And Aedion might have laughed again, for spite and defiance, had he not heard the prince say to someone in the hall, "The general is sick. See to it that he's attended to immediately."

No.

The thing must have smelled it on him.

Aedion could do nothing as a healer was summoned—an older woman named Amithy—and he was held down, too weak to fight back as she attended his wounds. She shoved a tonic down his throat that made him choke; his wound was washed and bound, and his shackles were shortened until he couldn't move his hands enough to rip out the stitching. The tonics kept coming, every hour, no matter how hard he bit, no matter how forcefully he tried to clamp his mouth shut.

So they saved him, and Aedion cursed and swore at Death for failing him, even as he silently prayed to Mala Light-Bringer to keep Aelin away from the party, away from the prince, and away from the king and his Wyrdstone collars.

The thing inside him left the dungeons and headed into the glass castle, steering his body like a ship. And now it forced him to be still as they stood before the man he often saw in those moments that pierced through the darkness.

The man was seated on a glass throne, smiling faintly as he said, "Bow."

The thing inside him yanked hard on their bond, lightning spearing his muscles, ordering them to obey. It was how he'd been forced to descend into those dungeons, where that golden-haired warrior had said her name—said her name so many times that he began screaming, even if he made no sound. He was still screaming as his muscles betrayed him yet again, bringing him to his knees, the tendons on his neck lashing with pain, forcing him to bow his head.

"Still resisting?" the man said, glancing at the dark ring on his finger as though it possessed the answer already. "I can feel both of you in there. Interesting."

Yes—that thing in the darkness was growing stronger, now able to reach through the invisible wall between them and puppet him, speak through him. But not entirely, not for long amounts of time. He patched up the holes as best he could, but it kept breaking through.

Demon. A demon prince.

And he saw that moment—over and over and over—when the woman he'd loved had lost her head. Hearing her name on the general's raspy tongue had made him start whaling on the other wall in his mind, the barrier that kept him locked in the dark. But the darkness in his mind was a sealed tomb.

The man on the throne said, "Report."

The command shuddered through him, and he spit out the details of his encounter, every word and action. And the thing—the *demon*—delighted in his horror at it.

"Clever of Aedion to try to quietly die on me," the man said. "He must think his cousin has a good chance of arriving at your party, then, if he's so desperate to rob us of our entertainment."

He kept silent, as he had not been instructed to speak. The man looked him over, those black eyes full of delight. "I should have done this years ago. I don't know why I wasted so much time waiting to see whether you'd have any power. Foolish of me."

He tried to speak, tried to move, tried to do anything with that mortal body of his. But the demon gripped his mind like a fist, and the muscles of his face slid into a smile as he said, "It is my pleasure to serve, Majesty."

CHAPTER
11

The Shadow Market had operated along the banks of the Avery for as long as Rifthold had existed. Maybe longer. Legend claimed it had been built on the bones of the god of truth so that it would keep the vendors and would-be thieves honest. Chaol supposed it was ironic, considering there was no god of truth. As far as he knew. Contraband, illicit substances, spices, clothes, flesh: the market catered to any and all clientele, if they were brave or foolish or desperate enough to venture inside.

When he'd first come here weeks ago, Chaol had been all of those things as he climbed down the half-rotted wooden stairs from a crumbling section of the docks into the embankment itself, where alcoves and tunnels and shops were tunneled into the riverbank.

Cloaked, armed figures patrolled the long, broad quay that served as the only path to the market. During rainy periods, the Avery would often rise high enough to flood the quay, and sometimes unlucky merchants and shoppers drowned inside the labyrinth of the Shadow Market. During drier months, you never knew what or who you might find selling their wares or meandering through the dirty, damp tunnels.

The market was packed tonight, even after a day of rain. A small relief. And another small relief as thunder reverberated through the subterranean warren, setting everyone murmuring. The vendors and lowlifes would be too busy preparing for the storm to take notice of Chaol and Nesryn as they strode down one of the main passageways.

The thunder rattled the hanging lanterns of colored glass—strangely beautiful, as if someone had once been determined to give this place some loveliness—that served as the main lights in the brown caverns, casting plenty of those shadows the market was so notorious for. Shadows for dark dealings, shadows to slip a knife between the ribs or to spirit someone away.

Or for conspirators to meet.

No one had bothered them as they'd slipped through one of the rough holes that served as an entrance to the Shadow Market's tunnels. They connected to the sewers somewhere—and he would bet that the more established vendors possessed their own secret exits beneath their stalls or shops. Vendor after vendor had set up stalls of wood or stone, with some wares displayed on tables or crates or in baskets, but most valuable goods hidden. A spice dealer offered everything from saffron to cinnamon—but even the most fragrant spices couldn't conceal the cloyingly sweet stench of the opium stashed beneath his displays.

Once, long ago, Chaol might have cared about the illegal substances, about the vendors selling whatever they pleased. He might have bothered to try to shut this place down.

Now, they were nothing but resources. As a city guard, Nesryn probably felt the same way. Even if, just by being in here, she was jeopardizing her own safety. This was a neutral zone—but its denizens didn't take kindly to authority.

He didn't blame them. The Shadow Market had been one of the first places the King of Adarlan had purged after magic vanished, seeking out vendors who claimed to have banned books or still-working charms and potions, as well as magic-wielders desperate for a cure or a glimmer of magic. The punishments hadn't been pretty.

Chaol almost heaved a sigh of relief when he spotted the two cloaked figures with a spread of knives for sale at a makeshift stand tucked into a dark corner. Exactly where they'd planned, and they'd done a hell of a job making it look authentic.

Nesryn slowed her steps, pausing at various vendors, no more than a bored shopper killing time until the rain ceased. Chaol kept close to her, his weapons and prowling gait enough to deter any foolish pickpockets from trying their luck. The punch he'd taken to his ribs earlier that night made maintaining his crawling pace and scowl all the easier.

He and a few others had interrupted a Valg commander in the midst of dragging a young man into the tunnels. And Chaol had been so damn distracted by Dorian, by what Aelin had said and done, that he'd been sloppy. So he'd earned that blow to the ribs, and the painful reminder of it each time he drew breath. No distractions; no slip-ups. Not when there was so much to do.

At last, Chaol and Nesryn paused by the little stall, staring down at the dozen knives and short swords displayed across the threadbare blanket.

"This place is even more depraved than the rumors suggested," Brullo said from the shadows of his hood. "I feel like I should cover poor Ress's eyes in half these chambers."

Ress chuckled. "I'm nineteen, old man. Nothing here surprises me." Ress glanced at Nesryn, who was fingering one of the curved blades. "Apologies, Lady—"

"I'm twenty-two," she said flatly. "And I think we city guards see a great deal more than you palace princesses."

What Chaol could see of Ress's face flushed. He could have sworn even Brullo was smiling. And for a moment, he couldn't breathe under the crushing weight that pushed in on him. There had been a time when this teasing was normal, when he'd sat in public with his men and laughed.

When he hadn't been two days away from unleashing hell on the castle that had once been his home.

"Any news?" he managed to say to Brullo, who was watching him too closely, as if his old mentor could see the agony ripping through him.

"We got the layout of the party this morning," Brullo said tightly. Chaol picked up a blade as Brullo reached into the pocket of his cloak. He made a good show of examining the dagger, then holding up a few fingers as if haggling for it. Brullo went on, "The new Captain of the Guard spread us all out—none of us in the Great Hall itself." The Weapons Master held up his own fingers, leaning forward, and Chaol shrugged, reaching into his cloak for the coins.

"You think he suspects anything?" Chaol said, handing over the coins. Nesryn closed in, blocking any outside view as Chaol's hand met Brullo's and coppers crunched against paper. The small, folded maps were in Chaol's pocket before anyone noticed.

"No," Ress answered. "The bastard just wants to demean us. He probably thinks some of us are loyal to you, but we'd be dead if he suspected any of us in particular."

"Be careful," Chaol said.

He sensed Nesryn tensing a heartbeat before another female voice drawled, "Three coppers for a Xandrian blade. If I'd known there was a sale happening, I would have brought more money."

Every muscle in Chaol's body locked up as he discovered Aelin now standing at Nesryn's side. Of course. Of course she'd tracked them here.

"Holy gods," Ress breathed.

Beneath the shadows of her dark hood, Aelin's grin was nothing short of wicked. "Hello, Ress. Brullo. Sorry to see your palace jobs aren't paying you enough these days."

The Weapons Master was glancing between her and the passageways. "You didn't say she was back," he said to Chaol.

Aelin clicked her tongue. "Chaol, it seems, likes to keep information to himself."

He clenched his fists at his sides. "You're drawing too much attention to us."

"Am I?" Aelin lifted a dagger, weighing it in her hands with expert ease. "I need to talk to Brullo and my old friend Ress. Since you refused to let me come the other night, this was the only way."

So typical of her. Nesryn had taken a casual step away, monitoring the carved tunnels. Or avoiding the queen.

Queen. The word struck him again. A queen of the realm was in the Shadow Market, in head-to-toe black, and looking more than happy to start slitting throats. He hadn't been wrong to fear her reunion with Aedion—what they might do together. And if she had her magic . . .

"Take off your hood," Brullo said quietly. Aelin looked up.

"Why, and no."

"I want to see your face."

Aelin went still.

But Nesryn turned back and leaned a hand on the table. "I saw her face last night, Brullo, and it's as pretty as before. Don't you have a wife to ogle, anyway?"

Aelin snorted. "I think I rather like you, Nesryn Faliq."

Nesryn gave Aelin a half smile. Practically beaming, coming from her.

Chaol wondered whether Aelin would like Nesryn if she knew about their history. Or whether the queen would even care.

Aelin tugged back her hood only far enough for the light to hit her face. She winked at Ress, who grinned. "I missed you, friend," she said. Color stained Ress's cheeks.

Brullo's mouth tightened as Aelin looked at him again. For a moment, the Weapons Master studied her. Then he murmured, "I see." The queen stiffened almost imperceptibly. Brullo bowed his head, ever so slightly. "You're going to rescue Aedion."

Aelin pulled her hood into place and inclined her head in confirmation, the swaggering assassin incarnate. "I am."

Ress swore filthily under his breath.

Aelin leaned closer to Brullo. "I know I'm asking a great deal of you—"

"Then don't ask it," Chaol snapped. "Don't endanger them. They risk enough."

"That's not your call to make," she said.

Like hell it wasn't. "If they're discovered, we lose our inside source of information. Not to mention their lives. What do you plan to do about Dorian? Or is it only Aedion you care about?"

They were all watching far too closely.

Her nostrils flared. But Brullo said, "What is it you require of us, Lady?"

Oh, the Weapons Master definitely knew, then. He must have seen Aedion recently enough to have recognized those eyes, that face and coloring, the moment she pulled back her hood. Perhaps he had suspected it for months now. Aelin said softly, "Don't let your men be stationed at the southern wall of the gardens."

Chaol blinked. Not a request or an order—but a warning.

Brullo's voice was slightly hoarse as he said, "Anywhere else we should avoid?"

She was already backing away, shaking her head as if she were a disinterested buyer. "Just tell your men to pin a red flower on their uniforms. If anyone asks, say it's to honor the prince on his birthday. But wear them where they can easily be seen."

Chaol glanced at her hands. Her dark gloves were clean. How much blood would stain them in a few days? Ress loosed a breath and said to her, "Thank you."

It wasn't until she'd vanished into the crowd with a jaunty swagger that Chaol realized thanks were indeed in order.

Aelin Galathynius was about to turn the glass palace into a killing field, and Ress, Brullo, and his men had all been spared.

She still hadn't said anything about Dorian. About whether *he* would be spared. Or saved.

Aelin had known she had eyes on her from the moment she'd left the Shadow Market after finishing some shopping of her own. She strode right into the Royal Bank of Adarlan anyway.

She had business to attend to, and though they'd been minutes away from closing for the day, the Master of the Bank had been more than happy to assist her with her inquiries. He never once questioned the fake name her accounts were under.

As the Master talked about her various accounts and the interest they'd gathered over the years, she took in the details of his office: thick, oak-paneled walls, pictures that had revealed no hidey-holes in the bare minute she'd had to snoop while he summoned his secretary to bring in tea, and ornate furniture that cost more than most citizens of Rifthold made in a lifetime, including a gorgeous mahogany armoire where many of his wealthiest clients' files—including hers—were kept, locked up with a little gold key he kept on his desk.

She'd risen as he again scuttled through the double doors of his office to withdraw the sum of money she would take with her that night. While he was in the anteroom, giving the order to his secretary, Aelin had casually made her way over to his desk, surveying the papers stacked and strewn about, the various gifts from clients, keys, and a little portrait of a woman who could be either a wife or a daughter. With men like him, it was impossible to tell.

He'd returned just as she casually slid a hand into the pocket of her cloak. She made small talk about the weather until the secretary appeared, a little box in hand. Dumping the contents into her coin purse with as much grace as she could muster, Aelin had thanked the secretary and the Master and breezed out of the office.

She took side streets and alleys, ignoring the stench of rotting flesh that even the rain couldn't conceal. Two—she'd counted *two* butchering blocks in once-pleasant city squares.

The bodies left for the crows had been mere shadows against the pale stone walls where they'd been nailed.

Aelin wouldn't risk capturing one of the Valg until after Aedion was saved—if she made it out alive—but that didn't mean she couldn't get a head start on it.

⌒

A chill fog had blanketed the world the night before, seeping in through every nook and cranny. Nestled under layers of quilts and down blankets, Aelin rolled over in bed and stretched a hand across the mattress, reaching lazily for the warm male body beside hers.

Cold, silken sheets slid against her fingers.

She opened an eye.

This wasn't Wendlyn. The luxurious bed bedecked in shades of cream and beige belonged to her apartment in Rifthold. And the other half of the bed was neatly made, its pillows and blankets undisturbed. Empty.

For a moment, she could see Rowan there—that harsh, unforgiving face softened into handsomeness by sleep, his silver hair glimmering in the morning light, so stark against the tattoo stretching from his left temple down his neck, over his shoulder, all the way to his fingertips.

Aelin loosed a tight breath, rubbing her eyes. Dreaming was bad enough. She would not waste energy missing him, wishing he were here to talk everything through, or to just have the comfort of waking up beside him and knowing he existed.

She swallowed hard, her body too heavy as she rose from the bed.

She had told herself once that it wasn't a weakness to need Rowan's help, to *want* his help, and that perhaps there was a kind of strength in acknowledging that, but . . . He wasn't a crutch, and she never wanted him to become one.

Still, as she downed her cold breakfast, she wished she hadn't felt such a strong need to prove that to herself weeks ago.

Especially when word arrived via urchin banging on the warehouse door that she'd been summoned to the Assassins' Keep. Immediately.

CHAPTER 12

An emotionless guard delivered the duke's summons, and Manon—who had been about to take Abraxos for a solo ride—ground her teeth for a good five minutes as she paced the aerie floor.

She was not a dog to be called for, and neither were her witches. Humans were for sport and blood and the occasional, very rare siring of witchlings. Never commanders; never superiors.

Manon stormed down from the aerie, and as she hit the base of the tower stairs, Asterin fell into step behind her. "I was just coming to get you," her Second murmured, her golden braid bouncing. "The duke—"

"I know what the duke wants," Manon snapped, her iron teeth out.

Asterin lifted an eyebrow, but kept silent.

Manon checked her growing inclination to start eviscerating. The duke summoned her endlessly for meetings with the tall, thin man who called himself Vernon and who looked at Manon with not nearly enough fear and respect. She could hardly get in a few hours of training with the Thirteen, let alone be airborne for long periods of time, without being called for.

She breathed in through her nose and out her mouth, again and again, until she could retract her teeth and nails.

Not a dog, but not a brash fool, either. She was Wing Leader, and had been heir of the Clan for a hundred years. She could handle this mortal pig who would be worm food in a few decades—and then she could return to her glorious, wicked, immortal existence.

Manon flung open the doors to the duke's council room, earning her a glance from the guards posted outside—a glance that held no reaction, no emotion. Human in shape, but nothing more.

The duke was studying a giant map spread across his table, his companion or advisor or jester, Lord Vernon Lochan, standing at his side. Down a few seats, staring at the dark glass surface, sat Kaltain, unmoving save for the flutter of her white throat as she breathed. The brutal scar on her arm had somehow darkened into a purplish red. Fascinating.

"What do you want?" Manon demanded.

Asterin took up her place by the door, arms crossed.

The duke pointed to the chair across from him. "We have matters to discuss."

Manon remained standing. "My mount is hungry, and so am I. I suggest telling me swiftly, so I can get on with my hunt."

Lord Vernon, dark-haired, slim as a reed, and clothed in a bright-blue tunic that was far too clean, looked Manon over. Manon bared her teeth at him in silent warning. Vernon just smiled and said, "What's wrong with the food we provide, Lady?"

Manon's iron teeth slid down. "I don't eat food made by mortals. And neither does my mount."

The duke at last lifted his head. "Had I known you would be so picky, I would have asked for the Yellowlegs heir to be made Wing Leader."

Manon casually flicked her nails out. "I think you would find Iskra Yellowlegs to be an undisciplined, difficult, and useless Wing Leader."

Vernon slid into a chair. "I've heard about the rivalry between Witch Clans. Got something against the Yellowlegs, Manon?"

Asterin let out a low growl at the informal address.

"You mortals have your rabble," Manon said. "We have the Yellowlegs."

"What an elitist," Vernon muttered to the duke, who snorted.

A line of cold flame went down Manon's spine. "You have five minutes, duke."

Perrington rapped his knuckles on the glass table. "We are to begin . . . experimenting. As we look to the future, we need to expand our numbers—to improve the soldiers we already have. You witches, with your history, allow us the chance to do just that."

"Explain."

"I am not in the business of explaining every last detail of my plans," the duke said. "All I need you to do is give me a Blackbeak coven under your command to test."

"Test *how?*"

"To determine whether they are compatible for breeding with our allies from another realm—the Valg."

Everything stopped. The man had to be mad, but—

"Not breed as humans do, of course. It would be an easy, relatively painless procedure—a bit of stone sewn just beneath the belly button. The stone allows them in, you see. And a child born of Valg and witch blood-lines . . . You can understand what an investment that would be. You witches value your offspring so ardently."

Both men were smiling blandly, waiting for her acceptance.

The Valg—the demons that had bred with the Fae to create the witches—somehow returned, and in contact with the duke and the king . . . She shut down the questions. "You have thousands of humans here. Use them."

"Most are not innately gifted with magic and compatible with the Valg, as you witches are. And only witches have Valg blood already flowing in their veins."

Did her grandmother know of this? "We are to be your army, not your whores," Manon said with lethal quiet. Asterin came up to her side, her face tight and pale.

"Pick a coven of Blackbeaks," was the duke's only reply. "I want them ready in a week. Interfere with this, Wing Leader, and I'll make dog meat of your precious mount. Perhaps do the same for your Thirteen."

"You touch Abraxos, and I'll peel the skin from your bones."

The duke went back to his map and waved a hand. "Dismissed. Oh—and go down to the aerial blacksmith. He sent word that your latest batch of blades are ready for inspection."

Manon stood there, calculating the weight of the black glass table—if she could flip it over and use the shards to slowly, deeply cut up both men.

Vernon flicked his brows up in a silent, taunting move, and it was enough to send Manon turning away—out the door before she could do something truly stupid.

They were halfway to her room when Asterin said, "What are you going to do?"

Manon didn't know. And she couldn't ask her grandmother, not without looking unsure or incapable of following orders. "I'll figure it out."

"But you're not going to give a Blackbeak Coven over to him for this—this breeding."

"I don't know." Maybe it wouldn't be bad—to join their bloodline with the Valg. Maybe it'd make their forces stronger. Maybe the Valg would know how to break the Crochan curse.

Asterin grabbed her by the elbow, nails digging in. Manon blinked at the touch, at the outright *demand* in it. Never before had Asterin even come *close* to—

"You cannot allow this to happen," Asterin said.

"I've had enough of orders for one day. You give me another, and you'll find your tongue on the floor."

Asterin's face went splotchy. "Witchlings are sacred—*sacred*, Manon. We do not give them away, not even to other Clans."

It was true. Witchlings were so rare, and all of them female, as a gift from the Three-Faced Goddess. They were sacred from the moment the mother showed the first signs of pregnancy to when they came of age at sixteen. To harm a pregnant witch, to harm her unborn witchling or her daughter, was a breach of code so profound that there was no amount of suffering that could be inflicted upon the perpetrator to match the hein-ousness of the crime. Manon herself had participated in the long, long executions twice now, and the punishment had never seemed enough.

Human children didn't count—human children were as good as veal to some of the Clans. Especially the Yellowlegs. But witchlings . . . there was no greater pride than to bear a witch-child for your Clan; and no greater shame than to lose one.

Asterin said, "What coven would you pick?"

"I haven't decided." Perhaps she'd pick a lesser coven—just in case—before allowing a more powerful one to join with the Valg. Maybe the demons would give their dying race the shot of vitality they had so desper-ately needed for the past few decades. Centuries.

"And if they object?"

Manon hit the stairs to her personal tower. "The only person who objects to anything these days, Asterin, is you."

"It's not right—"

Manon sliced out with a hand, tearing through the fabric and skin right above Asterin's breasts. "I'm replacing you with Sorrel."

Asterin didn't touch the blood pooling down her tunic.

Manon began walking again. "I warned you the other day to stand down, and since you've chosen to ignore me, I have no use for you in those meetings, or at my back." Never—not once in the past hundred years—had she changed their rankings. "As of right now, you are Third. Should you prove yourself to possess a shred of control, I'll reconsider."

"Lady," Asterin said softly.

Manon pointed to the stairs behind. "You get to be the one to tell the others. *Now.*"

"Manon," Asterin said, a plea in her voice that Manon had never heard before.

Manon kept walking, her red cloak stifling in the stairwell. She did not particularly care to hear what Asterin had to say—not when her grandmother had made it clear that any step out of line, any disobedience, would earn them all a brutal and swift execution. The cloak around her would never allow her to forget it.

"I'll see you at the aerie in an hour," Manon said, not bothering to look back as she entered her tower.

And smelled a human inside.

The young servant knelt before the fireplace, a brush and dustpan in her hands. She was trembling only slightly, but the tang of her fear had already coated the room. She'd likely been panicked from the moment she'd set foot inside the chamber.

The girl ducked her head, her sheet of midnight hair sliding over her pale face—but not before Manon caught the flash of assessment in her dark eyes.

"What are you doing in here?" Manon said flatly, her iron nails clicking against each other—just to see what the girl would do.

"C-c-cleaning," the girl stammered—too brokenly, too perfectly. Subservient, docile, and terrified, exactly the way the witches preferred. Only the scent of fear was real.

Manon retracted her iron teeth.

The servant eased to her feet, wincing in pain. She shifted enough that the threadbare, homespun skirts of her dress swayed, revealing a thick chain between her ankles. The right ankle was mangled, her foot twisted on its side, glossy with scar tissue.

Manon hid her predator's smile. "Why would they give me a cripple for a servant?"

"I-I only follow orders." The voice was watery, unremarkable.

Manon snorted and headed for the nightstand, her braid and bloodred cloak flowing behind her. Slowly, listening, she poured herself some water.

The servant gathered her supplies quickly and deftly. "I can come back when it won't disturb you, Lady."

"Do your work, mortal, and then be gone." Manon turned to watch the girl finish.

The servant limped through the room, meek and breakable and unworthy of a second glance.

"Who did that to your leg?" Manon asked, leaning against the bedpost.

The servant didn't even lift her head. "It was an accident." She gathered the ashes into the pail she'd lugged up here. "I fell down a flight of stairs when I was eight, and there was nothing to be done. My uncle didn't trust healers enough to let them into our home. I was lucky to keep it."

"Why the chains?" Another flat, bored question.

"So I couldn't ever run away."

"You would never have gotten far in these mountains, anyway."

There—the slight stiffening in her thin shoulders, the valiant effort to hide it.

"Yes," the girl said, "but I grew up in Perranth, not here." She stacked the logs she must have hauled in, limping more with every step. The trek down—hauling the heavy pail of ashes—would be another misery, no doubt. "If you have need of me, just call for Elide. The guards will know where to find me."

Manon watched every single limping step she took toward the door.

Manon almost let her out, let her think she was free, before she said, "No one ever punished your uncle for his stupidity about healers?"

Elide looked over her shoulder. "He's Lord of Perranth. No one could."

"Vernon Lochan is your uncle." Elide nodded. Manon cocked her head, assessing that gentle demeanor, so carefully constructed. "Why did your uncle come here?"

"I don't know," Elide breathed.

"Why bring *you* here?"

"I don't know," she said again, setting down the pail. She shifted, leaning her weight onto her good leg.

Manon said too softly, "And who assigned you to this room?"

She almost laughed when the girl's shoulders curved in, when she lowered her head farther. "I'm not—not a spy. I swear it on my life."

"Your life means nothing to me," Manon said, pushing off the bedpost and prowling closer. The servant held her ground, so convincing in her role of submissive human. Manon poked an iron-tipped nail beneath Elide's chin, tilting her head up. "If I catch you spying on me, Elide Lochan, you'll find yourself with *two* useless legs."

The stench of her fear stuffed itself down Manon's nose. "My lady, I—I swear I won't t-touch—"

"Leave." Manon sliced her nail underneath Elide's chin, leaving a trickle of blood in its wake. And just because, Manon pulled back and sucked Elide's blood off her iron nail.

It was an effort to keep her face blank as she tasted the blood. The truth it told.

But Elide had seen enough, it seemed, and the first round of their game was over. Manon let the girl limp out, that heavy chain clinking after her.

Manon stared at the empty doorway.

It had been amusing, at first, to let the girl think Manon had been fooled by her cowering, sweet-tongued, harmless act. Then Elide's heritage had been revealed—and Manon's every predatory instinct had kicked in as she monitored the way the girl hid her face so her reactions would be veiled, the way she told Manon what she wanted to hear. As though she was feeling out a potential enemy.

The girl might still be a spy, Manon told herself, turning toward the desk, where Elide's scent was strongest.

Sure enough, the sprawling map of the continent held traces of Elide's cinnamon-and-elderberries scent in concentrated spots. Fingerprints.

A spy for Vernon, or one with her own agenda? Manon had no idea.

But anyone with witch-blood in their veins was worth keeping an eye on.

Or Thirteen.

The smoke of countless forges stung Manon's eyes enough that she blinked her clear eyelid into place upon landing in the heart of the war camp to the sound of pounding hammers and crackling flames. Abraxos hissed, pacing in a tight circle that set the dark-armored soldiers who'd spotted her landing on edge. They found another place to be when Sorrel landed in the mud beside Manon a moment later, her bull snarling at the nearest group of onlookers.

Abraxos let out a snarl of his own, directed at Sorrel's mount, and Manon gave him a sharp nudge with her heels before dismounting. "No fighting," she growled at him, taking in the little clearing amid the roughly built shelters for the blacksmiths. The clearing was reserved for the wyvern riders, complete with deeply rooted posts around its perimeter to tie their mounts. Manon didn't bother, though Sorrel tied up hers, not trusting the creature.

Having Sorrel in Asterin's position was . . . strange. As if the balance of the world had shifted to one side. Even now, their wyverns were skittish around each other, though neither male had yet launched into outright combat. Abraxos usually made space for Asterin's sky-blue female—even brushed up against her.

Manon didn't wait for Sorrel to wrangle her bull before striding into the blacksmith's lair, the building little more than a sprawl of wooden posts and a makeshift roof. The forges—sleeping giants of stone—provided the light, and around them men hammered and heaved and shoveled and honed.

The aerial blacksmith was already waiting just past the first post, gesturing to them with a scarred, red hand. On the table before the muscled, middle-aged man lay an array of blades—Adarlanian steel, glossy from polishing. Sorrel remained beside Manon as she paused before the spread, picked up a dagger, and weighed it in her hands.

"Lighter," Manon said to the blacksmith, who watched her with dark, keen eyes. She plucked up another dagger, then a sword, weighing them as well. "I need lighter weapons for the covens."

The blacksmith's eyes narrowed slightly, but he picked up the sword she'd set down and weighed it as she had. He cocked his head, tapping at the decorated hilt and shaking his head.

"I don't care whether it's pretty," Manon said. "There's only one end that matters to me. Cut down on the frills and maybe you'll shave off some weight."

He glanced to where Wind-Cleaver peeked over her back, its hilt dull and ordinary. But she'd seen him admire the blade itself—the real masterpiece—when they met the other week.

"Only you mortals care whether the blade looks good," she said. His eyes flashed, and she wondered whether he would have told her off—if he'd had the tongue to do so. Asterin, through whatever way she charmed or terrified people into yielding information, had learned that the man's tongue had been cut out by one of the generals here, to keep him from spilling their secrets. He must not be able to write or read, then. Manon wondered what other things they held against him—maybe a family—to keep such a skilled man their prisoner.

Perhaps it was because of that, but she said, "The wyverns will be bearing enough weight during battle. Between our armor, weapons, supplies, and the wyverns' armor, we need to find places to lighten the load. Or else they won't stay airborne for long."

The blacksmith braced his hands on his hips, studying the weapons he'd made, and held up a hand to motion her to wait while he hurried deeper into the maze of fire and molten ore and anvils.

The strike and clang of metal on metal was the only sound as Sorrel weighed one of the blades herself. "You know I support any decision you make," she said. Sorrel's brown hair was pulled tightly back, her tan face— probably pretty for mortals—steady and solid as ever. "But Asterin . . ."

Manon stifled a sigh. The Thirteen hadn't dared show any reaction when Manon had taken Sorrel for this visit before the hunt. Vesta had kept close to Asterin in the aerie, though—out of solidarity or silent outrage, Manon didn't know. But Asterin had met Manon's stare and nodded—gravely, but she had nodded.

"Do you not want to be Second?" Manon said.

"It is an honor to be your Second," Sorrel said, her rough voice cutting through the hammers and fires. "But it was also an honor to be your Third. You know Asterin toes a fine line with wildness on a good day. Stuff her in this castle, tell her she can't kill or maim or hunt, tell her to keep away from the men . . . She's bound to be on edge."

"We're all on edge." Manon had told the Thirteen about Elide—and wondered if the girl's keen eyes would notice that she now had a coven of witches sniffing after her.

Sorrel heaved a breath, her powerful shoulders lifting. She set down the dagger. "At the Omega, we knew our place and what was expected of us. We had a routine; we had purpose. Before that, we hunted the Crochans. Here, we are no more than weapons waiting to be used." She gestured to the useless blades on the table. "Here, your grandmother is not around to . . . influence things. To provide strict rules; to instill fear. She would make that duke's life a living hell."

"Are you saying that I'm a poor leader, Sorrel?" A too-quiet question.

"I'm saying the Thirteen know why your grandmother made you kill the Crochan for that cloak." Dangerous—such dangerous ground.

"I think you sometimes forget what my grandmother can do."

"Trust me, Manon, we don't," Sorrel said softly as the blacksmith appeared, a set of blades in his powerful arms. "And more than any of us, Asterin has never for a second forgotten what your grandmother is capable of."

Manon knew she could demand more answers—but she also knew that Sorrel was stone, and stone would not break. So she faced the approaching blacksmith as he laid his other examples on the table, her stomach tight.

With hunger, she told herself. With hunger.

CHAPTER 13

Aelin didn't know whether she should be comforted by the fact that despite the changes two years had heaped upon her life, despite the hells she'd walked through, the Assassins' Keep hadn't altered. The hedges flanking the towering wrought-iron fence around the property were the exact same height, still trimmed with masterful precision; the curving gravel drive beyond still bore the same gray stones; and the sweeping manor home was still pale and elegant, its polished oak doors gleaming in the midmorning sunlight.

No one on the quiet residential street paused to look at the house that held some of the fiercest assassins in Erilea. For years now, the Assassins' Keep had remained anonymous, unremarkable, one of many palatial homes in a wealthy southwestern district of Rifthold. Right under the King of Adarlan's nose.

The iron gates were open, and the assassins disguised as common watchmen were unfamiliar to her as she strolled down the drive. But they didn't stop her, despite the suit and weapons she wore, despite the hood covering her features.

Night would have been better for sneaking across the city. Another test—to see if she could make it here in daylight without attracting too much attention. Thankfully, most of the city was preoccupied with preparations for the prince's birthday celebrations the next day: vendors were already out, selling everything from little cakes to flags bearing the Adarlanian wyvern to blue ribbons (to match the prince's eyes, of course). It made her stomach turn.

Getting here undetected had been a minor test, though, compared to the one looming before her. And the one waiting tomorrow.

Aedion—every breath she took seemed to echo his name. *Aedion, Aedion, Aedion.*

But she shoved away the thought of him—of what might have already been done to him in those dungeons—as she strode up the expansive front steps of the Keep.

She hadn't been in this house since the night everything had gone to hell.

There, to her right, were the stables where she'd knocked Wesley unconscious as he tried to warn her about the trap that had been laid for her. And there, a level up, looking out over the front garden, were the three windows of her old bedroom. They were open, the heavy velvet curtains blowing in the cool spring breeze, as if the room were being aired out for her. Unless Arobynn had given her quarters to someone else.

The carved oak doors swung open as she hit the top step, revealing a butler she'd never seen before, who bowed nonetheless and gestured behind him. Just past the grand marble foyer, the double doors of Arobynn's study were open wide.

She didn't glance at the threshold as she passed over it, sweeping into the house that had been a haven and a prison and a hellhole.

Gods, this house. Beneath the vaulted ceilings and glass chandeliers of the entry hall, the marble floors were polished so brightly that she could see her own dark reflection as she walked.

Not a soul in sight, not even wretched Tern. They were either out or under orders to stay away until this meeting was done—as though Arobynn didn't want to be overheard.

The smell of the Keep wrapped around her, tugging at her memory. Fresh-cut flowers and baking bread barely masked the tang of metal, or the lightning-crisp feeling of violence throughout.

Every step toward that ornate study had her bracing herself.

There he was, seated at the massive desk, his auburn hair like molten steel in the sunlight pouring in from the floor-to-ceiling windows flanking one side of the wood-paneled room. She shut out the information she'd learned in Wesley's letter and kept her posture loose, casual.

But she couldn't help glancing at the rug before the desk—a movement Arobynn either noted or expected. "A new rug," he said, looking up from the papers before him. "The bloodstains on the other one never really came out."

"Pity," she said, slumping into one of the chairs before his desk, trying not to look at the chair beside hers, where Sam had usually sat. "The other rug was prettier."

Until her blood had soaked it when Arobynn had beaten her for ruining his slave trade agreement, making Sam watch the entire time. And when she was unconscious, he'd beaten Sam into oblivion, too.

She wondered which of the scars on Arobynn's knuckles were from those beatings.

She heard the butler approach, but didn't deign to look at him as Arobynn said, "We're not to be disturbed." The butler murmured his understanding, and the study doors clicked shut.

Aelin slung a leg over the arm of her chair. "To what do I owe this summoning?"

Arobynn rose, a fluid movement limned with restrained power, and came around the desk to lean against its edge. "I merely wanted to see how you were doing the day before your grand event." His silver eyes flickered. "I wanted to wish you luck."

"And to see if I was going to betray you?"

"Why would I ever think that?"

"I don't think you want to get into a conversation about trust right now."

"Certainly not. Not when you need all your focus for tomorrow. So many little things that could go wrong. Especially if you're caught."

She felt the dagger of the implied threat slide between her ribs. "You know I don't break easily under torture."

Arobynn crossed his arms over his broad chest. "Of course not. I expect nothing less from my protégée than to shield me if the king catches you."

So that explained the summons.

"I never asked," Arobynn went on. "*Will* you be doing this as Celaena?"

As good a time as any to cast a bored glance around the study, ever the irreverent protégée. Nothing on the desk, nothing on the shelves, not even a box that might contain the Amulet of Orynth. She allowed herself one sweep before turning indolent eyes on him. "I hadn't planned on leaving a calling card."

"And what explanation will you give your cousin when you are reunited? The same you gave the noble captain?" She didn't want to know how he was aware of that disaster. She hadn't told Lysandra—since Lysandra still had no idea who she was. She'd think about it later.

"I'll tell Aedion the truth."

"Well, let's hope that's excuse enough for him."

It was a physical effort to clamp down on her retort. "I'm tired and don't feel like having a verbal sparring match today. Just tell me what you want so I can go soak in my tub." Not a lie. Her muscles ached from tracking Valg foot soldiers across Rifthold the night before.

"You know my facilities are at your disposal." Arobynn pinned his attention on her right leg, slung over the arm of the chair, as if he'd somehow figured out that it was giving her trouble. As if he knew that the fight at the Vaults had somehow aggravated the old wound she'd received during her duel with Cain. "My healer could rub down that leg for you. I wouldn't want you to be in pain. Or handicapped for tomorrow."

Training kept her features bored. "You truly do like hearing yourself talk, don't you?"

A sensual laugh. "Fine—no verbal sparring."

She waited, still lounging in the chair.

Arobynn ran an eye down the suit, and when his gaze met hers, there was only a cold, cruel killer staring out at her. "I have it on good authority that you've been monitoring patrols of the king's guard—but leaving them undisturbed. Have you forgotten our little bargain?"

She smiled a little. "Of course not."

"Then why is my promised demon not in my dungeon?"

"Because I'm not capturing one until after Aedion is freed."

A blink.

"These things might lead the king right to you. To us. I'm not jeopardizing Aedion's safety to satisfy your morbid curiosity. And who's to say you won't forget to help me when you're busy playing with your new toy?"

Arobynn pushed off the desk and approached, bending over her chair close enough to share breath. "I'm a man of my word, Celaena."

Again, that name.

He took a step back and cocked his head. "Though you, on the other hand . . . I recall you promising to kill Lysandra years ago. I was surprised when she returned unharmed."

"You did your best to ensure that we hated each other. I figured why not go the opposite way for once? Turns out she's not nearly as spoiled and selfish as you made me believe." Ever the petulant protégée, ever the smart-ass. "Though if you want me to kill her, I'll gladly turn my attention to that instead of the Valg."

A soft laugh. "No need. She serves me well enough. Replaceable, though, should you decide you'd like to uphold your promise."

"Was that the test, then? To see if I follow through on my promises?" Beneath her gloves, the mark she'd carved into her palm burned like a brand.

"It was a present."

"Stick with jewelry and clothes." She rose and glanced down at her suit. "Or useful things."

His eyes followed hers and lingered. "You fill it out better than you did at seventeen."

And that was quite enough. She clicked her tongue and turned away, but he gripped her arm—right where those invisible blades would snap out. He knew it, too. A dare; a challenge.

"You will need to lie low with your cousin once he escapes tomorrow," Arobynn said. "Should you decide not to fulfill your end of the bargain . . . you'll find out very quickly, Celaena darling, how deadly this city can be for those on the run—even fire-breathing bitch-queens."

"No more declarations of love or offers to walk over coals for me?"

A sensual laugh. "You were always my favorite dance partner." He came close enough to graze his lips against hers if she should sway a fraction of an inch. "If you want me to whisper sweet nothings into your ear, Majesty, I'll do just that. But you'll still get me what I need."

She didn't dare pull back. There was always such a gleaming in his silver eyes—like the cold light before dawn. She'd never been able to look away from it.

He angled his head, the sun catching in his auburn hair. "What about the prince, though?"

"Which prince?" she said carefully.

Arobynn gave a knowing smile, retreating a few inches. "There are three princes, I suppose. Your cousin, and then the two that now share Dorian Havilliard's body. Does the brave captain know that his friend is currently being devoured by one of those demons?"

"Yes."

"Does he know that you might decide to do the smart thing and put the king's son down before he can become a threat?"

She held his stare. "Why don't you tell me? You're the one who's been meeting with him."

His answering chuckle sent ice skittering over her bones. "So the captain has a hard time sharing with you. He seems to share everything just fine with his former lover—that Faliq girl. Did you know that her father makes the best pear tarts in the entire capital? He's even supplying some for the prince's birthday. Ironic, isn't it?"

It was her turn to blink. She'd known Chaol had at least one lover other than Lithaen, but . . . Nesryn? And how convenient for him not to tell her, especially when he'd thrown whatever nonsense he believed about her and Rowan in her face. *Your faerie prince*, he'd snapped. She doubted Chaol had done anything with the young woman since she'd left for Wendlyn, but . . . But she was feeling exactly what Arobynn wanted her to feel.

"Why don't you stay out of our business, Arobynn?"

"Don't you want to know why the captain came to me again last night?"

Bastards, both of them. She'd warned Chaol not to tangle with Arobynn. To reveal that she didn't know or to conceal that vulnerability . . . Chaol wouldn't jeopardize her safety or her plans for tomorrow, regardless of what information he kept from her. She smirked at Arobynn. "No. I was the one who sent him there." She sauntered toward the study doors. "You must truly be bored if you summoned me merely to taunt me."

A glimmer of amusement. "Good luck tomorrow. All the plans are in place, in case you were worried."

"Of course they are. I'd expect nothing less from you." She flung open one of the doors and waved her hand in lazy dismissal. "See you around, Master."

Aelin visited at the Royal Bank again on her way home, and when she returned to her apartment, Lysandra was waiting, as they'd planned.

Even better, Lysandra had brought food. Lots of food.

Aelin plunked down at the kitchen table where Lysandra currently lounged.

The courtesan was gazing toward the wide window above the kitchen sink. "You do realize you've got a shadow on the roof next door, don't you?"

"He's harmless." And useful. Chaol had men watching the Keep, the palace gates, and the apartment—all to monitor Arobynn. Aelin cocked her head. "Keen eyes?"

"Your master taught me a few tricks over the years. To protect myself, of course." *To protect his investment*, was what she didn't need to say. "You read the letter, I take it?"

"Every damn word."

Indeed, she'd read through Wesley's letter again and again, until she had memorized the dates and names and accounts, until she had seen so much fire that she was glad her magic was currently stifled. It changed little of her plans, but it helped. Now she knew she wasn't wrong, that the names on her own list were correct. "I'm sorry I couldn't keep it," Aelin said. "Burning it was the only way to stay safe."

Lysandra just nodded, picking at a piece of lint on the bodice of her rust-colored gown. The red sleeves were loose and billowing, with tight black velvet cuffs and gold buttons that glinted in the morning light as she reached for one of the hothouse grapes Aelin had bought yesterday. An elegant gown, but modest.

"The Lysandra I knew used to wear far less clothing," Aelin said.

Lysandra's green eyes flickered. "The Lysandra you knew died a long time ago."

So had Celaena Sardothien. "I asked you to meet me today so we could . . . talk."

"About Arobynn?"

"About you."

Elegant brows narrowed. "And when do we get to talk about you?"

"What do you want to know?"

"What are you doing in Rifthold? Aside from rescuing the general tomorrow."

Aelin said, "I don't know you well enough to answer that question."

Lysandra merely cocked her head. "Why Aedion?"

"He's more useful to me alive than dead." Not a lie.

Lysandra tapped a manicured nail on the worn table. After a moment she said, "I used to be so jealous of you. Not only did you have Sam but also Arobynn . . . I was such a fool, believing that he gave you everything and denied you nothing, hating you because I always knew, deep down, that I was just a pawn for him to use against you—a way to make you fight for his affection, to keep you on your toes, to hurt you. And I enjoyed it, because I thought it was better to be someone's pawn than nothing at all." Her hand shook as she raised it to brush back a strand of her hair. "I think I would have continued on that way for my whole life. But then—then Arobynn killed Sam and arranged for your capture, and . . . and summoned me the night you were hauled to Endovier. Afterward, on the carriage ride home, I just cried. I didn't know why. But Wesley was in the carriage with me. That was the night that everything changed between us." Lysandra glanced at the scars around Aelin's wrists, then at the tattoo marring her own.

Aelin said, "The other night, you didn't just come to warn me about Arobynn."

When Lysandra raised her head, her eyes were frozen. "No," she said with soft savagery. "I came to help you destroy him."

"You must trust me a great deal to have said that."

"You wrecked the Vaults," Lysandra said. "It was for Sam, wasn't it? Because those people—they all worked for Rourke Farran, and were there when . . ." She shook her head. "It's all for Sam, whatever you have planned for Arobynn. Besides, if you betray me, there's little that can hurt me more than what I've already endured."

Aelin leaned back in her chair and crossed her legs, trying not to think about the darkness the woman across from her had survived.

"I went too long without demanding retribution. I have no interest in forgiveness."

Lysandra smiled—and there was no joy in it. "After he murdered Wesley, I lay awake in his bed and thought about killing him right there. But it didn't seem like enough, and the debt didn't belong only to me."

For a moment, Aelin couldn't say anything. Then she shook her head. "You honestly mean to imply that you've been waiting for me this whole time?"

"You loved Sam as much as I loved Wesley."

Her chest hollowed out, but she nodded. Yes, she'd loved Sam—more than she'd ever loved anyone. Even Chaol. And reading in Wesley's letter exactly what Arobynn had ordered Rourke Farran to do to Sam had left a raging wound in the core of her. Sam's clothes were still in the two bottom drawers of her dresser, where Arobynn had indeed unpacked them. She'd worn one of his shirts to bed these past two nights.

Arobynn would pay.

"I'm sorry," Aelin said. "For the years I spent being a monster toward you, for whatever part I played in your suffering. I wish I'd been able to see myself better. I wish I'd seen *everything* better. I'm sorry."

Lysandra blinked. "We were both young and stupid, and should have seen each other as allies. But there's nothing to prevent us from seeing each other that way now." Lysandra gave her a grin that was more wolfish than refined. "If you're in, I'm in."

That fast—that easily—the offer of friendship was tossed her way. Rowan might have been her dearest friend, her *carranam*, but . . . she missed female companionship. Deeply. Though an old panic rose up at the thought of Nehemia not being there anymore to provide it— and part of her wanted to throw the offer back in Lysandra's face just because she *wasn't* Nehemia—she forced herself to stare down that fear.

Aelin said hoarsely, "I'm in."

Lysandra heaved a sigh. "Oh, thank the gods. Now I can talk to someone about clothes without being asked how so-and-so would approve of it, or gobble down a box of chocolates without someone telling me I'd better watch my figure—tell me you like chocolates. You do, right? I remember stealing a box from your room once when you were out killing someone. They were delicious."

Aelin waved a hand toward the boxes of goodies on the table. "You brought chocolate—as far as I'm concerned, you're my new favorite person."

Lysandra chuckled, a surprisingly deep, wicked sound—probably a laugh she never let Arobynn or her clients hear. "Some night soon, I'll sneak back in here and we can eat chocolates until we vomit."

"We're such refined, genteel ladies."

"Please," Lysandra said, waving a manicured hand, "you and I are nothing but wild beasts wearing human skins. Don't even try to deny it."

The courtesan had no idea how close she was to the truth. Aelin wondered how the woman would react to her other form—to the elongated canines. Somehow, she doubted Lysandra would call her a monster for it—or for the flames at her command.

Lysandra's smile flickered. "Everything's set for tomorrow?"

"Is that worry I detect?"

"You're just going to waltz into the palace and think a different hair color will keep you from being noticed? You trust Arobynn that much?"

"Do you have a better idea?"

Lysandra's shrug was the definition of nonchalance. "I happen to know a thing or two about playing different roles. How to turn eyes away when you don't want to be seen."

"I *do* know how to be stealthy, Lysandra. The plan is sound. Even if it was Arobynn's idea."

"What if we killed two birds with one stone?"

She might have dismissed it, might have shut her down, but there was such a wicked, feral gleam in the courtesan's eyes.

So Aelin rested her forearms on the table. "I'm listening."

CHAPTER 14

For every person Chaol and the rebels saved, it seemed there were always several more who made it to the butchering block.

The sun was setting as he and Nesryn crouched on a rooftop flanking the small square. The only people who'd bothered to watch were the typical lowlifes, content to breathe in the misery of others. That didn't bother him half as much as the decorations that had been put up in honor of Dorian's birthday tomorrow: red and gold streamers and ribbons hung across the square like a net, while baskets of blue and white flowers bordered its outer edges. A charnel house bedecked in late-spring cheer.

Nesryn's bowstring groaned as she pulled it back farther.

"Steady," he warned her.

"She knows what she's doing," Aelin muttered from a few feet away.

Chaol cut her a glance. "Remind me why you're here?"

"I wanted to help—or is this an Adarlanians-only rebellion?"

Chaol stifled his retort and turned his glare onto the square below.

Tomorrow, everything he cared about depended on her. Antagonizing her wouldn't be smart, even if it killed him to leave Dorian in her hands. But—

"About tomorrow," he said tightly, not taking his attention off the execution about to unfold. "You don't touch Dorian."

"Me? Never," Aelin purred.

"It's not a joke. You. Don't. Hurt. Him."

Nesryn ignored them and angled her bow to the left. "I can't get a clear shot at any of them."

Three men now stood before the block, a dozen guards around them. The boards of the wooden platform were already deeply stained with red from weeks of use. Gatherers monitored the massive clock above the execution platform, waiting for the iron hand to hit the six o'clock evening marker. They'd even tied gold and crimson ribbons to the clock's lower rim. Seven minutes now.

Chaol made himself look at Aelin. "Do you think you'll be able to save him?"

"Maybe. I'll try." No reaction in her eyes, in her posture.

Maybe. *Maybe.* He said, "Does Dorian actually matter, or is he a pawn for Terrasen?"

"Don't even start with that." For a moment he thought she was done, but then she spat, "Killing him, Chaol, would be a mercy. Killing him would be a gift."

"I can't make the shot," Nesryn said again—a bit more sharply.

"Touch him," Chaol said, "and I'll make sure those bastards down there find Aedion."

Nesryn silently turned to them, slackening her bow. It was the only card he had to play, even if it made him a bastard as well.

The wrath Chaol found in Aelin's eyes was world-ending.

"You bring my court into this, Chaol," Aelin said with lethal softness, "and I don't care what you were to me, or what you have done to help me. You betray them, you hurt them, and I don't care how long it takes, or how far you go: I'll burn you and your gods-damned kingdom to ash. Then you'll learn just how much of a monster I can be."

Too far. He'd gone too far.

"We're not enemies," Nesryn said, and though her face was calm, her eyes darted between them. "We have enough shit to worry about tomorrow. And right now." She pointed with her arrow toward the square. "Five minutes until six. Do we go down there?"

"Too public," Aelin said. "Don't risk exposing yourself. There's another patrol a quarter mile away, headed in this direction."

Of course she knew about it. "Again," Chaol said, "why are you here?" She'd just . . . snuck up on them. With far too much ease.

Aelin studied Nesryn a bit too thoughtfully. "How good's your accuracy, Faliq?"

"I don't miss," Nesryn said.

Aelin's teeth gleamed. "My kind of woman." She gave Chaol a knowing smile.

And he knew—he knew that she was aware of the history between them. And she didn't particularly care. He couldn't tell whether or not it was a relief.

"I'm debating ordering Arobynn's men off the mission tomorrow," Aelin said, those turquoise eyes fixed on Nesryn's face, on her hands, on her bow. "I want Faliq on wall duty instead."

"No," Chaol said.

"Are you her keeper?" He didn't deign to respond. Aelin crooned, "I thought so."

But Nesryn wouldn't be on wall duty—and neither would he. He was too recognizable to risk being close to the palace, and Aelin and her piece-of-shit master had apparently decided he'd be better off running interference along the border of the slums, making sure the coast was clear. "Nesryn has her orders already."

In the square, people began swearing at the three men who were watching the clock with pale, gaunt faces. Some of the onlookers even threw bits of spoiled food at them. Maybe this city did deserve Aelin Galathynius's flames. Maybe Chaol deserved to burn, too.

He turned back to the women.

"Shit," Aelin swore, and he looked behind him in time to see the guards shove the first victim—a sobbing, middle-aged man—toward the block, using the pommels of their swords to knock his knees out from under him. They weren't waiting until six. Another prisoner, also middle-aged, began shaking, and a dark stain spread across the front of his pants. Gods.

Chaol's muscles were locked, and even Nesryn couldn't draw her bow fast enough as the ax rose.

A thud silenced the city square. People applauded—*applauded*. The sound covered the second thud of the man's head falling and rolling away.

Then Chaol was in another room, in the castle that had once been his home, listening to the thud of flesh and bone on marble, red mist coating the air, Dorian screaming—

Oath-breaker. Liar. Traitor. Chaol was all of those things now, but not to Dorian. Never to his true king.

"Take out the clock tower in the garden," he said, the words barely audible. He felt Aelin turn toward him. "And magic will be free. It was a spell—three towers, all built of Wyrdstone. Take out one, and magic is free."

She glanced northward without so much as a blink of surprise, as though she could see all the way to the glass castle. "Thank you," she murmured. That was it.

"It's for Dorian's sake." Perhaps cruel, perhaps selfish, but true. "The king is expecting you tomorrow," he went on. "What if he stops caring about the public knowing and unleashes his magic on you? You know what happened with Dorian."

She scanned the roof tiles as if reading her mental map of the celebration—the map he'd given her. Then she swore. "He could lay traps for me—and Aedion. With the Wyrdmarks, he could write out spells on the floor or in the doors, keyed to me or Aedion, and we would be helpless—the exact same way I trapped that thing in the library. Shit," she breathed. "*Shit.*"

Gripping her slackened bow, Nesryn said, "Brullo told us the king has his best men escorting Aedion from the dungeons to the hall—perhaps spelling those areas, too. *If* he spells them."

"*If* is too big a gamble to make. And it's too late to change our plans," Aelin said. "If I had those gods-damned books, I could maybe find some sort of protection for me and Aedion, some spell, but I won't have enough time tomorrow to grab them from my old rooms. The gods know if they're even still there."

"They're not," Chaol said. Aelin's brows flicked up. "Because I have them. I grabbed them when I left the castle."

Aelin pursed her lips in what he could have sworn was reluctant appreciation. "We don't have much time." She began climbing over the roof and out of sight. "There are two prisoners left," she clarified. "And I think those streamers would look better with some Valg blood on them, anyway."

Nesryn remained on the rooftop while Aelin went to another across the square—faster than Chaol had thought possible. That left him on street level.

He hurried as swiftly as he could through the crowd, spotting his three men gathered near the other edge of the platform—ready.

The clock struck six just as Chaol positioned himself, after making sure two more of his men were waiting down a narrow alley. Just as the guards finally cleared away the body of the first prisoner and dragged forward the second. The man was sobbing, begging them as he was forced to kneel in the puddle of his friend's blood.

The executioner lifted his ax.

And a dagger, courtesy of Aelin Galathynius, went clean through the executioner's throat.

Black blood sprayed—some onto the streamers, as Aelin had promised. Before the guards could shout, Nesryn opened fire from the other direction. That was all the distraction Chaol needed as he and his men surged toward the platform amid the panicking, fleeing crowd. Nesryn and Aelin had both fired again by the time he hit the stage, the wood treacherously slick with blood. He grabbed the two prisoners and roared at them to *run, run, run!*

His men were blade-to-blade with the guards as he rushed the stumbling prisoners down the steps and into the safety of the alley—and the rebels waiting beyond.

Block after block they fled, leaving the chaos of the square behind, until they hit the Avery, and Chaol set about attaining them a boat.

Nesryn found him leaving the docks an hour later, unharmed but splattered with dark blood. "What happened?"

"Pandemonium," Nesryn said, scanning the river under the setting sun. "Everything fine?"

He nodded. "And you?"

"Both of us are fine." A kindness, he thought with a flicker of shame, that she knew he couldn't bring himself to ask about Aelin. Nesryn turned away, heading back in the direction she'd come.

"Where are you going?" he asked.

"To wash and change—and then go tell the family of the man who died."

It was protocol, even if it was horrible. Better to have the families genuinely mourn than risk being looked on any longer as rebel sympathizers. "You don't have to do that," he said. "I'll send one of the men."

"I'm a city guard," she said plainly. "My presence won't be unexpected. And besides," she said, her eyes glinting with her usual faint amusement, "you yourself said I don't exactly have a line of suitors waiting outside my father's house, so what else do I have to do with myself tonight?"

"Tomorrow's an important day," he said, even as he cursed himself for the words he'd spat the other night. An ass—that's what he'd been, even if she'd never let on that it bothered her.

"I was just fine before you came along, Chaol," she said—tired, possibly bored. "I know my limits. I'll see you tomorrow."

But he said, "Why go to the families yourself?"

Nesryn's dark eyes shifted toward the river. "Because it reminds me what I have to lose if I'm caught—or if we fail."

Night fell, and Aelin knew she was being followed as she stalked from rooftop to rooftop. Right now, even hours later, hitting the street was the most dangerous thing she could possibly do, given how pissed off the guards were after she and the rebels had stolen their prisoners right out from under them.

And she knew *that* because she'd been listening to them curse and hiss for the past hour as she trailed a patrol of black-uniformed guards on the route she'd noted the night before: along the docks, then keeping to the shadows off the main drag of taverns and brothels in the slums, and then near—but keeping a healthy distance from—the riverside Shadow Market. Interesting to learn how their route did or didn't change when chaos erupted—what hidey-holes they rushed to, what sort of formations they used.

What streets were left unmonitored when all hell broke loose.

As it would tomorrow, with Aedion.

But Arobynn's claims had been right—matching the maps Chaol and Nesryn had made, too.

She'd known that if she told Chaol why she'd shown up at the execution, he would get in the way somehow—send Nesryn to follow her, perhaps. She'd needed to see how skilled they were—*all* the parties that would be so crucial in tomorrow's events—and then see this.

Just as Arobynn had told her, each guard wore a thick black ring, and they moved with jerks and twitches that made her wonder how well the demons squatting inside their bodies were adjusting. Their leader, a pale man with night-dark hair, moved the most fluidly, like ink in water, she thought.

She had left them to stalk toward another part of the city while she continued on toward where the craftsman district jutted out into the curve of the Avery, until all was silent around her and the scent of those rotting corpses faded away.

Atop the roof of a glass-blowing warehouse, the tiles still warm from the heat of the day or the massive furnaces inside, Aelin surveyed the empty alley below.

The infernal spring rain began again, tinkling on the sloped roof, the many chimneys.

Magic—Chaol had told her how to free it. So easy, and yet—a monumental task. In need of careful planning. After tomorrow, though—if she survived—she'd set about doing it.

She shimmied down a drainpipe on the side of a crumbling brick building, splashing down a bit too loudly in a puddle of what she hoped was rain. She whistled as she strolled down the empty alley, a jaunty little tune she'd overheard at one of the slums' many taverns.

Still, she was honestly a little surprised that she got nearly halfway down the alley before a patrol of the king's guards stepped into her path, their swords like quicksilver in the dark.

The commander of the patrol—the demon inside him—looked at her and smiled as though it already knew what her blood tasted like.

Aelin grinned right back at him, flicking her wrists and sending the blades shooting out of her suit. "Hello, gorgeous."

Then she was upon them, slicing and twirling and ducking.

Five guards were dead before the others could even move.

The blood they leaked wasn't red, though. It was black, and slid down the sides of her blades, dense and shining as oil. The stench, like curdled milk and vinegar, hit her as hard as the clashing of their swords.

The reek grew, overpowering the lingering smoke from the glass factories around them, worsening as Aelin dodged the demon's blow and swiped low. The man's stomach opened up like a festering wound, and black blood and the gods knew what else sloshed onto the street.

Disgusting. Almost as bad as what wafted from the sewer grate at the other end of the alley—already open. Already oozing that too-familiar darkness.

The rest of the patrol closed in. Her wrath became a song in her blood as she ended them.

When blood and rain lay in puddles on the broken cobblestones, when Aelin stood in a field of fallen men, she began slicing.

Head after head tumbled away.

Then she leaned against the wall, waiting. Counting.

They did not rise.

Aelin stalked from the alley, kicking shut the sewer grate, and vanished into the rainy night.

Dawn broke, the day clear and warm. Aelin had been up half the night scouring the books Chaol had saved, including her old friend *The Walking Dead*.

Reciting what she'd learned in the quiet of her apartment, Aelin donned the clothes Arobynn had sent over, checking and rechecking that there were no surprises and everything was where she needed it to be. She let each step, each reminder of her plan anchor her, keep her from dwelling too long on what would come when the festivities began.

And then she went to save her cousin.

CHAPTER
15

Aedion Ashryver was ready to die.

Against his will, he'd recovered over the past two days, the fever breaking after sunset last night. He was strong enough to walk—albeit slowly—as they escorted him to the dungeon's washroom, where they chained him down to wash and scrub him, and even risked shaving him, despite his best efforts to slit his own throat on the razor.

It appeared that they wanted him presentable for the court when they cut off his head with his own blade, the Sword of Orynth.

After cleaning his wounds, they shoved him into pants and a loose white shirt, yanked back his hair, and dragged him up the stairs. Guards with dark uniforms flanked him three deep on both sides, four in front and behind, and every door and exit had one of the bastards posted by it.

He was too drained from dressing to provoke them into putting a sword through him, so he let them lead him through the towering doors into the ballroom. Red and gold banners hung from the rafters, springtime blossoms covered every table, and an archway of hothouse roses had been crafted over the dais from which the royal family would watch the festivities before his execution. The windows and doors beyond the platform where he would be killed opened onto one of the gardens, a guard stationed every other foot, others positioned in the garden itself. If the king wanted to set a trap for Aelin, he certainly hadn't bothered to be very subtle about it.

It was civilized of them, Aedion realized as he was shoved up the wooden steps of the platform, to give him a stool to sit on. At least he wouldn't have to lounge on the floor like a dog while he watched them all pretend that they weren't here just to see his head roll. And a stool, he realized with grim satisfaction, would make a good-enough weapon when the time came.

So Aedion let them chain him in the shackles anchored to the floor of the platform. Let them put the Sword of Orynth on display a few feet behind him, its scarred bone pommel glinting in the morning light.

It was just a matter of finding the right moment to meet the end of his own choosing.

CHAPTER 16

The demon made him sit on a dais, on a throne beside a crowned woman who had not noticed that the thing using his mouth wasn't the person who had been born of her flesh. To his other side lounged the man who controlled the demon inside him. And in front of him, the ballroom was full of tittering nobility who could not see that he was still in here, still screaming.

The demon had broken a little farther through the barrier today, and it now looked through his eyes with an ancient, glittering malice. It was starved for this world.

Perhaps the world deserved to be devoured by the thing.

Maybe it was that traitorous thought alone that had caused such a hole to rip in the barrier between them. Maybe it was winning. Maybe it had already won.

So he was forced to sit on that throne, and speak with words that were not his own, and share his eyes with something from another realm, who gazed at his sunny world with ravenous, eternal hunger.

The costume itched like hell. The paint all over her didn't help.

Most of the important guests had arrived in the days preceding the party, but those who dwelled inside the city or in the outlying foothills now formed a glittering line stretching through the massive front doors. Guards were posted there, checking invitations, asking questions, peering into faces none too keen to be interrogated. The entertainers, vendors, and help, however, were ordered to use one of the side entrances.

That was where Aelin had found Madam Florine and her troupe of dancers, clad in costumes of black tulle and silk and lace, like liquid night in the midmorning sun.

Shoulders back, core tight, arms loose at her sides, Aelin eased into the middle of the flock. With her hair dyed a ruddy shade of brown and her face coated in the heavy cosmetics the dancers all wore, she blended in well enough that none of the others looked her way.

She focused entirely on her role of trembling novice, on looking more interested in how the other dancers perceived her than in the six guards stationed at the small wooden door in the side of the stone wall. The castle hallway beyond was narrow—good for daggers, bad for swords, and deadly for these dancers if she got into trouble.

If Arobynn had indeed betrayed her.

Head down, Aelin subtly monitored the first test of trust.

The chestnut-haired Florine walked along her line of dancers like an admiral aboard a ship.

Aging but beautiful, Florine's every movement was layered with a grace that Aelin herself had never been able to replicate, no matter how many lessons she'd had with her while growing up. The woman had been the most celebrated dancer in the empire—and since her retirement, she remained its most valued teacher. *Instructor Overlord*, Aelin had called her in the years that she'd trained under the woman, learning the most fashionable dances and ways to move and hone her body.

Florine's hazel eyes were on the guards ahead as she paused beside

Aelin, a frown on her thin lips. "You still need to work on your posture," the woman said.

Aelin met Florine's sidelong gaze. "It's an honor to be an understudy for you, Madam. I do hope Gillyan soon recovers from her illness."

The guards waved through what looked to be a troupe of jugglers, and they inched forward.

"You look in good-enough spirits," Florine murmured.

Aelin made a show of ducking her head, curling in her shoulders, and willing a blush to rise to her cheeks—the new understudy, bashful at the compliments of her mistress. "Considering where I was ten months ago?"

Florine sniffed, and her gaze lingered on the thin bands of scars across Aelin's wrists that even the painted whorls couldn't conceal. They'd raised the top of the dancers' open-backed costumes, but even so, and even with the body paint, the upper ends of her tattoo-covered scars peeked through.

"If you think I had anything to do with the events that led up to that—"

Aelin's words were barely louder than the crunch of silk shoes on gravel as she said, "You'd already be dead if you had." It wasn't a bluff. When she'd written her plans on that ship, Florine's name had been one that she'd written down—and then crossed out, after careful consideration.

Aelin continued, "I trust you made the proper adjustments?" Not just the slight change in the costumes to accommodate the weapons and supplies Aelin would need to smuggle in—all paid for by Arobynn, of course. No, the big surprises would come later.

"A bit late to be asking that, isn't it?" Madam Florine purred, the dark jewels at her neck and ears glimmering. "You must trust me a great deal to have even appeared."

"I trust that you like getting paid more than you like the king." Arobynn had given a massive sum to pay off Florine. She kept an eye on the guards as she said, "And since the Royal Theater was shut down by His Imperial Majesty, I trust we both agree that what was done to those musicians was a crime as unforgivable as the massacres of the slaves in Endovier and Calaculla."

She knew she'd gambled correctly when she saw agony flicker in Florine's eyes.

"Pytor was my friend," Florine whispered, the color leeching from her tan cheeks. "There was no finer conductor, no greater ear. He made my career. He helped me establish all this." She waved a hand to encompass the dancers, the castle, the prestige she'd acquired. "I miss him."

There was nothing calculated, nothing cold, when Aelin put a hand over her own heart. "I will miss going to hear him conduct the *Stygian Suite* every autumn. I will spend the rest of my life knowing that I may never again hear finer music, never again experience a shred of what I felt sitting in that theater while he conducted."

Madam Florine wrapped her arms around herself. Despite the guards ahead, despite the task that neared with every tick of the clock, it took Aelin a moment to be able to speak again.

But that hadn't been what made Aelin agree to Arobynn's plan—to trust Florine.

Two years ago, finally free of Arobynn's leash but nearly beggared thanks to paying her debts, Aelin had continued to take lessons with Florine not only to keep current with the popular dances for her work but also to keep flexible and fit. Florine had refused to take her money.

Moreover, after each lesson Florine had allowed Aelin to sit at the pianoforte by the window and play until her fingers were sore, since she had been forced to leave her beloved instrument at the Assassins' Keep. Florine had never mentioned it, never made her feel like it was charity. But it had been a kindness when Aelin had desperately needed one.

Aelin said under her breath, "You've memorized the preparations for you and your girls?"

"Those who wish to flee may come on the ship Arobynn hired. I have made space for all, just in case. If they're stupid enough to stay in Rifthold, then they deserve their fate."

Aelin hadn't risked being seen meeting with Florine until now, and Florine hadn't even dared to pack her belongings for fear of being discovered. She would take only what she could carry with her to the performance—money, jewels—and flee to the docks the moment chaos erupted. There was a good chance she wouldn't make it out of the palace—and neither would her girls, despite the escape plans provided by Chaol and Brullo and the cooperation of the kinder guards.

Aelin found herself saying, "Thank you."

Florine's mouth quirked to the side. "Now there's something you never learned from your master."

The dancers at the front of the line reached the guards, and Florine sighed loudly and strutted toward them, bracing her hands on her narrow hips, power and grace lining every step closer to the black-uniformed guard studying a long list.

One by one, he looked over the dancers, comparing them with the list he bore. Checking rosters—detailed ones.

But thanks to Ress having broken into the barracks last night and adding a fake name along with her description, Aelin would be on the list.

They inched closer, Aelin keeping toward the back of the group to buy time to note details.

Gods, this castle—the same in every possible way, but different. Or maybe it was she who was different.

One by one the dancers were allowed between the blank-faced guards and hurried down the narrow castle hallway, giggling and whispering to one another.

Aelin rose up onto her toes to study the guards at the doors, no more than the novice scrunching her face in impatient curiosity.

Then she saw them.

Written across the threshold stones in dark paint were Wyrdmarks. They'd been beautifully rendered, as though merely decorative, but—

They must be at every door, every entrance.

Sure enough, even the windows a level up had small, dark symbols on them, no doubt keyed to Aelin Galathynius, to alert the king to her presence or to trap her in place long enough to be captured.

A dancer elbowed Aelin in the stomach to get her to stop leaning on her shoulder to peer over their heads. Aelin gaped at the girl—and then let out an *oomph* of pain.

The dancer glared over her shoulder, mouthing to shut up.

Aelin burst into tears.

Loud, blubbering, *hu-hu-hu* tears. The dancers froze, the one ahead of her stepping back, glancing to either side.

"T-that hurt," Aelin said, clutching her stomach.

"I didn't do anything," the woman hissed.

Aelin kept crying.

Ahead, Florine ordered her dancers to step aside, and then her face was in Aelin's. "What in the name of every god in the realm is this nonsense about?"

Aelin pointed a shaking finger at the dancer. "She h-hit me."

Florine whirled on the wide-eyed dancer who was already proclaiming her innocence. Then followed a series of accusations, insults, and more tears—now from the dancer, weeping over her surely ruined career.

"W-water," Aelin blubbered to Florine. "I need a glass of waaater." The guards had begun pushing toward them. Aelin squeezed Florine's arm hard. "*N-now.*"

Florine's eyes sparked, and she faced the guards who approached, barking her demands. Aelin held her breath, waiting for the strike, the slap . . . but there was one of Ress's friends—one of Chaol's friends, wearing a red flower pinned to his breast, as she'd asked—running off to get water. Exactly where Chaol had said he'd be, just in case something went wrong. Aelin clung to Florine until the water appeared—a bucket and ladle, the best the man could come up with. He wisely didn't meet her gaze.

With a little sob of thanks, Aelin grabbed both from his hands. They were shaking slightly.

She gave Florine a subtle nudge with her foot, urging her forward.

"Come with me," seethed Florine, dragging her to the front of the line. "I've had enough of this idiocy, and you've nearly wrecked your makeup."

Careful not to spill the water, Aelin allowed Florine to pull her to the stone-faced guard at the doors. "My foolish, useless understudy, Dianna," she said to the guard with flawless steel in her voice, unfazed by the black-eyed demon looking out at her.

The man studied the list in his hands, scanning, scanning—

And crossed off a name.

Aelin took a shivering sip of water from the ladle, and then dunked it back into the bucket.

The guard looked once more at Aelin—and she willed her lower lip to wobble, the tears to well again as the demon inside devoured her with his eyes. As if all these lovely dancers were dessert.

"Get in," the man grunted, jerking his chin to the hall behind him.

With a silent prayer, Aelin stepped toward the Wyrdmarks written over the threshold stones.

And tripped, sending the bucket of water spraying over the marks.

She wailed as she hit the ground, knees barking in genuine pain, and Florine was instantly upon her, demanding she stop being so clumsy and such a crybaby, and then shoving her in—shoving her over the ruined marks.

And into the glass castle.

CHAPTER 17

Once Florine and the rest of the dancers were allowed in, they were all stuffed down a narrow servants' hallway. In a matter of moments, the door at the far end would open into the side of the ballroom and they would flutter out like butterflies. Black, glittering butterflies, here to perform the "Handmaidens of Death" dance from one of the more popular symphonies.

They weren't stopped or questioned by anyone else, though the guards in every hall watched them like hawks. And not the shape-shifting Fae Prince kind.

So few of Chaol's men were present. No sign of Ress or Brullo. But everyone was where Chaol had promised they would be, based on Ress and Brullo's information.

A platter of honey-roasted ham with crackling sage was carried past on a servant's shoulder, and Aelin tried not to appreciate it, to savor the scents of the food of her enemy. Even if it was damn fine food.

Platter after platter went by, hauled by red-faced servants, no doubt winded from the trek up from the kitchens. Trout with hazelnuts, crisped asparagus, tubs of freshly whipped cream, pear tarts, meat pies—

Aelin cocked her head, watching the line of servants. A half smile grew on her face. She waited for the servants to return with empty hands, on their return journey to the kitchens. Finally the door opened again, and a slim servant in a crisp white apron filed into the dim hall, the loose strands of her inky hair falling out of her braid as she hurried to retrieve the next tray of pear tarts from the kitchen.

Aelin kept her face blank, disinterested, as Nesryn Faliq glanced her way.

Those dark, upturned eyes narrowed slightly—surprise or nerves, Aelin couldn't tell. But before she could decide how to deal with it, one of the guards signaled to Florine that it was time.

Aelin kept her head down, even as she felt the demon within the man rake its attention over her and the others. Nesryn was gone—vanished down the stairs—when Aelin turned back.

Florine strode down the line of dancers waiting by the door, her hands clasped behind her. "Backs straight, shoulders back, necks uplifted. You are light, you are air, you are grace. Do not disappoint me."

Florine took up the basket of black glass flowers she'd had her steadiest dancer carry in, each exquisite bloom flickering like an ebony diamond in the dim hall light. "If you break these before it is time to throw them down, you are finished. They cost more than you're worth, and there are no extras."

One by one, she handed the flowers down the line, each of them sturdy enough not to snap in the next few minutes.

Florine reached Aelin, the basket empty. "Watch them, and learn," she said loud enough for the demon guard to hear, and put a hand on Aelin's shoulder, ever the consoling teacher. The other dancers, now shifting on their feet, rolling their heads and shoulders, didn't look in her direction.

Aelin nodded demurely, as if trying to hide bitter tears of disappointment, and ducked out of line to stand at Florine's side.

Trumpets blasted in through the cracks around the door, and the crowd cheered loud enough to make the floor rumble.

"I peeked into the Great Hall," Florine said so quietly Aelin could barely hear her. "To see how the general is faring. He is gaunt and pale, but alert. Ready—for you."

Aelin went still.

"I always wondered where Arobynn found you," Florine murmured, staring at the door as if she could see through it. "Why he took such pains to break you to his will, more so than all the others." The woman closed her eyes for a moment, and when she opened them, steel gleamed there. "When you shatter the chains of this world and forge the next, remember that art is as vital as food to a kingdom. Without it, a kingdom is nothing, and will be forgotten by time. I have amassed enough money in my miserable life to not need any more—so you will understand me clearly when I say that wherever you set your throne, no matter how long it takes, I will come to you, and I will bring music and dancing."

Aelin swallowed hard. Before she could say anything, Florine left her standing at the back of the line and strolled to the door. She paused before it, looking down the line at each dancer. She spoke only when her eyes met Aelin's. "Give our king the performance he deserves."

Florine opened the door, flooding the hallway with light and music and the scent of roasted meats.

The other dancers sucked in a collective breath and sprang forward, one by one, waving those dark glass flowers overhead.

As she watched them go, Aelin willed the blood in her veins into black fire. Aedion—her focus was on Aedion, not on the tyrant seated at the front of the room, the man who had murdered her family, murdered Marion, murdered her people. If these were her last moments, then at least she would go down fighting, to the sound of exquisite music.

It was time.

One breath—another.

She was the heir of fire.

She *was* fire, and light, and ash, and embers. She was Aelin Fireheart, and she bowed for no one and nothing, save the crown that was hers by blood and survival and triumph.

Aelin squared her shoulders and slipped into the bejeweled crowd.

Aedion had been watching the guards in the hours he'd been chained to the stool, and had figured out who best to attack first, who favored a certain side or leg, who might hesitate when faced with the Wolf of the North, and, most importantly, who was impulsive and stupid enough to finally run him through despite the king's command.

The performances had begun, drawing the attention of the crowd that had been shamelessly gawking at him, and as the two dozen women floated and leaped and twirled into the wide space between the dais and his execution platform, for a moment Aedion felt . . . bad for interrupting. These women had no cause to be caught up in the bloodshed he was about to unleash.

It did seem fitting, though, that their sparkling costumes were of darkest black, accented with silver—Death's Handmaidens, he realized. That was who they portrayed.

It was as much a sign as anything. Perhaps the dark-eyed Silba would offer him a kind death instead of a cruel one at the blood-drenched hands of Hellas. Either way, he found himself smiling. Death was death.

The dancers were tossing fistfuls of black powder, coating the floor with it—representing ashes of the fallen, probably. One by one, they made pretty little spins and bowed before the king and his son.

Time to move. The king was distracted by a uniformed guard whispering in his ear; the prince was watching the dancers with bored disinterest, and the queen was chatting with whichever courtier she favored that day.

The crowd clapped and cooed over the unfolding performance. They'd all come in their finery—such careless wealth. The blood of an empire had paid for those jewels and silks. The blood of his people.

An extra dancer was moving through the crowd: some understudy, no doubt trying to get a better view of the performance. And he might not have thought twice about it, had she not been taller than the others—bigger, curvier, her shoulders broader. She moved more heavily, as if somehow rooted innately to the earth. The light hit her, shining through the lace of the costume's sleeves to reveal swirls and whorls of markings on her skin. Identical to the paint on the dancers' arms and chests, save for her back, where the paint was a little darker, a little different.

Dancers like that didn't have tattoos.

Before he could see more, between one breath and the next, as a cluster of ladies in massive ball gowns blocked her from sight, she vanished behind a curtained-off doorway, walking right past the guards with a sheepish smile, as if she were lost.

When she emerged again not a minute later, he only knew it was her from the build, the height. The makeup was gone, and her flowing tulle skirt had disappeared—

No—not disappeared, he realized as she slipped back through the doorway without the guards so much as looking at her. The skirt had been reversed into a silken cape, its hood covering her ruddy brown hair, and she moved . . . moved like a swaggering man, parading for the ladies around him.

Moved closer to him. To the stage.

The dancers were still tossing their black powder everywhere, circling around and around, flitting their way across the marble floor.

None of the guards noticed the dancer-turned-noble prowling toward him. One of the courtiers did—but not to cry an alarm. Instead, he shouted a name—a man's name. And the dancer in disguise turned, lifting a hand in greeting toward the man who'd called and giving a cocky grin.

She wasn't just in disguise. She'd become someone else completely.

Closer and closer she strutted, the music from the gallery orchestra rising into a clashing, vibrant finale, each note higher than the last as the dancers raised their glass roses above their heads: a tribute to the king, to Death.

The disguised dancer stopped outside the ring of guards flanking Aedion's stage, patting herself down as if checking for a handkerchief that had gone missing, muttering a string of curses.

An ordinary, believable pause—no cause for alarm. The guards went back to watching the dancers.

But the dancer looked up at Aedion beneath lowered brows. Even disguised as an aristo man, there was wicked, vicious triumph in her turquoise-and-gold eyes.

Behind them, across the hall, the dancers shattered their roses on the floor, and Aedion grinned at his queen as the entire world went to hell.

CHAPTER
18

It wasn't just the glass flowers that had been rigged with a reactive powder, quietly purchased by Aelin at the Shadow Market. Every bit of sparkling dust the dancers had tossed about had been full of it. And it was worth every damned silver she'd spent as smoke erupted through the room, igniting the powder they'd been scattering everywhere.

The smoke was so thick she could barely see more than a foot ahead, and blended perfectly with the gray cloak that had doubled as the skirt of her costume. Just as Arobynn had suggested.

Screaming halted the music. Aelin was already moving for the nearby stage as the clock tower—that clock tower that would save or damn them all—struck noon.

There was no black collar around Aedion's neck, and that was all she needed to see, even as relief threatened to wobble her knees. Before the clock's first strike finished, she had drawn the daggers built into the bodice of her costume—all the silver thread and beading masking the steel on her—and slashed one across the throat of the nearest guard.

Aelin spun and shoved him into the man closest to him as she plunged her other blade deep into the gut of a third.

Florine's voice rose above the crowd, ushering her dancers *out-out-out*.

The second strike of the clock tower sounded, and Aelin yanked her dagger from the belly of the groaning guard, another surging at her from the smoke.

The rest would go to Aedion on instinct, but they'd be slowed by the crowds, and she was already close enough.

The guard—one of those black-uniformed nightmares—stabbed with his sword, a direct attack to her chest. Aelin parried the thrust aside with one dagger, spinning into his exposed torso. Hot, reeking blood shot onto her hand as she shoved her other blade into his eye.

He was still falling as she ran the last few feet to the wooden platform and hurled herself onto it, rolling, keeping low until she was right up under two other guards who were still trying to wave away the veils of smoke. They screamed as she disemboweled them both in two swipes.

The fourth strike of the clock sounded, and there was Aedion, the three guards around him impaled by shards of his stool.

He was huge—even bigger up close. A guard charged for them out of the smoke, and Aelin shouted "*Duck!*" before throwing her dagger at the man's approaching face. Aedion barely moved fast enough to avoid the blow, and the guard's blood splattered on the shoulder of her cousin's tunic.

She lunged for the chains around Aedion's ankles, sheathing her remaining blade at her side.

A jolt shocked through her, and blue light seared her vision as the Eye flared. She didn't dare pause, not even for a heartbeat. Whatever spell the king had put on Aedion's chains burned like blue fire as she sliced open her forearm with her dagger and used her blood to draw the symbols she'd memorized on the chains: *Unlock*.

The chains thudded to the ground.

Seventh strike of the clock.

The screaming shifted into something louder, wilder, and the king's voice boomed over the panicking crowd.

A guard rushed at them, his sword out. Another benefit of the smoke: too risky to start firing arrows. But she'd only give Arobynn credit if she got out of this alive.

She unsheathed another blade, hidden in the lining of her gray cloak. The guard went down clutching at his throat, now split ear to ear. Then she whirled to Aedion, pulled the long chain of the Eye from around her neck, and threw it over his head. She opened her mouth, but he gasped out, "The sword."

And that's when she noticed the blade displayed behind his stool. The Sword of Orynth.

Her father's blade.

She'd been too focused on Aedion, on the guards and the dancers, to realize what blade it was.

"*Stay close,*" was all she said as she grabbed the sword from the stand and shoved it into his hands. She didn't let herself think too much about the weight of that blade, or about how it had even gotten there. She just grasped Aedion by the wrist and raced across the platform toward the patio windows, where the crowd was shrieking and guards were trying to establish a line.

The clock issued its ninth strike. She'd unlock Aedion's hands as soon as they got to the garden; they didn't have another second to spend in the suffocating smoke.

Aedion staggered but kept upright, close behind as she leaped off the platform into the smoke, right where Brullo claimed two guards would hold their position. One died with a dagger to the spine, the other a blow to the side of the neck. She squeezed the hilts of her daggers against the slippery blood now coating them—and every inch of her.

His sword gripped in both hands, Aedion jumped down beside her, and his knees buckled.

He was injured, but not from any wound she could see. She'd discerned as much in the moments she'd weaved through the crowd, altering her demeanor as Lysandra had instructed. The paleness of Aedion's face had nothing to do with fear, nor did his shallow breaths. They'd hurt him.

It made killing these men very, very easy.

The crowd was bottlenecking by the patio doors, just as she had calculated. All it took was her shouting "*Fire! Fire!*" and the screaming turned frantic.

The crowd began shattering the windows and the glass doors, trampling one another and the guards. People grabbed buckets to douse the flames, water spraying everywhere and splashing away the Wyrdmarks on the thresholds.

The smoke billowed out ahead, leading the way into the garden. Aelin pushed Aedion's head down as she shoved him into the mass of fleeing courtiers and servants. Thrashing, squeezing, shouting, ripping at her clothes, until—until the noontime sun blinded her.

Aedion hissed. Weeks in the dungeons had probably wrecked his eyes. "Just hold on to me," she said, putting his massive hand on her shoulder. He gripped her hard, his chains knocking against her as she waded through the crowd and into open, clear air beyond.

The clock tower bellowed its twelfth and final strike as Aelin and Aedion skidded to a halt before a line of six guards blocking the entrance to the garden hedges.

Aelin stepped out of Aedion's grip, and her cousin swore as his eyes adjusted enough to see what now lay between them and escape. "Don't get in my way," she said to him, then launched herself at the guards.

Rowan had taught her a few new tricks.

She was a whirling cloud of death, a queen of shadows, and these men were already carrion.

Slashing and ducking and twirling, Aelin gave herself completely to that killing calm, until the blood was a mist around her and the gravel was slick with it. Four of Chaol's men came racing up—then ran the other way. Allies or just smart, she didn't care.

And when the last of those black-uniformed guards had slumped to the bloody ground, she surged for Aedion. He'd been gaping—but he let out a low, dark laugh as he stumbled into a sprint beside her, into the hedges.

Archers—they had to clear the archers who were sure to begin firing as soon as the smoke vanished.

They dashed around and between the hedges she'd traversed dozens of times during her stay here, when she'd run every morning with Chaol. "*Faster*, Aedion," she breathed, but he was already lagging. She paused and sliced into her blood-soaked wrist with a dagger before sketching the unlocking Wyrdmarks on each of his manacles. Again, light flared and burned. But then the cuffs sprang open silently.

"Nice trick," he panted, and she yanked the chains off him. She was about to chuck the metal aside when the gravel crunched behind them.

Not the guards, and not the king.

It was with no small amount of horror that she found Dorian strolling toward them.

CHAPTER 19

"Going somewhere?" Dorian said, his hands in the pockets of his black pants.

The man who spoke those words was not her friend—she knew that before he'd even opened his mouth. The collar of his ebony tunic was unbuttoned, revealing the glimmering Wyrdstone torque at the base of his throat.

"Unfortunately, Your Highness, we have another party to get to." She marked the slender red maple to the right, the hedges, the glass palace towering beyond them. They were too deep in the garden to be shot at, but every wasted second was as good as signing her own death sentence. And Aedion's.

"Pity," said the Valg prince inside Dorian. "It was just getting exciting."

He struck.

A wave of black lashed for her, and Aedion shouted in warning. Blue flared before her, deflecting the assault from Aedion, but she was shoved back a step, as if by a hard, dark wind.

When the black cleared, the prince stared. Then he gave a lazy, cruel smile. "You warded yourself. Clever, lovely human thing."

She'd spent all morning painting every inch of her body with Wyrdmarks in her own blood, mixed with ink to hide the color.

"Aedion, run for the wall," she breathed, not daring to take her eyes off the prince.

Aedion did no such thing. "He's not the prince—not anymore."

"I know. Which is why you need to—"

"Such heroics," said the thing squatting in her friend. "Such foolish hope, to think you can get away."

Like an asp, he struck again with a wall of black-tainted power. It knocked her clean into Aedion, who grunted in pain but set her upright. Her skin began tickling beneath her costume, as if the blood-wards were flaking off with each assault. Useful, but short-lived. Precisely why she hadn't wasted them on getting into the castle.

They had to get out of here—*now*.

She shoved the chains into Aedion's hands, took the Sword of Orynth from him, and stepped toward the prince.

Slowly, she unsheathed the blade. Its weight was flawless, and the steel shone as brightly as it had the last time she'd seen it. In her father's hands.

The Valg prince snapped another whip of power at her, and she stumbled but kept walking, even as the blood-wards beneath her costume crumbled away.

"One sign, Dorian," she said. "Just give me one sign that you're in there."

The Valg prince laughed low and harsh, that beautiful face twisted with ancient brutality. His sapphire eyes were empty as he said, "I am going to destroy everything you love."

She raised her father's sword in both hands, advancing still.

"You'd never do it," the thing said.

"Dorian," she repeated, her voice breaking. "You are *Dorian*." Seconds—she had seconds left to give him. Her blood dripped onto the gravel, and she let it pool there, her eyes fixed on the prince as she began tracing a symbol with her foot.

The demon chuckled again. "Not anymore."

She gazed into those eyes, at the mouth she'd once kissed, at the friend she'd once cared for so deeply, and begged, "Just one sign, Dorian."

But there was nothing of her friend in that face, no hesitation or twinge of muscle against the attack as the prince lunged.

Lunged, and then froze as he passed over the Wyrdmark she'd drawn on the ground with her foot—a quick and dirty mark to hold him. It wouldn't last for more than a few moments, but that was all she needed as he was forced to his knees, thrashing and pushing against the power. Aedion quietly swore.

Aelin raised the Sword of Orynth over Dorian's head. One strike. Just one to cleave through flesh and bone, to spare him.

The thing was roaring with a voice that didn't belong to Dorian, in a language that did not belong in this world. The mark on the ground flared, but held.

Dorian looked up at her, such hatred on his beautiful face, such malice and rage.

For Terrasen, for their future, she could do this. She could end this threat here and now. End *him*, on his birthday—not a day past twenty. She would suffer for it later, grieve later.

Not one more name would she etch into her flesh, she'd promised herself. But for her kingdom . . . The blade dipped as she decided, and—

Impact slammed into her father's sword, knocking her off balance as Aedion shouted.

The arrow ricocheted into the garden, hissing against the gravel as it landed.

Nesryn was already approaching, another arrow drawn, pointed at Aedion. "Strike the prince, and I'll shoot the general."

Dorian let out a lover's laugh.

"You're a shit spy," Aelin snapped at her. "You didn't even try to remain hidden when you watched me inside."

"Arobynn Hamel told the captain you were going to try to kill the prince today," Nesryn said. "Put your sword down."

Aelin ignored the command. *Nesryn's father makes the best pear tarts in the capital.* She supposed Arobynn had tried to warn her—and she'd been too distracted by everything else to contemplate the veiled message. Stupid. So profoundly *stupid* of her.

Only seconds left before the wards failed.

"You lied to us," Nesryn said. The arrow remained pointed at Aedion, who was sizing up Nesryn, his hands curling as if he were imagining his fingers wrapped around her throat.

"You and Chaol are fools," Aelin said, even as a part of her heaved in relief, even as she wanted to admit that what she'd been about to do made her a fool as well. Aelin lowered the sword to her side.

The thing inside Dorian hissed at her, "You will regret this moment, girl."

Aelin just whispered, "I know."

Aelin didn't give a shit what happened to Nesryn. She sheathed the sword, grabbed Aedion, and ran.

Aedion's breath was like shards of glass in his lungs, but the blood-covered woman—*Aelin*—was tugging him along, cursing at him for being so slow. The garden was enormous, and shouts rose over the hedges behind them, closing in.

Then they were at a stone wall already Wyrdmarked in blood, and there were strong hands reaching down to help him up and over. He tried to tell her to go first, but she was shoving at his back and then his legs, pushing him up as the two men atop the wall grunted with his weight. The wound in his ribs stretched and burned in agony. The world grew bright and spun as the hooded men eased him down to the quiet city street on the other side. He had to brace a hand against the wall to keep from slipping in the pooled blood of the downed royal guards beneath. He recognized none of their faces, some still set in silent screams.

There was the hiss of a body on stone, and then his cousin swung down beside him, wrapping her gray cloak around her bloody costume, slinging the hood over her blood-spattered face. She had another cloak in her hands, courtesy of the wall patrol. He could hardly stand upright as she wrapped it around him and shoved the hood over his head.

"*Run,*" she said. The two men atop the wall remained there, bows groaning as they were drawn. No sign of the young archer from the garden.

Aedion stumbled, and Aelin swore, darting back to wrap an arm around his middle. And damn his strength for failing him now, he put his arm around her shoulders, leaning on her as they hurried down the too-quiet residential street.

Shouts were now erupting behind, accented by the whiz and thud of arrows and the bleating of dying men.

"Four blocks," she panted. "Just four blocks."

That didn't seem nearly far enough away to be safe, but he had no breath to tell her. Keeping upright was task enough. The stitches in his side had split, but—holy gods, they'd cleared the palace grounds. A miracle, a miracle, a mir—

"*Hurry, you hulking ass!*" she barked.

Aedion forced himself to focus and willed strength to his legs, to his spine.

They reached a street corner bedecked in streamers and flowers, and Aelin glanced in either direction before rushing through the intersection. The clash of steel on steel and the screams of wounded men shattered through the city, setting the throngs of merry-faced revelers around them to murmuring.

But Aelin continued down the street, and then down another. At the third, she slowed her steps and rocked into him, beginning to sing a bawdy tune in a very off-key, drunken voice. And thus they became two ordinary citizens out to celebrate the prince's birthday, staggering from one tavern to the next. No one paid them any heed—not when all eyes were fixed on the glass castle towering behind them.

The swaying made his head spin. If he fainted . . . "One more block," she promised.

This was all some hallucination. It had to be. No one would actually have been stupid enough to try to rescue him—and especially not his own queen. Even if he'd seen her cut down half a dozen men like so many stalks of wheat.

"Come on, come on," she panted, scanning the decorated street, and he knew she wasn't talking to him. People were milling about, pausing to ask what the palace commotion was about. Aelin led them through the crowd, mere cloaked and stumbling drunks, right up to the black carriage-for-hire that pulled along the curb as though it had been waiting. The door sprang open.

His cousin shoved him inside, right onto the floor, and shut the door behind her.

⁓

"They're already stopping every carriage at the major intersections," Lysandra said as Aelin pried open the hidden luggage compartment beneath one of the benches. It was big enough to fit a very tightly curled person, but Aedion was absolutely massive, and—

"In. Get in, *now*," she ordered, and didn't wait for Aedion to move before she heaved him into the compartment. He groaned. Blood had started seeping from his side, but—he'd live.

That is, if *any* of them lived through the next few minutes. Aelin shut the panel beneath the cushion, wincing at the thud of wood on flesh, and grabbed the wet rag Lysandra had pulled from an old hatbox.

"Are you hurt?" Lysandra asked as the carriage started into a leisurely pace through the reveler-clogged streets.

Aelin's heart was pounding so wildly that she thought she would vomit, but she shook her head as she wiped her face. So much blood—then the remnants of her makeup, then more blood.

Lysandra handed her a second rag to wipe down her chest, neck, and hands, and then held out the loose, long-sleeved green dress she'd brought. "Now, now, now," Lysandra breathed.

Aelin ripped her bloodied cloak away and tossed it to Lysandra, who rose to shove it into the compartment beneath her own seat as Aelin shimmied into the dress. Lysandra's fingers were surprisingly steady as she buttoned up the back, then made quick work of Aelin's hair, handed her a pair of gloves, and slung a jeweled necklace around her throat. A fan was pressed into her hands the moment the gloves were on, concealing any trace of blood.

The carriage halted at the sound of harsh male voices. Lysandra had just rolled up the curtains when stomping steps approached, followed by four of the king's guard peering into the carriage with sharp, merciless eyes.

Lysandra thrust open the window. "Why are we being stopped?"

The guard yanked open the door and stuck his head in. Aelin noticed a smudge of blood on the floor a moment before he did and flinched back, covering it with her skirts.

"Sir!" Lysandra cried. "An explanation is necessary *at once!*"

Aelin waved her fan with a lady's horror, praying that her cousin kept quiet in his little compartment. On the street beyond, some revelers had paused to watch the inspection—wide-eyed, curious, and not at all inclined to help the two women inside the carriage.

The guard looked them over with a sneer, the expression deepening as his eyes alighted on Lysandra's tattooed wrist. "I owe you nothing, whore." He spat out another filthy word at both of them, and then shouted, "Search the compartment in the back."

"We are on our way to an *appointment*," Lysandra hissed, but he slammed the door in her face. The carriage jostled as the men leaped onto the back and opened the rear compartment. After a moment, someone slammed a hand onto the side of the carriage and shouted, "*Move on!*"

They didn't dare stop looking offended, didn't dare stop fanning themselves for the next two blocks, or the two after that, until the driver thumped the top of the carriage twice. All clear.

Aelin jumped off the bench and flung open the compartment. Aedion had vomited, but he was awake and looking more than a bit put out as she beckoned him to emerge. "One more stop, and then we're there."

"Quick," said Lysandra, peering casually out the window. "The others are almost here."

The alley was barely wide enough to fit both of the carriages that ambled toward each other, no more than two large vehicles slowing to avoid colliding as they passed. Lysandra flung open the door just as they were aligned with the other carriage, and Chaol's tight face appeared across the way as he did the same.

"Go, go, go," she said to Aedion, shoving him over the small gap between the coaches. He stumbled, grunting as he landed against the captain. Lysandra said behind her, "I'll be there soon. Good luck."

Aelin leaped into the other carriage, shutting the door behind her, and they continued on down the street.

She was breathing so hard that she thought she'd never get enough air. Aedion slumped onto the floor, keeping low.

Chaol said, "Everything all right?"

She could only manage a nod, grateful he didn't push for any other answers. But it wasn't all right. Not at all.

The carriage, driven by one of Chaol's men, took them another few blocks, right to the border of the slums, where they got out on a deserted, decrepit street. She trusted Chaol's men—but only so far. Taking Aedion right to her apartment seemed like asking for trouble.

With Aedion sagging between them, she and Chaol hurried down the next several blocks, taking the long way back to the warehouse to dodge any tail, listening so hard they barely breathed. But then they were at the warehouse, and Aedion managed to stand long enough for Chaol to slide the door open before they rushed inside, into the dark and safety at last.

Chaol took Aelin's place at Aedion's side as she lingered by the door. Grunting at the weight, he managed to get her cousin up the stairs. "He's got an injury along his ribs," she said as she forced herself to wait—to monitor the warehouse door for any signs of pursuers. "It's bleeding." Chaol gave her a confirming nod over his shoulder.

When her cousin and the captain were almost to the top of the stairs, when it became clear no one was about to burst in, she followed them. But pausing had cost her; pausing had let the razor-sharp focus slip, let every thought she'd kept at bay come sweeping in. Every step she took was heavier than the last.

One foot up, then the next, then the next.

By the time she made it to the second floor, Chaol had taken Aedion into the guest bedroom. The sound of running water gurgled out to greet her.

Aelin left the front door unlocked for Lysandra, and for a moment, she just stood in her apartment, bracing a hand on the back of the couch, staring at nothing.

When she was certain she could move again, she strode into her bedroom. She was naked before she reached the bathing chamber, and she sat herself right in the cold, dry tub before she turned on the water.

Once she emerged, clean and wearing one of Sam's old white shirts and a pair of his undershorts, Chaol was waiting for her on the couch. She didn't dare look at his face—not yet.

Lysandra popped her head in from the guest room. "I'm just finishing cleaning him up. He should be fine, if he doesn't burst the stitches again. No infection, thank the gods."

Aelin lifted a limp hand in thanks, also not daring to look into the room behind Lysandra to see the massive figure lying on the bed, a towel around his waist. If Chaol and the courtesan had been introduced, she didn't particularly care.

There was no good place to have this talk with Chaol, so she just stood in the center of the room and watched as the captain rose from his seat, his shoulders tight.

"What happened?" he demanded.

She swallowed once. "I killed a lot of people today. I'm not in the mood to analyze it."

"That's never bothered you before."

She couldn't dredge up the energy to even feel the sting of the words. "The next time you decide you don't trust me, try not to prove it at a time when my life or Aedion's is on the line."

A flash of his bronze eyes told her he'd somehow already seen Nesryn. Chaol's voice was hard and cold as ice as he said, "You tried to *kill* him. You said you'd try to get him out, to help him, and you tried to kill him."

The bedroom where Lysandra was working had gone silent.

Aelin let out a low snarl. "You want to know what I did? I gave him one minute. I gave up *one minute* of my escape to him. Do you understand what can happen in one minute? Because I gave one to Dorian when he attacked Aedion and me today—to *capture us*. I gave him a minute, in which the fate of my entire kingdom could have changed forever. I chose the son of my enemy."

He gripped the back of the sofa as though physically restraining himself. "You're a liar. You've always *been* a liar. And today was no exception. You had a sword over his head."

"I did," she spat. "And before Faliq arrived to wreck everything, I was going to do it. I should have done it, as anyone with common sense would have, because Dorian is *gone*."

And there was her breaking heart, fracturing at the monster she'd seen living in Dorian's eyes, the demon that would hunt her and Aedion down, that would stalk her dreams.

"I do not owe you an apology," she said to Chaol.

"Don't talk down to me like you're my queen," he snapped.

"No, I'm not your queen. But you are going to have to decide soon whom you serve, because the Dorian you knew is gone forever. Adarlan's future does not depend on him anymore."

The agony in Chaol's eyes hit her like a physical blow. And she wished she had mastered herself better when explaining it, but . . . she needed him to understand the risk she'd taken, and the danger he'd let Arobynn manipulate him into putting her in. He had to know that there was a hard line that she must draw, and that she would hold, to protect her own people.

So she said, "Go to the roof and take the first watch."

Chaol blinked.

"I'm not your queen, but I'm going to attend to my cousin right now. And since I hope Nesryn is lying low, someone needs to take the watch. Unless you'd like for us all to be caught unawares by the king's men."

Chaol didn't bother replying as he turned on his heel and strode out. She listened to him storming up the stairs and onto the roof, and it was only then that she loosed a breath and scrubbed at her face.

When she lowered her hands, Lysandra was standing in the guest bedroom doorway, her eyes wide. "What do you mean, *queen*?"

Aelin winced, swearing under her breath.

"That's exactly the word I'd use," Lysandra said, her face pale.

Aelin said, "My name—"

"Oh, I know what your real name is, *Aelin*."

Shit. "You understand why I had to keep it a secret."

"Of course I do," Lysandra said, pursing her lips. "You don't know me, and more lives than yours are at stake."

"No—I *do* know you." Gods, why were the words so damn hard to get out? The longer the hurt flickered in Lysandra's eyes, the wider the gap across the room felt. Aelin swallowed. "Until I had Aedion back, I wasn't going to take any chances. I knew I would have to tell you the moment you saw us in a room together."

"And Arobynn knows." Those green eyes were hard as chips of ice.

"He's always known. This—this changes nothing between us, you know. Nothing."

Lysandra glanced behind her, to the bedroom where Aedion now lay unconscious, and loosed a long breath. "The resemblance *is* uncanny. Gods, the fact that you went undiscovered for so many years boggles the mind." She studied Aedion again. "Even though he's a handsome bastard, it'd be like kissing you." Her eyes were still hard, but—a flicker of amusement gleamed there.

Aelin grimaced. "I could have lived without knowing that." She shook her head. "I don't know why I was ever nervous you would start bowing and scraping."

Light and understanding danced in Lysandra's eyes. "Where would the fun be in that?"

CHAPTER 20

Several days after running into the Wing Leader, Elide Lochan's ankle was sore, her lower back a tight knot, and her shoulders aching as she took the last step into the aerie. At least she'd made it without encountering any horrors in the halls—though the climb had nearly killed her.

She hadn't grown accustomed to the steep, endless steps of Morath in the two months since she'd been dragged to this horrible place by Vernon. Just completing her daily tasks made her ruined ankle throb with pain she hadn't experienced in years, and today was the worst yet. She would have to scrounge up some herbs from the kitchen tonight to soak her foot; maybe even some oils, if the ornery cook was feeling generous enough.

Compared with some of the other denizens of Morath, he was fairly mild. He tolerated her presence in the kitchen, and her requests for herbs—especially when she oh-so-sweetly offered to clean a few dishes or prepare meals. And he never blinked twice when she inquired about when the next shipment of food and supplies would come in, because *Oh, she'd loved his whatever-fruit pie, and it would be so nice to have it again.* Easy to flatter, easy to trick. Making people see and hear what they wanted to: one of the many weapons in her arsenal.

A gift from Anneith, the Lady of Wise Things, Finnula had claimed—the only gift, Elide often thought, that she'd ever received, beyond her old nursemaid's good heart and wits.

She'd never told Finnula that she often prayed to the Clever Goddess to bestow another gift on those who made the years in Perranth a living hell: death, and not the gentle sort. Not like Silba, who offered peaceful ends, or Hellas, who offered violent, burning ones. No, deaths at Anneith's hands—at the hands of Hellas's consort—were brutal, bloody, and slow.

The kind of death Elide expected to receive at any moment these days, from the witches who prowled the halls or from the dark-eyed duke, his lethal soldiers, or the white-haired Wing Leader who'd tasted her blood like fine wine. She'd had nightmares about it ever since. That is, when she could sleep at all.

Elide had needed to rest twice on her way to the aerie, and her limp was deep by the time she reached the top of the tower, bracing herself for the beasts and the monsters who rode them.

An urgent message had come for the Wing Leader while Elide was cleaning her room—and when Elide explained that the Wing Leader was not there, the man heaved a sigh of relief, shoved the letter in Elide's hand, and said to find her.

And then the man had run.

She should have suspected it. It had taken two heartbeats to note and catalog the man's details, his tells and ticks. Sweaty, his face pale, pupils diluted—he'd sagged at the sight of Elide when she opened the door. Bastard. Most men, she'd decided, were bastards of varying degrees. Most of them were monsters. None worse than Vernon.

Elide scanned the aerie. Empty. Not even a handler to be seen.

The hay floor was fresh, the feeding troughs full of meat and grain. But the food was untouched by the wyverns whose massive, leathery bodies loomed beyond the archways, perched on wooden beams jutting over the plunge as they surveyed the Keep and the army below like thir-teen mighty lords. Limping as close as she dared to one of the massive openings, Elide peered out at the view.

It was exactly as the Wing Leader's map had depicted it in the spare moments when she could sneak a look.

They were surrounded by ashy mountains, and though she'd been in a prison wagon for the long journey here, she had taken note of the forest she spied in the distance and the rushing of the massive river they had passed days before they ascended the broad, rocky mountain road. In the middle of nowhere—that's where Morath was, and the view before her confirmed it: no cities, no towns, and an entire army surrounding her. She shoved back the despair that crept into her veins.

She had never seen an army before coming here. Soldiers, yes, but she'd been eight when her father passed her up onto Vernon's horse and kissed her good-bye, promising to see her soon. She hadn't been in Orynth to witness the army that seized its riches, its people. And she'd been locked in a tower at Perranth Castle by the time the army reached her family's lands and her uncle became the king's ever-faithful servant and stole her father's title.

Her title. Lady of Perranth—that's what she should have been. Not that it mattered now. There wasn't much of Terrasen's court left to belong to. None of them had come for her in those initial months of slaughter. And in the years since, none had remembered that she existed. Perhaps they assumed she was dead—like Aelin, that wild queen-who-might-have-been. Perhaps they were all dead themselves. And maybe, given the dark army now spread before her, that was a mercy.

Elide gazed across the flickering lights of the war camp, and a chill went down her spine. An army to crush whatever resistance Finnula had once whispered about during the long nights they were locked in that tower in Perranth. Perhaps the white-haired Wing Leader herself would lead that army, on the wyvern with shimmering wings.

A fierce, cool wind blew into the aerie, and Elide leaned into it, gulping it down as if it were fresh water. There had been so many nights in Perranth when only the wailing wind had kept her company. When she could have sworn it sang ancient songs to lull her into sleep. Here . . . here the wind was a colder, sleeker thing—serpentine, almost. *Entertaining such fanciful things will only distract you*, Finnula would have chided. She wished her nurse were here.

But wishing had done her no good these past ten years, and Elide, Lady of Perranth, had no one coming for her.

Soon, she reassured herself—soon the next caravan of supplies would crawl up the mountain road, and when it went back down, Elide would be stowed away in one of the wagons, free at long last. And then she would run somewhere far, far away, where they'd never heard of Terrasen or Adarlan, and leave these people to their miserable continent. A few weeks—then she might stand a chance of escaping.

If she survived until then. If Vernon didn't decide he truly did have some wicked purpose in dragging her here. If she didn't wind up with those poor people, caged inside the surrounding mountains, screaming for salvation every night. She'd overheard the other servants whisper about the dark, fell things that went on under those mountains: people being splayed open on black stone altars and then forged into something new, something *other*. For what wretched purpose, Elide had not yet learned, and mercifully, beyond the screaming, she'd never encountered whatever was being broken and pieced together beneath the earth. The witches were bad enough.

Elide shuddered as she took another step into the vast chamber. The crunching of hay under her too-small shoes and the clank of her chains were the only sounds. "W-Wing Lea—"

A roar blasted through the air, the stones, the floor, so loud that her head swam and she cried out. Tumbling back, her chains tangled as she slipped on the hay.

Hard, iron-tipped hands dug into her shoulders and kept her upright.

"If you are not a spy," a wicked voice purred in her ear, "then why are you here, Elide Lochan?"

Elide wasn't faking it when her hand shook as she held out the letter, not daring to move.

The Wing Leader stepped around her, circling Elide like prey, her long white braid stark against her leather flying gear.

The details hit Elide like stones: eyes like burnt gold; a face so impossibly beautiful that Elide was struck dumb by it; a lean, honed body; and a steady, fluid grace in every movement, every breath, that suggested the Wing Leader could easily use the assortment of blades on her. Human only in shape—immortal and predatory in every other sense.

Fortunately, the Wing Leader was alone. Unfortunately, those gold eyes held nothing but death.

Elide said, "Th-this came for you." The stammer—that was faked. People usually couldn't wait to get away when she stammered and stuttered. Though she doubted the people who ran this place would care about the stammer if they decided to have some fun with a daughter of Terrasen. If Vernon handed her over.

The Wing Leader held Elide's gaze as she took the letter.

"I'm surprised the seal isn't broken. Though if you were a good spy, you would know how to do it without breaking the wax."

"If I were a good spy," Elide breathed, "I could also read."

A bit of truth to temper the witch's distrust.

The witch blinked, and then sniffed, as if trying to detect a lie. "You speak well for a mortal, and your uncle is a lord. Yet you cannot read?"

Elide nodded. More than the leg, more than the drudgery, it was that miserable shortcoming that hounded her. Her nurse, Finnula, couldn't read—but Finnula had been the one to teach her how to take note of things, to listen, and to think. During the long days when they'd had nothing to do but needlepoint, her nurse had taught her to mark the little details—each stitch—while also never losing sight of the larger image. *There will come a day when I am gone, Elide, and you will need to have every weapon in your arsenal sharp and ready to strike.*

Neither of them had thought that Elide might be the one who left first. But she would not look back, not even for Finnula, once she ran. And when she found that new life, that new place . . . she would never gaze northward, to Terrasen, and wonder, either.

She kept her eyes on the ground. "I—I know basic letters, but my lessons stopped when I was eight."

"At your uncle's behest, I assume." The witch paused, rotating the envelope and showing the jumble of letters to her, tapping on them with an iron nail. "This says 'Manon Blackbeak.' You see anything like this again, bring it to me."

Elide bowed her head. Meek, submissive—just the way these witches liked their humans. "Of-of course."

"And why don't you stop pretending to be a stammering, cowering wretch while you're at it."

Elide kept her head bent low enough that her hair hopefully covered any glimmer of surprise. "I've tried to be pleasing—"

"I smelled your human fingers all over my map. It was careful, cunning work, not to put one thing out of order, not to touch anything but the map . . . Thinking of escaping after all?"

"Of course not, mistress." Oh, gods. She was so, so dead.

"Look at me."

Elide obeyed. The witch hissed, and Elide flinched as she shoved Elide's hair out of her eyes. A few strands fell to the ground, sliced off by the iron nails. "I don't know what game you're playing—if you're a spy, if you're a thief, if you're just looking out for yourself. But do not pretend that you are some meek, pathetic little girl when I can see that vicious mind working behind your eyes."

Elide didn't dare drop the mask.

"Was it your mother or father who was related to Vernon?"

Strange question—but Elide had known for a while she would do anything, say anything, to stay alive and unharmed. "My father was Vernon's elder brother," she said.

"And where did your mother come from?"

She didn't give that old grief an inch of room in her heart. "She was low-born. A laundress."

"*Where* did she come from?"

Why did it matter? The golden eyes were fixed on her, unyielding. "Her family was originally from Rosamel, in the northwest of Terrasen."

"I know where it is." Elide kept her shoulders bowed, waiting. "Get out."

Hiding her relief, Elide opened her mouth to make her good-byes, when another roar set the stones vibrating. She couldn't conceal her flinch.

"It's just Abraxos," Manon said, a hint of a smile forming on her cruel mouth, a bit of light gleaming in those golden eyes. Her mount must make her happy, then—if witches could be happy. "He's hungry."

Elide's mouth went dry.

At the sound of his name, a massive triangular head, scarred badly around one eye, poked into the aerie.

Elide's knees wobbled, but the witch went right up to the beast and placed her iron-tipped hands on his snout. "You swine," the witch said. "You need the whole mountain to know you're hungry?"

The wyvern huffed into her hands, his giant teeth—oh, gods, some of them were *iron*—so close to Manon's arms. One bite, and the Wing Leader would be dead. One bite, and yet—

The wyvern's eyes lifted and met Elide's. Not looked at, but *met*, as if . . .

Elide kept perfectly still, even though every instinct was roaring at her to run for the stairs. The wyvern nudged past Manon, the floor shuddering beneath him, and sniffed in Elide's direction. Then those giant, depthless eyes moved down—to her legs. No, to the chain.

There were so many scars all over him—so many brutal lines. She did not think Manon had made them, not with the way she spoke to him. Abraxos was smaller than the others, she realized. Far smaller. And yet the Wing Leader had picked him. Elide tucked that information away, too. If Manon had a soft spot for broken things, perhaps she would spare her as well.

Abraxos lowered himself to the ground, stretching out his neck until his head rested on the hay not ten feet from Elide. Those giant black eyes stared up at her, almost doglike.

"Enough, Abraxos," Manon hissed, grabbing a saddle from the rack by the wall.

"How do they—exist?" Elide breathed. She'd heard stories of wyverns and dragons, and she remembered glimpses of the Little Folk and the Fae, but . . .

Manon hauled the leather saddle over to her mount. "The king made them. I don't know how, and it doesn't matter."

The King of Adarlan *made* them, like whatever was being made inside those mountains. The man who had shattered her life, murdered her parents, doomed her to *this* . . . *Don't be angry*, Finnula had said, *be smart*. And soon the king and his miserable empire wouldn't be her concern, anyway.

Elide said, "Your mount doesn't seem evil." Abraxos's tail thumped on the ground, the iron spikes in it glinting. A giant, lethal dog. With wings.

Manon huffed a cold laugh, strapping the saddle into place. "No. However he was made, something went wrong with that part."

Elide didn't think that constituted going *wrong*, but kept her mouth shut.

Abraxos was still staring up at her, and the Wing Leader said, "Let's go hunt, Abraxos."

The beast perked up, and Elide jumped back a step, wincing as she landed hard on her ankle. The wyvern's eyes shot to her, as if aware of the pain. But the Wing Leader was already finishing with the saddle, and didn't bother to look in her direction as Elide limped out.

⁓

"You soft-hearted worm," Manon hissed at Abraxos once the cunning, many-faced girl was gone. The girl might be hiding secrets, but her lineage wasn't one of them. She had no idea that witch-blood flowed strong in her mortal veins. "A crippled leg and a few chains, and you're in love?"

Abraxos nudged her with his snout, and Manon gave him a firm but gentle slap before leaning against his warm hide and ripping open the letter addressed in her grandmother's handwriting.

Just like the High Witch of the Blackbeak Clan, it was brutal, to the point, and unforgiving.

Do not disobey the duke's orders. Do not question him. If there is another letter from Morath about your disobedience, I will fly down there myself and hang you by your intestines, with your Thirteen and that runt of a beast beside you.

Three Yellowlegs and two Blueblood covens are arriving tomorrow. See to it there are no fights or trouble. I do not need the other Matrons breathing down my neck about their vermin.

Manon turned the paper over, but that was it. Crunching it in a fist, she sighed.

Abraxos nudged at her again, and she idly stroked his head.

Made, made, made.

That was what the Crochan had said before Manon slit her throat. *You were made into monsters.*

She tried to forget it—tried to tell herself that the Crochan had been a fanatic and a preachy twat, but . . . She ran a finger down the deep red cloth of her cloak.

The thoughts opened up like a precipice before her, so many all at once that she stepped back. Turned away.

Made, made, made.

Manon climbed into the saddle and was glad to lose herself in the sky.

"Tell me about the Valg," Manon said, shutting the door to the small chamber behind her.

Ghislaine didn't look up from the book she was poring over. There was a stack of them on the desk before her, and another beside the narrow bed. Where the eldest and cleverest of her Thirteen had gotten them from, who she'd likely gutted to steal them, Manon didn't care.

"Hello, and come right in, why don't you" was the response.

Manon leaned against the door and crossed her arms. Only with books, only when *reading*, was Ghislaine so snappish. On the battlefield, in the air, the dark-skinned witch was quiet, easy to command. A solid soldier, made more valuable by her razor-sharp intelligence, which had earned her the spot among the Thirteen.

Ghislaine shut the book and twisted in her seat. Her black, curly hair was braided back, but even the plait couldn't keep it entirely contained. She narrowed her sea-green eyes—the shame of her mother, as there wasn't a trace of gold in them. "Why would you want to know about the Valg?"

"Do *you* know about them?"

Ghislaine pivoted on her chair until she was sitting backward in it, her legs straddling the sides. She was in her flying leathers, as if she couldn't be bothered to remove them before falling into one of her books. "Of course I know about the Valg," she said with a wave of her hand—an impatient, *mortal* gesture.

It had been an exception—an unprecedented exception—when Ghislaine's mother had convinced the High Witch to send her daughter to a mortal school in Terrasen a hundred years ago. She had learned magic and book-things and whatever else mortals were taught, and when Ghislaine had returned twelve years later, the witch had been . . . different. Still a Blackbeak, still bloodthirsty, but somehow more human. Even now, a century later, even after walking on and off killing fields, that sense of impatience, of *life* clung to her. Manon had never known what to make of it.

"Tell me everything."

"There's too much to tell you in one sitting," Ghislaine said. "But I'll give you the basics, and if you want more, you can come back."

An order, but this was Ghislaine's space, and books and knowledge were her domain. Manon motioned with an iron-tipped hand for her sentinel to go on.

"Millennia ago, when the Valg broke into our world, witches did not exist. It was the Valg, and the Fae, and humans. But the Valg were . . . demons, I suppose. They wanted our world for their own, and they thought a good way to get it would be to ensure that their offspring could survive here. The humans weren't compatible—too breakable. But the Fae... The Valg kidnapped and stole whatever Fae they could, and because your eyes are getting that glazed look, I'm just going to jump to the end and say the offspring became us. Witches. The Ironteeth took after our Valg ancestors more, while the Crochans got more of the Fae traits. The people of these lands didn't want us here, not after the war, but the Fae King Brannon didn't think it was right to hunt us all down. So he gave us the Western Wastes, and there we went, until the witch wars made us exiles again."

Manon picked at her nails. "And the Valg are . . . wicked?"

"*We* are wicked," Ghislaine said. "The Valg? Legend has it that they're the origin of evil. They are blackness and despair incarnate."

"Sounds like our kind of people." And maybe good ones indeed to ally with, to breed with.

But Ghislaine's smile faded. "No," she said softly. "No, I do not think they would be our kind of people at all. They have no laws, no codes. They would see the Thirteen as weak for our bonds and rules—as something to break for amusement."

Manon stiffened slightly. "And if the Valg were ever to return here?"

"Brannon and the Fae Queen Maeve found ways to defeat them—to send them back. I would hope that someone would find a way to do so again."

More to think about.

She turned, but Ghislaine said, "That's the smell, isn't it? The smell here, around some of the soldiers—like it's wrong, from another world. The king found some way to bring them here and stuff them into human bodies."

She hadn't thought *that* far, but ... "The duke described them as allies."

"That word does not exist for the Valg. They find the alliance useful, but will honor it only as long as it remains that way."

Manon debated the merits of ending the conversation there, but said, "The duke asked me to pick a Blackbeak coven for him to experiment on.

To allow him to insert some sort of stone in their bellies that will create a Valg-Ironteeth child."

Slowly, Ghislaine straightened, her ink-splattered hands hanging slack on either side of the chair. "And do you plan to obey, Lady?"

Not a question from a scholar to a curious student, but from a sentinel to her heir.

"The High Witch has given me orders to obey the duke's every command." But maybe . . . maybe she would write her grandmother another letter.

"Who will you pick?"

Manon opened the door. "I don't know. My decision is due in two days."

Ghislaine—whom Manon had seen glut herself on the blood of men—had paled by the time Manon shut the door.

Manon didn't know how, didn't know if the guards or the duke or Vernon or some eavesdropping human filth said something, but the next morning, the witches all knew. She knew better than to suspect Ghislaine. None of the Thirteen talked. Ever.

But everyone knew about the Valg, and about Manon's choice.

She strode into the dining hall, its black arches glinting in the rare morning sun. Already, the pounding of the forges was ringing out in the valley below, made louder by the silence that fell as she strode between the tables, headed for her seat at the front of the room.

Coven after coven watched, and she met their gazes, teeth out and nails drawn, Sorrel a steady force of nature at her back. It wasn't until Manon slid into her place beside Asterin—and realized it was now the wrong place, but didn't move—that chatter resumed in the hall.

She pulled a hunk of bread toward her but didn't touch it. None of them ate the food. Breakfast and dinner were always for show, to have a presence here.

The Thirteen didn't say a word.

Manon stared each and every one of them down, until they dropped their eyes. But when her gaze met Asterin's, the witch held it. "Do you have something you want to say," Manon said to her, "or do you just want to start swinging?"

Asterin's eyes flicked over Manon's shoulder. "We have guests."

Manon found the leader of one of the newly arrived Yellowlegs covens standing at the foot of the table, eyes downcast, posture unthreatening— complete submission.

"What?" Manon demanded.

The coven leader kept her head low. "We would request your consideration for the duke's task, Wing Leader."

Asterin stiffened, along with many of the Thirteen. The nearby tables had also gone silent. "And why," Manon asked, "would you want to do that?"

"You will force us to do your drudgery work, to keep us from glory on the killing fields. That is the way of our Clans. But we might win a different sort of glory in this way."

Manon held in her sigh, weighing, contemplating. "I will consider it."

The coven leader bowed and backed away. Manon couldn't decide whether she was a fool or cunning or brave.

None of the Thirteen spoke for the rest of breakfast.

⁓

"And what coven, Wing Leader, have you selected for me?"

Manon met the duke's stare. "A coven of Yellowlegs under a witch named Ninya arrived earlier this week. Use them."

"I wanted Blackbeaks."

"You're getting Yellowlegs," Manon snapped. Down the table, Kaltain did not react. "They volunteered."

Better than Blackbeaks, she told herself. Better that the Yellowlegs had offered themselves.

Even if Manon could have refused them.

She doubted Ghislaine was wrong about the nature of the Valg, but . . . Maybe this could work to their advantage, depending on how the Yellowlegs fared.

The duke flashed his yellowing teeth. "You toe a dangerous line, Wing Leader."

"All witches have to, in order to fly wyverns."

Vernon leaned forward. "These wild, immortal things are so diverting, Your Grace."

Manon gave him a long, long look that told Vernon that one day, in a shadowy hallway, he would find himself with the claws of this wild, immortal thing in his belly.

Manon turned to go. Sorrel—not Asterin—stood stone-faced by the door. Another jarring sight.

Then Manon turned back to the duke, the question forming even as she willed herself not to say it. "To what end? Why do all of this—why ally with the Valg, why raise this army . . . Why?" She could not understand it. The continent already belonged to them. It made no sense.

"Because we can," the duke said simply. "And because this world has too long dwelled in ignorance and archaic tradition. It is time to see what might be improved."

Manon made a show of contemplating and then nodding as she strode out.

But she had not missed the words—*this world*. Not *this land*, not *this continent*.

This world.

She wondered whether her grandmother had considered the idea that they might one day have to fight to keep the Wastes—fight the very men who had helped them take back their home.

And wondered what would become of these Valg-Ironteeth witchlings in that world.

CHAPTER 21

He had tried.

When the blood-soaked woman had spoken to him, when those turquoise eyes had seemed so familiar, he had tried to wrest away control of his body, his tongue. But the demon prince in him had held firm, delighting in his struggle.

He had sobbed with relief when she trapped it and raised an ancient blade over his head. Then she had hesitated—and then that other woman had fired an arrow, and she had put down the sword and left.

Left him still trapped with the demon.

He could not remember her name—refused to remember her name, even as the man on the throne questioned him about the incident. Even as he returned to the exact spot in the garden and prodded the discarded shackles lying in the gravel. She had left him, and with good reason. The demon prince had wanted to feed on her, and then hand her over.

But he wished she had killed him. He hated her for not killing him.

CHAPTER 22

Chaol left his watch on the roof of Aelin's apartment the moment the hooded head of one of the rebels appeared and signaled that he would take over. Thank the gods.

He didn't bother stopping in the apartment to see how Aedion was holding up. Each of his pounding steps on the wooden stairs accented the raging, thunderous beat of his heart, until it was all he could hear, all he could feel.

With the other rebels lying low or monitoring the city and Nesryn gone to make sure her father wasn't in danger, Chaol found himself alone as he stalked through the city streets. Everyone had their orders; everyone was where they were supposed to be. Nesryn had already told him Ress and Brullo had given her the signal that all was clear on their end—and now . . .

Liar. Aelin was and had always been a gods-damned liar. She was as much an oath-breaker as he was. Worse.

Dorian wasn't gone. He wasn't. And he didn't give a shit how much

Aelin trumpeted about *mercy* for Dorian, or that she said it was a weakness not to kill him. The weakness lay in his death—that's what he should have said. The weakness lay in giving up.

He stormed down an alley. He should have been hiding as well, but the roaring in his blood and bones was unrelenting. A sewer grate rang beneath his feet. He paused, and peered into the blackness below.

There were still things to do—so many things to do, so many people to keep from harm. And now that Aelin had yet again humiliated the king, he had no doubt that the Valg would round up more people as punishment, as a statement. With the city still in an uproar, perhaps it was the perfect time for him to strike. To even the odds between them.

No one saw as he climbed into the sewer, closing the lid overhead.

Tunnel after tunnel, his sword gleaming in the afternoon light streaming in through the grates, Chaol hunted those Valg pieces of filth, his steps near-silent. They usually kept to their nests of darkness, but every now and then, stragglers prowled the tunnels. Some of their nests were small—only three or four of them guarding their prisoners—or meals, he supposed. Easy enough for him to ambush.

And wouldn't it be wonderful to see those demon heads roll.

Gone. Dorian is gone.

Aelin didn't know everything. Fire or beheading couldn't be the only choices. Maybe he would keep one of the Valg commanders alive, see just how far gone the man inside of the demon truly was. Maybe there was another way—there *had* to be another way . . .

Tunnel after tunnel after tunnel, all the usual haunts, and no sign of them.

Not one.

Chaol hurried into a near-run as he headed for the largest nest he knew of, where they'd always been able to find civilians in need of rescuing, if they were lucky enough to catch the guards unawares. He would save them—because they deserved it, and because he *had* to keep at it, or else he would crumble and—

Chaol stared at the gaping mouth of the main nest.

Watery sunlight filtering from above illuminated the gray stones and the little river at the bottom. No sign of the telltale darkness that usually smothered it like a dense fog.

Empty.

The Valg soldiers had vanished. And taken their prisoners with them.

He didn't think they'd gone into hiding from fear.

They'd moved on, concealing themselves and their prisoners, as a giant, laughing go-to-hell to every rebel who'd actually thought they were winning this secret war. To Chaol.

He should have thought of pitfalls like this, should have considered what might happen when Aelin Galathynius made a fool of the king and his men.

He should have considered the cost.

Maybe *he* was the fool.

There was a numbness in his blood as he emerged from the sewers onto a quiet street. It was the thought of sitting in his ramshackle apartment, utterly alone with that numbness, that sent him southward, trying to avoid the streets that still teemed with panicked people. Everyone demanded to know what had happened, who had been killed, who had done it. The decorations and baubles and food vendors had been entirely forgotten.

The sounds eventually died away, the streets clearing out as he reached a residential district where the homes were of modest size but elegant, well kept. Little streams and fountains of water from the Avery flowed throughout, lending themselves to the surplus of blooming spring flowers at every gate, windowsill, and tiny lawn.

He knew the house from the smell alone: fresh-baked bread, cinnamon, and some other spice he couldn't name. Taking the alley between the two pale-stoned houses, he kept to the shadows as he approached the back door, peering through the pane of glass to the kitchen within. Flour coated a large worktable, along with baking sheets, various mixing bowls, and—

The door swung open, and Nesryn's slim form filled the entryway. "What are you doing here?"

She was back in her guard's uniform, a knife tucked behind her thigh. She'd no doubt spotted an intruder approaching her father's house and readied herself.

Chaol tried to ignore the weight pushing down on his back, threatening to snap him in two. Aedion was free—they'd accomplished that much. But how many other innocents had they doomed today?

Nesryn didn't wait for his reply before she said, "Come in."

$\smile$

"The guards came and went. My father sent them on their way with pastries."

Chaol glanced up from his own pear tart and scanned the kitchen. Bright tiles accented the walls behind the counters in pretty shades of blue, orange, and turquoise. He'd never been to Sayed Faliq's house before, but he'd known where it was—just in case.

He'd never let himself consider what that "just in case" might entail. Showing up like a stray dog at the back door hadn't been it.

"They didn't suspect him?"

"No. They just wanted to know whether he or his workers saw anyone who looked suspicious before Aedion's rescue." Nesryn pushed another pastry—this one almond and sugar—toward him. "Is the general all right?"

"As far as I know."

He told her about the tunnels, the Valg.

Nesryn only said, "So we'll find them again. Tomorrow."

He waited for her to pace, to shout and swear, but she remained steady—calm. Some tight part of him uncoiled.

She tapped a finger on the wooden table—lovingly worn, as if the kneading of a thousand loaves of bread had smoothed it out. "Why did you come here?"

"For distraction." There was a suspicious gleam in those midnight eyes of hers—enough so that he said, "Not for that."

She didn't even blush, though his own cheeks burned. If she had offered, he probably would have said yes. And hated himself for it.

"You're welcome here," she said, "but surely your friends at the apartment—the general, at least—would provide better company."

"Are they my friends?"

"You and Her Majesty have done a great job trying to be anything but."

"It's hard to be friends without trust."

"You *are* the one who went to Arobynn again, even after she warned you not to."

"And he was right," Chaol said. "He said she would promise not to touch Dorian, and then do the opposite." And he would be forever grateful for the warning shot Nesryn had fired.

Nesryn shook her head, her dark hair glimmering. "Let's just imagine that Aelin is right. That Dorian is gone. What then?"

"She's not right."

"Let's just imagine—"

He slammed his fist on the table hard enough to rattle his glass of water. "*She's not right!*"

Nesryn pursed her lips, even as her eyes softened. "Why?"

He scrubbed at his face. "Because then it's all for nothing. Everything that happened . . . it's all for *nothing*. You wouldn't understand."

"I wouldn't?" A cold question. "You think that I don't understand what's at stake? I don't care about your prince—not the way you do. I care about what he represents for the future of this kingdom, and for the future of people like my family. I won't allow another immigrant purge to happen. I don't ever want my sister's children coming home with broken noses again because of their foreign blood. You told me Dorian would fix the world, make it better. But if he's gone, if *we* made the mistake today in keeping him alive, then I will find another way to attain that future. And another one after that, if I have to. I will keep getting back up, no matter how many times those butchers shove me down."

He'd never heard so many words from her at once, had never . . . never even known she had a sister. Or that she was an aunt.

Nesryn said, "Stop feeling sorry for yourself. Stay the course, but also plot another one. Adapt."

His mouth had gone dry. "Were you ever hurt? For your heritage?"

Nesryn glanced toward the roaring hearth, her face like ice. "I became a city guard because not a single one of them came to my aid the day the other schoolchildren surrounded me with stones in their hands. Not one, even though they could hear my screaming." She met his stare again. "Dorian Havilliard offers a better future, but the responsibility also lies with us. With how common people choose to act."

True—so true, but he said, "I won't abandon him."

She sighed. "You're even more hardheaded than the queen."

"Would you expect me to be anything else?"

A half smile. "I don't think I would like you if you were anything but a stubborn ass."

"You actually admit to liking me?"

"Did last summer not tell you enough?"

Despite himself, Chaol laughed.

"Tomorrow," Nesryn said. "Tomorrow, we continue on."

He swallowed. "Stay the course, but plot a new path." He could do that; he could try it, at least.

"See you in the sewers bright and early."

CHAPTER 23

Aedion rose to consciousness and took in every detail that he could without opening his eyes. A briny breeze from a nearby open window tickled his face; fishermen were shouting their catches a few blocks away; and—and someone was breathing evenly, deeply, nearby. Sleeping.

He opened an eye to find that he was in a small, wood-paneled room decorated with care and a penchant for the luxurious. He knew this room. Knew this apartment.

The door across from his bed was open, revealing the great room beyond—clean and empty and bathed in sunshine. The sheets he slept between were crisp and silken, the pillows plush, the mattress impossibly soft. Exhaustion coated his bones, and pain splintered through his side, but dully. And his head was infinitely clearer as he looked toward the source of that even, deep breathing and beheld the woman asleep in the cream-colored armchair beside the bed.

Her long, bare legs were sprawled over one of the rolled arms, scars of every shape and size adorning them. She rested her head against the wing, her shoulder-length golden hair—the ends stained a reddish brown, as if a cheap dye had been roughly washed out—strewn across her face. Her mouth was slightly open as she dozed, comfortable in an oversized white shirt and what looked to be a pair of men's undershorts. Safe. Alive.

For a moment, he couldn't breathe.

Aelin.

He mouthed her name.

As if she heard it, she opened her eyes—coming fully alert as she scanned the doorway, the room beyond, then the bedroom itself for any danger. And then finally, finally she looked at him and went utterly still, even as her hair shifted in the gentle breeze.

The pillow beneath his face had become damp.

She just stretched out her legs like a cat and said, "I'm ready to accept your thanks for my spectacular rescue at any time, you know."

He couldn't stop the tears leaking down his face, even as he rasped, "Remind me never to get on your bad side."

A smile tugged at her lips, and her eyes—their eyes—sparkled. "Hello, Aedion."

Hearing his name on her tongue snapped something loose, and he had to close his eyes, his body barking in pain as it shook with the force of the tears trying to get out of him. When he'd mastered himself, he said hoarsely, "Thank you for your spectacular rescue. Let's never do it again."

She snorted, her eyes lined with silver. "You're exactly the way I dreamed you'd be."

Something in her smile told him that she already knew—that Ren or Chaol had told her about him, about being Adarlan's Whore, about the Bane. So all he could say was, "You're a little taller than I'd imagined, but no one's perfect."

"It's a miracle the king managed to resist executing you until yesterday."

"Tell me he's in a rage the likes of which have never been seen before."

"If you listen hard enough, you can actually hear him shrieking from the palace."

Aedion laughed, and it made his wound ache. But the laugh died as he looked her over from head to toe. "I'm going to throttle Ren and the captain for letting you save me alone."

"And here we go." She looked at the ceiling and sighed loudly. "A minute of pleasant conversation, and then the territorial Fae bullshit comes raging out."

"I waited an extra thirty seconds."

Her mouth quirked to the side. "I honestly thought you'd last ten."

He laughed again, and realized that though he'd loved her before, he'd merely loved the memory—the princess taken away from him. But the woman, the queen—the last shred of family he had . . .

"It was worth it," he said, his smile fading. "You were worth it. All these years, all the waiting. You're worth it." He'd known the moment she had looked up at him as she stood before his execution block, defiant and wicked and wild.

"I think that's the healing tonic talking," she said, but her throat bobbed as she wiped at her eyes. She lowered her feet to the floor. "Chaol said you're even meaner than I am most of the time."

"Chaol is already on his way to being throttled, and you're not helping."

She gave that half smile again. "Ren's in the North—I didn't get to see him before Chaol convinced him to go there for his own safety."

"Good," he managed to say, and patted the bed beside him. Someone had stuffed him into a clean shirt, so he was decent enough, but he managed to haul himself halfway into a sitting position. "Come here."

She glanced at the bed, at his hand, and he wondered whether he'd crossed some line, assumed some bond between them that no longer existed—until her shoulders slumped and she uncoiled from the chair in a smooth, feline motion before plopping down on the mattress.

Her scent hit him. For a second, he could only breathe it deep into his lungs, his Fae instincts roaring that this was his family, this was his queen, this was *Aelin*. He would have known her even if he were blind.

Even if there was another scent entwined with hers. Staggeringly powerful and ancient and—male. Interesting.

She plumped up the pillows, and he wondered if she knew how much it meant to him, as a demi-Fae male, to have her lean over to straighten his blankets, too, then run a sharp, critical eye down his face. To fuss over him.

He stared right back, scanning for any wounds, any sign that the blood on her the other day hadn't belonged only to those men. But save for a few shallow, scabbed cuts on her left forearm, she was unharmed.

When she seemed assured that he wasn't about to die, and when he was assured the wounds on her arm weren't infected, she leaned back on the pillows and folded her hands over her abdomen. "Do you want to go first, or should I?"

Outside, gulls were crying to each other, and that soft, briny breeze kissed his face. "You," he whispered. "Tell me everything."

So she did.

They talked and talked, until Aedion's voice became hoarse, and then Aelin bullied him into drinking a glass of water. And then she decided that he was looking peaky, so she padded to the kitchen and dug up some beef broth and bread. Lysandra, Chaol, and Nesryn were nowhere to be seen, so they had the apartment to themselves. Good. Aelin didn't feel like sharing her cousin right now.

As Aedion devoured his food, he told her the unabridged truth of what had happened to him these past ten years, just as she'd done for him. And when they were both finished telling their stories, when their souls were drained and grieving—but gilded with growing joy—she nestled down across from Aedion, her cousin, her friend.

They'd been forged of the same ore, two sides of the same golden, scarred coin.

She'd known it when she spied him atop the execution platform. She couldn't explain it. No one could understand that instant bond, that soul-deep assurance and rightness, unless they, too, had experienced it. But she owed no explanations to anyone—not about Aedion.

They were still sprawled on the bed, the sun now settling into late afternoon, and Aedion was just staring at her, blinking, as if he couldn't quite believe it.

"Are you ashamed of what I've done?" she dared to ask.

His brow creased. "Why would you ever think that?"

She couldn't quite look him in the eye as she ran a finger down the blanket. "Are you?"

Aedion was silent long enough that she lifted her head—but found him gazing toward the door, as though he could see through it, across the city, to the captain. When he turned to her, his handsome face was open—soft in a way she doubted many ever saw. "Never," he said. "I could never be ashamed of you."

She doubted that, and when she twisted away, he gently grabbed her chin, forcing her eyes to him.

"You survived; I survived. We're together again. I once begged the gods to let me see you—if only for a moment. To see you and know you'd made it. Just once; that was all I ever hoped for."

She couldn't stop the tears that began slipping down her face.

"Whatever you had to do to survive, whatever you did from spite or rage or selfishness . . . I don't give a damn. You're here—and you're perfect. You always were, and you always will be."

She hadn't realized how much she needed to hear that.

She flung her arms around him, careful of his injuries, and squeezed him as tightly as she dared. He wrapped an arm around her, the other bracing them, and buried his face in her neck.

"I missed you," she whispered onto him, breathing in his scent—that male warrior's scent she was just learning, remembering. "Every day, I missed you."

Her skin grew damp beneath his face. "Never again," he promised.

It was honestly no surprise that after Aelin had trashed the Vaults, a new warren of sin and debauchery had immediately sprung up in the slums.

The owners weren't even trying to pretend it wasn't a complete imitation of the original—not with a name like the Pits. But while its predecessor had at least provided a tavern-like atmosphere, the Pits didn't bother. In an underground chamber hewn from rough stone, you paid for your alcohol with your cover charge—and if you wanted to drink, you had to brave the casks in the back and serve yourself. Aelin found herself somewhat inclined to like the owners: they operated by a different set of rules.

But some things remained the same.

The floors were slick and reeking of ale and piss and worse, but Aelin had anticipated that. What she hadn't expected, exactly, was the deafening noise. The rock walls and close quarters magnified the wild cheers from the fighting pits the place had been named after, where onlookers were betting on the brawls within.

Brawls like the one she was about to participate in.

Beside her, Chaol, cloaked and masked, shifted on his feet. "This is a terrible idea," he murmured.

"You said you couldn't find the Valg nests, anyway," she said with equal quiet, tucking a loose strand of her hair—dyed red once more—back under her hood. "Well, here are some lovely commanders and minions, just waiting for you to track them home. Consider it Arobynn's form of an apology." Because he knew that she would bring Chaol with her tonight. She'd guessed as much, debated not bringing the captain, but in the end she needed him here, needed to be here herself, more than she needed to upend Arobynn's plans.

Chaol sliced a glare in her direction, but then shifted his attention to the crowd around them, and said again, "This is a terrible idea."

She followed his stare toward Arobynn, who stood across the sandy pit in which two men were fighting, now so bloodied up she couldn't tell who was in worse shape. "He summons, I answer. Just keep your eyes open."

It was the most they'd said to each other all night. But she had other things to worry about.

It had taken just one minute in this place to understand why Arobynn had summoned her.

The Valg guards flocked to the Pits—not to arrest and torture, but to watch. They were interspersed among the crowd, hooded, smiling, cold.

As if the blood and rage fueled them.

Beneath her black mask, Aelin focused on her breathing.

Three days after his rescue, Aedion was still injured badly enough that he remained bedridden, one of Chaol's most trusted rebels watching over the apartment. But she needed someone at her back tonight, so she'd asked Chaol and Nesryn to come. Even if she knew it would play into Arobynn's plans.

She'd tracked them down at a covert rebel meeting, to no one's delight.

Especially when, apparently, the Valg had vanished with their victims and couldn't be found despite days of tracking them. One look at Chaol's pursed lips had told her exactly whose *antics* he thought were to blame for it. So she was glad to talk to Nesryn instead, if only to take her mind off the new task pressing on her, its chiming now a mocking invitation from the glass castle. But destroying the clock tower—freeing magic—had to wait.

At least she'd been right about Arobynn wanting Chaol here, the Valg clearly an offering meant to entice the captain to continue trusting and confiding in him.

Aelin sensed Arobynn's arrival at her side moments before his red hair slid into her peripheral vision.

"Any plans to wreck this establishment, too?"

A dark head appeared at his other side, along with the wide-eyed male stares that followed it everywhere. Aelin was grateful for the mask that hid the tightness in her face as Lysandra inclined her head in greeting. Aelin made a good show of looking Lysandra up and down, and then turned to Arobynn, dismissing the courtesan as if she were no more than a bit of ornamentation.

"I just cleaned the suit," Aelin drawled to Arobynn. "Wrecking this shit-hole would only mess it up again."

Arobynn chuckled. "In case you were wondering, a certain celebrated dancer was on a ship heading south with all her dancers before word of your escapades even reached the docks." The roar of the crowd nearly drowned out his words. Lysandra frowned at a reveler who nearly spilled his ale on the skirts of her mint-and-cream gown.

"Thank you," Aelin said, and meant it. She didn't bring up Arobynn's little game of playing her and Chaol against each other—not when that was precisely what he wanted. Arobynn gave her a smile smug enough to make her ask, "Is there a particular reason that my services are necessary here tonight, or is this another present of yours?"

"After you so gleefully wrecked the Vaults, I'm now in the market for a new investment. The owners of the Pits, despite being public about *wanting* an investor, are hesitant to accept my offer. Participating tonight will go a long way toward convincing them of my considerable assets and . . . what I might bring to the table." And make a threat to the owners, to show off his deadly arsenal of assassins—and how they might help turn an even higher profit with fixed fights against trained killers. She knew exactly what he would say next. "Alas, my fighter fell through," Arobynn went on. "I needed a replacement."

"And who am I fighting as, exactly?"

"I told the owners you were trained by the Silent Assassins of the Red Desert. You remember them, don't you? Give the pit-lord whatever name you want."

Prick. She'd never forget those months in the Red Desert. Or who had sent her there.

She jerked her chin at Lysandra. "Aren't you a little fussy for this sort of place?"

"And here I was thinking you and Lysandra had become friends after your dramatic rescue."

"Arobynn, let's go watch somewhere else," Lysandra murmured. "The fight's ending."

She wondered what it was like to have to endure the man who had slaughtered your lover. But Lysandra's face was a mask of worried, wary mindlessness—another skin she wore as she idly cooled herself with a gorgeous fan of lace and ivory. So out of place in this cesspit.

"Pretty, isn't it? Arobynn gave it to me," Lysandra said, noticing her attention.

"A small trinket for such a tremendously talented lady," Arobynn said, leaning down to kiss Lysandra's bare neck.

Aelin clamped down on her disgust so hard that she choked on it.

Arobynn sauntered off into the crowd like a snake through the grass, catching the eye of the willowy pit-lord. When he was deep enough into the crowd, Aelin stepped closer to Lysandra. The courtesan glanced away from her, and Aelin knew it wasn't an act.

So softly no one could hear, Aelin said, "Thank you—for the other day."

Lysandra kept her eyes on the crowd and the bloodied fighters around them. They landed on the Valg, and she quickly looked at Aelin again, shifting so that the crowd formed a wall between her and the demons across the pit. "Is he all right?"

"Yes—just resting and eating as much as he can," Aelin said. And now that Aedion was safe . . . she would soon have to begin fulfilling her little favor to Arobynn. Though she doubted her former master had long to live once Aedion recovered and found out what sort of danger Arobynn was putting her in. Let alone what he'd done to her throughout the years.

"Good," Lysandra said, the crowd keeping them cocooned.

Arobynn clapped the pit-lord on the shoulder and stalked back toward them. Aelin tapped her foot until the King of the Assassins was between them again.

Chaol subtly moved within earshot, a hand on his sword.

Aelin just braced her hands on her hips. "Who shall my opponent be?"

Arobynn inclined his head toward a pack of the Valg guards. "Whichever one of them you desire. I just hope you choose one in less time than it's taken you to decide which one to hand over to me."

So that was what this was about. Who had the upper hand. And if she refused, with the debt unpaid . . . He could do worse. So much worse.

"You're insane," Chaol said to Arobynn, following his line of sight.

"So he speaks," Arobynn purred. "You're welcome, by the way—for the little tip." He flicked his gaze toward the gathered Valg. So they were a gift for the captain, then.

Chaol glared. "I don't need you to do my work—"

"Stay out of it," Aelin snapped, hoping Chaol would understand the ire wasn't for him. He turned back toward the blood-splattered sand, shaking his head. Let him be mad; she had plenty to rage at him for anyway.

The crowd died down, and the pit-lord called for the next fighter.

"You're up," Arobynn said, smiling. "Let's see what those things are capable of."

Lysandra squeezed his arm, as if pleading for him to let it go. "I would keep back," Aelin said to her, cracking her neck. "You wouldn't want to get blood on that pretty dress."

Arobynn chuckled. "Put on a good show, would you? I want the owners impressed—and pissing themselves."

Oh, she would put on a show. After days cooped up in the apartment at Aedion's side, she had energy to spare.

And she didn't mind spilling some Valg blood.

She shoved through the crowd, not daring to draw more attention to Chaol by saying good-bye. People took one look at her and backed away. With the suit, the boots, and the mask, she knew she was Death incarnate.

Aelin dropped into a swagger, her hips shifting with each step, rolling her shoulders as if loosening them. The crowd grew louder, restless.

She sidled up to the willowy pit-lord, who looked her over and said, "No weapons."

She merely cocked her head and lifted her arms, turning in a circle, and even allowed the pit-lord's little minion to pat her down with his sweaty hands to prove that she was unarmed.

As far as they could tell.

"Name," the pit-lord demanded. Around her, gold was already flashing.

"Ansel of Briarcliff," she said, the mask distorting her voice to a gravelly rasp.

"Opponent."

Aelin looked across the pit, to the crowd gathered, and pointed. "Him."

The Valg commander was already grinning at her.

CHAPTER 24

Chaol didn't know what the hell to think as Aelin leaped into the pit, landing on her haunches. But the crowd had seen whom she'd pointed to and was already in a frenzy, shoving to the front, passing gold as last-minute bets were made.

He had to plant his heels to keep from being knocked over the open lip of the pit. No ropes or railings here. If you fell in, you were fair game. A small part of him was glad Nesryn was on watch in the back. And a smaller part of him was glad for a night without more fruitless hunting for the new Valg nests. Even if it meant dealing with Aelin for a few hours. Even if Arobynn Hamel had given him this little *gift*. A gift that, he hated to admit, he sorely needed and did appreciate. But that was no doubt how Arobynn operated.

Chaol wondered what the price would be. Or whether his fear of a potential price was payment enough for the King of the Assassins.

Dressed head to toe in black, Aelin was a living shadow, pacing like a jungle cat on her side of the pit as the Valg commander jumped in. He could have sworn the ground shuddered.

They were both insane—Aelin *and* her master. Arobynn had said to choose any one of the Valg. She'd picked their leader.

They'd barely spoken since their fight after Aedion's rescue. Frankly, she didn't deserve a word out of him, but when she'd hunted him down an hour ago, interrupting a meeting that was so secret that they'd disclosed the location to the rebel leaders only an hour before . . . Maybe he was a fool, but he couldn't in good conscience say no. If only because Aedion would have slaughtered him for it.

But since the Valg were here . . . Yes, this night had been useful after all.

The pit-lord began shouting the rules. Simply: there were none, save for no blades. Just hands and feet and wits.

Gods above.

Aelin stilled her pacing, and Chaol had to elbow an overeager man in the stomach to keep from being shoved into the pit.

The Queen of Terrasen was in a fighting pit in the slums of Rifthold. No one here, he'd wager, would believe it. He was hardly able to believe it himself.

The pit-lord roared for the match to begin, and then—

They moved.

The commander lunged with a punch so swift most men would have had their heads spun around. But Aelin dodged and caught his arm in one hand, locking it into a hold he knew was bone-snapping. As the commander's face twisted with pain, she drove her knee up into the side of his head.

It was so fast, so brutal, even the crowd didn't know what the hell had happened until the commander was staggering back, and Aelin was dancing on her toes.

The commander laughed, straightening. It was the only break Aelin gave him before she went on the offensive.

She moved like a midnight storm. Whatever training she'd had in Wendlyn, whatever that prince had taught her . . . Gods help them all.

Punch after punch, block, lunge, duck, spin . . . The crowd was a writhing thing, foaming at the mouth at the swiftness, the skill.

Chaol had seen her kill. It had been a while since he'd seen her fight for the enjoyment of it.

And she was enjoying the hell out of this.

An opponent worthy of her, he supposed as she locked her legs around the commander's head and rolled, flipping him.

Sand sprayed around them. She wound up on top, driving her fist down into the man's cold, handsome face—

Only to be hurled off with a twist so swift that Chaol could hardly follow the movement. Aelin hit the bloodied sand and uncoiled to her feet just as the commander attacked once more.

Then they were again a blur of limbs and blows and darkness.

Across the pit, Arobynn was wide-eyed, grinning, a starving man before a feast. Lysandra clung to his side, her knuckles white as she gripped his arm. Men were whispering in Arobynn's ear, their eyes locked on the pit, as hungry as Arobynn. Either the owners of the Pits or prospective clients, bargaining for the use of the woman fighting with such wild wrath and wicked delight.

Aelin landed a kick to the commander's stomach that sent him slamming into the rock wall. He slumped, gasping for air. The crowd cheered, and Aelin flung out her arms, turning in a slow circle, Death triumphant.

The crowd's answering roar made Chaol wonder if the ceiling would come crashing down.

The commander hurtled for her, and Aelin whirled, catching him and locking his arms and neck into a hold not easily broken. She looked at Arobynn, as if in question.

Her master glanced at the wide-eyed, ravenous men beside him—then nodded to her.

Chaol's stomach turned over. Arobynn had seen enough. Proved enough.

It hadn't even been a fair fight. Aelin had let it go on because Arobynn had *wanted* it to go on. And once she took out that clock tower and her magic was back . . . What checks would there be against her? Against Aedion, and that Fae Prince of hers, and all the warriors like them? A new world, yes. But a world in which the ordinary human voice would be nothing more than a whisper.

Aelin twisted the commander's arms, and the demon shrieked in pain, and then—

Then Aelin was staggering back, clutching at her forearm, at the blood shining bright through the shred in her suit.

It was only when the commander whirled, blood slipping down his chin, his eyes pitch black, that Chaol understood. He'd bitten her. Chaol hissed through his teeth.

The commander licked his lips, his bloody grin growing. Even with the crowd, Chaol could hear the Valg demon say, "I know what you are now, you half-breed bitch."

Aelin lowered the hand she'd clapped on her arm, blood shining on her dark glove. "Good thing I know what you are, too, prick."

End it. She had to end it *now*.

"What's your name?" she said, circling the demon commander.

The demon inside the man's body chuckled. "You cannot pronounce it in your human tongue." The voice skittered down Chaol's veins, icing them.

"So condescending for a mere grunt," she crooned.

"I should bring you down to Morath myself, half-breed, and see how much you talk then. See what you make of all the delicious things we do to your kind."

Morath—Duke Perrington's Keep. Chaol's stomach turned leaden. That was where they brought the prisoners who weren't executed. The ones who vanished in the night. To do the gods knew what with them.

Aelin didn't give him time to say anything more, and Chaol again wished he could see her face, if only to know what the hell was going on in her head as she tackled the commander. She slammed his considerable weight into the sand and grabbed his head.

Crack went the commander's neck.

Her hands lingering on either side of the demon's face, Aelin stared at the empty eyes, at the open mouth. The crowd screamed its triumph.

Aelin panted, her shoulders hunched, and then she straightened, brushing the sand off the knees of her suit.

She gazed up at the pit-lord. "Call it."

The man blanched. "Victory is yours."

She didn't bother looking up again as she knocked her boot against the stone wall, freeing a thin, horrible blade.

Chaol was grateful for the screams of the crowd as she stomped it down through the neck of the commander. Again. Again.

In the dim lighting, no one else could tell the stain in the sand wasn't the right color.

No one but the stone-faced demons gathered around them, marking Aelin, watching each movement of her leg as she severed the commander's head from his body and then left it in the sand.

Aelin's arms were trembling as she took Arobynn's hand and was hauled out of the pit.

Her master crushed her fingers in a lethal grip, pulling her close in what anyone else would have thought was an embrace. "That's twice now, darling, you haven't delivered. I said *unconscious*."

"Bloodlust got the better of me, it seems." She eased back, her left arm aching from the vicious bite the thing had given her. Bastard. She could almost feel its blood seeping through the thick leather of her boot, feel the weight of the gore clinging onto the toe.

"I expect results, *Ansel*—and soon."

"Don't worry, *Master*." Chaol was making his way toward a darkened corner, Nesryn a shadow behind him, no doubt readying to track the Valg once they left. "You'll get what's owed to you." Aelin looked toward Lysandra, whose attention wasn't on the corpse being hauled out of the pit by the grunts, but fixed—with predatory focus—on the other Valg guards sneaking out.

Aelin cleared her throat, and Lysandra blinked, her expression smoothing into unease and repulsion.

Aelin made to slip out, but Arobynn said, "Aren't you the least bit curious where we buried Sam?"

He'd known his words would register like a blow. He'd had the upper hand, the sure-kill shot, the entire time. Even Lysandra recoiled a bit.

Aelin slowly turned. "Is there a price for learning that information?"

A flick of his attention to the pit. "You just paid it."

"I wouldn't put it past you to give me a fake location and have me bring stones to the wrong grave."

Not flowers—never flowers in Terrasen. Instead, they carried small stones to graves to mark their visits, to tell the dead that they still remembered.

Stones were eternal—flowers were not.

"You wound me with such accusations." Arobynn's elegant face told another story. He closed the distance between them, and said so quietly that Lysandra couldn't hear, "Do you think you will not have to pay up at some point?"

She bared her teeth. "Is that a threat?"

"It is a suggestion," he said smoothly, "that you remember what my considerable influences are, and what I might have to offer you and yours during a time when you are desperate for so many things: money, fighters . . ." A glance at the vanishing captain and Nesryn. "Things your friends need, too."

For a price—always for a price. "Just tell me where you buried Sam and let me leave. I need to clean my shoes."

He smiled, satisfied that he'd won and she'd accepted his little offering—no doubt soon to make another bargain, and then another, for whatever she needed from him. He named the location, a small graveyard by the river's edge. Not in the crypts of the Assassins' Keep, where most of them were entombed. Likely meant as an insult to Sam—not realizing Sam wouldn't have wanted to be buried in the Keep anyway.

Still, she choked out, "Thank you." And then she made herself look at Lysandra and drawl, "I hope he's paying you enough."

Lysandra's attention, however, was on the long scar marring Arobynn's neck—the scar Wesley had left. But Arobynn was too busy smiling at Aelin to notice. "We'll be seeing each other again soon," he said. Another threat. "Hopefully when you've upheld your end of the bargain."

The hard-faced men who had been at Arobynn's side during the fight still lingered several feet away. The owners of the Pits. They gave her a slight nod that she didn't return. "Tell your new partners I'm officially retired," she said by way of farewell.

It was an effort of will to leave Lysandra with him in that hellhole.

She could feel the Valg sentries monitoring her, feel their indecision and malice, and hoped that Chaol and Nesryn didn't run into trouble as she vanished into the open, cool night air.

She hadn't asked them to come just to watch her back, but to make them realize precisely how stupid they'd been in trusting a man like Arobynn Hamel. Even if Arobynn's gift was the reason they were now able to track the Valg back to wherever they were squatting.

She just hoped that despite her former master's gift, they at last understood that she should have killed Dorian that day.

CHAPTER 25

Elide was washing dishes, carefully listening to the cook complain about the next scheduled shipment of supplies. A few wagons would arrive in two weeks, it seemed, carrying wine and vegetables and perhaps, if they were lucky, salted meat. Yet it wasn't what was coming that interested her, but how it was carried, what sort of wagons might bear it. And where Elide might best hide in one.

That was when one of the witches walked in.

Not Manon, but the one named Asterin, golden-haired with eyes like a star-flecked night and a wildness in her very breath. Elide had long ago noted how quick she was to grin, and had marked the moments when Asterin thought no one was looking and gazed across the horizon, her face tight. Secrets—Asterin was a witch with secrets. And secrets made people deadly.

Elide kept her head down, shoulders tucked in, as the kitchen quieted in the Third's presence. Asterin just swaggered right up to the cook, who had gone pale as death. He was a loud, kind man most days, but a coward at heart.

"Lady Asterin," he said, and everyone—Elide included—bowed.

The witch smiled—with white, normal teeth, thank the gods. "I was thinking I might help with the dishes."

Elide's blood chilled. She felt the eyes of everyone in the kitchen fix on her.

"As much as we appreciate it, Lady—"

"Are you rejecting my offer, mortal?" Elide didn't dare to turn around. Beneath the soapy water, her pruny hands shook. She fisted them. Fear was useless; fear got you killed.

"N-no. Of course, Lady. We—and Elide—will be glad for the help."

And that was that.

The clatter and chaos of the kitchen slowly resumed, but conversation remained hushed. They were all watching, waiting—either for Elide's blood to spill on the gray stones, or to overhear anything juicy from the ever-smiling lips of Asterin Blackbeak.

She felt each step the witch took toward her—unhurried, but powerful.

"You wash. I'll dry," the sentinel said at her side.

Elide peeked out from behind the curtain of her hair. Asterin's black-and-gold eyes glittered.

"Th-thank you," she made herself stammer.

The amusement in those immortal eyes grew. Not a good sign.

But Elide continued her work, passing the witch the pots and plates.

"An interesting task, for a lord's daughter," Asterin observed, quietly enough that no one else in the bustling kitchen could hear.

"I'm happy to help."

"That chain says otherwise."

Elide didn't falter with the washing; didn't let the pot in her hands slip an inch. Five minutes, and then she could murmur some explanation and run.

"No one else in this place is chained up like a slave. What makes you so dangerous, Elide Lochan?"

Elide gave a little shrug. An interrogation—that's what this was. Manon had called her a spy. It seemed her sentinel had decided to assess what level of threat she posed.

"You know, men have always hated and feared our kind," Asterin went on. "It's rare for them to catch us, to kill us, but when they do . . . Oh, they delight in such horrible things. In the Wastes, they've made machines to break us apart. The fools never realized that all they needed to do to torture our kind, to make us beg"—she glanced down at Elide's legs— "was to chain us. Keep us tied to the earth."

"I'm sorry to hear that."

Two of the fowl-pluckers had hooked their hair behind their ears in a futile attempt to overhear them. But Asterin knew how to keep her voice low.

"You're, what—fifteen? Sixteen?"

"Eighteen."

"Small for your age." Asterin gave her a look that made Elide wonder if she could see through the homespun dress to the bandage she used to flatten her full breasts into an unnoticeable chest. "You must have been eight or nine when magic fell."

Elide scrubbed at the pot. She'd finish it and go. Talking about magic around these people, so many of them eager to sell any bit of information to the dread-lords who ruled this place . . . It would earn her a trip to the gallows.

"The witchlings who were your age at the time," the sentinel went on, "never even had a chance to fly. The power doesn't set in until their first bleeding. At least now they have the wyverns. But it's not the same, is it?"

"I wouldn't know."

Asterin leaned in close, an iron skillet in her long, deadly hands. "But your uncle does, doesn't he?"

Elide made herself smaller and bought herself a few more seconds of time as she pretended to consider. "I don't understand."

"You've never heard the wind calling your name, Elide Lochan? Never felt it tug at you? You've never listened to it and yearned to fly toward the horizon, to foreign lands?"

She'd spent most of her life locked in a tower, but there had been nights, wild storms . . .

Elide managed to get the last bit of burnt food off the pot and rinsed it, handing it to the witch before wiping her hands on her apron. "No, Lady. I don't see why I would."

Even if she *did* want to flee—wanted to run to the other end of the world and wash her hands of these people forever. But it had nothing to do with the whispering wind.

Asterin's black eyes seemed to devour her whole. "You would hear that wind, girl," she said with expert quiet, "because anyone with Ironteeth blood does. I'm surprised your mother never told you. It's passed on through the maternal line."

Witch-blood. *Ironteeth* blood. In her veins—in her *mother's* lineage.

It wasn't possible. Her blood flowed red; she had no iron teeth or nails. Her mother had been the same. If there was ancestry, it was so old that it had been forgotten, but . . .

"My mother died when I was a child," she said, turning away and nodding her farewell to the head cook. "She never told me anything."

"Pity," Asterin said.

The servants all gawked at Elide as she limped out, their questioning eyes telling her enough: they hadn't heard. A small relief, then.

Gods—oh, gods. Witch-blood.

Elide took the stairs up, each movement sending shooting pains through her leg. Was that why Vernon had kept her chained? To keep her from flying off if she ever showed a lick of power? Was that why the windows in that tower in Perranth had been barred?

No—no. She was human. Fully human.

But at the very moment these witches had gathered, when she'd heard those rumors about the demons who wanted to . . . to . . . *breed*, Vernon had brought her here. And had become very, very close with Duke Perrington.

She prayed to Anneith with every step upward, prayed to the Lady of Wise Things that she was wrong, that the Third was wrong. It wasn't until she reached the foot of the Wing Leader's tower that Elide realized she had no idea where she was going.

She had nowhere to go at all. No one to run to.

The delivery wagons wouldn't arrive for another few weeks. Vernon could hand her over whenever he wished. Why hadn't he done so immediately? What was he waiting for? To see if the first of the experiments worked before offering her as a bargaining chip for more power?

If she *was* such a valuable commodity, she'd have to go farther than she'd suspected to escape Vernon. Not just to the Southern Continent, but beyond, to lands she'd never heard of. But with no money, how would she? No money—except for the bags of coins the Wing Leader left scattered around her room. She peered up the stairs stretching into the gloom. Maybe she could use the money to bribe someone—a guard, a lower-coven witch—to get her out. Immediately.

Her ankle barked in pain as she hurried up the staircase. She wouldn't take an entire bag, but rather a few coins from each, so the Wing Leader wouldn't notice.

Mercifully, the witch's room was empty. And the various bags of coins had been left out with a carelessness only an immortal witch more interested in bloodshed could achieve.

Elide carefully set about stuffing coins into her pocket, the binding around her breasts, and her shoe so that they wouldn't be discovered all at once, so they wouldn't jingle.

"Are you out of your mind?"

Elide froze.

Asterin was leaning against the wall, her arms crossed.

⌒

The Third was smiling, each of those razor-sharp iron teeth glinting in the afternoon light.

"Bold, mad little thing," the witch said, circling Elide. "Not as docile as you pretend, eh?"

Oh, gods.

"To steal from our Wing Leader . . ."

"Please," Elide whispered. Begging—maybe that would work. "Please—I need to leave this place."

"Why?" A glance at the pouch of money clenched in Elide's hands.

"I heard what they're doing with the Yellowlegs. My uncle—if I have . . . if I have your blood, I can't let him use me like that."

"Running away because of Vernon . . . At least now we know you're not his spy, witchling." The witch grinned, and it was almost as terrifying as one of Manon's smiles.

That was why she'd ambushed her with the knowledge: to see where Elide would run to after.

"Don't call me that," Elide breathed.

"Is it so bad to be a witch?" Asterin spread her fingers, appreciating her iron nails in the dim light.

"I'm not a witch."

"What are you, then?"

"Nothing—I'm nobody. I'm nothing."

The witch clicked her tongue. "Everybody is something. Even the most common witch has her coven. But who has your back, Elide Lochan?"

"No one." Only Anneith, and Elide sometimes thought even that could be her imagination.

"There is no such thing as a witch being alone."

"I'm not a witch," she said again. And once she got away, once she left this festering empire, she'd be no one at all.

"No, she's certainly not a witch," Manon snapped from the doorway, gold eyes cold. "Start talking. Now."

Manon had endured a fairly shitty day, which was saying something, given her century of existence.

The Yellowlegs coven had been implanted in a subterranean chamber of the Keep, the room carved into the mountain rock itself. Manon had taken one sniff of that bed-lined room and walked right back out again. The Yellowlegs didn't want her there, anyway, while they were cut open by men, while that bit of stone was sewn inside them. No, a Blackbeak had no place in a room where Yellowlegs were vulnerable, and she'd likely make them vicious and lethal as a result.

So she'd gone to training, where Sorrel had kicked her ass in hand-to-hand combat. Then there had been not one, not two, but *three* different fights to break apart between the various covens, including the Bluebloods, who were somehow *excited* about the Valg. They had gotten their noses broken by suggesting to a Blackbeak coven that it was their divine *duty* not just to go through with the implantation but also to go so far as to physically mate with the Valg.

Manon didn't blame her Blackbeaks for shutting down the talk. But she'd had to dole out equal punishment between the two groups.

And then this. Asterin and Elide in her rooms, the girl wide-eyed and reeking of terror, her Third seeming to try to convince the girl to join their ranks.

"Start talking *now.*"

Temper—she knew she should rein it in, but the room smelled like human fear, and this was *her* space.

Asterin stepped in front of the girl. "She's not a spy for Vernon, Manon."

Manon did them the honor of listening as Asterin told her what had happened. When she finished, Manon crossed her arms. Elide was cowering by the bathing chamber door, the bag of coins still gripped in her hands.

"Where does the line get drawn?" Asterin said quietly.

Manon flashed her teeth. "Humans are for eating and rutting and bleeding. Not helping. If she's got witch-blood in her, it's a drop. Not enough to make her our own." Manon stalked toward her Third. "You are one of the Thirteen. You have duties and obligations, and yet this is how you spend your time?"

Asterin held her ground. "You said to keep an eye on her, and I did. I got to the bottom of things. She's barely past being a witchling. You want Vernon Lochan bringing her down to that chamber? Or over to one of the other mountains?"

"I don't give a shit what Vernon does with his human pets."

But once the words were out, they tasted foul.

"I brought her here so you could know—"

"You brought her here as a prize to win back your position."

Elide was still trying her best to vanish through the wall.

Manon snapped her fingers in the girl's direction. "I'm escorting you back to your room. Keep the money, if you want. My *Third* has an aerie full of wyvern shit to clean out."

"Manon," Asterin began.

"*Wing Leader*," Manon growled. "When you've stopped acting like a simpering mortal, you may again address me as Manon."

"And yet you tolerate a wyvern who sniffs flowers and makes puppy eyes at this girl."

Manon almost struck her—almost went for her throat. But the girl was watching, listening. So Manon grabbed Elide by the arm and yanked her toward the door.

Elide kept her mouth shut as Manon led her down the stairs. She didn't ask how the Wing Leader knew where her room was.

She wondered if Manon would kill her once they reached it.

Wondered if she'd beg and grovel for mercy when the time came.

But after a while, the witch said, "If you try to bribe anyone here, they'll just turn you in. Save the money for when you run."

Elide hid the shaking in her hands and nodded.

The witch gave her a sidelong glance, her golden eyes shimmering in the torchlight. "Where the hell would you have run to, anyway? There's nothing within a hundred miles. The only way you would stand a chance is if you got on the . . ." Manon snorted. "The supply wagons."

Elide's heart sank. "Please—please don't tell Vernon."

"Don't you think if Vernon wanted to use you like that, he'd have done it already? And why make you play servant?"

"I don't know. He likes games; he might be waiting for one of you to confirm what I am."

Manon fell silent again—until they rounded a corner.

Elide's stomach dropped down to her feet when she beheld who stood in front of her door as if she'd summoned him by mere thought.

Vernon was wearing his usual vibrant tunic—today a Terrasen green—and his brows rose at the sight of Manon and Elide.

"What are you doing here?" Manon snapped, coming to a stop in front of Elide's little door.

Vernon smiled. "Visiting my beloved niece, of course."

Though Vernon was taller, Manon seemed to look down her nose at him, seemed *bigger* than him as she kept her grip on Elide's arm and said, "For what purpose?"

"I was hoping to see how you two were getting along," her uncle purred. "But . . ." He looked at the hand Manon had around Elide's wrist. And the door beyond them. "It seems I needn't have worried."

It took Elide longer to catch it than Manon, who bared her teeth and said, "I'm not in the habit of forcing my servants."

"Only slaughtering men like pigs, correct?"

"Their deaths equate to their behavior in life," Manon replied with a kind of calm that made Elide wonder whether she should start running.

Vernon let out a low laugh. He was so unlike her father, who had been warm and handsome and broad-shouldered—a year past thirty when he was executed by the king. Her uncle had watched that execution and smiled. And then come to tell her all about it.

"Allying yourself with the witches?" Vernon asked Elide. "How ruthless of you."

Elide lowered her eyes to the ground. "There is nothing to ally against, Uncle."

"Perhaps I kept you too sheltered for all those years, if you believe that's so."

Manon cocked her head. "Say your piece and be gone."

"Careful, Wing Leader," Vernon said. "You know precisely where your power ends."

Manon shrugged. "I also know precisely where to bite."

Vernon grinned and bit the air in front of him. His amusement honed itself into something ugly as he turned to Elide. "I wanted to check on you. I know how hard today was."

Her heart stopped. Had someone told him about the conversation in the kitchens? Had there been a spy in the tower just now?

"Why would it be hard for her, human?" Manon's stare was as cold as iron.

"This date is always difficult for the Lochan family," Vernon said. "Cal Lochan, my brother, was a traitor, you know. A rebel leader for the few months after Terrasen was inherited by the king. But he was caught like the rest of them and put down. Difficult for us to curse his name and still miss him, isn't it, Elide?"

It hit her like a blow. How had she forgotten? She hadn't said the prayers, hadn't beseeched the gods to look after him. Her father's deathday, and she had forgotten him, as surely as the world had forgotten her. Keeping her head down wasn't an act now, even with the Wing Leader's eyes on her.

"You're a useless worm, Vernon," Manon said. "Go spew your nonsense elsewhere."

"Whatever would your grandmother say," Vernon mused, stuffing his hands into his pockets, "about such . . . behavior?" Manon's growl chased after him as he sauntered down the hall.

Manon flung open Elide's door, revealing a room barely big enough for a cot and a pile of clothes. She hadn't been permitted to bring any belongings, none of the keepsakes that Finnula had hidden all these years: the small doll her mother had brought back from a trip to the Southern Continent, her father's seal ring, her mother's ivory comb—the first gift Cal Lochan had given Marion the Laundress while courting her. Apparently, Marion the Ironteeth Witch would have been a better name.

Manon shut the door with a backward kick.

Too small—the room was too small for two people, especially when one of them was ancient and dominated the space just by breathing. Elide slumped onto the cot, if only to put more air between her and Manon.

The Wing Leader stared at her for a long moment, and then said, "You can choose, witchling. Blue or red."

"What?"

"Does your blood run blue or red? You decide. If it runs blue, it turns out I have jurisdiction over you. Little shits like Vernon can't do as they will to my kind—not without my permission. If your blood runs red . . . Well, I don't particularly care about humans, and seeing what Vernon does with you might be entertaining."

"Why would you offer this?"

Manon gave her a half smile, all iron teeth and no remorse. "Because I can."

"If my blood runs . . . blue, won't it confirm what Vernon suspects? Won't he act?"

"A risk you'll have to take. He can try to act on it—and learn where it gets him."

A trap. And Elide was the bait. Claim her heritage as a witch, and if Vernon took her to be implanted, Manon could have the grounds to kill him.

She had a feeling Manon might hope for that. It was not just a risk; it was a suicidal, *stupid* risk. But better than nothing.

The witches, who lowered their eyes for no man . . . Until she could get away, perhaps she might learn a thing or two about what it was like to have fangs and claws. And how to use them.

"Blue," she whispered. "My blood runs blue."

"Good choice, witchling," Manon said, and the word was a challenge and an order. She turned away, but glanced over her shoulder. "Welcome to the Blackbeaks."

Witchling. Elide stared after her. She had likely just made the biggest mistake of her life, but . . . it was strange.

Strange, that feeling of belonging.

CHAPTER 26

"I'm not about to keel over dead," Aedion said to his cousin, his queen, as she helped him walk around the roof. This was their third rotation, the moon shimmering on the tiles beneath them. It was an effort to keep upright, not from the steady throb in his side, but from the fact that Aelin—*Aelin*—was beside him, an arm around his waist.

A cool night breeze laced with the plume of smoke on the horizon wrapped around him, chilling the sweat on his neck.

But he angled his face away from the smoke, breathing in another, better smell. And found the source of it frowning up at him. Aelin's exquisite scent soothed him, awakened him. He'd never get sick of that scent. It was a miracle.

But her frown—*that* was not a miracle. "What?" he demanded. It had been a day since she'd fought in the Pits—a day of more sleeping. Tonight, under cover of darkness, was the first he'd been able to get out of bed. If he were cooped up for another moment, he'd start tearing down the walls.

He'd had enough of cages and prisons.

"I'm making my professional assessment," she said, keeping pace beside him.

"As an assassin, queen, or pit-brawler?"

Aelin gave him a grin—the sort that told him she was debating kicking his ass. "Don't be jealous that you didn't get a shot at those Valg bastards."

It wasn't that. She'd been fighting *Valg* last night, while he'd lain in bed, unaware she was in any sort of danger at all. He tried to convince himself that despite the peril, despite how she'd returned reeking of blood and injured from where one of them had bitten her, she'd at least learned that Morath was where the people with magic were being turned into Valg vessels.

Tried to convince himself, and failed. But—he had to give her space. He wouldn't be an overbearing, territorial Fae bastard, as she liked to call them.

"And if I pass your assessment," Aedion said at last, "will we go directly to Terrasen, or are we waiting here for Prince Rowan?"

"Prince Rowan," she said, rolling her eyes. "You keep needling me for details about *Prince Rowan*—"

"You befriended one of the greatest warriors in history—perhaps the greatest warrior alive. Your father, and his men, all told me stories about Prince Rowan."

"What?"

Oh, he'd been waiting to drop this particular gem of information. "Warriors in the North still talk about him."

"Rowan's never been to this continent."

She said it with such casualness—*Rowan*. She really had no clue who she now considered a member of her court, who she'd freed from his oath to Maeve. Who she frequently referred to as a pain in her ass.

Rowan was the most powerful full-blooded Fae male alive. And his scent was all over her. Yet she had no gods-damned idea.

"Rowan Whitethorn is a legend. And so is his—what do you call them?"

"Cadre," she said glumly.

"The six of them . . ." Aedion loosed a breath. "We used to tell stories about them around fires. Their battles and exploits and adventures."

She sighed through her nose. "Please, *please* don't ever tell him that. I'll never hear the end of it, and he'll use it in every argument we have."

Honestly, Aedion didn't know what he would say to the male— because there were many, many things to say. Expressing his admiration would be the easy part. But when it came to thanking him for what he'd done for Aelin this spring, or what, exactly, Rowan expected as a member of their court—if the Fae Prince expected to be offered the blood oath, then . . . It was an effort to keep from tightening his grip on Aelin.

Ren already knew that the blood oath was Aedion's by right, and any other child of Terrasen would know, too. So first thing Aedion would do when the prince arrived would be to make sure he understood that little fact. It wasn't like in Wendlyn, where warriors were offered the oath whenever their ruler pleased.

No—since Brannon had founded Terrasen, its kings and queens had picked only *one* of their court to swear the blood oath, usually at their coronation or soon after. Just one, for their entire lives.

Aedion had no interest in yielding the honor, even to the legendary warrior-prince.

"*Anyway,*" Aelin said sharply as they rounded the corner of the roof again, "we're not going to Terrasen—not yet. Not until you're well enough to travel hard and fast. Right now, we need to get the Amulet of Orynth from Arobynn."

Aedion was half tempted to hunt down her former master and rip him to shreds as he interrogated him about where the amulet was kept, but he could play along with her plan.

He was still weak enough that until now, he'd barely been able to stand long enough to piss. Having Aelin help him the first time had been awkward enough that he couldn't even go until she started singing a bawdy tune at the top of her lungs and turned on the sink faucet, all the while helping him stand over the toilet.

"Give me another day or two, and I'll help you hunt down one of those demon pricks for him." Rage slammed into him, as hard as any physical blow. The King of the Assassins had demanded she put herself in such danger—as if her life, as if the fate of their kingdom, were a gods-damned game to him.

But Aelin . . . Aelin had struck that bargain. For him.

Again, breathing became hard. How many scars would she add to that lithe, powerful body because of him?

Then Aelin said, "You're not going to hunt the Valg with me."

Aedion stumbled a step. "Oh, yes, I am."

"No, you're not," she said. "One, you're too recognizable—"

"Don't even start."

She observed him for a long moment, as if assessing his every weakness and strength. At last she said, "Very well."

He almost sagged in relief. "But after all that—the Valg, the amulet," Aedion pushed, "will we free magic?" A nod. "I assume you have a plan." Another nod. He gritted his teeth. "Do you care to share it?"

"Soon," she said sweetly.

Gods help him. "And after completing your mysterious, wonderful plan, we'll go to Terrasen." He didn't want to ask about Dorian. He'd seen the anguish on her face that day in the garden.

But if she couldn't put the princeling down, he'd do it. He wouldn't enjoy it, and the captain might very well kill him in return, but to keep Terrasen safe, he'd cut off Dorian's head.

Aelin nodded. "Yes, we'll go, but—you have only one legion."

"There are men who would fight, and other territories that might come if you call."

"We can discuss this later."

He leashed his temper. "We need to be in Terrasen before the summer is out—before the snow starts falling in autumn, or else we wait until spring." She nodded distantly. Yesterday afternoon, she'd dispatched the letters Aedion had asked her to write to Ren, the Bane, and the remaining loyal lords of Terrasen, letting them know they'd been reunited, and that anyone with magic in their veins was to lie low. He knew the remaining lords—the old, cunning bastards—wouldn't appreciate orders like that, even from their queen. But he had to try.

"And," he added, because she really was going to shut him down about this, "we'll need money for that army."

She said quietly, "I know."

Not an answer. Aedion tried again. "Even if men agree to fight on their honor alone, we stand a better chance of having greater numbers if we can pay them. Not to mention feeding our forces, and arming and supplying them." For years now, he and the Bane had traversed from tavern to tavern, quietly raising funds for their own efforts. It still killed him to see the poorest of his people plunk hard-earned coins into the pans they'd passed around, to see the hope in their gaunt, scarred faces. "The King of Adarlan emptied our royal coffers; it was one of the first things he did. The only money we have comes from whatever our people can donate—which isn't much—or whatever is granted by Adarlan."

"Another way of keeping control all these years," she murmured.

"Our people are beggared. They don't have two coppers to rub together these days, let alone to pay taxes."

"I wouldn't raise taxes to pay for a war," she said sharply. "And I'd rather not whore ourselves to foreign nations for loans, either. Not yet, anyway." Aedion's throat tightened at the bitterness coating her tone as they both considered the other way money and men could be obtained. But he couldn't bring himself to mention selling her hand in marriage to a wealthy foreign kingdom—not yet.

So he just said, "It's something to start contemplating. If magic is indeed freed, we could recruit the wielders to our side—offer them training, money, shelter. Imagine a soldier who can kill with blade and magic. It could turn the tide of a battle."

Shadows flickered in her eyes. "Indeed."

He weighed her posture, the clarity of her gaze, her tired face. Too much—she'd already faced and survived too much.

He'd seen the scars—the tattoos that covered them—peeking over the collar of her shirt every now and then. He hadn't yet dared to ask to see them. The bandaged bite on her arm was nothing compared to that pain, and the many others she hadn't mentioned, the scars all over her. The scars all over both of them.

"And then," he said, clearing his throat, "there's the blood oath." He'd had endless hours in bed to compile this list. She stiffened enough that Aedion quickly added, "You don't have to—not yet. But when you're ready, I'm ready."

"You still want to swear it to me?" Her voice was flat.

"Of course I do." He damned caution to hell and said, "It was my right then—and now. It can wait until we get to Terrasen, but it's going to be me who takes it. No one else."

Her throat bobbed. "Right." A breathless answer that he couldn't read.

She let go of him and stalked toward one of the little training areas to test out her injured arm. Or maybe she wanted to get away from him— maybe he'd broached the topic the wrong way.

He might have hobbled off the roof had the door not opened and the captain appeared.

Aelin was already striding toward Chaol with predatory focus. He'd hate to be on the receiving end of that gait. "What is it?" she said.

He'd hate to be on the receiving end of that greeting, too.

Aedion limped for them as Chaol kicked the door shut behind him. "The Shadow Market is gone."

Aelin drew up short. "What do you mean?"

The captain's face was tight and pale. "The Valg soldiers. They went to the market tonight and sealed the exits with everyone inside. Then they *burnt* it. The people who tried to escape through the sewers found garrisons of soldiers waiting there, swords ready."

That explained the smoke in the air, the plume on the horizon. Holy gods. The king had to have lost his mind entirely—had to have stopped caring what the general public thought.

Aelin's arms slackened at her sides. "Why?" The slight tremor in her voice had Aedion's hackles rising, those Fae instincts roaring to shut the captain up, to rip out his throat, to end the cause of her pain and fear—

"Because it got out that the rebels who freed *him*"—Chaol sent a cutting glance in Aedion's direction—"were meeting in the Shadow Market to buy supplies."

Aedion reached her side, close enough now to see the tightness of the captain's face, the gauntness that hadn't been there weeks ago. The last time they'd spoken.

"And I suppose you blame me?" Aelin said with midnight softness.

A muscle flickered on the captain's jaw. He didn't even nod a greeting to Aedion, or acknowledge the months they'd spent working together, what had happened in that tower room—

"The king could have ordered their slaughter by any means," Chaol said, the slender scar on his face stark in the moonlight. "But he chose fire."

Aelin went impossibly still.

Aedion snarled. "You're a prick for suggesting the attack was a message for her."

Chaol at last turned his attention toward him. "You think it's not true?"

Aelin cocked her head. "You came all this way to fling accusations in my face?"

"*You* told me to stop by tonight," Chaol retorted, and Aedion was half tempted to punch his teeth down his throat for the tone he used. "But I came to ask why you haven't moved on the clock tower. How many more innocent people are going to be caught in the crossfire of this?"

It was an effort to keep his mouth shut. He didn't need to speak for Aelin, who said with flawless venom, "Are you suggesting that I don't care?"

"You risked everything—multiple lives—to get out *one* man. I think you find this city and its citizens to be expendable."

Aelin hissed, "Need I remind you, *Captain*, that you went to Endovier and did not blink at the slaves, at the mass graves? Need I remind you that I was starved and chained, and you let Duke Perrington force me to the ground at Dorian's feet while you did *nothing*? And now you have the nerve to accuse *me* of not caring, when many of the people in this city have profited off the blood and misery of the very people *you* ignored?"

Aedion stifled the snarl working its way up his throat. The captain had never said that about the initial meeting with his queen. Never said he hadn't stepped in while she was manhandled, humiliated. Had the captain even flinched at the scars on her back, or merely examined them as though she were some prize animal?

"You don't get to blame me," Aelin breathed. "You don't get to blame me for the Shadow Market."

"This city still needs protecting," Chaol snapped.

Aelin shrugged, heading for the roof door. "Or maybe this city should burn," she murmured. A chill went down Aedion's spine, even though he knew she'd said it to piss off the captain. "Maybe the world should burn," she added, and stalked off the roof.

Aedion turned to the captain. "You want to pick a fight, you come to me, not her."

The captain just shook his head and stared across the slums. Aedion followed his gaze, taking in the capital twinkling around them.

He'd hated this city from the very first time he'd spotted the white walls, the glass castle. He'd been nineteen, and had bedded and reveled his way from one end of Rifthold to the other, trying to find something, anything, to explain why Adarlan thought it was so gods-damned superior, why Terrasen had fallen to its knees before these people. And when Aedion had finished with the women and the parties, after Rifthold had dumped its riches at his feet and begged him for *more, more, more,* he'd still hated it—even more than before.

And all that time, and every time after, he'd had no idea that what he truly sought, what his shredded heart still dreamed of, was dwelling in a house of killers mere blocks away.

At last, the captain said, "You look more or less in one piece."

Aedion gave him a wolf's grin. "And you won't be, if you speak to her that way again."

Chaol shook his head. "Did you learn anything about Dorian while you were in the castle?"

"You insult my queen and yet have the nerve to ask me for that information?"

Chaol rubbed his brows with his thumb and forefinger. "Please—just tell me. Today has been bad enough."

"Why?"

"I've been hunting the Valg commanders in the sewers since the fight in the Pits. We tracked them to their new nests, thank the gods, but found no sign of humans being held prisoner. Yet more people have vanished than ever—right under our noses. Some of the other rebels want to abandon Rifthold. Establish ourselves in other cities in anticipation of the Valg spreading."

"And you?"

"I don't leave without Dorian."

Aedion didn't have the heart to ask if that meant alive or dead. He sighed. "He came to me in the dungeons. Taunted me. There was no sign of the man inside him. He didn't even know who Sorscha was." And then, maybe because he was feeling particularly kind, thanks to the golden-haired blessing in the apartment beneath, Aedion said, "I'm sorry—about Dorian."

Chaol's shoulders sagged, as if an invisible weight pushed against them. "Adarlan needs to have a future."

"So make yourself king."

"I'm not fit to be king." The self-loathing in those words made Aedion pity the captain despite himself. Plans—Aelin had plans for everything, it seemed. She had invited the captain over tonight, he realized, not to discuss anything with her, but for this very conversation. He wondered when she would start confiding in him.

These things took time, he reminded himself. She was used to a lifetime of secrecy; learning to depend on him would take a bit of adjustment.

"I can think of worse alternatives," Aedion said. "Like Hollin."

"And what will you and Aelin do about Hollin?" Chaol asked, gazing toward the smoke. "Where do you draw the line?"

"We don't kill children."

"Even ones who already show signs of corruption?"

"You don't get the right to fling that sort of horseshit in our faces—not when *your* king murdered our family. Our people."

Chaol's eyes flickered. "I'm sorry."

Aedion shook his head. "We're not enemies. You can trust us—trust Aelin."

"No, I can't. Not anymore."

"Then it's your loss," Aedion said. "Good luck."

It was all he really had to offer the captain.

⁓

Chaol stormed out of the warehouse apartment and across the street to where Nesryn was leaning against a building, arms crossed. Beneath the shadows of her hood, her mouth quirked to the side. "What happened?"

He continued down the street, his blood roaring in his veins. "Nothing."

"What did they say?" Nesryn kept up with him, meeting him step for step.

"None of your business, so drop it. Just because we work together doesn't mean you're entitled to know everything that goes on in my life."

Nesryn stiffened almost imperceptibly, and part of Chaol flinched, already yearning to take the words back.

But it was true. He'd destroyed everything the day he fled the castle—and maybe he'd taken to hanging around with Nesryn because there was no one else who didn't look at him with pity in their eyes.

Maybe it had been selfish of him to do it.

Nesryn didn't bother with a good-bye before vanishing down an alley.

At least he couldn't hate himself any more than he already did.

Lying to Aedion about the blood oath was . . . awful.

She would tell him—she would find a way to tell him. When things were less new. When he stopped looking at her as though she were a gods-damned miracle and not a lying, cowardly piece of shit.

Maybe the Shadow Market *had* been her fault.

Crouched on a rooftop, Aelin shook off the cloak of guilt and temper that had been smothering her for hours and turned her attention to the alley below. Perfect.

She'd tracked several different patrols tonight, noting which of the commanders wore black rings, which seemed more brutal than the rest, which didn't even try to move like humans. The man—or was he a demon now?—hauling open a sewer grate in the street below was one of the milder ones.

She'd wanted to shadow this commander to wherever he made his nest, so she could at least give Chaol that information—prove to him how invested she was in the welfare of this piss-poor city.

This commander's men had headed for the glowing glass palace, the thick river fog casting the entire hillside in greenish light. But he had veered away, going deeper into the slums and to the sewers beneath them.

She watched him disappear through the sewer grate, then nimbly climbed off the roof, hurrying for the closest entrance that would connect to his. Swallowing that old fear, she quietly entered the sewers a block or two down from where he'd climbed in, and listened carefully.

Dripping water, the reek of refuse, the scurrying of rats . . .

And splashing steps ahead, around the next big intersection of tunnels. Perfect.

Aelin kept her blades concealed in her suit, not wanting them to rust in the sewer dampness. She clung to the shadows, her steps soundless as she neared the crossroads and peered around the corner. Sure enough, the Valg commander was striding down the tunnel, his back to her, headed deeper into the system.

When he was far enough ahead, she slipped around the corner, keeping to the darkness, avoiding the patches of light that shone through the overhead grates.

Tunnel after tunnel, she trailed him, until he reached a massive pool.

It was surrounded by crumbling walls covered in grime and moss, so ancient that she wondered if they'd been among the first built in Rifthold.

But it wasn't the man kneeling before the pool, its waters fed by rivers snaking in from either direction, that made her breath catch and panic flood her veins.

It was the creature that emerged from the water.

CHAPTER 27

The creature rose, its black stone body cutting through the water with hardly a ripple.

The Valg commander knelt before it, head down, not moving a muscle as the horror uncoiled to its full height.

Her heart leaped into a wild beat, and she willed it to calm as she took in the details of the creature that now stood waist-deep in the pool, water dripping off its massive arms and elongated, serpentine snout.

She'd seen it before.

One of eight creatures carved into the clock tower itself; eight gargoyles that she'd once sworn had . . . watched her. Smiled at her.

Was there currently one missing from the clock tower, or had the statues been molded after this monstrosity?

She willed strength to her knees. A faint blue light began pulsing from beneath her suit—shit. The Eye. Never a good sign when it flared—never, never, never.

She put a hand over it, smothering the barely perceptible glow.

"Report," the thing hissed through a mouth of dark stone teeth. Wyrdhound—that's what she would call it. Even if it didn't look remotely like a dog, she had the feeling the gargoyle-*thing* could track and hunt as well as any canine. And obeyed its master well.

The commander kept his head lowered. "No sign of the general, or those who helped him get away. We received word that he'd been spotted heading down the southern road, riding with five others for Fenharrow. I sent two patrols after them."

She could thank Arobynn for that.

"Keep looking," the Wyrdhound said, the dim light glinting on the iridescent veins running through its obsidian skin. "The general was injured—he can't have gotten far."

The creature's voice stopped her cold.

Not the voice of a demon, or a man.

But the king.

She didn't want to know what sort of things he'd done in order to see through this thing's eyes, speak through its mouth.

A shudder crawled down her spine as she backed down the tunnel. The water running beside the raised walkway was shallow enough that the creature couldn't possibly swim there, but . . . she didn't dare breathe too loudly.

Oh, she'd give Arobynn his Valg commander, all right. Then she'd let Chaol and Nesryn hunt them all into extinction.

But not until she had the chance to speak to one on her own.

~

It took Aelin ten blocks to stop the shaking in her bones, ten blocks to debate whether she would even tell them what she'd seen and what she had planned—but walking in the door and seeing Aedion pacing by the window was enough to set her on edge again.

"Would you look at that," she drawled, throwing back her hood. "I'm alive and unharmed."

"You said two hours—you were gone four."

"I had things to do—things that only *I* can do. So to accomplish those things, I needed to go out. You're in no shape to be in the streets, especially if there's danger—"

"You swore there wasn't any danger."

"Do I look like an oracle? There is always danger—*always*."

That wasn't even the half of it.

"You reek of the gods-damned sewers," Aedion snapped. "Want to tell me what you were doing *there*?"

No. Not really.

Aedion rubbed at his face. "Do you understand what it was like to sit on my ass while you were gone? You said two hours. What was I supposed to think?"

"Aedion," she said as calmly as she could, and pulled off her filthy gloves before taking his broad, callused hand. "I get it. I do."

"What were you doing that was so important it couldn't wait a day or two?" His eyes were wide, pleading.

"Scouting."

"You're good at this, aren't you—half truths."

"One, just because you're . . . *you*, it doesn't entitle you to information about everything I do. *Two*—"

"There you go with the *lists* again."

She squeezed his hand hard enough to shatter a lesser man's bones. "If you don't like my lists, then don't pick fights with me."

He stared at her; she stared right back.

Unyielding, unbreakable. They'd been cut from the same cloth.

Aedion loosed a breath and looked at their joined hands—then opened his to examine her scarred palm, crisscrossed with the marks of her vow to Nehemia and the cut she'd made the moment she and Rowan became *carranam*, their magic joining them in an eternal bond.

"It's hard not to think all of your scars are my fault."

Oh. *Oh.*

SARAH J. MAAS

It took her a breath or two, but she managed to cock her chin at a devious angle and say, "Please. Half of these scars I rightly deserved." She showed him a small scar down the inside of her forearm. "See that one? A man in a tavern sliced me open with a bottle after I cheated him in a round of cards and tried to steal his money."

A choked sound came from him.

"You don't believe me?"

"Oh, I believe you. I didn't know you were so bad at cards that you had to resort to cheating." Aedion chuckled quietly, but the fear lingered.

So she peeled back the collar of her tunic to reveal a thin necklace of scars. "Baba Yellowlegs, Matron of the Yellowlegs Witch-Clan, gave me these when she tried to kill me. I cut off her head, then cut her corpse into little bits, then shoved it all into the oven of her wagon."

"I wondered who killed Yellowlegs." She could have embraced him for that sentence alone—for the lack of fear or disgust in those eyes.

She walked to the buffet table and pulled out a bottle of wine from inside the cabinet. "I'm surprised you beasts didn't drink all my good alcohol these past months." She frowned at the cabinet. "Looks like one of you got into the brandy."

"Ren's grandfather," Aedion said, tracking her movements from his spot by the window. She opened the bottle of wine and didn't bother with a glass as she slumped onto the couch and swigged.

"This one," she said, pointing to a jagged scar by her elbow. Aedion came around the couch to sit beside her. He took up nearly half of the damn thing. "The Pirate Lord of Skull's Bay gave that to me after I trashed his entire city, freed his slaves, and looked damn good while doing it."

Aedion took the bottle of wine and drank from it. "Has anyone ever taught you humility?"

"You didn't learn it, so why should I?"

Aedion laughed, and then showed her his left hand. Several of the fingers were crooked. "In the training camps, one of those Adarlanian

238

bastards broke every finger when I mouthed off. Then he broke them in a second place because I wouldn't stop swearing at him after."

She whistled through her teeth, even as she marveled at the bravery, the defiance. Even as pride for her cousin mingled with the slightest tinge of shame for herself. Aedion yanked up his shirt to reveal a muscled abdomen where a thick, jagged slash plunged from his ribs to his belly button. "Battle near Rosamel. Six-inch serrated hunting knife, curved on the tip. Rutting prick got me here"—he pointed to the top, then dragged his finger down—"and sliced south."

"Shit," she said. "How the hell are you still breathing?"

"Luck—and I was able to move as he dragged it down, keeping him from gutting me. At least I learned the value of shielding after that."

So they went on through the evening and the night, passing the wine between them.

One by one, they told the stories of the wounds accumulated in the years spent apart. And after a while, she peeled off her suit and turned to show him her back—to show him the scars, and the tattoos she'd had etched over them.

When she again reclined on the couch, Aedion showed her the scar across his left pectoral, from the first battle he'd fought, when he'd finally been able to win back the Sword of Orynth—her father's sword.

He padded to what she now considered his room, and when he returned, he held the sword in his hands as he knelt. "This belongs to you," he said hoarsely. Her swallow was loud in her ears.

She folded Aedion's hands around the scabbard, even as her heart fractured at the sight of her father's blade, at what he had done to attain it, to save it. "It belongs to you, Aedion."

He didn't lower the blade. "It was just for safekeeping."

"It belongs to you," she said again. "There is no one else who deserves it." Not even her, she realized.

Aedion took a shuddering breath and bowed his head.

"You're a sad drunk," she told him, and he laughed.

Aedion set the sword on the table behind him and slumped back onto the couch. He was large enough that she was nearly popped off her own cushion, and she glared at him as she straightened. "Don't break my couch, you hulking brute."

Aedion ruffled her hair and stretched his long legs out before him. "Ten years, and that's the treatment I get from my beloved cousin."

She elbowed him in the ribs.

Two more days passed, and Aedion was going out of his mind, especially as Aelin kept sneaking out only to return covered in filth and reeking to Hellas's fiery realm. Going to the rooftop for fresh air wasn't the same as going *out*, and the apartment was small enough that he was starting to contemplate sleeping in the warehouse downstairs to have some sense of space.

He always felt that way, though—whether in Rifthold or Orynth or at the finest of palaces—if he went too long without walking through forests or fields, without the kiss of the wind on his face. Gods above, he'd even take the Bane's war camp over this. It had been too long since he'd seen his men, laughed with them, listened to and secretly envied their stories about their families, their homes. But no longer—not now that his own family had been returned to him; not now that *Aelin* was his home.

Even if the walls of *her* home now pushed on him.

He must have looked as caged as he felt, because Aelin rolled her eyes when she came back into the apartment that afternoon.

"All right, all right," she said, throwing up her hands. "I'd rather have you wreck yourself than destroy my furniture from boredom. You're worse than a dog."

Aedion bared his teeth in a smile. "I aim to impress."

So they armed and cloaked themselves and made it two steps outside before he detected a female scent—like mint and some spice he couldn't identify—approaching them. Fast. He'd caught that scent before, but couldn't place it.

Pain whipped his ribs as he reached for his dagger, but Aelin said, "It's Nesryn. Relax."

Indeed, the approaching woman lifted a hand in greeting, though she was cloaked so thoroughly that Aedion could see nothing of the pretty face beneath.

Aelin met her halfway down the block, moving with ease in that wicked black suit of hers, and didn't bother waiting for Aedion as she said, "Is something wrong?"

The woman's attention flicked from Aedion to his queen. He hadn't forgotten that day at the castle—the arrow she'd fired and the one she'd pointed at him. "No. I came to deliver the report on the new nests we've found. But I can return later, if you two are busy."

"We were just going out," Aelin said, "to get the general a drink."

Nesryn's shoulder-length night-dark hair shifted beneath her hood as she cocked her head. "You want an extra set of eyes watching your back?"

Aedion opened his mouth to say no, but Aelin looked contemplative. She glanced over her shoulder at him, and he knew she was assessing his condition to decide whether she might indeed want another sword among them. If Aelin were in the Bane, he might have tackled her right there.

Aedion drawled to the young rebel, "What I want is a pretty face that doesn't belong to my cousin. Looks like you'll do the trick."

"You're insufferable," Aelin said. "And I hate to tell you, Cousin, but the captain wouldn't be very pleased if you made a move on Faliq."

"It's not like that," Nesryn said tightly.

Aelin lifted a shoulder. "It would make no difference to me if it was." The bare, honest truth.

Nesryn shook her head. "I wasn't considering you, but—it's not like that. I think he's content to be miserable." The rebel waved a hand in dismissal. "We could die any day, any hour. I don't see a point in brooding."

"Well, you're in luck, Nesryn Faliq," Aelin said. "Turns out I'm as sick of my cousin as he is of me. We could use some new company."

Aedion sketched a bow to the rebel, the motion making his ribs positively ache, and gestured to the street ahead. "After you."

Nesryn stared him down, as though she could see exactly where his injury was groaning in agony, and then followed after the queen.

Aelin took them to a truly disreputable tavern a few blocks away. With impressive swagger and menace, she kicked out a couple of thieves sitting at a table in the back. They took one look at her weapons, at that utterly wicked suit of hers, and decided they liked having their organs inside their bodies.

The three of them stayed at the taproom until last call, hooded so heavily they could hardly recognize one another, playing cards and refusing the many offers to join other players. They didn't have money to waste on real games, so for currency they used some dried beans that Aedion sweet-talked the harried serving girl into bringing them.

Nesryn barely spoke as she won round after round, which Aedion supposed was good, given that he hadn't quite decided if he wanted to kill her for that arrow she'd fired. But Aelin asked her questions about her family's bakery, about life for her parents on the Southern Continent, about her sister and her nieces and nephews. When at last they left the drinking hall, none of them having dared to get inebriated in public, and none of them too eager to go to sleep just yet, they meandered through the alleys of the slums.

Aedion savored every step of freedom. He'd been locked in that cell for weeks. It had hit an old wound, one he hadn't spoken about to Aelin or anyone else, though his highest-ranking warriors in the Bane knew, if only because they'd helped him exact his revenge years after the fact. Aedion was still brooding about it when they strode down a narrow, foggy alley, its dark stones silvered with the light of the moon peeking out above.

He picked up the scrape of boots on stone before his companions did, his Fae ears catching the sound, and threw out an arm in front of Aelin and Nesryn, who froze with expert silence.

He sniffed the air, but the stranger was downwind. So he listened.

Just one person, judging from the near-silent footfalls that pierced through the wall of fog. Moving with a predator's ease that made Aedion's instincts rise to the forefront.

Aedion palmed his fighting knives as the male's scent hit him—unwashed, but with a hint of pine and snow. And then he smelled *Aelin* on the stranger, the scent complex and layered, woven into the male himself.

The male emerged from the fog; tall—maybe taller than Aedion himself, if only by an inch—powerfully built, and heavily armed both above and beneath his pale gray surcoat and hood.

Aelin took a step forward.

One step, as if in a daze.

She loosed a shuddering breath, and a small, whimpering noise came out of her—a sob.

And then she was sprinting down the alley, flying as though the winds themselves pushed at her heels.

She flung herself on the male, crashing into him hard enough that anyone else might have gone rocking back into the stone wall.

But the male grabbed her to him, his massive arms wrapping around her tightly and lifting her up. Nesryn made to approach, but Aedion stopped her with a hand on her arm.

Aelin was laughing as she cried, and the male was just holding her, his hooded head buried in her neck. As if he were breathing her in.

"Who is that?" Nesryn asked.

Aedion smiled. "Rowan."

CHAPTER 28

She was shaking from head to toe, and couldn't stop crying, not as the full weight of missing Rowan crashed into her, the weight of these weeks alone. "How did you get here? How did you *find* me?" Aelin withdrew far enough to study the harsh face shadowed by his hood, the tattoo peeking out along the side of it, and the grim line of his smile.

He was here, he was here, he was here.

"You made it clear my kind wouldn't be welcome on your continent," he said. Even the sound of his voice was a balm and a blessing. "So I stowed away on a ship. You'd mentioned a home in the slums, so when I arrived this evening, I wandered until I picked up your scent." He scanned her with a warrior's unflinching assessment, his mouth tight. "You have a lot to tell me," he said, and she nodded. Everything—she wanted to tell him everything. She gripped him harder, savoring the corded muscle of his forearms, the eternal strength of him. He brushed back a loose strand of her hair, his callused fingers scraping against her cheek in the lightest caress. The gentleness of it made her choke on another sob. "But you're not hurt," he said softly. "You're safe?"

She nodded again and buried her face in his chest. "I thought I gave you an order to stay in Wendlyn."

"I had my reasons, best spoken somewhere secure," he said onto her hood. "Your friends at the fortress say hello, by the way. I think they miss having an extra scullery maid. Especially Luca—*especially* in the mornings."

She laughed, and squeezed him. He was here, and he wasn't something she'd made up, some wild dream she'd had, and—

"Why are you crying?" he asked, trying to push her back far enough to read her face again.

But she held on to him, so fiercely she could feel the weapons beneath his clothes. It would all be fine, even if it went to hell, so long as he was here with her. "I'm crying," she sniffled, "because you smell so rutting bad my eyes are watering."

Rowan let out a roar of laughter that made the vermin in the alley go silent. She at last pulled away, flashing a grin. "Bathing isn't an option for a stowaway," he said, releasing her only to flick her nose. She gave him a playful shove, but he glanced down the alley, where Nesryn and Aedion were waiting. He'd likely been monitoring every move they made. And if he had deemed them a true threat to her safety, they'd have been dead minutes ago. "Are you just going to make them stand there all night?"

"Since when are you a stickler for manners?" She slung an arm around his waist, unwilling to let go of him lest he turn into wind and vanish. His casual arm around her shoulders was a glorious, solid weight as they approached the others.

If Rowan fought Nesryn, or even Chaol, there would be no contest. But Aedion . . . She hadn't seem him fight yet—and from the look her cousin was giving Rowan, despite all of his professed admiration, she wondered if Aedion was also wondering who'd emerge from that fight alive. Rowan stiffened a bit beneath her grip.

Neither male broke their stare as they neared.

Territorial nonsense.

Aelin squeezed Rowan's side hard enough that he hissed and pinched her shoulder right back. Fae warriors: invaluable in a fight—and raging pains in her ass at all other times. "Let's get inside," she said.

Nesryn had retreated slightly to observe what was sure to be a battle of warrior-arrogance for the ages. "I'll see you later," the rebel said to none of them in particular, the corners of her mouth twitching upward before she headed off into the slums.

Part of Aelin debated calling her back—the same part that had made her invite Nesryn along. The woman had seemed lonely, a bit adrift. But Faliq had no reason to stay. Not right now.

Aedion fell into step in front of her and Rowan, silently leading the way back to the warehouse.

Even through his layers of clothes and weapons, Rowan's muscles were tense beneath her fingers as he monitored Rifthold. She debated asking him what, exactly, he picked up with those heightened senses, what layers of the city she might never know existed. She didn't envy him his excellent sense of smell, not in the slums, at least. But it wasn't the time or place to ask—not until they got to safety. Until she talked to him. Alone.

Rowan examined the warehouse without comment before stepping aside to let her go in front of him. She'd forgotten how beautifully he moved that powerful body of his—a storm given flesh.

Tugging him by the hand, she led him up the stairs and into the great room. She knew he had taken in every detail, every entrance and exit and method of escape, by the time they were halfway across it.

Aedion stood before the fireplace, hood still on, hands still within easy reach of his weapons. She said over her shoulder to her cousin as they passed, "Aedion, meet Rowan. Rowan, meet Aedion. His Highness needs a bath or I'll vomit if I have to sit next to him for more than a minute."

She offered no other explanation before dragging Rowan into her bedroom and shutting the door behind them.

Aelin leaned against the door as Rowan paused in the center of the bedroom, his face darkened by the shadows of his heavy gray hood. The space between them went taut, every inch of it crackling.

She bit her bottom lip as she took him in: the familiar clothes; the assortment of wicked weapons; the immortal, preternatural stillness. His presence alone stole the air from the room, from her lungs.

"Take off your hood," he said with a soft growl, his eyes fixed on her mouth.

She crossed her arms. "You show me yours and I'll show you mine, Prince."

"From tears to sass in a few minutes. I'm glad the month apart hasn't dimmed your usual good spirits." He yanked back his hood, and she started.

"Your hair! You cut it all off!" She pulled off her own hood as she crossed the distance between them. Indeed, the long silver-white hair was now cropped short. It made him look younger, made his tattoo stand out more, and . . . fine, it made him more handsome, too. Or maybe that was just her missing him.

"Since you seemed to think that we would be doing a good amount of fighting here, shorter hair is more useful. Though I can't say that *your* hair might be considered the same. You might as well have dyed it blue."

"Hush. Your hair was so *pretty*. I was hoping you'd let me braid it one day. I suppose I'll have to buy a pony instead." She cocked her head. "When you shift, will your hawk form be plucked, then?"

His nostrils flared, and she clamped her lips together to keep from laughing.

He surveyed the room: the massive bed she hadn't bothered to make that morning, the marble fireplace adorned with trinkets and books, the open door to the giant closet. "You weren't lying about your taste for luxury."

"Not all of us enjoy living in warrior-squalor," she said, grabbing his hand again. She remembered these calluses, the strength and size of his hands. His fingers closed around hers.

Though it was a face she'd memorized, a face that had haunted her dreams these past few weeks . . . it was new, somehow. And he just looked at her, as if he were thinking the same thing.

He opened his mouth, but she pulled him into the bathroom, lighting a few candles by the sink and on the ledge above the tub. "I meant it about the bath," she said, twisting the faucets and plugging the drain. "You stink."

Rowan watched as she bent to grab a towel from the small cabinet by the toilet. "Tell me everything."

She plucked up a green vial of bath salts and another of bath oil and dumped in generous amounts of each, turning the rushing water milky and opaque. "I will, when you're soaking in the bath and don't smell like a vagrant."

"If memory serves, *you* smelled even worse when we first met. And I didn't shove you into the nearest trough in Varese."

She glared. "Funny."

"You made my eyes water for the entire damn journey to Mistward."

"Just *get in*." Chuckling, he obeyed. She shrugged off her own cloak, then began unstrapping her various weapons as she headed out of the bathroom.

She might have taken longer than usual to remove her weapons, peel off her suit, and change into a loose white shirt and pants. By the time she finished, Rowan was in the bath, the water so clouded she could see nothing of the lower body beneath.

The powerful muscles of his scarred back shifted as he scrubbed at his face with his hands, then his neck, then his chest. His skin had deepened to a golden brown—he must have spent time outdoors these past weeks. Without clothing, apparently.

He splashed water on his face again, and she started into movement, reaching for the washcloth she'd set on the sink. "Here," she said a bit hoarsely.

He just dunked it in the milky water and attacked his face, the back of his neck, the strong column of his throat. The full tattoo down his left arm gleamed with the water sliding off him.

Gods, he took up the entire bathtub. She mutely handed him her favorite lavender-scented soap, which he sniffed at, sighed in resignation, and then began using.

She took a seat on the curved lip of the tub and told him everything that had happened since they'd left. Well, mostly everything. He washed while she spoke, scrubbing himself down with brutal efficiency. He lifted the lavender soap to his hair, and she squeaked.

"You don't use that in your hair," she hissed, jolting from her perch to reach for one of the many hair tonics lining the little shelf above the bath. "Rose, lemon verbena, or . . ." She sniffed the glass bottle. "Jasmine." She squinted down at him.

He was staring up at her, his green eyes full of the words he knew he didn't have to say. *Do I look like I care what you pick?*

She clicked her tongue. "Jasmine it is, you buzzard."

He didn't object as she took up a place at the head of the tub and dumped some of the tonic into his short hair. The sweet, night-filled scent of jasmine floated up, caressing and kissing her. Even Rowan breathed it in as she scrubbed the tonic into his scalp. "I could still probably braid this," she mused. "Very teensy-tiny braids, so—" He growled, but leaned back against the tub, his eyes closed. "You're no better than a house cat," she said, massaging his head. He let out a low noise in his throat that might very well have been a purr.

Washing his hair was intimate—a privilege she doubted he'd ever allowed many people; something she'd never done for anyone else. But lines had always been blurred for them, and neither of them had particularly cared. He'd seen every bare inch of her several times, and she'd seen *most* of him. They'd shared a bed for months. On top of that, they were *carranam*. He'd let her inside his power, past his inner barriers, to where half a thought from her could have shattered his mind. So washing his hair, touching him . . . it was an intimacy, but it was essential, too.

"You haven't said anything about your magic," she murmured, her fingers still working his scalp.

He tensed. "What about it?"

Fingers in his hair, she leaned down to peer at his face. "I take it it's gone. How does it feel to be as powerless as a mortal?"

He opened his eyes to glare. "It's not funny."

"Do I look like I'm laughing?"

"I spent the first few days sick to my stomach and barely able to move. It was like having a blanket thrown over my senses."

"And now?"

"And now I'm dealing with it."

She poked him in the shoulder. It was like touching velvet-wrapped steel. "Grumpy, grumpy."

He gave a soft snarl of annoyance, and she pursed her lips to keep the smile in. She pushed down on his shoulders, beckoning him to dunk under the water. He obeyed, and when he emerged, she rose from the tiles and grabbed the towel she'd left on the sink. "I'm going to find you some clothes."

"I have—"

"Oh, no. Those are going right to the laundress. And you'll get them back only if she can make them smell decent again. Until then, you'll wear whatever I give you."

She handed him the towel, but didn't let go as his hand closed around it. "You've become a tyrant, Princess," he said.

She rolled her eyes and released the towel, turning as he stood in a mighty movement, water sloshing everywhere. It was an effort not to peek over her shoulder.

Don't you even dare, a voice hissed in her head.

Right. She'd call *that* voice Common Sense—and she'd listen to it from now on.

Striding into her closet, she went to the dresser in the back and knelt before the bottom drawer, opening it to reveal folded men's undershorts, shirts, and pants.

For a moment, she stared at Sam's old clothes, breathing in the faint smell of him clinging to the fabric. She hadn't mustered the strength to go to his grave yet, but—

"You don't have to give those to me," Rowan said from behind her. She started a bit, and twisted in place to face him. He was so damn stealthy.

Aelin tried not to look too jolted by the sight of him with the towel wrapped around his hips, at the tan and muscled body that gleamed with the oils of the bath, at the scars crisscrossing it like the stripes of a great cat. Even Common Sense was at a loss for words.

Her mouth was a little dry as she said, "Clean clothes are scarce in the house right now, and these are of no use sitting here." She pulled out a shirt and held it up. "I hope it fits." Sam had been eighteen when he died; Rowan was a warrior honed by three centuries of training and battle.

She pulled out undershorts and pants. "I'll get you proper clothes tomorrow. I'm pretty sure you'll start a riot if the women of Rifthold see you walking down the streets in nothing but a towel."

Rowan huffed a laugh and strode to the clothes hanging along one wall of the closet: dresses, tunics, jackets, shirts . . . "You wore all this?" She nodded and uncoiled to her feet. He flicked through some of the dresses and embroidered tunics. "These are . . . very beautiful," he admitted.

"I would have pegged you for a proud member of the anti-finery crowd."

"Clothes are weapons, too," he said, pausing on a black velvet gown. Its tight sleeves and front were unadorned, the neckline skimming just beneath the collarbones, unremarkable save for the tendrils of embroidered, shimmering gold creeping over the shoulders. Rowan angled the dress to look at the back—the true masterpiece. The gold embroidery continued from the shoulders, sweeping to form a serpentine dragon, its maw roaring toward the neck, the body curving down until the narrow tail formed the border of the lengthened train. Rowan loosed a breath. "I like this one best."

She fingered the solid black velvet sleeve. "I saw it in a shop when I was sixteen and bought it immediately. But when the dress was delivered a few weeks later, it seemed too . . . old. It overpowered the girl I was. So I never wore it, and it's hung here for three years."

He ran a scarred finger down the golden spine of the dragon. "You're not that girl anymore," he said softly. "Someday, I want to see you wear this."

She dared to look up at him, her elbow brushing his forearm. "I missed you."

His mouth tightened. "We weren't apart that long."

Right. To an immortal, several weeks were nothing. "So? Am I not allowed to miss you?"

"I once told you that the people you care about are weapons to be used against you. Missing me was a foolish distraction."

"You're a real charmer, you know that?" She hadn't expected tears or emotion, but it would have been nice to know he'd missed her at least a fraction as badly as she had. She swallowed, her spine locking, and pushed Sam's clothes into his arms. "You can get dressed in here."

She left him in the closet, and went right to the bathroom, where she splashed cold water on her face and neck.

She returned to her bedroom to find him frowning.

Well, the pants fit—barely. They were too short, and did wonders for showing off his backside, but— "The shirt is too small," he said. "I didn't want to rip it."

He handed it to her, and she looked a bit helplessly at the shirt, then at his bare torso. "I'll go out first thing." She sighed sharply through her nose. "Well, if you don't mind meeting Aedion shirtless, I suppose we should go say hello."

"We need to talk."

"Good talk or bad talk?"

"The kind that will make me glad you don't have access to your power so you don't spew flames everywhere."

Her stomach tightened, but she said, "That was *one* incident, and if you ask me, your absolutely *wonderful* former lover deserved it."

More than deserved it. The encounter with the visiting group of high-born Fae at Mistward had been miserable, to say the least. And when Rowan's former lover had refused to stop touching him, despite his request to do so, when she'd threatened to have Aelin whipped for stepping in . . . Well, Aelin's new favorite nickname—*fire-breathing bitch-queen*—had been fairly accurate during that dinner.

A twitch of his lips, but shadows flickered in Rowan's eyes.

Aelin sighed again and looked at the ceiling. "Now or later?"

"Later. It can wait a bit."

She was half tempted to demand he tell her whatever it was, but she turned toward the door.

⌒

Aedion rose from his seat at the kitchen table as Aelin and Rowan entered. Her cousin looked Rowan over with an appreciative eye and said, "You never bothered to tell me how handsome your faerie prince is, Aelin." Aelin scowled. Aedion just jerked his chin at Rowan. "Tomorrow morning, you and I are going to train on the roof. I want to know everything you know."

Aelin clicked her tongue. "All I've heard from your mouth these past few days is *Prince Rowan this* and *Prince Rowan that*, and yet *this* is what you decide to say to him? No bowing and scraping?"

Aedion slid back into his chair. "If Prince Rowan wants formalities, I can grovel, but he doesn't look like someone who particularly cares."

With a flicker of amusement in his green eyes, the Fae Prince said, "Whatever my queen wants."

Oh, please.

Aedion caught the words, too. *My* queen.

The two princes stared at each other, one gold and one silver, one her twin and one her soul-bonded. There was nothing friendly in the stares, nothing human—two Fae males locked in some unspoken dominance battle.

She leaned against the sink. "If you're going to have a pissing contest, can you at least do it on the roof?"

Rowan looked at her, brows high. But it was Aedion who said, "She says we're no better than dogs, so I wouldn't be surprised if she actually believes we'd piss on her furniture."

Rowan didn't smile, though, as he tilted his head to the side and sniffed.

"Aedion needs a bath, too, I know," she said. "He insisted on smoking a pipe at the taproom. He said it gave him an air of dignity."

Rowan's head was still angled as he asked, "Your mothers were cousins, Prince, but who sired you?"

Aedion lounged in his chair. "Does it matter?"

"Do you know?" Rowan pressed.

Aedion shrugged. "She never told me—or anyone."

"I'm guessing you have some idea?" Aelin asked.

Rowan said, "He doesn't look familiar to you?"

"He looks like me."

"Yes, but—" He sighed. "You met his father. A few weeks ago. Gavriel."

Aedion stared at the shirtless warrior, wondering if he'd strained his injuries too much tonight and was now hallucinating.

The prince's words sank in. Aedion just kept staring. A wicked tattoo in the Old Language stretched down the side of Rowan's face and along his neck, shoulder, and muscled arm. Most people would take one look at that tattoo and run in the other direction.

Aedion had seen plenty of warriors in his day, but this male was a Warrior—law unto himself.

Just like Gavriel. Or so the legends claimed.

Gavriel, Rowan's friend, one of his cadre, whose other form was a mountain lion.

"He asked me," Aelin murmured. "He asked me how old I was, and seemed relieved when I said nineteen."

Nineteen was too young, apparently, to be Gavriel's daughter, though she looked so similar to the woman he'd once bedded. Aedion didn't remember his mother well; his last memories were of a gaunt, gray face as she sighed her final breath. As she refused the Fae healers who could have cured the wasting sickness in her. But he had heard she'd once looked almost identical to Aelin and her mother, Evalin.

Aedion's voice was hoarse as he asked, "The Lion is my father?"

A nod from Rowan.

"Does he know?"

"I bet seeing Aelin was the first time he wondered if he'd sired a child with your mother. He probably still doesn't have any idea, unless that prompted him to start looking."

His mother had never told anyone—anyone but Evalin—who his father was. Even when she was dying, she'd kept it to herself. She'd refused those Fae healers because of it.

Because they might identify him—and if Gavriel knew he had a son . . . If Maeve knew . . .

An old ache ripped through him. She'd kept him safe—had *died* to keep him out of Maeve's hands.

Warm fingers slid around his hand and squeezed. He hadn't realized how cold he was.

Aelin's eyes—their eyes, the eyes of their mothers—were soft. Open. "This changes nothing," she said. "About who you are, what you mean to me. Nothing."

But it did. It changed everything. Explained everything: the strength, the speed, the senses; the lethal, predatory instincts he'd always struggled to keep in check. Why Rhoe had been so hard on him during his training.

Because if Evalin knew who his father was, then Rhoe certainly did, too. And Fae males, even half-Fae males, were deadly. Without the control Rhoe and his lords had drilled into him from an early age, without the focus . . . They'd known. And kept it from him.

Along with the fact that after he swore the blood oath to Aelin one day . . . he might very well remain young while she grew old and died.

Aelin brushed her thumb against the back of his hand, and then pivoted toward Rowan. "What does this mean where Maeve is concerned? Gavriel is bound through the blood oath, so would she have a claim on his offspring?"

"Like hell she does," Aedion said. If Maeve tried to claim him, he'd rip out her throat. His mother had *died* for fear of the Fae Queen. He knew it in his bones.

Rowan said, "I don't know. Even if she thought so, it would be an act of war to steal Aedion from you."

"This information doesn't leave this room," Aelin said. Calm. Calculating—already sorting through every plan. The other side of their fair coin. "It's ultimately your choice, Aedion, whether to approach Gavriel. But we have enough enemies gathering around us as it is. I don't need to start a war with Maeve."

But she would. She would go to war for him. He saw it in her eyes.

It nearly knocked the breath from him. Along with the thought of what the carnage would be like on both sides, if the Dark Queen and the heir of Mala Fire-Bringer collided.

"It stays with us," Aedion managed to say. He could feel Rowan assessing and weighing him and bit back a snarl. Slowly, Aedion lifted his gaze to meet the prince's.

The sheer dominance in that stare was like being hit in the face with a stone.

Aedion held it. Like hell he'd back down; like hell he'd yield. And there *would* be a yielding—somewhere, at some point. Probably when Aedion took that blood oath.

Aelin clicked her tongue at Rowan. "Stop doing that alpha-male nonsense. Once was enough."

Rowan didn't so much as blink. "I'm not doing anything." But the prince's mouth quirked into a smile, as if saying to Aedion, *You think you can take me, cub?*

Aedion grinned. *Any place, any time, Prince.*

Aelin muttered, "Insufferable," and gave Rowan a playful shove in the arm. He didn't move an inch. "Are you *actually* going to get into a pissing contest with every person we meet? Because if that's the case, then it'll take us an hour just to make it down one block of this city, and I doubt the residents will be particularly happy."

Aedion fought the urge to take a deep breath as Rowan broke his stare to give their queen an incredulous look.

She crossed her arms, waiting.

"It'll take time to adjust to a new dynamic," Rowan admitted. Not an apology, but from what Aelin had told him, Rowan didn't often bother with such things. She looked downright shocked by the small concession, actually.

Aedion tried to lounge in his chair, but his muscles were taut, his blood thrumming in his veins. He found himself saying to the prince, "Aelin never said anything about sending for you."

"Does she answer to you, General?" A dangerous, quiet question. Aedion knew that when males like Rowan spoke softly, it usually meant violence and death were on their way.

Aelin rolled her eyes. "You know he didn't mean it that way, so don't pick a fight, you prick."

Aedion stiffened. He could fight his own battles. If Aelin thought he needed protecting, if she thought Rowan was the superior warrior—

Rowan said, "I'm blood-sworn to you—which means several things, one of which being that I don't particularly care for the questioning of others, even your cousin."

The words echoed in his head, his heart.

Blood-sworn.

Aelin went pale.

Aedion asked, "What did he just say?"

Rowan had taken the blood oath to Aelin. *His* blood oath.

Aelin squared her shoulders, and said clearly, steadily, "Rowan took the blood oath to me before I left Wendlyn."

A roaring sound went through him. "You let him do *what?*"

Aelin exposed her scarred palms. "As far as I knew, Aedion, you were loyally serving the king. As far as I knew, I was never going to see you again."

"*You let him take the blood oath to you?*" Aedion bellowed.

She had lied to his face that day on the roof.

He had to get out, out of his skin, out of this apartment, out of this gods-damned city. Aedion lunged for one of the porcelain figurines atop the hearth mantel, needing to shatter *something* to just get that roaring out of his system.

She flung out a vicious finger, advancing on him. "You break one thing, you shatter just *one* of my possessions, and I will shove the shards down your rutting throat."

A command—from a queen to her general.

Aedion spat on the floor, but obeyed. If only because ignoring that command might very well shatter something far more precious.

He instead said, "How *dare* you? How dare you let him take it?"

"I dare because it is *my* blood to give away; I dare because you did not exist for me then. Even if neither of you had taken it yet, I would still give it to him because he is my *carranam*, and he has earned my unquestioning loyalty!"

Aedion went rigid. "And what about *our* unquestioning loyalty? What have you done to earn that? What have you done to save our people since you've returned? Were you ever going to tell me about the blood oath, or was that just another of your many lies?"

Aelin snarled with an animalistic intensity that reminded him she, too, had Fae blood in her veins. "Go have your temper tantrum somewhere else. Don't come back until you can act like a human being. Or half of one, at least."

Aedion swore at her, a filthy, foul curse that he immediately regretted. Rowan lunged for him, knocking back his chair hard enough to flip it over, but Aelin threw out a hand. The prince stood down.

That easily, she leashed the mighty, immortal warrior.

Aedion laughed, the sound brittle and cold, and smiled at Rowan in a way that usually made men throw the first punch.

But Rowan just set his chair upright, sat down, and leaned back, as if he already knew where he'd strike Aedion's death blow.

Aelin pointed at the door. "Get the hell out. I don't want to see you again for a good while."

The feeling was mutual.

All his plans, everything he'd worked for . . . Without the blood oath he was just a general; just a landless prince of the Ashryver line.

Aedion stalked to the front door and flung it open so hard he almost ripped it off its hinges.

Aelin didn't call after him.

CHAPTER 29

Rowan Whitethorn debated for a good minute if it was worthwhile to hunt down the demi-Fae prince and tear him into bloody ribbons for what he'd called Aelin, or if he was better off here, with his queen, while she paced in front of her bedroom fireplace. He understood—he really did—why the general was enraged. He'd have felt the same. But it wasn't a good-enough excuse. Not even close.

Perched on the edge of the plush mattress, he watched her move.

Even without her magic, Aelin was a living wildfire, more so now with the red hair—a creature of such roaring emotions that he could sometimes only watch her and marvel.

And her face.

That gods-damned face.

While they'd been in Wendlyn, it had taken him a while to realize she was beautiful. Months, actually, to really notice it. And for these past few weeks, against his better judgment, he'd thought often about that face—especially that smart-ass mouth.

But he hadn't remembered just how stunning she was until she'd taken off her hood earlier, and it had struck him stupid.

These weeks apart had been a brutal reminder of what life had been like until he had found her drunk and broken on that rooftop in Varese. The nightmares had started the very night she'd left—such relentless dreams that he'd nearly vomited when he flung himself out of them, Lyria's screaming ringing in his ears. The memory of it sent cold licking down his spine. But even that was burned away by the queen before him.

Aelin was well on her way to wearing a track in the rug before the fireplace.

"If that's any indication of what to expect from our court," Rowan said at last, flexing his fingers in an attempt to dislodge the hollow shakiness he hadn't been able to master since his magic had been smothered, "then we'll never have a dull moment."

She flung out a hand in a dismissive wave of irritation. "Don't tease me right now." She scrubbed at her face and huffed a breath.

Rowan waited, knowing she was gathering the words, hating the pain and sorrow and guilt on every line of her body. He'd sell his soul to the dark god to never have her look like that again.

"Every time I turn around," she said, approaching the bed and leaning against the carved post, "I feel like I'm one wrong move or word away from leading them to ruin. People's lives—*your* life—depend on me. There's no room for error."

There it was, the weight that had been slowly crushing her. It killed him that he'd have to add to it when he told her the news he carried—the reason he'd disobeyed her first order to him.

He could offer her nothing but the truth. "You will make mistakes. You will make decisions, and sometimes you will regret those choices. Sometimes there won't be a right choice, just the best of several bad options. I don't need to tell you that you can do this—you know you can. I wouldn't have sworn the oath to you if I didn't think you could."

She slid onto the bed beside him, her scent caressing him. Jasmine, and lemon verbena, and crackling embers. Elegant, feminine, and utterly wild. Warm, and steadfast—unbreakable, his queen.

Save for the weakness they both shared: that bond between them.

For in his nightmares, he sometimes heard Maeve's voice over the crack of a whip, cunning and cold. *Not for all the world, Aelin? But what about for Prince Rowan?*

He tried not to think about it: the fact that Aelin would hand over one of the Wyrdkeys for him. He locked that knowledge up so tightly that it could escape only in his dreams, or when he woke reaching across a cold bed for a princess who was thousands of miles away.

Aelin shook her head. "It was so much easier being alone."

"I know," he said, clamping down on the instinct to sling his arm around her shoulders and tuck her in close. He focused on listening to the city around them instead.

He could hear more than mortal ears, but the wind no longer sang its secrets to him. He no longer felt it tugging at him. And stuck in his Fae body, unable to shift . . . Caged. Restless. Made worse by the fact that he couldn't shield this apartment from any enemy attacks while they were here.

Not powerless, he reminded himself. He had been bound head to toe in iron before and had still killed. He could keep this apartment secure— the old-fashioned way. He was just . . . off-balance. *At a time when being off-balance could be fatal to her.*

For a while, they sat there in silence.

"I said some appalling things to him," she said.

"Don't worry about it," he said, unable to help the growl. "He said some equally appalling things to you. Your tempers are evenly matched."

She let out a breathy chuckle. "Tell me about the fortress—what it was like when you went back to help rebuild."

So he did, until he got to the knowledge he'd been holding in all night.

"Just say it," she said, with a direct, unyielding sort of look. He wondered if she realized that for all she complained about *his* alpha nonsense, she was pure-blooded alpha herself.

Rowan took a long breath. "Lorcan's here."

She straightened. "That's why you came."

Rowan nodded. And why keeping his distance was the smarter move; Lorcan was wicked and cunning enough to use their bond against them. "I caught his scent sneaking around near Mistward and tracked it to the coast, then onto a ship. I picked up his trail when I docked this evening." Her face was pale, and he added, "I made sure to cover my tracks before hunting you down."

Over five centuries old, Lorcan was the strongest male in the Fae realm, equal only to Rowan himself. They'd never been true friends, and after the events of a few weeks ago, Rowan would have liked nothing more than to slit the male's throat for leaving Aelin to die at the hands of the Valg princes. He might very well get the chance to do that—soon.

"He doesn't know you well enough to immediately pick up your scent," Rowan went on. "I'd bet good money that he got on that boat just to drag me here so I'd lead him to you." But it was better than letting Lorcan find her while he remained in Wendlyn.

Aelin swore with creative colorfulness. "Maeve probably thinks we'll also lead him right to the third Wyrdkey. Do you think she gave him the order to put us down—either to get the key, or afterward?"

"Maybe." The thought was enough to shoot icy rage through him. "I won't let that happen."

Her mouth quirked to the side. "You think I could take him?"

"If you had your magic, possibly." Irritation rippled in her eyes—enough so that he knew something else nagged at her. "But without magic, in your human form . . . You'd be dead before you could draw your sword."

"He's that good."

He gave her a slow nod.

She looked him over with an assassin's eye. "Could *you* take him?"

"It'd be so destructive, I wouldn't risk it. You remember what I told you about Sollemere." Her face tightened at the mention of the city he and Lorcan had obliterated at Maeve's request nearly two centuries ago. It was a stain that would forever linger, no matter what he told himself about how corrupt and evil its residents had been. "Without our magic, it's hard to call who'd win. It would depend on who wanted it more."

Lorcan, with his unending cold rage and a talent for killing gifted to him by Hellas himself, never allowed himself to lose. Battles, riches, females—Lorcan always won, at any cost. Once, Rowan might have let him win, let Lorcan end him just to put a stop to his own miserable life, but now . . . "Lorcan makes a move against you, and he dies."

She didn't blink at the violence that laced every word. Another part of him—a part that had been knotted from the moment she left—uncoiled like some wild animal stretching out before a fire. Aelin cocked her head. "Any idea where he'd hide?"

"None. I'll start hunting him tomorrow."

"No," she said. "Lorcan will easily find us without you hunting him. But if he expects me to lead him to the third key so he can bring it back to Maeve, then maybe . . ." He could almost see the wheels turning in her head. She let out a hum. "I'll think about that tomorrow. Do you think Maeve wants the key merely to keep me from using it, or to use it herself?"

"You know the answer to that."

"Both, then." Aelin sighed. "The question is, will she try to use us to hunt down the other two keys, or does she have another one of your cadre out searching for them now?"

"Let's hope she hasn't sent anyone else."

"If Gavriel knew that Aedion is his son . . ." She glanced toward the bedroom door, guilt and pain flickering on her lovely features. "Would he follow Maeve, even if it meant hurting or killing Aedion in the process? Is her control over him that strong?"

It had been a shock earlier to realize whose son lounged at the kitchen table. "Gavriel . . ." He'd seen the warrior with lovers over the centuries, and seen him leave them at Maeve's order. He'd also seen him ink the names of his fallen men onto his flesh. And of all his cadre, only Gavriel had stopped that night to help Aelin against the Valg.

"Don't answer now," Aelin cut in with a yawn. "We should go to bed."

Rowan had surveyed every inch of the apartment within moments of arriving, but he asked as casually as he could, "Where should I sleep?"

She patted the bed behind them. "Just like old times."

He clenched his jaw. He'd been bracing himself for this all night—for weeks now. "It's not like the fortress, where no one thinks twice about it."

"And what if I want you to stay in here with me?"

He didn't allow those words to sink in fully, the idea of being in that bed. He'd worked too damn hard at shutting out those thoughts. "Then I'll stay. On the couch. But you need to be clear to the others about what my staying in here means."

There were so many lines that needed to be held. She was off-limits—completely off-limits, for about a dozen different reasons. He'd thought he would be able to deal with it, but—

No, he would deal with it. He'd find a way to deal with it, because he wasn't a fool, and he had some gods-damned self-control. Now that Lorcan was in Rifthold, tracking them, hunting for the Wyrdkey, he had bigger things to worry about.

She shrugged, irreverent as always. "Then I'll issue a royal decree about my honorable intentions toward you over breakfast."

Rowan snorted. Though he didn't want to, he said, "And—the captain."

"What about him?" she said too sharply.

"Just consider how he might interpret things."

"Why?" She'd done an excellent job of not mentioning him at all.

But there was enough anger, enough pain in that one word, that Rowan couldn't back down. "Tell me what happened."

She didn't meet his eyes. "He said what occurred here—to my friends, to him and Dorian, while I was away in Wendlyn—that it was my fault. And that I was a monster."

For a moment, a blinding, blistering wrath shot through him. It was instinct to lunge for her hand, to touch the face that remained down-turned. But he held himself in check. She still didn't look at him as she said, "Do you think—"

"Never," he said. "Never, Aelin."

At last she met his stare, with eyes that were too old, too sad and tired to be nineteen. It had been a mistake to ever call her a girl—and there were indeed moments when Rowan forgot how young she truly was. The woman before him shouldered burdens that would break the spine of someone three times her age. "If you're a monster, I'm a monster," he said with a grin broad enough to show off his elongated canines.

She let out a rough laugh, close enough that it warmed his face. "Just sleep in the bed," she said. "I don't feel like digging up bedding for the couch."

Maybe it was the laugh, or the silver lining her eyes, but he said, "Fine." Fool—he was such a stupid fool when it came to her. He made himself add, "But it sends a message, Aelin."

She lifted her brows in a way that usually meant fire was going to start flickering—but none came. Both of them were trapped in their bodies, stranded without magic. He'd adapt; he'd endure.

"Oh?" she purred, and he braced himself for the tempest. "And what message *does* it send? That I'm a whore? As if what I do in the privacy of my own room, with *my* body, is anyone's concern."

"You think I don't agree?" His temper slipped its leash. No one else had ever been able to get under his skin so fast, so deep, in the span of a few words. "But *things are different now*, Aelin. You're a queen of the realm. We have to consider how it looks, what impact it might have on our relationships with people who find it to be improper. Explaining that it's for your safety—"

"Oh, please. My safety? You think Lorcan or the king or whoever the hell else has it in for me is going to slither through the window in the middle of the night? I *can* protect myself, you know."

"Gods above, I know you can." He'd never been in doubt of that.

Her nostrils flared. "This is one of the stupidest fights we've ever had. All thanks to *your* idiocy, I might add." She stalked toward her closet, her hips swishing as if to accentuate every word as she snapped, "Just get in bed."

He loosed a tight breath as she and those hips vanished into the closet. *Boundaries. Lines. Off-limits.*

Those were his new favorite words, he reminded himself as he grimaced at the silken sheets, even as the huff of her breath still touched his cheek.

Aelin heard the bathroom door close, then running water as Rowan washed up with the toiletries she'd left out for him.

Not a monster—not for what she'd done, not for her power, not when Rowan was there. She'd thank the gods every damn day for the small mercy of giving her a friend who was her match, her equal, and who would never look at her with horror in his eyes. No matter what happened, she'd always be grateful for that.

But . . . *Improper.*

Improper indeed.

He didn't know how improper she could be.

She opened the top drawer of the oak dresser. And slowly smiled.

Rowan was in bed by the time she strutted toward the bathroom. She heard, rather than saw, him jolt upright, the mattress groaning as he barked, "What in hell is *that*?"

She kept going toward the bathroom, refusing to apologize or look down at the pink, delicate, *very* short lace nightgown. When she emerged, face washed and clean, Rowan was sitting up, arms crossed over his bare chest. "You forgot the bottom part."

She merely blew out the candles in the room one by one. His eyes tracked her the entire time. "There is no bottom part," she said, flinging back the covers on her side. "It's starting to get *so* hot, and I hate sweating when I sleep. Plus, you're practically a furnace. So it's either this or I sleep naked. You can sleep in the bathtub if you have a problem with it."

His growl rattled the room. "You've made your point."

"Hmm." She slid into bed beside him, a healthy, *proper* distance away.

For a few heartbeats, there was only the sound of rustling blankets as she nestled down.

"I need to fill in the ink a bit more in a few places," he said flatly.

She could barely see his face in the dark. "What?"

"Your tattoo," he said, staring at the ceiling. "There are a few spots I need to fill in at some point."

Of course. He wasn't like other men—not even close. There was so little she could do to jar him, taunt him. A naked body was a naked body. Especially hers.

"Fine," she said, turning so that her back was to him.

They were silent again. Then Rowan said, "I've never seen—clothing like that."

She rolled over. "You mean to tell me the females in Doranelle don't have scandalous nightclothes? Or anywhere else in the world?"

His eyes gleamed like an animal's in the dark. She'd forgotten what it was like to be Fae, to have one foot always in the forest. "My encounters with other females usually didn't involve parading around in nightclothes."

"And what clothes did they involve?"

"Usually, none at all."

She clicked her tongue, shoving away the image. "Having had the utter delight of meeting Remelle this spring, I have a hard time believing *she* didn't subject you to clothing parades."

He turned his face toward the ceiling again. "We're not talking about this."

She chuckled. Aelin: one, Rowan: zero.

She was still smiling when he asked, "Are all your nightclothes like that?"

"So curious about my negligees, Prince. Whatever would the others say? Maybe you should issue a decree to clarify." He growled, and she grinned into her pillow. "Yes, I have more, don't worry. If Lorcan is going to murder me in my sleep, I might as well look good."

"Vain until the bitter end."

She pushed back against the thought of Lorcan, of what Maeve might want, and said, "Is there a specific color you'd like me to wear? If I'm going to scandalize you, I should at least do it in something you like."

"You're a menace."

She laughed again, feeling lighter than she had in weeks, despite the news Rowan had given her. She was fairly certain they were done talking for the night when his voice rumbled across the bed. "Gold. Not yellow—real, metallic gold."

"You're out of luck," she said into her pillow. "I would never own anything so ostentatious."

She could almost feel him smiling at her as she fell asleep.

Thirty minutes later, Rowan was still staring up at the ceiling, teeth gritted as he calmed the roaring in his veins that was steadily shredding through his self-control.

That gods-damned nightgown.

Shit.

He was in such deep, unending shit.

Rowan was asleep, his massive body half covered with blankets, as dawn streamed in through the lace curtains. Silently rising, Aelin stuck out her tongue at him as she shrugged on her pale-blue silk robe, tied her already-fading red hair into a knot atop her head, and padded into the kitchen.

Until the Shadow Market had burned to cinders, that miserable merchant there had been making a small fortune off all the bricks of dye she'd kept buying. Aelin winced at the thought of having to track down the vendor again—the woman had seemed the sort who would have escaped the flames. And would now charge double, triple, on her already overpriced dyes to make up for her lost goods. And since Lorcan could track her by scent alone, changing the color of her hair would have no impact on him. Though she supposed that with the king's guard on the lookout for her . . . Oh, it was too damn early to consider the giant pile of horseshit that had become her life.

Groggy, she made tea mostly by muscle memory. She started on toast, and prayed they had eggs left in the cooling box—they did. And bacon, to her delight. In this house, food tended to vanish as soon as it came in.

One of the biggest pigs of all approached the kitchen on immortal-silent feet. She braced herself as, arms full of food, she nudged the small cooling box shut with a hip.

Aedion eyed her warily while she went to the small counter beside the stove and began pulling down bowls and utensils. "There are mushrooms somewhere," he said.

"Good. Then you can clean and cut them. And you get to chop the onion."

"Is that punishment for last night?"

She cracked the eggs one by one into a bowl. "If that's what you think is an acceptable punishment, sure."

"And is making breakfast at this ungodly hour your self-imposed punishment?"

"I'm making breakfast because I'm sick of you burning it and making the whole house smell."

Aedion laughed quietly and came up beside her to begin slicing the onion.

"You stayed on the roof the whole time you were out, didn't you?" She yanked an iron skillet from the rack over the stove, set it on a burner, and chucked a thick pat of butter onto its dark surface.

"You kicked me out of the apartment, but not the warehouse, so I figured I might as well make myself useful and take watch." The twisty, bendy Old Ways manner of warping orders. She wondered what the Old Ways had to say about queenly propriety.

She grabbed a wooden spoon and pushed the melting butter around a bit. "We both have atrocious tempers. You know I didn't mean what I said, about the loyalty thing. Or about the half-human thing. You know none of that matters to me." Gavriel's son—holy gods. But she would keep her mouth shut about it until Aedion felt like broaching the subject.

"Aelin, I'm ashamed of what I said to you."

"Well, that makes two of us, so let's leave it at that." She whisked the eggs, keeping an eye on the butter. "I—I understand, Aedion, I really do, about the blood oath. I knew what it meant to you. I made a mistake not telling you. I don't normally admit to that kind of thing, but . . . I should have told you. And I'm sorry."

He sniffed at the onions, his expert slicing leaving a neat heap of them on one end of the cutting board, and then started on the small brown mushrooms. "That oath meant everything to me. Ren and I used to be at each other's throats because of it when we were children. His father hated me because I was the one favored to take it."

She took the onions from him and chucked them into the butter, sizzling filling the kitchen. "There's nothing that says you can't take the oath, you know. Maeve has several blood-sworn members in her court." Who were now making Aelin's life a living hell. "You can take it, and so can Ren—only if you want to, but . . . I won't be upset if you don't want to."

"In Terrasen, there was only one."

She stirred the onions. "Things change. New traditions for a new court. You can swear it right now if you wish."

Aedion finished the mushrooms and set down the knife as he leaned against the counter. "Not now. Not until I see you crowned. Not until we can be in front of a crowd, in front of the world."

She dumped in the mushrooms. "You're even more dramatic than I am."

Aedion snorted. "Hurry up with the eggs. I'm going to die of starvation."

"Make the bacon, or you don't get to eat any."

Aedion could hardly move fast enough.

CHAPTER 30

There was a room deep below the stone castle that the demon lurking inside him liked to visit.

The demon prince even let him out sometimes, through the eyes that might have once been his.

It was a room cloaked in endless night. Or maybe the darkness was from the demon.

But they could see; they had always been able to see in the blackness. Where the demon prince had come from, so little light existed that it had learned to hunt in the shadows.

There were pedestals arranged in the round room in an elegant curve, each topped with a black pillow. And on each pillow sat a crown.

Kept down here like trophies—kept in darkness. Like him.

A secret room.

The prince stood in the center of it, surveying the crowns.

The demon had taken control of the body completely. He'd let him, after that woman with the familiar eyes had failed to kill him.

He waited for the demon to leave the room, but the demon prince spoke instead. A hissing, cold voice that came from between the stars, speaking to him—only to him.

The crowns of the conquered nations, the demon prince said. *More will be added soon. Perhaps the crowns of other worlds, too.*

He did not care.

You should care—you will enjoy it as we rip the realms to shreds.

He backed away, tried to retreat into a pocket of darkness where even the demon prince couldn't find him.

The demon laughed. *Spineless human. No wonder she lost her head.*

He tried to shut out the voice.

Tried to.

He wished that woman had killed him.

CHAPTER 31

Manon stormed into Perrington's massive war tent, shoving aside the heavy canvas flap so violently that her iron nails slashed through the material. "Why are my Thirteen being denied access to the Yellowlegs coven? Explain. *Now.*"

As the last word snapped out of her, Manon stopped dead.

Standing in the center of the dim tent, the duke whirled toward her, his face dark—and, Manon had to admit with a thrill, a bit terrifying. "*Get out,*" he said, his eyes flaring like embers.

But Manon's attention was fixed on what—who—stood beyond the duke.

Manon stepped forward, even as the duke advanced on her.

Her black, filmy dress like woven night, Kaltain was facing a kneeling, trembling young soldier, her pale hand outstretched toward his contorted face.

And all over her, an unholy aura of dark fire burned.

"What is that?" Manon said.

"*Out*," the duke barked, and actually had the nerve to lunge for Manon's arm. She swiped with her iron nails, sidestepping the duke without so much as glancing at him. All her focus, every pore of her, was pinned on the dark-haired lady.

The young soldier—one of Perrington's own—was silently sobbing as tendrils of that black fire floated from Kaltain's fingertips and slithered over his skin, leaving no marks. The human turned pain-filled gray eyes to Manon. *Please*, he mouthed.

The duke snatched for Manon again, and she darted past him. "Explain this."

"You do not give orders, Wing Leader," the duke snapped. "Now get out."

"What is that?" Manon repeated.

The duke surged for her, but then a silken female voice breathed, "Shadowfire."

Perrington froze, as if surprised she had spoken.

"Where does this shadowfire come from?" Manon demanded. The woman was so small, so thin. The dress was barely more than cobwebs and shadows. It was cold in the mountain camp, even for Manon. Had she refused a cloak, or did they just not care? Or perhaps, with this fire . . . Perhaps she did not need one at all.

"From me," Kaltain said, in a voice that was dead and hollow and yet vicious. "It has always been there—asleep. And now it has been awoken. Shaped anew."

"What does it do?" Manon said. The duke had stopped to observe the young woman, like he was figuring out some sort of puzzle, like he was waiting for something else.

Kaltain smiled faintly at the soldier shaking on the ornate red carpet, his golden-brown hair shimmering in the light of the dimmed lantern above him. "It does this," she whispered, and curled her delicate fingers.

The shadowfire shot from her hand and wrapped around the soldier like a second skin.

He opened his mouth in a silent scream—convulsing and thrashing, tipping his head back to the ceiling of the tent and sobbing in quiet, unheard agony.

But no burns marred his skin. As if the shadowfire summoned only pain, as if it tricked the body into thinking it was being incinerated.

Manon didn't take her eyes away from the man spasming on the carpet, tears of blood now leaking from his eyes, his nose, his ears. Quietly she asked the duke, "Why are you torturing him? Is he a rebel spy?"

Now the duke approached Kaltain, peering at her blank, beautiful face. Her eyes were wholly fixed on the young man, enthralled. She spoke again. "No. Just a simple man." No inflection, no sign of empathy.

"Enough," the duke said, and the fire vanished from Kaltain's hand. The young man sagged on the carpet, panting and weeping. The duke pointed to the curtains in the back of the tent, which no doubt concealed a sleeping area. "Lie down."

Like a doll, like a ghost, Kaltain turned, that midnight gown swirling with her, and stalked toward the heavy red curtains, slipping through them as if she were no more than mist.

The duke walked over to the young man and knelt before him on the ground. The captive lifted his head, blood and tears mingling on his face. But the duke's eyes met Manon's as he put his massive hands on either side of his soldier's face.

And snapped his neck.

The death-crunch shuddered through Manon like the twanging of a harp. Normally, she would have chuckled.

But for a heartbeat she felt warm, sticky blue blood on her hands, felt the hilt of her knife imprinted against her palm as she gripped it hard and slashed it across the throat of that Crochan.

The soldier slumped to the carpet as the duke rose. "What is it that you want, Blackbeak?"

Like the Crochan's death, this had been a warning. Keep her mouth shut.

But she planned to write to her grandmother. Planned to tell her everything that had happened: this, and that the Yellowlegs coven hadn't been seen or heard from since entering the chamber beneath the Keep. The Matron would fly down here and start shredding spines.

"I want to know why we have been blocked from the Yellowlegs coven. They are under my jurisdiction, and as such, I have the right to see them."

"It was successful; that's all you need to know."

"You're to tell your guards immediately to grant me and mine permission to enter." Indeed, dozens of guards had blocked her path—and short of killing her way through, Manon had no way in.

"You choose to ignore my orders. Why should I follow yours, Wing Leader?"

"You won't have a gods-damned army to ride those wyverns if you lock them all up for your *breeding* experiments."

They were warriors—they were Ironteeth witches. They weren't chattel to be bred. They weren't to be experimented upon. Her grandmother would slaughter him.

The duke merely shrugged. "I told you I wanted Blackbeaks. You refused to give them to me."

"Is this punishment?" The words snapped out of her. The Yellowlegs were still Ironteeth, after all. Still under her command.

"Oh, no. Not at all. But if you disobey my orders again, the next time, it might be." He cocked his head, and the light gilded his dark eyes. "There are princes, you know—among the Valg. Powerful, cunning princes, capable of splattering people on walls. They've been very keen to test themselves against your kind. Perhaps they'll pay a visit to your barracks. See who survives the night. It'd be a good way to weed out the lesser witches. I have no use for weak soldiers in my armies, even if it decreases your numbers."

For a moment, there was a roaring silence in her head. A threat.

A threat from this *human*, this man who had lived but a fraction of her existence, this mortal *beast*—

Careful, a voice said in her head. *Proceed with cunning.*

So Manon allowed herself to nod slightly in acquiescence, and asked, "And what of your other ... activities? What goes on beneath the mountains circling this valley?"

The duke studied her, and she met his gaze, met every inch of blackness within it. And found something slithering inside that had no place in this world. At last he said, "You do not wish to learn what is being bred and forged under those mountains, Blackbeak. Don't bother sending your scouts in. They won't see daylight again. Consider yourself warned."

The human worm clearly didn't know precisely how skilled her Shadows were, but she wasn't about to correct him, not when it could be used to her advantage one day. Yet whatever did go on inside those mountains wasn't her concern—not with the Yellowlegs and the rest of the legion to deal with. Manon jerked her chin toward the dead soldier. "What do you plan to use this shadowfire for? Torture?"

A flash of ire at yet another question. The duke said tightly, "I have not yet decided. For now, she will experiment like this. Perhaps later, she will learn to incinerate the armies of our enemies."

A flame that did not leave burns—loosed upon thousands. It would be glorious, even if it was grotesque. "And are there armies of enemies gathering? Will you use this shadowfire on them?"

The duke again cocked his head, the scars on his face thrown into stark contrast in the dim lantern light. "Your grandmother didn't tell you, then."

"About what?" she bit out.

The duke strode toward the curtained-off part of the room. "About the weapons she has been making for me—for you."

"What weapons?" She didn't bother wasting time with tactical silence.

The duke just grinned at her as he disappeared, the curtains swinging enough to reveal Kaltain lying on a low bed covered in furs, her thin, pale arms at her sides, her eyes open and unseeing. A shell. A weapon.

Two weapons—Kaltain, and whatever her grandmother was making.

That was why the Matron had stayed in the Fangs with the other High Witches.

If the three of them were combining their knowledge, wisdom, and cruelty to develop a weapon to use against the mortal armies . . .

A shiver skidded down Manon's spine as she glanced once more at the broken human on the rug.

Whatever this new weapon was, whatever the three High Witches came up with . . .

The humans wouldn't stand a chance.

⁓

"I want you all spreading the word to the other covens. I want sentinels on constant surveillance at the entrances to the barracks. Three-hour watch rotations, no longer—we don't need anyone passing out and letting the enemy slip in. I've dispatched a letter to the Matron already."

Elide awoke with a jolt inside the aerie, warm and rested and not daring to breathe. It was still dark, but the moonlight was gone, dawn far off. And in the blackness, she could faintly make out the gleam of snow-white hair and the flicker of a few sets of iron teeth and nails. Oh, gods.

She'd planned to sleep for only an hour. She must have slept for at least four. Abraxos didn't move behind her, his wing still shielding her.

Since that encounter with Asterin and Manon, every hour, waking or sleeping, had been a nightmare for Elide, and even days afterward she caught herself holding her breath at odd moments, when the shadow of the fear gripped her by the throat. The witches hadn't bothered with her, even though she'd claimed her blood ran blue. But neither had Vernon.

But tonight . . . she'd been limping back to her room, the stairwell dark and quiet—too quiet, even with the scraping of her chains on the floor. And by her door, a pocket of utter silence, as if even the dust mites had held their breath. Someone was inside her room. Waiting for her.

So she'd kept walking, all the way to the moonlit aerie, where her uncle wouldn't dare go. The wyverns of the Thirteen had been curled up on the floor like cats or perched on their posts over the drop. To her left, Abraxos had watched her from where he'd sprawled on his belly, his depthless eyes wide, unblinking. When she'd come close enough to smell the carrion on his breath, she'd said, "I need somewhere to sleep. Just for tonight."

His tail moved slightly, the iron spikes clinking on the stones. Wagging. Like a dog—sleepy, but pleased to see her. There was no growl to be heard, no glint of iron teeth readying to gulp her down in two bites. She would *rather* be gobbled down than face whoever had been in her room.

Elide had slid down against the wall, tucking her hands under her armpits and curling her knees to her chest. Her teeth began clacking against each other, and she curled tighter. It was so cold in here that her breath clouded in front of her.

Hay crunched, and Abraxos sidled closer.

Elide had tensed—might have sprung to her feet and bolted. The wyvern had extended one wing toward her as if in invitation. To sit beside him.

"Please don't eat me," she'd whispered.

He'd huffed, as if to say, *You wouldn't be much of a mouthful.*

Shivering, Elide rose. He seemed bigger with every step. But that wing remained extended, as if she were the animal in need of calming.

As she reached his side, she could hardly breathe as she extended a hand and stroked the curving, scaly hide. It was surprisingly soft, like worn leather. And toasty, as if he were a furnace. Carefully, aware of the head he angled to watch her every move, she sat down against him, her back instantly warmed.

That wing had gracefully lowered, folding down until it became a wall of warm membrane between her and the chill wind. She'd leaned farther into his softness and delightful heat, letting it sink into her bones.

She hadn't even realized that she'd tumbled into sleep. And now . . . *they* were here.

Abraxos's reek must be concealing her own human scent, or else the Wing Leader would have found her by now. Abraxos kept still enough that she wondered if he knew that, too.

The voices moved toward the center of the aerie, and Elide gauged the distance between Abraxos and the door. Perhaps she could slip away before they noticed—

"Keep it quiet; keep it secret. If anyone reveals our defenses, they die at my hand."

"As you will it," Sorrel said.

Asterin said, "Do we tell the Yellowlegs and Bluebloods?"

"No," Manon said, her voice like death and bloodshed. "Blackbeaks only."

"Even if another coven winds up volunteering for the next round?" Asterin said.

Manon gave a snarl that made the hair on Elide's neck rise. "We can only tug so much at the leash."

"Leashes can snap," Asterin challenged.

"So can your neck," Manon said.

Now—now, while they were fighting. Abraxos remained unmoving, as if not daring to draw attention to himself while Elide prepared to hurry out. But the chains . . . Elide sat back down and carefully, slowly, lifted her foot just a little off the floor, holding the chains so they wouldn't drag. With one foot and one hand, she began pushing herself across the stones, sliding for the door.

"This shadowfire," Sorrel mused, as if trying to diffuse the brewing storm between the Wing Leader and her cousin. "Will he use it on us?"

"He seemed inclined to think it could be used on entire armies. I wouldn't put it past him to hold it over our heads."

Closer and closer, Elide edged for the open doorway.

She was almost there when Manon crooned, "If you had any backbone, Elide, you would have stayed beside Abraxos until we left."

CHAPTER 32

Manon had spotted Elide sleeping against Abraxos the moment they'd entered the aerie, and she'd become aware of her presence moments before that—tracking her from scent alone up the stairs. If Asterin and Sorrel had noticed, they made no comment.

The servant girl was sitting on her ass, almost to the doorway, one foot in the air to keep her chains from dragging. Smart, even if she'd been too stupid to realize how well they saw in the dark.

"There was someone in my room," Elide said, lowering her foot and standing.

Asterin stiffened. "Who?"

"I don't know," Elide said, keeping near the doorway, even if it would do her no good. "It didn't seem wise to go inside."

Abraxos had tensed, his tail shifting over the stones. The useless beast was worried for the girl. Manon narrowed her eyes at him. "Isn't your kind supposed to eat young women?"

He glared at her.

Elide held her ground as Manon prowled closer. And Manon, despite herself, was impressed. She looked at the girl—really looked at her.

A girl who was not afraid to sleep against a wyvern, who had enough common sense to tell when danger might be approaching . . . Perhaps that blood really did run blue.

"There is a chamber beneath this castle," Manon said, and Asterin and Sorrel fell into rank behind her. "Inside it is a coven of Yellowlegs witches, all taken by the duke to . . . create demon offspring. I want you to get into that chamber. I want you to tell me what's happening in there."

The human went pale as death. "I can't."

"You can, and you will," Manon said. "You're mine now." She felt Asterin's attention on her—the disapproval and surprise. Manon went on, "You find a way into that chamber, you give me the details, you keep *quiet* about what you learn, and you live. If you betray me, if you tell anyone . . . then we'll toast to you at your wedding party to a handsome Valg husband, I suppose."

The girl's hands were shaking. Manon smacked them down to her sides. "We do not tolerate cowards in the Blackbeak ranks," she hissed. "Or did you think your protection was free?" Manon pointed to the door. "You're to stay in my chambers if your own are compromised. Go wait at the bottom of the stairs."

Elide glanced behind Manon to her Second and Third, as if she was considering begging them to help. But Manon knew that their faces were stony and unyielding. Elide's terror was a tang in Manon's nose as she limped away. It took her far too long to get down the stairs, that wasted leg of hers slowing her to a crone's pace. Once she was at the bottom, Manon turned to Sorrel and Asterin.

"She could go to the duke," Sorrel said. As Second, she had the right to make that remark—to think through all threats to the heir.

"She's not that ruthless."

Asterin clicked her tongue. "That was why you spoke, knowing she was here."

Manon didn't bother nodding.

"If she's caught?" Asterin asked. Sorrel glanced sharply at her. Manon didn't feel like reprimanding. It was on Sorrel to sort out the dominance between them now.

"If she's caught, then we'll find another way."

"And you have no qualms about them killing her? Or using that shadowfire on her?"

"Stand down, Asterin," Sorrel ground out.

Asterin did no such thing. "You should be asking these questions, *Second*."

Sorrel's iron teeth snapped down. "It is because of your questioning that you're now Third."

"Enough," Manon said. "Elide is the only one who might get into that chamber and report. The duke has his grunts under orders not to let a single witch near. Even the Shadows can't get close enough. But a servant girl, cleaning up whatever mess . . ."

"You were the one waiting in her room," Asterin said.

"A dose of fear goes a long way in humans."

"Is she human, though?" Sorrel asked. "Or do we count her among us?"

"It makes no difference if she's human or witch-kind. I'd send whoever was the most qualified down into those chambers, and at this moment, only Elide can gain access to them."

Cunning—that was how she would get around the duke, with his schemes and his weapons. She might work for his king, but she would not tolerate being left ignorant.

"I need to know what's happening in those chambers," Manon said. "If we lose one life to do that, then so be it."

"And what then?" Asterin asked, despite Sorrel's warning. "Once you learn, what then?"

Manon hadn't decided. Again, that phantom blood coated her hands.

Follow orders—or else she and the Thirteen would be executed. Either by her grandmother or by the duke. After her grandmother read her letter, maybe it would be different. But until then—

"Then we continue as we've been commanded," Manon said. "But I will not be led into this with a blindfold over my eyes."

~

Spy.

A spy for the Wing Leader.

Elide supposed it was no different than being a spy for herself—for her own freedom.

But learning about the supply wagons' arrival *and* trying to get into that chamber while also going about her duties . . . Maybe she would get lucky. Maybe she could do both.

Manon had a pallet of hay brought up to her room, setting it near the fire to warm Elide's mortal bones, she'd said. Elide hardly slept that first night in the witch's tower. When she stood to use the privy, convinced that the witch was asleep, she'd made it two steps before Manon had said, "Going somewhere?"

Gods, her voice. Like a snake hidden up a tree.

She'd stammered out an explanation about needing the bathing room. When Manon hadn't replied, Elide had stumbled out. She'd returned to find the witch asleep—or at least her eyes were closed.

Manon slept naked. Even with the chill. Her white hair cascaded down her back, and there wasn't a part of the witch that didn't seem lean with muscle or flecked with faint scarring. No part that wasn't a reminder of what Manon would do to her if she failed.

Three days later, Elide made her move. The exhaustion that had tugged relentlessly on her vanished as she clutched the armful of linens she'd taken from the laundry and peered down the hallway.

Four guards stood at the door to the stairwell.

It had taken her three days of helping in the laundry, three days of chatting up the laundresses, to learn if linens were ever needed in the chamber at the bottom of those stairs.

No one wanted to talk to her the first two days. They just eyed her and told her where to haul things or when to singe her hands or what to scrub until her back hurt. But yesterday—yesterday she had seen the torn, blood-soaked clothes come in.

Blue blood, not red.

Witch-blood.

Elide kept her head down, working on the soldiers' shirts she'd been given once she'd proved her skill with a needle. But she noted which laundresses intercepted the clothes. And then she kept working through the hours it took to clean and dry and press them, staying later than most of the others. Waiting.

She was nobody and nothing and belonged to no one—but if she let Manon and the Blackbeaks think she accepted their claim on her, she might very well still get free once those wagons arrived. The Blackbeaks didn't care about her—not really. Her heritage was convenient for them. She doubted they would notice when she vanished. She'd been a ghost for years now, anyway, her heart full of the forgotten dead.

So she worked, and waited.

Even when her back was aching, even when her hands were so sore they shook, she marked the laundress who hauled the pressed clothes out of the chamber and vanished.

Elide memorized every detail of her face, of her build and height. No one noticed when she slipped out after her, carrying an armful of linens for the Wing Leader. No one stopped her as she trailed the laundress down hall after hall until she reached this spot.

Elide peered down the hall again just as the laundress came up out of the stairwell, arms empty, face drawn and bloodless.

The guards didn't stop her. Good.

The laundress turned down another hall, and Elide loosed the breath she'd been holding.

Turning toward Manon's tower, she silently thought through her plan over and over.

If she was caught . . .

Perhaps she should throw herself from one of the balconies rather than face one of the dozens of awful deaths awaiting her.

No—no, she would endure. She had survived when so many—nearly everyone she'd loved—had not. When her kingdom had not. So she would survive for them, and when she left, she would build herself a new life far away in their honor.

Elide hobbled up a winding stairwell. Gods, she hated stairs.

She was about halfway up when she heard a man's voice that stopped her cold.

"The duke said you spoke—why will you not say a word to me?"

Vernon.

Silence greeted him.

Back down the stairs—she should go right back down the stairs.

"So beautiful," her uncle murmured to whomever it was. "Like a moonless night."

Elide's mouth went dry at the tone in his voice.

"Perhaps it's fate that we ran into each other here. He watches you so closely." Vernon paused. "Together," he said quietly, reverently. "Together, we shall create wonders that will make the world tremble."

Such dark, intimate words, filled with such . . . *entitlement*. She didn't want to know what he meant.

Elide took as silent a step as she could down the stairs. She had to get away.

"Kaltain," her uncle rumbled, a demand and a threat and a promise.

The silent young woman—the one who never spoke, who never looked at anything, who had such marks on her. Elide had seen her only a few times. Had seen how little she responded. Or fought back.

And then Elide was walking up the stairs.

Up and up, making sure her chains clanked as loudly as possible. Her uncle fell silent.

She rounded the next landing, and there they were.

Kaltain had been shoved up against the wall, the neck of that too-flimsy gown tugged to the side, her breast nearly out. There was such emptiness on her face—as if she weren't even there at all. Vernon stood a few paces away. Elide clutched her linens so hard she thought she'd shred them. Wished she had those iron nails, for once.

"Lady Kaltain," she said to the young woman, barely a few years older than she.

She did not expect her own rage. Did not expect herself to go on to say, "I was sent to find you, Lady. This way, please."

"Who sent for her?" Vernon demanded.

Elide met his gaze. And did not bow her head. Not an inch. "The Wing Leader."

"The Wing Leader isn't authorized to meet with her."

"And you are?" Elide set herself between them, though it would do no good should her uncle decide to use force.

Vernon smiled. "I was wondering when you'd show your fangs, Elide. Or should I say your iron teeth?"

He knew, then.

Elide stared him down and put a light hand on Kaltain's arm. She was as cold as ice.

She didn't even look at Elide.

"If you'd be so kind, Lady," Elide said, tugging on that arm, clutching the laundry with her other hand. Kaltain mutely started into a walk.

Vernon chuckled. "You two could be sisters," he said casually.

"Fascinating," Elide said, guiding the lady up the steps—even as the effort to keep balanced made her leg throb in agony.

"Until next time," her uncle said from behind them, and she didn't want to know who he meant.

In silence, her heart pounding so wildly that she thought she might vomit, Elide led Kaltain up to the next landing, and let go of her long enough to open the door and guide her into the hall.

The lady paused, staring at the stone, at nothing.

"Where do you need to go?" Elide asked her softly.

The lady just stared. In the torchlight, the scar on her arm was gruesome. Who had done that?

Elide put a hand on the woman's elbow again. "Where can I take you that is safe?"

Nowhere—there was nowhere here that was safe.

But slowly, as if it took her a lifetime to remember how to do it, the lady slid her eyes to Elide.

Darkness and death and black flame; despair and rage and emptiness.

And yet—a kernel of understanding.

Kaltain merely walked away, that dress hissing on the stones. There were bruises that looked like fingerprints around her other arm. As if someone had gripped her too hard.

This place. These *people*—

Elide fought her nausea, watching until the woman vanished around a corner.

Manon was seated at her desk, staring at what appeared to be a letter, when Elide entered the tower. "Did you get into the chamber?" the witch said, not bothering to turn around.

Elide swallowed hard. "I need you to get me some poison."

CHAPTER
33

Standing in a wide clearing among the stacks of crates, Aedion blinked against the late-morning sun slanting through the windows high up in the warehouse. He was already sweating, and in dire need of water as the heat of the day turned the warehouse suffocating.

He didn't complain. He'd demanded to be allowed to help, and Aelin had refused.

He'd insisted he was fit to fight, and she had merely said, "Prove it."

So here they were. He and the Fae Prince had been going through a workout routine with sparring sticks for the past thirty minutes, and it was thoroughly kicking his ass. The wound on his side was one wrong move away from splitting, but he gritted through it.

The pain was welcome, considering the thoughts that had kept him up all night. That Rhoe and Evalin had never told him, that his mother had died to conceal the knowledge of who sired him, that he was half Fae—and that he might not know for another decade how he would age. If he would outlast his queen.

And his father—Gavriel. *That* was a whole other path to be explored. Later. Perhaps it'd be useful, if Maeve made good on the threat she posed, now that one of his father's legendary companions was hunting Aelin in this city.

Lorcan.

Shit. The stories he'd heard about Lorcan had been full of glory and gore—mostly the latter. A male who didn't make mistakes, and who was ruthless with those who did.

Dealing with the King of Adarlan was bad enough, but having an immortal enemy at their backs . . . Shit. And if Maeve ever saw fit to send Gavriel over here . . . Aedion would find a way to endure it, as he'd found a way to endure everything in his life.

Aedion was finishing a maneuver with the stick that the prince had shown him twice now when Aelin paused her own exercising. "I think that's enough for today," she said, barely winded.

Aedion stiffened at the dismissal already in her eyes. He'd been waiting all morning for this. For the past ten years, he had learned everything he could from mortals. If warriors came to his territory, he'd use his considerable charms to convince them to teach him what they knew. And whenever he'd ventured outside of his lands, he'd made a point to glean as much as he could about fighting and killing from whoever lived there. So pitting himself against a purebred Fae warrior, direct from Doranelle, was an opportunity he couldn't waste. He wouldn't let his cousin's pity wreck it.

"I heard a story," Aedion drawled to Rowan, "that you killed an enemy warlord using a table."

"Please," Aelin said. "Who the hell told you that?"

"Quinn—your uncle's Captain of the Guard. He was an admirer of Prince Rowan's. He knew all the stories."

Aelin slid her eyes to Rowan, who smirked, bracing his sparring stick on the floor. "You can't be serious," she said. "What—you squashed him to death like a pressed grape?"

Rowan choked. "No, I didn't squash him like a grape." He gave the queen a feral smile. "I ripped the leg off the table and impaled him with it."

"Clean through the chest and into the stone wall," Aedion said.

"Well," said Aelin, snorting, "I'll give you points for resourcefulness, at least."

Aedion rolled his neck. "Let's get back to it."

But Aelin gave Rowan a look that pretty much said, *Don't kill my cousin, please. Call it off.*

Aedion gripped the wooden sparring stick tighter. "I'm fine."

"A week ago," Aelin said, "you had one foot in the Afterworld. Your wound is still healing. We're done for today, and you're not coming out."

"I know my limits, and I say I'm fine."

Rowan's slow grin was nothing short of lethal. An invitation to dance.

And that primal part of Aedion decided it didn't want to flee from the predator in Rowan's eyes. No, it very much wanted to stand its ground and roar back.

Aelin groaned, but kept her distance. *Prove it*, she'd said. Well, he would.

Aedion gave no warning as he attacked, feinting right and aiming low. He'd killed men with that move—sliced them clean in half. But Rowan dodged him with brutal efficiency, deflecting and positioning to the offensive, and that was all that Aedion managed to see before he brought up his stick on pure instinct. Bracing himself against the force of Rowan's blow had his side bleating in pain, but he kept focused—even though Rowan had almost knocked the stick from his hands.

He managed to strike the next blow himself. But as Rowan's lips tugged upward, Aedion had the feeling that the prince was toying with him.

Not for amusement—no, to prove some point. Red mist coated his vision.

Rowan went to sweep his legs out, and Aedion stomped hard enough on Rowan's stick that it snapped in two. As it did, Aedion twisted, lunging to bring his own stick straight into Rowan's face. Gripping the two pieces in either hand, the Fae warrior dodged, going low, and—

Aedion didn't see the second blow coming to his legs. Then he was blinking at the wooden beams of the ceiling, gasping for breath as the pain from his wound arced through his side.

Rowan snarled down at him, one piece of the stick angled to cut his throat while the other pushed against his abdomen, ready to spill his guts.

Holy burning hell.

Aedion had known he'd be fast, and strong, but this . . . Having Rowan fight alongside the Bane might very well decide battles in any sort of war.

Gods, his side hurt badly enough he thought he might be bleeding.

The Fae Prince spoke so quietly that even Aelin couldn't hear. "Your queen gave you an order to stop—for your own good. Because she needs you healthy, and because it pains her to see you injured. Do not ignore her command next time."

Aedion was wise enough not to snap a retort, nor to move as the prince dug in the tips of his sticks a little harder. "And," Rowan added, "if you ever speak to her again the way you did last night, I'll rip out your tongue and shove it down your throat. Understand?"

With the stick at his neck, Aedion couldn't nod without impaling himself on the jagged end. But he breathed, "Understood, Prince."

Aedion opened his mouth again as Rowan backed away, about to say something he would surely regret, when a bright hello sounded.

They all whirled, weapons up, as Lysandra closed the rolling door behind her, boxes and bags in her arms. She had an uncanny way of sneaking into places unnoticed.

Lysandra took two steps, that stunning face grave, and stopped dead as she beheld Rowan.

Then his queen was suddenly moving, snatching some of the bags from Lysandra's arms and steering her into the apartment a level above.

Aedion eased from where he'd been sprawled on the ground.

"Is that Lysandra?" Rowan asked.

"Not too bad on the eyes, is she?"

Rowan snorted. "Why is she here?"

Aedion gingerly prodded the wound in his side, making sure it was indeed intact. "She probably has information about Arobynn."

Whom Aedion would soon begin hunting, once his gods-damned wound was finally healed, regardless of whether Aelin deemed him fit. And then he'd cut the King of the Assassins into little, tiny pieces over many, many days.

"Yet she doesn't want you to hear it?"

Aedion said, "I think she finds everyone but Aelin boring. Biggest disappointment of my life." A lie, and he didn't know why he said it.

But Rowan smiled a bit. "I'm glad she found a female friend."

Aedion marveled for a heartbeat at the softness in the warrior's face. Until Rowan shifted his eyes toward him and they were full of ice. "Aelin's court will be a new one, different from any other in the world, where the Old Ways are honored again. You're going to learn them. And I'm going to teach you."

"I know the Old Ways."

"You're going to learn them again."

Aedion's shoulders pushed back as he rose to his full height. "I'm the general of the Bane, and a prince of both Ashryver and Galathynius houses. I'm not some untrained foot soldier."

Rowan gave a sharp nod of agreement—and Aedion supposed he should be flattered. Until Rowan said, "My cadre, as Aelin likes to call them, was a lethal unit because we stuck together and abided by the same code. Maeve might be a sadist, but she ensured that we all understood and followed it. Aelin would never force us into anything, and our code will be different—better—than Maeve's. You and I are going to form the backbone of this court. We will shape and decide our own code."

"What? Obedience and blind loyalty?" He didn't feel like getting a lecture. Even if Rowan was right, and every word out of the prince's mouth was one that Aedion had dreamed of hearing for a decade. He should have been the one to initiate this conversation. Gods above, he'd *had* this conversation with Ren weeks ago.

Rowan's eyes glittered. "To protect and serve."

"Aelin?" He could do that; he had already planned on doing that.

"Aelin. And each other. And Terrasen." No room for argument, no hint of doubt.

A small part of Aedion understood why his cousin had offered the prince the blood oath.

~

"Who is that?" Lysandra said too innocently as Aelin escorted her up the stairs.

"Rowan," Aelin said, kicking open the apartment door.

"He's spectacularly built," she mused. "I've never been with a Fae male. Or female, for that matter."

Aelin shook her head to try to clear the image from her mind. "He's—" She swallowed. Lysandra was grinning, and Aelin hissed, setting down the bags on the great room floor and shutting the door. "Stop that."

"Hmm," was all Lysandra said, dropping her boxes and bags beside Aelin's. "Well, I have two things. One, Nesryn sent me a note this morning saying that you had a new, very muscled guest staying and to bring some clothes. So I brought clothes. Looking at our guest, I think Nesryn undersold him a good deal, so the clothes might be tight—not that I'm objecting to *that* one bit—but he can use them until you get others."

"Thank you," she said, and Lysandra waved a slender hand. She'd thank Faliq later.

"The other thing I brought you is news. Arobynn received a report last night that two prison wagons were spotted heading south to Morath—chock full of all those missing people."

She wondered if Chaol knew, and if he had tried to stop it. "Does he know that former magic-wielders are being targeted?"

A nod. "He's been tracking which people disappear and which get sent south in the prison wagons. He's looking into all his clients' lineages now, no matter how the families tried to conceal their histories after magic was banned, to see if he can use anything to his advantage. It's something to consider when dealing with him . . . given your talents."

Aelin chewed on her lip. "Thank you for telling me that, too."

Fantastic. Arobynn, Lorcan, the king, the Valg, the key, Dorian . . . She had half a mind to stuff her face with every remaining morsel of food in the kitchen.

"Just prepare yourself." Lysandra glanced at a small pocket watch. "I need to go. I have a lunch appointment." No doubt why Evangeline wasn't with her.

She was almost to the door when Aelin said, "How much longer—until you're free of your debts?"

"I still have a great deal to pay off, so—a while." Lysandra paced a few steps, and then caught herself. "Clarisse keeps adding money as Evangeline grows, claiming that someone so beautiful would have made her double, triple what she originally told me."

"That's despicable."

"What can I do?" Lysandra held up her wrist, where the tattoo had been inked. "She'll hunt me until the day I die, and I can't run with Evangeline."

"I could dig Clarisse a grave no one would ever discover," Aelin said. And meant it.

Lysandra knew she meant it, too. "Not yet—not now."

"You say the word, and it's done."

Lysandra's smile was a thing of savage, dark beauty.

⁓

Standing before a crate in the cavernous warehouse, Chaol studied the map Aelin had just handed him. He focused on the blank spots—trying not to stare at the warrior-prince on guard by the door.

It was hard to avoid doing so when Rowan's presence somehow sucked out all the air in the warehouse.

Then there was the matter of the delicately pointed ears peeking out from the short silver hair. *Fae*—he'd never seen one other than Aelin in those brief, petrifying moments. And Rowan . . . Conveniently, in all her storytelling, Aelin had forgotten to mention that the prince was so handsome.

A handsome Fae Prince, whom she'd spent months living and training with—while Chaol's own life fell apart, while people *died* because of her actions—

Rowan was watching Chaol as if he might be dinner. Depending on his Fae form, that might not be too far wrong.

Every instinct was screaming at him to run, despite the fact that Rowan had been nothing but polite. Distant and intense, but polite. Still, Chaol didn't need to see the prince in action to know that he would be dead before he could even draw his sword.

"You know, he won't bite," Aelin crooned.

Chaol leveled a stare at her. "Can you just explain what these maps are for?"

"Anything you, Ress, or Brullo can fill in regarding these gaps in the castle defenses would be appreciated," she said. Not an answer. There was no sign of Aedion among the stacked crates, but the general was probably listening from somewhere nearby with his keen Fae hearing.

"For you to bring down the clock tower?" Chaol asked, folding up the map and tucking it into the inner pocket of his tunic.

"Maybe," she said. He tried not to bristle. But there was something settled about her now—as if some invisible tension in her face had vanished. He tried not to look toward the door again.

"I haven't heard from Ress or Brullo for a few days," he said instead. "I'll make contact soon."

She nodded, pulling out a second map—this one of the labyrinthine network of the sewers—and weighted down the ends with whatever small blades she had on her. A good number of them, apparently.

"Arobynn learned that the missing prisoners were taken to Morath last night. Did you know?"

Another failure that fell on his shoulders—another disaster. "No."

"They can't have gotten far. You could gather a team and ambush the wagons."

"I know I could."

"Are you going to?"

He laid a hand on the map. "Did you bring me here to prove a point about my uselessness?"

She straightened. "I asked you to come because I thought it would be helpful for the both of us. We're both—we're both under a fair amount of pressure these days."

Her turquoise-and-gold eyes were calm—unfazed.

Chaol said, "When do you make your move?"

"Soon."

Again, not an answer. He said as evenly as he could, "Anything else I should know?"

"I'd start avoiding the sewers. It's your death warrant if you don't."

"There are people trapped down there—we've found the nests, but no sign of the prisoners. I won't abandon them."

"That's all well and good," she said, and he clenched his teeth at the dismissal in her tone, "but there are worse things than Valg grunts patrolling the sewers, and I bet they won't turn a blind eye to anyone in their territory. I would weigh the risks if I were you." She dragged a hand through her hair. "So are you going to ambush the prison wagons?"

"Of course I am." Even though the rebels' numbers were down. So many of their people were either fleeing the city altogether or refusing to risk their necks in an increasingly futile battle.

Was that concern flickering in her eyes? But she said, "They use warded locks on the wagons. And the doors are reinforced with iron. Bring the right tools."

He drew in a breath to snap at her about talking down to him, but—

She would know about the wagons; she'd spent weeks in one.

He couldn't quite meet her stare as he straightened up to go.

"Tell Faliq that Prince Rowan says thank you for the clothes," Aelin said.

What the hell was she talking about? Perhaps it was another jab.

So he made for the door, where Rowan stepped aside with a murmured farewell. Nesryn had told him she'd spent the evening with Aedion and Aelin, but he hadn't realized they might be . . . friends. He hadn't considered that Nesryn might wind up unable to resist the allure of Aelin Galathynius.

Though he supposed that Aelin was a queen. She did not falter. She did not do anything but plow ahead, burning bright.

Even if it meant killing Dorian.

They hadn't spoken of it since the day of Aedion's rescue. But it still hung between them. And when she went to free magic . . . Chaol would again have the proper precautions in place.

Because he did not think she would put her sword down the next time.

CHAPTER 34

Aelin knew she had things to do—vital things, terrible things—but she could sacrifice one day.

Keeping to the shadows whenever possible, she spent the afternoon showing Rowan the city, from the elegant residential districts to the markets crammed with vendors selling goods for the summer solstice in two weeks.

There was no sign or scent of Lorcan, thank the gods. But the king's men were posted at a few busy intersections, giving Aelin an opportunity to point them out to Rowan. He studied them with trained efficiency, his keen sense of smell enabling him to pick out which ones were still human and which were inhabited by lesser Valg demons. From the look on his face, she honestly felt a little bad for any guard that came across him, demon or human. A little, but not much. Especially given that their presence alone somewhat ruined her plans for a peaceful, quiet day.

She wanted to show Rowan the good parts of the city before dragging him into its underbelly.

So she took him to one of Nesryn's family's bakeries, where she went so far as to buy a few of those pear tarts. At the docks, Rowan even convinced her to try some pan-fried trout. She'd once sworn never to eat fish, and had cringed as the fork had neared her mouth, but—the damned thing was delicious. She ate her entire fish, then snuck bites of Rowan's, to his snarling dismay.

Here—Rowan was here with her, in Rifthold. And there was so much more she wanted him to see, to learn about what her life had been like. She'd never wanted to share any of it before.

Even when she'd heard the crack of a whip after lunch as they cooled themselves by the water, she'd wanted him with her to witness it. He'd silently stood with a hand on her shoulder as they watched the cluster of chained slaves hauling cargo onto one of the ships. Watched—and could do nothing.

Soon, she promised herself. Putting an end to *that* was a high priority.

They meandered back through the market stalls, one after another, until the smell of roses and lilies wafted by, the river breeze sweeping petals of every shape and color past their feet as the flower girls shouted about their wares.

She turned to him. "If you were a gentleman, you'd buy me—"

Rowan's face had gone blank, his eyes hollow as he stared at one of the flower girls in the center of the square, a basket of hothouse peonies on her thin arm. Young, pretty, dark-haired, and— Oh, gods.

She shouldn't have brought him here. Lyria had sold flowers in the market; she'd been a poor flower girl before Prince Rowan had spotted her and instantly known she was his mate. A faerie tale—until she'd been slaughtered by enemy forces. Pregnant with Rowan's child.

Aelin clenched and unclenched her fingers, any words lodged in her throat. Rowan was still staring at the girl, who smiled at a passing woman, aglow with some inner light.

"I didn't deserve her," Rowan said quietly.

Aelin swallowed hard. There were wounds in both of them that had yet to heal, but this one . . . Truth. As always, she could offer him one truth in exchange for another. "I didn't deserve Sam."

He looked at her at last.

She'd do anything to get rid of the agony in his eyes. Anything.

His gloved fingers brushed her own, then dropped back to his side.

She clenched her hand into a fist again. "Come. I want to show you something."

Aelin scrounged up some dessert from the street vendors while Rowan waited in a shadowed alley. Now, sitting on one of the wooden rafters in the gilded dome of the darkened Royal Theater, Aelin munched on a lemon cookie and swung her legs in the open air below. The space was the same as she remembered it, but the silence, the darkness . . .

"This used to be my favorite place in the entire world," she said, her words too loud in the emptiness. Sunlight poured in from the roof door they'd broken into, illuminating the rafters and the golden dome, gleaming faintly off the polished brass banisters and the bloodred curtains of the stage below. "Arobynn owns a private box, so I went any chance I could. The nights I didn't feel like dressing up or being seen, or maybe the nights I had a job and only an hour free, I'd creep in here through that door and listen."

Rowan finished his cookie and gazed at the dark space below. He'd been so quiet for the past thirty minutes—as if he'd pulled back into a place where she couldn't reach him.

She nearly sighed with relief as he said, "I've never seen an orchestra— or a theater like this, crafted around sound and luxury. Even in Doranelle, the theaters and amphitheaters are ancient, with benches or just steps."

"There's no place like this anywhere, perhaps. Even in Terrasen."

"Then you'll have to build one."

"With what money? You think people are going to be happy to starve while I build a theater for my own pleasure?"

"Perhaps not right away, but if you believe one would benefit the city, the country, then do it. Artists are essential."

Florine had said as much. Aelin sighed. "This place has been shut down for months, and yet I swear I can still hear the music floating in the air."

Rowan angled his head, studying the dark with those immortal senses. "Perhaps the music does live on, in some form."

The thought made her eyes sting. "I wish you could have heard it—I wish you had been there to hear Pytor conduct the *Stygian Suite*. Sometimes, I feel like I'm still sitting down in that box, thirteen years old and weeping from the sheer glory of it."

"You cried?" She could almost see the memories of their training this spring flash in his eyes: all those times music had calmed or unleashed her magic. It was a part of her soul—as much as he was.

"The final movement—every damn time. I would go back to the Keep and have the music in my mind for days, even as I trained or killed or slept. It was a kind of madness, loving that music. It was why I started playing the pianoforte—so I could come home at night and make my poor attempt at replicating it."

She'd never told anyone that—never taken anyone here, either.

Rowan said, "Is there a pianoforte in here?"

⌒

"I haven't played in months and months. And this is a horrible idea for about a dozen different reasons," she said for the tenth time as she finished rolling back the curtains on the stage.

She'd stood here before, when Arobynn's patronage had earned them invitations to galas held on the stage for the sheer thrill of walking on sacred space. But now, amid the gloom of the dead theater, lit with the single candle Rowan had found, it felt like standing in a tomb.

The chairs of the orchestra were still arranged as they probably had been the night the musicians had walked out to protest the massacres in

Endovier and Calaculla. They were all still unaccounted for—and considering the array of miseries the king now heaped upon the world, death would have been the kindest option.

Clenching her jaw, Aelin leashed the familiar, writhing anger.

Rowan was standing beside the pianoforte near the front right of the stage, running a hand over the smooth surface as if it were a prize horse.

She hesitated before the magnificent instrument. "It seems like sacrilege to play that thing," she said, the word echoing loudly in the space.

"Since when are you the religious type, anyway?" Rowan gave her a crooked smile. "Where should I stand to best hear it?"

"You might be in for a lot of pain at first."

"Self-conscious today, too?"

"If Lorcan's snooping about," she grumbled, "I'd rather he not report back to Maeve that I'm lousy at playing." She pointed to a spot on the stage. "There. Stand there, and stop talking, you insufferable bastard."

He chuckled, and moved to the spot she'd indicated.

She swallowed as she slid onto the smooth bench and folded back the lid, revealing the gleaming white and black keys beneath. She positioned her feet on the pedals, but made no move to touch the keyboard.

"I haven't played since before Nehemia died," she admitted, the words too heavy.

"We can come back another day, if you want." A gentle, steady offer.

His silver hair glimmered in the dim candlelight. "There might not be another day. And—and I would consider my life very sad indeed if I never played again."

He nodded and crossed his arms. A silent order.

She faced the keys and slowly set her hands on the ivory. It was smooth and cool and waiting—a great beast of sound and joy about to be awakened.

"I need to warm up," she blurted, and plunged in without another word, playing as softly as she could.

Once she had started seeing the notes in her mind again, when muscle memory had her fingers reaching for those familiar chords, she began.

It was not the sorrowful, lovely piece she had once played for Dorian, and it was not the light, dancing melodies she'd played for sport; it was not the complex and clever pieces she had played for Nehemia and Chaol. This piece was a celebration—a reaffirmation of life, of glory, of the pain and beauty in breathing.

Perhaps that was why she'd gone to hear it performed every year, after so much killing and torture and punishment: as a reminder of what she was, of what she struggled to keep.

Up and up it built, the sound breaking from the pianoforte like the heart-song of a god, until Rowan drifted over to stand beside the instrument, until she whispered to him, *"Now,"* and the crescendo shattered into the world, note after note after note.

The music crashed around them, roaring through the emptiness of the theater. The hollow silence that had been inside her for so many months now overflowed with sound.

She brought the piece home to its final explosive, triumphant chord.

When she looked up, panting slightly, Rowan's eyes were lined with silver, his throat bobbing. Somehow, after all this time, her warrior-prince still managed to surprise her.

He seemed to struggle for words, but he finally breathed, "Show me— show me how you did that."

So she obliged him.

⌒

They spent the better part of an hour seated together on the bench, Aelin teaching him the basics of the pianoforte—explaining the sharps and flats, the pedals, the notes and chords. When Rowan heard someone at last coming to investigate the music, they slipped out. She stopped at the Royal Bank, warning Rowan to wait in the shadows across the street as she again sat in the Master's office while one of his underlings rushed in and out on her business. She eventually left with another bag of gold— vital, now that there was one more mouth to feed and body to clothe—and found Rowan exactly where she'd left him, pissed off that she'd refused to let him accompany her. But he'd raise too many questions.

"So you're using your own money to support us?" Rowan asked as they slipped down a side street. A flock of beautifully dressed young women passed by on the sunny avenue beyond the alley and gaped at the hooded, powerfully built male who stormed past—and then all turned to admire the view from behind. Aelin flashed her teeth at them.

"For now," she said to him.

"And what will you do for money later?"

She glanced sidelong at him. "It'll be taken care of."

"By whom?"

"Me."

"Explain."

"You'll find out soon enough." She gave him a little smile that she knew drove him insane.

Rowan made to grab her by the shoulder, but she ducked away from his touch. "Ah, ah. Better not move too swiftly, or someone might notice." He snarled, the sound definitely not human, and she chuckled. Annoyance was better than guilt and grief. "Just be patient and don't get your feathers ruffled."

CHAPTER 35

Gods, he hated the smell of their blood.

But damn if it wasn't a glorious thing to be covered in when two dozen Valg lay dead around him, and good people were finally safe.

Drenched in Valg blood from head to toe, Chaol Westfall searched for a clean bit of fabric with which to wipe down his black-stained blade, but came up empty. Across the hidden clearing, Nesryn was doing the same.

He'd killed four; she'd taken down seven. Chaol knew only because he'd been watching her the entire time; she'd paired off with someone else during the ambush. He'd apologized for snapping at her the other night, but she'd just nodded—and still teamed up with another rebel. But now . . . She gave up trying to wipe down her blade and looked toward him.

Her midnight eyes were bright, and even with her face splattered in black blood, her smile—relieved, a bit wild with the thrill of the fight, their victory—was . . . beautiful.

The word clanged through him. Chaol frowned, and the expression was instantly wiped from her face. His mind was always a jumble after a fight, as if it had been spun around and around and twisted upside down, and then given a heavy dose of liquor. But he strode toward her. They'd done this—together, they'd saved these people. More at once than they'd ever rescued before, and with no loss of life beyond the Valg.

Gore and blood were splattered on the grassy forest floor, the only remnants of the decapitated Valg bodies that had already been hauled away and dumped behind a boulder. When they left, they'd pay the bodies' former owners the tribute of burning them.

Three of his group had set to unchaining the huddled prisoners now seated in the grass. The Valg bastards had stuffed so many of them into the two wagons that Chaol had nearly gagged at the smell. Each wagon had only a small, barred window high up on the wall, and a man had fainted inside. But all of them were safe now.

He wouldn't stop until the others still hidden in the city were out of harm's way as well.

A woman reached up with her filthy hands—her nails split and finger-tips swollen as if she'd tried to claw her way out of whatever hellhole she'd been kept in. "Thank you," she whispered, her voice hoarse. Probably from screaming that had gone unanswered.

Chaol's throat tightened as he gave the woman's hands a gentle squeeze, mindful of her near-broken fingers, and stepped to where Nesryn was now wiping her blade on the grass. "You fought well," he told her.

"I know I did." Nesryn looked over her shoulder at him. "We need to get them to the river. The boats won't wait forever."

Fine—he didn't expect warmth or camaraderie after a battle, despite that smile, but . . . "Maybe once we're back in Rifthold, we can go for a drink." He needed one. Badly.

Nesryn rose from her crouch, and he fought the urge to wipe a splatter of black blood from her tan cheek. The hair she'd tied back had come loose, and the warm forest breeze set the strands floating past her face. "I thought we were friends," she said.

"We are friends," he said carefully.

"Friends don't spend time with each other only when they're feeling sorry for themselves. Or bite each other's heads off for asking difficult questions."

"I told you I was sorry for snapping the other night."

She sheathed her blade. "I'm fine with distracting each other for whatever reason, Chaol, but at least be honest about it."

He opened his mouth to object, but . . . maybe she was right. "I do like your company," he said. "I wanted to go for a drink to celebrate—not . . . brood. And I'd like to go with you."

She pursed her lips. "That was the most half-assed attempt at flattery I've ever heard. But fine—I'll join you." The worst part was that she didn't even sound mad—she genuinely meant it. He could go drinking with or without her, and she wouldn't particularly care. The thought didn't sit well.

Personal conversation decidedly over, Nesryn surveyed the clearing, the wagon, and the carnage. "Why now? The king has had ten years to do this; why the sudden rush to get these people all down to Morath? What's it building to?"

Some of the rebels turned their way. Chaol studied the bloody aftermath as if it were a map.

"Aelin Galathynius's return might have started it," Chaol said, aware of those who listened.

"No," Nesryn said simply. "Aelin announced herself barely two months ago. Something this large . . . It's been in the works for a long, long time."

Sen—one of the leaders with whom Chaol met regularly—said, "We should consider yielding the city. Move to other places where their foothold isn't as secure; maybe try to establish a border somehow. If Aelin Galathynius is lingering near Rifthold, we should meet with her—maybe head for Terrasen, push Adarlan out, and hold the line."

"We can't abandon Rifthold," Chaol said, glancing at the prisoners being helped to their feet.

"It might be suicide to stay," Sen challenged. Some of the others nodded their agreement.

Chaol opened his mouth, but Nesryn said, "We need to head for the river. Fast."

He gave her a grateful look, but she was already moving.

⁓

Aelin waited until everyone was asleep and the full moon had risen before climbing out of bed, careful not to jostle Rowan.

She slipped into the closet and dressed swiftly, strapping on the weapons she'd casually dumped there that afternoon. Neither male had commented when she'd plucked Damaris from the dining table, claiming she wanted to clean it.

She strapped the ancient blade onto her back along with Goldryn, the two hilts peeking over either shoulder as she stood in front of the closet mirror and hastily braided back her hair. It was short enough now that braiding had become a nuisance, and the front bits slipped out, but at least it wasn't in her face.

She crept from the closet, a spare cloak in hand, past the bed where Rowan's tattooed torso gleamed in the light of the full moon leaking in from the window. He didn't stir as she snuck from the bedroom and out of the apartment, no more than a shadow.

CHAPTER 36

It didn't take long for Aelin to set her trap. She could feel the eyes monitoring her as she found the patrol led by one of the more sadistic Valg commanders.

Thanks to Chaol and Nesryn's reports, she knew their new hideouts. What Chaol and Nesryn didn't know—what she had spent these nights sneaking out to track on her own—was which sewer entrances the commanders used when going to speak to one of the Wyrdhounds.

They seemed to prefer the most ancient waterways to swimming through the filth of the more recent main tunnels. She'd been getting as close as she dared, which usually was not near enough to overhear anything.

Tonight, she slipped down into the sewers after the commander, her steps nearly silent on the slick stones, trying to stifle her nausea at the stench. She'd waited until Chaol, Nesryn, and their top lieutenants were out of the city, chasing down those prison wagons, if only so no one would get in her way again. She couldn't risk it.

As she walked, keeping far enough behind the Valg commander that he wouldn't hear, she began speaking softly.

"I got the key," she said, a sigh of relief passing over her lips.

Twisting her voice just as Lysandra had showed her, she replied in a male tenor, "You brought it with you?"

"Of course I did. Now show me where you wanted to hide it."

"Patience," she said, trying not to smile too much as she turned down a corner, creeping along. "It's just up this way."

On she went, offering whispers of conversation, until she neared the crossroads where the Valg commanders liked to meet with their Wyrdhound overseer and fell silent. There, she dumped the spare cloak she'd brought, and then backtracked to a ladder leading up to the street.

Aelin's breath caught as she pushed against the grate, and it mercifully gave.

She heaved herself onto the street, her hands unsteady. For a moment, she contemplated lying there on the filthy, wet cobblestones, savoring the free air around her. But he was too close. So she silently sealed the grate again.

It took only a minute before near-silent boots scraped on stone below, and a figure moved past the ladder, heading to where she'd left the cape, tracking her as he'd done all night.

As she'd let him do all night.

And when Lorcan walked right into that den of Valg commanders and the Wyrdhound that had come to retrieve their reports, when the clash of weapons and roar of dying filled her ears, Aelin merely sauntered down the street, whistling to herself.

Aelin was striding down an alley three blocks from the warehouse when a force akin to a stone wall slammed her face-first into the side of a brick building.

"You little *bitch*," Lorcan snarled in her ear.

Both of her arms were somehow already pinned behind her back, his legs digging hard enough into hers that she couldn't move them.

"Hello, Lorcan," she said sweetly, turning her throbbing face as much as she could.

From the corner of her eye, she could make out cruel features beneath his dark hood, along with onyx eyes and matching shoulder-length hair, and—damn. Elongated canines shone far too near her throat.

One hand gripped her arms like a steel vise; Lorcan used the other to push her head against the damp brick so hard her cheek scraped. "You think that was funny?"

"It was worth a shot, wasn't it?"

He reeked of blood—that awful, otherworldly Valg blood. He pushed her face a little harder into the wall, his body an immovable force against her. "I'm going to kill you."

"Ah, about that," she said, and shifted her wrist just enough for him to feel the blade she'd flicked free in the moment before she'd sensed his attack—the steel now resting against his groin. "Immortality seems like a long, long time to go without your favorite body part."

"I'll rip out your throat before you can move."

She pressed the blade harder against him. "*Big* risk to take, isn't it?"

For a moment, Lorcan remained unmoving, still shoving her into the wall with the force of five centuries of lethal training. Then cool air nipped at her neck, her back. By the time she whirled, Lorcan was several paces away.

In the darkness, she could barely make out the granite-hewn features, but she remembered enough from that day in Doranelle to guess that beneath his hood, the unforgiving face was livid. "Honestly," she said, leaning against the wall, "I'm a little surprised you fell for it. You must think I'm truly stupid."

"Where's Rowan?" he sneered. His close-fitting dark clothes, armored with black metal at the forearms and shoulders, seemed to gobble up the dim light. "Still warming your bed?"

She didn't want to know how Lorcan knew that. "Isn't that all you pretty males are good for?" She looked him up and down, marking the many weapons both visible and concealed. Massive—as massive as Rowan and Aedion. And utterly unimpressed by her. "Did you kill all of them? There were only three by my count."

"There were six of them, and one of those stone *demons*, you bitch, and you knew it."

So he had found a way to kill one of the Wyrdhounds. Interesting— and good. "You know, I'm really rather tired of being called that. You'd think five centuries would give you enough time to come up with something more creative."

"Come a little closer, and I'll show you just what five centuries can do."

"Why don't I show you what happens when you whip my friends, you spineless prick?"

Violence danced across those brutal features. "Such a big mouth for someone without her fire tricks."

"Such a big mouth for someone who needs to mind his surroundings."

Rowan's knife was angled along Lorcan's throat before he could so much as blink.

She'd been wondering how long it would take him to find her. He'd probably awakened the moment she pushed back the covers. "Start talking," Rowan ordered Lorcan.

Lorcan gripped his sword—a mighty, beautiful weapon that she had no doubt had ended many lives on killing fields in distant lands. "You don't want to get into this fight right now."

"Give me a good reason not to spill your blood," Rowan said.

"If I die, Maeve will offer aid to the King of Adarlan against you."

"Bullshit," Aelin spat.

"Friends close but enemies closer, right?" Lorcan said.

Slowly, Rowan let go of him and stepped away. All three of them monitored every movement the others made, until Rowan was at Aelin's side, his teeth bared at Lorcan. The aggression pouring off the Fae Prince was enough to make her jumpy.

"You made a fatal mistake," Lorcan said to her, "the moment you showed my queen that vision of you with the key." He flicked his black eyes to Rowan. "And *you*. You stupid fool. Allying yourself—*binding* yourself to a mortal queen. What will you do, Rowan, when she grows old and dies? What about when she looks old enough to be your mother? Will you still share her bed, still—"

"That's enough," Rowan said softly. She didn't let one flicker of the emotions that shot through her show, didn't dare to even think about them for fear Lorcan could smell them.

Lorcan just laughed. "You think you beat Maeve? She *allowed* you to walk out of Doranelle—both of you."

Aelin yawned. "Honestly, Rowan, I don't know how you put up with him for so many centuries. Five minutes and I'm bored to tears."

"Watch yourself, girl," Lorcan said. "Maybe not tomorrow, maybe not in a week, but someday you will trip up. And I'll be waiting."

"Really—you Fae males and your dramatic speeches." She turned to walk away, a move she could make only because of the prince standing between them. But she looked back over her shoulder, dropping all pretense of amusement, of boredom. Let that killing calm rise close enough to the surface that she knew there was nothing human in her eyes as she said to Lorcan, "I will never forget, not for one moment, what you did to him that day in Doranelle. Your miserable existence is at the bottom of my priority list, but one day, Lorcan . . ." She smiled a little. "One day, I'll come to claim that debt, too. Consider tonight a warning."

⁓

Aelin had just unlocked the warehouse door when Rowan's deep voice purred from behind, "Busy night, Princess?"

She hauled open the door, and the two of them slipped into the near-black warehouse, illuminated only by a lantern near the back stairs. She took her time locking the sliding door behind her. "Busy, but enjoyable."

"You're going to have to try a lot harder to sneak past me," Rowan said, the words laced with a growl.

"You and Aedion are insufferable." Thank the gods Lorcan hadn't seen Aedion—hadn't scented his heritage. "I was perfectly safe." Lie. She hadn't been sure whether Lorcan would even show up—or whether he would fall for her little trap.

Rowan poked her cheek gently, and pain rippled. "You're lucky scraping you is all he did. The next time you sneak out to pick a fight with Lorcan, you will *tell me* beforehand."

"I will do no such thing. It's my damn business, and—"

"It's *not* just your business, not anymore. You will take me along with you the next time."

"The next time I sneak out," she seethed, "if I catch you following me like some overprotective nursemaid, I will—"

"You'll *what*?" He stepped up close enough to share breath with her, his fangs flashing.

In the light of the lantern, she could clearly see his eyes—and he could see hers as she silently said, *I don't know what I'll do, you bastard, but I'll make your life a living hell for it.*

He snarled, and the sound stroked down her skin as she read the unspoken words in his eyes. *Stop being stubborn. Is this some attempt to cling to your independence?*

And so what if it is? she shot back. *Just—let me do these things on my own.*

"I can't promise that," he said, the dim light caressing his tan skin, the elegant tattoo.

She punched him in the bicep—hurting herself more than him. "Just because you're older and stronger doesn't mean you're entitled to order me around."

"It's exactly because of those things that I can do whatever I please."

She let out a high-pitched sound and went to pinch his side, and he grabbed her hand, squeezing it tightly, dragging her a step closer to him. She tilted her head back to look at him.

For a moment, alone in that warehouse with nothing but the crates keeping them company, she allowed herself to take in his face, those green eyes, the strong jaw.

Immortal. Unyielding. Blooded with power.

"Brute."

"Brat."

She loosed a breathy laugh.

"Did you really lure Lorcan into a sewer with one of those creatures?"

"It was such an easy trap that I'm actually disappointed he fell for it."

Rowan chuckled. "You never stop surprising me."

"He hurt you. I'm never going to forgive that."

"Plenty of people have hurt me. If you're going to go after every one, you'll have a busy life ahead of you."

She didn't smile. "What he said—about me getting old—"

"Don't. Just—don't start with that. Go to sleep."

"What about you?"

He studied the warehouse door. "I wouldn't put it past Lorcan to return the favor you dealt him tonight. He forgets and forgives even less easily than you do. Especially when someone threatens to cut off his manhood."

"At least I said it would be a *big* mistake," she said with a fiendish grin. "I was tempted to say 'little.'"

Rowan laughed, his eyes dancing. "Then you definitely would have been dead."

CHAPTER 37

There were men screaming in the dungeons.

He knew because the demon had forced him to take a walk there, past every cell and rack.

He thought he might know some of the prisoners, but he couldn't remember their names; he could never remember their names when the man on the throne ordered the demon to watch their interrogation. The demon was happy to oblige. Day after day after day.

The king never asked them any questions. Some of the men cried, some screamed, and some stayed silent. Defiant, even. Yesterday, one of them—young, handsome, familiar—had recognized him and begged. He'd begged for mercy, insisted he knew nothing, and wept.

But there was nothing he could do, even as he watched them suffer, even as the chambers filled with the reek of burning flesh and the coppery tang of blood. The demon savored it, growing stronger each day it went down there and breathed in their pain.

He added their suffering to the memories that kept him company, and let the demon take him back to those dungeons of agony and despair the next day, and the next.

CHAPTER 38

Aelin didn't dare to go back to the sewers—not until she was certain Lorcan was out of the area and the Valg weren't lurking about.

The next night, they were all eating a dinner Aedion had scraped together from whatever was lying around the kitchen when the front door opened and Lysandra breezed in with a chirped hello that had them all releasing the weapons they'd grabbed.

"How do you *do* that?" Aedion demanded as she paraded into the kitchen.

"What a miserable-looking meal," was all Lysandra said, peering over Aedion's shoulder at the spread of bread, pickled vegetables, cold eggs, fruit, dried meat, and leftover breakfast pastries. "Can't any of you cook?"

Aelin, who'd been swiping grapes off Rowan's plate, snorted. "Breakfast, it seems, is the only meal any of us are decent at. And this one"—she jabbed a thumb in Rowan's direction—"only knows how to cook meat on a stick over a fire."

Lysandra nudged Aelin down the bench and squeezed onto the end, her blue dress like liquid silk as she reached for some bread. "Pathetic—utterly pathetic for such esteemed and mighty leaders."

Aedion braced his arms on the table. "Make yourself at home, why don't you."

Lysandra kissed the air between them. "Hello, General. Good to see you're looking well."

Aelin would have been content to sit back and watch—until Lysandra turned those uptilted green eyes toward Rowan. "I don't think we were introduced the other day. Her Queenliness had something rather urgent to tell me."

A sly cat's glance in Aelin's direction.

Rowan, seated on Aedion's right, cocked his head to the side. "Do you need an introduction?"

Lysandra's smile grew. "I like your fangs," she said sweetly.

Aelin choked on her grape. Of course Lysandra did.

Rowan gave a little grin that usually sent Aelin running. "Are you studying them so you can replicate them when you take my form, shape-shifter?"

Aelin's fork froze in midair.

"Bullshit," Aedion said.

All amusement had vanished from the courtesan's face.

Shape-shifter.

Holy gods. What was fire magic, or wind and ice, compared to shape-shifting? Shifters: spies and thieves and assassins able to demand any price for their services; the bane of courts across the world, so feared that they'd been hunted nearly to extinction even before Adarlan had banned magic.

Lysandra plucked up a grape, examined it, and then flicked her eyes to Rowan. "Perhaps I'm just studying you to know where to sink *my* fangs if I ever get my gifts back."

Rowan laughed.

It explained so much. *You and I are nothing but beasts wearing human skins.*

Lysandra turned her attention to Aelin. "No one knows this. Not even Arobynn." Her face was hard. A challenge and a question lay in those eyes.

Secrets—Nehemia had kept secrets from her, too. Aelin didn't say anything.

Lysandra's mouth tightened as she turned to Rowan. "How'd you know?"

A shrug, even as Aelin felt his attention on her and knew he could read the emotions biting at her. "I met a few shifters, centuries ago. Your scents are the same."

Lysandra sniffed at herself, but Aedion murmured, "So *that's* what it is."

Lysandra looked at Aelin again. "Say something."

Aelin held up a hand. "Just—just give me a moment." A moment to sort out one friend from another—the friend she had loved and who had lied to her at every chance, and the friend she had hated and who she had kept secrets from herself . . . hated, until love and hate had met in the middle, fused by loss.

Aedion asked, "How old were you when you found out?"

"Young—five or six. I knew even then to hide it from everyone. It wasn't my mother, so my father must have had the gift. She never mentioned him. Or seemed to miss him."

Gift—interesting choice of words. Rowan said, "What happened to her?"

Lysandra shrugged. "I don't know. I was seven when she beat me, then threw me out of the house. Because we lived here—in this city—and that morning, for the first time, I'd made the mistake of shifting in her presence. I don't remember why, but I remember being startled enough that I changed into a hissing tabby right in front of her."

"Shit," Aedion said.

"So you're a full-powered shifter," Rowan said.

"I'd known what I was for a long time. From even before that moment,

I knew that I could change into any creature. But magic was outlawed here. And everyone, in every kingdom, was distrustful of shape-shifters. How could they not be?" A low laugh. "After she kicked me out, I was left on the streets. We were poor enough that it was hardly different, but—I spent the first two days crying on the doorstep. She threatened to turn me in to the authorities, so I ran, and I never saw her again. I even went back to the house months later, but she was gone—moved away."

"She sounds like a wonderful person," Aedion said.

Lysandra hadn't lied to her. Nehemia had lied outright, kept things that were vital. What Lysandra was . . . They were even: after all, she hadn't told Lysandra she was queen.

"How'd you survive?" Aelin asked at last, her shoulders relaxing. "A seven-year-old on the streets of Rifthold doesn't often meet a happy end."

Something sparked in Lysandra's eyes, and Aelin wondered if she had been waiting for the blow to fall, waiting for the order to get out. "I used my abilities. Sometimes I was human; sometimes I wore the skins of other street children with high standing in their packs; sometimes I became an alley cat or a rat or a gull. And then I learned that if I made myself prettier—if I made myself beautiful—when I begged for money, it came far faster. I was wearing one of those beautiful faces the day magic fell. And I've been stuck in it ever since."

"So this face," Aelin said, "isn't your real face? Your real body?"

"No. And what kills me is that I can't remember what my real face was. That was the danger of shifting—that you would forget your real form, because it's the memory of it that guides the shifting. I remember being plain as a dormouse, but . . . I don't remember if my eyes were blue or gray or green; I can't remember the shape of my nose or my chin. And it was a child's body, too. I don't know what I would look like now, as a woman."

Aelin said, "And this was the form that Arobynn spotted you in a few years later."

Lysandra nodded and picked at an invisible fleck of lint on her dress. "If magic is free again—would you be wary of a shape-shifter?"

So carefully phrased, so casually asked, as if it weren't the most important question of all.

Aelin shrugged and gave her the truth. "I'd be *jealous* of a shape-shifter. Shifting into any form I please would come in rather handy." She considered it. "A shape-shifter would make a powerful ally. And an even more entertaining friend."

Aedion mused, "It would make a difference on a battlefield, once magic is freed."

Rowan just asked, "Did you have a favorite form?"

Lysandra's grin was nothing short of wicked. "I liked anything with claws and big, big fangs."

Aelin swallowed her laugh. "Is there a reason behind this visit, Lysandra, or are you here just to make my friends squirm?"

All amusement faded as Lysandra held up a velvet sack that sagged with what looked to be a large box. "What you requested." The box thumped as she set the sack onto the worn wooden table.

Aelin slid the sack toward herself, even as the males raised their brows and subtly sniffed at the box within. "Thank you."

Lysandra said, "Arobynn is going to call in your favor tomorrow, to be delivered the following night. Be ready."

"Good." It was an effort to keep her face blank.

Aedion leaned forward, glancing between them. "Does he expect only Aelin to deliver it?"

"No—all of you, I think."

Rowan said, "Is it a trap?"

"Probably, in some way or another," Lysandra said. "He wants you to deliver it and then join him for dinner."

"Demons and dining," Aelin said. "A delightful combination."

Only Lysandra smiled.

"Will he poison us?" Aedion asked.

Aelin scratched at a piece of dirt on the table. "Poison isn't Arobynn's style. If he were to do anything to the food, it would be to add some drug that would incapacitate us while he had us moved wherever he wanted. It's the control that he loves," she added, still staring at the table, not quite feeling like seeing what was written on Rowan's or Aedion's face. "The pain and fear, yes—but the power is what he really thrives on." Lysandra's face had lost its softness, her eyes cold and sharp—a reflection of Aelin's own, no doubt. The only person who could understand, who had also learned firsthand exactly how far that lust for control went. Aelin rose from her seat. "I'll walk you to your carriage."

She and Lysandra paused among the stacks of crates in the warehouse.

"Are you ready?" Lysandra asked, crossing her arms.

Aelin nodded. "I'm not sure the debt could ever be paid for what he . . . what they all did. But it will have to be enough. I'm running out of time."

Lysandra pursed her lips. "I won't be able to risk coming here again until afterward."

"Thank you—for everything."

"He could still have a few tricks up his sleeve. Be on your guard."

"And you be on yours."

"You're not . . . mad that I didn't tell you?"

"Your secret could get you killed just as easily as mine, Lysandra. I just felt . . . I don't know. If anything, I wondered if I'd done something wrong, something to make you not trust me enough to tell me."

"I wanted to—I've been dying to."

Aelin believed her. "You risked those Valg guards for me—for Aedion that day we rescued him," Aelin said. "They'd probably be beside themselves if they learned there was a shifter in this city." And that night at the Pits, when she'd kept turning away from the Valg and hiding behind Arobynn . . . It had been to avoid their notice. "You have to be insane."

"Even before I knew who you were, Aelin, I knew that what you were working toward . . . It was worth it."

"What is?" Her throat tightened.

"A world where people like me don't have to hide." Lysandra turned away, but Aelin grabbed her by the hand. Lysandra smiled a bit. "Times like these, I wish I had your particular skill set instead."

"Would you do it if you could? About two nights from now, I mean."

Lysandra gently let go of her hand. "I've thought about it every single day since Wesley died. I would do it, and gladly. But I don't mind if you do it. You won't hesitate. I find that comforting, somehow."

The invitation arrived by street urchin at ten o'clock the next morning.

Aelin stared at the cream-colored envelope on the table before the fireplace, its red wax seal imprinted with crossed daggers. Aedion and Rowan, peering over her shoulders, studied the box it had come with. Both males sniffed—and frowned.

"It smells like almonds," Aedion said.

She pulled out the card. A formal invitation for dinner tomorrow at eight—for her and two guests—and a request for the favor owed to him.

His patience was at an end. But in typical Arobynn fashion, dumping the demon at his doorstep wouldn't be enough. No—she'd deliver it on his terms.

The dinner was late enough in the day to give her time to stew.

There was a note at the end of the invitation, in an elegant yet efficient scrawl.

A gift—and one I hope you'll wear tomorrow night.

She chucked the card onto the table and waved a hand to Aedion or Rowan to open the box as she walked to the window and looked out toward the castle. It was blindingly bright in the morning sun, glimmering as though it had been crafted from pearl and gold and silver.

The slither of ribbon, the thud of the box lid opening, and—

"What the hell is that?"

She glanced over her shoulder. Aedion held a large glass bottle in his hands, full of amber liquid.

She said flatly, "Perfumed skin oil."

"Why does he want you to wear it?" Aedion asked too quietly.

She looked out the window again. Rowan stalked over and perched on the armchair behind her, a steady force at her back. Aelin said, "It's just another move in the game we've been playing."

She'd have to rub it into her skin. His scent.

She told herself that she'd expected nothing less, but . . .

"And you're going to use it?" Aedion spat.

"Tomorrow, our one goal is to get the Amulet of Orynth from him. Agreeing to wear that oil will put him on unsure footing."

"I don't follow."

"The invitation is a threat," Rowan replied for her. She could feel him inches away, was aware of his movements as much as her own. "Two companions—he knows how many of us are here, knows who you are."

"And you?" Aedion asked.

The fabric of his shirt sighed against Rowan's skin as he shrugged. "He's probably figured out by now that I'm Fae."

The thought of Rowan facing Arobynn, and what Arobynn might try to do—

"And what about the demon?" Aedion demanded. "He expects us to bring it over in all our finery?"

"Another test. And yes."

"So when do we go catch ourselves a Valg commander?"

Aelin and Rowan glanced at each other. "You're staying here," she said to Aedion.

"Like hell I am."

She pointed to his side. "If you hadn't been a hotheaded pain in my ass and torn your stitches when you sparred with Rowan, you could have come. But you're still on the mend, and I'm not going to risk exposing your wounds to the filth in the sewers just so you can feel better about yourself."

Aedion's nostrils flared as he reined in his temper. "You're going to face a *demon*—"

"She'll be taken care of," Rowan said.

"I can take care of myself," she snapped. "I'm going to get dressed." She grabbed her suit from where she'd left it drying over an armchair before the open windows.

Aedion sighed behind her. "Please—just be safe. And Lysandra is to be trusted?"

"We'll find out tomorrow," she said. She trusted Lysandra—she wouldn't have let her near Aedion otherwise—but Lysandra wouldn't necessarily know if Arobynn was using her.

Rowan lifted his brows. *Are you all right?*

She nodded. *I just want to get through these two days and be done with it.*

"That will never stop being strange," Aedion muttered.

"Deal with it," she told him, carrying the suit into the bedroom. "Let's go hunt ourselves a pretty little demon."

CHAPTER 39

"Dead as dead can be," Aelin said, toeing the upper half of the Wyrdhound's remains. Rowan, crouching over one of the bottom bits, growled his confirmation. "Lorcan doesn't pull punches, does he?" she said, studying the reeking, blood-splattered sewer crossroads. There was hardly anything left of the Valg captains, or the Wyrdhound. In a matter of moments, Lorcan had massacred them all as if they were chattel. Gods above.

"Lorcan probably spent the entire fight imagining each of these creatures was you," Rowan said, rising from his crouch bearing a clawed arm. "The stone skin seems like armor, but inside it's just flesh." He sniffed at it, and snarled in disgust.

"Good. And thank you, Lorcan, for finding that out for us." She strode to Rowan, taking the heavy arm from him, and waved at the prince with the creature's stiff fingers.

"Stop that," he hissed.

She wriggled the demon's fingers a bit more. "It'd make a good back-scratcher."

Rowan only frowned.

"Killjoy," she said, and chucked the arm onto the torso of the Wyrdhound. It landed with a heavy thump and click of stone. "So, Lorcan can bring down a Wyrdhound." Rowan snorted at the name she'd coined. "And once it's down, it seems like it stays down. Good to know."

Rowan eyed her warily. "This trap wasn't just to send Lorcan a message, was it?"

"These things are the king's puppets," she said, "so his Grand Imperial Majesty now has a read on Lorcan's face and smell, and I suspect he will not be very pleased to have a Fae warrior in his city. Why, I'd bet that Lorcan is currently being pursued by the seven other Wyrdhounds, who no doubt have a score to settle on behalf of their king *and* their fallen brother."

Rowan shook his head. "I don't know whether to throttle you or clap you on the back."

"I think there's a long line of people who feel the same way." She scanned the sewer-turned-charnel-house. "I needed Lorcan's eyes else-where tonight and tomorrow. And I needed to know whether these Wyrdhounds could be killed."

"Why?" He saw too much.

Slowly, she met his gaze. "Because I'm going to use their beloved sewer entrance to get into the castle—and blow up the clock tower right from under them."

Rowan let out a low, wicked chuckle. "That's how you're going to free magic. Once Lorcan kills the last of the Wyrdhounds, you're going in."

"He really should have killed me, considering the world of trouble that's now hunting him through this city."

Rowan bared his teeth in a feral smile. "He had it coming."

Cloaked, armed, and masked, Aelin leaned against the stone wall of the abandoned building while Rowan circled the bound Valg commander in the center of the room.

"*You've signed your death warrant, you maggots,*" the thing inside the guard's body said.

Aelin clicked her tongue. "You must not be a very good demon to be captured so easily."

It had been a joke, really. Aelin had picked the smallest patrol led by the mildest of the commanders. She and Rowan had ambushed the patrol just before midnight in a quiet part of the city. She'd barely killed two guards before the rest were dead at Rowan's hand—and when the commander tried to run, the Fae warrior had caught him within heartbeats.

Rendering him unconscious had been the work of a moment. The hardest part had been dragging his carcass across the slums, into the building, and down into the cellar, where they'd chained him to a chair.

"I'm—not a demon," the man hissed, as if every word burned him.

Aelin crossed her arms. Rowan, bearing both Goldryn and Damaris, circled the man, a hawk closing in on prey.

"Then what's the ring for?" she said.

A gasp of breath—human, labored. "To enslave us—corrupt us."

"And?"

"*Come closer, and I might tell you.*" His voice *changed* then, deeper and colder.

"What's your name?" Rowan asked.

"*Your human tongues cannot pronounce our names, or our language,*" the demon said.

She mimicked, "Your human tongues cannot pronounce our names. I've heard that one before, unfortunately." Aelin let out a low laugh as the creature inside the man seethed. "What is your name—your *real* name?"

The man thrashed, a violent jerking motion that made Rowan step closer. She carefully monitored the battle between the two beings inside that body. At last it said, "Stevan."

"Stevan," she said. The man's eyes were clear, fixed on her. "Stevan," she said again, louder.

"*Quiet,*" the demon snapped.

"Where are you from, Stevan?"

"*Enough of*—Melisande."

"Stevan," she repeated. It hadn't worked on the day of Aedion's escape—it hadn't been enough then, but now . . . "Do you have a family, Stevan?"

"Dead. All of them. *Just as you will be.*" He stiffened, slumped, stiffened, slumped.

"Can you take off the ring?"

"*Never,*" the thing said.

"Can you come back, Stevan? If the ring is gone?"

A shudder that left his head hanging between his shoulders. "I don't want to, even if I could."

"Why?"

"The things—things I did, we did . . . *He liked to watch while I took them, while I ripped them apart.*"

Rowan stopped his circling, standing beside her. Despite his mask, she could almost see the look on his face—the disgust and pity.

"Tell me about the Valg princes," Aelin said.

Both man and demon were silent.

"Tell me about the Valg princes," she ordered.

"*They are darkness, they are glory, they are eternal.*"

"Stevan, tell me. Is there one here—in Rifthold?"

"Yes."

"Whose body is it inhabiting?"

"The Crown Prince's."

"Is the prince in there, as you are in there?"

"I never saw him—never spoke to him. If—if it's a prince inside him . . . I can't hold out, can't stand this thing. If it's a prince . . . *the prince will have broken him, used and taken him.*"

Dorian, Dorian . . .

The man breathed, "Please," his voice so empty and soft compared to that of the thing inside him. "Please—just end it. I can't hold it."

"Liar," she purred. "You gave yourself to it."

"No choice," the man gasped out. "They came to our homes, our families. They said the rings were part of the uniform, so we had to wear them." A shudder went through him, and something ancient and cold smiled at her. "*What* are *you, woman?*" It licked its lips. "*Let me taste you. Tell me what you are.*"

Aelin studied the black ring on its finger. Cain—once upon a time, months and lifetimes ago, Cain had fought the thing inside him. There had been a day, in the halls of the castle, when he'd looked hounded, hunted. As if, despite the ring . . .

"I am death," she said simply. "Should you want it."

The man sagged, the demon vanishing. "Yes," he sighed. "Yes."

"What would you offer me in exchange?"

"Anything," the man breathed. "Please."

She looked at his hand, at his ring, and reached into her pocket. "Then listen carefully."

⁓

Aelin awoke, drenched in sweat and twisted in the sheets, fear clenching her like a fist.

She willed herself to breathe, to blink—to look at the moon-bathed room, to turn her head and see the Fae Prince slumbering across the bed.

Alive—not tortured, not dead.

Still, she reached a hand out over the sea of blankets between them and touched his bare shoulder. Rock-hard muscle encased in velvet-soft skin. Real.

They'd done what they needed to, and the Valg commander was locked in another building, ready and waiting for tomorrow night, when they would bring him to the Keep, Arobynn's favor at last fulfilled. But the words of the demon rang through her head. And then they blended with the voice of the Valg prince that had used Dorian's mouth like a puppet.

I will destroy everything that you love. A promise.

Aelin loosed a breath, careful not to disturb the Fae Prince sleeping beside her. For a moment, it was hard to pull back the hand touching his arm—for a moment, she was tempted to stroke her fingers down the curve of muscle.

But she had one last thing to do tonight.

So she withdrew her hand.

And this time, he didn't wake when she crept out of the room.

It was almost four in the morning when she slipped back into the bedroom, her boots clutched in one hand. She made it all of two steps—two immensely heavy, exhausted steps—before Rowan said from the bed, "You smell like ash."

She just kept going, until she'd dropped her boots off in the closet, stripped down into the first shirt she could find, and washed her face and neck.

"I had things to do," she said as she climbed into bed.

"You were stealthier this time." The rage simmering off him was almost hot enough to burn through the blankets.

"This wasn't particularly high risk." Lie. Lie, lie, lie. She'd just been lucky.

"And I suppose you're not going to tell me until you want to?"

She slumped against the pillows. "Don't get pissy because I out-stealthed you."

His snarl reverberated across the mattress. "It's not a joke."

She closed her eyes, her limbs leaden. "I know."

"Aelin—"

She was already asleep.

Rowan wasn't pissy.

No, pissy didn't cover a fraction of it.

The rage was still riding him the next morning, when he awoke before she did and slipped into her closet to examine the clothes she'd shucked off. Dust and metal and smoke and sweat tickled his nose, and there were streaks of dirt and ash on the black cloth. Only a few daggers lay scattered nearby—no sign of Goldryn or Damaris having been moved from where he'd dumped them on the closet floor last night. No whiff of Lorcan, or the Valg. No scent of blood.

Either she hadn't wanted to risk losing the ancient blades in a fight, or she hadn't wanted the extra weight.

She was sprawled across the bed when he emerged, his jaw clenched. She hadn't even bothered to wear one of those ridiculous nightgowns. She must have been exhausted enough not to bother with anything other than that oversized shirt. *His* shirt, he noticed with no small amount of male satisfaction.

It was enormous on her. It was so easy to forget how much smaller she was than him. How mortal. And how utterly unaware of the control he had to exercise every day, every hour, to keep her at arm's length, to keep from touching her.

He glowered at her before striding out of the bedroom. In the mountains, he would have made her go on a run, or chop wood for hours, or pull extra kitchen duty.

This apartment was too small, too full of males used to getting their own way and a queen used to getting hers. Worse, a queen hell-bent on keeping secrets. He'd dealt with young rulers before: Maeve had dispatched him to enough foreign courts that he knew how to get them to heel. But Aelin . . .

She'd taken him out to hunt *demons*. And yet this task, whatever she had done, required even him to be kept in ignorance.

Rowan filled the kettle, focusing on each movement—if only to keep from throwing it through the window.

"Making breakfast? How domestic of you." Aelin leaned against the doorway, irreverent as always.

"Shouldn't you be sleeping like the dead, considering your busy night?"

"Can we *not* get into a fight about it before my first cup of tea?"

With lethal calm, he set the kettle on the stove. "After tea, then?"

She crossed her arms, sunlight kissing the shoulder of her pale-blue robe. Such a creature of luxury, his queen. And yet—yet she hadn't bought a single new thing for herself lately. She loosed a breath, and her shoulders slumped a bit.

The rage roaring through his veins stumbled. And stumbled again when she chewed on her lip. "I need you to come with me today."

"Anywhere you need to go," he said. She looked toward the table, at the stove. "To Arobynn?" He hadn't forgotten for one second where they would be going tonight—what she would be facing.

She shook her head, then shrugged. "No—I mean, yes, I want you to come tonight, but . . . There's something else I need to do. And I want to do today, before everything happens."

He waited, restraining himself from going to her, from asking her to tell him more. That had been their promise to each other: space to sort out their own miserable lives—to sort out how to share them. He didn't mind. Most of the time.

She rubbed at her brows with her thumb and forefinger, and when she squared her shoulders—those silk-clad shoulders that bore a weight he'd do anything to relieve—she lifted her chin. "There's a grave I need to visit."

⁓

She didn't have a black gown fit for mourning, but Aelin figured Sam would have preferred to see her in something bright and lovely anyway. So she wore a tunic the color of spring grass, its sleeves capped with dusty golden velvet cuffs. *Life*, she thought as she strode through the small, pretty graveyard overlooking the Avery. The clothes Sam would have wanted her to wear reminded her of life.

The graveyard was empty, but the headstones and grass were well kept, and the towering oaks were budding with new leaves. A breeze coming in off the glimmering river set them sighing and ruffled her unbound hair, which was back now to its normal honey-gold.

Rowan had stayed near the little iron gate, leaning against one of those oaks to keep passersby on the quiet city street behind them from noticing him. If they did, his black clothes and weapons painted him as a mere bodyguard.

She had planned to come alone. But this morning she'd awoken and just . . . needed him with her.

The new grass cushioned each step between the pale headstones bathed in the sunlight streaming down.

She picked up pebbles along the way, discarding the misshapen and rough ones, keeping those that gleamed with bits of quartz or color. She clutched a fistful of them by the time she approached the last line of graves at the edge of the large, muddy river flowing lazily past.

It was a lovely grave—simple, clean—and on the stone was written:

SAM CORTLAND

BELOVED

Arobynn had left it blank—unmarked. But Wesley had explained in his letter how he'd asked the tombstone carver to come. She approached the grave, reading it over and over.

Beloved—not just by her, but by many.

Sam. Her Sam.

For a moment, she stared at that stretch of grass, at the white stone. For a moment she could see that beautiful face grinning at her, yelling at her, loving her. She opened her fist of pebbles and picked out the three loveliest—two for the years since he'd been taken from her, one for what they'd been together. Carefully, she placed them at the apex of the head-stone's curve.

Then she sat down against the stone, tucking her feet beneath her, and rested her head against the smooth, cool rock.

"Hello, Sam," she breathed onto the river breeze.

She said nothing for a time, content to be near him, even in this form. The sun warmed her hair, a kiss of heat along her scalp. A trace of Mala, perhaps, even here.

She began talking, quietly and succinctly, telling Sam about what had happened to her ten years ago, telling him about these past nine months. When she was done, she stared up at the oak leaves rustling overhead and dragged her fingers through the soft grass.

"I miss you," she said. "Every day, I miss you. And I wonder what you would have made of all this. Made of me. I think—I think you would have been a wonderful king. I think they would have liked you more than me, actually." Her throat tightened. "I never told you—how I felt. But I loved you, and I think a part of me might always love you. Maybe you were my mate, and I never knew it. Maybe I'll spend the rest of my life wondering about that. Maybe I'll see you again in the Afterworld, and then I'll know for sure. But until then . . . until then I'll miss you, and I'll wish you were here."

She would not apologize, nor say it was her fault. Because his death wasn't her fault. And tonight . . . tonight she would settle that debt.

She wiped at her face with the back of her sleeve and got to her feet. The sun dried her tears. She smelled the pine and snow before she heard him, and when she turned, Rowan stood a few feet away, staring at the headstone behind her.

"He was—"

"I know who he was to you," Rowan said softly, and held out his hand. Not to take hers, but for a stone.

She opened her fist, and he sorted through the pebbles until he found one—smooth and round, the size of a hummingbird's egg. With a gentleness that cracked her heart, he set it on the headstone beside her own pebbles.

"You're going to kill Arobynn tonight, aren't you?" he said.

"After the dinner. When he's gone to bed. I'm going back to the Keep and ending it."

She'd come here to remind herself—remind herself why that grave before them existed, and why she had those scars on her back.

"And the Amulet of Orynth?"

"An endgame, but also a distraction."

The sunlight danced on the Avery, nearly blinding. "You're ready to do it?"

She looked back at the gravestone, and at the grass concealing the coffin beneath. "I have no choice but to be ready."

CHAPTER
40

Elide spent two days on voluntary kitchen duty, learning where and when the laundresses ate and who brought their food. By that point, the head cook trusted her enough that when she volunteered to bring the bread up to the dining hall, he didn't think twice.

No one noticed when she sprinkled the poison onto a few rolls of bread. The Wing Leader had sworn it wouldn't kill—just make the laundress sick for a few days. And maybe it made her selfish for placing her own survival first, but Elide didn't hesitate as she dumped the pale powder onto some of the rolls, blending it into the flour that dusted them.

Elide marked one roll in particular to make sure she gave it to the laundress she'd noted days before, but the others would be given out at random to the other laundresses.

Hell—she was likely going to burn in Hellas's realm forever for this.

But she could think about her damnation when she had escaped and was far, far away, beyond the Southern Continent.

Elide limped into the raucous dining hall, a quiet cripple with yet another platter of food. She made her way down the long table, trying to keep the weight off her leg as she leaned in again and again to deposit rolls onto plates. The laundress didn't even bother to thank her.

The next day, the Keep was abuzz with the news that a third of the laundresses were sick. It must have been the chicken at dinner, they said. Or the mutton. Or the soup, since only some of them had had it. The cook apologized—and Elide had tried not to apologize to *him* when she saw the terror in his eyes.

The head laundress actually looked relieved when Elide limped in and volunteered to help. She told her to pick any station and get to work.

Perfect.

But guilt pushed down on her shoulders as she went right to that woman's station.

She worked all day, and waited for the bloodied clothes to arrive.

When they finally did, there was not as much blood as before, but more of a substance that looked like vomit.

Elide almost vomited herself as she washed them all. And wrung them out. And dried them. And pressed them. It took hours.

Night was falling when she folded the last of them, trying to keep her fingers from shaking. But she went up to the head laundress and said softly, no more than a nervous girl, "Should—should I bring them back?"

The woman smirked. Elide wondered if the other laundress had been sent down there as a punishment.

"There's a stairwell over that way that will take you to the subterranean levels. Tell the guards you're Misty's replacement. Bring the clothes to the second door on the left and drop them outside." The woman looked at Elide's chains. "Try to run out, if you can."

Elide's bowels had turned to water by the time she reached the guards.

But they didn't so much as question her as she recited what the head laundress had said.

Down, down, down she walked, into the gloom of the spiral stairwell. The temperature plummeted the farther she descended.

And then she heard the moaning.

Moans of pain, of terror, of despair.

She held the basket of clothes to her chest. A torch flickered ahead.

Gods, it was so cold here.

The stairs widened toward the bottom, flaring out into a straight descent and revealing a broad hallway, lit with torches and lined with countless iron doors.

The moans were coming from behind them.

Second door on the left. It was gouged with what looked like claw marks, pushing out from within.

There were guards down here—guards and strange men, patrolling up and down, opening and closing the doors. Elide's knees wobbled. No one stopped her.

She set the basket of laundry in front of the second door and rapped quietly. The iron was so cold that it burned. "Clean clothes," she said against the metal. It was absurd. In this place, with these people, they still insisted on clean clothes.

Three of the guards had paused to watch. She pretended not to notice—pretended to back away slowly, a scared little rabbit.

Pretended to catch her mangled foot on something and slip.

But it was real pain that roared through her leg as she went down, her chains snapping and tugging at her. The floor was as cold as the iron door.

None of the guards made to help her up.

She hissed, clutching her ankle, buying as much time as she could, her heart thundering-thundering-thundering.

And then the door cracked open.

Manon watched Elide vomit again. And again.

A Blackbeak sentinel had found her curled in a ball in a corner of a random hallway, shaking, a puddle of piss beneath her. Having heard that the servant was now Manon's property, the sentinel had dragged her up here.

Asterin and Sorrel stood stone-faced behind Manon as the girl puked into the bucket again—only bile and spittle this time—and at last raised her head.

"Report," Manon said.

"I saw the chamber," Elide rasped.

They all went still.

"*Something* opened the door to take the laundry, and I saw the chamber beyond."

With those keen eyes of hers, she'd likely seen too much.

"Out with it," Manon said, leaning against the bedpost. Asterin and Sorrel lingered by the door, monitoring for eavesdroppers.

Elide stayed on the floor, her leg twisted out to the side. But the eyes that met Manon's sparked with a fiery temper that the girl rarely revealed.

"The thing that opened the door was a beautiful man—a man with golden hair and a collar around his neck. But he was *not* a man. There was nothing human in his eyes." One of the princes—it had to be. "I—I'd pretended to fall so I could buy myself more time to see who opened the door. When he saw me on the ground, he smiled at me—and this *darkness* leaked out of him . . ." She lurched toward the bucket and leaned over it, but didn't vomit. After another moment, she said, "I managed to look past him into the room behind."

She stared at Manon, then at Asterin and Sorrel. "You said they were to be . . . implanted."

"Yes," Manon said.

"Did you know how many times?"

"What?" Asterin breathed.

"Did you know," Elide said, her voice uneven with rage or fear, "how many times they were each to be implanted with offspring before they were let go?"

Everything went quiet in Manon's head. "Go on."

Elide's face was white as death, making her freckles look like dried, splattered blood. "From what I saw, they've delivered at least one baby each. And are already about to give birth to another."

"That's impossible," Sorrel said.

"The witchlings?" Asterin breathed.

Elide really did vomit again this time.

When she was done, Manon mastered herself enough to say, "Tell me about the witchlings."

"They are not witchlings. They are not babies," Elide spat, covering her face with her hands as if to rip out her eyes. "They are *creatures*. They are *demons*. Their skin is like black diamond, and they—they have these snouts, with teeth. *Fangs.* Already, they have fangs. And not like yours." She lowered her hands. "They have teeth of black stone. There is nothing of you in them."

If Sorrel and Asterin were horrified, they showed nothing.

"What of the Yellowlegs?" Manon demanded.

"They have them chained to tables. Altars. And they were sobbing. They were begging the man to let them go. But they're . . . they're so close to giving birth. And then I ran. I ran from there as fast as I could, and . . . oh, gods. *Oh, gods.*" Elide began weeping.

Slowly, slowly Manon turned to her Second and Third.

Sorrel was pale, her eyes raging.

But Asterin met Manon's gaze—met it with a fury that Manon had never seen directed at her. "You let them do this."

Manon's nails flicked out. "These are my orders. This is our task."

"It is an abomination!" Asterin shouted.

Elide paused her weeping. And backed away to the safety of the fireplace.

Then there were tears—*tears*—in Asterin's eyes.

Manon snarled. "Has your heart softened?" The voice might as well have been her grandmother's. "Do you have no stomach for—"

"*You let them do this!*" Asterin bellowed.

Sorrel got right into Asterin's face. "Stand down."

Asterin shoved Sorrel away so violently that Manon's Second went crashing into the dresser. Before Sorrel could recover, Asterin was inches from Manon.

"You gave him those witches. You gave him witches!"

Manon lashed out, her hand wrapping around Asterin's throat. But Asterin gripped her arm, digging in her iron nails so hard that blood ran.

For a moment, Manon's blood dripping on the floor was the only sound.

Asterin's life should have been forfeited for drawing blood from the heir.

Light glinted off Sorrel's dagger as she approached, ready to tear it into Asterin's spine if Manon gave the order. Manon could have sworn Sorrel's hand wobbled slightly.

Manon met Asterin's gold-flecked black eyes. "You do not question. You do not demand. You are no longer Third. Vesta will replace you. You—"

A harsh, broken laugh. "You're not going to do anything about it, are you? You're not going to free them. You're not going to fight for them. For us. Because what would Grandmother say? Why hasn't she answered your letters, Manon? How many have you sent now?" Asterin's iron nails dug in harder, shredding flesh. Manon embraced the pain.

"Tomorrow morning at breakfast, you will receive your punishment," Manon hissed, and shoved her Third away, sending Asterin staggering toward the door. Manon let her bloodied arm hang at her side. She'd need to bind it up soon. The blood—on her palm, on her fingers—felt so familiar . . .

"If you try to free them, if you do anything stupid, Asterin Blackbeak," Manon went on, "the next punishment you'll receive will be your own execution."

Asterin let out another joyless laugh. "You would not have disobeyed even if it had been Blackbeaks down there, would you? Loyalty, obedience, brutality—that is what you are."

"Leave while you can still walk," Sorrel said softly.

Asterin whirled toward the Second, and something like hurt flashed across her face.

Manon blinked. Those *feelings* . . .

Asterin turned on her heel and left, slamming the door behind her.

Elide had managed to clear her head by the time she offered to clean and bandage Manon's arm.

What she'd seen today, both in this room and in that chamber below . . .

You let them do this. She didn't blame Asterin for it, even if it had shocked her to see the witch lose control so completely. She had never seen any of them react with anything but cool amusement, indifference, or raging bloodlust.

Manon hadn't said a word since she'd ordered Sorrel away, to follow Asterin and keep her from doing something profoundly stupid.

As if saving those Yellowlegs witches might be foolish. As if that sort of mercy was reckless.

Manon was staring at nothing as Elide finished applying the salve and reached for the bandages. The puncture wounds were deep, but not bad enough to warrant stiches. "Is your broken kingdom worth it?" Elide dared to ask.

Those burnt-gold eyes shifted toward the darkened window.

"I do not expect a human to understand what it is like to be an immortal with no homeland. To be cursed with eternal exile." Cold, distant words.

Elide said, "My kingdom was conquered by the King of Adarlan, and everyone I loved was executed. My father's lands and my title were stolen from me by my uncle, and my best chance of safety now lies in sailing to the other end of the world. I understand what it is like to wish—to hope."

"It is not hope. It is survival."

Elide gently rolled a bandage around the witch's forearm. "It is hope for your homeland that guides you, that makes you obey."

"And what of your future? For all your talk of hope, you seem resigned to fleeing. Why not return to your kingdom—to fight?"

Perhaps the horror she'd witnessed today gave her the courage to say, "Ten years ago, my parents were murdered. My father was executed on a butchering block in front of thousands. But my mother . . . My mother died defending Aelin Galathynius, the heir to the throne of Terrasen. She bought Aelin time to run. They followed Aelin's tracks to the frozen river, where they said she must have fallen in and drowned.

"But you see, Aelin had fire magic. She could have survived the cold. And Aelin . . . Aelin never really liked me or played with me because I was so shy, but . . . I never believed them when they said she was dead. Every day since then, I've told myself that she got away, and that she's still out there, biding her time. Growing up, growing strong, so that she might one day come to save Terrasen. And you are my enemy—because if she returns, she will fight you.

"But for ten years, until I came here, I endured Vernon because of her. Because of the hope that she got away, and my mother's sacrifice wasn't in vain. I thought that one day, Aelin would come to save me—would remember I existed and rescue me from that tower." There it was, her great secret, which she had never dared tell anyone, even her nursemaid. "Even though . . . even though she never came, even though I'm here now, I can't let go of that. And I think that is why you obey. Because you have been hoping every day of your miserable, hideous life that you'll get to go home."

Elide finished wrapping the bandage and stepped back. Manon was staring at her now.

"If this Aelin Galathynius were indeed alive, would you try to run to her? Fight with her?"

"I would fight with tooth and claw to get to her. But there are lines I would not cross. Because I don't think I could face her if . . . if I couldn't face myself for what I'd done."

Manon said nothing. Elide stepped away, heading to the bathing room to wash her hands.

The Wing Leader said from behind her, "Do you believe monsters are born, or made?"

From what she'd seen today, she would say some creatures were very much born evil. But what Manon was asking . . . "I'm not the one who needs to answer that question," Elide said.

CHAPTER 41

The oil was sitting on the edge of the bathtub, gleaming like amber in the afternoon light.

Naked, Aelin stood before it, unable to reach for the bottle.

It was what Arobynn wanted—for her to think of him as she rubbed the oil into every inch of her skin. For her breasts, her thighs, her neck to smell like almond—*his* chosen scent.

His scent, because he knew that a Fae male had come to stay with her, and all signs pointed to their being close enough for scent to matter to Rowan.

She closed her eyes, steeling herself.

"Aelin," Rowan said through the door.

"I'm fine," she said. Only a few more hours. And then everything would change.

She opened her eyes and reached for the oil.

It took Rowan a jerk of his chin to get Aedion to follow him to the roof. Aelin was still in her room dressing, but Rowan wasn't going far. He would hear any enemies on the street long before they had a chance to get into the apartment.

Despite the Valg prowling the city, Rifthold was one of the milder capitals he'd encountered—its people mostly prone to avoiding trouble. Perhaps from fear of being noticed by the monster who dwelled in that godawful glass castle. But Rowan would keep his guard up all the same— here, in Terrasen, or wherever else their paths might lead.

Aedion was now lounging in a small chair one of them had dragged up here at some point. Gavriel's son—a surprise and a shock every time he saw that face or caught a whiff of his scent. Rowan couldn't help but wonder if Aelin had sent the Wyrdhounds hunting after Lorcan not just to keep him from tracking her and to pave the way for her to free magic but also to keep him from getting close enough to Aedion to detect his lineage.

Aedion crossed his legs with a lazy grace that probably served to hide his speed and strength from opponents. "She's going to kill him tonight, isn't she?"

"After the dinner and whatever Arobynn plans to do with the Valg commander. She's going to circle back and put him down."

Only a fool would think Aedion's grin sprang from amusement. "That's my girl."

"And if she decides to spare him?"

"It's her decision to make."

Smart answer. "What if she were to say we could take care of it?"

"Then I'd hope you'd join me for a hunt, Prince."

Another smart answer, and what he'd been waiting to hear. Rowan said, "And when the time comes?"

"You took the blood oath," Aedion said, and there wasn't any hint of a challenge in his eyes—only the truth, spoken warrior to warrior. "I get Arobynn's killing blow."

"Fair enough."

Primal wrath flickered in Aedion's face. "It's not going to be quick, and it's not going to be clean. That man has many, many debts to pay before he meets his end."

By the time Aelin emerged, the males were talking in the kitchen, already dressed. On the street outside the apartment, the Valg commander was bound, blindfolded, and locked in the trunk of the carriage Nesryn had acquired.

Aelin squared her shoulders, shaking loose the breath that had become a tight knot in her chest, and crossed the room, each step bringing her too quickly toward their inevitable departure.

Aedion, facing her in a fine tunic of deep green, was the first to notice. He let out a low whistle. "Well, if you didn't already scare the living shit out of me, you've certainly done it now."

Rowan turned to her.

He went completely and utterly still as he took in the dress.

The black velvet hugged every curve and hollow before pooling at her feet, revealing each too-shallow breath as Rowan's eyes grazed over her body. Down, then up—to the hair she'd swept back with golden bat-wing-shaped combs that rose above either side of her head like a primal headdress; to the face she'd kept mostly clean, save for a sweep of kohl along her upper eyelid and the deep red lips she'd painstakingly colored.

With the burning weight of Rowan's attention upon her, she turned to show them the back—the roaring golden dragon clawing up her body. She looked over her shoulder in time to see Rowan's eyes again slide south, and linger.

Slowly, his gaze lifted to hers. And she could have sworn that hunger— ravenous hunger—flickered there.

"Demons and dining," Aedion said, clapping Rowan on the shoulder. "We should go."

Her cousin passed her by with a wink. When she turned back to Rowan, still breathless, only cool observation remained on his face.

"You said you wanted to see me in this dress," she said a bit hoarsely.

"I hadn't realized the effect would be so . . ." He shook his head. He took in her face, her hair, the combs. "You look like—"

"A queen?"

"The fire-breathing bitch-queen those bastards claim you are."

She chuckled, waving a hand toward him: the formfitting black jacket that showed off those powerful shoulders, the silver accents that matched his hair, the beauty and elegance of the clothes that made an enthralling contrast with the tattoo down the side of his face and neck. "You don't look too bad yourself, Prince."

An understatement. He looked . . . she couldn't stop staring, that's how he looked.

"Apparently," he said, walking toward her and offering an arm, "we both clean up well."

She gave him a sly grin as she took his elbow, the scent of almonds wrapping around her again. "Don't forget your cloak. You'd feel rather guilty when all those poor mortal women combust at the sight of you."

"I'd say likewise, but I think you'd enjoy seeing men bursting into flames as you strutted by."

She winked at him, and his chuckle echoed through her bones and blood.

CHAPTER 42

The front gates of the Assassins' Keep were open, the gravel drive and manicured lawn lit with shimmering glass lamps. The pale stone estate itself was bright, beautiful, and inviting.

Aelin had told them what to expect on the carriage ride over, but even as they came to a stop at the foot of the steps, she looked at the two males crammed in with her and said, "Be on your guard, and keep your fat mouths shut. Especially with the Valg commander. No matter what you hear or see, just *keep your fat mouths shut.* No psychotic territorial bullshit."

Aedion chuckled. "Remind me to tell you tomorrow how charming you are."

But she wasn't in the mood to laugh.

Nesryn jumped down from the driver's seat and opened the carriage door. Aelin stepped out, leaving her cloak behind, and didn't dare look to the house across the street—to the roof where Chaol and a few rebels were providing backup in case things went very, very wrong.

She was halfway up the marble steps when the carved oak doors swung open, flooding the threshold with golden light. It wasn't the butler standing there, smiling at her with too-white teeth.

"Welcome home," Arobynn purred.

He beckoned them into the cavernous entry hall. "And welcome to your friends." Aedion and Nesryn moved around the carriage to the trunk in the back. Her cousin's nondescript sword was drawn as they opened the compartment and yanked out the chained, hooded figure.

"Your favor," Aelin said as they hauled him to his feet. The Valg commander thrashed and stumbled in their grip as they led him toward the house, the hood over his head swaying this way and that. A low, vicious hissing noise crept out from under the coarse-knit fibers.

"I would have preferred the servants' door for our guest," Arobynn said tightly. He was in green—green for Terrasen, though most would assume it was to offset his auburn hair. A way to confuse their assumptions about his intentions, his allegiance. He wore no weapons she could see, and there was nothing but warmth in those silver eyes as he held out his hands to her, as if Aedion wasn't now tugging a demon up the front steps. Behind them, Nesryn steered the carriage away.

She could feel Rowan bristling, sense Aedion's disgust, but she blocked them out.

She took Arobynn's hands—dry, warm, callused. He squeezed her fingers gently, peering into her face. "You look ravishing, but I'd expect nothing less. Not even a bruise after trapping our guest. Impressive." He leaned closer, sniffing. "And you smell divine, too. I'm glad my gift was put to good use."

From the corner of her eye, she saw Rowan straighten, and she knew he'd slid into the killing calm. Neither Rowan nor Aedion wore visible weapons save for the single blade her cousin now had out—but she knew they were both armed beneath their clothes, and knew Rowan would snap Arobynn's neck if he so much as blinked wrong at her.

It was that thought alone that made her smile at Arobynn. "You look well," she said. "I suppose you already know my companions."

He faced Aedion, who was busy digging his sword into the commander's side as a gentle reminder to keep moving. "I haven't had the pleasure of meeting your cousin."

She knew Arobynn took in every detail as Aedion came closer, pushing his charge before him; trying to find any weakness, anything to use to his advantage. Aedion just continued into the house, the Valg commander stumbling across the threshold. "You've recovered well, General," Arobynn said. "Or should I call you 'Your Highness,' in honor of your Ashryver lineage? Whichever you prefer, of course."

She knew then that Arobynn had no plans to let the demon—and Stevan—leave this house alive.

Aedion gave Arobynn a lazy grin over his shoulder. "I don't give a shit what you call me." He shoved the Valg commander farther inside. "Just take this rutting *thing* off my hands."

Arobynn smiled blandly, unfazed—he'd calculated Aedion's hatred. With deliberate slowness, he turned to Rowan.

"You, I don't know," Arobynn mused, having to lift his head to see Rowan's face. He made a show of looking Rowan over. "It's been an age since I saw one of the Fae. I don't remember them being quite so large."

Rowan moved deeper into the entry hall, every step laced with power and death, coming to a stop at her side. "You can call me Rowan. That's all you need to know." He cocked his head to the side, a predator assessing prey. "Thank you for the oil," he added. "My skin was a little dry."

Arobynn blinked—as much surprise as he'd show.

It took her a moment to process what Rowan had said, and to realize that the almond smell hadn't just been coming from her. He'd worn it, too.

Arobynn flicked his attention to Aedion and the Valg commander. "Third door on the left—take him downstairs. Use the fourth cell."

Aelin didn't dare look at her cousin as he dragged Stevan along. There was no sign of the other assassins—not even a servant. Whatever Arobynn had planned . . . he didn't want any witnesses.

Arobynn trailed after Aedion, his hands in his pockets.

But Aelin remained in the hall for a moment, looking at Rowan.

His brows were high as she read the words in his eyes, his posture. *He never specified that only you had to wear it.*

Her throat tightened and she shook her head.

What? he seemed to ask.

You just . . . She shook her head again. *Surprise me sometimes.*

Good. I'd hate for you to get bored.

Despite herself, despite what was to come, a smile tugged on her lips as Rowan took her hand and gripped it tightly.

When she turned to head into the dungeons, her smile faded as she found Arobynn watching.

Rowan was about a hair's breadth from ripping out the King of the Assassins' throat as he led them down, down, down into the dungeons.

Rowan kept a step behind Aelin while they descended the long, curving stone staircase, the reek of mildew and blood and rust growing stronger with each step. He'd been tortured enough, and done enough torturing himself, to know what this place was.

To know what sort of training Aelin had received down here.

A girl—she'd been a girl when the red-haired bastard a few steps ahead had brought her here and taught her how to cut up men, how to keep them alive while she did it, how to make them scream and plead. How to end them.

There was no part of her that disgusted him, no part of her that scared him, but the thought of her in this place, with these smells, in this darkness . . .

With every step down the stairs, Aelin's shoulders seemed to droop, her hair seeming to grow duller, her skin paler.

This was where she'd last seen Sam, he realized. And her master knew it.

"We use this for most of our meetings—harder to eavesdrop or be caught unawares," Arobynn said to no one in particular. "Though it also has other uses, as you'll soon see." He opened door after door, and it seemed to Rowan that Aelin was counting them, waiting, until—

"Shall we?" Arobynn said, gesturing toward the cell door.

Rowan touched her elbow. Gods, his self-control had to be in shreds tonight; he couldn't stop making excuses to touch her. But this touch was essential. Her eyes met his, dim and cold. *You give the word—just one damn word and he's dead, and then we can search this house from top to bottom for that amulet.*

She shook her head as she entered the cell, and he understood it well enough. *Not yet. Not yet.*

She'd almost balked on the stairs to the dungeons, and it was only the thought of the amulet, only the warmth of the Fae warrior at her back that made her put one foot in front of the other and descend into the dark stone interior.

She would never forget this room.

It still haunted her dreams.

The table was empty, but she could see him there, broken and almost unrecognizable, the scent of gloriella clinging to his body. Sam had been tortured in ways she hadn't even known until she read Wesley's letter. The worst of it had been requested by Arobynn. Requested, as punishment for Sam's loving her—punishment for tampering with Arobynn's belongings.

Arobynn sauntered into the room, hands in his pockets. Rowan's sharp sniff told her enough about what this place smelled like.

Such a dark, cold room where they'd put Sam's body. Such a dark, cold room where she'd vomited and then lain beside him on that table for hours and hours, unwilling to leave him.

Where Aedion now chained Stevan to the wall.

"Get out," Arobynn said simply to Rowan and Aedion, who stiffened. "The two of you can wait upstairs. We don't need unnecessary distractions. And neither does our guest."

"Over my rotting corpse," Aedion snapped. Aelin shot him a sharp look.

"Lysandra is waiting for you in the drawing room," Arobynn said with expert politeness, his eyes now fixed on the hooded Valg chained to the wall. Stevan's gloved hands tugged at the chains, his incessant hissing rising with impressive violence. "She'll entertain you. We'll be up for dinner shortly."

Rowan was watching Aelin very, very carefully. She gave him a slight nod.

Rowan met Aedion's gaze—the general stared right back.

Honestly, had she been anywhere else, she might have pulled up a chair to watch this latest little dominance battle. Thankfully, Aedion just turned toward the stairs. A moment later, they were gone.

Arobynn stalked to the demon and snatched the hood from his head.

Black, rage-filled eyes glared at them and blinked, scanning the room.

"We can do this the easy way, or the hard way," Arobynn drawled.

Stevan just smiled.

Aelin listened to Arobynn interrogate the demon, demanding to know what it was, where it had come from, what the king wanted. After thirty minutes and minimal slicing, the demon was talking about anything and everything.

"*How* does the king control you?" Arobynn pushed.

The demon laughed. "Wouldn't you like to know."

Arobynn half turned to her, holding up his dagger, a trickle of dark blood sliding down the blade. "Would you like to do the honors? This is for your benefit, after all."

She frowned at her dress. "I don't want to get blood on it."

Arobynn smirked and slashed his dagger down the man's pectoral. The demon screeched, drowning out the pitter-patter of blood on the stones. "The ring," it panted after a moment. "We've all got them." Arobynn paused, and Aelin cocked her head. "Left—left hand," it said.

Arobynn yanked off the man's glove, revealing the black ring.

"How?"

"He has a ring, too—uses it to control us all. Ring goes on, and it doesn't come off. We do what he says, whatever he says."

"Where did he get the rings from?"

"Made 'em, I don't know." The dagger came closer. "I swear! We wear the rings, and he makes a cut on our arms—licks our blood so it's in him, and then he can control us however he wants. It's the blood that links us."

"And what does he plan to do with you all, now that you're invading my city?"

"We're searching for the general. I won't—won't tell anyone he's here . . . Or that *she's* here, I swear. The rest—the rest I don't know." His eyes met hers—dark, pleading.

"Kill him," she said to Arobynn. "He's a liability."

"Please," Stevan said, his eyes still holding hers. She looked away.

"He does seem to have run out of things to tell me," Arobynn mused.

Swift as an adder, Arobynn lunged for him, and Stevan screamed so loudly it hurt her ears as Arobynn sliced off his finger—and the ring that held it—in one brutal movement. "Thank you," Arobynn said above Stevan's screaming, and then slashed his knife across the man's throat.

Aelin stepped clear of the spray of blood, holding Stevan's stare as the light faded from his gaze. When the spray had slowed, she frowned at Arobynn. "You could have killed him and *then* cut off the ring."

"Where would the fun be in that?" Arobynn held up the bloody finger and pried off the ring. "Lost your bloodlust?"

"I'd dump that ring in the Avery if I were you."

"The king is enslaving people to his will with these things. I plan to study this one as best I can." Of course he did. He pocketed the ring and inclined his head toward the door. "Now that we're even, darling . . . shall we eat?"

It was an effort to nod with Stevan's still-bleeding body sagging from the wall.

Aelin was seated to Arobynn's right, as she'd always been. She'd expected Lysandra to be across from her, but instead the courtesan was beside her. No doubt meant to reduce her options to two: deal with her longtime rival, or talk to Arobynn. Or something like that.

She had bid hello to Lysandra, who'd been keeping Aedion and Rowan company in the drawing room, keenly aware of Arobynn on her heels as she shook Lysandra's hand, subtly passing over the note she'd kept hidden in her dress all night.

The note was gone by the time Aelin leaned in to kiss the courtesan's cheek, the peck of someone not entirely thrilled to be doing so.

Arobynn had seated Rowan to his left, with Aedion beside the warrior. The two members of her court were separated by the table to keep them from reaching her, and to leave her unprotected from Arobynn. Neither had asked what happened in the dungeon.

"I have to say," Arobynn mused as their first course—tomato and basil soup, courtesy of vegetables grown in the hothouse in the back—was cleared away by silent servants who had been summoned now that Stevan had been dealt with. Aelin recognized some, though they didn't look at her. They had never looked at her, even when she was living here. She knew they wouldn't dare whisper a word about who dined at this table tonight. Not with Arobynn as their master. "You're a rather quiet group. Or has my protégée scared you into silence?"

Aedion, who had watched every bite she took of that soup, lifted an eyebrow. "You want us to make small talk after you just interrogated and butchered a demon?"

Arobynn waved a hand. "I'd like to hear more about you all."

"Careful," she said too quietly to Arobynn.

The King of the Assassins straightened the silverware flanking his plate. "Shouldn't I be concerned about who my protégée is living with?"

"You weren't concerned about who I was living with when you had me shipped off to Endovier."

A slow blink. "Is that what you think I did?"

Lysandra stiffened beside her. Arobynn noted the movement—as he noted every movement—and said, "Lysandra can tell you the truth: I fought tooth and nail to free you from that prison. I lost half my men to the effort, all of them tortured and killed by the king. I'm surprised your friend the captain didn't tell you. Such a pity he's on rooftop watch tonight."

He missed nothing, it seemed.

Arobynn looked to Lysandra—waiting. She swallowed and murmured, "He did try, you know. For months and months."

It was so convincing that Aelin might have believed it. Through some miracle, Arobynn had no idea that the woman had been meeting with them in secret. Some miracle—or Lysandra's own wits.

Aelin drawled to Arobynn, "Do you plan on telling me why you insisted we stay for dinner?"

"How else would I get to see you? You would have just dumped that thing on my doorstep and left. And we learned so much—so much that we could use, together." The chill down her spine wasn't faked. "Though I have to say, this *new* you is much more . . . subdued. I suppose for Lysandra that's a good thing. She always looks at the hole you left in the entry wall when you threw that dagger at her head. I kept it there as a little reminder of how much we all missed you."

Rowan was watching her, an asp ready to strike. But his brows bunched slightly, as if to say, *You really threw a dagger at her head?*

Arobynn began talking about a time Aelin had brawled with Lysandra and they'd rolled down the stairs, scratching and yowling like cats, so Aelin looked at Rowan a moment longer. *I was a tad hotheaded.*

I'm beginning to admire Lysandra more and more. Seventeen-year-old Aelin must have been a delight to deal with.

She fought the twitching in her lips. *I would pay good money to see seventeen-year-old Aelin meet seventeen-year-old Rowan.*

His green eyes glittered. Arobynn was still talking. *Seventeen-year-old Rowan wouldn't have known what to do with you. He could barely speak to females outside his family.*

Liar—I don't believe that for a second.

It's true. You would have scandalized him with your nightclothes—even with that dress you have on.

She sucked on her teeth. *He would probably have been even more scandalized to learn I'm not wearing any undergarments beneath this dress.*

The table rattled as Rowan's knee banged into it.

Arobynn paused, but continued when Aedion asked about what the demon had told him.

You can't be serious, Rowan seemed to say.

Did you see any place where this dress might hide them? Every line and wrinkle would show.

Rowan shook his head subtly, his eyes dancing with a light that she'd only recently come to glimpse—and cherish. *Do you delight in shocking me?*

She couldn't stop her smile. *How else am I supposed to keep a cranky immortal entertained?*

His grin was distracting enough that it took her a moment to notice the silence, and that everyone was staring at them—waiting.

She glanced at Arobynn, whose face was a mask of stone. "Did you ask me something?"

There was only calculating ire in his silver eyes—which might have once made her start begging for mercy. "I asked," Arobynn said, "if you've had fun these past few weeks, wrecking my investment properties and ensuring that all my clients won't touch me."

CHAPTER 43

Aelin leaned back in her chair. Even Rowan was staring at her now, surprise and annoyance written on his face. Lysandra was doing a good job of feigning shock and confusion—even though it had been she who had fed Aelin the details, who had made her plan so much better and broader than it had been when Aelin scribbled it out on that ship.

"I don't know what you're talking about," she said with a little smile.

"Oh?" Arobynn swirled his wine. "You mean to tell me that when you wrecked the Vaults beyond repair, it wasn't a move against my investment in that property—and my monthly cut of their profits? Don't pretend it was just vengeance for Sam."

"The king's men showed up. I had no choice but to fight for my life." After she'd led them directly from the docks to the pleasure hall, of course.

"And I suppose it was an accident that the lockbox was hacked open so its contents could be snatched up by the crowd."

It had worked—worked so spectacularly that she was surprised Arobynn had lasted this long without going for her throat.

"You know how those lowlifes get. A little chaos, and they turn into animals foaming at the mouth."

Lysandra cringed; a stellar performance of a woman witnessing a betrayal.

"Indeed," Arobynn said. "But especially the lowlifes at establishments from which I receive a handsome monthly sum, correct?"

"So you invited me and my friends here tonight to fling accusations at me? Here I was, thinking I'd become your personal Valg hunter."

"You deliberately disguised yourself as Hinsol Cormac, one of my most loyal clients and investors, when you freed your cousin," Arobynn snapped. Aedion's eyes widened slightly. "I could dismiss it as coincidence, except a witness says he called out Cormac's name at the prince's party, and Cormac *waved* to him. The witness told the king that, too—that he saw Cormac heading toward Aedion right before the explosions happened. And what a coincidence that the very day Aedion disappeared, two carriages, belonging to a business that Cormac and I own *together*, went missing—carriages Cormac then told all my clients and partners that *I* used to get Aedion to safety when *I* freed the general that day by impersonating him, because I, apparently, have become a *gods-damned rebel sympathizer strutting about town at all hours of the day*."

She dared a look at Rowan, whose face remained carefully blank, but saw the words there anyway. *You wicked, clever fox.*

And here you were, thinking the red hair was just for vanity.

I shall never doubt again.

She turned to Arobynn. "I can't help it if your prissy clients turn on you at the slightest hint of danger."

"Cormac has fled the city, and continues to drag my name through the mud. It's a miracle the king hasn't come to haul me to his castle."

"If you're worried about losing money, you could always sell the house, I suppose. Or stop using Lysandra's services."

Arobynn hissed, and Rowan and Aedion reached casually under the table for their hidden weapons. "What will it take, *dearest*, for you to stop being such a raging pain in my ass?"

There they were. The words she'd wanted to hear, the reason she'd been so careful not to wreck him altogether but merely to annoy him just enough.

She picked at her nails. "A few things, I think."

⁓

The sitting room was oversized and made to entertain parties of twenty or thirty, with couches and chairs and chaises spread throughout. Aelin lounged in an armchair before the fire, Arobynn across from her, fury still dancing in his eyes.

She could feel Rowan and Aedion in the hall outside, monitoring every word, every breath. She wondered whether Arobynn knew they'd disobeyed his command to remain in the dining room; she doubted it. They were stealthier than ghost leopards, those two. But she didn't want them in here, either—not until she'd done what she needed to do.

She crossed one leg over the other, revealing the simple black velvet shoes she wore, and her bare legs.

"So all of this was punishment—for a crime I didn't commit," Arobynn said at last.

She ran a finger down the rolled arm of the chair. "First thing, Arobynn: let's not bother with lies."

"I suppose you've told your friends the truth?"

"My court knows everything there is to know about me. And they know everything you've done, too."

"Casting yourself as the victim, are you? You're forgetting that it didn't take much encouragement to put those knives in your hands."

"I am what I am. But it doesn't erase the fact that you knew very well who I was when you found me. You took my family necklace off me, and told me that anyone who came looking for me would wind up killed by my enemies." She didn't dare let her breathing hitch, didn't let him consider the words too much as she plowed ahead. "You wanted to shape me into your own weapon—why?"

"Why not? I was young and angry, and my kingdom had just been conquered by that bastard king. I believed I could give you the tools you needed to survive, to someday defeat him. That *is* why you've come back, isn't it? I'm surprised you and the captain haven't killed him yet—isn't that what he wants, why he tried to work with me? Or are you claiming that kill for yourself?"

"You honestly expect me to believe that your end goal was to have me avenge my family and reclaim my throne."

"Who would you have become without me? Some pampered, quaking princess. Your beloved cousin would have locked you up in a tower and thrown away the key. I *gave* you your freedom—I gave you the ability to bring down men like Aedion Ashryver with a few blows. And all I get for it is contempt."

She clenched her fingers, feeling the weight of the pebbles she'd carried that morning to Sam's grave.

"So what else do you have in store for me, O Mighty Queen? Shall I save you the trouble and tell you how else you might continue to be a thorn in my side?"

"You know the debt isn't anywhere near paid."

"Debt? For what? For trying to free you from Endovier? And when that didn't work, I did the best I could. I bribed those guards and officials with money from my own coffers so that they wouldn't hurt you beyond repair. All the while, I tried to find ways to get you out—for a year straight."

Lies and truth, as he'd always taught her. Yes, he'd bribed the officials and guards to ensure she would still be functioning when he eventually freed her. But Wesley's letter had explained in detail just how little effort Arobynn had put forth once it became clear she was headed for Endovier. How he'd adjusted his plans—embracing the idea of her spirit being broken by the mines.

"And what about Sam?" she breathed.

"Sam was murdered by a sadist, whom my useless bodyguard got it into his head to kill. You know I couldn't allow that to go unpunished, not when we needed the new Crime Lord to continue working with us."

Truth and lies, lies and truth. She shook her head and looked toward the window, ever the confused and conflicted protégée falling for Arobynn's poisoned words.

"Tell me what I need to do to make you *understand*," he said. "Do you know why I had you capture that demon? So that *we* could attain its knowledge. So you and I could take on the king, learn what he knows. Why do you think I let you in that room? Together—we'll bring that monster down *together*, before we're all wearing those rings. Your friend the captain can even join in, free of charge."

"You expect me to believe a word you say?"

"I have had a long, long while to think on the wretched things I've done to you, Celaena."

"*Aelin*," she snapped. "My name is Aelin. And you can start proving you've mended your ways by giving me back my family's gods-damned amulet. Then you can prove it some more by giving me your resources—by letting me use your men to get what I need."

She could see the wheels turning in that cold and cunning head. "In what capacity?"

No word about the amulet—no denying he had it.

"You want to take down the king," she murmured, as if to keep the two Fae males outside the door from hearing. "Then let's take down the king. But we do it my way. The captain and my court stay out of it."

"What's in it for me? These are dangerous times, you know. Why, just today, one of the top opiate dealers was caught by the king's men and killed. Such a pity; he escaped the slaughter at the Shadow Market only to be caught buying dinner a few blocks away."

More nonsense to distract her. She merely said, "I won't send a tip to the king about this place—about how you operate and who your clients are. Or mention the demon in your dungeon, its blood now a permanent stain." She smiled a little. "I've tried; their blood doesn't wash away."

"Threats, *Aelin*? And what if I make threats of my own? What if I mention to the king's guard that his missing general and his Captain of the Guard are frequently visiting a certain warehouse? What if I let it slip that a Fae warrior is wandering his city? Or, worse, that his mortal enemy is living in the slums?"

"I suppose it'll be a race to the palace, then. It's too bad the captain has men stationed by the castle gates, messages in hand, ready for the signal to send them this very night."

"You'd have to get out of here alive to give that signal."

"The signal is us not returning, I'm afraid. All of us."

Again, that cold stare. "How cruel and ruthless you've become, my love. But will you become a tyrant as well? Perhaps you should start slipping rings onto the fingers of your followers."

He reached into his tunic. She kept her posture relaxed as a golden chain glinted around his long white fingers, and then a tinkling sounded, and then—

The amulet was exactly as she remembered it.

It had been with a child's hands that she'd last held it, and with a child's eyes that she'd last seen the cerulean blue front with the ivory stag and the golden star between its antlers. The immortal stag of Mala Fire-Bringer, brought over to these lands by Brannon himself and set free in Oakwald Forest. The amulet glinted in Arobynn's hands as he removed it from his neck.

The third and final Wyrdkey.

It had made her ancestors mighty queens and kings; had made Terrasen untouchable, a powerhouse so lethal no force had ever breached its borders. Until she'd fallen into the Florine River that night—until this man had removed the amulet from around her neck, and a conquering army had swept through. And Arobynn had risen from being a local lord of assassins to crown himself this continent's unrivaled king of their

Guild. Perhaps his power and influence derived solely from the neck-lace—*her* necklace—that he'd worn all these years.

"I've become rather attached to it," Arobynn said as he handed it over.

He'd known she would ask for it tonight, if he was wearing it. Perhaps he'd planned to offer it to her all along, just to win her trust—or get her to stop framing his clients and interrupting his business.

Keeping her face neutral was an effort as she reached for it.

Her fingers grazed the golden chain, and she wished then and there that she'd never heard of it, never touched it, never been in the same room with it. *Not right*, her blood sang, her bones groaned. *Not right, not right, not right.*

The amulet was heavier than it looked—and warm from his body, or from the boundless power dwelling inside of it.

The Wyrdkey.

Holy gods.

That quickly, that easily, he'd handed it over. How Arobynn hadn't felt it, noticed it . . . Unless you needed magic in your veins to feel it. Unless it never . . . *called* to him as it did to her now, its raw power brushing up against her senses like a cat rubbing along her legs. How had her mother, her father—any of them—never felt it?

She almost walked out right then and there. But she slid the Amulet of Orynth around her neck, its weight becoming heavier still—a force pressing down on her bones, spreading through her blood like ink in water. *Not right.*

"Tomorrow morning," she said coldly, "you and I are going to talk again. Bring your best men, or whoever is licking your boots these days. And then we're going to plan." She rose from the chair, her knees wobbling.

"Any other requests, Your Majesty?"

"You think I don't realize you have the upper hand?" She willed calm to her veins, her heart. "You've agreed to help me far too easily. But I like this game. Let's keep playing it."

His answering smile was serpentine.

Each step toward the door was an effort of will as she forced herself not to think about the thing thudding between her breasts. "If you betray us tonight, Arobynn," she added, pausing before the door, "I'll make what was done to Sam seem like a mercy compared to what I do to you."

"Learned some new tricks these past few years, have you?"

She smirked, taking in the details of how he looked at this exact moment: the sheen of his red hair, his broad shoulders and narrow waist, the scars on his hands, and those silver eyes, so bright with challenge and triumph. They'd probably haunt her dreams until the day she died.

"One more thing," Arobynn said.

It was an effort to lift a brow as he came close enough to kiss her, embrace her. But he just took her hand in his, his thumb caressing her palm. "I'm going to enjoy having you back," he purred.

Then, faster than she could react, he slid the Wyrdstone ring onto her finger.

CHAPTER 44

The hidden dagger Aelin had drawn clattered to the wooden floor the moment the cool black stone slid against her skin. She blinked at the ring, at the line of blood that had appeared on her hand beneath Arobynn's sharp thumbnail as he raised her hand to his mouth and brushed his tongue along the back of her palm.

Her blood was on his lips as he straightened.

Such a silence in her head, even now. Her face stopped working; her heart stopped working.

"Blink," he ordered her.

She did.

"Smile."

She did.

"Tell me why you came back."

"To kill the king; to kill the prince."

Arobynn leaned in close, his nose grazing her neck. "Tell me that you love me."

"I love you."

"My name—say my name when you tell me that you love me."

"I love you, Arobynn Hamel."

His breath warmed her skin as he huffed a laugh onto her neck, then brushed a kiss where it met her shoulder. "I think I'm going to like this."

He pulled back, admiring her blank face, her features, now empty and foreign. "Take my carriage. Go home and sleep. Do not tell anyone of this; do not show your friends the ring. And tomorrow, report here after breakfast. We have plans, you and I. For our kingdom, and Adarlan."

She just stared, waiting.

"Do you understand?"

"Yes."

He lifted her hand again and kissed the Wyrdstone ring. "Good night, Aelin," he murmured, his hand grazing her backside as he shooed her out.

⁓

Rowan was trembling with restrained rage as they took Arobynn's carriage home, none of them speaking.

He'd heard every word uttered inside that room. So had Aedion. He'd seen the final touch Arobynn had made, the proprietary gesture of a man convinced that he had a new, very shiny toy to play with.

But Rowan didn't dare grab for Aelin's hand to see the ring.

She didn't move; she didn't speak. She just sat there and stared at the wall of the carriage.

A perfect, broken, obedient doll.

I love you, Arobynn Hamel.

Every minute was an agony, but there were too many eyes on them— too many, even as they finally reached the warehouse and climbed out. They waited until Arobynn's carriage had driven off before Rowan and Aedion flanked the queen as she slipped inside the warehouse and up the stairs.

The curtains were already shut inside the house, a few candles left burning. The flames caught on the golden dragon embroidered on the back of that remarkable gown, and Rowan didn't dare breathe as she just stood in the center of the room. A slave awaiting orders.

"Aelin?" Aedion said, his voice hoarse.

Aelin lifted her hands in front of her and turned.

She pulled off the ring. "So *that* was what he wanted. I honestly expected something grander."

Aelin slapped the ring down on the small table behind the couch.

Rowan frowned at it. "He didn't check Stevan's other hand?"

"No," she said, still trying to clear the horror of betrayal from her mind. Trying to ignore the *thing* hanging from her neck, the abyss of power that beckoned, beckoned—

Aedion snapped, "One of you needs to explain *now*."

Her cousin's face was drained of color, his eyes so wide that the whites shone all around them as he glanced from the ring to Aelin and back again.

She'd held it together during the carriage ride, maintaining the mask of the puppet Arobynn believed she'd become. She crossed the room, keeping her arms at her sides to avoid chucking the Wyrdkey against the wall. "I'm sorry," she said. "You couldn't know—"

"I could have rutting known. You really think I can't keep my mouth shut?"

"Rowan didn't even know until last night," she snapped.

Deep in that abyss, thunder rumbled.

Oh, gods. Oh, *gods*—

"Is that supposed to make me feel better?"

Rowan crossed his arms. "It is, considering the fight we had about it."

Aedion shook his head. "Just . . . explain."

Aelin picked up the ring. Focus. She could focus on this conversation, until she could safely hide the amulet. Aedion couldn't know what she carried, what weapon she'd claimed tonight. "In Wendlyn, there was a moment when Narrok . . . came back. When he warned me. And thanked me for ending him. So I picked the Valg commander who seemed to have the least amount of control over the human's body, out of hope that the man might be in there, wishing for redemption in some form." Redemption for what the demon had made him do, hoping to die knowing he'd done one good thing.

"Why?"

Speaking normally was an effort. "So I could offer him the mercy of death and freedom from the Valg, if he would only tell Arobynn all the wrong information. He tricked Arobynn into thinking that a bit of blood could control these rings—and that the ring he bore was the real thing." She held up the ring. "I got the idea from you, actually. Lysandra has a very good jeweler, and had a fake made. The real thing I cut off the Valg commander's finger. If Arobynn had taken off his other glove, he would have found him without a digit."

"You'd need weeks to plan all that—"

Aelin nodded.

"But why? Why bother with any of it? Why not just kill the prick?"

Aelin set down the ring. "I had to know."

"Know what? That Arobynn is a monster?"

"That there was no redeeming him. I knew, but . . . It was his final test. To show his hand."

Aedion hissed. "He would have made you into his own personal figurehead—he *touched*—"

"I know what he touched, and what he wanted to do." She could still feel that touch on her. It was nothing compared to the hideous weight pressing against her chest. She rubbed her thumb across the scabbed-over slice on her hand. "So now we know."

Some small, pathetic part of her wished she didn't.

Still in their finery, Aelin and Rowan stared at the amulet lying on the low table before the darkened fireplace in her bedroom.

She'd taken it off the moment she entered the room—Aedion having gone to the roof to take watch—and slumped onto the couch facing the table. Rowan took a seat beside her a heartbeat later. For a minute, they said nothing. The amulet gleamed in the light of the two candles Rowan had lit.

"I was going to ask you to make sure it wasn't a fake; that Arobynn hadn't switched it somehow," Rowan said at last, his eyes fixed on the Wyrdkey. "But I can feel it—a glimmer of whatever is inside that thing."

She braced her forearms on her knees, the black velvet of her dress softly caressing. "In the past, people must have assumed that feeling came from the magic of whoever was wearing it," she said. "With my mother, with Brannon . . . it would never have been noticed."

"And your father and uncle? They had little to no magic, you said."

The ivory stag seemed to stare at her, the immortal star between its horns flickering like molten gold. "But they had presence. What better place to hide this thing than around the neck of a swaggering royal?"

Rowan tensed as she reached for the amulet and flipped it over as quickly as she could. The metal was warm, its surface unmarred despite the millennia that had passed since its forging.

There, exactly as she'd remembered, were carved three Wyrdmarks.

"Any idea what those mean?" Rowan said, shifting close enough that his thigh grazed hers. He moved away an inch, though it did nothing to stop her from feeling the heat of him.

"I've never seen—"

"That one," Rowan said, pointing to the first one. "I've seen that one. It burned on your brow that day."

"Brannon's mark," she breathed. "The mark of the bastard-born—the nameless."

"No one in Terrasen *ever* looked into these symbols?"

"If they did, it was never revealed—or they wrote it in their personal accounts, which were stored in the Library of Orynth." She chewed on the inside of her lip. "It was one of the first places the King of Adarlan sacked."

"Maybe the librarians smuggled out the rulers' accounts first—maybe they got lucky."

Her heart sank a bit. "Maybe. We won't know until we return to Terrasen." She tapped her foot on the carpet. "I need to hide this." There was a loose floorboard in her closet under which she stashed money, weapons, and jewelry. It would be good enough for now. And Aedion wouldn't question it, since she couldn't risk wearing the damn thing in public anyway, even under her clothes—not until she was back in Terrasen. She stared down at the amulet.

"So do it," he said.

"I don't want to touch it."

"If it was that easy to trigger, your ancestors would have figured out what it was."

"You pick it up," she said, frowning.

He just gave her a look.

She bent down, willing her mind blank while she lifted the amulet off the table. Rowan stiffened as if bracing himself, despite his reassurance.

The key was a millstone in her hand, but that initial sense of wrongness, of an abyss of power . . . It was quiet. Slumbering.

She made quick work of pulling back the rug in her closet and yanking loose the floorboard. She felt Rowan come up behind her, peering over her shoulder where she knelt and into the small compartment.

She had picked up the amulet to drop it into the little space when a thread tugged inside her—no, not a thread, but . . . a wind, as if some force barreled from Rowan *into* her, as if their bond were a living thing, and she could feel what it was to *be* him—

She dropped the amulet into the compartment. It thudded only once, a dead weight.

"What?" Rowan asked.

She twisted to peer up at him. "I felt—I felt you."

"How?"

So she told him—about his essence sliding into her, of feeling like she wore his skin, if only for a heartbeat.

He didn't look entirely pleased. "That sort of ability could be a helpful tool for later."

She scowled. "Typical warrior-brute thinking."

He shrugged. Gods, how did he handle it, the weight of his power? He could crush bones into dust even without his magic; he could bring this whole building down with a few well-placed blows.

She'd known—of course she'd known—but to *feel* it . . . The most powerful purebred Fae male in existence. To an ordinary human, he was as alien as the Valg.

"But I think you're right: it can't just blindly act on my will," she said at last. "Or else my ancestors would have razed Orynth to the ground anytime they were royally pissed off. I—I think these things might be neutral by nature; it's the bearer who guides how they are used. In the hands of someone pure of heart, it would only be beneficial. That was how Terrasen thrived."

Rowan snorted as she replaced the wooden plank, tamping it down with the heel of her hand. "Trust me, your ancestors weren't utterly holy." He offered her a hand up, and she tried not to stare at it as she gripped it. Hard, callused, unbreakable—nearly impossible to kill. But there was a gentleness to his grip, a care reserved only for those he cherished and protected.

"I don't think any of them were assassins," she said as he dropped her hand. "The keys can corrupt an already black heart—or amplify a pure one. I've never heard anything about hearts that are somewhere in between."

"The fact that you worry says enough about your intentions."

She stepped all around the area to ensure that no creaking boards gave away the hiding place. Thunder rumbled above the city. "I'm going to pretend that's not an omen," she muttered.

"Good luck with that." He nudged her with an elbow as they reentered the bedroom. "We'll keep an eye on things—and if you appear to be heading toward Dark Lorddom, I promise to bring you back to the light."

"Funny." The little clock on her nightstand chimed, and thunder boomed again through Rifthold. A swift-moving storm. Good—maybe it would clear her head, too.

She went to the box Lysandra had brought her and pulled out the other item.

"Lysandra's jeweler," Rowan said, "is a very talented person."

Aelin held up a replica of the amulet. She'd gotten the size, coloring, and weight almost perfect. She set it on her vanity like a discarded piece of jewelry. "Just in case anyone asks where it went."

The downpour had softened to a steady drizzle by the time the clock struck one, yet Aelin hadn't come down from the roof. She'd gone up there to take over Aedion's watch, apparently—and Rowan had waited, biding his time as the clock neared midnight and then passed it. Chaol had come by to give Aedion a report on the movements of Arobynn's men, but slipped back out around twelve.

Rowan was done waiting.

She was standing in the rain, facing westward—not toward the glowing castle to her right, not toward the sea at her back, but across the city.

He didn't mind that she'd gotten that glimpse into him. He wanted to tell her that he didn't care what she knew about him, so long as it didn't scare her away—and would have told her before if he still hadn't been so stupidly distracted by how she looked tonight.

The lamplight glinted off the combs in her hair and along the golden dragon on the dress.

"You'll ruin that dress standing out here in the rain," he said.

She half turned toward him. The rain had left streaks of kohl down her face, and her skin was as pale as a fish's belly. The look in her eyes—guilt, anger, agony—hit him like a blow to the gut.

She turned again toward the city. "I was never going to wear this dress again, anyway."

"You know I'll take care of it tonight," he said, stepping beside her, "if you don't want to be the one to do it." And after what that bastard had tried to do to her, what he'd *planned* to do to her . . . He and Aedion would take a long, long time ending Arobynn's life.

She gazed across the city, toward the Assassins' Keep. "I told Lysandra she could do it."

"Why?"

She wrapped her arms around herself, hugging tight. "Because more than me, more than you or Aedion, Lysandra deserves to be the one who ends him."

It was true. "Will she be needing our assistance?"

She shook her head, spraying droplets of rain off the combs and the damp strands of hair that had come loose. "Chaol went to ensure everything goes fine."

Rowan allowed himself a moment to look at her—at the relaxed shoulders and uplifted chin, the grip she had on her elbows, the curve of her nose against the streetlight, the thin line of her mouth.

"It feels wrong," she said, "to still wish that there had been some other way." She took an uneven breath, the air clouding in front of her. "He was a bad man," she whispered. "He was going to enslave me to his will, use me to take over Terrasen, maybe make himself king—maybe sire my—" She shuddered so violently that light shimmered off the gold in her dress. "But he also . . . I also owe him my life. All this time I thought it would be a relief, a joy to end him. But all I feel is hollow. And tired."

She was like ice when he slid an arm around her, folding her into his side. Just this once—just this once, he would let himself hold her. If he'd been asked to put down Maeve, and one of his cadre had done it instead— if Lorcan had done it—he would have felt the same.

She twisted slightly to peer up at him, and though she tried to hide it, he could see the fear in her gaze, and the guilt. "I need you to hunt down Lorcan tomorrow. See if he's accomplished the little task I gave him."

If he'd killed those Wyrdhounds. Or been killed by them. So she could at last free magic.

Gods. Lorcan was his enemy now. He shut out the thought. "And if it's necessary to eliminate him?"

He watched her throat bob as she swallowed. "It's your call then, Rowan. Do as you see fit."

He wished she'd told him one way or another, but giving him the choice, respecting their history enough to allow him to make that decision . . . "Thank you."

She rested her head against his chest, the tips of the bat-wing combs digging into him enough that he eased them one at a time from her hair. The gold was slick and cold in his hands, and as he admired the crafts-manship, she murmured, "I want you to sell those. And burn this dress."

"As you wish," he said, pocketing the combs. "Such a pity, though. Your enemies would have fallen to their knees if they ever saw you in it."

He'd almost fallen to his knees when he'd first seen her earlier tonight.

She huffed a laugh that might have been a sob and wrapped her arms around his waist as if trying to steal his warmth. Her sodden hair tumbled down, the scent of her—jasmine and lemon verbena and crackling embers—rising above the smell of almonds to caress his nose, his senses.

Rowan stood with his queen in the rain, breathing in her scent, and let her steal his warmth for as long as she needed.

⁓

The rain lightened to a soft sprinkle, and Aelin stirred from where Rowan held her. From where she'd been standing, soaking up his strength, thinking.

She twisted slightly to take in the strong lines of his face, his cheekbones gilded with the rain and the light from the street. Across the city, in a room she knew too well, Arobynn was hopefully bleeding out. Hopefully dead.

A hollow thought—but also the clicking of a lock finally opened.

Rowan turned his head to look at her, rain dripping off his silver hair. His features softened a bit, the harsh lines becoming more inviting—vulnerable, even. "Tell me what you're thinking," he murmured.

"I'm thinking that the next time I want to unsettle you, all I need to do is tell you how rarely I wear undergarments."

His pupils flared. "Is there a *reason* you do that, Princess?"

"Is there any reason *not* to?"

He flattened his hand against her waist, his fingers contracting once as if debating letting her go. "I pity the foreign ambassadors who will have to deal with you."

She grinned, breathless and more than a little reckless. Seeing that dungeon room tonight, she'd realized she was tired. Tired of death, and of waiting, and of saying good-bye.

She lifted a hand to cup Rowan's face.

So smooth, his skin, the bones beneath strong and elegant.

She waited for him to pull back, but he just stared at her—stared *into* her in that way he always did. Friends, but more. So much more, and she'd known it longer than she wanted to admit. Carefully, she stroked her thumb across his cheekbone, his face slick with the rain.

It hit her like a stone—the wanting. She was a fool to have dodged it, denied it, even when a part of her had screamed it every morning that she'd blindly reached for the empty half of the bed.

She lifted her other hand to his face and his eyes locked onto hers, his breathing ragged as she traced the lines of the tattoo along his temple.

His hands tightened slightly on her waist, his thumbs grazing the bottom of her ribcage. It was an effort not to arch into his touch.

"Rowan," she breathed, his name a plea and a prayer. She slid her fingers down the side of his tattooed cheek, and—

Faster than she could see, he grabbed one wrist and then the other, yanking them away from his face and snarling softly. The world yawned open around her, cold and still.

He dropped her hands as if they were on fire, stepping away, those green eyes flat and dull in a way she hadn't seen for some time now. Her throat closed up even before he said, "Don't do that. Don't—touch me like that."

There was a roaring in her ears, a burning in her face, and she swallowed hard. "I'm sorry."

Oh, gods.

He was over three hundred years old. Immortal. And she—she . . .

"I didn't mean—" She backed away a step, toward the door on the other side of the roof. "I'm sorry," she repeated. "It was nothing."

"Good," he said, going for the roof door himself. "Fine."

Rowan didn't say anything else as he stalked downstairs. Alone, she scrubbed at her wet face, at the oily smear of cosmetics.

Don't touch me like that.

A clear line in the sand. A line—because he was three hundred years old, and immortal, and had lost his flawless mate, and she was . . . She was young and inexperienced and his *carranam* and queen, and he wanted nothing more than that. If she hadn't been so foolish, so stupidly unaware, maybe she would have realized that, understood that though she'd seen his eyes shine with hunger—hunger for *her*—it didn't mean he wanted to act on it. Didn't mean he might not hate himself for it.

Oh, gods.

What had she done?

⌒

The rain sliding down the windows cast slithering shadows on the wooden floor, on the painted walls of Arobynn's bedroom.

Lysandra had been watching it for some time now, listening to the steady rhythm of the storm and to the breathing of the man sleeping beside her. Utterly unconscious.

If she were to do it, it would have to be now—when his sleep was deepest, when the rain covered up most sounds. A blessing from Temis, Goddess of Wild Things, who had once watched over her as a shape-shifter and who never forgot the caged beasts of the world.

Three words—that was all that had been written on the note Aelin slipped her earlier that night; a note still tucked into the hidden pocket of her discarded underwear.

He's all yours.

A gift, she knew—a gift from the queen who had nothing else to give a no-name whore with a sad story.

Lysandra turned onto her side, staring now at the naked man sleeping inches away, at the red silk of his hair spilled across his face.

He'd never once suspected who had fed Aelin the details about Cormac. But that had always been her ruse with Arobynn—the skin she'd worn since childhood. He had never thought otherwise of her vapid and vain behavior, never bothered to. If he had, he wouldn't keep a knife under his pillow and let her sleep in this bed with him.

He hadn't been gentle tonight, and she knew she would have a bruise on her forearm from where he'd gripped her too tightly. Victorious, smug, a king certain of his crown, he hadn't even noticed.

At dinner, she'd seen the expression flash across his face when he caught Aelin and Rowan smiling at each other. All of Arobynn's jabs and stories had failed to find their mark tonight because Aelin had been too lost in Rowan to hear.

She wondered whether the queen knew. Rowan did. Aedion did. And Arobynn did. He had understood that with Rowan, she was no longer afraid of him; with Rowan, Arobynn was now utterly unnecessary. Irrelevant.

He's all yours.

After Aelin had left, as soon as he'd stopped strutting about the house, convinced of his absolute mastery over the queen, Arobynn had called in his men.

Lysandra hadn't heard the plans, but she knew the Fae Prince would be his first target. Rowan would die—Rowan *had* to die. She'd seen it in Arobynn's eyes as he watched the queen and her prince holding hands, grinning at each other despite the horrors around them.

Lysandra slid her hand beneath the pillow as she sidled up to Arobynn, nestling against him. He didn't stir; his breathing remained deep and steady.

He'd never had trouble sleeping. The night he'd killed Wesley he slept like the dead, unaware of the moments when even her iron will couldn't keep the silent tears from falling.

She would find that love again—one day. And it would be deep and unrelenting and unexpected, the beginning and the end and eternity, the kind that could change history, change the world.

The hilt of the stiletto was cool in her hand, and as Lysandra rolled back over, no more than a restless sleeper, she pulled it with her.

Lightning gleamed on the blade, a flicker of quicksilver.

For Wesley. For Sam. For Aelin.

And for herself. For the child she'd been, for the seventeen-year-old on her Bidding night, for the woman she'd become, her heart in shreds, her invisible wound still bleeding.

It was so very easy to sit up and slice the knife across Arobynn's throat.

CHAPTER 45

The man strapped to the table was screaming as the demon ran its hands down his bare chest, its nails digging in and leaving blood in their wake.

Listen to him, the demon prince hissed. *Listen to the music he makes.*

Beyond the table, the man who usually sat on the glass throne said, "Where are the rebels hiding?"

"I don't know, I don't know!" the man shrieked.

The demon ran a second nail down the man's chest. There was blood everywhere.

Do not cringe, spineless beast. Watch; savor.

The body—the body that might once have been his—had betrayed him entirely. The demon gripped him tightly, forcing him to watch as his own hands gripped a cruel-looking device, fitting it onto the man's face, and began tightening.

"Answer me, rebel," the crowned man said.

The man screamed as the mask tightened.

He might have begun screaming, too—might have begun begging the demon to stop.

Coward—human coward. Do you not taste his pain, his fear?

He could, and the demon shoved every bit of delight it felt into him.

Had he been able to vomit, he would have. Here there was no such thing. Here there was no escape.

"Please," the man on the table begged. *"Please!"*

But his hands did not stop.

And the man went on screaming.

CHAPTER 46

Today, Aelin decided, was already forfeited to hell, and there was no use even trying to salvage it—not with what she had to do next.

Armed to the teeth, she tried not to think about Rowan's words from the night before as they took the carriage across the city. But she heard them beneath every clop of the horses' hooves, just as she'd heard them all night long while she lay awake in bed, trying to ignore his presence. *Don't touch me like that.*

She sat as far from Rowan as she could get without hanging out the carriage window. She'd spoken to him, of course—distantly and quietly—and he'd given her clipped answers. Which made the ride truly delightful. Aedion, wisely, didn't ask about it.

She needed to be clear-headed, relentless, in order to endure the next few hours.

Arobynn was dead.

Word had come an hour ago that Arobynn had been found murdered. Her presence was requested immediately by Tern, Harding, and Mullin, the three assassins who had seized control of the Guild and estate until everything was sorted out.

She'd known last night, of course. Hearing it confirmed was a relief—that Lysandra had done it, and survived it, but . . .

Dead.

The carriage pulled up in front of the Assassins' Keep, but Aelin didn't move. Silence fell as they looked up at the pale stone manor looming above. But Aelin closed her eyes, breathing in deep.

One last time—you have to wear this mask one last time, and then you can bury Celaena Sardothien forever.

She opened her eyes, her shoulders squaring and her chin lifting, even as the rest of her went fluid with feline grace.

Aedion gaped, and she knew there was nothing of the cousin he'd come to know in her face. She glanced at him, then Rowan, a cruel smile spreading as she leaned over to open the carriage door.

"Don't get in my way," she told them.

She swept from the carriage, her cloak flapping in the spring wind as she stormed up the steps of the Keep and kicked open the front doors.

CHAPTER 47

"What the *rutting hell* happened?" Aelin roared as the front doors to the Assassins' Keep banged behind her. Aedion and Rowan followed on her heels, both concealed beneath heavy hoods.

The front hall was empty, but a glass crashed from the closed sitting room, and then—

Three males, one tall, one short and slender, and one monstrously muscled, stalked into the hall. Harding, Tern, and Mullin. She bared her teeth at the men—Tern in particular. He was the smallest, oldest, and the most cunning, the ringleader of their little group. He'd probably hoped that she'd kill Arobynn that night they ran into each other in the Vaults.

"Start talking now," she hissed.

Tern braced his feet apart. "Not unless you do the same."

Aedion let out a low growl as the three assassins looked over her companions. "Never mind the guard dogs," she snapped, drawing their attention back to her. "Explain yourselves."

There was a muffled sob from the sitting room behind the men, and she flicked her eyes over Mullin's towering shoulder. "Why are those two pieces of whoring trash in this house?"

Tern glowered. "Because Lysandra was the one who woke up screaming next to his body."

Her fingers curled into claws. "Was she, now?" she murmured, such wrath in her eyes that even Tern stepped aside as she stalked into the sitting room.

Lysandra was slumped in an armchair, a handkerchief pressed to her face. Clarisse, her madam, stood behind the chair, her face pale and tight.

Blood stained Lysandra's skin and matted her hair, and patches had soaked through the thin silk robe that did little to hide her nakedness.

Lysandra jerked upright, her eyes red and face splotchy. "I didn't—I swear I didn't—"

A spectacular performance. "Why the hell should I believe you?" Aelin drawled. "You're the only one with access to his room."

Clarisse, golden-haired and aging gracefully for a woman in her forties, clicked her tongue. "Lysandra would never harm Arobynn. Why would she, when he was doing so much to pay off her debts?"

Aelin cocked her head at the madam. "Did I ask for your gods-damned opinion, *Clarisse*?"

Poised for violence, Rowan and Aedion kept silent, though she could have sworn a hint of shock flashed in their shadowed eyes. Good. Aelin flicked her attention to the assassins. "Show me where you found him. *Now*."

Tern gave her a long look, considering her every word. *A valiant effort*, she thought, *to try to catch me in knowing more than I should*. The assassin pointed to the sweeping stairs visible through the open sitting room doors. "In his room. We moved his body downstairs."

"You moved it before I could study the scene myself?"

It was tall, quiet Harding who said, "You were told only as a courtesy." *And to see if I'd done it.*

She stalked from the sitting room, pointing a finger behind her at Lysandra and Clarisse. "If either of them tries to run," she said to Aedion, "gut them."

Aedion's grin shone from beneath his hood, his hands hovering within casual reach of his fighting knives.

Arobynn's bedroom was a bloodbath. And there was nothing feigned as she paused on the threshold, blinking at the blood-drenched bed and the blood pooled on the floor.

What the hell had Lysandra *done* to him?

She clenched her hands against their trembling, aware that the three assassins at her back could see it. They were monitoring her every breath and blink and swallow. "How?"

Mullin grunted. "Someone sliced his throat open and let him choke to death on his own blood."

Her stomach turned—honestly turned. Lysandra, it seemed, hadn't been content to let him go quickly. "There," she said, and her throat closed. She tried again. "There's a footprint in the blood."

"Boots," Tern said at her side. "Big—probably male." He gave Aelin's slender feet a pointed look. Then he studied Rowan's feet where the prince loomed behind her, even though he'd probably already examined them. The little shit. Of course, the footprints Chaol had deliberately left were made with boots different from what any of them wore.

"The lock shows no sign of tampering," she said, touching the door. "Does the window?"

"Go check," Tern said.

She would have to walk through Arobynn's blood to reach it. "Just tell me," she said quietly. Wearily.

"Lock's broken from the outside," Harding said, and Tern shot him a glare.

She stepped back into the cool darkness of the hall. Rowan silently kept his distance, his Fae heritage still undetected beneath that hood— and it would remain that way so long as he didn't open his mouth to reveal his elongated canines. Aelin said, "No one reported signs of anything being amiss?"

Tern shrugged. "There was a storm. The murderer probably waited until then to kill him." He gave her another long look, wicked violence dancing in his dark eyes.

"Why don't you just say it, Tern? Why don't you ask me where I was last night?"

"We know where you were," Harding said, coming to tower over Tern. There was nothing kind on his long, bland face. "Our eyes saw you at home all night. You were on the roof of your house, and then you went to bed."

Exactly as she'd planned.

"Are you telling me that detail because you'd like me to hunt down your little *eyes* and blind them?" Aelin replied sweetly. "Because after I sort out *this* mess, that's exactly what I plan to do."

Mullin sighed sharply through his nose and glared at Harding, but said nothing. He was always a man of few words—perfect for dirty work.

"You don't touch our men, and we won't touch yours," Tern said.

"I don't make bargains with piece-of-shit, second-rate assassins," she chirped, and gave him a nasty smile as she swept down the hall, past her old room, and down the stairs, Rowan a step behind.

She gave Aedion a nod as she entered the sitting room. He kept up his watchful position, still smiling like a wolf. Lysandra hadn't moved an inch. "You can go," she said to her. Lysandra's head snapped up.

"What?" Tern barked.

Aelin pointed to the door. "Why would these two money-grubbing whores kill their biggest client? If anything," she said over her shoulder, "I'd think you three would have more to gain."

Before they could start barking, Clarisse coughed pointedly.

"*Yes?*" Aelin hissed.

Clarisse's face was deathly pale, but she held her head high as she said, "If you would allow it, the Master of the Bank will be here soon to read

Arobynn's will. Arobynn . . ." She dabbed at her eyes, the perfect portrait of grief. "Arobynn informed me that we were named. We would like to remain until it has been read."

Aelin grinned. "Arobynn's blood hasn't yet dried on that bed, and you're already swooping in for your bequest. I don't know why I'm surprised. Maybe I've dismissed you as his murderer too soon, if you're that eager to snatch whatever he's left you."

Clarisse paled again, and Lysandra began shaking. "Please, Celaena," Lysandra begged. "We didn't—I would never—"

Someone knocked on the front door.

Aelin slid her hands into her pockets. "Well, well. What good timing."

The Master of the Bank looked as if he might vomit at the sight of blood-covered Lysandra, but then he sighed with something like relief when he spied Aelin. Lysandra and Clarisse now sat in twin armchairs while the Master took a seat behind the little writing desk before the towering bay windows, Tern and his cronies hovering like vultures. Aelin leaned against the wall beside the doorway, arms crossed, Aedion flanking her left side and Rowan her right.

As the Master went on and on with his condolences and apologies, she felt Rowan's eyes on her.

He took a step nearer, as if to brush his arm against hers. She sidled out of reach.

Rowan was still staring at her when the Master opened a sealed envelope and cleared his throat. He spouted some legal jargon and offered his condolences again, which gods-damned Clarisse had the audacity to accept as though she were Arobynn's widow.

Then came the long list of Arobynn's assets—his business investments, his properties, and the enormous, outrageous fortune left in his account. Clarisse was practically drooling on the carpet, but Arobynn's three assassins kept their faces carefully neutral.

"It is my will," the Master read, "that the sole beneficiary of all my fortune, assets, and holdings should be my heir, Celaena Sardothien."

Clarisse whipped around in her chair, fast as an adder. *"What?"*

"Bullshit," Aedion blurted.

Aelin just stared at the Master, her mouth a bit open, her hands falling slack to her sides. "Say that again," she breathed.

The Master gave a nervous, watery smile. "Everything—all of it, is left to you. Well, except for . . . this sum to Madam Clarisse, to settle his debts." He showed Clarisse the paper.

"That's impossible," the madam hissed. "He *promised* I was in that will."

"And you are," Aelin drawled, pushing off the wall to peer over Clarisse's shoulder at the small number. "Don't get greedy, now."

"Where are the duplicates?" Tern demanded. "Have you inspected them?" He stormed around the table to examine the will.

The Master flinched, but held up the parchment—signed by Arobynn and utterly legal. "We verified the copies in our vaults this morning. All identical, all dated from three months ago."

When she'd been in Wendlyn.

She stepped forward. "So, aside from that teensy sum for Clarisse . . . all of this—this house, the Guild, the other properties, his fortune—it's all mine?"

The Master nodded again, already scrambling to pack up his case. "Congratulations, Miss Sardothien."

Slowly, she turned her head toward Clarisse and Lysandra. "Well, if that's the case . . ." She bared her teeth in a vicious smile. "Get your whoring, blood-sucking carcasses the *hell* off my property."

The Master choked.

Lysandra couldn't move fast enough as she rushed for the door. Clarisse, however, remained seated. "How *dare* you—" the madam began.

"Five," Aelin said, holding up five fingers. She lowered one, and reached for her dagger with her other hand. "Four." Another. "Three."

Clarisse hauled ass from the room, bustling after a sobbing Lysandra.

Then Aelin looked at the three assassins. Their hands hung limp at their sides, fury and shock and—wisely enough—something like fear on their faces.

She said too quietly, "You held Sam back while Arobynn beat me into oblivion, and then didn't raise a finger to stop it when Arobynn beat him, too. I don't know what role you played in his death, but I will never forget the sounds of your voices outside my bedroom door as you fed me the details about Rourke Farran's house. Was it easy for you three? To send me to that sadist's house, knowing what he'd done to Sam and what he was aching to do to me? Were you just following orders, or were you more than happy to volunteer?"

The Master had recoiled in his chair, trying to make himself as invisible as possible in a room full of professional killers.

Tern's lip curled. "We don't know what you're talking about."

"Pity. I might have been willing to listen to some paltry excuses." She looked at the clock on the mantel. "Pack your clothes and get the hell out. Right now."

They blinked. "What?" Tern said.

"Pack your clothes," she said, enunciating each word. "Get the hell out. Right now."

"This is our home," Harding said.

"Not anymore." She picked at her nails. "Correct me if I'm wrong, Master," she purred, and the man cringed at the attention. "I own this house and everything in it. Tern, Harding, and Mullin haven't yet paid back their debts to poor Arobynn, so I own everything they have here—even their clothes. I'm feeling generous, so I'll let them keep those, since their taste is shit-awful anyway. But their weapons, their client lists, the Guild . . . All of that is mine. I get to decide who's in and who's out. And since these three saw fit to accuse *me* of murdering my master, I say they're out. If they try to work again in this city, on this continent, then by law and by the laws of the Guild, I have the right to hunt them down and chop them into itty-bitty pieces." She batted her eyelashes. "Or am I wrong?"

The Master's gulp was audible. "You are correct."

Tern took a step toward her. "You can't—you can't do this."

"I can, and I will. Queen of the Assassins sounds so nice, doesn't it?" She waved to the door. "See yourselves out."

Harding and Mullin made to move, but Tern flung his arms out, stopping them. "What the hell do you want from us?"

"Honestly, I wouldn't mind seeing you three gutted and hanging from the chandeliers by your insides, but I think it would ruin these very beautiful carpets that I'm now the owner of."

"You can't just toss us out. What will we do? Where will we go?"

"I hear hell is particularly nice at this time of year."

"Please—please," Tern said, his breath coming fast.

She stuffed her hands into her pockets and surveyed the room. "I suppose . . ." She made a thoughtful sound. "I suppose I could *sell* you the house, and the land, and the Guild."

"You *bitch*—" Tern spat, but Harding stepped forward. "How much?" he asked.

"How much were the property and the Guild valued at, Master?"

The Master looked like a man walking up to the gallows as he opened his file again and found the sum. Astronomical, outrageous, impossible for the three of them to pay.

Harding ran a hand through his hair. Tern had turned a spectacular shade of purple.

"I take it you don't have that much," Aelin said. "Too bad. I was going to offer to sell it all to you at face value—no markup."

She made to turn away, but Harding said, "Wait. What if we all paid together—the three of us and the others. So we all owned the house and the Guild."

She paused. "Money's money. I don't give a shit where you get it from, so long as it's given to me." She angled her head toward the Master. "Can you have the papers drawn up today? Providing they come through with the money, of course."

"This is insane," Tern murmured to Harding.

Harding shook his head. "Be quiet, Tern. Just—be quiet."

"I . . . ," the Master said. "I—I can have them made up and ready within three hours. Will that be adequate time for you to provide proof of sufficient funds?"

Harding nodded. "We'll find the others and tell them."

She smiled at the Master and at the three men. "Congratulations on your new freedom." She pointed to the door again. "And as I am mistress of this house for another three hours . . . *get out.* Go find your friends, get your money together, and then sit on the curb like the trash you are until the Master returns."

They wisely obeyed, Harding clamping down on Tern's hand to keep him from giving her a vulgar gesture. When the Master of the Bank left, the assassins spoke to their colleagues, and every inhabitant of the house filed outside one by one, even the servants. She didn't care what the neighbors made of it.

Soon the giant, beautiful manor house was empty save for her, Aedion, and Rowan.

They silently followed as she walked through the door to the lower levels and descended into the dark to see her master one last time.

Rowan didn't know what to make of it. A whirlwind of hate and rage and violence, that was what she'd become. And none of these piss-poor assassins had been surprised—not even a blink at her behavior. From Aedion's pale face, he knew the general was thinking the same thing, contemplating the years she'd spent as that unyielding and vicious creature. Celaena Sardothien—that was who she'd been then, and who she'd become today.

He hated it. Hated that he couldn't reach her when she was that person. Hated that he'd snapped at her last night, had panicked at the touch of her hands. Now she'd shut him out entirely. This person she'd become today had no kindness, no joy.

He followed her down into the dungeons, where candles lit a path toward the room where her master's body was being kept. She was still swaggering, hands in her pockets, not caring that Rowan lived or breathed or even existed. *Not real*, he told himself. *An act.*

But she'd avoided him since last night, and today she had actually stepped away from his touch when he'd dared to reach for her. *That* had been real.

She strode through the open door into the same room where Sam had lain. Red hair spilled out from underneath the white silk sheet covering the naked body on the table, and she paused before it. Then she turned to Rowan and Aedion.

She stared at them, waiting. Waiting for them to—

Aedion swore. "You switched the will, didn't you?"

She gave a small, cold smile, her eyes shadowed. "You said you needed money for an army, Aedion. So here's your money—all of it, and every coin for Terrasen. It was the least Arobynn owed us. That night I fought at the Pits, we were only there because I'd contacted the owners days before and told them to send out subtle feelers to Arobynn about investing. He took the bait—didn't even question the timing of it. But I wanted to make sure he quickly earned back all the money he lost when I trashed the Vaults. So we wouldn't be denied one coin owed to us."

Holy burning hell.

Aedion shook his head. "How—how the hell did you even do it?"

She opened her mouth, but Rowan said quietly, "She snuck into the bank—all those times that she slipped out in the middle of the night. And used all those daytime meetings with the Master of the Bank to get a better sense of the layout, where things were kept." This woman, this queen of his . . . A familiar thrill raced through his blood. "You burned the originals?"

She didn't even look at him. "Clarisse would have been a very rich woman, and Tern would have become King of the Assassins. And you know what I would have received? The Amulet of Orynth. That was all he left me."

"That was how you knew he truly had it—and where he kept it," Rowan said. "From reading the will."

She shrugged again, dismissing the shock and admiration he couldn't keep from his face. Dismissing *him*.

Aedion scrubbed at his face. "I don't even know what to say. You should have told me so I didn't act like a gawking fool up there."

"Your surprise needed to be genuine; even Lysandra didn't know about the will." Such a distant answer—closed and heavy. Rowan wanted to shake her, demand she talk to him, *look* at him. But he wasn't entirely sure what he would do if she wouldn't let him near, if she pulled away again while Aedion was watching.

Aelin turned back to Arobynn's body and flipped the sheet away from his face, revealing a jagged wound that sliced across his pale neck.

Lysandra had mangled him.

Arobynn's face had been arranged in an expression of calm, but from the blood Rowan had seen in the bedroom, the man had been very much awake while he choked on his own blood.

Aelin peered down at her former master, her face blank save for a slight tightening around her mouth. "I hope the dark god finds a special place for you in his realm," she said, and a shiver went down Rowan's spine at the midnight caress in her tone.

She extended a hand behind her to Aedion. "Give me your sword."

Aedion drew the Sword of Orynth and handed it to her. Aelin gazed down at the blade of her ancestors as she weighed it in her hands.

When she raised her head, there was only icy determination in those remarkable eyes. A queen exacting justice.

Then she lifted her father's sword and severed Arobynn's head from his body.

It rolled to the side with a vulgar thud, and she smiled grimly at the corpse.

"Just to be sure," was all she said.

PART TWO

Queen of Light

CHAPTER 48

Manon beat Asterin in the breakfast hall the morning after her outburst regarding the Yellowlegs coven. No one asked why; no one dared.

Three unblocked blows.

Asterin didn't so much as flinch.

When Manon was finished, the witch just stared her down, blue blood gushing from her broken nose. No smile. No wild grin.

Then Asterin walked away.

The rest of the Thirteen monitored them warily. Vesta, now Manon's Third, looked half inclined to sprint after Asterin, but a shake of Sorrel's head kept the red-haired witch still.

Manon was off-kilter all day afterward.

She'd told Sorrel to stay quiet about the Yellowlegs, but wondered if she should tell Asterin to do the same.

She hesitated, thinking about it.

You let them do this.

The words danced around and around in Manon's head, along with that preachy little speech Elide had made the night before. *Hope*. What drivel.

The words were still dancing when Manon stalked into the duke's council chamber twenty minutes later than his summons demanded.

"Do you delight in offending me with your tardiness, or are you incapable of telling time?" the duke said from his seat. Vernon and Kaltain were at the table, the former smirking, the latter staring blankly ahead. No sign of shadowfire.

"I'm an immortal," Manon said, taking a seat across from them as Sorrel stood guard by the doors, Vesta in the hall outside. "Time means nothing to me."

"A little sass from you today," Vernon said. "I like it."

Manon leveled a cold look at him. "I missed breakfast this morning, human. I'd be careful if I were you."

The lord only smiled.

She leaned back in her chair. "Why did you summon me this time?"

"I need another coven."

Manon kept her face blank. "What of the Yellowlegs you already have?"

"They are recovering well and will be ready for visitors soon."

Liar.

"A Blackbeak coven this time," the duke pressed.

"Why?"

"Because I want one, and you'll provide one, and that's all you need to know."

You let them do this.

She could feel Sorrel's gaze on the back of her head.

"We're not whores for your men to use."

"You are sacred vessels," the duke said. "It is an honor to be chosen."

"I find that a very male thing to assume."

A flash of yellowing teeth. "Pick your strongest coven, and send them downstairs."

"That will require some consideration."

"Do it fast, or I will pick myself."

You let them do this.

"And in the meantime," the duke said as he rose from his seat in a swift, powerful movement, "prepare your Thirteen. I have a mission for you."

Manon sailed on a hard, fast wind, pushing Abraxos even as clouds gathered, even as a storm broke around the Thirteen. Out. She had to get out, had to remember the bite of the wind on her face, what unchecked speed and unlimited strength were like.

Even if the rush of it was somewhat diminished by the rider she held in front of her, her frail body bundled up against the elements.

Lightning cleaved the air so close by that Manon could taste the tang of the ether, and Abraxos veered, plunging into rain and cloud and wind. Kaltain didn't so much as flinch. Shouts burst from the men riding with the rest of the Thirteen.

Thunder cracked, and the world went numb with the sound. Even Abraxos's roar was muted in her dulled ears. The perfect cover for their ambush.

You let them do this.

The rain soaking through her gloves turned to warm, sticky blood.

Abraxos caught an updraft and ascended so fast that Manon's stomach dropped. She held Kaltain tightly, even though the woman was harnessed in. Not one reaction from her.

Duke Perrington, riding with Sorrel, was a cloud of darkness in Manon's peripheral vision as they soared through the canyons of the White Fangs, which they had so carefully mapped all these weeks.

The wild tribes would have no idea what was upon them until it was too late.

She knew there was no way to outrun this—no way to avoid it.

Manon kept flying through the heart of the storm.

When they reached the village, blended into the snow and rock, Sorrel swooped in close enough for Kaltain to hear Perrington. "The houses. Burn them all."

Manon glanced at the duke, then at her charge. "Should we land—"

"From here," the duke ordered, and his face became grotesquely soft as he spoke to Kaltain. "Do it now, pet."

Below, a small female figure slipped out of one of the heavy tents. She looked up, shouting.

Dark flames—shadowfire—engulfed her from head to toe. Her scream was carried to Manon on the wind.

Then there were others, pouring out as the unholy fire leaped upon their houses, their horses.

"All of them, Kaltain," the duke said over the wind. "Keep circling, Wing Leader."

Sorrel met Manon's stare. Manon quickly looked away and reeled Abraxos back around the pass where the tribe had been camped. There were rebels among them; Manon knew because she'd tracked them herself.

Shadowfire ripped through the camp. People dropped to the ground, shrieking, pleading in tongues Manon didn't understand. Some fainted from the pain; some died from it. The horses were bucking and scream-ing—such wretched sounds that even Manon's spine stiffened.

Then it vanished.

Kaltain sagged in Manon's arms, panting, gasping down raspy breaths.

"She's done," Manon said to the duke.

Irritation flickered on his granite-hewn face. He observed the people running about, trying to help those who were weeping or unconscious— or dead. Horses fled in every direction.

"Land, Wing Leader, and put an end to it."

Any other day, a good bloodletting would have been enjoyable. But at his order . . .

She'd scouted this tribe for him.

You let them do this.

Manon barked the command to Abraxos, but his descent was slow—as if giving her time to reconsider. Kaltain was shuddering in Manon's arms, nearly convulsing. "What's wrong with you?" Manon said to the woman, half wondering if she should stage an accident that would end with the woman's neck snapped on the rocks.

Kaltain said nothing, but the lines of her body were locked tight, as if frozen despite the fur she'd been wrapped in.

Too many eyes—there were too many eyes on them for Manon to kill her. And if she was so valuable to the duke, Manon had no doubt he'd take one—or all—of the Thirteen as retribution. "Hurry, Abraxos," she said, and he picked up his pace with a snarl. She ignored the disobedience, the disapproval, in the sound.

They landed on a flattened bit of mountain ledge, and Manon left Kaltain in Abraxos's care as she stomped through the sleet and snow toward the panicking village.

The Thirteen silently fell into rank behind her. She didn't glance at them; part of her didn't dare to see what might be on their faces.

The villagers halted as they beheld the coven standing atop the rock outcropping jutting over the hollow where they'd made their home.

Manon drew Wind-Cleaver. And then the screaming started anew.

CHAPTER
49

By midafternoon, Aelin had signed all the documents the Master of the Bank brought over, abandoned the Keep to its horrible new owners, and Aedion *still* hadn't wrapped his mind around everything that she had done.

Their carriage deposited them at the edge of the slums, and they kept to the shadows as they made their way home, silent and unseen. Yet when they reached the warehouse, Aelin kept walking toward the river several blocks away without so much as a word. Rowan took a step to follow, but Aedion cut him off.

He must have had a death wish, because Aedion even raised his brows a bit at the Fae Prince before he sauntered down the street after her. He'd heard their little fight on the roof last night thanks to his open bedroom window. Even now, he honestly couldn't decide if he was amused or enraged by Rowan's words—*Don't touch me like that*—when it was obvious the warrior-prince felt quite the opposite. But Aelin—gods above, Aelin was still figuring it out.

She was stomping down the street with delightful temper as she said, "If you've come along to reprimand—oh." She sighed. "I don't suppose I can convince you to turn around."

"Not a chance in hell, sweetheart."

She rolled her eyes and continued on. They walked silently for block after block until they reached the glimmering brown river. A decrepit, filthy length of cobblestone walkway ran along the water's edge. Below, abandoned and crumbling posts were all that was left of an ancient dock.

She stared out across the muddy water, crossing her arms. The afternoon light was nearly blinding as it reflected off the calm surface. "Out with it," she said.

"Today—who you were today . . . that wasn't entirely a mask."

"That bothers you? You saw me cut down the king's men."

"It bothers me that the people we met today didn't bat an eye at that person. It bothers me that you *were* that person for a time."

"What do you want me to tell you? Do you want me to apologize for it?"

"No—gods, no. I just . . ." The words were coming out all wrong. "You know that when I went to those war camps, when I became general . . . I let the lines blur, too. But I was still in the North, still home, among our people. You came here instead, and had to grow up with those piece-of-shit men, and . . . I wish I'd been here. I wish Arobynn had somehow found me, too, and raised us together."

"You were older. You never would have let Arobynn take us. The moment he looked away, you would have grabbed me and run."

True—very true, but . . . "The person you were today, and a few years ago—that person had no joy, or love."

"Gods, I had *some*, Aedion. I wasn't a complete monster."

"Still, I just wanted you to know all that."

"That you feel guilty that I became an assassin while you endured the war camps and battlefields?"

"That I wasn't *there*. That you had to face those people alone." He added, "You came up with that whole plan by yourself and didn't trust any of us with it. You took on the burden of getting that money. I could have found a way—gods, I would have married whatever wealthy princess or empress you asked me to, if they promised men and money."

"I'm *never* going to sell you off like chattel," she snapped. "And we have enough now to pay for an army, don't we?"

"Yes." And then some. "But that's beside the point, Aelin." He took a breath. "The point is—I should have been there then, but I *am* here now. I'm healed. Let me share this burden."

She tipped her head back, savoring the breeze off the river. "And what could I ever ask of you that I couldn't do myself?"

"That's the problem. Yes, you can do most things on your own. That doesn't mean you have to."

"Why should I risk your life?" The words were clipped.

Ah. *Ah.* "Because I'm still more expendable than you are."

"Not to me." The words were barely more than a whisper.

Aedion put a hand on her back, his own reply clogged in his throat. Even with the world going to hell around them, just hearing her say that, standing here beside her—it was a dream.

She stayed silent, so he mastered himself enough to say, "What, exactly, are we going to do now?"

She glanced at him. "I'm going to free magic, take down the king, and kill Dorian. The order of the last two items on that list could be flipped, depending on how it all goes."

His heart stopped. "What?"

"Was something about that not clear?"

All of it. Every damn part of it. He had no doubt she would do it— even the part about killing her friend. If Aedion objected, she'd only lie and cheat and trick him.

"What and when and *how*?" he asked.

"Rowan's working on the first leg of it."

"That sounds a lot like, 'I have more secrets that I'm going to spring on you whenever I feel like stopping your heart dead in your chest.'"

But her answering smile told him he would get nowhere with her. He couldn't decide if it charmed or disappointed him.

Rowan was half-asleep in bed by the time Aelin returned hours later, murmuring good night to Aedion before slipping into her room. She didn't so much as glance in his direction as she began unbuckling her weapons and piling them on the table before the unlit hearth.

Efficient, quick, quiet. Not a sound from her.

"I went hunting for Lorcan," he said. "I tracked his scent around the city, but didn't see him."

"Is he dead, then?" Another dagger clattered onto the table.

"The scent was fresh. Unless he died an hour ago, he's still very much alive."

"Good," she said simply as she walked into the open closet to change. Or just to avoid looking at him some more.

She emerged moments later in one of those flimsy little nightgowns, and all the thoughts went right out of his damn head. Well, apparently she'd been mortified by their earlier encounter—but not enough to wear something more matronly to bed.

The pink silk clung to her waist and slid over her hips as she approached the bed, revealing the glorious length of her bare legs, still lean and tan from all the time they'd spent outdoors this spring. A strip of pale yellow lace graced the plunging neckline, and he tried—gods damn him, he honestly tried—not to look at the smooth curve of her breasts as she bent to climb into bed.

He supposed any lick of self-consciousness had been flayed from her under the whips of Endovier. Even though he'd tattooed over the bulk of the scars on her back, their ridges remained. The nightmares, too—when she'd still startle awake and light a candle to drive away the blackness they'd shoved her into, the memory of the lightless pits they'd used for punishment. His Fireheart, shut in the dark.

He owed the overseers of Endovier a visit.

Aelin might have an inclination to punish anyone who'd hurt him, but she didn't seem to realize that he—and Aedion, too—might also have scores to settle on her behalf. And as an immortal, he had infinite patience where those monsters were concerned.

Her scent hit him as she unbound her hair and nestled into the pile of pillows. That scent had always struck him, had always been a call and a challenge. It had shaken him so thoroughly from centuries encased in ice that he'd hated her at first. And now . . . now that scent drove him out of his mind.

They were both really damn lucky that she currently couldn't shift into her Fae form and smell what was pounding through his blood. It had been hard enough to conceal it from her until now. Aedion's knowing looks told him enough about what her cousin had detected.

He'd seen her naked before—a few times. And gods, yes, there *had* been moments when he'd considered it, but he'd mastered himself. He'd learned to keep those useless thoughts on a short, short leash. Like that time she'd moaned at the breeze he sent her way on Beltane—the arch of her neck, the parting of that mouth of hers, the *sound* that came out of her—

She was now lying on her side, her back to him.

"About last night," he said through his teeth.

"It's fine. It was a mistake."

Look at me. Turn over and look *at me.*

But she remained with her back to him, the moonlight caressing the silk bunched over the dip of her waist, the slope of her hip.

His blood heated. "I didn't mean to—snap at you," he tried.

"I know you didn't." She tugged the blanket up as if she could feel the weight of his gaze lingering on that soft, inviting place between her neck and shoulder—one of the few places on her body that wasn't marked with scars or ink. "I don't even know what happened, but it's been a strange few days, so let's just chalk it up to that, all right? I need to sleep."

He debated telling her that it was *not* all right, but he said, "Fine."

Moments later, she was indeed asleep.

He rolled onto his back and stared up at the ceiling, tucking a hand beneath his head.

He needed to sort this out—needed to get her to just *look* at him again, so he could try to explain that he hadn't been prepared. Having her touch the tattoo that told the story of what he'd done and how he'd lost Lyria . . . He hadn't been ready for what he felt in that moment. The desire hadn't been what shook him at all. It was just . . . Aelin had driven him insane these past few weeks, and yet he hadn't considered what it would be like to have her look at him with interest.

It wasn't at all the way it had been with the lovers he'd taken in the past: even when he'd cared for them, he hadn't really *cared*. Being with them had never made him think of that flower market. Never made him remember that he was alive and touching another woman while Lyria— Lyria was dead. Slaughtered.

And Aelin . . . If he went down that road, and if something happened to her . . . His chest seized at the thought.

So he needed to sort it out—needed to sort himself out, too, no matter what he wanted from her.

Even if it was agony.

⁓

"This wig is horrible," Lysandra hissed, patting her head as she and Aelin elbowed their way into the packed bakery alongside a nicer stretch of the docks. "It won't stop itching."

"Quiet," Aelin hissed back. "You only have to wear it for another few minutes, not your whole damn life."

Lysandra opened her mouth to complain some more, but two gentlemen approached, boxes of baked goods in hand, and gave them appreciative nods. Both Lysandra and Aelin had dressed in their finest, frilliest dresses, no more than two wealthy women on an afternoon stroll through the city, monitored by two bodyguards each.

Rowan, Aedion, Nesryn, and Chaol were leaning against the wooden dock posts outside, discreetly watching them through the large glass window of the shop. They were clothed and hooded in black, wearing two separate coats of arms—both fake, acquired from Lysandra's stash for when she met with secretive clients.

"That one," Aelin said under her breath as they pushed through the lunchtime crowd, fixing her attention on the most harried-looking woman behind the counter. The best time to come here, Nesryn had said, was when the workers were too busy to really note their clientele and would want them out of the way as quickly as possible. A few gentlemen parted to let them pass, and Lysandra cooed her thanks.

Aelin caught the eye of the woman behind the counter.

"What can I get you, miss?" Polite, but already sizing up the customers clustering behind Lysandra.

"I want to talk to Nelly," Aelin said. "She was to make me a brambleberry pie."

The woman narrowed her eyes. Aelin flashed a winning smile.

The woman sighed and hustled through the wooden door, allowing a glimpse of the chaos of the bakery behind it. A moment later she came back out, giving Aelin a *She'll be out in a minute* look and going right to another customer.

Fine.

Aelin leaned against one of the walls and crossed her arms. Then she lowered them. A lady didn't loiter.

"So Clarisse has no idea?" Aelin said under her breath, watching the bakery door.

"None," Lysandra said. "And any tears she shed were for her own losses. You should have seen her raging when we got into the carriage with those few coins. You're not frightened of having a target on your back?"

"I've had a target on my back since the day I was born," Aelin said. "But I'll be gone soon enough, and I'll never be Celaena again, anyway."

Lysandra let out a little hum. "You know I could have done this for you on my own."

"Yes, but two ladies asking questions are less suspicious than one." Lysandra gave her a knowing look. Aelin sighed. "It's hard," she admitted. "To let go of the control."

"I wouldn't know."

"Well, you're close to paying off your debts, aren't you? You'll be free soon."

A casual shrug. "Not likely. Clarisse increased all of our debts since she got shut out of Arobynn's will. It seems she made some advance purchases and now has to pay for them."

Gods—she hadn't even considered that. Hadn't even *thought* about what it might mean for Lysandra and the other girls. "I'm sorry for any extra burden it's caused you."

"To have seen the look on Clarisse's face when the will was read, I'll gladly endure another few years of this."

A lie, and they both knew it. "I'm sorry," Aelin said again. And because it was all she could offer, she added, "Evangeline looked well and happy just now. I could see if there was a way to take her when we go—"

"And drag an eleven-year-old girl across kingdoms and into a potential war? I think not. Evangeline will remain with me. You don't need to make me promises."

"How are you feeling?" Aelin asked. "After the other night."

Lysandra watched three young women giggle to one another as they passed a handsome young man. "Fine. I can't quite believe I got away with it, but . . . We both pulled it off, I suppose."

"Do you regret doing it?"

"No. I regret . . . I regret that I didn't get to tell him what I really thought of him. I regret that I didn't tell him what I'd done with you—to see the betrayal and shock in his eyes. I did it so fast, and had to go for the throat, and after I did, I just rolled over and listened—until it was done, but . . ." Her green eyes were shadowed. "Do you wish you had been the one to do it?"

"No."

And that was that.

She glanced at her friend's saffron-and-emerald gown. "That dress suits you." She jerked her chin toward Lysandra's chest. "And does wonders for them, too. The poor men in here can't stop looking."

"Trust me, having larger ones isn't a blessing. My back hurts all the time." Lysandra frowned down at her full breasts. "As soon as I get my powers back, these things will be the first to go."

Aelin chuckled. Lysandra would get her powers back—once that clock tower was gone. She tried not to let the thought sink in. "Really?"

"If it wasn't for Evangeline, I think I'd just turn into something with claws and fangs and live in the wilderness forever."

"No more luxury for you?"

Lysandra pulled a bit of lint off Aelin's sleeve. "Of course I like luxury—you think I don't love these gowns and jewels? But in the end . . . they're replaceable. I've come to value the people in my life more."

"Evangeline is lucky to have you."

"I wasn't just talking about her," Lysandra said, and she chewed on her full lip. "You—I'm grateful for you."

Aelin might have said something back, something to adequately convey the flicker of warmth in her heart, had a slim, brown-haired woman not emerged from the kitchen door. Nelly.

Aelin pushed off the wall and flounced up to the counter, Lysandra in tow. Nelly said, "You came to see me about a pie?"

Lysandra smiled prettily, leaning close. "Our supplier of pies, it seems, vanished with the Shadow Market." She spoke so softly that even Aelin could barely hear. "Rumor has it you know where he is."

Nelly's blue eyes shuttered. "Don't know anything about that."

Aelin delicately placed her purse on the counter, leaning in so that the other customers and workers couldn't see as she slid it toward Nelly, making sure the coins clinked. Heavy coins. "We are very, very hungry for . . . pie," Aelin said, letting some desperation show. "Just tell us where he went."

"No one escaped the Shadow Market alive."

Good. Just as Nesryn had assured them, Nelly didn't talk easily. It would be too suspicious for Nesryn to ask Nelly about the opium dealer, but two vapid, spoiled rich women? No one would think twice.

Lysandra set another coin purse on the counter. One of the other workers glanced their way, and the courtesan said, "We'd like to place an order." The worker focused on her customer again, unfazed. Lysandra's smile turned feline. "So tell us where to pick it up, Nelly."

Someone barked Nelly's name from the back, and Nelly glanced between them, sighing. She leaned forward and whispered, "They got out through the sewers."

"We heard guards were down there, too," Aelin said.

"Not down far enough. A few went to the catacombs beneath. Still hiding out down there. Bring your guards, but don't let 'em wear their sigils. Not a place for rich folk."

Catacombs. Aelin had never heard of catacombs *beneath* the sewers. Interesting.

Nelly withdrew, striding back into the bakery. Aelin looked down at the counter.

Both bags of coins were gone.

They slipped out of the bakery unnoticed and fell into step with their four bodyguards.

"Well?" Nesryn murmured. "Was I right?"

"Your father should fire Nelly," Aelin said. "Opium addicts are piss-poor employees."

"She makes good bread," Nesryn said, and then fell back to where Chaol was walking behind them.

"What'd you learn?" Aedion demanded. "And do you care to explain *why* you needed to know about the Shadow Market?"

"Patience," Aelin said. She turned to Lysandra. "You know, I bet the men around here would cut out their snarling if you turned into a ghost leopard and snarled back at them."

Lysandra's brows rose. "Ghost leopard?"

Aedion swore. "Do me a favor and never turn into one of those."

"What are they?" Lysandra said. Rowan chuckled under his breath and stepped a bit closer to Aelin. She tried to ignore it. They'd barely spoken all morning.

Aedion shook his head. "Devils cloaked in fur. They live up in the Staghorns, and during the winter they creep down to prey on livestock. As big as bears, some of them. Meaner. And when the livestock runs out, they prey on us."

Aelin patted Lysandra's shoulder. "Sounds like your kind of creature."

Aedion went on, "They're white and gray, so you can barely make them out against the snow and rock. You can't really tell they're on you until you're staring right into their pale green eyes . . ." His smile faltered as Lysandra fixed *her* green eyes on him and cocked her head.

Despite herself, Aelin laughed.

"Tell us why we're here," Chaol said as Aelin climbed over a fallen wooden beam in the abandoned Shadow Market. Beside her, Rowan held a torch high, illuminating the ruins—and the charred bodies. Lysandra had gone back to the brothel, escorted by Nesryn; Aelin had swiftly changed into her suit in an alley, and stashed her gown behind a discarded crate, praying no one snatched it before she could return.

"Just be quiet for a moment," Aelin said, tracing the tunnels by memory.

Rowan shot her a glance, and she lifted a brow. *What?*

"You've come here before," Rowan said. "You came to search the ruins." *That's why you smelled of ash, too.*

Aedion said, "Really, Aelin? Don't you ever sleep?"

Chaol was watching her now, too, though maybe that was to avoid looking at the bodies littered around the halls. "What *were* you doing here the night you interrupted my meeting with Brullo and Ress?"

Aelin studied the cinders of the oldest stalls, the soot stains, the smells. She paused before one shop whose wares were now nothing but ash and twisted bits of metal. "Here we are," she trilled, and strode into the hewn-rock stall, its stones burned black.

"It still smells like opium," Rowan said, frowning. Aelin brushed her foot over the ashy ground, kicking away cinders and debris. It had to be somewhere—ah.

She swept away more and more, the ash staining her black boots and suit. At last a large, misshapen stone appeared beneath her feet, a worn hole near its edge.

She said casually, "Did you know that in addition to dealing opium, this man was rumored to sell hellfire?"

Rowan whipped his gaze to her.

Hellfire—nearly impossible to attain or make, mostly because it was so lethal. Just a vat of it could take out half of a castle's retainer wall.

"He would never talk to me about it, of course," Aelin went on, "no matter how many times I came here. He claimed he didn't have it, yet he had some of the ingredients around the shop—all very rare—so . . . There must have been a supply of it here."

She hauled open the stone trapdoor to reveal a ladder descending into the gloom. None of the males spoke as the reek of the sewers unfurled.

She crouched, sliding onto the first rung, and Aedion tensed, but he wisely said nothing about her going first.

Smoke-scented darkness enveloped her as she climbed down, down, down, until her feet hit smooth rock. The air was dry, despite their proximity to the river. Rowan came next, dropping his torch onto the ancient stones to reveal a cavernous tunnel—and bodies.

Several bodies, some of them nothing but dark mounds in the distance, cut down by the Valg. There were fewer to the right, toward the Avery.

They'd probably anticipated an ambush at the river mouth and gone the other way—to their doom.

Not waiting for Aedion or Chaol to climb down, Aelin began following the tunnel, Rowan silent as a shadow at her side—looking, listening. After the stone door groaned closed above, she said into the darkness, "When the king's men set this place alight, if the fire had hit that supply . . . Rifthold probably wouldn't be here anymore. At least not the slums, and probably more."

"Gods above," Chaol murmured from a few paces behind.

Aelin paused at what looked like an ordinary grate in the sewer floor. But no water ran beneath, and only dusty air floated up to meet her.

"That's how you're planning to blow up the clock tower—with hellfire," Rowan said, crouching at her side. He made to grab her elbow as she reached for the grate, but she sidled out of range. "Aelin—I've seen it used, seen it wreck cities. It can literally *melt* people."

"Good. So we know it works, then."

Aedion snorted, peering down into the gloom beyond the grate. "So what? You think he kept his supply down there?" If he had a professional opinion about hellfire, he kept it to himself.

"These sewers were too public, but he had to keep it near the market," Aelin said, yanking on the grate. It gave a little, and Rowan's scent caressed her as he leaned to help haul it off the opening.

"It smells like bones and dust down there," Rowan said. His mouth quirked to the side. "But you suspected that already."

Chaol said from a few feet behind, "That's what you wanted to know from Nelly—where he was hiding. So he can sell it to you."

Aelin lit a bit of wood from Rowan's torch. She carefully poised it just beneath the lip of the hole before her, the flame lighting a drop of about ten feet, with cobblestones beneath.

A wind pushed from behind, toward the hole. Into it.

She set aside the flame and sat on the lip of the hole, her legs swinging in the dimness beneath. "What Nelly doesn't know yet is that the opium monger was actually caught two days ago. Killed on sight by the king's men. You know, I do think Arobynn sometimes had no idea whether he really wanted to help me or not." It had been his casual mention of it at dinner that had set her thinking, planning.

Rowan murmured, "So his supply in the catacombs is now unguarded."

She peered into the gloom below. "Finders keepers," she said, and jumped.

CHAPTER 50

"How did those lowlifes keep this place a secret?" Aelin breathed as she turned to Chaol.

The four of them stood atop a small staircase, the cavernous space beyond them illuminated in flickering gold by the torches Aedion and Rowan bore.

Chaol was shaking his head, surveying the space. Not a sign of scavengers, thank the gods. "Legend has it that the Shadow Market was built on the bones of the god of truth."

"Well, they got the bones part right."

In every wall, skulls and bones were artfully arranged—and every wall, even the ceiling, had been formed from them. Even the floor at the foot of the stairs was laid with bones of varying shapes and sizes.

"These aren't ordinary catacombs," Rowan said, setting down his torch. "This was a temple."

Indeed, altars, benches, and even a dark reflection pool lay in the massive space. Still more sprawled away into shadow.

"There's writing on the bones," Aedion said, striding down the steps and onto the bone floor. Aelin grimaced.

"Careful," Rowan said as Aedion went to the nearest wall. Her cousin lifted a hand in lazy dismissal.

"It's in every language—all in different handwriting," Aedion marveled, holding his torch aloft as he moved along the wall. "Listen to this one here: 'I am a liar. I am a thief. I took my sister's husband and laughed while I did it.'" A pause. He silently read another. "None of this writing . . . I don't think these were good people."

Aelin scanned the bone temple. "We should be quick," she said. "Really damn quick. Aedion, you take that wall; Chaol, the center; Rowan, the right. I'll grab the back. Careful of where you wave your fire." Gods help them if they unwittingly placed a torch near the hellfire.

She took a step down, and then another. Then the last one, onto the bone floor.

A shudder crawled through her, and she glanced at Rowan out of instinct. His tight face told her all she needed to know. But he still said, "This is a bad place."

Chaol strode past them, his sword out. "Then let's find this hellfire supply and get out."

Right.

All around them, the empty eyes of the skulls in the walls, in the structures, the pillars in the center of the room, seemed to watch.

"Seems like this god of truth," Aedion called from his wall, "was more of a Sin-Eater than anything. You should read some of the things people wrote—the horrible things they did. I think this was a place for them to be buried, and to confess on the bones of other sinners."

"No wonder no one wanted to come here," Aelin muttered as she strode off into the dark.

The temple went on and on, and they found supplies—but no whisper of scavengers or other residents. Drugs, money, jewelry, all hidden inside skulls and within some of the bone crypts on the floor. But no hellfire.

Their cautious steps on the bone floor were the only sounds.

Aelin moved deeper and deeper into the gloom. Rowan soon cleared his side of the temple and joined her in the back, exploring the alcoves and little hallways that branched off into the slumbering dark. "The language," Aelin said to him. "It gets older and older the farther back we go. The way they spell the words, I mean."

Rowan twisted toward her from where he'd been carefully opening a sarcophagus. She doubted an ordinary man would be able to shift the stone lid. "Some of them even date their confessions. I just saw one from seven hundred years ago."

"Makes you seem young, doesn't it?"

He gave her a wry smile. She quickly looked away.

The bone floor clicked as he stepped toward her. "Aelin."

She swallowed hard, staring at a carved bone near her head. *I killed a man for sport when I was twenty and never told anyone where I buried him. I kept his finger bone in a drawer.*

Dated nine hundred years ago.

Nine hundred—

Aelin studied the darkness beyond. If the Shadow Market dated back to Gavin, then this place had to have been built before it—or around the same time.

The god of truth . . .

She drew Damaris from across her back, and Rowan tensed. "What is it?"

She examined the flawless blade. "The Sword of Truth. That's what they called Damaris. Legend said the bearer—Gavin—could see the truth when he wielded it."

"And?"

"Mala blessed Brannon, and she blessed Goldryn." She peered into the gloom. "What if there was a god of truth—a Sin-Eater? What if he blessed Gavin, and this sword?"

Rowan now stared toward the ancient blackness. "You think Gavin used this temple."

Aelin weighed the mighty sword in her hands. "What sins did you confess to, Gavin?" she whispered into the dark.

Deep into the tunnels they went, so far that when Aedion's triumphant cry of "Found it!" reached Aelin and Rowan, she could barely hear it. And barely cared.

Not when she stood before the back wall—the wall behind the altar of what had no doubt been the original temple. Here the bones were nearly crumbling with age, the writing almost impossible to read.

The wall behind the altar was of pure stone—white marble—and carved in Wyrdmarks.

And in the center was a giant rendering of the Eye of Elena.

Cold. It was so cold in here that their breath clouded in front of them, mingling.

"Whoever this god of truth was," Rowan murmured, as if trying not to be overheard by the dead, "he was not a benevolent sort of deity."

No; with a temple built from the bones of murderers and thieves and worse, she doubted this god had been a particular favorite. No wonder he'd been forgotten.

Aelin stepped up to the stone.

Damaris turned icy in her hand—so frigid her fingers splayed, and she dropped the sword on the altar floor and backed away. Its clang against the bones was like thunder.

Rowan was instantly at her side, his swords out.

The stone wall before them groaned.

It began shifting, the symbols rotating, altering themselves. From the flicker of her memory she heard the words: *It is only with the Eye that one can see rightly.*

"Honestly," Aelin said as the wall at last stopped rearranging itself from the proximity of the sword. A new, intricate array of Wyrdmarks had formed. "I don't know why these coincidences keep surprising me."

"Can you read it?" Rowan asked. Aedion called their names, and Rowan called back, telling them both to come.

Aelin stared up at the carvings. "It might take me some time."

"Do it. I don't think it was chance that we found this place."

Aelin shook off her shiver. No—nothing was ever chance. Not when it came to Elena and the Wyrdkeys. So she loosed a breath and began.

"It's . . . it's about Elena and Gavin," she said. "The first panel here"—she pointed to a stretch of symbols—"describes them as the first King and Queen of Adarlan, how they were mated. Then . . . then it jumps back. To the war."

Footsteps sounded and light flickered as Aedion and Chaol reached them. Chaol whistled.

"I have a bad feeling about this," Aedion said. He frowned at the giant rendering of the Eye, and then at the one around Aelin's neck.

"Get comfortable," she said.

Aelin read a few more lines, deciphering and decoding. So hard—the Wyrdmarks were so damn hard to read. "It describes the demon wars with the Valg that had been left here after the First War. And . . ." She read the line again. "And the Valg this time were led . . ." Her blood chilled. "By one of the three kings—the king who remained trapped here after the gate was sealed. It says that to look upon a king—to look upon a Valg king was to gaze into . . ." She shook her head. "Madness? Despair? I don't know that symbol. He could take any form, but he appeared to them now as a handsome man with golden eyes. The eyes of the Valg kings."

She scanned the next panel. "They did not know his true name, so they called him Erawan, the Dark King."

Aedion said, "Then Elena and Gavin battled him, your magic necklace saved their asses, and Elena called him by his true name, distracting him enough for Gavin to slay him."

"Yes, yes," Aelin said, waving a hand. "But—no."

"No?" Chaol said.

Aelin read further, and her heart skipped a beat. "What is it?" Rowan demanded, as if his Fae ears had noted her heart's stutter.

She swallowed hard, running a shaking finger under a line of symbols. "This . . . this is Gavin's confessional. From his deathbed."

None of them spoke.

Her voice trembled as she said, "They did not slay him. Not by sword, or fire, or water, or might could Erawan be slain or his body be destroyed. The Eye . . ." Aelin touched her hand to the necklace; the metal was warm. "The Eye contained him. Only for a short time. No—not contained. But . . . put him to sleep?"

"I have a very, *very* bad feeling about this," Aedion said.

"So they built him a sarcophagus of iron and some sort of indestructible stone. And they put it in a sealed tomb beneath a mountain—a crypt so dark . . . so dark that there was no air, no light. Upon the labyrinth of doors," she read, "they put symbols, unbreakable by any thief or key or force."

"You're saying that they never killed Erawan," Chaol said.

Gavin had been Dorian's childhood hero, she recalled. And the story had been a lie. *Elena* had lied to her—

"Where did they bury him?" Rowan asked softly.

"They buried him . . ." Her hands shook so badly that she lowered them to her sides. "They buried him in the Black Mountains, and built a keep atop the tomb, so that the noble family who dwelled above might forever guard it."

"There are no Black Mountains in Adarlan," Chaol said.

Aelin's mouth went dry. "Rowan," she said quietly. "How do you say 'Black Mountains' in the Old Language?"

A pause, and then a loosened breath.

"Morath," Rowan said.

She turned to them, her eyes wide. For a moment, they all just stared at one another.

"What are the odds," she said, "that the king is sending his forces down to Morath by mere coincidence?"

"What are the odds," Aedion countered, "that our illustrious king has acquired a key that can unlock any door—even a door between worlds—and his second in command happens to own the very place where Erawan is buried?"

"The king is insane," Chaol said. "If he plans to raise Erawan—"

"Who says he hasn't already?" Aedion asked.

Aelin glanced at Rowan. His face was grim. *If there is a Valg king in this world, we need to move fast. Get those Wyrdkeys and banish them all back to their hellhole.*

She nodded. "Why now, though? He's had the two keys for at least a decade. Why bring the Valg over now?"

"It would make sense," Chaol said, "if he's doing it in anticipation of raising Erawan again. To have an army ready for him to lead."

Aelin's breathing was shallow. "The summer solstice is in ten days. If we bring magic down on the solstice, when the sun is strongest, there's a good chance my power will be greater then, too." She turned to Aedion. "Tell me you found a lot of hellfire."

His nod wasn't as reassuring as she'd hoped.

CHAPTER 51

Manon and her Thirteen stood around a table in a room deep within the witches' barracks.

"You know why I called you here," Manon said. None of them replied; none of them sat. They'd barely spoken to her since butchering that tribe in the White Fangs. And then today—more news. More requests.

"The duke asked me to pick another coven to use. A Blackbeak coven." Silence.

"I'd like your suggestions."

They didn't meet her eyes. Didn't utter a word.

Manon snapped down her iron teeth. *"You would dare defy me?"*

Sorrel cleared her throat, attention on the table. "Never you, Manon. But we defy that human worm's right to use our bodies as if they were his own."

"Your High Witch has given orders that will be *obeyed*."

"You might as well name the Thirteen," Asterin said, the only one of them holding Manon's gaze. Her nose was still swollen and bruised from the beating. "For we would sooner that be our fate than hand over our sisters."

"And you all agree with this? That you wish to breed demon offspring until your bodies break apart?"

"We are Blackbeaks," Asterin said, her chin high. "We are no one's slaves, and will not be used as such. If the price for that is never returning to the Wastes, then so be it."

None of the others so much as flinched. They'd all met—they'd discussed this beforehand. What to say to her.

As if she were in need of managing.

"Was there anything else you all decided in your little council meeting?"

"There are . . . things, Manon," Sorrel said. "Things you need to hear."

Betrayal—this was what mortals called betrayal.

"I don't give a shit about what you fools dared believe I *need* to hear. The only thing I need to hear is the sound of you saying *Yes, Wing Leader.* And the name of a *gods-damned coven.*"

"Pick one yourself," Asterin snapped.

The witches shifted. Not a part of the plan, was it?

Manon stalked around the table to Asterin, past the other witches who didn't dare turn to face her. "You have been nothing but a waste from the minute you set foot in this Keep. I don't care if you have flown at my side for a century—I am going to put you down like the yapping dog you are—"

"Do it," Asterin hissed. "*Rip my throat out.* Your grandmother will be so proud that you finally did."

Sorrel was at Manon's back.

"Is that a challenge?" Manon said too quietly.

Asterin's gold-flecked black eyes danced. "It's a—"

But the door opened and shut.

A young man with golden hair now stood in the room, his black stone collar gleaming in the torchlight.

He shouldn't have gotten in.

There had been witches everywhere, and she'd set sentinels from another coven to guard the halls so that none of the duke's men could catch them unawares.

As one, the Thirteen turned toward the handsome young man.

And as one, they flinched as he smiled, and a wave of darkness crashed into them.

Darkness without end, darkness even Manon's eyes couldn't penetrate, and—

And Manon was again standing before that Crochan witch, a dagger in her hand.

"We pity you . . . for what you do to your children . . . You force them to kill and hurt and hate until there is nothing left inside of them—of you. That is why you are here," the Crochan wept . . . *"Because of the threat you posed to the monster you call grandmother when you chose mercy and you saved your rival's life."*

Manon violently shook her head, blinking. Then it was gone. There was only darkness, and the Thirteen, shouting to one another, struggling, and—

A golden-haired young man had been in that room with the Yellowlegs, Elide had said.

Manon started prowling through the darkness, navigating the room by memory and smell. Some of her Thirteen were nearby; some had backed against the walls. And the otherworldly reek of the man, of the demon inside him—

The smell wrapped around her fully, and Manon drew Wind-Cleaver.

Then there he was, chuckling as someone—Ghislaine—started screaming. Manon had never heard that sound. She'd never heard any of them scream with . . . with fear. And pain.

Manon hurtled into a blind sprint and tackled him to the ground. No sword—she didn't want a sword for this execution.

Light cracked around her, and there was his handsome face, and that collar. "Wing Leader," he grinned, in a voice that was not from this world.

Manon's hands were around his throat, squeezing, her nails ripping through his skin.

"Were you sent here?" she demanded.

Her eyes met his—and the ancient malice in them shrank back. "Get away," he hissed.

Manon did no such thing. *"Were you sent here?"* she roared.

The young man surged up, but then Asterin was there, pinning his legs. "Make him bleed," she said from behind Manon.

The creature continued thrashing. And in the darkness, some of the Thirteen were still shouting in agony and terror. *"Who sent you?"* Manon bellowed.

His eyes shifted—turning blue, turning clear. It was with a young man's voice that he said, "Kill me. Please—please kill me. Roland—my name was Roland. Tell my—"

Then blackness spread across his eyes again, along with pure panic at whatever he beheld in Manon's face, and in Asterin's over her shoulder. The demon inside the man shrieked: *"Get away!"*

She'd heard and seen enough. Manon squeezed harder, her iron nails shredding through mortal flesh and muscle. Black, reeking blood coated her hand, and she ripped harder into him, until she got to the bone and slashed through it, and his head thumped against the floor.

Manon could have sworn he sighed.

The darkness vanished, and Manon was instantly on her feet, gore dripping from her hands as she surveyed the damage.

Ghislaine sobbed in the corner, all the color leeched from her rich, dark skin. Thea and Kaya were both tearstained and silent, the two lovers gaping at each other. And Edda and Briar, both of her Shadows, both born and raised in darkness . . . they were on their hands and knees, puking. Right alongside the green-eyed demon twins, Faline and Fallon.

The rest of the Thirteen were unharmed. Still flush with color, some panting from the momentary surge of rage and energy, but . . . Fine.

Had only some of them been targeted?

Manon looked at Asterin—at Sorrel, and Vesta, and Lin, and Imogen. Then at the ones that had been drained.

They all met her gaze this time.

Get away, the demon had screamed—as if in surprise and terror.

After looking her in the eyes.

Those who had been affected . . . their eyes were ordinary colors. Brown and blue and green. But the ones who hadn't . . .

Black eyes, flecked with gold.

And when he'd looked at Manon's eyes . . .

Gold eyes had always been prized among Blackbeaks. She'd never wondered why.

But now wasn't the time. Not with this reeking blood soaking into her skin.

"This was a reminder," Manon said, her voice bouncing hollowly off the stones. She turned from the room. Leave them to each other. "Get rid of that body."

⁓

Manon waited until Kaltain was alone, drifting up one of the forgotten spiraling staircases of Morath, before she pounced.

The woman didn't flinch as Manon pinned her against the wall, her iron nails digging into Kaltain's pale, bare shoulders. "Where does the shadowfire come from?"

Dark, empty eyes met hers. "From me."

"Why you? What magic is it? Valg power?"

Manon studied the collar around the woman's thin throat.

Kaltain gave a small, dead smile. "It was mine—to start. Then it was . . . melded with another source. And now it is the power of every world, every life."

Nonsense. Manon pushed her harder into the dark stone. "How do you take that collar off?"

"It does not come off."

Manon bared her teeth. "And what do you want with us? To put collars on us?"

"They want kings," Kaltain breathed, her eyes flickering with some strange, sick delight. "Mighty kings. Not you."

More drivel. Manon growled—but then there was a delicate hand on her wrist.

And it burned.

Oh, *gods*, it burned, and her bones were melting, her iron nails had become molten ore, her blood was boiling—

Manon leaped back from Kaltain, and only gripping her wrist told her that the injuries weren't real. "I'm going to kill you," Manon hissed.

But shadowfire danced on Kaltain's fingertips even as the woman's face went blank again. Without a word, as if she had done nothing, Kaltain walked up the stairs and vanished.

Alone in the stairwell, Manon cradled her arm, the echo of pain still reverberating through her bones. Slaughtering that tribe with Wind-Cleaver, she told herself, had been a mercy.

CHAPTER 52

As they left the Sin-Eater's temple, Chaol marveled at how strange it was to be working with Aelin and her court. How strange it was to not be fighting her for once.

He shouldn't have even gone with them, given how much there was to do. Half the rebels had left Rifthold, more fleeing every day, and those who remained were pushing to relocate to another city. He'd kept them in line as much as he could, relying on Nesryn to back him up whenever they started to bring up his own past with the king. There were still people going missing, being executed—still people whom they rescued as often as they could from the butchering blocks. He would keep doing it until he was the last rebel left in this city; he would stay to help them, to protect them. But if what they'd learned about Erawan was true . . .

Gods help them all.

Back on the city street, he turned in time to see Rowan offer a helping hand to pull Aelin out of the sewers. She seemed to hesitate, but then gripped it, her hand swallowed by his.

A team, solid and unbreaking.

The Fae Prince hoisted her up and set her on her feet. Neither of them immediately let go of the other.

Chaol waited—waited for that twist and tug of jealousy, for the bile of it to sting him.

But there was nothing. Only a flickering relief, perhaps, that . . .

That Aelin had Rowan.

He must be feeling truly sorry for himself, he decided.

Footsteps sounded, and they all went still, weapons drawn, just as—

"I've been looking for you for an hour," Nesryn said, hurrying out of the alley shadows. "What's—" She noticed their grim faces. They'd left the hellfire down there, hidden in a sarcophagus, for safekeeping—and to keep themselves from being melted should things go very wrong.

He was surprised Aelin had let him know that much—though *how* she planned to get into the castle, she hadn't told him.

Just tell Ress and Brullo and the others to stay the hell away from the clock tower was her only warning so far. He'd almost demanded to know what her plans were for the other innocents in the castle, but . . . It had been nice. To have one afternoon with no fighting, with no one hating him. To feel like he was part of their unit.

"I'll fill you in later," Chaol said to her. But Nesryn's face was pale. "What is it?"

Aelin, Rowan, and Aedion stalked up to them with that unnatural, immortal silence.

Nesryn squared her shoulders. "I received word from Ren. He got into some minor trouble on the border, but he's fine. He has a message for you—for us." She brushed back a strand of her inky hair. Her hand trembled slightly.

Chaol braced himself, fought against the urge to put a hand on her arm. "The king," Nesryn went on, "has been building an army down in Morath, under Duke Perrington's supervision. The Valg guards around Rifthold are the first of them. More are coming up this way."

Valg footsoldiers, then. Morath, it seemed, might very well be their first or last battleground.

Aedion cocked his head, the Wolf incarnate. "How many?"

"Too many," Nesryn said. "We haven't gotten a full count. Some are camped inside mountains surrounding the war camp—never out all at once, never in full sight. But it's an army greater than any he's assembled before."

Chaol's palms became slick with sweat.

"And more than that," Nesryn said, her voice hoarse, "the king now has an aerial cavalry of Ironteeth witches—a host three thousand strong—who have been secretly training in the Ferian Gap to ride wyverns that the king has somehow managed to create and breed."

Gods above.

Aelin lifted her head, gazing up at the brick wall as if she could see that aerial army there, the movement revealing the ring of scars around her neck.

Dorian—they needed Dorian on the throne. Needed this shut down.

"You are certain of this?" Aedion said.

Rowan was staring at Nesryn, his face the portrait of a cold, calculating warrior, and yet—yet he'd somehow moved closer to Aelin.

Nesryn said tightly, "We lost many spies to attain that information."

Chaol wondered which of them had been her friends.

Aelin spoke, her voice flat and hard. "Just to make sure I have it right: we are now facing three thousand bloodthirsty Ironteeth witches on wyverns. And a host of deadly soldiers gathering in the south of Adarlan, likely to cut off any alliance between Terrasen and the southern kingdoms."

Leaving Terrasen stranded. *Say it*, Chaol silently beseeched her. *Say that you need Dorian—free and alive.*

Aedion mused, "Melisande might be capable of uniting with us." He pinned Chaol with an assessing stare—a general's stare. "Do you think your father knows about the wyverns and witches? Anielle is the closest city to the Ferian Gap."

His blood chilled. Was that why his father had been so keen to get him home? He sensed Aedion's next question before the general spoke. "He doesn't wear a black ring," Chaol said. "But I doubt you'd find him a pleasant ally—if he bothered to ally with you at all."

"Things to consider," Rowan said, "should we need an ally to punch through the southern lines." Gods, they were actually talking about this. War—war was coming. And they might not all survive it.

"So what are they waiting for?" Aedion said, pacing. "Why not attack now?"

Aelin's voice was soft—cold. "Me. They're waiting for me to make my move."

None of them contradicted her.

Chaol's voice was strained as he shoved aside his swarming thoughts. "Anything else?"

Nesryn reached into her tunic and pulled out a letter. She handed it to Aedion. "From your second in command. They all worry for you."

"There's a tavern down the block. Give me five minutes, and I'll have a reply for you," Aedion said, already striding away. Nesryn followed him, giving Chaol a silent nod. The general said over his shoulder to Rowan and Aelin, his heavy hood concealing any telltale features, "I'll see you at home."

Meeting over.

But Aelin suddenly said, "Thank you."

Nesryn paused, somehow knowing the queen had spoken to her.

Aelin put a hand on her heart. "For all that you're risking—thank you."

Nesryn's eyes flickered as she said, "Long live the queen."

But Aelin had already turned away.

Nesryn met Chaol's gaze, and he followed after her and Aedion.

An indestructible army, possibly led by Erawan, if the King of Adarlan were insane enough to raise him.

An army that could crush any human resistance.

But . . . but maybe not if they allied with magic-wielders.

That is, if the magic-wielders, after all that had been done to them, even wanted to bother saving their world.

⁓

"Talk to me," Rowan said from behind her as Aelin stormed down street after street.

She couldn't. She couldn't form the thoughts, let alone the words.

How many spies and rebels had lost their lives to get that information? And how much worse would it feel when *she* sent people to their deaths— when she had to watch her soldiers butchered by those monsters? If Elena had thrown her a bone tonight, somehow leading that opium monger to the Sin-Eater's temple so that they might find it, she wasn't feeling particularly grateful.

"Aelin," Rowan said, quietly enough for only her and the alley rats to hear.

She'd barely survived Baba Yellowlegs. How would *anyone* survive an army of witches trained in combat?

He gripped her elbow, forcing her to stop. "We'll face this together," he breathed, his eyes shining bright and canines gleaming. "As we have in the past. To whatever end."

She trembled—trembled like a gods-damned coward—and yanked free, stalking away. She didn't even know where she was going—only that she had to walk, had to find a way to sort herself out, sort the world out, before she stopped moving, or else she would never move again.

Wyverns. Witches. A new, even bigger army. The alley pressed in on her, sealing as tightly as one of those flooded sewer tunnels.

"Talk to me," Rowan said again, keeping a respectful distance behind.

She knew these streets. A few blocks down, she would find one of the Valg sewer entrances. Maybe she'd jump right in and hack a few of them to pieces. See what they knew about the Dark King Erawan, and whether he was still slumbering under that mountain.

Maybe she wouldn't bother with questions at all.

There was a strong, broad hand at her elbow, yanking her back against a hard male body.

But the scent wasn't Rowan's.

And the knife at her throat, the blade pressing so hard that her skin stung and split . . .

"Going somewhere, Princess?" Lorcan breathed into her ear.

Rowan had thought he knew fear. He had thought he could face any danger with a clear head and ice in his veins.

Until Lorcan appeared from the shadows, so fast that Rowan hadn't even scented him, and put that knife against Aelin's throat.

"You move," Lorcan snarled in Aelin's ear, "and you die. You speak, and you die. Understand?"

Aelin said nothing. If she nodded, she'd slice her throat open on the blade. Blood was shining there already, just above her collarbone, filling the alley with its scent.

The smell of it alone sent Rowan sliding into a frozen, murderous calm.

"*Understand?*" Lorcan hissed, jostling her enough that her blood flowed a bit faster. Still she said nothing, obeying his order. Lorcan chuckled. "Good. I thought so."

The world slowed and spread around Rowan with sharp clarity, revealing every stone of the buildings and the street, and the refuse and rubbish around them. Anything to give him an advantage, to use as a weapon.

If he'd had his magic, he would have choked the air from Lorcan's lungs by now, would have shattered through Lorcan's own dark shields with half a thought. If he'd had his magic, he would have had a shield of their own around them from the start, so this ambush could never happen.

Aelin's eyes met his.

And fear—that was genuine fear shining there.

She knew she was in a compromised position. They both knew that no matter how fast he was, she was, Lorcan's slice would be faster.

Lorcan smiled at Rowan, his dark hood off for once. No doubt so that Rowan could see every bit of triumph in Lorcan's black eyes. "No words, Prince?"

"Why?" was all Rowan could ask. Every action, every possible plan still left him too far away. He wondered whether Lorcan realized that if he killed her, Lorcan himself would be next. Then Maeve. And maybe the world, for spite.

Lorcan craned his head to look at Aelin's face. Her eyes narrowed to slits. "Where is the Wyrdkey?"

Aelin tensed, and Rowan willed her not to speak, not to taunt Lorcan. "We don't have it," Rowan said. Rage—unending, cataclysmic rage—pounded through him.

Exactly what Lorcan wanted. Exactly how Rowan had witnessed the demi-Fae warrior manipulate their enemies for centuries. So Rowan locked that rage down. Tried to, at least.

"I could snap this neck of yours so easily," Lorcan said, grazing his nose against the side of her throat. Aelin went rigid. The possessiveness in that touch alone half blinded him with feral wrath. It was an effort to stifle it again as Lorcan murmured onto her skin, "You're so much better when you don't open that hideous mouth."

"We don't have the key," Rowan said again. He'd slaughter Lorcan in the way only immortals learned and liked to kill: slowly, viciously, creatively. Lorcan's suffering would be thorough.

"What if I told you we were working for the same side?" Lorcan said.

"I'd tell you that Maeve works for only one side: her own."

"Maeve didn't send me here."

Rowan could almost hear the words Aelin was struggling to keep in. *Liar. Piece-of-shit liar.*

"Then who did?" Rowan demanded.

"I left."

"If we're on the same side, then put your rutting knife down," Rowan growled.

Lorcan chuckled. "I don't want to hear the princess yapping. What I have to say applies to both of you." Rowan waited, taking every second to assess and reassess their surroundings, the odds. At last, Lorcan loosened the blade slightly. Blood slid down Aelin's neck, onto her suit. "You made the mistake of your short, pathetic mortal life when you gave Maeve that ring."

Through the lethal calm, Rowan felt the blood drain from his face.

"You should have known better," Lorcan said, still gripping Aelin around the waist. "You should have known she wasn't some sentimental fool, pining after her lost love. She had plenty of things from Athril— why would she want his ring? His ring, and not Goldryn?"

"Stop dancing around it and tell us what it is."

"But I'm having so much fun."

Rowan leashed his temper so hard that he choked on it.

"The ring," Lorcan said, "wasn't some family heirloom from Athril. She *killed* Athril. She wanted the keys, and the ring, and he refused, and she killed him. While they fought, Brannon stole them away, hiding the ring with Goldryn and bringing the keys here. Didn't you ever wonder why the ring was in that scabbard? A demon-hunting sword—and a ring to match."

"If Maeve wants to kill demons," Rowan said, "we won't complain."

"The ring doesn't kill them. It grants immunity from their power. A ring forged by Mala herself. The Valg could not harm Athril when he wore it."

Aelin's eyes widened even more, the scent of her fear shifting to something far deeper than dread of bodily harm.

"The bearer of that ring," Lorcan went on, smiling at the terror coating her smell, "need never fear being enslaved by Wyrdstone. You handed her your own immunity."

"That doesn't explain why you left."

Lorcan's face tightened. "She slaughtered her lover for the ring, for the keys. She will do far worse to attain them now that they are on the playing board again. And once she has them . . . My queen will make herself a god."

"So?" The knife remained too close to Aelin's neck to risk attacking.

"It will destroy her."

Rowan's rage stumbled. "You plan to get the keys—to keep them from her."

"I plan to destroy the keys. You give me your Wyrdkey," Lorcan said, opening the fist he'd held against Aelin's abdomen, "and I'll give you the ring."

Sure enough, in his hand shone a familiar gold ring.

"You shouldn't be alive," Rowan said. "If you had stolen the ring and fled, she would have killed you already." It was a trap. A pretty, clever trap.

"I move quickly."

Lorcan *had* been hauling ass out of Wendlyn. It didn't prove anything, though.

"The others—"

"None of them know. You think I trust them not to say anything?"

"The blood oath makes betrayal impossible."

"I'm doing this for *her* sake," Lorcan said. "I'm doing this because I do not wish to see my queen become a demon herself. I am obeying the oath in that regard."

Aelin was bristling now, and Lorcan closed his fingers around the ring again. "You're a fool, Rowan. You think only of the next few years, decades. What I am doing is for the sake of the centuries. For eternity. Maeve will send the others, you know. To hunt you. To kill you both. Let tonight be a reminder of your vulnerability. You will never know peace for a single moment. Not one. And even if we don't kill Aelin of the Wildfire . . . time will."

Rowan shut out the words.

Lorcan peered at Aelin, his black hair shifting with the movement. "Think it over, Princess. What is immunity worth in a world where your enemies are waiting to shackle you, where one slip could mean becoming their eternal slave?"

Aelin just bared her teeth.

Lorcan shoved her away, and Rowan was already moving, lunging for her.

She whirled, the built-in blades in her suit flashing free.

But Lorcan was gone.

After deciding that the slices on her neck were shallow and that she was in no danger of dying from them, Rowan didn't talk to her for the rest of the journey home.

If Lorcan was right . . . No, he wasn't right. He was a liar, and his bargain reeked of Maeve's tricks.

Aelin pressed a handkerchief to her neck as they walked, and by the time they reached the apartment, the wounds had clotted. Aedion, mercifully, was already in bed.

Rowan strode right into their bedroom.

She followed him in, but he reached the bathroom and quietly shut the door behind him.

Running water gurgled a heartbeat later. A bath.

He'd done a good job concealing it, and his rage had been . . . she'd never seen someone that wrathful. But she'd still seen the terror on his face. It had been enough to make her master her own fear as fire started crackling in her veins. And she'd tried—gods damn it, she'd tried—to find a way out of that hold, but Lorcan . . . Rowan had been right. Without her magic, she was no match for him.

He could have killed her.

All she had been able to think about, in spite of her kingdom, in spite of all she still had to do, was the fear in Rowan's eyes.

And that it would be a shame if he never knew . . . if she never told him . . .

Aelin cleaned her neck in the kitchen, washed the little bit of blood from her suit and hung it in the living room to dry, then pulled on one of Rowan's shirts and climbed into bed.

She barely heard any splashing. Maybe he was just lying in the tub, staring at nothing with that hollow expression he'd worn since Lorcan had removed the knife from her throat.

Minutes passed, and she shouted good night to Aedion, whose echoing good night rumbled through the walls.

Then the bathroom door opened, a veil of steam rippled out, and Rowan appeared, a towel slung low across his hips. She took in the muscled abdomen, the powerful shoulders, but—

But the emptiness in those eyes.

She patted the bed. "Come here."

He stood there, his eyes lingering on her scabbed neck.

"We both are experts at clamming up, so let's make an agreement to talk right now like even-tempered, reasonable people."

He didn't meet her gaze as he padded toward the bed and slumped down beside her, stretching out over the blankets. She didn't even reprimand him for getting the sheets wet—or mention that he could have taken half a minute to put on some clothes.

"Looks like our days of fun are over," she said, propping her head with a fist and staring down at him. He gazed blankly at the ceiling. "Witches, dark lords, Fae Queens . . . If we make it through this alive, I'm going to take a nice, long vacation."

His eyes were cold.

"Don't shut me out," she breathed.

"Never," he murmured. "That's not—" He rubbed his eyes with his thumb and forefinger. "I failed you tonight." His words were a whisper in the darkness.

"Rowan—"

"He got close enough to kill you. If it had been another enemy, they might have." The bed rumbled as he took a shuddering sigh and lowered his hand from his eyes. The raw emotion there made her bite her lip. Never—*never* did he let her see those things. "I failed you. I swore to protect you, and I failed tonight."

"Rowan, it's fine—"

"It's *not* fine." His hand was warm as it clamped on her shoulder. She let him turn her onto her back, and found him half on top of her as he peered into her face.

His body was a massive, solid force of nature above hers, but his eyes—the panic lingered. "I broke your trust."

"You did no such thing. Rowan, you told him you wouldn't hand over the key."

He sucked in a breath, his broad chest expanding. "I would have. Gods, Aelin—he had me, and he didn't even know it. He could have waited another minute and I would have told him, ring or no ring. Erawan, witches, the king, Maeve . . . I would face all of them. But losing you . . ." He bowed his head, his breath warming her mouth as he closed his eyes. "I failed you tonight," he murmured, his voice hoarse. "I'm sorry."

His pine-and-snow scent wrapped around her. She should move away, roll out of reach. *Don't touch me like that.*

Yet there he was, his hand a brand on her bare shoulder, his body nearly covering hers. "You have nothing to be sorry for," she whispered. "I trust you, Rowan."

He gave her a barely perceptible nod.

"I missed you," he said quietly, his gaze darting between her mouth and eyes. "When I was in Wendlyn. I lied when I said I didn't. From the moment you left, I missed you so much I went out of my mind. I was *glad* for the excuse to track Lorcan here, just to see you again. And tonight, when he had that knife at your throat . . ." The warmth of his callused finger bloomed through her as he traced a path over the cut on her neck. "I kept thinking about how you might never know that I missed you with only an ocean between us. But if it was death separating us . . . I would find you. I don't care how many rules it would break. Even if I had to get all three keys myself and open a gate, I would find you again. Always."

She blinked back the burning in her eyes as he reached between their bodies and took her hand, guiding it up to lay against his tattooed cheek.

It was an effort to remember how to breathe, to focus on anything but that smooth, warm skin. He didn't tear his eyes away from hers as she grazed her thumb along his sharp cheekbone. Savoring each stroke, she caressed his face, that tattoo, never breaking his stare, even as it stripped her naked.

I'm sorry, he still seemed to say.

She kept her stare locked on his as she let go of his face and slowly, making sure he understood every step of the way, tilted her head back until her throat was arched and bared before him.

"Aelin," he breathed. Not in reprimand or warning, but . . . a plea. It sounded like a plea. He lowered his head to her exposed neck and hovered a hair's breadth away.

She arched her neck farther, a silent invitation.

Rowan let out a soft groan and grazed his teeth against her skin.

One bite, one movement, was all it would take for him to rip out her throat.

His elongated canines slid along her flesh—gently, precisely. She clenched the sheets to keep from running her fingers down his bare back and drawing him closer.

He braced one hand beside her head, his fingers twining in her hair.

"No one else," she whispered. "I would never allow anyone else at my throat." Showing him was the only way he'd understand that trust, in a manner that only the predatory, Fae side of him would comprehend. "No one else," she said again.

He let out another low groan, answer and confirmation and request, and the rumble echoed inside her. Carefully, he closed his teeth over the spot where her lifeblood thrummed and pounded, his breath hot on her skin.

She shut her eyes, every sense narrowing on that sensation, on the teeth and mouth at her throat, on the powerful body trembling with restraint above hers. His tongue flicked against her skin.

She made a small noise that might have been a moan, or a word, or his name. He shuddered and pulled back, the cool air kissing her neck. Wildness—pure wildness sparked in those eyes.

Then he thoroughly, brazenly surveyed her body, his nostrils flaring delicately as he scented exactly what she wanted.

Her breathing turned ragged as he dragged his stare to hers—hungry, feral, unyielding.

"Not yet," he said roughly, his own breathing uneven. "Not now."

"Why?" It was an effort to remember speech with him looking at her like that. Like he might eat her alive. Heat pounded through her core.

"I want to take my time with you—to learn . . . every inch of you. And this apartment has very, very thin walls. I don't want to have an audience," he added as he leaned down again, brushing his mouth over the cut at the base of her throat, "when I make you moan, Aelin."

Oh, by the Wyrd. She was in trouble. So much rutting trouble. And when he said her name like that . . .

"This changes things," she said, hardly able to get the words out.

"Things have been changing for a while already. We'll deal with it." She wondered how long his resolve to wait would last if she lifted her face to claim his mouth with her own, if she ran her fingers down the groove of his spine. If she touched him lower than that. But—

Wyverns. Witches. Army. Erawan.

She loosed a heavy breath. "Sleep," she mumbled. "We should sleep."

He swallowed again, slowly peeling himself away from her and strode to the closet to dress. Honestly, it was an effort not to leap after him and rip that damn towel away.

Maybe she should make Aedion go stay somewhere else. Just for a night.

And then she would burn in hell for all eternity for being the most selfish, awful person to ever grace the earth.

She forced herself to put her back to the closet, not trusting herself to so much as look at Rowan without doing something infinitely stupid.

Oh, she was in *so* much gods-damned trouble.

CHAPTER 53

Drink, the demon prince coaxed in a lover's croon. *Savor it.*

The prisoner was sobbing on the floor of the dungeon cell, his fear and pain and memories leaking from him. The demon prince inhaled them as though they were opium.

Delicious.

It was.

He hated himself, cursed himself.

But the despair coming from the man as his worst memories ripped him to shreds . . . it was intoxicating. It was strength; it was life.

He had nothing and no one, anyway. If he got the chance, he would find a way to end it. For now, this was eternity, this was birth and death and rebirth.

So he drank the man's pain, his fear, his sorrow.

And he learned to like it.

CHAPTER 54

Manon stared at the letter that the trembling messenger had just delivered. Elide was trying her best to look as though she wasn't observing every flick of Manon's eyes across the page, but it was hard not to stare when the witch snarled with every word she read.

Elide lay on her pallet of hay, the fire already dying down to embers, and groaned as she sat up, her sore body aching. She'd found a water skein in the larder, and had even asked the cook if she could take it for the Wing Leader. He didn't dare object. Or begrudge her the two little bags of nuts she had also nabbed "for the Wing Leader." Better than nothing.

She'd stored it all under her pallet, and Manon hadn't noticed. Any day now, the wagon would be arriving with supplies. When it left, Elide would be on it. And never have to deal with any of this darkness again.

Elide reached for the pile of logs and added two to the fire, sending sparks shooting up in a wave. She was about to lie down again when Manon said from the desk, "In three days, I'll be heading out with my Thirteen."

"To where?" Elide dared ask. From the violence with which the Wing Leader had read the letter, it couldn't be anywhere pleasant.

"To a forest in the North. To—" Manon caught herself and moved across the floor, her steps light but powerful as she came to the hearth and chucked the letter in. "I'll be gone for at least two days. If I were you, I'd suggest using that time to lie low."

Elide's stomach twisted at the thought of what, exactly, it might mean for the Wing Leader's protection to be thousands of miles away. But there was no point in telling Manon that. She wouldn't care, even if she'd claimed Elide as one of her kind.

It meant nothing, anyway. She wasn't a witch. She'd be escaping soon. She doubted anyone here would really think twice about her disappearance.

"I'll lie low," Elide said.

Perhaps in the back of a wagon, as it made its way out of Morath and to freedom beyond.

It took three whole days to prepare for the meeting.

The Matron's letter had contained no mention of the breeding and slaughter of witches. In fact, it was as if her grandmother hadn't received any of Manon's messages. As soon as Manon got back from this little mission, she'd start questioning the Keep's messengers. Slowly. Painfully.

The Thirteen were to fly to coordinates in Adarlan—smack in the middle of the kingdom, just inside the tangle of Oakwald Forest—and arrive a day before the arranged meeting to establish a safe perimeter.

For the King of Adarlan was to at last see the weapon her grand-mother had been building, and apparently wanted to inspect Manon as well. He was bringing his son, though Manon doubted it was for guarding his back in the way that the heirs protected their Matrons. She didn't particularly care—about any of it.

A stupid, useless meeting, she'd almost wanted to tell her grandmother. A waste of her time.

At least seeing the king would provide an opportunity to meet the man who was sending out these orders to destroy witches and make monstrosities of their witchlings. At least she would be able to tell her grandmother in person about it—maybe even witness the Matron make mincemeat of the king once she learned the truth about what he'd done.

Manon climbed into the saddle, and Abraxos walked out onto the post, adjusting to the latest armor the aerial blacksmith had crafted— finally light enough for the wyverns to manage, and now to be tested on this trip. Wind bit at her, but she ignored it. Just as she'd ignored her Thirteen.

Asterin wouldn't speak to her—and none of them had spoken about the Valg prince that the duke had sent to them.

It had been a test, to see who would survive, and to remind her what was at stake.

Just as unleashing shadowfire on that tribe had been a test.

She still couldn't pick a coven. And she wouldn't, until she'd spoken to her grandmother.

But she doubted that the duke would wait much longer.

Manon gazed into the plunge, at the ever-growing army sweeping across the mountains and valleys like a carpet of darkness and fire—so many more soldiers hidden beneath it. Her Shadows had reported that very morning about spotting lean, winged creatures with twisted human forms soaring through the night skies—too swift and agile to track before they vanished into the heavy clouds and did not return. The majority of Morath's horrors, Manon suspected, had yet to be revealed. She wondered if she'd command them, too.

She felt the eyes of her Thirteen on her, waiting for the signal.

Manon dug her heels into Abraxos's side, and they free-fell into the air.

The scar on her arm ached.

It always ached—more than the collar, more than the cold, more than the duke's hands on her, more than anything that had been done to her. Only the shadowfire was a comfort.

She had once believed that she'd been born to be queen.

She had since learned that she'd been born to be a wolf.

The duke had even put a collar on her like a dog, and had shoved a demon prince inside her.

She'd let it win for a time, curling up so tightly inside herself that the prince forgot she was there.

And she waited.

In that cocoon of darkness, she bided her time, letting him think her gone, letting them do what they wanted to the mortal shell around her. It was in that cocoon where the shadowfire began to flicker, fueling her, feeding her. Long ago, when she was small and clean, flames of gold had crackled at her fingers, secret and hidden. Then they had vanished, as all good things had vanished.

And now they had returned—reborn within that dark shell as phantom fire.

The prince inside her did not notice when she began to nibble at him.

Bit by bit, she stole morsels of the otherworldly creature that had taken her body for its skin, who did such despicable things with it.

The creature noticed the day she took a bigger bite—big enough that it screamed in agony.

Before it could tell anyone, she leaped upon it, tearing and ripping with her shadowfire until only ashes of malice remained, until it was no more than a whisper of thought. Fire—it did not like fire of any kind.

For weeks now, she had been here. Waiting again. Learning about the flame in her veins—how it bled into the thing in her arm and reemerged as shadowfire. The thing spoke to her sometimes, in languages she had never heard, that had maybe never existed.

The collar remained around her neck, and she let them order her around, let them touch her, hurt her. Soon enough—soon enough she would find true purpose, and then she would howl her wrath at the moon.

She'd forgotten the name she'd been given, but it made no difference. She had only one name now:

Death, devourer of worlds.

CHAPTER
55

Aelin fully believed in ghosts.

She just didn't think they usually came out during the day.

Rowan's hand clamped onto her shoulder right before sunrise. She took one look at his tight face and braced herself. "Someone's broken into the warehouse."

Rowan was out of the room, armed and fully ready to shed blood before Aelin could grab her own weapons. Gods above—he *moved* like the wind, too. She could still feel his canines at her throat, rasping against her skin, pressing down lightly—

On near-silent feet, she went after him, finding him and Aedion standing before the apartment door, blades in hand, their muscled, scarred backs rigid. The windows—they were their best options for escape if it was an ambush. She reached the two males just as Rowan eased open the door to reveal the gloom of the stairwell.

Collapsed in a heap, Evangeline was sobbing on the stair landing, her scarred face deathly pale and those citrine eyes wide with terror as she peered up at Rowan and Aedion. Hundreds of pounds of lethal muscle and bared teeth—

Aelin shoved past them, taking the stairs by twos and threes until she reached the girl. She was clean—not a scratch on her. "Are you hurt?"

She shook her head, her red-gold hair catching the light of the candle that Rowan brought down. The staircase shuddered with every step he and Aedion took.

"Tell me," Aelin panted, silently praying it wasn't as bad as it seemed. "Tell me everything."

"They took her, they took her, they took her."

"Who?" Aelin said, brushing back the girl's hair, wondering whether she would panic if she held her.

"The king's men," Evangeline whispered. "They came with a letter from Arobynn. Said it was in Arobynn's will that they be told about Lysandra's b-b-bloodline."

Aelin's heart stopped dead. Worse—far worse than what she'd braced for—

"They said she was a shape-shifter. They *took* her, and they were going to take me, too, but she fought them, and she made me run, and Clarisse wouldn't help—"

"Where did they take her?"

Evangeline sobbed. "I don't know. Lysandra said I was to come here if anything ever happened; she told me to tell you to *run*—"

She couldn't breathe, couldn't think. Rowan knelt down beside them and slid his arms around the girl, scooping her up, his hand so big that it nearly enveloped the entire back of her head. Evangeline buried her face in his tattooed chest, and Rowan murmured wordless sounds of comfort.

He met Aelin's eyes over the girl's head. *We need to be out of this house in ten minutes—until we figure out if he betrayed you, too.*

As if he'd heard it, Aedion edged past them, going to the warehouse window that Evangeline had somehow slipped in through. Lysandra, it seemed, had taught her charge a few things.

Aelin scrubbed at her face and braced a hand on Rowan's shoulder as she stood, his skin warm and soft beneath her callused fingers. "Nesryn's father. We'll ask him to look after her today."

Arobynn had done this. A final card up his sleeve.

He'd known. About Lysandra—about their friendship.

He didn't like to share his belongings.

Chaol and Nesryn burst into the warehouse a level below, and Aedion was halfway to them before they even realized he was there.

They had more news. One of Ren's men had contacted them moments ago: a meeting was to take place tomorrow in Oakwald, between the king, Dorian, and the Wing Leader of his aerial cavalry.

With a delivery of one new prisoner headed for Morath.

"You have to get her out of the tunnels," Aelin said to Chaol and Nesryn, as she stormed down the stairs. "Right now. You're human; they won't notice you at first. You're the only ones who can go into that darkness."

Chaol and Nesryn exchanged glances.

Aelin stalked up to them. *You have to get her out right now.*

For a heartbeat, she wasn't in the warehouse. For a heartbeat, she was standing in a beautiful bedroom, before a bloody bed and the wrecked body splayed upon it.

Chaol held out his hands. "We're better off spending the time setting up an ambush."

The sound of his voice . . . The scar on his face was stark in the dim light. Aelin clenched her fingers into a fist, her nails—the nails that had shredded his face—digging in. "They could be feeding on her," she managed to say.

Behind her, Evangeline let out a sob. If they made Lysandra endure what Aelin had endured when she fought the Valg prince . . . "Please," Aelin said, her voice breaking on the word.

Chaol noticed, then, where her eyes had focused on his face. He paled, his mouth opening.

But Nesryn reached for her hand, her slim, tan fingers cool against Aelin's clammy palms. "We will get her back. We will save her. Together."

Chaol just held Aelin's gaze, his shoulders squaring as he said, "Never again."

She wanted to believe him.

CHAPTER 56

A few hours later, seated on the floor of a ramshackle inn on the opposite side of Rifthold, Aelin peered at a map they'd marked with the meeting's location spot—about half a mile from the temple of Temis. The tiny temple was just inside the cover of Oakwald, perched atop a towering slice of rock in the middle of a deep ravine. It was accessible only via two dangling footbridges attached to either side of the ravine, which had spared it from invading armies over the years. The surrounding forest would likely be empty, and if wyverns were flying in, they would no doubt arrive under cover of darkness the night before. Tonight.

Aelin, Rowan, Aedion, Nesryn, and Chaol sat around the map, sharpening and polishing their blades as they talked over their plan. They'd given Evangeline to Nesryn's father, along with more letters for Terrasen and the Bane—and the baker hadn't asked any questions. He'd only kissed his youngest daughter on the cheek and announced that he and Evangeline would bake special pies for their return.

If they returned.

"What if she has a collar or a ring on?" Chaol asked from across their little circle.

"Then she loses a head or a finger," Aedion said baldly.

Aelin shot him a look. "You don't make that call without me."

"And Dorian?" Aedion asked.

Chaol was staring at the map as if he would burn a hole through it. "Not my call," Aelin said tightly.

Chaol's eyes flashed to hers. "You don't touch him."

It was a terrible risk, to bring them all within range of a Valg prince, but . . . "We paint ourselves in Wyrdmarks," Aelin said. "All of us. To ward against the prince."

In the ten minutes it had taken them to grab their weapons, clothes, and supplies from the warehouse apartment, she'd remembered to get her books on Wyrdmarks, which now sat on the little table before the sole window in the room. They'd rented three for the night: one for Aelin and Rowan, one for Aedion, and the other for Chaol and Nesryn. The gold coin she'd slapped onto the innkeeper's counter had been enough to pay for at least a month. And his silence.

"Do we take out the king?" Aedion said.

"We don't engage," Rowan replied, "until we know for sure we can kill the king and neutralize the prince with minimal risk. Getting Lysandra out of that wagon comes first."

"Agreed," Aelin said.

Aedion's gaze settled on Rowan. "When do we leave?"

Aelin wondered at his yielding to the Fae Prince.

"I don't want those wyverns or witches sniffing us out," Rowan said, the commander bracing for the battlefield. "We arrive just before the meeting takes place—long enough to find advantageous spots and to locate their scouts and sentries. The witches' sense of smell is too keen to risk discovery. We move in fast."

She couldn't decide whether or not she was relieved.

The clock chimed noon. Nesryn rose to her feet. "I'll order lunch."

Chaol got up, stretching. "I'll help you bring it up." Indeed, in a place like this, they would get no kitchen-to-room service. Though in a place like this, Aelin supposed, Chaol might very well be going to keep an eye on Faliq's back. Good.

Once they left, Aelin picked up one of Nesryn's blades and began polishing it: a decent dagger, but not great. If they lived past tomorrow, maybe she would buy her a better one as a thank-you.

"Too bad Lorcan's a psychotic bastard," she said. "We could use him tomorrow." Rowan's mouth tightened. "What will he do when he finds out about Aedion's heritage?"

Aedion set down the dagger he'd been honing. "Will he even care?"

Halfway through polishing a short sword, Rowan paused. "Lorcan might not give a shit—or he might find Aedion intriguing. But he would more likely be interested in how Aedion's existence can be used against Gavriel."

She eyed her cousin, his golden hair now seeming more proof of his ties to Gavriel than to her. "Do you want to meet him?" Perhaps she'd brought this up only to keep from thinking about tomorrow.

A shrug. "I'd be curious, but I'm not in any rush. Not unless he's going to drag his cadre over here to help with the fighting."

"Such a pragmatist." She faced Rowan, who was back at work on the sword. "Would they ever be convinced to help, despite what Lorcan said?" They had provided aid once—during the attack on Mistward.

"Unlikely," Rowan said, not looking up from the blade. "Unless Maeve decides that sending you succor is the next move in whatever game she's playing. Maybe she'll want to ally with you to kill Lorcan for his betrayal." He mused, "Some of the Fae who used to dwell here might still be alive and in hiding. Perhaps they could be trained—or already have training."

"I wouldn't count on it," Aedion said. "The Little Folk I've seen and felt in Oakwald. But the Fae . . . Not a whisper of them there." He didn't meet Rowan's eyes, and instead started cleaning Chaol's final unsharpened blade. "The king wiped them out too thoroughly. I would bet any survivors are stuck in their animal forms."

Aelin's body became heavy with a familiar grief. "We'll figure all that out later."

If they lived long enough to do so.

⌒

For the rest of the day and well into the evening, Rowan planned their course of action with the same efficiency she'd come to expect and cherish. But it didn't feel comforting now—not when the danger was so great, and everything could change in a matter of minutes. Not when Lysandra might already be beyond saving.

"You should be sleeping," Rowan said, his deep voice rumbling across the bed and along her skin.

"The bed's lumpy," Aelin said. "I hate cheap inns."

His low laugh echoed in the near-dark of the room. She'd rigged the door and window to alert them to any intruder, but with the ruckus coming from the seedy tavern downstairs, they would have a hard time hearing anyone in the hall. Especially when some of the rooms were rented by the hour.

"We'll get her back, Aelin."

The bed was much smaller than hers—small enough that her shoulder brushed his as she turned over. She found him already facing her, his eyes gleaming in the dark. "I can't bury another friend."

"You won't."

"If anything ever happened to you, Rowan—"

"Don't," he breathed. "Don't even say it. We dealt with that enough the other night."

He lifted a hand—hesitated, and then brushed back a strand of hair that had fallen across her face. His callused fingers scraped against her cheekbone, then caressed the shell of her ear.

It was foolish to even start down this road, when every other man she'd let in had left some wound, in one way or another, accidentally or not.

There was nothing soft or tender on his face. Only a predator's glittering gaze. "When we get back," he said, "remind me to prove you wrong about every thought that just went through your head."

She lifted an eyebrow. "Oh?"

He gave her a sly smile that made thinking impossible. Exactly what he wanted—to distract her from the horrors of tomorrow. "I'll even let you decide how I tell you: with words"—his eyes flicked once to her mouth—"or with my teeth and tongue."

A thrill went through her blood, pooling in her core. Not fair—not fair at all to tease her like that. "This miserable inn is rather loud," she said, daring to slide a hand over his bare pectoral, then up to his shoulder. She marveled at the strength beneath her palm. He shuddered, but his hands remained at his sides, clenched and white knuckled. "It's too bad Aedion could still probably hear through the wall."

She gently scraped her nails across his collarbone, marking him, claiming him, before leaning in to press her mouth to the hollow of his throat. His skin was so smooth, so invitingly warm.

"Aelin," he groaned.

Her toes curled at the roughness in his voice. "Too bad," she murmured against his neck. He growled, and she chuckled quietly as she rolled back over and closed her eyes, her breathing easier than it had been moments before. She'd get through tomorrow, regardless of what happened. She wasn't alone—not with him, and not with Aedion also beside her.

She was smiling when the mattress shifted, steady footsteps padded toward the dresser, and the sounds of splashing filled the room as Rowan dunked the pitcher of cold water over himself.

CHAPTER 57

"I can smell them all right," Aedion said, his whisper barely audible as they crept through the underbrush, each of them clothed in green and brown to remain concealed in the dense forest. He and Rowan walked several paces ahead of Aelin, arrows loosely nocked in their bows as they picked out the way with their keen hearing and smell.

If she had her damn Fae form, she could be helping instead of lingering behind with Chaol and Nesryn, but—

Not a useful thought, she told herself. She would make do with what she had.

Chaol knew the forest best, having come hunting this way with Dorian countless times. He'd laid out a path for them the night before, but had yielded leading to the two Fae warriors and their impeccable senses. His steps were unfaltering on the leaves and moss beneath their boots, his face drawn but steady. Focused.

Good.

They passed through the trees of Oakwald so silently that the birds didn't stop their chirping.

Brannon's forest. Her forest.

She wondered if its denizens knew what blood flowed in her veins, and hid their little party from the horrors waiting ahead. She wondered if they'd somehow help Lysandra when it came time.

Rowan paused ten feet ahead and pointed to three towering oaks. She halted, her ears straining as she scanned the forest.

Growls and roars of beasts that sounded far too large rumbled toward them, along with the scrape of leathery wings on stone.

Bracing herself, she hurried to where Rowan and Aedion were waiting by the oak trees, her cousin pointing skyward to indicate their next movement.

Aelin took the center tree, hardly disturbing a leaf or twig as she climbed. Rowan waited until she'd reached a high branch before coming up after her—in about the same amount of time she had done it, she noted a bit smugly. Aedion took the tree to the right, with Chaol and Nesryn scaling the left. They all kept climbing, as smoothly as snakes, until the foliage blocked their view of the ground below and they could see into a little meadow up ahead.

Holy gods.

The wyverns were enormous. Enormous, vicious, and . . . and those were indeed saddles on their backs. "Poisoned barbs on the tail," Rowan mouthed in her ear. "With that wingspan, they can probably fly hundreds of miles a day."

He would know, she supposed.

Only thirteen wyverns were grounded in the meadow. The smallest of them was sprawled on his belly, face buried in a mound of wildflowers. Iron spikes gleamed on his tail in lieu of bone, scars covered his body like a cat's stripes, and his wings . . . she knew the material grafted there. Spidersilk. That much of it must have cost a fortune.

The other wyverns were all normal, and all capable of ripping a man in half in one bite.

They would be dead within moments against *one* of these things. But an army three thousand strong? Panic pushed in.

I am Aelin Ashryver Galathynius—

"That one—I bet she's the Wing Leader," Rowan said, pointing now to the women gathered at the edge of the meadow.

Not women. Witches.

They were all young and beautiful, with hair and skin of every shade and color. But even from the distance, she picked out the one Rowan had pointed to. Her hair was like living moonlight, her eyes like burnished gold.

She was the most beautiful person Aelin had ever seen.

And the most horrifying.

She moved with a swagger that Aelin supposed only an immortal could achieve, her red cloak snapping behind her, the riding leathers clinging to her lithe body. A living weapon—that's what the Wing Leader was.

The Wing Leader prowled through the camp, inspecting the wyverns and giving orders Aelin's human ears couldn't hear. The other twelve witches seemed to track her every movement, as if she were the axis of their world, and two of them followed behind her especially closely. Lieutenants.

Aelin fought to keep her balance on the wide bough.

Any army that Terrasen might raise would be annihilated. Along with the friends around her.

They were all so, so dead.

Rowan put a hand on her waist, as if he could hear the refrain pounding through her with every heartbeat. "You took down one of their Matrons," he said in her ear, barely more than a rustling leaf. "You can take down her inferiors."

Maybe. Maybe not, given the way the thirteen witches in the clearing moved and interacted. They were a tight-knit, brutal unit. They did not look like the sort that took prisoners.

If they did, they likely ate them.

Would they fly Lysandra to Morath once the prison wagon arrived? If so . . . "Lysandra doesn't get within thirty feet of the wyverns." If she got hauled onto one of them, then it would already be too late.

"Agreed," Rowan murmured. "Horses approaching from the north. And more wings from the west. Let's go."

The Matron, then. The horses would be the king and the prison wagon. And Dorian.

Aedion looked ready to start ripping out witch throats as they reached the ground and slunk through the forest again, heading for the clearing. Nesryn had an arrow nocked in her bow as she slipped into the brush to provide cover, her face grave—ready for anything. At least that made one of them.

Aelin fell into step beside Chaol. "No matter what you see or hear, do not move. We need to assess Dorian before we act. Just one of those Valg princes is lethal."

"I know," he said, refusing to meet her stare. "You can trust me."

"I need you to make sure Lysandra gets out. You know this forest better than any of us. Get her somewhere safe."

Chaol nodded. "I promise." She didn't doubt it. Not after this winter.

She reached out, paused—and then put a hand on his shoulder. "I won't touch Dorian," she said. "I swear it."

His bronze eyes flickered. "Thank you."

They kept moving.

Aedion and Rowan had them all doubling back to the area they'd scouted earlier, a little outcropping of boulders with enough brush for them to crouch unseen and observe everything that was happening in the clearing.

Slowly, like lovely wraiths from a hell-realm, the witches appeared.

The white-haired witch strode to greet an older, black-haired female who could only be the Matron of the Blackbeak Clan. Behind the Matron, a cluster of witches hauled a large covered wagon, much like the one the Yellowlegs had once parked before the glass palace. The wyverns must have carried it between them. It looked ordinary—painted black and blue and yellow—but Aelin had a feeling that she didn't want to know what was inside.

Then the royal party arrived.

She didn't know where to look: at the King of Adarlan, at the small, too-familiar prison wagon in the center of the riders . . .

Or at Dorian, riding at his father's side, that black collar around his neck and nothing human in his face.

CHAPTER 58

Manon Blackbeak hated this forest.

The trees were unnaturally close—so close that they'd had to leave the wyverns behind in order to make their way to the clearing a half mile from the crumbling temple. At least the humans hadn't been stupid enough to pick the temple itself as a meeting site. It was too precariously perched, the ravine too open to spying eyes. Yesterday, Manon and the Thirteen had scouted all the clearings within a mile radius, weighing them for their visibility, accessibility, and cover, and finally settled on this one. Near enough to where the king had originally demanded they meet— but a far more protected spot. Rule one of dealing with mortals: never let them pick the exact location.

First, her grandmother and her escort coven strode through the trees from wherever they'd landed, a covered wagon in tow, no doubt carrying the weapon she'd created. She assessed Manon with a slashing glance and merely said, "Keep silent and out of our way. Speak only when spoken to. Don't cause trouble, or I'll rip out your throat."

Later, then. She would talk to her grandmother about the Valg later.

The king was late, and his party made enough gods-damned noise as they traipsed through the woods that Manon heard them a good five minutes before the king's massive black warhorse appeared around the bend in the path. The other riders flowed behind him like a dark shadow.

The scent of the Valg slithered along her body.

They'd brought a prison wagon with them, containing a prisoner to be transferred to Morath. Female, from the smell of her—and strange. She'd never come across that scent before: not Valg, not Fae, not entirely human. Interesting.

But the Thirteen were warriors, not couriers.

Her hands behind her back, Manon waited as her grandmother glided toward the king, monitoring his human-Valg entourage while they surveyed the clearing. The man closest to the king didn't bother glancing around. His sapphire eyes went right to Manon, and stayed there.

He would have been beautiful were it not for the dark collar around his throat and the utter coldness in his perfect face.

He smiled at Manon as though he knew the taste of her blood.

She stifled the urge to bare her teeth and shifted her focus to the Matron, who had now stopped before the mortal king. Such a reek from these people. How was her grandmother not grimacing as she stood before them?

"Your Majesty," her grandmother said, her black robes like liquid night as she gave the slightest of bobs. Manon shut down the bark of protest in her throat. Never—*never* had her grandmother bowed or curtsied or so much as nodded for another ruler, not even the other Matrons.

Manon shoved the outrage down deep as the king dismounted in one powerful movement. "High Witch," he said, angling his head in not quite a bow, but enough to show some kernel of acknowledgment. A massive sword hung at his side. His clothes were dark and rich, and his face . . .

Cruelty incarnate.

Not the cold, cunning cruelty that Manon had honed and delighted in, but base, brute cruelty, the kind that sent all those men to break into her cottages, thinking her in need of a lesson.

This was the man to whom they were to bow. To whom her grandmother had lowered her head a fraction of an inch.

Her grandmother gestured behind her with an iron-tipped hand, and Manon lifted her chin. "I present to you my granddaughter, Manon, heir of the Blackbeak Clan and Wing Leader of your aerial cavalry."

Manon stepped forward, enduring the raking gaze of the king. The dark-haired young man who had ridden at his side dismounted with fluid grace, still smirking at her. She ignored him.

"You do your people a great service, Wing Leader," the king said, his voice like granite.

Manon just stared at him, keenly aware of the Matron judging her every move.

"Aren't you going to say anything?" the king demanded, his thick brows—one scarred—high.

"I was told to keep my mouth shut," Manon said. Her grandmother's eyes flashed. "Unless you'd prefer I get on my knees and grovel."

Oh, there would certainly be hell to pay for that remark. Her grandmother turned to the king. "She's an arrogant thing, but you'll find no deadlier warrior."

But the king was smiling—though it didn't reach his dark eyes. "I don't think you've ever groveled for anything in your life, Wing Leader."

Manon gave him a half smile in return, her iron teeth out. Let his young companion wet himself at the sight. "We witches aren't born to grovel before humans."

The king chuckled mirthlessly and faced her grandmother, whose iron-tipped fingers had curved as if she were imagining them around Manon's throat. "You chose our Wing Leader well, Matron," he said, and then gestured to the wagon painted with the Ironteeth banner. "Let us see what you've brought for me. I hope it will be equally impressive—and worth the wait."

Her grandmother grinned, revealing iron teeth that had begun to rust in some spots, and ice licked up Manon's spine. "This way."

Shoulders back, head high, Manon waited at the bottom of the wagon steps to follow the Matron and the king inside, but the man—so much taller and wider than she up close—frowned at the sight of her. "My son can entertain the Wing Leader."

And that was it—she was shut out as he and her grandmother vanished within. Apparently, she wasn't to see this weapon. At least, not as one of the first, Wing Leader or not. Manon took a breath and checked her temper.

Half of the Thirteen encircled the wagon for the Matron's safety, while the others dispersed to monitor the royal party around them. Knowing their place, their inadequacy in the face of the Thirteen, the escort coven faded back into the tree line. Black-uniformed guards watched them all, some armed with spears, some with crossbows, some with vicious swords.

The prince was now leaning against a gnarled oak. Noticing her attention, he gave her a lazy grin.

It was enough. King's son or not, she didn't give a damn.

Manon crossed the clearing, Sorrel behind her. On edge, but keeping her distance.

There was no one in earshot as Manon stopped a few feet away from the Crown Prince. "Hello, princeling," she purred.

⁓

The world kept slipping out from underneath Chaol's feet, so much so that he grabbed a handful of dirt just to remember where he was and that this was real, not some nightmare.

Dorian.

His friend; unharmed, but—but not Dorian.

Not even close to Dorian, as the prince smirked at that beautiful, white-haired witch.

The face was the same, but the soul gazing out of those sapphire eyes had not been created in this world.

Chaol squeezed the dirt harder.

He had run. He had run from Dorian, and let *this* happen.

It hadn't been hope that he carried when he fled, but stupidity.

Aelin had been right. It would be a mercy to kill him.

With the king and Matron occupied . . . Chaol glanced toward the wagon and then at Aelin, lying on her stomach in the brush, a dagger out. She gave him a quick nod, her mouth a tight line. Now. If they were going to make their move to free Lysandra, it would have to be now.

And for Nehemia, for the friend vanished beneath a Wyrdstone collar, he would not falter.

⁓

The ancient, cruel demon squatting inside him began thrashing as the white-haired witch sauntered up to him.

It had been content to sneer from afar. *One of us, one of ours,* it hissed to him. *We made it, so we'll take it.*

Every step closer made her unbound hair shimmer like moonlight on water. But the demon began scrambling away as the sun lit up her eyes.

Not too close, it said. *Do not let the witchling too close. The eyes of the Valg kings—*

"Hello, princeling," she said, her voice bedroom-soft and full of glorious death.

"Hello, witchling," he said.

And the words were his own.

For a moment he was so stunned that he blinked. *He* blinked. The demon inside of him recoiled, clawing at the walls of his mind. *Eyes of the Valg kings, eyes of our masters,* it shrieked. *Do not touch that one!*

"Is there a reason you're smiling at me," she said, "or shall I interpret it as a death wish?"

Do not speak to it.

He didn't care. Let this be another dream, another nightmare. Let this new, lovely monster devour him whole. He had nothing beyond the here and now.

"Do I need a reason to smile at a beautiful woman?"

"I'm not a woman." Her iron nails glinted as she crossed her arms. "And you . . ." She sniffed. "Man or demon?"

"Prince," he said. That's what the thing inside him was; he had never learned its name.

Do not speak to it!

He cocked his head. "I've never been with a witch."

Let her rip out his throat for that. End it.

A row of iron fangs snapped down over her teeth as her smile grew. "I've been with plenty of men. You're all the same. Taste the same." She looked him over as if he were her next meal.

"I dare you," he managed to say.

Her eyes narrowed, the gold like living embers. He'd never seen anyone so beautiful.

This witch had been crafted from the darkness between the stars.

"I think not, Prince," she said in her midnight voice. She sniffed again, her nose crinkling slightly. "But would you bleed red, or black?"

"I'll bleed whatever color you tell me to."

Step away, get away. The demon prince inside him yanked so hard he took a step. But not away. Toward the white-haired witch.

She let out a low, vicious laugh. "What is your name, Prince?"

His name.

He didn't know what that was.

She reached out, her iron nails glimmering in the dappled sunlight. The demon's screaming was so loud in his head that he wondered if his ears would bleed.

Iron clinked against stone as she grazed the collar around his neck. Higher—if she just slashed higher—

"Like a dog," she murmured. "Leashed to your master."

She ran a finger along the curve of the collar, and he shuddered—in fear, in pleasure, in anticipation of the nails tearing into his throat.

"What is your name." A command, not a question, as eyes of pure gold met his.

"Dorian," he breathed.

Your name is nothing, your name is mine, the demon hissed, and a wave of that human woman's screaming swept him away.

Crouched in the brush just twenty feet from the prison wagon, Aelin froze.

Dorian.

It couldn't have been. There wasn't a chance of it, not when the voice that Dorian had spoken with was so empty, so hollow, but—

Beside her, Chaol's eyes were wide. Had he heard the slight shift?

The Wing Leader cocked her head, her iron-tipped hand still touching the Wyrdstone collar. "Do you want me to kill you, Dorian?"

Aelin's blood went cold.

Chaol tensed, his hand going to his sword. Aelin gripped the back of his tunic in silent reminder. She had no doubt that across the clearing, Nesryn's arrow was already pointed with lethal accuracy at the Wing Leader's throat.

"I want you to do lots of things to me," the prince said, raking his eyes along the witch's body.

The humanity was gone again. She'd imagined it. The way the king had acted . . . That was a man who held pure control over his son, confident that there was no struggle inside.

A soft, joyless laugh, and then the Wing Leader released Dorian's collar. Her red cloak flowed around her on a phantom wind as she stepped back. "Come find me again, Prince, and we'll see about that."

A Valg prince inhabited Dorian—but Aelin's nose did not bleed in its presence, and there was no creeping fog of darkness. Had the king muted its powers so his son could deceive the world around him? Or was that battle still being waged inside the prince's mind?

Now—they had to move *now*, while the Matron and the king remained in that painted wagon.

Rowan cupped his hands to his mouth and signaled with a bird's call, so lifelike that none of the guards shifted. But across the clearing, Aedion and Nesryn heard, and understood.

She didn't know how they managed to accomplish it, but a minute later, the wyverns of the High Witch's coven were roaring with alarm, the trees shuddering with the sound. Every guard and sentinel turned toward the racket, away from the prison wagon.

It was all the distraction Aelin needed.

She'd spent two weeks in one of those wagons. She knew the bars of the little window, knew the hinges and the locks. And Rowan, fortunately, knew exactly how to dispatch the three guards stationed at the back door without making a sound.

She didn't dare breathe too loudly as she climbed the few steps to the back of the wagon, pulled out her lock-picking kit, and set to work. One look over here, one shift of the wind—

There—the lock sprang open, and she eased back the door, bracing for squeaky hinges. By some god's mercy, it made no sound, and the wyverns went on bellowing.

Lysandra was curled against the far corner, bloody and dirty, her short nightgown torn and her bare legs bruised.

No collar. No ring on either hand.

Aelin bit back her cry of relief and flicked her fingers to tell the courtesan to *hurry*—

On near-silent feet, Lysandra hurtled past her, right into the speckled brown-and-green cloak Rowan was holding out. Two heartbeats later she was down the steps and into the brush. Another beat, and the dead guards were inside the wagon with the door locked. Aelin and Rowan slipped back into the forest amid the roars of the wyverns.

Lysandra was shivering where she knelt in the thicket, Chaol before her, inspecting her wounds. He mouthed to Aelin that she was fine and helped the courtesan rise to her feet before hauling her deeper into the woods.

It had taken less than two minutes—and thank the gods, because a moment later the painted wagon's door was flung open and the Matron and king stormed out to see what the noise was about.

A few paces from Aelin, Rowan monitored every step, every breath their enemy took. There was a flash of movement beside her, and then Aedion and Nesryn were there, dirty and panting, but alive. The grin on Aedion's face faltered as he peered back at the clearing behind them.

The king stalked to the heart of the clearing, demanding answers.

Butchering bastard.

And for a moment, they were again in Terrasen, at that dinner table in her family's castle, where the king had eaten her family's food, drunk their finest wine, and then he'd tried to shatter her mind.

Aedion's eyes met hers, his body trembling with restraint—waiting for her order.

She knew she might live to regret it, but Aelin shook her head. Not here—not now. There were too many variables, and too many players on the board. They had Lysandra. It was time to go.

The king told his son to get onto his horse and barked orders to the others as the Wing Leader backed away from the prince with a casual, lethal grace. The Matron waited across the clearing, her voluminous black robes billowing despite her stillness.

Aelin prayed that she and her companions would never run into the Matron—at least not without an army behind them.

Whatever the king had seen inside the painted wagon had been important enough that they hadn't risked letters about its specific details.

Dorian mounted his horse, his face cold and empty.

I'll come back for you, she'd promised him. She had not thought it would be in this way.

The king's party departed with eerie silence and efficiency, seemingly unaware that they were now missing three of their own. The stench of the Valg faded as they vanished, cleared away by a brisk wind as if Oakwald itself wanted to wipe away any trace.

Headed in the opposite direction, the witches prowled into the trees, lugging the wagon behind them with inhuman strength, until only the Wing Leader and her horrifying grandmother remained in the clearing.

The blow happened so fast that Aelin couldn't detect it. Even Aedion flinched.

The smack reverberated through the forest, and the Wing Leader's face snapped to the side to reveal four lines of blue blood now running down her cheek.

"Insolent fool," the Matron hissed. Lingering near the trees, the beautiful, golden-haired lieutenant observed every movement the Matron made—so intensely that Aelin wondered if she would go for the Matron's throat. "Do you wish to cost me everything?"

"Grandmother, I sent you letters—"

"I received your whining, sniveling letters. And I burned them. You are under orders to obey. Did you think my silence was not intentional? *Do as the duke says.*"

"How can you allow these—"

Another strike—four more lines bleeding down the witch's face. "You dare question me? Do you think yourself as good as a High Witch, now that you're Wing Leader?"

"No, Matron." There was no sign of that cocky, taunting tone of minutes before; only cool, lethal rage. A killer by birth and training. But the golden eyes turned toward the painted wagon—a silent question.

The Matron leaned in, her rusted iron teeth within shredding distance of her granddaughter's throat. "Ask it, Manon. Ask what's inside that wagon."

The golden-haired witch by the trees was ramrod straight.

But the Wing Leader—Manon—bowed her head. "You'll tell me when it's necessary."

"Go look. Let's see if it meets my granddaughter's standards."

With that, the Matron strode into the trees, the second coven of witches now waiting for her.

Manon Blackbeak didn't wipe away the blue blood sliding down her face as she walked up the steps of the wagon, pausing on the landing for only a heartbeat before entering the gloom beyond.

It was as good a sign as any to get the hell out. With Aedion and Nesryn guarding their backs, Aelin and Rowan hurried for the spot where Chaol and Lysandra would be waiting. Not without magic would she take on the king and Dorian. She didn't have a death wish—either for herself or her friends.

She found Lysandra standing with a hand braced against a tree, wide-eyed, breathing hard.

Chaol was gone.

CHAPTER
59

The demon seized control the moment the man who wielded the collar returned. It shoved him back into that pit of memory until he was the one screaming again, until he was small and broken and fragmented.

But those golden eyes lingered.

Come find me again, Prince.

A promise—a promise of death, of release.

Come find me again.

The words soon faded, swallowed up by screaming and blood and the demon's cold fingers running over his mind. But the eyes lingered—and that name.

Manon.

Manon.

Chaol couldn't let the king take Dorian back to the castle. He might never get this chance again.

He had to do it now. Had to kill him.

Chaol hurtled through the brush as quietly as he could, sword out, bracing himself.

A dagger through the eye—a dagger, and then—

Talking from ahead, along with the rustling of leaves and wood.

Chaol neared the party, beginning to pray, beginning to beg for forgiveness—for what he was about to do and for how he had run. He'd kill the king later; let that kill be his last. But this would be the kill that broke him.

He drew his dagger, cocking his arm. Dorian had been directly behind the king. One throw, to knock the prince off the horse, then a sweep of his sword, and it could be over. Aelin and the others could deal with the aftermath; he'd already be dead.

Chaol broke through the trees into a field, the dagger a burning weight in his hand.

It was not the king's party that stood there in the tall grass and sunlight.

Thirteen witches and their wyverns turned to him.

And smiled.

⁓

Aelin ran through the trees as Rowan tracked Chaol by scent alone.

If he got them killed, if he got them hurt—

They'd left Nesryn to guard Lysandra, ordering them to head for the forest across the nearby temple ravine and to wait under an outcropping of stones. Before herding Lysandra between the trees, Nesryn had tightly grabbed Aelin's arm and said, "Bring him back."

Aelin had only nodded before bolting.

Rowan was a streak of lightning through the trees, so much faster than her when she was stuck in this body. Aedion sprinted close behind him. She ran as quickly as she could, but—

The path veered away, and Chaol had taken the wrong fork. Where the hell had Chaol even been going?

She could scarcely draw breath fast enough. Then light flooded in through a break in the trees—the other side of the wide meadow.

Rowan and Aedion stood a few feet into the swaying grass, their swords out—but downcast.

She saw why a heartbeat later.

Not thirty feet from them, Chaol's lip bled down his chin as the white-haired witch held him against her, iron nails digging into his throat. The prison wagon was open beyond them to reveal the three dead soldiers inside.

The twelve witches behind the Wing Leader were all grinning with anticipatory delight as they took in Rowan and Aedion, then her.

"What's this?" the Wing Leader said, a killing light in her golden eyes. "Spies? Rescuers? Where did you take our prisoner?"

Chaol struggled, and she dug her nails in farther. He stiffened. A trickle of blood leaked down his neck and onto his tunic.

Oh, gods. Think—think, think, think.

The Wing Leader shifted those burnt-gold eyes to Rowan.

"Your kind," the Wing Leader mused, "I have not seen for a time."

"Let the man go," Rowan said.

Manon's smile revealed a row of flesh-shredding iron teeth, far, far too close to Chaol's neck. "I don't take orders from Fae bastards."

"Let him go," Rowan said too softly. "Or it will be the last mistake you make, Wing Leader."

In the field behind them, the wyverns were stirring, their tails lashing, wings shifting.

The white-haired witch peered at Chaol, whose breathing had turned ragged. "The king is not too far down the road. Perhaps I should hand you over to him." The cuts on her cheeks, scabbed in blue, were like brutal war paint. "He'll be furious to learn you stole his prisoner from me. Maybe you'll appease him, boy."

Aelin and Rowan shared all of one look before she stepped up to his side, drawing Goldryn. "If you want a prize to give to the king," Aelin said, "then take me."

"Don't," Chaol gasped out.

The witch and all twelve of her sentinels now fixed their immortal, deadly attention on Aelin.

Aelin dropped Goldryn into the grass and lifted her hands. Aedion snarled in warning.

"Why should I bother?" the Wing Leader said. "Perhaps we'll take you all to the king."

Aedion's sword lifted slightly. "You can try."

Aelin carefully approached the witch, her hands still up. "You enter into a fight with us, and you and your companions will die."

The Wing Leader looked her up and down. "Who are you." An order—not a question.

"Aelin Galathynius."

Surprise—and perhaps something else, something Aelin couldn't identify—sparked in the Wing Leader's golden eyes. "The Queen of Terrasen."

Aelin bowed, not daring to take her attention off the witch. "At your service."

Only three feet separated her from the Blackbeak heir.

The witch sliced a glance at Chaol, and then at Aedion and Rowan. "Your court?"

"What's it to you?"

The Wing Leader studied Aedion again. "Your brother?"

"My cousin, Aedion. Almost as pretty as me, wouldn't you say?"

The witch didn't smile.

But Aelin was now near enough, so close that the spatters of Chaol's blood lay in the grass before the tip of her boots.

⁓

The Queen of Terrasen.

Elide's hope had not been misplaced.

Even if the young queen was now toeing the dirt and grass, unable to keep still while she bargained for the man's life.

Behind her, the Fae warrior observed every flicker of movement.

He'd be the deadly one—the one to look out for.

It had been fifty years since she'd fought a Fae warrior. Bedded him, then fought him. He'd left the bones of her arm in pieces.

She'd just left him in pieces.

But he had been young, and arrogant, and barely trained.

This male . . . He might very well be capable of killing at least a few of her Thirteen if she so much as harmed a hair on the queen's head. And then there was the golden-haired one—as large as the Fae male, but possessing his cousin's bright arrogance and honed wildness. He might be problematic, if left alive too long.

The queen kept fidgeting her foot in the grass. She couldn't be more than twenty. And yet, she moved like a warrior, too—or she had, until the incessant shifting around. But she halted the movement, as if realizing that it gave away her nerves, her inexperience. The wind was blowing in the wrong direction for Manon to detect the queen's true level of fear. "Well, Wing Leader?"

Would the king put a collar around her fair neck, as he had the prince's? Or would he kill her? It made no difference. She would be a prize the king would welcome.

Manon shoved away the captain, sending him stumbling toward the queen. Aelin reached out with an arm, nudging him to the side—behind her. Manon and the queen stared at each other.

No fear in her eyes—in her pretty, mortal face.

None.

It'd be more trouble than it was worth.

Manon had bigger things to consider, anyway. Her grandmother approved. Approved of the breeding, the breaking of the witches.

Manon needed to get into the sky, needed to lose herself in cloud and wind for a few hours. Days. Weeks.

"I have no interest in prisoners or battling today," Manon said.

The Queen of Terrasen gave her a grin. "Good."

Manon turned away, barking at her Thirteen to get to their mounts.

"I suppose," the queen went on, "that makes you smarter than Baba Yellowlegs."

Manon stopped, staring straight ahead and seeing nothing of the grass or sky or trees.

Asterin whirled. "What do you know of Baba Yellowlegs?"

The queen gave a low chuckle, despite the warning growl from the Fae warrior.

Slowly, Manon looked over her shoulder.

The queen tugged apart the lapels of her tunic, revealing a necklace of thin scars as the wind shifted.

The scent—iron and stone and pure hatred—hit Manon like a rock to the face. Every Ironteeth witch knew the scent that forever lingered on those scars: Witch Killer.

Perhaps Manon would lose herself in blood and gore instead.

"You're carrion," Manon said, and lunged.

Only to slam face-first into an invisible wall.

And then freeze entirely.

"Run," Aelin breathed, snatching up Goldryn and bolting for the trees. The Wing Leader was frozen in place, her sentinels wide-eyed as they rushed to her.

Chaol's human blood wouldn't hold the spell for long.

"The ravine," Aedion said, not looking back from where he sprinted ahead with Chaol toward the temple.

They hurtled through the trees, the witches still in the meadow, still trying to break the spell that had trapped their Wing Leader.

"You," Rowan said as he ran beside her, "are one very lucky woman."

"Tell me that again when we're out of here," she panted, leaping over a fallen tree.

A roar of fury set the birds scattering from the trees, and Aelin ran faster. Oh, the Wing Leader was pissed. Really, really pissed.

Aelin hadn't believed for one moment that the witch would have let them walk away without a fight. She had needed to buy whatever time they could get.

The trees cleared, revealing a barren stretch of land jutting toward the deep ravine and the temple perched on the spit of rock in the center. On the other side, Oakwald sprawled onward.

Connected only by two chain-and-wood bridges, it was the sole way across the ravine for miles. And with the dense foliage of Oakwald blocking the wyverns, it was the only way to escape the witches, who would no doubt pursue on foot.

"*Hurry*," Rowan shouted as they made for the crumbling temple ruins.

The temple was small enough that not even the priestesses had dwelled here. The only decorations on the stone island were five weather-stained pillars and a crumbling, domed roof. Not even an altar—or at least one that had survived the centuries.

Apparently, people had given up on Temis long before the King of Adarlan came along.

She just prayed that the bridges on either side—

Aedion hurled himself to a stop before the first footbridge, Chaol thirty paces behind, Aelin and Rowan following. "Secure," Aedion said. Before she could bark a warning, he thundered across.

The bridge bounced and swayed, but held—held even as her damn heart stopped. Then Aedion was at the temple island, the single, thin pillar of rock carved out by the rushing river flowing far, far below. He waved Chaol on. "One at a time," he ordered. Beyond him the second bridge waited.

Chaol hurried through the stone pillars that flanked the entrance to the first bridge, the thin iron chains on the sides writhing as the bridge bounced. He kept upright, flying toward the temple, faster than she'd ever seen him run during all those morning exercises through the castle grounds.

Then Aelin and Rowan were at the columns, and— "Don't even try to argue," Rowan hissed, shoving her ahead of him.

Gods above, that was a wicked drop beneath them. The roar of the river was barely a whisper.

But she ran—ran because Rowan was waiting, and there were the witches breaking through the trees with Fae swiftness. The bridge bucked and swayed as she shot over the aging wooden planks. Ahead, Aedion had cleared the second bridge to the other side, and Chaol was now sprinting across it. Faster—she had to go faster. She leaped the final few feet onto the temple rock.

Ahead, Chaol exited the second bridge and drew his blade as he joined Aedion on the grassy cliff beyond, an arrow nocked in her cousin's bow— aimed at the trees behind her. Aelin lunged up the few stairs onto the bald temple platform. The entire circular space was barely more than thirty feet across, bordered on all sides by a sheer plunge—and death.

Temis, apparently, was not the forgiving sort.

She twisted to look behind. Rowan was running across the bridge, so fast that the bridge hardly moved, but—

Aelin swore. The Wing Leader had reached the posts, flinging herself over and jumping through the air to land a third of the way down the bridge. Even Aedion's warning shot went long, the arrow imbedding where any mortal *should* have landed. But not a witch. Holy burning hell.

"*Go*," Rowan roared at Aelin, but she palmed her fighting knives, bending her knees as—

As an arrow fired by the golden-haired lieutenant shot for Aelin from the other side of the ravine.

Aelin twisted to avoid it, only to find a second arrow from the witch already there, anticipating her maneuver.

A wall of muscle slammed into her, shielding her and shoving her to the stones.

And the witch's arrow went clean through Rowan's shoulder.

CHAPTER 60

For a moment, the world stopped.

Rowan slammed onto the temple stones, his blood spraying on the aging rock.

Aelin's scream echoed down the ravine.

But then he was up again, running and bellowing at her to *go*. Beneath the dark arrow protruding through his shoulder, blood already soaked his tunic, his skin.

If he had been one inch farther behind, it would have hit his heart.

Not forty paces down the bridge, the Wing Leader closed in on them. Aedion rained arrows on her sentinels with preternatural precision, keeping them at bay by the tree line.

Aelin wrapped an arm around Rowan and they raced across the temple stones, his face paling as the wound gushed blood. She might have still been screaming, or sobbing—there was such a roaring silence in her.

Her heart—it had been meant for *her* heart.

And he had taken that arrow for her.

The killing calm spread through her like hoarfrost. She'd kill them all. Slowly.

They reached the second bridge just as Aedion's barrage of arrows halted, his quiver no doubt emptied. She shoved Rowan onto the planks. "Run," she said.

"No—"

"*Run.*"

It was a voice that she'd never heard herself use—a queen's voice—that came out, along with the blind *yank* she made on the blood oath that bound them together.

His eyes flashed with fury, but his body moved as though she'd compelled him. He staggered across the bridge, just as—

Aelin whirled, drawing Goldryn and ducking just as the Wing Leader's sword swiped for her head.

It hit stone, the pillar groaning, but Aelin was already moving—not toward the second bridge but back toward the first one, on the witches' side.

Where the other witches, without Aedion's arrows to block them, were now racing from the cover of the woods.

"*You,*" the Wing Leader growled, attacking again. Aelin rolled—right through Rowan's blood—again dodging the fatal blow. She uncurled to her feet right in front of the first bridge, and two swings of Goldryn had the chains snapping.

The witches skidded to a stop at the lip of the ravine as the bridge collapsed, cutting them off.

The air behind her shifted, and Aelin moved—but not fast enough.

Cloth and flesh tore in her upper arm, and she barked out a cry as the witch's blade sliced her.

She whirled, bringing Goldryn up for the second blow.

Steel met steel and sparked.

Rowan's blood was at her feet, smeared across the temple stones.

Aelin Galathynius looked at Manon Blackbeak over their crossed swords and let out a low, vicious snarl.

Queen, savior, enemy, Manon didn't give a shit.

She was going to kill the woman.

Their laws demanded it; honor demanded it.

Even if she hadn't slaughtered Baba Yellowlegs, Manon would have killed her just for that spell she'd used to freeze her in place.

That was what she'd been doing with her feet. Etching some foul spell with the man's blood.

And now she was going to die.

Wind-Cleaver pressed against the queen's blade. But Aelin held her ground and hissed, "I'm going to rip you to shreds."

Behind them, the Thirteen gathered on the ravine's edge, cut off. One whistle from Manon had half of them scrambling for the wyverns. She didn't get to sound the second whistle.

Faster than a human had a right to be, the queen swept out a leg, sending Manon tripping back. Aelin didn't hesitate; she flipped the sword in her hand and lunged.

Manon deflected the blow, but Aelin got past her guard and pinned her, slamming her head against stones that were damp with the Fae warrior's blood. Splotches of dark bloomed in her vision.

Manon drew in breath for the second whistle—the one to call off Asterin and her arrows.

She was interrupted by the queen slamming her fist into Manon's face.

Black splintered further across her vision—but she twisted, twisted with every bit of her immortal strength, and they went flipping across the temple floor. The drop loomed, and then—

An arrow whizzed right for the queen's exposed back as she landed atop Manon.

Manon twisted again, and the arrow bounced off the pillar instead. She threw Aelin from her, but the queen was instantly on her feet again, nimble as a cat.

"*She's mine*," Manon barked across the ravine to Asterin.

The queen laughed, hoarse and cold, circling as Manon got to her feet.

Across the other side of the ravine, the two males were helping the wounded Fae warrior off the bridge, and the golden-haired warrior charged—

"Don't you dare, Aedion," Aelin said, throwing out a hand in the male's direction.

He froze halfway across the bridge. Impressive, Manon admitted, to have them under her command so thoroughly.

"Chaol, keep an eye on him," the queen barked.

Then, holding Manon's gaze, Aelin sheathed her mighty blade across her back, the giant ruby in the pommel catching in the midday light.

"Swords are boring," the queen said, and palmed two fighting knives.

Manon sheathed Wind-Cleaver along her own back. She flicked her wrists, the iron nails shooting out. She cracked her jaw, and her fangs descended. "Indeed."

The queen looked at the nails, the teeth, and grinned.

Honestly—it was a shame that Manon had to kill her.

Manon Blackbeak lunged, as swift and deadly as an adder.

Aelin darted back, dodging each swipe of those lethal iron nails. For her throat, for her face, for her guts. Back, and back, circling around the pillars.

It was only a matter of minutes before the wyverns arrived.

Aelin jabbed with her daggers, and the witch sidestepped her, only to slash with her nails, right at Aelin's neck.

Aelin spun aside, but the nails grazed her skin. Blood warmed her neck and shoulders.

The witch was so damn fast. And one hell of a fighter.

But Rowan and the others were across the second bridge.

Now she just had to get there, too.

Manon Blackbeak feinted left and slashed right.

Aelin ducked and rolled aside.

The pillar shuddered as those iron claws gouged four lines deep into the stone.

Manon hissed. Aelin made to drive her dagger into her spine; the witch lashed out with a hand and wrapped it clean around the blade.

Blue blood welled, but the witch bore down on the blade until it snapped into three pieces in her hand.

Gods above.

Aelin had the sense to go in low with her other dagger, but the witch was already there—and Aedion's shout rang in her ears as Manon's knee drove up into her gut.

The air knocked from her in a whoosh, but Aelin kept her grip on the dagger, even as the witch threw her into another pillar.

The stone column rocked against the blow, and Aelin's head cracked, agony arcing through her, but—

A slash, directly for her face.

Aelin ducked.

Again, the stone shuddered beneath the impact.

Aelin squeezed air into her body. *Move*—she had to keep moving, smooth as a stream, smooth as the wind of her *carranam*, bleeding and hurt across the way.

Pillar to pillar, she retreated, rolling and ducking and dodging.

Manon swiped and slashed, slamming into every column, a force of nature in her own right.

And then back around, again and again, pillar after pillar absorbing the blows that should have shredded her face, her neck. Aelin slowed her steps, let Manon think she was tiring, growing clumsy—

"*Enough*, coward," Manon hissed, making to tackle Aelin to the ground.

But Aelin swung around a pillar and onto the thin lip of bare rock beyond the temple platform, the drop looming, just as Manon collided with the column.

The pillar groaned, swayed—and toppled to the side, hitting the pillar beside it, sending them both cracking to the ground.

Along with the domed roof.

Manon didn't even have time to lunge out of the way as the marble crashed down on her.

One of the few remaining witches on the other side of the ravine screamed.

Aelin was already running, even as the rock island itself began trembling, as if whatever ancient force held this temple together had died the moment the roof crumbled.

Shit.

Aelin sprinted for the second bridge, dust and debris burning her eyes and lungs.

The island jolted with a thunderous *crack*, so violent that Aelin stumbled. But there were the posts and the bridge beyond, Aedion waiting on the other side—an arm held out, beckoning.

The island swayed again—wider and longer this time.

It was going to collapse beneath them.

There was a flicker of blue and white, a flash of red cloth, a glimmer of iron—

A hand and a shoulder, grappling with a fallen column.

Slowly, painfully, Manon heaved herself onto a slab of marble, her face coated in pale dust, blue blood leaking down her temple.

Across the ravine, cut off entirely, the golden-haired witch was on her knees. "*Manon!*"

I don't think you've ever groveled for anything in your life, Wing Leader, the king had said.

But there was a Blackbeak witch on her knees, begging whatever gods they worshipped; and there was Manon Blackbeak, struggling to rise as the temple island crumbled away.

Aelin took a step onto the bridge.

Asterin—that was the golden-haired witch's name. She screamed for Manon again, a plea to rise, to survive.

The island jolted.

The remaining bridge—the bridge to her friends, to Rowan, to safety—still held.

Aelin had felt it before: a thread in the world, a current running between her and someone else. She'd felt it one night, years ago, and had given a young healer the money to get the hell out of this continent. She'd felt the tug—and had decided to tug back.

Here it was again, that tug—toward Manon, whose arms buckled as she collapsed to the stone.

Her enemy—her new enemy, who would have killed her and Rowan if given the chance. A monster incarnate.

But perhaps the monsters needed to look out for each other every now and then.

"*Run!*" Aedion roared from across the ravine.

So she did.

Aelin ran for Manon, leaping over the fallen stones, her ankle wrenching on loose debris.

The island rocked with her every step, and the sunlight was scalding, as if Mala were holding that island aloft with every last bit of strength the goddess could summon in this land.

Then Aelin was upon Manon Blackbeak, and the witch lifted hate-filled eyes to her. Aelin hauled off stone after stone from her body, the island beneath them buckling.

"You're too good a fighter to kill," Aelin breathed, hooking an arm under Manon's shoulders and hauling her up. The rock swayed to the left—but held. Oh, gods. "If I die because of you, I'll beat the shit out of you in hell."

She could have sworn the witch let out a broken laugh as she got to her feet, nearly a dead weight in Aelin's arms.

"You—should let me die," Manon rasped as they limped over the rubble.

"I know, I know," Aelin panted, her sliced arm aching with the weight of the witch it supported. They hurried over the second bridge, the temple rock swaying to the right—stretching the bridge behind them tightly over the drop and the shining river far, far below.

Aelin tugged at the witch, gritting her teeth, and Manon stumbled into a staggering run. Aedion remained between the posts across the ravine, an arm still extended toward her—while his other lifted his sword high, ready for the Wing Leader's arrival. The rock behind them groaned.

Halfway—nothing but a death-plunge waiting for them. Manon coughed blue blood onto the wooden slats. Aelin snapped, "What the hell good are your beasts if they can't save you from this kind of thing?"

The island veered back in the other direction, and the bridge went taut—oh, shit—*shit*, it was going to snap. Faster they ran, until she could see Aedion's straining fingers and the whites of his eyes.

The rock cracked, so loudly it deafened her. Then came the tug and stretch of the bridge as the island began to crumble into dust, sliding to the side—

Aelin lunged the last few steps, gripping Manon's red cloak as the chains of the bridge snapped. The wooden slats dropped out from beneath them, but they were already leaping.

Aelin let out a grunt as she slammed into Aedion. She whirled to see Chaol grabbing Manon and hauling her over the lip of the ravine, her cloak torn and covered in dust, fluttering in the wind.

When Aelin looked past the witch, the temple was gone.

Manon gasped for air, concentrating on her breathing, on the cloudless sky above her.

The humans left her lying between the stone bridge posts. The queen hadn't even bothered to say good-bye. She'd just dashed for the injured Fae warrior, his name like a prayer on her lips.

Rowan.

Manon had looked up in time to see the queen fall to her knees before the injured warrior in the grass, demanding answers from the brown-haired man—Chaol—who pressed a hand to the arrow wound in Rowan's shoulder to stanch the bleeding. The queen's shoulders were shaking.

Fireheart, the Fae warrior murmured. Manon would have watched— would have, had she not coughed blood onto the bright grass and blacked out.

When she awoke, they were gone.

Only minutes had passed—because then there were booming wings, and Abraxos's roar. And there were Asterin and Sorrel, rushing for her before their wyverns had fully landed.

The Queen of Terrasen had saved her life. Manon didn't know what to make of it.

For she now owed her enemy a life debt.

And she had just learned how thoroughly her grandmother and the King of Adarlan intended to destroy them.

CHAPTER 61

The trek back through Oakwald was the longest journey of Aelin's miserable life. Nesryn had removed the arrow from Rowan's shoulder, and Aedion had found some herbs to chew and shove into the open wound to stanch the bleeding.

But Rowan still sagged against Chaol and Aedion as they hurried through the forest.

Nowhere to go. She had nowhere to take an injured Fae male in the capital city, in this entire shit-hole kingdom.

Lysandra was pale and shaking, but she'd squared her shoulders and offered to help carry Rowan when one of them tired. None of them accepted. When Chaol at last asked Nesryn to take over, Aelin glimpsed the blood soaking his tunic and hands—Rowan's blood—and nearly vomited.

Slower—every step was slower as Rowan's strength flagged.

"He needs to rest," Lysandra said gently. Aelin paused, the towering oaks pressing in around her.

Rowan's eyes were half-closed, his face drained of all color. He couldn't even lift his head.

She should have let the witch die.

"We can't just camp out in the middle of the woods," Aelin said. "He needs a healer."

"I know where we can take him," Chaol said. She dragged her eyes to the captain.

She should have let the witch kill him, too.

Chaol wisely averted his gaze and faced Nesryn. "Your father's country house—the man who runs it is married to a midwife."

Nesryn's mouth tightened. "She's not a healer, but—yes. She might have something."

"Do you understand," Aelin said very quietly to them, "that if I suspect they're going to betray us, they will die?"

It was true, and maybe it made her a monster to Chaol, but she didn't care.

"I know," Chaol said. Nesryn merely nodded, still calm, still solid.

"Then lead the way," Aelin said, her voice hollow. "And pray they can keep their mouths shut."

⌒

Joyous, frenzied barking greeted them, rousing Rowan from the half consciousness he'd fallen into during the last few miles to the little stone farmhouse. Aelin had barely breathed the entire time.

But despite herself, despite Rowan's injuries, as Fleetfoot raced across the high grass toward them, Aelin smiled a little.

The dog leaped upon her, licking and whining and wagging her feathery, golden tail.

She hadn't realized how filthy and bloody her hands were until she put them on Fleetfoot's shining coat.

Aedion grunted as he took all of Rowan's weight while Chaol and Nesryn jogged for the large, brightly lit stone house, dusk having fallen fully around them. Good. Fewer eyes to see as they exited Oakwald and crossed the freshly tilled fields. Lysandra tried to help Aedion, but he refused her again. She hissed at him and helped anyway.

Fleetfoot danced around Aelin, then noticed Aedion, Lysandra, and Rowan, and that tail became a bit more tentative. "Friends," she told her dog. She'd become huge since Aelin had last seen her. She wasn't sure why it surprised her, when everything else in her life had changed as well.

Aelin's assurance seemed good enough for Fleetfoot, who trotted ahead, escorting them to the wooden door that had opened to reveal a tall midwife with a no-nonsense face that took one look at Rowan and tightened.

One word. One damn word that suggested she might turn them in, and she was dead.

But the woman said, "Whoever put that bloodmoss on the wound saved his life. Get him inside—we need to clean it before anything else can be done."

It took a few hours for Marta, the housekeeper's wife, to clean, disinfect, and patch up Rowan's wounds. *Lucky*, she kept saying—*so lucky it didn't hit anything vital.*

Chaol didn't know what to do with himself other than carry away the bowls of bloodied water.

Aelin just sat on a stool beside the cot in the spare room of the elegant, comfortable house, and monitored every move Marta made.

Chaol wondered if Aelin knew that she was a bloodied mess. That she looked even worse than Rowan.

Her neck was brutalized, blood had dried on her face, her cheek was bruised, and the left sleeve of her tunic was torn open to reveal a vicious slice. And then there were the dust, dirt, and blue blood of the Wing Leader coating her.

But Aelin perched on the stool, never moving, only drinking water, snarling if Marta so much as looked at Rowan funny.

Marta, somehow, endured it.

And when the midwife was done, she faced the queen. With no clue at all who sat in her house, Marta said, "You have two choices: you can either go wash up in the spigot outside, or you can sit with the pigs all night. You're dirty enough that one touch could infect his wounds."

Aelin glanced over her shoulder at Aedion, who was leaning against the wall behind her. He nodded silently. He'd look after him.

Aelin rose and stalked out.

"I'll inspect your other friend now," Marta said, and hurried to where Lysandra had fallen asleep in the adjoining room, curled up on a narrow bed cot. Upstairs, Nesryn was busy dealing with the staff—ensuring their silence. But he'd seen the tentative joy on their faces when they'd arrived: Nesryn and the Faliq family had earned their loyalty long ago.

Chaol gave Aelin two minutes, and then followed her outside.

The stars were bright overhead, the full moon nearly blinding. The night wind whispered through the grass, barely audible over the clunk and sputter of the spigot.

He found the queen crouched before it, her face in the stream of water.

"I'm sorry," he said.

She rubbed at her face and heaved the lever until more water poured over her.

Chaol went on, "I just wanted to end it for him. You were right—all this time, you were right. But I wanted to do it myself. I didn't know it would . . . I'm sorry."

She released the lever and pivoted to look up at him.

"I saved my enemy's life today," she said flatly. She uncoiled to her feet, wiping the water from her face. And though he stood taller than her, he felt smaller as Aelin stared at him. No, not just Aelin. Queen Aelin Ashryver Galathynius, he realized, was staring at him. "They tried to shoot my . . . Rowan through the heart. And I saved her anyway."

"I know," he said. Her scream when that arrow had gone through Rowan . . .

"I'm sorry," he said again.

She gazed up at the stars—toward the North. Her face was so cold. "Would you truly have killed him if you'd had the chance?"

"Yes," Chaol breathed. "I was ready for that."

She slowly turned to him. "We'll do it—together. We'll free magic, then you and I will go in there and end it together."

"You're not going to insist I stay back?"

"How can I deny you that last gift to him?"

"Aelin—"

Her shoulders sagged slightly. "I don't blame you. If it had been Rowan with that collar around his neck, I would have done the same thing."

The words hit him in the gut as she walked away.

A monster, he'd called her weeks ago. He had believed it, and allowed it to be a shield against the bitter tang of disappointment and sorrow.

He was a fool.

They moved Rowan before dawn. By whatever immortal grace lingering in his veins, he'd healed enough to walk on his own, and so they slipped out of the lovely country house before any of the staff awoke. Aelin said good-bye only to Fleetfoot, who had slept curled by her side during the long night that she'd watched over Rowan.

Then they were off, Aelin and Aedion flanking Rowan, his arms slung over their shoulders as they hurried across the foothills.

The early-morning mist cloaked them as they made their way into Rifthold one last time.

CHAPTER 62

Manon didn't bother looking pleasant as she sent Abraxos slamming into the ground in front of the king's party. The horses whinnied and bucked while the Thirteen circled above the clearing in which they'd spotted the party.

"Wing Leader," the king said from astride his warhorse, not at all perturbed. Beside him, his son—Dorian—cringed.

Cringed the way that blond thing in Morath had when it attacked them.

"Was there something you wanted?" the king asked coolly. "Or a reason you look halfway to Hellas's realm?"

Manon dismounted Abraxos and walked toward the king and his son. The prince focused on his saddle, careful not to meet her eyes. "There are rebels in your woods," she said. "They took your little prisoner out of the wagon, and then tried to attack me and my Thirteen. I slaughtered them all. I hope you don't mind. They left three of your men dead in the wagon—though it seems their loss wasn't noticed."

The king merely said, "You came all this way to tell me that?"

"I came all this way to tell you that when I face your rebels, your enemies, I shall have no interest in prisoners. And the Thirteen are not a caravan to transport them as you will."

She stepped closer to the prince's horse. "Dorian," she said. A command and a challenge.

Sapphire eyes snapped to hers. No trace of otherworldly darkness.

Just a man trapped inside.

She faced the king. "You should send your son to Morath. It'd be his sort of place." Before the king could reply, Manon walked back to Abraxos.

She'd planned on telling the king about Aelin. About the rebels who called themselves Aedion and Rowan and Chaol.

But . . . they were human and could not travel swiftly—not if they were injured.

She owed her enemy a life debt.

Manon climbed into Abraxos's saddle. "My grandmother might be High Witch," she said to the king, "but I ride at the head of the armies."

The king chuckled. "Ruthless. I think I rather like you, Wing Leader."

"That weapon my grandmother made—the mirrors. You truly plan to use shadowfire with it?"

The king's ruddy face tightened with warning. The replica inside the wagon had been a fraction of the size of what was depicted in the plans nailed to the wall: giant, transportable battle towers, a hundred feet high, their insides lined with the sacred mirrors of the Ancients. Mirrors that were once used to build and break and mend. Now they would be amplifiers, reflecting and multiplying any power the king chose to unleash, until it became a weapon that could be aimed at any target. If the power were Kaltain's shadowfire . . .

"You ask too many questions, Wing Leader," the king said.

"I don't like surprises," was her only reply. Except this—this had been a surprise.

The weapon wasn't for winning glory or triumph or the love of battle.

It was for extermination. A full-scale slaughter that would involve little fighting at all. Any opposing army—even Aelin and her warriors—would be defenseless.

The king's face was turning purple with impatience.

But Manon was already taking to the skies, Abraxos beating his wings hard. She watched the prince until he was a speck of black hair.

And wondered what it was like to be trapped within that body.

⁓

Elide Lochan waited for the supply wagon. It didn't come.

A day late; two days late. She hardly slept for fear it would arrive when she was dozing. When she awoke on the third day, her mouth dry, it was already habit to hurry down to help in the kitchen. She worked until her leg nearly gave out.

Then, just before sunset, the whinny of horses and the clatter of wheels and the shouts of men bounced off the dark stones of the long Keep bridge.

Elide slipped from the kitchen before they could notice her, before the cook could conscript her into performing some new task. She hurried up the steps as best she could with her chain, her heart in her throat. She should have kept her things downstairs, should have found some hiding spot.

Up and up, into Manon's tower. She'd refilled the water skein each morning, and had amassed a little supply of food in a pouch. Elide threw open the door to Manon's room, surging for the pallet where she kept her supplies.

But Vernon was inside.

He sat on the edge of Manon's bed as if it were his own.

"Going somewhere, Elide?"

CHAPTER 63

"Where on earth could you be headed?" Vernon said as he stood, smug as a cat.

Panic bleated in her veins. The wagon—the *wagon*—

"Was that the plan all along? To hide among those witches, and then run?"

Elide backed toward the door. Vernon clicked his tongue.

"We both know there's no point in running. And the Wing Leader isn't going to be here anytime soon."

Elide's knees wobbled. Oh, gods.

"But is my beautiful, clever niece human—or witch-kind? Such an important question." He grabbed her by the elbow, a small knife in his hand. She could do nothing against the stinging slice in her arm, the red blood that welled. "Not a witch at all, it seems."

"I am a Blackbeak," Elide breathed. She would not bow to him, would not cower.

Vernon circled her. "Too bad they're all up north and can't verify it."

Fight, fight, fight, her blood sang—*do not let him cage you. Your mother went down fighting. She was a witch, and you are a witch, and you do not yield—you do not yield—*

Vernon lunged, faster than she could avoid in her chains, one hand gripping her under the arm while the other slammed her head into the wood so hard that her body just—stopped.

That was all he needed—that stupid pause—to pin her other arm, gripping both in his hand while the other now clenched on her neck hard enough to hurt, to make her realize that her uncle had once trained as her father had. "You're coming with me."

"No." The word was a whisper of breath.

His grip tightened, twisting her arms until they barked in pain. "Don't you know what a prize you are? What you might be able to do?"

He yanked her back, opening the door. No—no, she wouldn't let him take her, wouldn't—

But screaming would do her no good. Not in a Keep full of monsters. Not in a world where no one remembered she existed, or bothered to care. She stilled, and he took that as acquiescence. She could feel his smile at the back of her head as he nudged her into the stairwell.

"Blackbeak blood is in your veins—along with our family's generous line of magic." He hauled her down the stairs, and bile burned her throat. There was no one coming for her—because she had belonged to no one. "The witches don't have magic, not like us. But you, a hybrid of both lines . . ." Vernon gripped her arm harder, right over the cut he'd made, and she cried out. The sound echoed, hollow and small, down the stone stairwell. "You do your house a great honor, Elide."

⁓

Vernon left her in a freezing dungeon cell.

No light.

No sound, save for the dripping of water somewhere.

Shaking, Elide didn't even have the words to beg as Vernon tossed her inside. "You brought this upon yourself, you know," he said, "when you allied with that witch and confirmed my suspicions that their blood flows through your veins." He studied her, but she was gobbling down the details of the cell—anything, *anything* to get her out. She found nothing. "I'll leave you here until you're ready. I doubt anyone will notice your absence, anyway."

He slammed the door, and darkness swallowed her entirely.

She didn't bother trying the handle.

Manon was summoned by the duke the moment she set foot in Morath.

The messenger was cowering in the archway to the aerie, and could barely get the words out as he took in the blood and dirt and dust that still covered Manon.

She'd contemplated snapping her teeth at him just for trembling like a spineless fool, but she was drained, her head was pounding, and anything more than basic movement required far too much thought.

None of the Thirteen had dared say anything about her grand-mother—that she had approved of the breeding.

Sorrel and Vesta trailing mere steps behind her, Manon flung open the doors to the duke's council chamber, letting the slamming wood say enough about what she thought of being summoned immediately.

The duke—only Kaltain beside him—flicked his eyes over her. "Explain your . . . appearance."

Manon opened her mouth.

If Vernon heard that Aelin Galathynius was alive—if he suspected for one heartbeat the debt that Aelin might feel toward Elide's mother for saving her life, he might very well decide to end his niece's life. "Rebels attacked us. I killed them all."

The duke chucked a file of papers onto the table. They hit the glass and slid, spreading out in a fan. "For months now, you've wanted explanations.

Well, here they are. Status reports on our enemies, larger targets for us to strike . . . His Majesty sends his best wishes."

Manon approached. "Did he also send that demon prince into my barracks to attack us?" She stared at the duke's thick neck, wondering how easily the rough skin would tear.

Perrington's mouth twisted to the side. "Roland had outlived his usefulness. Who better to take care of him than your Thirteen?"

"I hadn't realized we were to be your executioners." She should indeed rip out his throat for what he'd tried to do. Beside him, Kaltain was wholly blank, a shell. But that shadowfire . . . Would she summon it if the duke were attacked?

"Sit and read the files, Wing Leader."

She didn't appreciate the command, and let out a snarl to tell him so, but she sat.

And read.

Reports on Eyllwe, on Melisande, on Fenharrow, on the Red Desert, and Wendlyn.

And on Terrasen.

According to the report, Aelin Galathynius—long believed to be dead—had appeared in Wendlyn and bested four of the Valg princes, including a lethal general in the king's army. Using fire.

Aelin had fire magic, Elide had said. *She could have survived the cold.*

But—but that meant that magic . . . Magic still worked in Wendlyn. And not here.

Manon would bet a great deal of the gold hoarded at Blackbeak Keep that the man in front of her—and the king in Rifthold—was the reason why.

Then a report of Prince Aedion Ashryver, former general of Adarlan, kin to the Ashryvers of Wendlyn, being arrested for treason. For associating with rebels. He had been rescued from his execution mere weeks ago by unknown forces.

Possible suspects: Lord Ren Allsbrook of Terrasen . . .

And Lord Chaol Westfall of Adarlan, who had loyally served the king as his Captain of the Guard until he'd joined forces with Aedion this past spring and fled the castle the day of Aedion's capture. They suspected the captain hadn't gone far—and that he would try to free his lifelong friend, the Crown Prince.

Free him.

The prince had taunted her, provoked her—as if trying to get her to kill him. And Roland had begged for death.

If Chaol and Aedion were both now with Aelin Galathynius, all working together . . .

They hadn't been in the forest to spy.

But to save the prince. And whoever that female prisoner had been. They'd rescued one friend, at least.

The duke and the king didn't know. They didn't know how close they'd been to all their targets, or how close their enemies had come to seizing their prince.

That was why the captain had come running.

He had come to kill the prince—the only mercy he believed he could offer him.

The rebels didn't know that the man was still inside.

"Well?" the duke demanded. "Any questions?"

"You have yet to explain the necessity of the weapon my grandmother is building. A tool like that could be catastrophic. If there's no magic, then surely obliterating the Queen of Terrasen can't be worth the risk of using those towers."

"Better to be overprepared than surprised. We have full control of the towers."

Manon tapped an iron nail on the glass table.

"This is a base of information, Wing Leader. Continue to prove yourself, and you will receive more."

Prove herself? She hadn't done anything lately to prove herself, except—except shred one of his demon princes and butcher that mountain tribe for no good reason. A shiver of rage went through her. Unleashing the prince in the barracks hadn't been a message, then, but a test. To see if she could hold up against his worst, and still obey.

"Have you picked a coven for me?"

Manon forced herself to give a dismissive shrug. "I was waiting to see who behaved themselves the best while I was away. It'll be their reward."

"You have until tomorrow."

Manon stared him down. "The moment I leave this room, I'm going to bathe and sleep for a day. If you or your little demon cronies bother me before then, you'll learn just how much I enjoy playing executioner. The day after that, I'll make my decision."

"You wouldn't be avoiding it, would you, Wing Leader?"

"Why should I bother handing out favors to covens that don't deserve them?" Manon didn't give herself one heartbeat to contemplate what the Matron was letting these men do as she gathered up the files, shoved them into Sorrel's arms, and strode out.

She had just reached the stairs to her tower when she spotted Asterin leaning against the archway, picking at her iron nails.

Sorrel and Vesta sucked in their breath.

"What is it?" Manon demanded, flicking out her own nails.

Asterin's face was a mask of immortal boredom. "We need to talk."

⁓

She and Asterin flew into the mountains, and she let her cousin lead—let Abraxos follow Asterin's sky-blue female until they were far from Morath. They alighted on a little plateau covered in purple and orange wildflowers, its grasses hissing in the wind. Abraxos was practically grunting with joy, and Manon, her exhaustion as heavy as the red cloak she wore, didn't bother to reprimand him.

They left their wyverns in the field. The mountain wind was surprisingly warm, the day clear and the sky full of fat, puffy clouds. She'd ordered Sorrel and Vesta to remain behind, despite their protests. If things had gotten to the point where Asterin could not be trusted to be alone with her . . . Manon did not want to consider it.

Perhaps that was why she had agreed to come.

Perhaps it was because of the scream Asterin had issued from the other side of the ravine.

It had been so like the scream of the Blueblood heir, Petrah, when her wyvern had been ripped to shreds. Like the scream of Petrah's mother when Petrah and her wyvern, Keelie, had tumbled into thin air.

Asterin walked to the edge of the plateau, the wildflowers swaying about her calves, her riding leathers shining in the bright sun. She unbraided her hair, shaking out the golden waves, then unbuckled her sword and daggers and let them thud to the ground. "I need you to listen, and not talk," she said as Manon came to stand beside her.

A high demand to make of her heir, but there was no challenge, no threat in it. And Asterin had never spoken to her like that. So Manon nodded.

Asterin stared out across the mountains—so vibrant here, now that they were far from the darkness of Morath. A balmy breeze flitted between them, ruffling Asterin's curls until they looked like sunshine given form.

"When I was twenty-eight, I was off hunting Crochans in a valley just west of the Fangs. I had a hundred miles to go before the next village, and when a storm rolled in, I didn't feel like landing. So I tried to outrace the storm on my broom, tried to fly over it. But the storm went on and on, up and up. I don't know if it was the lightning or the wind, but suddenly I was falling. I managed to get control of my broom long enough to land, but the impact was brutal. Before I blacked out, I knew my arm was broken in two different places, my ankle twisted beyond use, and my broom shattered."

Over eighty years ago—this had been over eighty years ago, and Manon had never heard of it. She'd been off on her own mission—where, she couldn't remember now. All those years she'd spent hunting Crochans had blurred together.

"When I awoke, I was in a human cabin, my broom in pieces beside the bed. The man who had found me said he'd been riding home through the storm and saw me fall from the sky. He was a young hunter—mostly of exotic game, which was why he had a cabin out in the deep wild. I think I would have killed him if I'd had any strength, if only because I wanted his resources. But I faded in and out of consciousness for a few days while my bones knitted together, and when I awoke again . . . he fed me enough that he stopped looking like food. Or a threat."

A long silence.

"I stayed there for five months. I didn't hunt a single Crochan. I helped him stalk game, found ironwood and began carving a new broom, and . . . And we both knew what I was, what he was. That I was long-lived and he was human. But we were the same age at that moment, and we didn't care. So I stayed with him until my orders bade me report back to Blackbeak Keep. And I told him . . . I said I'd come back when I could."

Manon could hardly think, hardly breathe over the silence in her head. She'd never heard of this. Not a whisper. For Asterin to have ignored her sacred duties . . . For her to have taken up with this human man . . .

"I was a month pregnant when I arrived back at Blackbeak Keep."

Manon's knees wobbled.

"You were already gone—off on your next mission. I told no one, not until I knew that the pregnancy would actually survive those first few months."

Not unexpected, as most witches lost their offspring during that time. For the witchling to grow past that threshold was a miracle in itself.

"But I made it to three months, then four. And when I couldn't hide it anymore, I told your grandmother. She was pleased, and ordered me on bed rest in the Keep, so nothing disturbed me or the witchling in my womb. I told her I wanted to go back out, but she refused. I knew better than to tell her I wanted to return to that cabin in the forest. I knew she'd kill him. So I remained in the tower for months, a pampered prisoner. You even visited, twice, and she didn't tell you I was there. Not until the witchling was born, she said."

A long, uneven breath.

It wasn't uncommon for witches to be overprotective of those carrying witchlings. And Asterin, bearing the Matron's bloodline, would have been a valued commodity.

"I made a plan. The moment I recovered from the birth, the moment they looked away, I'd take the witchling to her father and present her to him. I thought maybe a life in the forest, quiet and peaceful, would be better for my witchling than the bloodshed we had. I thought maybe it would be better . . . for me."

Asterin's voice broke on the last two words. Manon couldn't bring herself to look at her cousin.

"I gave birth. The witchling almost ripped me in two coming out. I thought it was because she was a fighter, because she was a true Blackbeak. And I was proud. Even as I was screaming, even as I was bleeding, I was so proud of her."

Asterin fell silent, and Manon looked at her at last.

Tears were rolling down her cousin's face, gleaming in the sunshine. Asterin closed her eyes and whispered into the wind. "She was stillborn. I waited to hear that cry of triumph, but there was only silence. Silence, and then your grandmother . . ." She opened her eyes. "Your grandmother struck me. She beat me. Again and again. All I wanted was to see my witchling, and she ordered them to have her burned instead. She refused to let me see her. I was a disgrace to every witch who had come before me; I was to blame for a defective witchling; I had dishonored the Blackbeaks; I had disappointed her. She screamed it at me again and again, and when I sobbed, she . . . she . . ."

Manon didn't know where to stare, what to do with her arms.

A stillborn was a witch's greatest sorrow—and shame. But for her grandmother . . .

Asterin unbuttoned her jacket and shrugged it off into the flowers. She removed her shirt, and the one beneath, until her golden skin glowed in the sunlight, her breasts full and heavy. Asterin turned, and Manon fell to her knees in the grass.

There, branded on Asterin's abdomen in vicious, crude letters was one word:

UNCLEAN

"She branded me. Had them heat up the iron in the same flame where my witchling burned and stamped each letter herself. She said I had no business ever trying to conceive a Blackbeak again. That most men would take one look at the word and run."

Eighty years. For eighty years she had hidden this. But Manon had seen her naked, had—

No. No, she hadn't. Not for decades and decades. When they were witchlings, yes, but . . .

"In my shame, I told no one. Sorrel and Vesta . . . Sorrel knew because she was in that room. Sorrel fought for me. Begged your grandmother. Your grandmother snapped her arm and sent her out. But after the Matron chucked me into the snow and told me to crawl somewhere and die, Sorrel found me. She got Vesta, and they brought me to Vesta's aerie deep in the mountains, and they secretly took care of me for the months that I . . . that I couldn't get out of bed. Then one day, I just woke up and decided to fight.

"I trained. I healed my body. I grew strong—stronger than I'd been before. And I stopped thinking about it. A month later I went hunting for Crochans, and walked back into the Keep with three of their hearts in a box. If your grandmother was surprised I hadn't died, she didn't show it. You were there that night I came back. You toasted in my honor, and said you were proud to have such a fine Second."

Still on her knees, the damp earth soaking into her pants, Manon stared at that hideous brand.

"I never went back to the hunter. I didn't know how to explain the brand. How to explain your grandmother, or apologize. I was afraid he'd treat me as your grandmother had. So I never went back." Her mouth wobbled. "I'd fly overhead every few years, just . . . just to see." She wiped at her face. "He never married. And even when he was an old man, I'd sometimes see him sitting on that front porch. As if he were waiting for someone."

Something . . . something was cracking and aching in Manon's chest, caving in on itself.

Asterin sat among the flowers and began pulling on her clothes. She was weeping silently, but Manon didn't know if she should reach out. She didn't know how to comfort, how to soothe.

"I stopped caring," Asterin said at last. "About anything and everything. After that, it was all a joke, and a thrill, and nothing scared me."

That wildness, that untamed fierceness . . . They weren't born of a free heart, but of one that had known despair so complete that living brightly, living violently, was the only way to outrun it.

"But I told myself"—Asterin finished buttoning her jacket—"I would dedicate my life wholly to being your Second. To serving *you*. Not your grandmother. Because I knew your grandmother had hidden me from you for a reason. I think she knew you would have fought for me. And whatever your grandmother saw in you that made her afraid . . . It was worth waiting for. Worth serving. So I have."

That day Abraxos had made the Crossing, when her Thirteen had looked ready to fight their way out should her grandmother give the order to kill her . . .

Asterin met her stare. "Sorrel, Vesta, and I have known for a very long time what your grandmother is capable of. We never said anything because we feared that if you knew, it could jeopardize you. The day you saved Petrah instead of letting her fall . . . You weren't the only one who understood why your grandmother made you slaughter that Crochan."

Asterin shook her head. "I am begging you, Manon. Do not let your grandmother and these men take our witches and use them like this. Do not let them turn our witchlings into monsters. What they've already done . . . I am begging you to help me undo it."

Manon swallowed hard, her throat achingly tight. "If we defy them, they will come after us, and they will kill us."

"I know. We all know. That's what we wanted to tell you the other night."

Manon looked at her cousin's shirt, as if she could see through to the brand beneath. "That is why you've been behaving this way."

"I am not foolish enough to pretend that I don't have a weak spot where witchlings are concerned."

This was why her grandmother had pushed for decades to have Asterin demoted.

"I don't think it's a weak spot," Manon admitted, and glanced over her shoulder to where Abraxos was sniffing at the wildflowers. "You're to be reinstated as Second."

Asterin bowed her head. "I am sorry, Manon."

"You have nothing to be sorry for." She dared add, "Are there others whom my grandmother treated this way?"

"Not in the Thirteen. But in other covens. Most let themselves die when your grandmother cast them out." And Manon had never been told. She had been *lied* to.

Manon gazed westward across the mountains. *Hope*, Elide had said— hope for a better future. For a home.

Not obedience, brutality, discipline. But hope.

"We need to proceed carefully."

Asterin blinked, the gold flecks in her black eyes glittering. "What are you planning?"

"Something very stupid, I think."

CHAPTER
64

Rowan barely remembered anything of the agonizing trip back to Rifthold. By the time they had snuck across the city walls and through the alleys to reach the warehouse, he was so exhausted that he'd hardly hit the mattress before unconsciousness dragged him under.

He awoke that night—or was it the next?—with Aelin and Aedion sitting on the side of the bed, talking.

"Solstice is in six days; we need to have everything lined up by then," she was saying to her cousin.

"So you're going to ask Ress and Brullo to just leave a back door open so you can sneak in?"

"Don't be so simpleminded. I'm going to walk in through the front door."

Of course she was. Rowan let out a groan, his tongue dry and heavy in his mouth.

She whirled to him, half lunging across the bed. "How are you feeling?" She brushed a hand over his forehead, testing for fever. "You seem all right."

"Fine," he grunted. His arm and shoulder ached. But he'd endured worse. The blood loss had been what knocked his feet out from under him—more blood than he'd ever lost at once, at least so quickly, thanks to his magic being stifled. He ran an eye over Aelin. Her face was drawn and pale, a bruise kissed her cheekbone, and four scratches marred her neck.

He was going to slaughter that witch.

He said as much, and Aelin smiled. "If you're in the mood for violence, then I suppose you're just fine." But the words were thick, and her eyes gleamed. He reached out with his good arm to grip one of her hands and squeezed tightly. "Please don't ever do that again," she breathed.

"Next time, I'll ask them not to fire arrows at you—or me."

Her mouth tightened and wobbled, and she rested her brow on his good arm. He lifted the other arm, sending burning pain shooting through him as he stroked her hair. It was still matted in a few spots with blood and dirt. She must not have even bothered with a full bath.

Aedion cleared his throat. "We've been thinking up a plan for freeing magic—and taking out the king and Dorian."

"Just—tell me tomorrow," Rowan said, a headache already blooming. The mere thought of explaining to them again that every time he'd seen hellfire used it had been more destructive than anyone could anticipate made him want to go back to sleep. Gods, without his magic . . . Humans were remarkable. To be able to survive without leaning on magic . . . He had to give them credit.

Aedion yawned—the lousiest attempt at one Rowan had ever seen— and excused himself.

"Aedion," Rowan said, and the general paused in the doorway. "Thank you."

"Anytime, brother." He walked out.

Aelin was looking between them, her lips pursed again.

"What?" he said.

She shook her head. "You're too nice when you're wounded. It's unsettling."

Seeing the tears shine in her eyes just now had nearly unsettled *him*. If magic had already been freed, those witches would have been ashes the moment that arrow hit him. "Go take a bath," he growled. "I'm not sleeping next to you while you're covered in that witch's blood."

She examined her nails, still slightly lined with dirt and blue blood. "Ugh. I've washed them ten times already." She rose from her seat on the side of the bed.

"Why," he asked. "Why did you save her?"

She dragged a hand through her hair. A white bandage around her upper arm peeked through her shirt with the movement. He hadn't even been conscious for that wound. He stifled the urge to demand to see it, assess the injury himself—and tug her close against him.

"Because that golden-haired witch, Asterin . . . ," Aelin said. "She screamed Manon's name the way I screamed yours."

Rowan stilled. His queen gazed at the floor, as if recalling the moment.

"How can I take away somebody who means the world to someone else? Even if she's my enemy." A little shrug. "I thought you were dying. It seemed like bad luck to let her die out of spite. And . . ." she snorted. "Falling into a ravine seemed like a pretty shitty way to die for someone who fights that spectacularly."

Rowan smiled, drinking in the sight of her: the pale, grave face; the dirty clothes; the injuries. Yet her shoulders were back, chin high. "You make me proud to serve you."

A jaunty slant to her lips, but silver lined her eyes. "I know."

⁓

"You look like shit," Lysandra said to Aelin. Then she remembered Evangeline, who stared at her wide-eyed, and winced. "Sorry."

Evangeline refolded her napkin in her lap, every inch the dainty little queen. "You said I'm not to use such language—and yet you do."

"I can curse," Lysandra said as Aelin suppressed a smile, "because I'm older, and I know when it's most effective. And right now, our friend looks like absolute shit."

Evangeline lifted her eyes to Aelin, her red-gold hair bright in the morning sun through the kitchen window. "You look even worse in the morning, Lysandra."

Aelin choked out a laugh. "Careful, Lysandra. You've got a hellion on your hands."

Lysandra gave her young ward a long look. "If you've finished eating the tarts clean off our plates, Evangeline, go onto the roof and raise hell for Aedion and Rowan."

"Take care with Rowan," Aelin added. "He's still on the mend. But pretend that he isn't. Men get pissy if you fuss."

A wicked gleam in her eye, Evangeline bounded for the front door. Aelin listened to make sure the girl did indeed go upstairs, and then turned to her friend. "She's going to be a handful when she's older."

Lysandra groaned. "You think I don't know that? Eleven years old, and she's already a tyrant. It's an endless stream of *Why?* and *I would prefer not to* and *why, why, why* and *no, I should not like to listen to your good advice, Lysandra.*" She rubbed her temples.

"A tyrant, but a brave one," Aelin said. "I don't think there are many eleven-year-olds who would do what she did to save you." The swelling had gone down, but bruises still marred Lysandra's face, and the small, scabbed cut near her lip remained an angry red. "And I don't think there are many nineteen-year-olds who would fight tooth and nail to save a child." Lysandra stared down at the table. "I'm sorry," Aelin said. "Even though Arobynn orchestrated it—I'm sorry."

"You came for me," Lysandra said so quietly that it was hardly a breath. "All of you—you came for me." She had told Nesryn and Chaol in detail of her overnight stay in a hidden dungeon beneath the city streets; already, the rebels were combing the sewers for it. She remembered little of the rest, having been blindfolded and gagged. Wondering if they would put a Wyrdstone ring on her finger had been the worst of it, she said. That dread would haunt her for a while.

"You thought we wouldn't come for you?"

"I've never had friends who cared what happened to me, other than Sam and Wesley. Most people would have let me be taken—dismissed me as just another whore."

"I've been thinking about that."

"Oh?"

Aelin reached into her pocket and pushed a folded piece of paper across the table. "It's for you. And her."

"We don't need—" Lysandra's eyes fell upon the wax seal. A snake in midnight ink: Clarisse's sigil. "What is this?"

"Open it."

Glancing between her and the paper, Lysandra cracked the seal and read the text.

"I, Clarisse DuVency, hereby declare that any debts owed to me by—"

The paper began shaking.

"Any debts owed to me by Lysandra and Evangeline are now paid in full. At their earliest convenience, they may receive the Mark of their freedom."

The paper fluttered to the table as Lysandra's hands slackened. She raised her head to look at Aelin.

"Och," Aelin said, even as her own eyes filled. "I hate you for being so beautiful, even when you cry."

"Do you know how much money—"

"Did you think I'd leave you enslaved to her?"

"I don't . . . I don't know what to say to you. I don't know how to thank you—"

"You don't need to."

Lysandra put her face in her hands and sobbed.

"I'm sorry if you wanted to do the proud and noble thing and stick it out for another decade," Aelin began.

Lysandra only wept harder.

"But you have to understand that there was no rutting way I was going to leave without—"

"Shut up, Aelin," Lysandra said through her hands. "Just—shut up." She lowered her hands, her face now puffy and splotchy.

Aelin sighed. "Oh, thank the gods. You *can* look hideous when you cry."

Lysandra burst out laughing.

Manon and Asterin stayed in the mountains all day and night after her Second revealed her invisible wound. They caught mountain goats for themselves and their wyverns and roasted them over a fire that night as they carefully considered what they might do.

When Manon eventually dozed off, curled against Abraxos with a blanket of stars overhead, her head felt clearer than it had in months. And yet something nagged at her, even in sleep.

She knew what it was when she awoke. A loose thread in the loom of the Three-Faced Goddess.

"You ready?" Asterin said, mounting her pale-blue wyvern and smiling—a real smile.

Manon had never seen that smile. She wondered how many people had. Wondered if she herself had ever smiled that way.

Manon gazed northward. "There's something I need to do." When she explained it to her Second, Asterin didn't hesitate to declare that she would go with her.

So they stopped by Morath long enough to get supplies. They let Sorrel and Vesta know the bare details, and instructed them to tell the duke she'd been called away.

They were airborne within an hour, flying hard and fast above the clouds to keep hidden.

Mile after mile they flew. Manon couldn't tell why that thread kept yanking, why it felt so urgent, but she pushed them hard, all the way to Rifthold.

⁓

Four days. Elide had been in this freezing, festering dungeon for four days.

It was so cold that she could hardly sleep, and the food they chucked in was barely edible. Fear kept her alert, prompting her to test the door, to watch the guards whenever they opened it, to study the halls behind them. She learned nothing useful.

Four days—and Manon had not come for her. None of the Blackbeaks had.

She didn't know why she expected it. Manon had forced her to spy on that chamber, after all.

She tried not to think about what might await her now.

Tried, and failed. She wondered if anyone would even remember her name when she was dead. If it would ever be carved anywhere.

She knew the answer. And knew there was no one coming for her.

CHAPTER 65

Rowan was more tired than he'd admit to Aelin or Aedion, and in the flurry of planning, he hardly had a moment alone with the queen. It had taken him two days of rest and sleeping like the dead before he was back on his feet and able to go through his training exercises without being winded.

After finishing his evening routine, he was so exhausted by the time he staggered into bed that he was asleep before Aelin had finished washing up. No, he hadn't given humans nearly enough credit all these years.

It would be such a damn relief to have his magic back—if their plan worked. Considering the fact that they were using hellfire, things could go very, very wrong. Chaol hadn't been able to meet with Ress or Brullo yet, but tried every day to get messages to them. The real difficulty, it seemed, was that over half the rebels had fled as more Valg soldiers poured in. Three executions a day was the new rule: sunrise, noon, and sunset. Former magic-wielders, rebels, suspected rebel sympathizers—Chaol and Nesryn managed to save some, but not all. The cawing of crows could now be heard on every street.

A male scent in the room snapped Rowan from sleep. He slid his knife out from under his pillow and sat up slowly.

Aelin slumbered beside him, her breathing deep and even, yet again wearing one of his shirts. Some primal part of him snarled in satisfaction at the sight, at knowing she was covered in his scent.

Rowan rolled to his feet, his steps silent as he scanned the room, knife at the ready.

But the scent wasn't inside. It was drifting in from beyond.

Rowan edged to the window and peered out. No one on the street below; no one on the neighboring rooftops.

Which meant Lorcan had to be on the roof.

His old commander was waiting, arms crossed over his broad chest. He surveyed Rowan with a frown, noting the bandages and his bare torso. "Should I thank you for putting on pants?" Lorcan said, his voice barely more than a midnight wind.

"I didn't want you to feel inadequate," Rowan replied, leaning against the roof door.

Lorcan huffed a laugh. "Did your queen claw you up, or are the wounds from one of those beasts she sent after me?"

"I was wondering who would ultimately win—you or the Wyrdhounds."

A flash of teeth. "I slaughtered them all."

"Why'd you come here, Lorcan?"

"You think I don't know that the heir of Mala Fire-Bringer is planning something for the summer solstice in two days? Have you fools considered my offer?"

A carefully worded question, to bait him into revealing what Lorcan had only guessed at. "Aside from drinking the first of the summer wine and being a pain in my ass, I don't think she's planning anything at all."

"So that's why the captain is trying to set up a meeting with guards at the palace?"

"How am I supposed to keep up with what he does? The boy used to serve the king."

"Assassins, whores, traitors—what fine company you keep these days, Rowan."

"Better than being a dog leashed by a psychotic master."

"Is that what you thought of us? All those years that we worked together, killed men and bedded females together? I never heard you complain."

"I didn't realize there was anything to complain about. I was as blind as you."

"And then a fiery princess flounced into your life, and you decided to change for her, right?" A cruel smile. "Did you tell her about Sollemere?"

"She knows everything."

"Does she now. I suppose her own history makes her even more understanding of the horrors you committed on our queen's behalf."

"*Your* queen's behalf. What is it, exactly, about Aelin that gets under your skin, Lorcan? Is it that she's not afraid of you, or is it that I walked away from you for her?"

Lorcan snorted. "Whatever you're planning, it won't work. You'll all die in the process."

That was highly likely, but Rowan said, "I don't know what you're talking about."

"You owe me more than that horseshit."

"Careful, Lorcan, or you'll sound like you care about someone other than yourself." As a discarded bastard child growing up on the back streets of Doranelle, Lorcan had lost that ability centuries before Rowan had even been born. He'd never pitied him for it, though. Not when Lorcan had been blessed in every other regard by Hellas himself.

Lorcan spat on the roof. "I was going to offer to bring your body back to your beloved mountain to be buried alongside Lyria once I finish with the keys. Now I'll just let you rot here. Alongside your pretty little princess."

He tried to ignore the blow, the thought of that grave atop his mountain. "Is that a threat?"

"Why would I bother? If you're truly planning something, I won't need to kill her—she can do that all on her own. Maybe the king will put her in one of those collars. Just like his son."

A chord of horror struck so deep in Rowan that his stomach turned. "Mind what you say, Lorcan."

"I bet Maeve would offer good coin for her. And if she gets her hands on that Wyrdkey . . . You can imagine just as well as I what sort of power Maeve would wield then."

Worse—so much worse than he could imagine if Maeve wanted Aelin not dead but enslaved. A weapon without limit in one hand, and the heir of Mala Fire-Bringer in her other. There would be no stopping her.

Lorcan read the hesitation, the doubt. Gold gleamed in his hand. "You know me, Prince. You know I'm the only one qualified to hunt down and destroy those keys. Let your queen take on the army gathering in the south—leave this task to me." The ring seemed to glow in the moonlight as Lorcan extended it. "Whatever she's planning, she'll need this. Or else you can say good-bye." Lorcan's eyes were chips of black ice. "We all know how well you handled saying it to Lyria."

Rowan leashed his rage. "Swear it."

Lorcan smiled, knowing he'd won.

"Swear that this ring grants immunity to the Valg, and I'll give it to you," Rowan said, and he pulled the Amulet of Orynth from his pocket.

Lorcan's focus snapped to the amulet, to the otherworldly strangeness it radiated, and swore.

A blade flashed, and then the scent of Lorcan's blood filled the air. He clenched his fist, lifting it. "I swear on my blood and honor that I have not deceived you in any of this. The ring's power is genuine."

Rowan watched the blood drip onto the roof. One drop; two; three.

Lorcan might have been a prick, but Rowan had never seen him break an oath before. His word was his bond; it had always been the one currency he valued.

They both moved at once, chucking the amulet and the ring into the space between them. Rowan caught the ring and swiftly pocketed it, but Lorcan just stared at the amulet in his hands, his eyes shadowed.

Rowan avoided the urge to hold his breath and stayed silent.

Lorcan slid the chain around his neck and tucked the amulet into his shirt. "You're all going to die. Carrying out this plan, or in the war that follows."

"You destroy those keys," Rowan said, "and there might not be a war." A fool's hope.

"There will be a war. It's too late to stop it now. Too bad that ring won't keep any of you from being spiked on the castle walls."

The image flashed through his head—made all the worse, perhaps, because of the times he'd seen it himself, done it himself. "What happened to you, Lorcan? What happened in your miserable existence to make you this way?" He'd never asked for the full story, had never cared to. It hadn't bothered him until now. Before, he would have stood beside Lorcan and taunted the poor fool who dared defy their queen. "You're a better male than this."

"Am I? I still serve my queen, even if she cannot see it. Who was the one who abandoned her the first time a pretty human thing opened her legs—"

"That is enough."

But Lorcan was gone.

Rowan waited a few minutes before going back downstairs, turning the ring over and over in his pocket.

Aelin was awake in the bed when he entered, the windows shut and curtained, the hearth dark. "Well?" she said, the word barely audible above the rustling of the blankets as he climbed in beside her.

His night-keen eyes allowed him to see the scarred palm she held out as he dropped the ring into it. She slid it onto her thumb, wriggled her fingers, and frowned when nothing particularly exciting happened. A laugh caught in his throat.

"How mad is Lorcan going to be," Aelin murmured as they lay down face-to-face, "when he eventually opens up that amulet, finds the Valg commander's ring inside, and realizes we gave him a fake?"

The demon ripped down the remaining barriers between their souls as though they were paper, until only one remained, a tiny shell of self.

He did not remember waking, or sleeping, or eating. Indeed, there were very few moments when he was even there, looking out through his eyes. Only when the demon prince fed on the prisoners in the dungeons— when he allowed him to feed, to drink alongside him—that was the only time he now surfaced.

Whatever control he'd had that day—

What day?

He could not remember a time when the demon had not been there inside of him.

And yet—

Manon.

A name.

Do not think of that one—do not think of her. The demon hated that name.

Manon.

Enough. We do not speak of them, the descendants of our kings.

Speak of whom?

Good.

"You're ready for tomorrow?" Aelin said to Chaol as they stood on the roof of her apartment, gazing toward the glass castle. In the setting sun, it was awash in gold and orange and ruby—as if it were already aflame.

Chaol prayed it wouldn't come to that, but . . . "As ready as I can be."

He'd tried not to look too hesitant, too wary, when he'd arrived minutes ago to run through tomorrow's plan one last time and Aelin had instead asked him to join her up here. Alone.

She was wearing a loose white shirt tucked into tight brown pants, her hair unbound, and hadn't even bothered to put on shoes. He wondered what her people would think of a barefoot queen.

Aelin braced her forearms on the roof rail, hooking one ankle over the other as she said, "You know that I won't unnecessarily endanger any lives."

"I know. I trust you."

She blinked, and shame washed through him at the shock on her face. "Do you regret," she said, "sacrificing your freedom to get me to Wendlyn?"

"No," he said, surprising himself to find it true. "Regardless of what happened between us, I was a fool to serve the king. I like to think I would have left someday."

He needed to say that to her—had needed to say it from the moment she'd returned.

"With me," she said, her voice hoarse. "You would have left with me—when I was just Celaena."

"But you were never just Celaena, and I think you knew that, deep down, even before everything happened. I understand now."

She studied him with eyes that were far older than nineteen. "You're still the same person, Chaol, that you were before you broke the oath to your father."

He wasn't sure whether or not that was an insult. He supposed he deserved it, after all he'd said and done.

"Maybe I don't want to be that person anymore," he said. That person—that stupidly loyal, useless person—had lost everything. His friend, the woman he loved, his position, his honor. Lost everything, with only himself to blame.

"I'm sorry," he said. "About Nehemia—about everything." It wasn't enough. It never would be.

But she gave him a grim smile, eyes darting to the faint scar on his cheek. "I'm sorry I mauled your face, then tried to kill you." She turned to the glass castle again. "It's still hard for me, to think about what happened this winter. But in the end I'm grateful you sent me to Wendlyn, and made that bargain with your father." She closed her eyes and took a shallow breath. When she opened her eyes, the setting sun filled them with liquid gold. Chaol braced himself. "It meant something to me. What you and I had. More than that, your friendship meant something to me. I never told you the truth about who I was because *I* couldn't face that truth. I'm sorry if what I said to you on the docks that day—that I'd pick you—made you think I'd come back, and it would all be fixed. Things changed. I changed."

He'd waited for this conversation for weeks now, months now—and he'd expected himself to yell, or pace, or just shut her out entirely. But there was nothing but calm in his veins, a steady, peaceful calm. "You deserve to be happy," he said. And meant it. She deserved the joy he so often glimpsed on her face when Rowan was near—deserved the wicked laughter she shared with Aedion, the comfort and teasing with Lysandra. She deserved happiness, perhaps more than anyone.

She flicked her gaze over his shoulder—to where Nesryn's slim silhouette filled the doorway onto the roof, where she'd been waiting for the past few minutes. "So do you, Chaol."

"You know she and I haven't—"

"I know. But you should. Faliq—Nesryn is a good woman. You deserve each other."

"This is assuming she has any interest in me."

A knowing gleam in those eyes. "She does."

Chaol again glanced toward Nesryn, who gazed at the river. He smiled a bit.

But then Aelin said, "I promise I'll make it quick and painless. For Dorian."

His breathing locked up. "Thank you. But—if I ask . . ." He couldn't say it.

"Then the blow is yours. Just say the word." She ran her fingers over the Eye of Elena, its blue stone gleaming in the sunset. "We do not look back, Chaol. It helps no one and nothing to look back. We can only go on."

There she was, that queen looking out at him, a hint of the ruler she was becoming. And it knocked the breath out of him, because it made him feel so strangely young—when she now seemed so old. "What if we go on," he said, "only to more pain and despair? What if we go on, only to find a horrible end waiting for us?"

Aelin looked northward, as if she could see all the way to Terrasen. "Then it is not the end."

"Only twenty of them left. I hope to hell they're ready tomorrow," Chaol said under his breath as he and Nesryn left a covert gathering of rebels at a run-down inn beside the fishing docks. Even inside the inn, the cheap ale hadn't been able to cover the reek of fish coming from both the guts still splattered on the wooden planks outside and the hands of the fishmongers who shared the tavern room.

"Better than only two—and they will be," Nesryn said, her steps light on the dock as they strode down the riverfront. Lanterns on the boats docked alongside the walkway bobbed and swayed with the current; from far across the Avery, the faint sound of music trickled from one of the pretty country estates on its banks. A party on the eve of the summer solstice.

Once, a lifetime ago, he and Dorian had gone to those parties, dropping by several in one night. He'd never enjoyed it, had only gone to keep Dorian safe, but . . .

He should have enjoyed it. He should have savored every second with his friend.

He'd never realized how precious the calm moments were.

But—but he wouldn't think about it, what he had to do tomorrow. What he'd say good-bye to.

SARAH J. MAAS

They walked in silence, until Nesryn turned down a side street and walked up to a small stone temple wedged between two market warehouses. The gray rock was worn, the columns flanking the entrance imbedded with various shells and bits of coral. Golden light spilled from the inside, revealing a round, open space with a simple fountain in its center.

Nesryn climbed the few steps and dropped a coin into the sealed bin beside a pillar. "Come with me."

And maybe it was because he didn't want to sit alone in his apartment and brood over what was to come tomorrow; maybe it was because visiting a temple, however useless, couldn't hurt.

Chaol followed her inside.

At this hour, the Sea God's temple was empty. A small door at the back of the space was padlocked. Even the priest and priestess had gone to sleep for a few hours before they had to awake ahead of the dawn, when the sailors and fishermen would make their offerings, reflect, or ask for blessings before setting off with the sun.

Two lanterns, crafted from sun-bleached coral, hung from the domed ceiling, setting the mother-of-pearl tiles above them glimmering like the surface of the sea. Nesryn took a seat on one of four benches set along the curved walls—a bench for each direction a sailor might journey in.

She picked south.

"For the Southern Continent?" Chaol asked, sitting beside her on the smooth wood.

Nesryn stared at the little fountain, the bubbling water the only sound. "We went to the Southern Continent a few times. Twice when I was a child, to visit family; once to bury my mother. Her whole life, I'd always catch her gazing south. As if she could see it."

"I thought only your father came from there."

"Yes. But she fell in love with it, and said it felt more like home than this place. My father never agreed with her, no matter how many times she begged him to move back."

"Do you wish he had?"

Her night-dark eyes shifted toward him. "I've never felt as though I had a home. Either here, or in the Milas Agia."

"The . . . god-city," he said, recalling the history and geography lessons that had been drilled into him. It was more frequently called by its other name—Antica—and was the largest city on the Southern Continent, home to a mighty empire in its own right, which claimed it had been built by the hands of gods. Also home to the Torre Cesme, the best mortal healers in the world. He'd never known Nesryn's family had been from the city itself.

"Where do you think home might be?" he asked.

Nesryn braced her forearms on her knees. "I don't know," she admitted, twisting her head to look back at him. "Any ideas?"

You deserve to be happy, Aelin had said earlier that night. An apology and a shove out the door, he supposed.

He didn't want to waste the calm moments.

So he reached for her hand, sliding closer as he interlaced their fingers. Nesryn stared at their hands for a heartbeat, then sat up. "Maybe once all this . . . once everything is over," Chaol said hoarsely, "we could figure that out. Together."

"Promise me," she breathed, her mouth shaking. Indeed, that was silver lining her eyes, which she closed long enough to master herself. Nesryn Faliq, moved to tears. "Promise me," she repeated, looking at their hands again, "that you will walk out of that castle tomorrow."

He'd wondered why she'd brought him in here. The Sea God—and the God of Oaths.

He squeezed her hand. She squeezed back.

Gold light rippled on the surface of the Sea God's fountain, and Chaol offered up a silent prayer. "I promise."

Rowan was in bed, casually testing his left shoulder with careful rotations. He'd pushed himself hard today while training, and soreness now throbbed in his muscles. Aelin was in her closet, preparing for bed—quiet, as she'd been all day and evening.

With two urns of hellfire now hidden a block away in an abandoned building, everyone should be tiptoeing around. One small accident, and they would be incinerated so thoroughly that no ash would remain.

But he'd made sure that wasn't her concern. Tomorrow, he and Aedion would be the ones bearing the urns through the network of sewer tunnels and into the castle itself.

Aelin had tracked the Wyrdhounds to their secret entrance—the one that fed right to the clock tower—and now that she'd tricked Lorcan into killing them all for her, the way would be clear for him and Aedion to plant the vats, set the fuses, and use their Fae swiftness to get the hell out before the tower exploded.

Then Aelin . . . Aelin and the captain would play their part, the most dangerous of all. Especially since they hadn't been able to get a message in to the palace beforehand.

And Rowan wouldn't be there to help her.

He'd gone over the plan with her again and again. Things could go wrong so easily, and yet she hadn't looked nervous as she downed her dinner. But he knew her well enough to see the storm brewing beneath the surface, to feel its charge even from across the room.

Rowan rotated his shoulder again, and soft footsteps sounded on the carpet. "I've been thinking," Rowan started, and then forgot everything he was going to say as he bolted upright in bed.

Aelin leaned against the closet doorway, clad in a nightgown of gold.

Metallic gold—as he'd requested.

It could have been painted on her for how closely it hugged every curve and dip, for all that it concealed.

A living flame, that's what she looked like. He didn't know where to look, where he wanted to touch first.

"If I recall correctly," she drawled, "*someone* said to remind him to prove me wrong about my hesitations. I think I had two options: words, or tongue and teeth."

A low growl rumbled in his chest. "Did I now."

She took a step, and the full scent of her desire hit him like a brick to the face.

He was going to rip that nightgown to shreds.

He didn't care how spectacular it looked; he wanted bare skin.

"Don't even think about it," she said, taking another step, as fluid as molten metal. "Lysandra lent it to me."

His heartbeat thundered in his ears. If he moved an inch, he'd be on her, would take her in his arms and begin learning just what made the Heir of Fire really burn.

But he got out of bed, risking all of one step, drinking down the sight of the long, bare legs; the curve of her breasts, peaked despite the balmy summer night; the bob of her throat as she swallowed.

"You said that things had changed—that we'd deal with it." Her turn to dare another step. Another. "I'm not going to ask you for anything you're not ready or willing to give."

He froze as she stopped directly before him, tipping back her head to study his face as her scent twined around him, awakening him.

Gods, that scent. From the moment he'd bitten her neck in Wendlyn, the moment he'd tasted her blood and loathed the beckoning wildfire that crackled in it, he'd been unable to get it out of his system. "Aelin, you deserve better than this—than me." He'd wanted to say it for a while now.

She didn't so much as flinch. "Don't tell me what I do and don't deserve. Don't tell me about tomorrow, or the future, or any of it."

He took her hand; her fingers were cold—shaking slightly. *What do you want me to tell you, Fireheart?*

She studied their joined hands, and the gold ring encircling her thumb. He squeezed her fingers gently. When she lifted her head, her eyes were blazing bright. "Tell me that we'll get through tomorrow. Tell me that we'll survive the war. Tell me—" She swallowed hard. "Tell me that even if I lead us all to ruin, we'll burn in hell together."

"We're not going to hell, Aelin," he said. "But wherever we go, we'll go together."

Her mouth wobbled slightly, and she released his hand only to brace her own on his chest. "Just once," she said. "I want to kiss you just once."

Every thought went out of his head. "That sounds like you're expecting not to do it again."

The flicker of fear in her eyes told him enough—told him that her behavior at dinner might have been mostly bravado to keep Aedion calm. "I know the odds."

"You and I have always relished damning the odds."

She tried and failed to smile. He leaned in, sliding a hand around her waist, the lace and silk smooth against his fingers, her body warm and firm beneath it, and whispered in her ear, "Even when we're apart tomorrow, I'll be with you every step of the way. And every step after—wherever that may be."

She sucked in a shuddering breath, and he pulled back far enough for them to share breath. Her fingers shook as she brushed them against his mouth, and his control nearly shredded apart right there.

"What are you waiting for?" he said, the words near guttural.

"Bastard," she murmured, and kissed him.

Her mouth was soft and warm, and he bit back a groan. His body went still—his entire world went still—at that whisper of a kiss, the answer to a question he'd asked for centuries. He realized he was staring only when she withdrew slightly. His fingers tightened at her waist.

"Again," he breathed.

She slid out of his grip. "If we live through tomorrow, you'll get the rest."

He didn't know whether to laugh or roar. "Are you trying to bribe me into surviving?"

She smiled at last. And damn if it didn't kill him, the quiet joy in her face.

They had walked out of darkness and pain and despair together. They were still walking out of it. So that smile . . . It struck him stupid every time he saw it and realized it was for him.

Rowan remained rooted to the center of the room as Aelin climbed into bed and blew out the candles. He stared at her through the darkness.

She said softly, "You make me want to live, Rowan. Not survive; not exist. *Live.*"

He didn't have the words. Not when what she said hit him harder and deeper than any kiss.

So he climbed into bed and held her tightly all through the night.

CHAPTER 66

Aelin ventured out at dawn to snag breakfast from the vendors in the main market of the slums. The sun was already warming the quiet streets, and her cloak and hood quickly turned stuffy. At least it was a clear day; at least that bit had gone right. Despite the crows cackling over the corpses in the execution squares.

The sword at her side was a dead weight. Too soon she'd be swinging it.

Too soon she'd face the man who had murdered her family and enslaved her kingdom. Too soon she would put an end to her friend's life.

Maybe she wouldn't even walk out of the castle alive.

Or perhaps she would walk out wearing a black collar of her own, if Lorcan had betrayed them.

Everything was prepared; every possible pitfall had been considered; every weapon had been sharpened.

Lysandra had taken Evangeline to have their tattoos formally stamped off yesterday, and then collected her belongings from the brothel. Now they were staying in an upscale inn across the city, paid for with the small savings

Lysandra had squirreled away for years. The courtesan had offered her help again and again, but Aelin ordered her to get the hell out of the city and to head for Nesryn's country home. The courtesan warned her to be careful, kissed both her cheeks, and set off with her ward—both of them beaming, both of them free. Hopefully they were on their way out now.

Aelin bought a bag of pastries and some meat pies, barely listening to the market around her, already abuzz with early revelers out to celebrate the solstice. They were more subdued than most years, but given the executions, she didn't blame them.

"Miss?"

She stiffened, going for her sword—and realized that the pie vendor was still waiting for his coppers.

He flinched and retreated a few steps behind his wooden cart.

"Sorry," she mumbled, dumping the coins into his outstretched hand.

The man gave her a wary smile. "Everyone's a bit jumpy this morning, it seems."

She half turned. "More executions?"

The vendor jerked his round chin toward a street leading off the market. "You didn't see the message on your way in?" She gave a sharp shake of the head. He pointed. She'd thought the crowd by the corner was watching some street performer. "Oddest thing. No one can make any sense of it. They say it's written in what looks like blood, but it's darker—"

Aelin was already heading toward the street the man had indicated, following the throng of people pressing to see it.

She trailed the crowd, weaving around curious revelers and vendors and common market guards until they all flowed around a corner into a brightly lit dead-end alley.

The crowd had gathered at the pale stone wall at its end, murmuring and milling about.

"What does it mean?" "Who wrote it?" "Sounds like bad news, especially on the solstice." "There are more, all saying the same thing, right near every major market in the city."

Aelin pushed through the crowd, an eye on her weapons and purse lest a pickpocket get any bad ideas, and then—

The message had been written in giant black letters, the reek coming off them sure enough that of Valg blood, as if someone with very, very sharp nails had ripped open one of the guards and used him as a paint bucket.

Aelin turned on her heel and ran.

She hurtled through the bustling city streets and the slums, alley after alley, until she reached Chaol's decrepit house and flung open the door, shouting for him.

The message on the wall had only been one sentence.

Payment for a life debt.

One sentence just for Aelin Galathynius; one sentence that changed everything:

WITCH KILLER—
THE HUMAN IS STILL INSIDE HIM

CHAPTER 67

Aelin and Chaol helped Rowan and Aedion carry the two urns of hellfire into the sewers, all of them barely breathing, none of them talking.

Now they stood in the cool, reeking dark, not daring a flame with the two vats sitting next to them on the stone walkway. Aedion and Rowan, with their Fae eyesight, wouldn't need a torch, anyway.

Rowan shook Chaol's hand, wishing him luck. When the Fae Prince turned to Aelin, she focused instead on a torn corner of his cloak—as if it had snagged on some long-ago obstacle and been ripped off. She kept staring at that ripped-off bit of cloak as she embraced him—quickly, tightly, breathing in his scent perhaps for the last time. His hands lingered on her as if he'd hold her a moment longer, but she turned to Aedion.

Ashryver eyes met her own, and she touched the face that was the other side of her fair coin.

"For Terrasen," she said to him.

"For our family."

"For Marion."

"For *us*."

Slowly, Aedion drew his blade and knelt, his head bowed as he lifted the Sword of Orynth. "Ten years of shadows, but no longer. Light up the darkness, Majesty."

She did not have room in her heart for tears, would not allow or yield to them.

Aelin took her father's sword from him, its weight a steady, solid reassurance.

Aedion rose, returning to his place beside Rowan.

She looked at them, at the three males who meant everything—more than everything.

Then she smiled with every last shred of courage, of desperation, of hope for the glimmer of that glorious future. "Let's go rattle the stars."

CHAPTER 68

Lysandra's carriage meandered through the packed city streets. Every block took thrice as long as usual, thanks to the streaming crowds headed to the markets and squares to celebrate the solstice. None of them were aware of what was to occur, or who was making her way across the city.

Lysandra's palms turned sweaty within her silk gloves. Evangeline, drowsy with the morning heat, dozed lightly, her head resting on Lysandra's shoulder.

They should have left last night, but . . . But she'd had to say good-bye.

Brightly dressed revelers pushed past the carriage, and the driver shouted to clear out of the street. Everyone ignored him.

Gods, if Aelin wanted an audience, she'd picked the perfect day for it.

Lysandra peered out the window as they halted in an intersection. The street offered a clear view of the glass palace, blinding in the midmorning sun, its upper spires like lances piercing the cloudless sky.

"Are we there yet?" Evangeline mumbled.

Lysandra stroked her arm. "A while yet, pet."

And she began praying—praying to Mala Fire-Bringer, whose holiday had dawned so bright and clear, and to Temis, who never forgot the caged things of this world.

But she was no longer in a cage. For Evangeline, she could stay in this carriage, and she could leave this city. Even if it meant leaving her friends behind.

Aedion gritted his teeth against the weight he held so delicately between his hands. It was going to be a damn long trek to the castle. Especially when they had to ease across waterways and over crumbling bits of stone that made even their Fae balance unsteady.

But this was the way the Wyrdhounds had come. Even if Aelin and Nesryn hadn't provided a detailed path, the lingering stench would have led the way.

"Careful," Rowan said over his shoulder as he hoisted the vat he carried higher and edged around a loose bit of rock. Aedion bit back his retort at the obvious order. But he couldn't blame the prince. One tumble, and they'd risk the various substances mixing inside.

A few days ago, not trusting Shadow Market quality, Chaol and Aedion had found an abandoned barn outside the city to test an urn barely a tenth the size of the ones they carried.

It had worked *too* well. As they'd hurried back to Rifthold before curious eyes could see them, the smoke could be seen for miles.

Aedion shuddered to think about what a vat this size—let alone two of them—might do if they weren't careful.

But by the time they rigged up the triggering mechanisms and ignited the wicks they would trail a long, long distance away . . . Well, Aedion just prayed he and Rowan were swift enough.

They entered a sewer tunnel so dark that it took even his eyes a moment to adjust. Rowan just continued ahead. They were damn lucky that Lorcan had killed those Wyrdhounds and cleared the way. Damn lucky that Aelin had been ruthless and clever enough to trick Lorcan into doing it for them.

He didn't stop to consider what might happen if that ruthlessness and cleverness failed her today.

They turned down another pathway, the reek now smothering. Rowan's sharp sniff was the only sign of his mutual disgust. The gateway.

The iron gates were in shambles, but Aedion could still make out the markings etched in them.

Wyrdmarks. Ancient, too. Perhaps this had once been a path Gavin had used to visit the Sin-Eater's temple unseen.

The otherworldly stench of the creatures pushed and pulled at Aedion's senses, and he paused, scanning the darkness of the looming tunnel.

Here the water ended. Past the gates, a broken, rocky path that looked more ancient than any they'd yet seen sloped up into the impenetrable gloom.

"Watch where you step," Rowan said, scanning the tunnel. "It's all loose stone and debris."

"I can see just as well as you," Aedion said, unable to stop the retort this time. He rotated his shoulder, the cuff of his tunic slipping up to reveal the Wyrdmarks Aelin had instructed them to paint in their own blood all over their torsos, arms, and legs.

"Let's go," was Rowan's only reply as he hauled his vat along as if it weighed nothing.

Aedion debated snapping a response, but . . . perhaps that was why the warrior-prince kept giving him stupid warnings. To piss him off enough to distract him—and maybe Rowan himself—from what was happening above them. What they carried between them.

The Old Ways—to look out for their queen and their kingdom—but also for each other.

Damn, it was almost enough to make him want to embrace the bastard.

So Aedion followed Rowan through the iron gates.

And into the castle catacombs.

⁓

Chaol's chains clanked, the manacles already rubbing his skin raw as Aelin tugged him down the crowded street, a dagger poised to sink into his side. One block remained until they reached the iron fence that surrounded the sloping hill on which the castle perched.

Crowds streamed past, not noticing the chained man in their midst or the black-cloaked woman who hauled him closer and closer to the glass castle.

"You remember the plan?" Aelin murmured, keeping her head down and her dagger pressed against his side.

"Yes," he breathed. It was the only word he could manage.

Dorian was still in there—still holding on. It changed everything. And nothing.

The crowds quieted near the fence, as if wary of the black-uniformed guards that surely monitored the entrance. The first obstacle they'd encounter.

Aelin stiffened almost imperceptibly and paused so suddenly that Chaol almost slammed into her. "Chaol—"

The crowd shifted, and he beheld the castle fence.

There were corpses hanging from the towering wrought-iron bars.

Corpses in red and gold uniforms.

"Chaol—"

He was already moving, and she swore and walked with him, pretending to lead him by the chains, keeping the dagger tight to his ribs.

He didn't know how he hadn't heard the crows jabbering as they picked at the dead flesh tied along each iron post. With the crowd, he hadn't thought to notice. Or maybe he'd just gotten used to the cawing in every corner of the city.

His men.

Sixteen of them. His closest companions, his most loyal guards.

The first one had the collar of his uniform unbuttoned, revealing a chest crisscrossed with welts and cuts and brands.

Ress.

How long had they tortured him—tortured all the men? Since Aedion's rescue?

He racked his mind to think of the last time they'd had contact. He'd assumed the difficulty was because they were lying low. Not because—because they were being—

Chaol noticed the man strung up beside Ress.

Brullo's eyes were gone, either from torture or the crows. His hands were swollen and twisted—part of his ear was missing.

Chaol had no sounds in his head, no feeling in his body.

It was a message, but not to Aelin Galathynius or Aedion Ashryver.

His fault. *His.*

He and Aelin didn't speak as they neared the iron gates, the death of those men lingering over them. Every step was an effort. Every step was too fast.

His fault.

"I'm sorry," Aelin murmured, nudging him closer to the gates, where black-uniformed guards were indeed monitoring every face that passed on the street. "I'm so sorry—"

"The plan," he said, his voice shaking. "We change it. Now."

"Chaol—"

He told her what he needed to do. When he finished, she wiped away her tears as she gripped his hand and said, "I'll make it count."

The tears were gone by the time they broke from the crowd, nothing between them and those familiar gates but open cobblestones.

Home—this had once been his home.

He did not recognize the guards standing watch at the gates he had once protected so proudly, the gates he had ridden through not even a year ago with an assassin newly freed from Endovier, her chains tied to his saddle.

Now she led him in chains through those gates, an assassin one last time.

Her walk became a swagger, and she moved with fluid ease toward the guards who drew their swords, their black rings gobbling up the sunlight.

Celaena Sardothien halted a healthy distance away and lifted her chin. "Tell His Majesty that his Champion has returned—and she's brought him one hell of a prize."

CHAPTER
69

Aelin's black cloak flowed behind her as she led the fallen Captain of the Guard through the shining halls of the palace. Hidden at her back was her father's sword, its pommel wrapped in black cloth. None of their ten-guard escort bothered to take her weapons.

Why would they, when Celaena Sardothien was weeks early for her expected return, and still loyal to king and crown?

The halls were so quiet. Even the queen's court was sealed and silent. Rumor had it the queen had been cloistered in the mountains since Aedion's rescue and had taken half her court with her. The rest had vanished as well, to escape either the rising summer heat—or the horrors that had come to rule their kingdom.

Chaol said nothing, though he put on a good show of looking furious, like a pursued man desperate to find a way back to freedom. No sign of the devastation that had been on his face upon finding his men hanging from the gates.

He jerked against the chains, and she leaned in close. "I don't think so, Captain," she purred. Chaol didn't deign a response.

The guards glanced at her. Wyrdmarks written in Chaol's blood covered her beneath her clothes, its human scent hopefully masking any hints of her heritage that the Valg might otherwise pick up. There were only two demons in this group—a small mercy.

So they went, up and up, into the glass castle itself.

The halls seemed too bright to contain such evil. The few servants they passed averted their eyes and scurried along. Had *everyone* fled since Aedion's rescue?

It was an effort to not look too long at Chaol as they neared the massive red-and-gold glass doors, already open to reveal the crimson-marbled floor of the king's council room.

Already open to reveal the king, seated on his glass throne.

And Dorian standing beside him.

Their faces.

They were faces that tugged at him.

Human filth, the demon hissed.

The woman—he recognized that face as she yanked back her dark hood and knelt before the dais on which he stood.

"Majesty," she said. Her hair was shorter than he remembered.

No—he did not remember. He did not know her.

And the man in chains beside her, bloodied and filthy . . .

Screaming, wind, and—

Enough, the demon snapped.

But their faces—

He did not know those faces.

He did not care.

The King of Adarlan, the murderer of her family, the destroyer of her kingdom, lounged in his glass throne. "Isn't this an interesting turn of events, Champion."

She smiled, hoping the cosmetics she'd dabbed around her eyes would mute the turquoise and gold of her irises, and that the drab shade of blond she'd dyed her hair would disguise its near-identical hue with Aedion's. "Do you want to hear an interesting story, Your Majesty?"

"Does it involve my enemies in Wendlyn being dead?"

"Oh, that, and much, much more."

"Why has word not arrived, then?"

The ring on his finger seemed to suck in the light. But she could spy no sign of the Wyrdkeys, couldn't *feel* them here, as she'd felt the presence of the one in the amulet.

Chaol was pale, and kept glancing at the floor of the room.

This was where everything had happened. Where they'd murdered Sorscha. Where Dorian had been enslaved. Where, once upon a time, she'd signed her soul away to the king under a fake name, a coward's name.

"Don't blame me for the piss-poor messengers," she said. "I sent word the day before I left." She pulled out two objects from her cloak and looked over her shoulder at the guards, jerking her chin at Chaol. "Watch him."

She strode to the throne and extended her hand to the king. He reached forward, the reek of him—

Valg. Human. Iron. Blood.

She dropped two rings into his palm. The clink of metal on metal was the only sound.

"The seal rings of the King and Crown Prince of Wendlyn. I'd have brought their heads, but . . . Immigration officials can get so pissy."

The king plucked up one of the rings, his face stony. Lysandra's jeweler had yet again done a stunning job of re-creating the royal crest of Wendlyn and then wearing down the rings until they looked ancient, like heirlooms. "And where were *you* during Narrok's attack on Wendlyn?"

"Was I supposed to be anywhere but hunting my prey?"

The king's black eyes bored into hers.

"I killed them when I could," she went on, crossing her arms, careful of the hidden blades in the suit. "Apologies for not making it the grand statement you wanted. Next time, perhaps."

Dorian hadn't moved a muscle, his features stone-cold above the collar around his neck.

"And how did you wind up with my Captain of the Guard in chains?"

Chaol was only gazing at Dorian, and she didn't think his distraught, pleading face was an act.

"He was waiting for me at the docks, like a good dog. When I saw that he was without his uniform, I got him to confess to everything. Every last little conspiratorial thing he's done."

The king eyed the captain. "Did he, now."

Aelin avoided the urge to check the grandfather clock ticking in the far corner of the room, or the position of the sun beyond the floor-to-ceiling window. Time. They needed to bide their time a bit longer. But so far, so good.

"I do wonder," the king mused, leaning back on his throne, "who has been conspiring more: the captain, or you, Champion. Or should I call you Aelin?"

CHAPTER 70

This place smelled like death, like hell, like the dark spaces between the stars.

Centuries of training kept Rowan's steps light, kept him focused on the lethal weight he carried as he and the general crept through the dry, ancient passageway.

The ascending stone path had been gouged by brutal claws, the space so dark that even Rowan's eyes were failing him. The general trailed close behind, making no sound save for the occasional pebble skittering from beneath his boots.

Aelin would be in the castle by now, the captain in tow as her ticket into the throne room.

Only a few minutes more, if they'd calculated right, and then they could ignite their deadly burden and get the hell out.

Minutes after, he'd be at her side, rife with magic that he'd use to choke the air clean out of the king's lungs. And then he'd enjoy watching as she burned him alive. Slowly.

Though he knew his satisfaction would pale in comparison to what the general would feel. What every child of Terrasen would feel.

They passed through a door of solid iron that had been peeled back as if massive, clawed hands had ripped it off its hinges. The walkway beyond was smooth stone.

Aedion sucked in a breath at the same moment the pounding struck Rowan's brain, right between his eyes.

Wyrdstone.

Aelin had warned him of the tower—that the stone had given her a headache, but this . . .

She had been in her human body then.

It was unbearable, as if his very blood recoiled at the wrongness of the stone.

Aedion cursed, and Rowan echoed it.

But there was a wide sliver in the stone wall ahead, and open air beyond it.

Not daring to breathe too loudly, Rowan and Aedion eased through the crack.

A large, round chamber greeted them, flanked by eight open iron doors. The bottom of the clock tower, if their calculations were correct.

The darkness of the chamber was nearly impenetrable, but Rowan didn't dare light the torch he'd brought with them. Aedion sniffed, a wet sound. Wet, because—

Blood dribbled down Rowan's lip and chin. A nosebleed.

"Hurry," he whispered, setting down his vat at the opposite end of the chamber.

Just a few more minutes.

Aedion stationed his vat of hellfire across from Rowan's at the chamber entrance. Rowan knelt, his head pounding, worse and worse with each throb.

He kept moving, shoving the pain down as he set the fuse wire and led it over to where Aedion crouched. The dripping of their nosebleeds on the black stone floor was the only sound.

"Faster," Rowan ordered, and Aedion snarled softly—no longer willing to be annoyed with warnings as a distraction. He didn't feel like telling the general he'd stopped doing it minutes ago.

Rowan drew his sword, making for the doorway through which they'd entered. Aedion backed toward him, unspooling the joined fuses as he went. They had to be far enough away before they could light it, or else they'd be turned to ash.

He sent up a silent prayer to Mala that Aelin was biding her time—and that the king was too focused on the assassin and the captain to consider sending anyone below.

Aedion reached him, unrolling inch after inch of fuse, the line a white streak through the dark. Rowan's other nostril began bleeding.

Gods, the smell of this place. The death and reek and misery of it. He could hardly think. It was like having his head in a vise.

They retreated into the tunnel, that fuse their only hope and salvation.

Something dripped onto his shoulder. An ear bleed.

He wiped it away with his free hand.

But it was not blood on his cloak.

Rowan and Aedion went rigid as a low growling filled the passage.

Something on the ceiling moved, then.

Seven somethings.

Aedion dropped the spool and drew his sword.

A piece of fabric—gray, small, worn—dropped from the maw of the creature clinging to the stone ceiling. His cloak—the missing corner of his cloak.

Lorcan had lied.

He hadn't killed the remaining Wyrdhounds.

He'd just given them Rowan's scent.

Aelin Ashryver Galathynius faced the King of Adarlan.

"Celaena, Lillian, Aelin," she drawled, "I don't particularly care what you call me."

None of the guards behind them stirred.

She could feel Chaol's eyes on her, feel the relentless attention of the Valg prince inside Dorian.

"Did you think," the king said, grinning like a wolf, "that I could not peer inside my son's mind and ask what he knows, what he saw the day of your cousin's rescue?"

She hadn't known, and she certainly hadn't planned on revealing herself this way. "I'm surprised it took you this long to notice who you'd let in by the front door. Honestly, I'm a little disappointed."

"So your people might say of you. What was it like, Princess, to climb into bed with my son? Your mortal enemy?" Dorian didn't so much as blink. "Did you end it with him because of the guilt—or because you'd gained a foothold in my castle and no longer needed him?"

"Is that fatherly concern I detect?"

A low laugh. "Why doesn't the captain stop pretending that he's stuck in those manacles and come a bit closer."

Chaol stiffened. But Aelin gave him a subtle nod.

The king didn't bother glancing at his guards as he said, "Get out."

As one, the guards left, sealing the door behind them. The heavy glass groaned shut, the floor shuddering. Chaol's shackles clattered to the ground, and he flexed his wrists.

"Such traitorous filth, dwelling in my own home. And to think I once had you in chains—once had you so close to execution, and had no idea what prize I instead sentenced to Endovier. The Queen of Terrasen—slave and my Champion." The king unfurled his fist to look at the two rings in his palm. He chucked them aside. They bounced on the red marble, pinging faintly. "Too bad you don't have your flames now, Aelin Galathynius."

Aelin tugged the cloth from the pommel of her father's blade and drew the Sword of Orynth.

"Where are the Wyrdkeys?"

"At least you're direct. But what shall you do to me, heir of Terrasen, if I do not tell you?" He gestured to Dorian, and the prince descended the steps of the dais, stopping at the bottom.

Time—she needed time. The tower wasn't down yet. "Dorian," Chaol said softly.

The prince didn't respond.

The king chuckled. "No running today, Captain?"

Chaol leveled his stare at the king, and drew Damaris—Aelin's gift to him.

The king tapped a finger on the arm of his throne. "What would the noble people of Terrasen say if they knew Aelin of the Wildfire had such a bloody history? If they knew that she had signed her services over to me? What hope would it give them to know that even their long-lost princess was corrupted?"

"You certainly like to hear yourself speak, don't you?"

The king's finger stilled on the throne. "I'll admit that I don't know how I didn't see it. You're the same spoiled child who strutted about her castle. And here I was, thinking I'd helped you. I saw into your mind that day, Aelin Galathynius. You loved your home and your kingdom, but you had such a wish to be ordinary, such a wish for freedom from your crown, even then. Have you changed your mind? I offered you freedom on a platter ten years ago, and yet you wound up a slave anyway. Funny."

Time, time, time. Let him talk . . .

"You had the element of surprise then," Aelin said. "But now we know what power you wield."

"Do you? Do you understand the cost of the keys? What you must become to use one?"

She tightened her grip on the Sword of Orynth.

"Would you like to go head-to-head with me, then, Aelin Galathynius? To see if the spells you learned, the books you stole from me, will hold out? Little tricks, Princess, compared to the raw power of the keys."

"Dorian," Chaol said again. The prince remained fixated on her, a hungry smile now on those sensuous lips.

"Let me demonstrate," the king said. Aelin braced herself, her gut clenching.

He pointed at Dorian. "Kneel."

The prince dropped to his knees. She hid her wince at the impact of bone on marble. The king's brows knotted. A darkness began to build, cracking from the king like forks of lightning.

"No," Chaol breathed, stepping forward. Aelin grabbed the captain by the arm before he could do something incredibly stupid.

A tendril of night slammed into Dorian's back and he arched, groaning.

"I think there is more that you know, Aelin Galathynius," the king said, that too-familiar blackness growing. "Things that perhaps only the heir of Brannon Galathynius might have learned."

The third Wyrdkey.

"You wouldn't dare," Aelin said. The prince's neck was taut as he panted, as the darkness whipped him.

Once—twice. Lashings.

She knew that pain. "He's your son—your heir."

"You forget, Princess," the king said, "that I have two sons."

Dorian screamed as another whip of darkness slashed his back. Black lightning flitted across his exposed teeth.

She lunged—and was thrown back by the very wards she'd drawn on her body. An invisible wall of that black pain lay around Dorian now, and his screams became unending.

Like a beast snapped from its leash, Chaol flung himself against it, roaring Dorian's name, the blood crumbling from the cuff of his jacket with each attempt.

Again. Again. Again.

Dorian was sobbing, darkness pouring out of his mouth, shackling his hands, branding his back, his neck—

Then it vanished.

The prince sagged to the floor, chest heaving. Chaol halted midstrike, his breathing ragged, face drawn.

"Rise," the king said.

Dorian got to his feet, his black collar gleaming as his chest heaved. "Delicious," the thing inside the prince said. Bile burned Aelin's throat.

"Please," Chaol said hoarsely to the king, and her heart cracked at the word, at the agony and desperation. "Free him. Name your price. I'll give you anything."

"Would you hand over your former lover, Captain? I see no use in losing a weapon if I don't gain one in return." The king waved a hand toward her. "You destroyed my general and three of my princes. I can think of a few other Valg who are aching to get their claws into you for that—who would very much enjoy the chance to slip into your body. It's only fair."

Aelin dared a glance toward the window. The sun climbed higher.

"You came into my family's home and murdered them in their sleep," Aelin said. The grandfather clock began chiming twelve. A heartbeat later, the miserable, off-kilter clanging of the clock tower sounded. "It's only *fair*," she said to the king as she backed a step toward the doors, "that I destroy you in return."

She tugged the Eye of Elena from under her suit. The blue stone glowed like a small star.

Not just a ward against evil.

But a key in its own right, that could be used to unlock Erawan's tomb.

The king's eyes went wide and he rose from his throne. "You've just made the mistake of your life, girl."

He might have a point.

The noontime bells were ringing.

Yet the clock tower still stood.

CHAPTER 71

Rowan swung his sword and the Wyrdhound fell back, howling as his blade pierced through stone and into the tender flesh beneath. But not enough to keep it down, to kill it. Another Wyrdhound leaped. Where they lunged, Rowan struck.

Side by side, he and Aedion had been pushed against a wall, conceding foot after foot of the passage—driven farther and farther from the spool of fuse Aedion had been forced to drop.

A clanging, miserable noise rang out.

In the span between clangs, Rowan slashed for two different Wyrdhounds, blows that would have disemboweled most creatures.

The clock tower. Noon.

The Wyrdhounds were herding them back, dodging sure-kill blows, keeping out of their reach.

To keep them from getting to the fuse.

Rowan swore and launched into an assault that engaged three of them at once, Aedion flanking him. The Wyrdhounds held their line.

Noon, he had promised Aelin. As the sun began to reach its apex on the solstice, they'd bring the tower crashing down.

The final clang of the clock tower sounded.

Noon had come and gone.

And his Fireheart, his queen, was in that castle above them—left with only her mortal training and wits to keep her alive. Perhaps not for much longer.

The thought was so abhorrent, so outrageous, that Rowan roared his fury, louder than the shrieks of the beasts.

The bellow cost his brother. One creature shot past Rowan's guard, leaping, and Aedion barked out a curse and staggered back. Rowan smelled Aedion's blood before he saw it.

It must have been a dinner bell to the Wyrdhounds, that demi-Fae blood. Four of them leaped for the general as one, their maws revealing flesh-shredding stone teeth.

The three others whirled for Rowan, and there was nothing he could do to get to that fuse.

To save the queen who held his heart in her scarred hands.

A few steps ahead of him, Chaol watched Aelin back toward the glass doors, just as they'd planned after seeing his men dead.

The king's attention was fixed on the Eye of Elena around her neck. She removed it, holding it in a steady hand. "Been looking for this, have you? Poor Erawan, locked in his little tomb for so long."

It was an effort to hold his position as Aelin kept retreating.

"Where did you find that?" the king seethed.

Aelin reached Chaol, brushing against him, a comfort and a thank-you and a good-bye as she continued past. "Turns out your ancestor didn't approve of your hobbies. We Galathynius women stick together, you know."

For the first time in his life, Chaol saw the king's face go slack. But then the man said, "And did that ancient fool tell you what will happen if you wield the other key you already possess?"

She was so close to the doors. "Let the prince go, or I'll destroy this right here, and Erawan can stay locked up." She slid the chain into her pocket.

"Very well," the king said. He looked at Dorian, who showed no sign of even remembering his own name, despite what the witch had written on the walls of their city. "Go. Retrieve her."

Darkness surged from Dorian, leaking like blood in water, and Chaol's head gave a burst of pain as—

Aelin ran, exploding through the glass doors.

Faster than he should be, Dorian raced after her, ice coating the floor, the room. The cold of it knocked the breath from him. But Dorian didn't glance once in his direction before he was gone.

The king took a step down the dais, his breath clouding in front of him.

Chaol lifted his sword, holding his position between the open doors and the conqueror of their continent.

The king took another step. "More heroic antics? Don't you ever get bored of them, Captain?"

Chaol did not yield. "You murdered my men. And Sorscha."

"And a good many more."

Another step. The king stared over Chaol's shoulder to the hallway where Aelin and Dorian had vanished.

"It ends now," Chaol said.

The Valg princes had been lethal in Wendlyn. But when inhabiting Dorian's body, with Dorian's magic . . .

Aelin hurtled down the hallway, glass windows flanking her, marble beneath—nothing but open sky around her.

And behind, charging after her like a black storm, was Dorian.

Ice spread from him, hoarfrost splintering along the windows.

The moment that ice hit her, Aelin knew she would not run another step.

She'd memorized every hallway and stairwell thanks to Chaol's maps. She pushed herself harder, praying that Chaol bought her time as she neared a narrow flight of stairs and hurled herself up, taking the steps by twos and threes.

Ice cracked along the glass right behind her, and cold bit at her heels.

Faster—*faster.*

Around and around, up and up she flew. It was past noon. If something had gone wrong with Rowan and Aedion . . .

She hit the top of the stairs, and ice made the landing so slick that she skidded, going sideways, going down—

She caught herself with a hand against the floor, her skin ripping open on the ice. She slammed into a glass wall and rebounded, then she was running again as the ice closed in around her.

Higher—she had to get higher.

And Chaol, facing the king—

She didn't let herself think about that. Spears of ice shot out from the walls, narrowly missing her sides.

Her breath was a flame in her throat.

"I told you," a cold male voice said from behind, not at all winded. Ice spiderwebbed across the windows on either side. "I told you that you would regret sparing me. That I would destroy everything you love."

She reached a glass-covered bridge that stretched between two of the highest spires. The floor was utterly transparent, so clear that she could see every inch of the plunge to the ground far, far below.

Hoarfrost coated the windows, groaning—

Glass exploded, and a cry shattered from her throat as it sliced into her back.

Aelin veered to the side, for the now-broken window, its too-small iron frame, and the drop beyond.

She flung herself through it.

CHAPTER 72

Bright, open air, the wind roaring in her ears, then—

Aelin landed on the open glass bridge a level below, her knees popping as she absorbed the impact and rolled. Her body shrieked in agony at the slices in her arms and back where bits of glass stuck clean through her suit, but she was already sprinting for the tower door at the other end of the bridge.

She looked in time to see Dorian hurtle right through the space she'd cleared, his eyes fixed on her.

Aelin flung open the door as the *boom* of Dorian hitting the bridge sounded.

She slammed the door behind her, but even that couldn't seal out the growing cold.

Just a little farther.

Aelin raced up the spiraling tower stairs, half sobbing through her gritted teeth.

Rowan. Aedion. Chaol.

Chaol—

The door shattered off its hinges at the base of the spire and cold exploded through, stealing her breath.

But Aelin had reached the top of the tower. Beyond it, another glass footbridge, thin and bare, stretched far across to one of the other spires.

It was still shaded as the sun crept across the other side of the building, the uppermost turrets of the glass castle surrounding and smothering her like a cage of darkness.

Aelin had gotten out, and taken Dorian with her.

Chaol had bought her that time, in one final attempt to save his friend and his king.

When she had burst into his house this morning, sobbing and laughing, she'd explained what the Wing Leader had written, the payment the witch had given in exchange for saving her life. Dorian was still in there, still fighting.

She had planned to take them both on at once, the king and the prince, and he had agreed to help her, to try to talk Dorian back into humanity, to try to convince the prince to fight. Until that moment he'd seen his men hanging from the gates.

Now he had no interest in talking.

If Aelin were to stand a chance—any chance—of freeing Dorian from that collar, she needed the king out of the picture. Even if it cost her the vengeance for her family and kingdom.

Chaol was glad to settle that score on her behalf—and on the behalf of many more.

The king looked at Chaol's sword, then at his face, and laughed.

"You'll kill me, Captain? Such dramatics."

They'd gotten away. Aelin had gotten Dorian out, her bluff so flawless even Chaol had believed the Eye in her hands was the real thing, with the way she'd angled it into the sun so the blue stone glowed. He had no idea where she'd put the real one. If she was even wearing it.

All of it—all that they had done, and lost, and fought for. All of it for this moment.

The king kept approaching, and Chaol held his sword before him, not yielding one step.

For Ress. For Brullo. For Sorscha. For Dorian. For Aelin, and Aedion, and their family, for the thousands massacred in those labor camps. And for Nesryn—who he'd lied to, who would wait for a return that wouldn't come, for time they wouldn't have together.

He had no regrets but that one.

A wave of black slammed into him, and Chaol staggered back a step, the marks of protection tingling on his skin.

"You lost," Chaol panted. The blood was flaking away beneath his clothes, itching.

Another wave of black, identical to the one that had struck Dorian— which Dorian hadn't been able to stand against.

Chaol felt it that time: the throb of unending agony, the whisper of pain to come.

The king approached. Chaol lifted his sword higher.

"Your wards are failing, boy."

Chaol smiled, tasting blood in his mouth. "Good thing steel lasts longer."

The sun through the windows warmed Chaol's back—as if in an embrace, as if in comfort. As if it to tell him it was time.

I'll make it count, Aelin had promised him.

He had bought her time.

A wave of black reared up behind the king, sucking the light out of the room.

Chaol spread his arms wide as the darkness hit him, shattered him, obliterated him until there was nothing but light—burning blue light, warm and welcoming.

Aelin and Dorian had gotten away. It was enough.

When the pain came, he was not afraid.

CHAPTER 73

It was going to kill her.

He wanted it to.

Her face—that *face*—

He neared the woman, step by step across the narrow, shaded bridge, the turrets high above them gleaming with blinding light.

Blood covered her arms, and she panted as she backed away from him, her hands out before her, a gold ring shining on her finger. He could smell her now—the immortal, mighty blood in her veins.

"Dorian," she said.

He did not know that name.

And he was going to kill her.

CHAPTER 74

Time. She needed to buy more time, or steal it, while the bridge still lay in shadow, while the sun slowly, slowly moved.

"Dorian," Aelin pleaded again.

"I'm going to rip you apart from the inside out," the demon said.

Ice spread across the bridge. The glass in her back shifted and ripped into her with each step she retreated toward the tower door.

Still the clock tower had not come down.

But the king had not yet arrived.

"Your father is currently in his council room," she said, fighting the pain splintering through her. "He is in there with Chaol—with your *friend*—and your father has likely already killed him."

"Good."

"Chaol," Aelin said, her voice breaking. Her foot slid against a patch of ice, and the world tilted as she steadied her balance. The drop to the ground hundreds of feet below hit her in the gut, but she kept her eyes on the prince even as agony rippled down her body again. "*Chaol.*

You sacrificed yourself. You let them put that collar on you—so he could get out."

"I'm going to let him put a collar on you, and then we can play."

She hit the tower door, fumbling for the latch.

But it was iced over.

She clawed at the ice, glancing between the prince and the sun that had begun to peek around the corner of the tower.

Dorian was ten steps away.

She whirled back around. "*Sorscha*—her name was Sorscha, and she loved you. You loved her. And *they* took her away from you."

Five steps.

There was nothing human in that face, no flicker of memory in those sapphire eyes.

Aelin began weeping, even as blood leaked down her nose from his nearness. "I came back for you. Just like I promised."

A dagger of ice appeared in his hand, its lethal tip glinting like a star in the sunlight. "I don't care," Dorian said.

She shoved a hand between them as if she could push him away, grabbing one of his own hands tight. His skin was so cold as he used the other to plunge the knife into her side.

⁓

Rowan's blood sprayed from his mouth as the creature slammed into him, knocking him to the ground.

Four were dead, but three remained between him and the fuse.

Aedion bellowed in pain and fury, holding the line, keeping the other three at bay as Rowan drove his blade home—

The creature flipped back, away out of reach.

The three beasts converged again, wild with the Fae blood now covering the passage. His blood. Aedion's. The general's face was already pale from the loss of it. They couldn't stand this much longer.

But he had to get that tower down.

As though they were of one mind, one body, the three Wyrdhounds lunged, driving him and Aedion apart, one leaping for the general, two snapping for him—

Rowan went down as stone jaws clamped onto his leg.

Bone snapped, and black crushed in—

He roared against the darkness that meant death.

Rowan slammed his fighting knife into the creature's eye, driving up and deep, just as the second beast lunged for his outstretched arm.

But something massive slammed into the creature, and it yelped as it was thrown against the wall. The dead one was hurled away a heartbeat later, and then—

And then there was Lorcan, swords out and swinging, a battle cry on his lips as he tore into the remaining creatures.

Rowan bellowed against the agony in his lower leg as he got to his feet, balancing his weight. Aedion was already up, his face a bloody mess but his eyes clear.

One of the creatures lunged for Aedion, and Rowan hurled his fighting knife—hurled it hard and true, right into its gaping mouth. The Wyrdhound hit the ground not six inches from the general's feet.

Lorcan was a whirlwind of steel, his fury unmatched. Rowan drew his other knife, readying to throw it—

Just as Lorcan drove his sword clean down into the creature's skull.

Silence—utter silence in the bloodied tunnel.

Aedion scrambled, limping and swaying, for the fuse twenty paces away. It was still attached to the spool.

"*Now*," Rowan barked. He didn't care if they didn't make it out. For all he knew—

A phantom pain lanced through his ribs, brutally violent and nauseating.

His knees buckled. Not pain from a wound of his—but another's.

No.

No, no, no, no, no.

He might have been screaming it, might have been roaring it, as he surged for the passage exit—as he felt that agony, that lick of cold.

Things had gone very, very wrong.

He made it another step before his leg gave out, and it was only that invisible bond, straining and fraying, that kept him conscious. A hard, blood-soaked body slammed into his, an arm wrapping around his waist, hauling him up. "*Run*, you stupid fool," Lorcan hissed, hauling him from the fuse.

Aedion was crouched over it, his bloody hands steady as he grasped the flint and struck.

Once. Twice.

Then a spark, and a flame that went roaring off into the darkness.

They ran like hell.

"*Faster*," Lorcan said, and Aedion caught up to them, taking Rowan's other arm and adding his strength and speed.

Down the passage. Past the broken iron gates, into the sewers.

There was not enough time and space between them and the tower.

And Aelin—

The bond stretched tighter, splintering. *No.*

Aelin—

They heard it before they felt it.

The utter lack of sound, like the world had paused. Followed by a cracking *boom*.

"*Move*," Lorcan said, a barked order that had Rowan blindly obeying just as he had for centuries.

Then the wind—the dry, burning wind that flayed his skin.

Then a flash of blinding light.

Then heat—such heat that Lorcan swore, shoving them into an alcove.

The tunnels shook; the *world* shook.

The ceilings came crashing down.

When the dust and debris cleared, when Rowan's body was singing with pain and joy and power, the way into the castle was blocked. And behind them, stretching into the gloom of the sewers, were a hundred Valg commanders and foot soldiers, armed and smiling.

⌒

Reeking to Hellas's realm with Valg blood, Manon and Asterin were soaring down the continent, back to Morath, when—

A soft wind, a shudder in the world, a silence.

Asterin barked a cry, her wyvern banking right as if the reins had been yanked. Abraxos loosed a yelp of his own, but Manon just peered down at the land, where birds were taking flight at the shimmer that seemed to rush past . . .

At the magic that now rippled through the world, free.

Darkness embrace her.

Magic.

Whatever had happened, however it had been freed, Manon didn't care.

That mortal, human weight vanished. Strength coursed through her, coating her bones like armor. Invincible, immortal, unstoppable.

Manon tipped her head back to the sky, spread her arms wide, and roared.

⌒

The Keep was in chaos. Witches and humans were running around, shouting.

Magic.

Magic was free.

Not possible.

But she could feel it, even with the collar around her neck and that scar on her arm.

The loosing of some great beast inside her.

A beast who purred at the shadowfire.

⌒

Aelin crawled away from the door stained with her blood, away from the Valg prince who laughed as she clutched at her side and inched across the bridge, her blood a smear behind her.

The sun was still creeping around that tower.

"Dorian," she said, her legs pushing against the glass, her blood dribbling out from between her freezing fingers, warming them. "Remember."

The Valg prince stalked her, smiling faintly as she collapsed onto her front in the center of the bridge. The shadowed spires of the glass castle loomed around her—a tomb. Her tomb.

"Dorian, *remember*," she gasped out. He'd missed her heart—barely.

"He said to retrieve you, but perhaps I'll have my fun first."

Two knives appeared in his hands, curved and vicious.

The sun began glinting just above the tower overhead.

"Remember Chaol," she begged. "Remember Sorscha. Remember me."

A *boom* shook the castle from somewhere on the other side of the building.

And then a great wind, a soft wind, a lovely wind, as if the heart-song of the world were carried on it.

She closed her eyes for a moment and pressed her hand against her side, drawing in a breath.

"We get to come back," Aelin said, pushing her hand harder and harder into her wound until the blood stopped, until it was only her tears that flowed. "Dorian, *we get to come back* from this loss—from this darkness. We get to come back, and I came back for you."

She was weeping now, weeping as that wind faded away and her wound knitted closed.

The prince's daggers had gone slack in his hands.

And on his finger, Athril's golden ring glowed.

"Fight it," she panted. The sun angled closer. "*Fight it*. We get to come back."

Brighter and brighter, the golden ring pulsed at his finger.

The prince staggered back a step, his face twisting. "*You human worm.*"

He had been too busy stabbing her to notice the ring she'd slipped onto his finger when she'd grabbed his hand as if to shove him away.

"Take it off," he growled, trying to touch it—and hissing as though it burned. "*Take it off!*"

Ice grew, spreading toward her, fast as the rays of sunlight that now shot between the towers, refracting across every glass parapet and bridge, filling the castle with Mala Fire-Bringer's glorious light.

The bridge—this bridge that she and Chaol had selected for this purpose, for this one moment at the apex of the solstice—was smack in the middle of it.

The light hit her, and it filled her heart with the force of an exploding star.

With a roar, the Valg prince sent a wave of ice for her, spears and lances aimed at her chest.

So Aelin flung her hands out toward the prince, toward her friend, and hurled her magic at him with everything she had.

CHAPTER 75

There was fire, and light, and darkness, and ice.

But the woman—the woman was there, halfway across the bridge, her hands out before her as she got to her feet.

No blood leaked from where the ice had stabbed her. Only clean, polished skin peeked through the black material of her suit.

Healed—with magic.

All around him there was so much fire and light, tugging at him.

We get to come back, she said. As if she knew what this darkness was, what horrors existed. *Fight it*.

A light was burning at his finger—a light that cracked *inside* him.

A light that cracked a sliver into the darkness.

Remember, she said.

Her flames tore at him, and the demon was screaming. But it did not hurt him. Her flames only kept the demon at bay.

Remember.

A sliver of light in the blackness.

A cracked doorway.

Remember.

Over the demon's screaming, he pushed—*pushed*, and looked out through its eyes. *His* eyes.

And saw Celaena Sardothien standing before him.

⁓

Aedion spat blood onto the debris. Rowan was barely remaining conscious as he leaned against the cave-in behind them, while Lorcan tried to cut a path through the onslaught of Valg fighters.

More and more poured in from the tunnels, armed and bloodthirsty, alerted by the blast.

Drained and unable to summon the full depths of their magic so soon, even Rowan and Lorcan wouldn't be able to keep the Valg occupied for long.

Aedion had two knives left. He knew they weren't getting out of these tunnels alive.

The soldiers came in like an unending wave, their hollow eyes lit with bloodlust.

Even down here, Aedion could hear the people screaming in the streets, either from the explosion or the magic returning to flood their land. That wind . . . he'd never smelled anything like it, never would again.

They'd taken out the tower. They'd done it.

Now his queen would have her magic. Maybe now she'd stand a chance.

Aedion gutted the Valg commander nearest him, black blood splattering on his hands, and engaged the two that stepped in to replace him. Behind him, Rowan's breaths were rasping. Too labored.

The prince's magic, draining with his blood loss, had begun faltering moments ago, no longer able to choke the air out of the soldiers' lungs. Now it was no more than a cold wind shoving against them, keeping the bulk at bay.

Aedion hadn't recognized Lorcan's magic as it had blasted from him in near-invisible dark winds. But where it struck, soldiers went down. And did not rise.

It, too, had now failed him.

Aedion could scarcely lift his sword arm. Just a little longer; just a few more minutes of keeping these soldiers engaged so that his queen could remain distraction-free.

With a grunt of pain, Lorcan was engulfed by half a dozen soldiers and shoved out of sight into the blackness.

Aedion kept swinging and swinging until there were no Valg before him, until he realized that the soldiers had pulled back twenty feet and regrouped.

A solid line of Valg foot soldiers, their numbers stretching away into the gloom, stood watching him, holding their swords. Waiting for the order to strike. Too many. Too many to escape.

"It's been an honor, Prince," Aedion said to Rowan.

Rowan's only reply was a rasping breath.

The Valg commander stalked to the front of the line, his own sword out. Somewhere back in the sewer, soldiers began screaming. Lorcan— that selfish prick—must have cut a path through them after all. And run.

"Charge on my mark," the commander said, his black ring glinting as he lifted a hand.

Aedion stepped in front of Rowan, useless as it would be. They'd kill Rowan once he was dead, anyway. But at least he'd go down fighting, defending his brother. At least he would have that.

People were still screaming on the street above—shrieking with blind terror, the sounds of their panic growing closer, louder.

"Steady," the commander said to the swordsmen.

Aedion took a breath—one of his last, he realized. Rowan straightened as best he could, stalwart against the death that now beckoned, and Aedion could have sworn the prince whispered Aelin's name. More shouting from the soldiers in the back; some in the front turning to see what the panic was about behind them.

Aedion didn't care. Not with a row of swords before them, gleaming like the teeth of some mighty beast.

The commander's hand came down.

And was ripped clean off by a ghost leopard.

For Evangeline, for her freedom, for her future.

Where Lysandra lunged, slashing with claws and fangs, soldiers died.

She'd made it halfway across the city before she got out of that carriage. She told Evangeline to take it all the way to the Faliqs' country house, to be a good girl and *stay safe*. Lysandra had sprinted two blocks toward the castle, not caring if she had little to offer them in their fight, when the wind slammed into her and a wild song sparkled in her blood.

Then she shed her human skin, that mortal cage, and *ran*, tracking the scents of her friends.

The soldiers in the sewer were screaming as she tore into them— a death for every day in hell, a death for the childhood taken from her and from Evangeline. She was fury, she was wrath, she was vengeance.

Aedion and Rowan were backed up against the cave-in, their faces bloody and gaping as she leaped upon the back of a sentry and shredded his spine clean out of his skin.

Oh, she *liked* this body.

More soldiers rushed into the sewers and Lysandra whirled toward them, giving herself wholly to the beast whose form she wore. She became death incarnate.

When there were none left, when blood soaked her pale fur—blood that tasted *vile*—she paused at last.

"The palace," Rowan gasped from where he'd slumped against the stones, Aedion pressing a hand to a wound in the Fae warrior's leg. Rowan pointed to the open sewer behind them, littered with gore. "*To the queen.*"

An order and a plea.

Lysandra nodded her furry head, that disgusting blood leaking from her maw, black gore in her fangs, and bolted back the way she'd come.

People screamed at the ghost leopard that shot down the street, sleek as an arrow, dodging whinnying horses and carriages.

The glass castle loomed, half shrouded by the smoking ruins of the clock tower, and light—*fire*—exploded between its turrets. *Aelin.*

Aelin was still alive, and fighting like hell.

The iron gates of the castle appeared ahead, strung with reeking corpses.

Fire and darkness slammed into each other atop the castle, and people fell silent as they pointed. Lysandra raced for the gates, and the crowd spied her at last, scrambling and bleating to get out of her way. They cleared a path right to the open entrance.

Revealing thirty Valg guards armed with crossbows lined up in front of it, ready to fire.

They all trained their weapons on her.

Thirty guards with bolts—and beyond them, an open path to the castle. To Aelin.

Lysandra leaped. The closest guard fired a clean, spiraling shot right for her chest.

She knew, with that leopard's senses, that it would hit home.

Yet Lysandra did not slow. She did not stop.

For Evangeline. For her future. For her freedom. For the friends who had come for her.

The bolt neared her heart.

And was knocked from the air by an arrow.

Lysandra landed on the guard's face and shredded it with her claws.

There was only one sharpshooter with that sort of aim.

Lysandra loosed a roar, and became a storm of death upon the guards nearest her while arrows rained on the rest.

When Lysandra dared look, it was in time to see Nesryn Faliq draw another arrow atop the neighboring rooftop, flanked by her rebels, and fire it clean through the eye of the final guard between Lysandra and the castle.

"*Go!*" Nesryn shouted over the panicking crowd.

Flame and night warred in the highest spires, and the earth shuddered.

Lysandra was already running up the sloped, curving path between the trees.

Nothing but the grass and the trees and the wind.

Nothing but this sleek, powerful body, her shape-shifter's heart burning, glowing, singing with each step, each curve she took, fluid and swift and *free*.

Faster and faster, every movement of that leopard's body a joy, even as her queen battled for her kingdom and their world high, high above.

CHAPTER 76

Aelin panted, fighting against the throbbing in her head.

Too soon; too much power too soon. She hadn't had time to draw it up the safe way, spiraling slowly to its depths.

Shifting into her Fae form hadn't helped—it had only made the Valg smell worse.

Dorian was on his knees, clawing at his hand, where the ring kept glowing, branding his flesh.

He sent darkness snapping for her again and again—and each time, she slammed it away with a wall of flame.

But her blood was heating.

"*Try*, Dorian," she begged, her tongue like paper in her parched mouth.

"*I will kill you, you Fae bitch.*"

A low laugh sounded behind her.

Aelin half turned—not daring to put her back to either of them, even if it meant exposing herself to the open fall.

The King of Adarlan stood in the open doorway at the other end of the bridge.

Chaol—

"Such a noble effort from the captain. To try to buy you time so you might save my son."

She'd tried—*tried*, but—

"*Punish her,*" the demon hissed from the other end of the bridge.

"Patience." But the king stiffened as he took in the gold ring burning on Dorian's hand. That harsh, brutal face tightened. "What have you done?"

Dorian thrashed, shuddering, and let out a scream that set her Fae ears ringing.

Aelin drew her father's sword. "You killed Chaol," she said, the words hollow.

"The boy didn't even land a single blow." He smirked at the Sword of Orynth. "I doubt you will, either."

Dorian went silent.

Aelin snarled, "*You killed him.*"

The king approached, his footfalls thudding on the glass bridge.

"My one regret," the king said to her, "is that I did not get to take my time."

She backed up a step—just one.

The king drew Nothung. "I'll take my time with you, though."

Aelin lifted her sword in both hands.

Then—

"What did you say?"

Dorian.

The voice was hoarse, broken.

The king and Aelin both turned toward the prince.

But Dorian's eyes were on his father, and they were burning like stars. "What did you say. About Chaol."

The king snapped. "*Silence.*"

"Did you kill him." Not a question.

Aelin's lips began trembling, and she tunneled down, down, down inside herself.

"And if I did?" the king said, brows high.

"Did you kill Chaol?"

The light at Dorian's hand burned and burned—

But the collar remained around his neck.

"*You*," the king snapped—and Aelin realized he meant her just as a spear of darkness shot for her so fast, too fast—

The darkness shattered against a wall of ice.

Dorian.

His name was Dorian.

Dorian Havilliard, and he was the Crown Prince of Adarlan.

And Celaena Sardothien—Aelin Galathynius, his friend . . . she had come back for him.

She faced him, an ancient sword in her hands.

"Dorian?" she breathed.

The demon inside him was screaming and pleading, ripping at him, trying to bargain.

A wave of black slammed into the shield of ice he'd thrown up between the princess and his father. Soon—soon the king would break through it.

Dorian lifted his hands to the Wyrdstone collar—cold, smooth, thrumming.

Don't, the demon shrieked. *Don't!*

There were tears running down Aelin's face as Dorian gripped the black stone encircling his throat.

And, bellowing his grief, his rage, his pain, he snapped the collar from his neck.

CHAPTER 77

The Wyrdstone collar broke in two—severing along a hairline fracture where the ring's power had sliced through.

Dorian was panting, and blood was running from his nose, but—

"Aelin," he gasped out, and the voice was his. It was him.

She ran, sheathing the Sword of Orynth, reaching his side as the wall of ice exploded beneath a hammer of darkness.

The king's power surged for them, and Aelin flung out a single hand. A shield of fire blasted into existence, and the darkness was shoved back.

"Neither of you are leaving here alive," the king said, his rough voice slithering through the fire.

Dorian sagged against her, and Aelin slipped a hand around his waist to hold him up.

Pain flickered in her gut, and a throbbing began in her blood. She couldn't hold out, not so unprepared, even as the sun held at its peak, as if Mala herself willed it to linger just a little longer to amplify the gifts she'd already showered on a Princess of Terrasen.

"Dorian," Aelin said, pain lancing down her spine as burnout neared.

He turned his head, an eye still on the wall of flickering flames. Such pain, and grief, and rage in those eyes. Yet, somehow, beneath it all—a spark of spirit. Of hope.

Aelin extended her hand—a question and an offer and a promise.

"To a better future," she said.

"You came back," he said, as if that were an answer.

They joined hands.

So the world ended.

And the next one began.

They were infinite.

They were the beginning and the ending; they were eternity.

The king standing before them gaped as the shield of flame died out to reveal Aelin and Dorian, hand in hand, glowing like newborn gods as their magic entwined.

"*You're mine*," the man raged. He became darkness; folded himself into the power he carried, as if he were nothing but malice on a dark wind.

He struck them, swallowed them.

But they held tighter to each other, past and present and future; flickering between an ancient hall in a mountain castle perched above Orynth, a bridge suspended between glass towers, and another place, perfect and strange, where they had been crafted from stardust and light.

A wall of night knocked them back. But they could not be contained.

The darkness paused for breath.

They erupted.

Rowan blinked against the sunlight as it poured from beyond Aedion.

Soldiers had infiltrated the sewers again, even after Lysandra had saved their sorry asses. Lorcan had rushed back, bloodied, and told them the way out was barred, and whatever way Lysandra had gotten in was now overrun.

With battlefield efficiency, Rowan had healed his leg as best he could with his remaining power. While he'd patched himself up, bone and skin knitting together hastily enough to make him bark in pain, Aedion and Lorcan clawed a path through the cave-in, just as the sewer had filled with the sounds of the soldiers rushing in. They'd hauled ass back to the castle grounds, where they hit another cave-in. Aedion had started ripping at the top of it, shouting and roaring at the earth as if his will alone could move it.

But now there was a hole. It was all Rowan needed.

Rowan shifted, his leg flashing in agony as he exchanged his limbs for wings and talons. He loosed a cry, shrill and raging. A white-tailed hawk soared out of the small opening, past Aedion.

Rowan did not linger as he took in his surroundings. They were some-where in the castle gardens, the glass castle looming beyond. The reek of the smoke from the ruin of the clock tower clogged his senses.

Light exploded from the uppermost castle spires, so bright that he was blinded for a moment.

Aelin.

Alive. *Alive.* He flapped, bending the wind to his will with the dregs of his magic, soaring faster and faster. He sent another wind toward the clock tower, rerouting the smoke toward the river, away from them.

Rowan rounded the corner of the castle.

He had no words for what he saw.

⁓

The King of Adarlan bellowed as Aelin and Dorian fractured his power. Together they broke down every spell, every ounce of evil that he'd bent and shackled to his command.

Infinite—Dorian's power was infinite.

They were full of light, of fire and starlight and sunshine. They over-flowed with it as they snapped the final tether on the king's power and cleaved his darkness away, burning it up until it was nothing.

The king fell to his knees, the glass bridge thudding with the impact.

Aelin released Dorian's hand. Cold emptiness flooded her so violently that she, too, fell to the glass floor, gulping down air, reeling herself back in, remembering who she was.

Dorian was staring at his father: the man who had broken him, enslaved him.

In a voice she had never heard, the king whispered, "My boy."

Dorian didn't react.

The king gazed up at his son, his eyes wide—bright—and said again, "My boy."

Then the king looked to where she was on her knees, gaping at him. "Have you come to save me at last, Aelin Galathynius?"

CHAPTER 78

Aelin Galathynius stared at the butcher of her family, her people, her continent.

"Don't listen to his lies," Dorian said, flat and hollow.

Aelin studied the king's hand, where the dark ring had been shattered away. Only a pale band of skin remained. "Who are you?" she said quietly.

Human—more and more, the king looked . . . human. Softer.

The king turned to Dorian, exposing his broad palms. "Everything I did—it was all to keep you safe. From him."

Aelin went still.

"I found the key," the king went on, the words tumbling out. "I found the key and brought it to Morath. And he . . . *Perrington*. We were young, and he took me under the Keep to show me the crypt, even though it was forbidden. But I opened it with the key . . ." Tears, real and clear, flowed down his ruddy face. "I opened it, and *he* came; he took Perrington's body—and . . ." He gazed at his bare hand. Watched it shake. "He let his minion take me."

"That's enough," Dorian said.

Aelin's heart stumbled. "Erawan is free," she breathed. And not only free—Erawan *was* Perrington. The Dark King himself had manhandled her, lived in this castle with her—and had never known, by luck or Fate or Elena's own protection, that she was here. *She* had never known, either—never detected it on him. Gods above, Erawan had forced her to bow that day in Endovier and neither of them had scented or marked what the other was.

The king nodded, setting his tears splattering on his tunic. "The Eye—you could have sealed him back in with the Eye . . ."

The look on the king's face when she'd revealed the necklace . . . He'd been seeing a tool not of destruction, but of salvation.

Aelin said, "How is it possible he's been inside Perrington all this time and no one noticed?"

"He can hide inside a body like a snail in its shell. But cloaking his presence also stifles his own abilities to scent others—like you. And now you are back—all the players in the unfinished game. The Galathynius line—and the Havilliard, which he has hated so fiercely all this time. Why he targeted my family, and yours."

"You butchered my kingdom," she managed to say. That night her parents died, there had been that *smell* in the room . . . The scent of the Valg. "You slaughtered millions."

"I tried to stop it." The king braced a hand on the bridge, as if to keep from collapsing under the weight of the shame now coating his words. "They could find you based on your magic alone, and wanted the strongest of you for themselves. And when you were born . . ." His craggy features crumpled as he again addressed Dorian. "You were so strong—so precious. I couldn't let them take you. I wrested control away for just long enough."

"To do what," Dorian said hoarsely.

Aelin glanced at the smoke wafting toward the river far beyond. "To order the towers built," she said, "and use that spell to banish magic." And now that they had freed magic . . . the magic-wielders would be sniffed out by every Valg demon in Erilea.

The king gasped a shuddering breath. "But he didn't know how I'd done it. He thought the magic vanished as punishment from our gods and knew nothing of why the towers were built. All this time I used my strength to keep the knowledge of it away from him—from them. All my strength—so I could not fight the demon, stop it when . . . when it did those things. I kept that knowledge safe."

"He's a liar," Dorian said, turning on his heel. There was no mercy in his voice. "I still wound up able to use my magic—it didn't protect me at all. He'll say anything."

The wicked will tell us anything to haunt our thoughts long after, Nehemia had warned her.

"I didn't know," the king pleaded. "Using my blood in the spell must have made my line immune. It was a mistake. I'm sorry. *I'm sorry*. My boy—Dorian—"

"You don't get to call him that," Aelin snapped. "You came to my home and murdered my family."

"I came to find you. *I came to have you burn it out of me!*" the king sobbed. "Aelin of the Wildfire. I tried to get you to do it. But your mother knocked you unconscious before you could kill me, and the demon . . . The demon became devoted to wiping out your line after that, so no fire could ever cleanse him from me."

Aelin's blood turned to ice. No—no, it couldn't be true, couldn't be right.

"All of it was to find you," the king said to her. "So you could save me—so you could end me at last. Please. Do it." The king was weeping now, and his body seemed to waste away bit by bit, his cheeks hollowing out, his hands thinning.

As if his life force and the demon prince inside him had indeed been bonded—and one could not exist without the other.

"Chaol is alive," the king murmured through his emaciated hands, lowering them to reveal red-rimmed eyes, already milky with age. "Broken, but I didn't make the kill. There was—a light around him. I left him alive."

A sob ripped from her throat. She had hoped, had tried to give him a shot at survival—

"You are a liar," Dorian said again, his voice cold. So cold. "And you deserve this." Light sparked at Dorian's fingertips.

Aelin mouthed his name, trying to reel herself back in, gather her wits. The demon inside the king had hunted her not because of the threat Terrasen posed—but for the fire in her veins. The fire that could end them both.

She lifted a hand as Dorian stepped toward his father. They had to ask more, learn more—

The Crown Prince tipped his head back to the sky and roared, and it was the battle cry of a god.

Then the glass castle shattered.

CHAPTER
79

The bridge exploded from beneath her, and the world turned into shards of flying glass.

Aelin plummeted into open air, towers crashing down around her.

She flung out her magic in a cocoon, burning through the glass as she fell and fell and fell.

People were screaming—screaming as Dorian brought the castle down for Chaol, for Sorscha, and sent a tidal wave of glass rushing toward the city lying below.

Down and down Aelin went, the ground surging up, the buildings around her rupturing, the light so bright on all the fragments—

Aelin pulled out every last drop of her magic as the castle collapsed, the lethal wave of glass cascading toward Rifthold.

Wildfire raced for the gates, raced against the wind, against death.

And as the wave of glass crested the iron gates, shredding through the corpses tied there as if they were paper, a wall of fire erupted before it, shooting sky-high, spreading wide. Halting it.

A wind shoved against her, brutal and unforgiving, her bones groaning as it pushed her up, not down. She didn't care—not when she yielded the entirety of her magic, the entirety of her being, to holding the barrier of flame now shielding Rifthold. A few more seconds, then she could die.

The wind tore at her, and it sounded like it was roaring her name.

Wave after wave of glass and debris slammed into her wildfire.

But she kept that wall of flame burning—for the Royal Theater. And the flower girls at the market. For the slaves and the courtesans and the Faliq family. For the city that had offered her joy and pain, death and rebirth, for the city that had given her music, Aelin kept that wall of fire burning bright.

There was blood raining down among the glass—blood that sizzled on her little cocoon of flame, reeking of darkness and pain.

The wind kept blowing until it swept that dark blood away.

Still Aelin held the shield around the city, held on to the final promise she'd made to Chaol.

I'll make it count.

She held on until the ground rose up to meet her—

And she landed softly in the grass.

Then darkness slammed into the back of her head.

The world was so bright.

Aelin Galathynius groaned as she pushed herself onto her elbows, the small hill of grass beneath her untouched and vibrant. Only a moment—she'd been out for only a moment.

She raised her head, her skull throbbing as she shoved her unbound hair from her eyes and looked at what she had done.

What Dorian had done.

The glass castle was gone.

Only the stone castle remained, its gray stones warming under the midday sun.

And where a cascade of glass and debris should have destroyed a city, a massive, opaque wall glittered.

A wall of glass, its upper lip curved as if it indeed had been a cresting wave.

The glass castle was gone. The king was dead. And Dorian—

Aelin scrambled up, her arms buckling under her. There, not three feet away, was Dorian, sprawled on the grass, eyes closed.

But his chest was rising and falling.

Beside him, as if some benevolent god had indeed been looking after them, lay Chaol.

His face was bloody, but he breathed. No other wounds that she could detect.

She began shaking. She wondered if he had noticed when she'd slipped the real Eye of Elena into his pocket as she'd fled the throne room.

The scent of pine and snow hit her, and she realized how they had survived the fall.

Aelin got to her feet, swaying.

The sloping hill down to the city had been demolished, its trees and lampposts and greenery shredded by the glass.

She didn't want to know about the people who had been on the grounds—or in the castle.

She forced herself to walk.

Toward the wall. Toward the panicked city beyond. Toward the new world that beckoned.

Two scents converged, then a third. A strange, wild scent that belonged to everything and nothing.

But Aelin did not look at Aedion, or Rowan, or Lysandra as she descended the hill to the city.

Every step was an effort, every breath a trial to pull herself back from the brink, to hold on to the here and now, and what had to be done.

Aelin approached the towering glass wall that now separated the castle from the city, that separated death from life.

She punched a battering ram of blue flame through it.

More yelling arose as the flame ate away at the glass, forming an archway.

The people beyond, crying and holding one another or gripping their heads or covering their mouths, went quiet as she strode through the door she'd made.

The gallows still stood just beyond the wall. It was the only raised surface that she could see.

Better than nothing.

Aelin ascended the butchering block, her court falling into rank behind her. Rowan was limping, but she didn't allow herself to examine him, to even ask if he was all right. Not yet.

Aelin kept her shoulders back, her face grave and unyielding as she stopped at the edge of the platform.

"Your king is dead," she said. The crowd stirred. "Your prince lives."

"All hail Dorian Havilliard," someone shouted down the street. No one else echoed it.

"My name is Aelin Ashryver Galathynius," she said. "And I am the Queen of Terrasen."

The crowd murmured; some onlookers stepped away from the platform.

"Your prince is in mourning. Until he is ready, this city is mine."

Absolute silence.

"If you loot, if you riot, if you cause one lick of trouble," she said, looking a few in the eye, "I will find you, and I will burn you to ash." She lifted a hand, and flames danced at her fingertips. "If you revolt against your new king, if you try to take his castle, then this wall"—she gestured with her burning hand—"will turn to molten glass and flood your streets, your homes, your throats."

Aelin lifted her chin, her mouth cutting a hard, unforgiving line as she surveyed the crowd filling the streets, people craning to see her, see the Fae ears and elongated canines, see the flames flickering around her fingers.

"I killed your king. His empire is over. Your slaves are now free people. If I catch you holding on to your slaves, if I hear of any household keeping them captive, you are dead. If I hear of you whipping a slave, or trying to sell one, you are dead. So I suggest that you tell your friends, and families, and neighbors. I suggest that you act like reasonable, intelligent people. And I suggest that you stay on your best behavior until your king is ready to greet you, at which time I swear on my crown that I will yield control of this city to him. If anyone has a problem with it, you can take it up with my court." She motioned behind her. Rowan, Aedion, and Lysandra—bloodied, battered, filthy—grinned like hellions. "Or," Aelin said, the flames winking out on her hand, "you can take it up with me."

Not a word. She wondered whether they were breathing.

But Aelin didn't care as she strode off the platform, back through the gate she'd made, and all the way up the barren hillside to the stone castle.

She was barely inside the oak doors before she collapsed to her knees and wept.

CHAPTER
80

Elide had been in the dungeon so long that she'd lost track of time.

But she'd felt that ripple in the world, could have sworn she heard the wind singing her name, heard panicked shouts—and then nothing.

No one explained what it was, and no one came. No one was coming for her.

She wondered how long Vernon would wait before he gave her to one of those things. She tried counting meals to track time, but the food they gave her was the same for breakfast and dinner, and her meal times changed around . . . As if they wanted her to lose track. As if they wanted her to fold herself into the darkness of the dungeon so that when they came for her, she'd be willing, desperate just to see the sun again.

The door to her cell clicked open, and she staggered to her feet as Vernon slipped inside. He left the door ajar behind him, and she blinked at the torchlight as it stung her eyes. The stone hallway beyond was empty. He probably hadn't brought guards with him. He knew how futile running would be for her.

"I'm glad to see they've been feeding you. A shame about the smell, though."

She refused to be embarrassed by it. Smell was the least of her concerns.

Elide pressed herself against the slick, freezing stone wall. Maybe if she got lucky, she'd find a way to get the chain around his throat.

"I'll send someone to clean you up tomorrow." Vernon began to turn, as if his inspection were done.

"For what?" she managed to ask. Her voice was already hoarse with disuse.

He looked over his thin shoulder. "Now that magic has returned . . ."

Magic. That was what the ripple had been.

"I want to learn what lies dormant in your bloodline—*our* bloodline. The duke is even more curious what will come of it."

"Please," she said. "I'll disappear. I'll never bother you. Perranth is yours—it's all yours. You've won. Just let me go."

Vernon clicked his tongue. "I do like it when you beg." He glanced into the hall beyond and snapped his fingers. "Cormac."

A young man stepped into view.

He was a man of unearthly beauty, with a flawless face beneath his red hair, but his green eyes were cold and distant. Horrific.

There was a black collar around his throat.

Darkness leaked from him in tendrils. And as his eyes met with hers . . .

Memories tugged at her, horrible memories, of a leg that had slowly broken, of years of terror, of—

"Leash it," Vernon snapped. "Or she'll be no fun for you tomorrow."

The red-haired young man sucked the darkness back into himself, and the memories stopped.

Elide vomited her last meal onto the stones.

Vernon chuckled. "Don't be so dramatic, Elide. A little incision, a few stitches, and you'll be perfect."

The demon prince smiled at her.

"You'll be given into his care afterward, to make sure that everything takes as it should. But with magic so strong in your bloodline, how could it not? Perhaps you'll outshine those Yellowlegs. After the first time," Vernon mused, "maybe His Highness will even perform his own experiments with you. The acquaintance that sold him out mentioned in his letter that Cormac enjoyed . . . playing with young women, when he lived in Rifthold."

Oh, gods. Oh, gods. "Why?" she begged. "*Why?*"

Vernon shrugged. "Because I can."

He walked out of the cell, taking the demon prince—her betrothed—with him.

As soon as the door clicked shut, Elide bolted for it, yanking on the handle, tugging until the metal bit into her hands and rubbed them raw, begging Vernon, begging *anyone*, to hear her, remember her.

But there was no one.

Manon was more than ready to fall into bed at last. After all that had happened . . . She hoped that the young queen was lingering around Rifthold, and had understood the message.

The halls of the Keep were in an uproar, bustling with messengers who avoided looking at her. Whatever it was, she didn't care. She wanted to bathe, and then sleep. For days.

When she awoke, she'd tell Elide what she'd learned about her queen. The final piece of the life debt she owed.

Manon shouldered into her room. Elide's pallet of hay was tidy, the room spotless. The girl was probably skulking about somewhere, spying on whoever seemed most useful to her.

Manon was halfway to the bathing room when she noticed the smell. Or lack of it.

Elide's scent was worn—stale. As if she hadn't been here for days.

Manon looked toward the fire. No embers. She reached a hand over it. Not a hint of warmth.

Manon scanned the room.

No signs of a struggle. But . . .

Manon was out the door the next moment, headed back downstairs.

She made it three steps before her prowl turned into a full-on sprint. She took the stairs two and three at a time and leaped the last ten feet onto the landing, the impact shuddering through her legs, now strong, so wickedly strong, with magic returned.

If there had been a time for Vernon to get back at her for taking Elide from him, it would have been while she was away. And if magic ran in Elide's family along with the Ironteeth blood in her veins . . . Its return might have awakened something.

They want kings, Kaltain had said that day.

Hall after hall, stairwell after stairwell, Manon ran, her iron nails sparking as she gripped corners to swing herself around. Servants and guards darted out of her way.

She reached the kitchens moments later, iron teeth out. Everyone went dead silent as she leaped down the stairs, heading right for the head cook. "*Where is she?*"

The man's ruddy face went pale. "W-who?"

"The girl—Elide. Where is she?"

The cook's spoon clattered to the floor. "I don't know; I haven't seen her in days, Wing Leader. She sometimes volunteers at the laundry, so maybe—"

Manon was already sprinting out.

The head laundress, a haughty bull, snorted and said she hadn't seen Elide, and perhaps the cripple had gotten what was coming to her. Manon left her screaming on the floor, four lines gouged across her face.

Manon hurtled up the stairs and across an open stone bridge between two towers, the black rock smooth against her boots.

She had just reached the other side when a woman shouted from the opposite end of the bridge, "Wing Leader!"

Manon slammed to a stop so hard she almost collided with the tower wall. When she whirled, a human woman in a homespun gown was running for her, reeking of whatever soaps and detergents they used in the laundry.

The woman gulped down great breaths of air, her dark skin flushed. She had to brace her hands on her knees to catch her breath, but then she lifted her head and said, "One of the laundresses sees a guard who works in the Keep dungeons. She said that Elide's locked up down there. No one's allowed in but her uncle. Don't know what they're planning to do, but it can't be good."

"What dungeons?" There were three different ones here—along with the catacombs in which they kept the Yellowlegs coven.

"She didn't know. He'll only tell her so much. Some of us girls were trying to—to see if there was anything to be done, but—"

"Tell no one that you spoke to me." Manon turned. Three dungeons, three possibilities.

"Wing Leader," the young woman said. Manon looked over her shoulder. The woman put a hand on her heart. "Thank you."

Manon didn't let herself think about the laundress's gratitude, or what it meant for those weak, helpless humans to have even considered trying to rescue Elide on their own.

She did not think that woman's blood would be watery or taste of fear.

Manon launched into a sprint—not to the dungeon, but to the witches' barracks.

To the Thirteen.

CHAPTER 81

Elide's uncle sent two stone-faced female servants down to scrub her, both bearing buckets of water. She tried to fight when they stripped her, but the women were walls of iron. Any sort of Blackbeak blood in Elide's veins, she realized, had to be the diluted kind. When she was naked before them, they dumped the water on her and attacked her with their brushes and soaps, not even hesitating as they washed her *everywhere*, even when she shrieked at them to stop.

A sacrificial offering; a lamb to the slaughter.

Shaking, weak from the effort of fighting them, Elide had hardly any strength to retaliate as they dragged combs through her hair, yanking hard enough that her eyes watered. They left it unbound, and dressed her in a plain green robe. With nothing beneath.

Elide begged them, over and over. They might as well have been deaf.

When they left, she tried to squeeze out the cell door after them. The guards shoved her back in with a laugh.

Elide backed up until she was pressed against the wall of her cell.

Every minute was closer to her last.

A stand. She'd make a stand. She was a Blackbeak, and her mother had secretly been one, and they would both go down swinging. Force them to gut her, to kill her before they could touch her, before they could implant that stone inside her, before she could birth those monsters—

The door clicked open. Four guards appeared.

"The prince is waiting in the catacombs."

Elide dropped to her knees, shackles clanking. "Please. Please—"

"*Now.*"

Two of them shoved into the cell, and she couldn't fight back against the hands that grabbed under her arms and dragged her toward that door. Her bare feet tore on the stones as she kicked and thrashed, despite the chain, trying to claw free.

Closer and closer, they hauled her like a bucking horse toward the open cell door.

The two waiting guards sniggered, eyes on the flap of the robe that fell open as she kicked, revealing her thighs, her stomach, everything to them. Elide sobbed, even as she knew the tears would do her no good. They just laughed, devouring her with their eyes—

Until a hand with glittering iron nails shoved *through* the throat of one of them, puncturing it wholly. The guards froze, the one at the door whirling at the spray of blood—

He screamed as his eyes were slashed into ribbons by one hand, his throat shredded by another.

Both guards collapsed to the ground, revealing Manon Blackbeak standing behind them.

Blood ran down her hands, her forearms.

And Manon's golden eyes glowed as if they were living embers as she looked at the two guards gripping Elide. As she beheld the disheveled robe.

They released Elide to grab their weapons, and she sagged to the floor.

Manon just said, "You're already dead men."

And then she moved.

Elide didn't know if it was magic, but she'd never seen anyone in her life move like that, as if she were a phantom wind.

Manon snapped the neck of the first guard with a brutal crunch. As the second lunged for her, Elide scrambling out of the way, Manon only laughed—laughed and twirled away, moving behind him to plunge her hand into his back, into his body.

His shriek blasted through the cell. Flesh tore, revealing a white column of bone—his spine—which she gripped, her nails shredding deep, and broke in two.

Elide trembled—at the man who fell to the ground, bleeding and broken, and at the witch standing over him, bloodied and panting. The witch who had come for her.

"We need to run," Manon said.

Manon knew rescuing Elide would be a statement—and knew there were others who would want to make it with her.

But chaos had broken out in the Keep as she had raced to summon her Thirteen. News had come.

The King of Adarlan was dead. Destroyed by Aelin Galathynius.

She had shattered his glass castle, used her fire to spare the city from a deadly wave of glass, and declared Dorian Havilliard King of Adarlan.

The Witch Killer had done it.

People were in a panic; even the witches were looking to her for answers. What would they do now that the mortal king was dead? Where would they go? Were they free of their bargain?

Later—Manon would think of those things later. Now she had to act.

So she had found her Thirteen and ordered them to get the wyverns saddled and ready.

Three dungeons.

Hurry, Blackbeak, whispered a strange, soft female voice in her head that was at once old and young and wise. *You race against doom.*

Manon had hit the nearest dungeon, Asterin, Sorrel, and Vesta at her back, the green-eyed demon twins behind them. Men began dying—fast and bloody.

No use arguing—not when the men took one look at them and drew their weapons.

The dungeon held rebels of all kingdoms, who pleaded for death when they saw them, in such states of unspeakable torment that even Manon's stomach turned. But no sign of Elide.

They had swept the dungeon, Faline and Fallon lingering to make sure they hadn't missed anything.

The second dungeon held more of the same. Vesta stayed this time to sweep it again.

Faster, Blackbeak, that wise female voice begged her, as if there were only so much she might interfere. *Faster*—

Manon ran like hell.

The third dungeon was above the catacombs, and so heavily guarded that black blood became a mist around them as they launched themselves into tier after tier of soldiers.

Not one more. Not one more female would she allow them to take.

Sorrel and Asterin plunged into the soldiers, plowing a path for her. Asterin ripped out the throat of one man with her teeth while she gutted another with her nails. Black blood sprayed from Asterin's mouth as she pointed to the stairs ahead and roared, *"Go!"*

So Manon had left her Second and Third behind, leaping down the stairs, around and around. There had to be a secret entrance from these dungeons into the catacombs, some quiet way to transport Elide—

Faster, Blackbeak! that sage voice barked.

And as a little wind pushed at Manon's feet as if it could hurry her along, she knew that it was a goddess peering over her shoulder, a lady of wise things. Who perhaps had watched over Elide her entire life, muted without magic, but now that it was free . . .

Manon hit the lowest level of the dungeon, a mere floor above the catacombs. Sure enough, at the end of the hall, a door opened onto a descending staircase.

Between her and that staircase were two guards sniggering at an open cell door as a young woman begged for their mercy.

It was the sound of Elide's weeping—that girl of quiet steel and quick-silver wit who had not wept for herself or her sorry life, only faced it with grim determination—that made Manon snap entirely.

She killed those guards in the hall.

She saw what they had been laughing at: the girl gripped between two other guards, her robe tugged open to reveal her nakedness, the full extent of that ruined leg—

Her grandmother had sold them to these people.

She was a Blackbeak; she was no one's slave. No one's prize horse to breed.

Neither was Elide.

Her wrath was a song in her blood, and Manon had merely said, "You're already dead men," before she unleashed herself on them.

When she'd chucked the last guard's body onto the ground, when she was covered in black and blue blood, Manon looked at the girl on the floor.

Elide tugged her green robe shut, shaking so badly Manon thought she'd puke. She could smell vomit already in the cell. They had kept her here, in this rotting place.

"We need to run," Manon said.

Elide tried to rise, but couldn't so much as get to her knees.

Manon stalked to her, helping the girl to her feet, leaving a smear of blood on her forearm. Elide swayed, but Manon was looking at the old chain around her ankles.

With a swipe of her iron nails, she snapped through it.

She'd unlock the shackles later. "Now," Manon said, tugging Elide into the hall.

There were more soldiers shouting from the way she'd come, and

Asterin and Sorrel's battle cries rang out down the stairs. But behind them, from the catacombs below . . .

More men—Valg—curious about the clamor leaking in from above.

Bringing Elide into the melee might very well kill her, but if the soldiers from the catacombs attacked from behind . . . Worse, if they brought one of their princes . . .

Regret. It had been regret she'd felt that night she'd killed the Crochan. Regret and guilt and shame, for acting on blind obedience, for being a coward when the Crochan had held her head high and spoken truth.

They have made you into monsters. Made, Manon. And we feel sorry for you.

It was regret that she'd felt when she heard Asterin's tale. For not being worthy of trust.

And for what she had allowed to happen to those Yellowlegs.

She did not want to imagine what she might feel should she bring Elide to her death. Or worse.

Brutality. Discipline. Obedience.

It did not seem like a weakness to fight for those who could not defend themselves. Even if they weren't true witches. Even if they meant nothing to her.

"We're going to have to battle our way out," Manon said to Elide.

But the girl was wide-eyed, gaping at the cell doorway.

Standing there, her dress flowing around her like liquid night, was Kaltain.

CHAPTER 82

Elide stared at the dark-haired young woman.

And Kaltain stared back.

Manon let out a warning snarl. "Unless you want to die, get the rutting hell out of the way."

Kaltain, her hair unbound, her face pale and gaunt, said, "They are coming now. To find out why she has not yet arrived."

Manon's bloodied hand was sticky and damp as it clamped around Elide's arm and tugged her toward the door. The single step, the freedom of movement without that chain . . . Elide almost sobbed.

Until she heard the fighting ahead. Behind them, from the dark stairwell at the other end of the hall, the rushing feet of more men approached from far below.

Kaltain stepped aside as Manon pushed past.

"Wait," Kaltain said. "They will turn this Keep upside down looking for you. Even if you get airborne, they will send out riders after you and use your own people against you, Blackbeak."

Manon dropped Elide's arm. Elide hardly dared to breathe as the witch said, "How long has it been since you destroyed the demon inside that collar, Kaltain?"

A low, broken laugh. "A while."

"Does the duke know?"

"My dark liege sees what he wants to see." She shifted her eyes to Elide. Exhaustion, emptiness, sorrow, and rage danced there together. "Remove your robe and give it to me."

Elide backed up a step. "What?"

Manon looked between them. "You can't trick them."

"They see what they want to see," Kaltain said again.

The men closing in on either side grew nearer with every uneven heartbeat. "This is insane," Elide breathed. "It'll never work."

"Take off your robe and give it to the lady," Manon ordered. "Do it now."

No room for disobedience. So Elide listened, blushing at her own nakedness, trying to cover herself.

Kaltain merely let her black dress slip from her shoulders. It rippled on the ground.

Her body—what they had done to her body, the bruises on her, the thinness . . .

Kaltain wrapped herself in the robe, her face empty again.

Elide slid on the gown, its fabric horribly cold when it should have been warm.

Kaltain knelt before one of the dead guards—oh, gods, those were corpses lying there—and ran her hand over the hole in the guard's neck. She smeared and flicked blood over her face, her neck, her arms, the robe. She ran it through her hair, tugging it forward, hiding her face until bits of blood were all that could be seen, folding her shoulders inward, until—

Until Kaltain looked like Elide.

You could be sisters, Vernon had said. Now they could be twins.

"Please—come with us," Elide whispered.

Kaltain laughed quietly. "Dagger, Blackbeak."

Manon pulled out a dagger.

Kaltain sliced it deep into the hideous scarred lump in her arm. "In your pocket, girl," Kaltain said to her. Elide reached into the dress and pulled out a scrap of dark fabric, frayed and ripped at the edges, as if it had been torn from something.

Elide held it toward the lady as Kaltain reached into her arm, no expression of pain on that beautiful, bloodied face, and pulled out a glimmering sliver of dark stone.

Kaltain's red blood dripped off it. Carefully, the lady set it onto the scrap of fabric Elide held out, and folded Elide's fingers around it.

A dull, strange thudding pounded through Elide as she grasped the shard.

"What is that?" Manon asked, sniffing subtly.

Kaltain just squeezed Elide's fingers. "You find Celaena Sardothien. Give her this. No one else. *No one else.* Tell her that you can open any door, if you have the key. And tell her to remember her promise to me—to punish them all. When she asks why, tell her I said that they would not let me bring the cloak she gave me, but I kept a piece of it. To remember that promise she made. To remember to repay her for a warm cloak in a cold dungeon."

Kaltain stepped away.

"We can take you with us," Elide tried again.

A small, hateful smile. "I have no interest in living. Not after what they did. I don't think my body could survive without their power." Kaltain huffed a laugh. "I shall enjoy this, I think."

Manon tugged Elide to her side. "They'll notice you without the chains—"

"They'll be dead before they do," Kaltain said. "I suggest you run."

Manon didn't ask questions, and Elide didn't have time to say thank you before the witch grabbed her and they ran.

She was a wolf.

She was death, devourer of worlds.

The guards found her curled up in the cell, shuddering at the carnage. They didn't ask questions, didn't look twice at her face before they hauled her down the hall and into the catacombs.

Such screaming here. Such terror and despair. But the horrors under the other mountains were worse. So much worse. Too bad she would not have the opportunity to also spare them, slaughter them.

She was a void, empty without that sliver of power that built and ate and tore apart worlds inside of her.

His precious gift, his key, he had called her. A living gate, he promised. Soon, he had said he would add the other. And then find the third.

So that the king inside him might rule again.

They led her into a chamber with a table in the center. A white sheet covered it, and men watched as they shoved her onto the table—the altar. They chained her down.

With the blood on her, they did not notice the cut on her arm, or whose face she wore.

One of the men came forward with a knife, clean and sharp and gleaming. "This won't take but a few minutes."

Kaltain smiled up at him. Smiled broadly, now that they had brought her into the bowels of this hellhole.

The man paused.

A red-haired young man walked into the room, reeking of the cruelty born in his human heart and amplified by the demon inside him. He froze as he saw her.

He opened his mouth.

Kaltain Rompier unleashed her shadowfire upon them all.

This was not the ghost of shadowfire they had made her kill with—the reason why they had first approached her, lied to her when they invited her to that glass castle—but the real thing. The fire she had harbored since magic had returned—golden flame now turned to black.

The room became cinders.

Kaltain pushed the chains off her as though they were cobwebs and arose.

She disrobed as she walked out of the room. Let them see what had been done to her, the body they'd wasted.

She made it two steps into the hall before they noticed her, and beheld the black flames rippling off her.

Death, devourer of worlds.

The hallway turned to black dust.

She strode toward the chamber where the screaming was loudest, where female cries leaked through the iron door.

The iron did not heat, did not bend to her magic. So she melted an archway through the stones.

Monsters and witches and men and demons whirled.

Kaltain flowed into the room, spreading her arms wide, and became shadowfire, became freedom and triumph, became a promise hissed in a dungeon beneath a glass castle:

Punish them all.

She burned the cradles. She burned the monsters within. She burned the men and their demon princes. And then she burned the witches, who looked at her with gratitude in their eyes and embraced the dark flame.

Kaltain unleashed the last of her shadowfire, tipping her face to the ceiling, toward a sky she'd never see again.

She took out every wall and every column. As she brought it all crashing and crumbling around them, Kaltain smiled, and at last burned herself into ash on a phantom wind.

Manon ran. But Elide was so slow—so painfully slow with that leg.

If Kaltain unleashed her shadowfire before they got out . . .

Manon grabbed Elide and hauled her over a shoulder, the beaded dress cutting into Manon's hand as she sprinted up the stairs.

Elide didn't say a word as Manon reached the dungeon landing and beheld Asterin and Sorrel finishing off the last of the soldiers. *"Run!"* she barked.

They were coated in that black blood, but they'd live.

Up and up, they hurtled out of the dungeons, even as Elide became a weight borne on pure defiance of the death surely racing toward them from levels below.

There was a shudder—

"Faster!"

Her Second made it to the giant dungeon doors and hurled herself against them, heaving them open. Manon and Sorrel dashed through; Asterin shoved them sealed with a bang. It would only delay the flame a second, if that.

Up and up, toward the aerie.

Another shudder and a boom—

Screaming, and heat—

Down the halls they flew, as if the god of wind were pushing at their heels.

They hit the base of the aerie tower. The rest of the Thirteen were gathered in the stairwell, waiting.

"Into the skies," Manon ordered as they took the stairs, one after one, Elide so heavy now that she thought she'd drop her. Only a few more feet to the top of the tower, where the wyverns were hopefully saddled and prepared. They were.

Manon hurtled for Abraxos and shoved the shuddering girl into the saddle. She climbed up behind her as the Thirteen scrambled onto their mounts. Wrapping her arms around Elide, Manon dug her heels into Abraxos's side. *"Fly now!"* she roared.

Abraxos leaped through the opening, soaring up and out, the Thirteen leaping with them, wings beating hard, beating wildly—

Morath exploded.

Black flame erupted, taking out stone and metal, racing higher and higher. People shouted and then were silenced, as even rock melted.

The air hollowed out and ruptured in Manon's ears, and she curled her body around Elide's, twisting them so the heat of the blast singed her own back.

The aerie tower was incinerated, and crumbled away behind them.

The blast sent them tumbling, but Manon gripped the girl tight, clenching the saddle with her thighs as hot, dry wind blasted past them. Abraxos screeched, shifting and soaring into the gust.

When Manon dared to look, a third of Morath was a smoldering ruin.

Where those catacombs had once been—where those Yellowlegs had been tortured and broken, where they had bred monsters—there was nothing left.

CHAPTER
83

Aelin slept for three days.

Three days, while Rowan sat by her bed, healing his leg as best he could while the abyss of his power refilled.

Aedion assumed control of the castle, imprisoning any surviving guards. Most, Rowan had been viciously pleased to learn, had been killed in the storm of glass the prince had called down. Chaol had survived, by some miracle—probably the Eye of Elena, which they'd found tucked into his pocket. It was an easy guess who had put it there. Though Rowan honestly wondered if, when the captain woke up, he might wish he hadn't made it after all. He'd encountered enough soldiers who felt that way.

After Aelin had so spectacularly leashed the people of Rifthold, they found Lorcan waiting by the doors to the stone castle. The queen hadn't even noticed him as she sank to her knees and cried and cried, until Rowan scooped her into his arms and, limping slightly, carried her through the frenzied halls, servants dodging them as Aedion led the way to her old rooms.

It was the only place to go. Better to establish themselves in their enemy's former stronghold than retreat to the warehouse apartment.

A servant named Philippa was asked to look after the prince, who had been unconscious the last time Rowan had seen him—when he plummeted to earth and Rowan's wind stopped his fall.

He didn't know what had happened in the castle. Through her weeping, Aelin hadn't said anything.

She had been unconscious by the time Rowan reached her lavish suite of rooms, not even stirring as he kicked open the locked door. His leg had burned in pain, the rough healing he'd done barely holding the wound together, but he didn't care. He'd barely set Aelin on the bed before Lorcan's scent hit him again, and he whirled, snarling.

But there was already someone in Lorcan's face, blocking the warrior's path into the queen's bedchamber. Lysandra.

"May I help you?" the courtesan had said sweetly. Her dress was in shreds, and blood both black and red coated most of her, but she held her head high and her back straight. She'd made it as far as the upper levels of the stone castle before the glass one above it had exploded. And showed no plans of leaving anytime soon.

Rowan had thrown a shield of hard air around Aelin's room as Lorcan stared down at Lysandra, his blood-splattered face impassive. "Out of my way, shifter."

Lysandra had held up a slender hand—and Lorcan paused. The shape-shifter pressed her other hand against her stomach, her face blanching. But then she smiled and said, "You forgot to say 'please.'"

Lorcan's dark brows flattened. "I don't have time for this." He made to step around her, shove her aside.

Lysandra vomited black blood all over him.

Rowan didn't know whether to laugh or cringe as Lysandra, panting, gaped at Lorcan, and at the blood on his neck and chest. Slowly, too slowly, Lorcan looked down at himself.

She pressed a hand over her mouth. "I am—so sorry—"

Lorcan didn't even step out of the way as Lysandra vomited on him again, black blood and bits of gore now on the warrior and on the marble floor.

Lorcan's dark eyes flickered.

Rowan decided to do them both a favor and joined them in the antechamber, shutting the queen's bedroom door behind him as he stepped around the puddle of blood, bile, and gore.

Lysandra gagged again, and wisely darted to what looked to be a bathing room off the foyer.

All of the men and demons she'd wasted, it seemed, did not sit well in her human stomach. The sounds of her purging leaked out from beneath the bathing room door.

"You deserved that," Rowan said.

Lorcan didn't so much as blink. "That's the thanks I get?"

Rowan leaned against the wall, crossing his arms and keeping the weight off his now-healing leg. "You knew we'd try to use those tunnels," Rowan said, "and yet you lied about the Wyrdhounds being dead. I should rip out your gods-damned throat."

"Go ahead. Try."

Rowan remained against the door, calculating every move of his former commander. A fight right here, right now would be too destructive, and too dangerous with his queen unconscious in the room behind him. "I wouldn't have given a shit about it if it had just been me. But when you let me walk into that trap, you endangered my queen's life—"

"Looks like she did just fine—"

"—and the life of a brother in my court."

Lorcan's mouth tightened—barely.

"That's why you came to help, isn't it?" Rowan said. "You saw Aedion when we left the apartment."

"I did not know Gavriel's son would be in that tunnel with you. Until it was too late."

Of course, Lorcan would never have warned them about the trap after learning Aedion would be there. Not in a thousand years would Lorcan ever admit to a mistake.

"I wasn't aware that you even cared."

"Gavriel is still my brother," Lorcan said, his eyes flashing. "I would have faced him with dishonor if I had let his son die."

Only for honor, for the blood bond between them—not for saving this continent. The same twisted bond was leading him now to destroy the keys before Maeve could acquire them. Rowan had no doubt that Lorcan meant to do it, even if Maeve killed him for it later.

"What are you doing here, Lorcan? Didn't you get what you wanted?"

A fair question—and a warning. The male was now inside his queen's suite, closer than most people in her court would ever get. Rowan began a silent countdown in his head. Thirty seconds seemed generous. Then he would throw Lorcan out on his ass.

"It's not over," the warrior said. "Not even close."

Rowan lifted his brows. "Idle threats?" But Lorcan had only shrugged and walked out, covered in Lysandra's vomit, and did not look back before disappearing down the hall.

That had been three days ago. Rowan hadn't seen or scented Lorcan since. Lysandra, mercifully, had stopped hurling her guts up—or someone else's guts, he supposed. The shape-shifter had claimed a room across the hall, between the two chambers in which the Crown Prince and Chaol still slept.

After what Aelin and the Crown Prince had done, the magic they'd wielded together and alone, three days of sleep was hardly surprising.

Yet it drove Rowan out of his mind.

There were so many things he needed to say to her—though perhaps he would just ask how the hell she'd gotten stabbed in the side. She'd healed herself, and he wouldn't have even known were it not for the rips in the ribs, back, and arms of that black assassin's suit.

When the healer had inspected the sleeping queen, she'd found that Aelin had healed herself too quickly, too desperately—and had sealed her flesh around some shards of glass in her back. Watching as the healer stripped her naked, then began carefully opening the dozens of little wounds to dig out the glass almost made him tear down the walls.

Aelin slept through it, which he supposed was a mercy, given how deep the healer had to dig to get the glass out.

She's lucky it didn't hit anything permanent, the healer had said.

Once every shard was gone, Rowan had used his strained magic to slowly—so slowly, damn him—heal the wounds again. It left the tattoo on her back in ribbons.

He'd have to fill it in when she recovered. And teach her more about battlefield healing.

If she ever woke up.

Sitting in a chair beside her bed, Rowan toed off his boots and rubbed at the faint, lingering soreness in his leg. Aedion had just finished giving a report about the current status of the castle. Three days later, the general still hadn't spoken about what had happened—that he'd been willing to lay down his life to protect Rowan from the Valg foot soldiers, or that the King of Adarlan was dead. As far as the former, Rowan had thanked him for that in the only way he knew how: offering Aedion one of his own daggers, forged by the greatest of Doranelle's blacksmiths. Aedion had initially refused, insisting he needed no thanks, but had worn the blade at his side ever since.

But in regard to the latter . . . Rowan had asked, just once, what the general felt about the king being dead. Aedion had merely said he wished the bastard had suffered longer, but dead was dead, so it was fine by him. Rowan wondered if he truly meant it, but Aedion would tell him when he was good and ready. Not all wounds could be healed with magic. Rowan knew that too well. But they did heal. Eventually.

And the wounds on this castle, on the city—those would heal, too. He'd stood on battlefields after the killing had stopped, the earth still wet with blood, and lived to see the scars slowly heal, decade after decade, on the land, the people. So, too, would Rifthold heal.

Even if Aedion's latest report on the castle was grim. Most of the staff had survived, along with a few courtiers, but it seemed that a good number of those who had remained at court—courtiers Aedion had known to be worthless, scheming devils—hadn't made it. As if the prince had wiped clean the stain from his castle.

Rowan shuddered at the thought, gazing at the doors Aedion had vacated. The Crown Prince had such tremendous power. Rowan had never seen its like. He'd need to find a way to train it—hone it—or risk it destroying him.

And Aelin—that brilliant, insane fool—had taken a tremendous risk in weaving her power with his. The prince had raw magic that could be shaped into anything. Aelin could have burnt herself out in a second.

Rowan turned his head and glared at her.

And found Aelin glaring back.

"I save the world," Aelin said, her voice like gravel, "and yet I wake up to you being pissy."

"It was a group effort," Rowan said from a chair nearby. "And I'm pissy for about twenty different reasons, most of them having to do with you making some of the most reckless decisions I've ever—"

"Dorian," she blurted. "Is Dorian—"

"Fine. Asleep. He's been out as long as you."

"Chaol—"

"Asleep. Recovering. But alive."

A weight eased from her shoulders. And then . . . she looked at the Fae Prince and understood that he was unharmed, that she was in her old room, that they weren't in chains or collars, and that the king . . . What the king had said before he died . . .

"Fireheart," Rowan murmured, starting from his chair, but she shook her head. The movement made her skull throb.

She took a steadying breath, wiping at her eyes. Gods, her arm ached, her back ached, her side ached . . . "No more tears," she said. "No more weeping." She lowered her hands to the blankets. "Tell me—everything."

So he did. About the hellfire, and the Wyrdhounds, and Lorcan. And then the past three days, of organizing and healing and Lysandra scaring the living shit out of everyone by shifting into a ghost leopard anytime one of Dorian's courtiers stepped out of line.

When he'd finished, Rowan said, "If you can't talk about it, you don't—"

"I need to talk about it." To him—if only to him. The words tumbled out, and she did not cry as she explained what the king had said, what he'd claimed. What Dorian had still done. Rowan's face remained drawn, thoughtful, throughout. At last, she said, "Three days?"

Rowan nodded gravely. "Distracting Aedion with running the castle is the only way I've kept him from chewing on the furniture."

She met those pine-green eyes, and he opened his mouth again, but she made a small noise. "Before we say anything else . . ." She glanced at the door. "I need you to help me get to the bathing room. Or else I'm going to wet myself."

Rowan burst out laughing.

She glared at him again as she sat up, the movement agonizing, exhausting. She was naked save for the clean undergarments someone had stuffed her into, but she supposed she was decent enough. He'd seen every part of her, anyway.

Rowan was still chuckling as he helped her up, letting her lean against him as her legs—useless, wobbling like a newborn fawn—tried to work. It took her so long to go three steps that she didn't object when he swept her up and carried her to the bathing room. She growled when he tried to set her on the toilet itself, and he left with his hands upraised, his eyes dancing as if to say *Can you blame me for trying? You might very well fall into it instead.*

He laughed once more at the profanities in her eyes, and when she was done, she managed to stand and walk the three steps to the door before he hefted her in his arms again. No limp, she realized—his leg, mercifully, was mostly healed.

Her arms draped around him, she pressed her face into his neck as he carried her toward the bed, and breathed in his scent. When he made to set her down, she held on to him, a silent request.

So Rowan sat on the bed, holding her in his lap as he stretched out his legs and settled into the rows of pillows. For a moment, they said nothing.

Then, "So this was your room. And that was the secret passage."

A lifetime ago, a whole other person ago. "You don't sound impressed."

"After all your stories, it just seems so . . . ordinary."

"Most people would hardly call this castle ordinary."

A huff of laughter warmed her hair. She grazed her nose against the bare skin of his neck.

"I thought you were dying," he said roughly.

She held him tighter, even if it made her back ache. "I was."

"Please don't ever do that again."

It was her turn to puff out a laugh. "Next time, I'll just ask Dorian not to stab me."

But Rowan pulled back, scanning her face. "I felt it—I felt every second of it. I went out of my mind."

She brushed a finger along his cheek. "I thought something had gone wrong for you, too—I thought you might be dead, or hurt. And it killed me not to be able to go to you."

"Next time we need to save the world, we do it together."

She smiled faintly. "Deal."

He shifted his arm so he could brush her hair back. His fingers lingered along her jaw. "You make me want to live, too, Aelin Galathynius," he said. "Not exist—but live." He cupped her cheek, and took a steadying breath—as if he'd thought about every word these past three days, over and over again. "I spent centuries wandering the world, from empires to kingdoms to wastelands, never settling, never stopping—not for one moment. I was always looking toward the horizon, always wondering what waited across the next ocean, over the next mountain. But I think . . . I think that whole time, all those centuries, I was just looking for you."

He brushed away a tear that escaped her then, and Aelin gazed at the Fae Prince who held her—at her friend, who had traveled through darkness and despair and ice and fire with her.

She didn't know which one of them moved first, but then Rowan's mouth was on hers, and Aelin gripped his shirt, pulling him closer, claiming him as he claimed her.

His arms wrapped tighter around her, but gently—so careful of the wounds that ached. He brushed his tongue against hers, and she opened her mouth to him. Each movement of their lips was a whisper of what was to come once they were both healed, and a promise.

The kiss was slow—thorough. As if they had all the time in the world.

As if they were the only ones in it.

Realizing he'd forgotten to tell Rowan about the letter he'd received from the Bane, Aedion Ashryver walked into Aelin's suite of rooms in time to see that Aelin was awake—finally awake, and lifting her face to Rowan's. They were sitting on the bed, Aelin in Rowan's lap, the Fae warrior's arms locked around her as he looked at her the way she deserved to be looked at. And when they kissed, deeply, without hesitation—

Rowan didn't so much as glance Aedion's way before a wind snapped through the suite, slamming the bedroom door in Aedion's face.

Point taken.

A strange, ever-changing female scent hit him, and Aedion found Lysandra leaning against the hallway door. Tears gleamed in her eyes even as she smiled.

She gazed at the closed bedroom door, as if she could still see the prince and queen inside. "That," she said, more to herself than to him. "That is what I am going to find one day."

"A gorgeous Fae warrior?" Aedion said, shifting a bit.

Lysandra chuckled, wiping away her tears, and gave him a knowing look before walking away.

Apparently, Dorian's golden ring was gone—and Aelin knew exactly who had been responsible for the momentary blackness when she'd hit the ground as the castle collapsed, who had bestowed the unconsciousness courtesy of a blow to the back of her head.

She didn't know why Lorcan hadn't killed her, but she didn't particularly care—not when he was long gone. She supposed he'd never promised *not* to steal the ring back.

Though he'd also never made them verify that the Amulet of Orynth wasn't a fake. Too bad she wouldn't be there to see his face when he realized it.

The thought was enough to make Aelin smile the next day, despite the door she stood before—despite who waited behind it.

Rowan lingered at the end of the hallway, guarding the only way in or out. He gave her a nod, and even from the distance, she read the words in his eyes. *I'll be right here. One shout, and I'll be at your side.*

She rolled her eyes at him. *Overbearing, territorial Fae beast.*

She'd lost track of how long they'd kissed for, how long she'd lost herself in him. But then she'd taken his hand and laid it on her breast, and he'd growled in a way that made her toes curl and her back arch . . . and then wince at the remnant of pain flickering in her body.

He had pulled back at that wince, and when she'd tried to convince him to keep going, he'd told her that he had no interest in bedding an invalid, and since they'd already waited this long, she could cool her heels and wait some more. Until she was able to keep up with him, he'd added with a wicked grin.

Aelin shoved away the thought with another glare in Rowan's direction, loosed a steadying breath, and pushed down on the handle.

He was standing by the window overlooking the wrecked gardens where servants were struggling to repair the catastrophic damage he'd caused.

"Hello, Dorian," she said.

CHAPTER 84

Dorian Havilliard had awoken alone, in a room he didn't recognize.

But he was free, even though a pale band of skin now marred his neck.

For a moment, he had lain in bed, listening.

No screaming. No wailing. Just a few birds tentatively chirping outside the window, summer sunshine leaking in, and . . . silence. Peace.

There was such an emptiness in his head. A hollowness in him.

He'd even put a hand over his heart to see if it was beating.

The rest was a blur—and he lost himself in it, rather than think about that emptiness. He bathed, he dressed, and he spoke to Aedion Ashryver, who looked at him as if he had three heads and who was apparently now in charge of castle security.

Chaol was alive but still recovering, the general said. Not yet awake—and maybe that was a good thing, because Dorian had no idea how he'd face his friend, how he'd explain everything. Even when most of it was mere shards of memory, pieces he knew would further break him if he ever put them together.

A few hours later, Dorian was still in that bedroom, working up the nerve to survey what he'd done. The castle he'd destroyed; the people he'd killed. He'd seen the wall: proof of his enemy's power . . . and mercy.

Not his enemy.

Aelin.

"Hello, Dorian," she said. He turned from the window as the door shut behind her.

She lingered by the door, in a tunic of deep blue and gold, unbuttoned with careless grace at the neck, her hair loose at her shoulders, her brown boots scuffed. But the way she held herself, the way she stood with utter stillness . . . A queen looked out at him.

He didn't know what to say. Where to begin.

She prowled for the little sitting area where he stood. "How are you feeling?"

Even the way she talked was slightly different. He'd already heard what she'd said to his people, the threats she'd made and the order she'd demanded.

"Fine," he managed to say. His magic rumbled deep inside him, but it was barely more than a whisper, as if it was drained. As if it was as empty as him.

"You wouldn't be hiding in here, would you?" she said, slumping into one of the low chairs on the pretty, ornate rug.

"Your men put me in here so they could keep an eye on me," he said, remaining by the window. "I wasn't aware that I was allowed to leave." Perhaps that was a good thing—considering what the demon prince had made him do.

"You can leave whenever you please. This is your castle—your kingdom."

"Is it?" he dared ask.

"You're the King of Adarlan now," she said softly, but not gently. "Of course it is."

His father was dead. Not even a body was left to reveal what they'd done that day.

Aelin had publicly declared she'd killed him, but Dorian knew he'd ended his father when he shattered the castle. He had done it for Chaol, and for Sorscha, and he knew she'd claimed the kill because to tell his people . . . to tell his people that he'd killed his father—

"I still have to be crowned," he said at last. His father had stated such wild things in those last few moments; things that changed everything and nothing.

She crossed her legs, leaning back in her seat, but there was nothing casual in her face. "You say that like you hope it doesn't happen."

Dorian stifled the urge to touch his neck and confirm that the collar was still gone and clenched his hands behind his back. "Do I deserve to be king after all I did? After all that happened?"

"Only you can answer that question."

"Do you believe what he said?"

Aelin sucked on her teeth. "I don't know what to believe."

"Perrington's going to war with me—with us. My being king won't stop that army."

"We'll figure it out." She loosed a breath. "But your being king is the first step of it."

Beyond the window, the day was bright, clear. The world had ended and begun anew, and yet nothing at all had changed, either. The sun would still rise and fall, the seasons would still change, heedless of whether he was free or enslaved, prince or king, heedless of who was alive and who was gone. The world would keep moving on. It didn't seem right, somehow.

"She died," he said, his breathing ragged, the room crushing him. "Because of me."

Aelin got to her feet in a smooth movement and walked to where he stood by the window, only to tug him down onto the sofa beside her. "It is going to take a while. And it might never be right again. But you . . ." She gripped his hand, as if he hadn't used those hands to hurt and maim, to stab her. "You will learn to face it, and to endure it. What happened, Dorian, was not your fault."

"It was. I tried to *kill* you. And what happened to Chaol—"

"Chaol chose. He chose to buy you time—because your father was to blame. Your father, and the Valg prince inside him, did that to you, and to Sorscha."

He almost vomited at the name. It would dishonor her to never say it again, to never speak of her again, but he didn't know if he could let out those two syllables without a part of him dying over and over again.

"You're not going to believe me," Aelin went on. "What I've just said, you're not going to believe me. I know it—and that's fine. I don't expect you to. When you're ready, I'll be here."

"You're the Queen of Terrasen. You can't be."

"Says who? We are the masters of our own fates—*we* decide how to go forward." She squeezed his hand. "You're my friend, Dorian."

A flicker of memory, from the haze of darkness and pain and fear. *I came back for you.*

"You both came back," he said.

Her throat bobbed. "You pulled me out of Endovier. I figured I could return the favor."

Dorian looked at the carpet, at all the threads woven together. "What do I do now?" They were gone: the woman he'd loved—and the man he'd hated. He met her stare. No calculation, no coldness, no pity in those turquoise eyes. Just unflinching honesty, as there had been from the very start with her. "What do I do?"

She had to swallow before she said, "You light up the darkness."

Chaol Westfall opened his eyes.

The Afterworld looked an awful lot like a bedroom in the stone castle.

There was no pain in his body, at least. Not like the pain that had slammed into him, followed by warring blackness and blue light. And then nothing at all.

He might have yielded to the exhaustion that threatened to drag him back into unconsciousness, but someone—a man—let out a rasping breath, and Chaol turned his head.

There were no sounds, no words in him as he found Dorian seated in a chair beside the bed. Bruised shadows were smudged beneath his eyes; his hair was unkempt, as if he'd been running his hands through it, but— but beyond his unbuttoned jacket, there was no collar. Only a pale line marring his golden skin.

And his eyes . . . Haunted, but clear. Alive.

Chaol's vision burned and blurred.

She had done it. Aelin had done it.

Chaol's face crumpled.

"I didn't realize I looked that bad," Dorian said, his voice raw.

He knew then—that the demon inside the prince was gone.

Chaol wept.

Dorian surged from the chair and dropped to his knees beside the bed. He grabbed Chaol's hand, squeezing it as he pressed his brow against his. "You were dead," the prince said, his voice breaking. "I thought you were dead."

Chaol at last mastered himself, and Dorian pulled back far enough to scan his face. "I think I was," he said. "What—what happened?"

So Dorian told him.

Aelin had saved his city.

And saved his life, too, when she'd slipped the Eye of Elena into his pocket.

Dorian's hand gripped Chaol's a bit tighter. "How do you feel?"

"Tired," Chaol admitted, flexing his free hand. His chest ached from where the blast had hit him, but the rest of him felt—

He didn't feel anything.

He couldn't feel his legs. His toes.

"The healers that survived," Dorian said very quietly, "said you shouldn't even be alive. Your spine—I think my father broke it in a few places. They said Amithy might have been able to . . ." A flicker of rage. "But she died."

Panic, slow and icy, crept in. He couldn't move, couldn't—

"Rowan healed two of the injuries higher up. You would have been . . . paralyzed"—Dorian choked on the word—"from the neck down otherwise. But the lower fracture . . . Rowan said it was too complex, and he didn't dare trying to heal it, not when he could make it worse."

"Tell me there's a 'but' coming," Chaol managed to say.

If he couldn't walk—if he couldn't *move*—

"We won't risk sending you to Wendlyn, not with Maeve there. But the healers at the Torre Cesme could do it."

"I'm not going to the Southern Continent." Not now that he'd gotten Dorian back, not now that they'd all somehow survived. "I'll wait for a healer here."

"There are no healers left here. Not magically gifted ones. My father and Perrington wiped them out." Cold flickered in those sapphire eyes. Chaol knew that what his father had claimed, what Dorian had still done to him despite it, would haunt the prince for a while.

Not the prince—the king.

"The Torre Cesme might be your only hope of walking again," Dorian said.

"I'm not leaving you. Not again."

Dorian's mouth tightened. "You never left me, Chaol." He shook his head once, sending tears slipping down his face. "You never left me."

Chaol squeezed his friend's hand.

Dorian glanced toward the door a moment before a hesitant knock sounded, and smiled faintly. Chaol wondered just what Dorian's magic allowed him to detect, but then the king wiped away his tears and said, "Someone's here to see you."

The handle quietly lowered and the door cracked open, revealing a curtain of inky black hair and a tan, pretty face. Nesryn beheld Dorian and bowed deeply, her hair swaying with her.

Dorian rose to his feet, waving a hand in dismissal. "Aedion might be the new head of castle security, but Miss Faliq is my temporary Captain of the Guard. Turns out, the guards find Aedion's style of leadership to be . . . What's the word, Nesryn?"

Nesryn's mouth twitched, but her eyes were on Chaol, as if he were a miracle, as if he were an illusion. "Polarizing," Nesryn murmured, striding right for him, her gold-and-crimson uniform fitting her like a glove.

"There's never been a woman in the king's guard before," Dorian said, heading for the door. "And since you're now Lord Chaol Westfall, the King's Hand, I needed someone to fill the position. New traditions for a new reign."

Chaol broke Nesryn's wide-eyed stare to gape at his friend. "What?"

But Dorian was at the door, opening it. "If I have to be stuck with king duty, then you're going to be stuck right there with me. So go to the Torre Cesme and heal fast, Chaol. Because we've got work to do." The king's gaze flicked to Nesryn. "Fortunately, you already have a knowledgeable guide." Then he was gone.

Chaol stared up at Nesryn, who was holding a hand over her mouth.

"Turns out I wound up breaking my promise to you after all," he said. "Since I technically *can't* walk out of this castle."

She burst into tears.

"Remind me to never make a joke again," he said, even as the crushing, squeezing panic set in. His legs—no. No . . . They wouldn't be sending him to the Torre Cesme unless they knew there was a possibility he would walk again. He would accept no other alternative.

Nesryn's thin shoulders shook as she wept.

"Nesryn," he croaked. "Nesryn—please."

She slid onto the floor beside his bed and buried her face in her hands. "When the castle shattered," she said, her voice cracking, "I thought you were dead. And when I saw the glass coming for me, I thought *I'd* be dead. But then the fire came, and I prayed . . . I prayed she'd somehow saved you, too."

Rowan had been the one who'd done that, but Chaol wasn't about to correct her.

She lowered her hands, at last looking at his body beneath the blankets. "We will fix this. We will go to the Southern Continent, and I will *make* them heal you. I've seen the wonders they can do, and I know they can do it. And—"

He reached for her hand. "Nesryn."

"And now you're a lord," she went on, shaking her head. "You were a lord before, I mean, but—you are the king's second in command. I know it's—I know we—"

"We'll figure it out," Chaol said.

She met his stare at last. "I don't expect anything of you—"

"We'll figure it out. You might not even want a crippled man."

She pulled back. "Do not insult me by assuming I'm that shallow or fickle."

He choked on a laugh. "Let's have an adventure, Nesryn Faliq."

CHAPTER
85

Elide couldn't stop crying as the witches flew northward.

She didn't care that she was *flying*, or that death loomed on every side.

What Kaltain had done . . . She didn't dare open her clenched fist for fear the fabric and the little stone would be ripped away in the wind.

At sunset, they landed somewhere in Oakwald. Elide didn't care about that, either. She lay down and passed into a deep sleep, still wearing Kaltain's dress, that bit of cloak clutched in her hand.

Someone covered her with a cloak in the night, and when she awoke, there was a set of clothes—flying leathers, a shirt, pants, boots—beside her. The witches were sleeping, their wyverns a mass of muscle and death around them. None of them stirred as Elide strode to the nearest stream, stripped off that dress, and sat in the water, watching the two pieces of her loose chain swaying in the current until her teeth were chattering.

When she had dressed, the clothes a bit big, but warm, Elide tucked that scrap of cloak and the stone it contained into one of her inner pockets.

Celaena Sardothien.

She'd never heard that name—didn't know where to start looking. But to repay the debt she owed Kaltain . . .

"Don't waste your tears on her," Manon said from a few feet away, a pack dangling from her clean hands. She must have washed off the blood and dirt the night before. "She knew what she was doing, and it wasn't for your sake."

Elide wiped at her face. "She still saved our lives—and put an end to those poor witches in the catacombs."

"She did it for herself. To free herself. And she was entitled to. After what they did, she was entitled to rip the entire damn world to shreds."

Instead, she'd taken out a third of Morath.

Manon was right. Kaltain hadn't cared if they'd cleared the blast. "What do we do now?"

"We're going back to Morath," Manon said plainly. "But you're not."

Elide started.

"This is as far as we can take you without raising suspicions," Manon said. "When we return, if your uncle survived, I'll tell him you must have been incinerated in the blast."

And with that blast, all evidence of what Manon and her Thirteen had done to get Elide out of the dungeons would also have been erased.

But to leave her here . . . The world opened wide and brutal around her. "Where do I go?" Elide breathed. Endless woods and hills surrounded them. "I—I can't read, and I have no map."

"Go where you will, but if I were you, I'd head north, and stick to the forest. Stay out of the mountains. Keep going until you hit Terrasen."

That had never been part of the plan. "But—but the king—Vernon—"

"The King of Adarlan is dead," Manon said. The world stopped. "Aelin Galathynius killed him and shattered his glass castle."

Elide covered her mouth with a hand, shaking her head. Aelin . . . Aelin . . .

"She was aided," Manon went on, "by Prince Aedion Ashryver."

Elide began sobbing.

"And rumor has it Lord Ren Allsbrook is working in the North as a rebel."

Elide buried her face in her hands. Then there was a hard, iron-tipped hand on her shoulder.

A tentative touch.

"Hope," Manon said quietly.

Elide lowered her hands and found the witch smiling at her. Barely a tilt to her lips, but—a smile, soft and lovely. Elide wondered if Manon even knew she was doing it.

But to go to Terrasen . . . "Things will get worse, won't they," Elide said.

Manon's nod was barely perceptible.

South—she could still go south, run far, far away. Now that Vernon thought she was dead, no one would ever come looking for her. But Aelin was alive. And strong. And maybe it was time to stop dreaming of running. Find Celaena Sardothien—she would do that, to honor Kaltain and the gift she'd been given, to honor the girls like them, locked in towers with no one to speak for them, no one who remembered them.

But Manon had remembered her.

No—she would not run.

"Go north, Elide," Manon said, reading the decision in Elide's eyes and extending the pack. "They are in Rifthold, but I bet they won't be there for long. Get to Terrasen and lie low. Keep off the roads, avoid inns. There's money in that pack, but use it sparingly. Lie and steal and cheat if you have to, but get to Terrasen. Your queen will be there. I'd suggest not mentioning your mother's heritage to her."

Elide considered, shouldering the pack. "Having Blackbeak blood does not seem like such a horrible thing," she said quietly.

Those gold eyes narrowed. "No," Manon said. "No, it does not."

"How can I thank you?"

"It was a debt already owed," Manon said, shaking her head when Elide opened her mouth to ask more. The witch handed her three daggers, showing her where to tuck one into her boot, storing one in her pack, and then sheathing the other at her hip. Finally, she bade Elide to take off her boots, revealing the shackles she'd squeezed inside. Manon removed a small skeleton key and unlocked the chains, still clamped to her ankles.

Cool, soft air caressed her bare skin, and Elide bit her lip to keep from weeping again as she tugged her boots back on.

Through the trees, the wyverns were yawning and grumbling, and the sounds of the Thirteen laughing flitted past. Manon looked toward them, that faint smile returning to her mouth. When Manon turned back, the heir of the Blackbeak Witch-Clan said, "When war comes—which it will if Perrington survived—you should hope you do not see me again, Elide Lochan."

"All the same," Elide said, "I hope I do." She bowed to the Wing Leader.

And to her surprise, Manon bowed back.

"North," Manon said, and Elide supposed it was as much of a good-bye as she'd get.

"North," Elide repeated, and set off into the trees.

Within minutes, she'd passed beyond the sounds of the witches and their wyverns and was swallowed up by Oakwald.

She gripped the straps of her pack as she walked.

Suddenly, the animals went silent, and the leaves rustled and whispered. A moment later, thirteen great shadows passed overhead. One of them—the smallest—lingered, sweeping back a second time, as if in farewell.

Elide didn't know if Abraxos could see through the canopy, but she raised a hand in farewell anyway. A joyous, fierce cry echoed in response, and then the shadow was gone.

North.

To Terrasen. To fight, not run.

To Aelin and Ren and Aedion—grown and strong and alive.

She did not know how long it would take or how far she would have to walk, but she would make it. She would not look back.

Walking under the trees, the forest buzzing around her, Elide pressed a hand against the pocket inside her leather jacket, feeling the hard little lump tucked there. She whispered a short prayer to Anneith for wisdom, for guidance—and could have sworn a warm hand brushed her brow as if in answer. It straightened her spine, lifted her chin.

Limping, Elide began the long journey home.

CHAPTER
86

"This is the last of your clothes," Lysandra said, toeing the trunk that one of the servants had just dropped off. "I thought *I* had a shopping problem. Don't you ever throw anything away?"

From her perch on the velvet ottoman in the center of the enormous closet, Aelin stuck out her tongue. "Thank you for getting it all," she said. There was no point in unpacking the clothes Lysandra had brought from her old apartment, just as there was no point in returning there. It didn't help that Aelin couldn't bring herself to leave Dorian alone. Even if she'd finally managed to get him out of that room and walking around the castle.

He looked like the living dead, especially with that white line around his golden throat. She supposed he had every right to.

She'd been waiting for him outside of Chaol's room. When she heard Chaol speak at last, she had summoned Nesryn as soon as she'd mastered the tears of relief that had threatened to overwhelm her. After Dorian had emerged, when he'd looked at her and his smile had crumpled, she'd taken the king right back into his bedroom and sat with him for a good long while.

The guilt—that would be as heavy a burden for Dorian as his grief.

Lysandra put her hands on her hips. "Any other tasks for me before I retrieve Evangeline tomorrow?"

Aelin owed Lysandra more than she could begin to express, but—

She pulled a small box from her pocket.

"There's one more task," Aelin said, holding the box out to Lysandra. "You'll probably hate me for it later. But you can start by saying yes."

"Proposing to me? How unexpected." Lysandra took the box but didn't open it.

Aelin waved a hand, her heart pounding. "Just—open it."

With a wary frown, Lysandra opened the lid and cocked her head at the ring inside—the movement purely feline. "*Are* you proposing to me, Aelin Galathynius?"

Aelin held her friend's gaze. "There's a territory in the North, a small bit of fertile land that used to belong to the Allsbrook family. Aedion took it upon himself to inform me that the Allsbrooks have no use for it, so it's been sitting open for a while." Aelin shrugged. "It could use a lady."

The blood drained from Lysandra's face. "What."

"It's plagued by ghost leopards—hence the engraving on the ring. But I suppose if there were anyone capable of handling them, it'd be you."

Lysandra's hands shook. "And—and the key symbol above the leopard?"

"To remind you of who now holds your freedom. You."

Lysandra covered her mouth, staring at the ring, then at Aelin. "Are you out of your mind?"

"Most people would probably think so. But as the land was officially released by the Allsbrooks years ago, I can technically appoint you lady of it. With Evangeline as your heir, should you wish it."

Her friend had not voiced any plans for herself or her ward beyond retrieving Evangeline, had not asked to come with them, to start over in a new land, a new kingdom. Aelin had hoped it meant she wanted to join them in Terrasen, but—

Lysandra sank to the carpeted floor, staring at the box, at the ring.

"I know it'll be a great deal of work—"

"I don't deserve this. No one will *ever* want to serve me. Your people will resent you for appointing me."

Aelin slid onto the ground, knee to knee with her friend, and took the box from the shape-shifter's trembling hands. She pulled out the gold ring that she'd commissioned weeks ago. It had only been ready this morning, when Aelin and Rowan had slipped out to retrieve it, along with the real Wyrdkey.

"There is no one who deserves it more," Aelin said, grabbing her friend's hand and putting the ring on her finger. "There is no one else I'd want guarding my back. If my people cannot see the worth of a woman who sold herself into slavery for the sake of a child, who defended my court with no thought for her own life, then they are not my people. And they can burn in hell."

Lysandra traced a finger over the coat of arms that Aelin had designed. "What's the territory called?"

"I have no idea," Aelin said. "'Lysandria' sounds good. So does 'Lysandrius,' or maybe 'Lysandraland.'"

Lysandra gaped at her. "You *are* out of your mind."

"Will you accept?"

"I don't know the first thing about ruling a territory—about being a lady."

"Well, I don't know the first thing about ruling a kingdom. We'll learn together." She flashed her a conspirator's grin. "So?"

Lysandra gazed at the ring, then lifted her eyes to Aelin's face—and threw her arms around her neck, squeezing tight. She took that as a yes.

Aelin grimaced at the dull throb of pain, but held on. "Welcome to the court, Lady."

Aelin honestly wanted nothing more than to climb into bed that evening, hopefully with Rowan beside her. But as they finished up dinner—their first meal together as a court—a knock sounded on the door. Aedion was answering it before Aelin could so much as set down her fork.

He returned with Dorian in tow, the king glancing between them all. "I wanted to see if you'd eaten—"

Aelin pointed with her fork to the empty seat beside Lysandra. "Join us."

"I don't want to impose."

"Sit your ass down," she told the new King of Adarlan. That morning he'd signed a decree freeing all the conquered kingdoms from Adarlan's rule. She'd watched him do it, Aedion holding her hand tightly throughout, and wished that Nehemia had been there to see it.

Dorian moved to the table, amusement sparking in those haunted sapphire eyes. She introduced him again to Rowan, who bowed his head deeper than Aelin expected. Then she introduced Lysandra, explaining who she was and what she had become to Aelin, to her court.

Aedion watched them, his face tight, his lips a thin line. Their eyes met.

Ten years later, and they were all sitting together at a table again—no longer children, but rulers of their own territories. Ten years later, and here they were, friends despite the forces that had shattered and destroyed them.

Aelin looked at the kernel of hope glowing in that dining room and lifted her glass.

"To a new world," the Queen of Terrasen said.

The King of Adarlan lifted his glass, such endless shadows dancing in his eyes, but—there. A glimmer of life. "To freedom."

CHAPTER 87

The duke survived. So did Vernon.

A third of Morath had been blown out, and a good number of guards and servants with it, along with two covens and Elide Lochan.

A solid loss, but not nearly as devastating as it might have been. Manon herself had spilled three drops of her own blood in thanks to the Three-Faced Goddess that most of the covens had been out on a training exercise that day.

Manon stood in the duke's council chamber, hands behind her back as the man ranted.

A major setback, he hissed at the other men who were assembled: war leaders and councilmen. It would take months to repair Morath, and with so many of their supplies incinerated, they would have to put their plans on hold.

Day and night, men hauled away the stones piled high above the ruins of the catacombs—searching, Manon knew, for the body of a woman who was no more than ash, and the stone she'd borne. Manon had not even told her Thirteen who now limped northward with that stone.

"Wing Leader," the duke snapped, and Manon lazily turned her eyes toward him. "Your grandmother will be arriving in two weeks. I want your covens trained with the latest battle plans."

She nodded. "As you will it."

Battles. There would be battles, because even now that Dorian Havilliard was king, the duke had no plans to let go—not with this army. As soon as those witch towers were built and he found another source of shadowfire, Aelin Galathynius and her forces would be obliterated.

Manon quietly hoped that Elide would not be on those battlefields.

The council meeting was soon over, and Manon paused as she walked past Vernon on her way out. She put a hand on his shoulder, her nails digging into his skin, and he yelped as she brought her iron teeth close to his ear. "Just because she is dead, Lord, do not think that I will forget what you tried to do to her."

Vernon paled. "You can't touch me."

Manon dug her nails in deeper. "No, I can't," she purred into his ear. "But Aelin Galathynius is alive. And I hear that she has a score to settle." She yanked out her nails and squeezed his shoulder, setting the blood running down Vernon's green tunic before she stalked from the room.

<hr />

"What now?" Asterin said as they studied the new aerie they'd commandeered from one of the lesser covens. "Your grandmother arrives, and then we fight in this war?"

Manon gazed out the open archway to the ashy sky beyond. "For now, we stay. We wait for my grandmother to bring those towers."

She didn't know what she'd do when she saw her grandmother. She glanced sidelong at her Second. "That human hunter . . . How did he die?"

Asterin's eyes gleamed. For a moment she said nothing. Then: "He was old—very old. I think he went into the woods one day and lay down somewhere and never came back. He would have liked that, I think. I never found his body."

But she'd looked.

"What was it like?" Manon asked quietly. "To love."

For love was what it had been—what Asterin perhaps alone of all the Ironteeth witches had felt, had learned.

"It was like dying a little every day. It was like being alive, too. It was joy so complete it was pain. It destroyed me and unmade me and forged me. I hated it, because I knew I couldn't escape it, and knew it would forever change me. And that witchling . . . I loved her, too. I loved her in a way I cannot describe—other than to tell you that it was the most powerful thing I've ever felt, greater than rage, than lust, than magic." A soft smile. "I'm surprised you're not giving me the 'Obedience. Discipline. Brutality' speech."

Made into monsters.

"Things are changing," Manon said.

"Good," Asterin said. "We're immortals. Things should change, and often, or they'll get boring."

Manon lifted her brows, and her Second grinned.

Manon shook her head and grinned back.

CHAPTER 88

With Rowan circling high above the castle on watch, and with their departure scheduled for dawn, Aelin took it upon herself to make one last trip to Elena's tomb as the clock struck twelve.

Her plans, however, were ruined: the way to the tomb was blocked by rubble from the explosion. She'd spent fifteen minutes searching for a way in, with both her hands and her magic, but had no luck. She prayed Mort hadn't been destroyed—though perhaps the skull door knocker would have embraced his strange, immortal existence coming to an end at last.

The sewers of Rifthold, apparently, were as clear of the Valg as the castle tunnels and catacombs, as if the demons had fled into the night when the king had fallen. For the moment, Rifthold was safe.

Aelin emerged from the hidden passageway, wiping the dust off her. "You two make so much noise, it's ridiculous." With her Fae hearing, she'd detected them minutes ago.

Dorian and Chaol were seated before her fireplace, the latter in a special wheeled chair that they'd acquired for him.

The king looked at her pointed ears, the elongated canines, and lifted a brow. "You look good, Majesty." She supposed he hadn't really noticed that day on the glass bridge, and she'd been in her human form until now. She grinned.

Chaol turned his head. His face was gaunt, but a flicker of determination shone there. Hope. He would not let his injury destroy him.

"I always look good," Aelin said, plopping onto the armchair across from Dorian's.

"Find anything interesting down there?" Chaol asked.

She shook her head. "I figured it wouldn't hurt to look one last time. For old time's sake." And maybe bite Elena's head off. After she got answers to all her questions. But the ancient queen was nowhere to be found.

The three of them looked at each other, and silence fell.

Aelin's throat burned, so she turned to Chaol and said, "With Maeve and Perrington breathing down our necks, we might need allies sooner rather than later, especially if the forces in Morath block access to Eyllwe. An army from the Southern Continent could cross the Narrow Sea within a few days and provide reinforcements—push Perrington from the south while we hammer from the north." She crossed her arms. "So I'm appointing you an official Ambassador for Terrasen. I don't care what Dorian says. Make friends with the royal family, woo them, kiss their asses, do whatever you have to do. But we need that alliance."

Chaol glanced at Dorian in silent request. The king nodded, barely a dip of his chin. "I'll try." It was the best answer she could hope for. Chaol reached into the pocket of his tunic and chucked the Eye toward her. She caught it in a hand. The metal had been warped, but the blue stone remained. "Thank you," he said hoarsely.

"He was wearing that for months," Dorian said as she tucked the amulet into her pocket, "yet it never reacted—even in peril. Why now?"

Aelin's throat tightened. "Courage of the heart," she said. "Elena once told me that courage of the heart was rare—and to let it guide me. When Chaol chose to . . ." She couldn't form the words. She tried again. "I think that courage saved him, made the amulet come alive for him." It had been a gamble, and a fool's one, but—it had worked.

Silence fell again.

Dorian said, "So here we are."

"The end of the road," Aelin said with a half smile.

"No," Chaol said, his own smile faint, tentative. "The beginning of the next."

The following morning, Aelin yawned as she leaned against her gray mare in the castle courtyard.

Once Dorian and Chaol had left last night, Lysandra had entered and passed out in her bed with no explanation for why or what she'd been doing beforehand. And since she was utterly unconscious, Aelin had just climbed into bed beside her. She had no idea where Rowan had curled up for the night, but she wouldn't have been surprised to look out her window and spy a white-tailed hawk perched on the balcony rail.

At dawn, Aedion had burst in, demanding why they weren't ready to leave—to go *home*.

Lysandra had shifted into a ghost leopard and chased him out. Then she returned, lingering in her massive feline form, and again sprawled beside Aelin. They managed to get another thirty minutes of sleep before Aedion came back and chucked a bucket of water on them.

He was lucky to escape alive.

But he was right—they had little reason to linger. Not with so much to do in the North, so much to plan and heal and oversee.

They would travel until nightfall, where they'd pick up Evangeline at the Faliqs' country home and then continue north, hopefully uninterrupted, until they reached Terrasen.

Home.

She was going home.

Fear and doubt curled in her gut—but joy flickered alongside them.

They'd readied themselves quickly, and now all that was left, she supposed, was good-bye.

Chaol's injuries made taking the stairs impossible, but she'd crept into his room that morning to say good-bye—only to find Aedion, Rowan, and Lysandra already there, chatting with him and Nesryn. When they'd left, Nesryn following them out, the captain had merely squeezed Aelin's hand and said, "Can I see it?"

She knew what he meant, and had held up her hands before her.

Ribbons and plumes and flowers of red and gold fire danced through his room, bright and glorious and elegant.

Chaol's eyes had been lined with silver when the flames winked out. "It's lovely," he said at last.

She'd only smiled at him and left a rose of gold flame burning on his nightstand—where it would burn without heat until she was out of range.

And for Nesryn, who had been called away on captain duty, Aelin had left another gift: an arrow of solid gold, presented to her last Yulemas as a blessing of Deanna—her own ancestor. Aelin figured the sharpshooter would love and appreciate that arrow more than she ever would have, anyway.

"Do you need anything else? More food?" Dorian asked, coming to stand beside her. Rowan, Aedion, and Lysandra were already mounting their horses. They'd packed light, taking only the barest supplies. Mostly weapons, including Damaris, which Chaol had given to Aedion, insisting the ancient blade remain on these shores. The rest of their belongings would be shipped to Terrasen.

"With this group," Aelin said to Dorian, "it'll probably be a daily competition to see who can hunt the best."

Dorian chuckled. Silence fell, and Aelin clicked her tongue. "You're wearing the same tunic you had on a few days ago. I don't think I ever saw you wear the same thing twice."

A flicker in those sapphire eyes. "I think I have bigger things to worry about now."

"Will you—will you be all right?"

"Do I have any option but to be?"

She touched his arm. "If you need anything, send word. It'll be a few weeks before we reach Orynth, but—I suppose with magic returned, you can find a messenger to get word to me quickly."

"Thanks to you—and to your friends."

She glanced over her shoulder at them. They were all trying their best to look like they weren't eavesdropping. "Thanks to all of us," she said quietly. "And to you."

Dorian gazed toward the city horizon, the rolling green foothills beyond. "If you had asked me nine months ago if I thought . . ." He shook his head. "So much has changed."

"And will keep changing," she said, squeezing his arm once. "But . . . There are things that won't change. I will always be your friend."

His throat bobbed. "I wish I could see her, just one last time. To tell her . . . to say what was in my heart."

"She knows," Aelin said, blinking against the burning in her eyes.

"I'll miss you," Dorian said. "Though I doubt the next time we meet will be in such . . . civilized circumstances." She tried not to think about it. He gestured over her shoulder to her court. "Don't make them too miserable. They're only trying to help you."

She smiled. To her surprise, a king smiled back.

"Send me any good books that you read," she said.

"Only if you do the same."

She embraced him one last time. "Thank you—for everything," she whispered.

Dorian squeezed her, and then stepped away as Aelin mounted her horse and nudged it into a walk.

She moved to the head of the company, where Rowan rode a sleek black stallion. The Fae Prince caught her eye. *Are you all right?*

She nodded. *I didn't think saying good-bye would be so hard. And with everything that's to come—*

We'll face it together. To whatever end.

She reached across the space between them and took his hand, gripping it tightly.

They held on to each other as they rode down the barren path, through the gateway she'd made in the glass wall, and into the city streets, where people paused what they were doing and gaped or whispered or stared.

But as they rode out of Rifthold, that city that had been her home and her hell and her salvation, as she memorized each street and building and face and shop, each smell and the coolness of the river breeze, she didn't see one slave. Didn't hear one whip.

And as they passed by the domed Royal Theater, there was music—beautiful, exquisite music—playing within.

⁓

Dorian didn't know what awoke him. Perhaps it was that the lazy summer insects had stopped their nighttime buzzing, or perhaps it was the chilled wind that slithered into his old tower room, ruffling the curtains.

The moonlight gleaming on the clock revealed it was three in the morning. The city was silent.

He rose from the bed, touching his neck yet again—just to make sure. Whenever he woke from his nightmares, it took him minutes to tell if he was indeed awake—or if it was merely a dream and he was still trapped in his own body, enslaved to his father and that Valg prince. He had not told Aelin or Chaol about the nightmares. Part of him wished he had.

He could still barely remember what had happened while he'd worn that collar. He'd turned twenty—and had no recollection of it. There were only bits and pieces, glimpses of horror and pain. He tried not to think about it. Didn't *want* to remember. He hadn't told Chaol or Aelin that, either.

He already missed her, and the chaos and intensity of her court. He missed having anyone around at all. The castle was too big, too quiet. And Chaol was to leave in two days. He didn't want to think about what missing his friend would be like.

Dorian padded onto his balcony, needing to feel the river breeze on his face, to know that this was real and he was free.

He opened the balcony doors, the stones cool on his feet, and gazed out across the razed grounds. He'd done that. He loosed a breath, taking in the glass wall as it sparkled in the moonlight.

There was a massive shadow perched atop it. Dorian froze.

Not a shadow but a giant beast, its claws gripping the wall, its wings tucked into its body, shimmering faintly in the glow of the full moon. Shimmering like the white hair of the rider atop it.

Even from the distance, he knew she was staring right at him, her hair streaming to the side like a ribbon of moonlight, caught in the river breeze.

Dorian lifted a hand, the other rising to his neck. No collar.

The rider on the wyvern leaned down in her saddle, saying something to her beast. It spread its massive, glimmering wings and leaped into the air. Each beat of its wings sent a hollowed-out, booming gust of wind toward him.

It flapped higher, her hair streaming behind her like a glittering banner, until they vanished into the night, and he couldn't hear its wings beating anymore. No one sounded the alarm. As if the world had stopped paying attention for the few moments they'd looked at each other.

And through the darkness of his memories, through the pain and despair and terror he'd tried to forget, a name echoed in his head.

Manon Blackbeak sailed into the starry night sky, Abraxos warm and swift under her, the blazingly bright moon—the Mother's full womb— above her.

She didn't know why she'd bothered to go; why she'd been curious.

But there had been the prince, no collar to be seen around his neck.

And he had lifted his hand in greeting—as if to say *I remember you.*

The winds shifted, and Abraxos rode them, rising higher into the sky, the darkened kingdom below passing by in a blur.

Changing winds—a changing world.

Perhaps a changing Thirteen, too. And herself.

She didn't know what to make of it.

But Manon hoped they'd all survive it.

She hoped.

CHAPTER
89

For three weeks they rode straight north, keeping off the main roads and out of the villages. There was no need to announce that Aelin was on her way back to Terrasen. Not until she saw her kingdom for herself and knew what she faced, both from within and from what gathered down in Morath. Not until she had somewhere safe to hide the great, terrible thing in her saddlebag.

With her magic, no one noticed the Wyrdkey's presence. But Rowan would occasionally glance at the saddlebag and angle his head in inquiry. Each time, she'd silently tell him she was fine, and that she hadn't noticed anything strange regarding the amulet. Or regarding the Eye of Elena, which she again wore at her throat. She wondered if Lorcan was indeed on his way to hunt down the second and third keys, perhaps where Perrington—Erawan—had held them all along. If the king hadn't been lying.

She had a feeling Lorcan would start looking in Morath. And prayed the Fae warrior would defy the odds stacked against him and emerge triumphant. It would certainly make her life easier. Even if he'd one day come to kick her ass for deceiving him.

The summer days grew cooler the farther north they rode. Evangeline, to her credit, kept pace with them, never complaining about having to sleep on a bedroll night after night. She seemed perfectly happy to curl up with Fleetfoot, her new protector and loyal friend.

Lysandra used the journey to test out her abilities—sometimes flying with Rowan overhead, sometimes running as a pretty black dog alongside Fleetfoot, sometimes spending days in her ghost leopard form and pouncing on Aedion whenever he least expected it.

Three weeks of grueling travel—but also three of the happiest weeks Aelin had ever experienced. She would have preferred a little more privacy, especially with Rowan, who kept looking at her in that way that made her want to combust. Sometimes when no one was watching, he'd sneak up behind her and nuzzle her neck or tug at her earlobe with his teeth, or just slide his arms around her and hold her against him, breathing her in.

One night—just one gods-damned night with him was all she wanted.

They didn't dare stop at an inn, so she was left to burn, and to endure Lysandra's quiet teasing.

The terrain grew steeper, hillier, and the world turned lush and green and bright, the rocks becoming jagged granite outcroppings.

The sun had barely risen as Aelin walked beside her horse, sparing it from having to carry her up a particularly steep hill. She was already on her second meal of the day—already sweaty and dirty and cranky. Fire magic, it turned out, came in rather handy while traveling, keeping them warm on the chill nights, lighting their fires, and boiling their water. She would have killed for a tub big enough to fill with water and bathe in, but luxuries could wait.

"It's just up this hill," Aedion said from her left.

"What is?" she asked, finishing her apple and chucking the remains behind her. Lysandra, wearing the form of a crow, squawked in outrage as the core hit her. "Sorry," Aelin called.

Lysandra cawed and soared skyward, Fleetfoot barking merrily at her as Evangeline giggled from atop her shaggy pony.

Aedion pointed to the hillcrest ahead. "You'll see."

Aelin looked at Rowan, who had been scouting ahead for part of the morning as a white-tailed hawk. Now he walked beside her, guiding his black stallion along. He lifted his brows at her silent demand for information. *I'm not going to tell you.*

She glowered at him. *Buzzard.*

Rowan grinned. But with every step, Aelin did the calculations about what day it was, and—

They crested the hill and halted.

Aelin released the reins and took a staggering step, the emerald grass soft underfoot.

Aedion touched her shoulder. "Welcome home, Aelin."

A land of towering mountains—the Staghorns—spread before them, with valleys and rivers and hills; a land of untamed, wild beauty.

Terrasen.

And the smell—of pine and snow . . . How had she never realized that Rowan's scent was of Terrasen, of home? Rowan came close enough to graze her shoulder and murmured, "I feel as if I've been looking for this place my entire life."

Indeed—with the wicked wind flowing fast and strong between the gray, jagged Staghorns in the distance, with the dense spread of Oakwald to their left, and the rivers and valleys sprawling toward those great northern mountains—it was paradise for a hawk. Paradise for her.

"Right there," Aedion said, pointing to a small, weather-worn granite boulder carved with whorls and swirls. "Once we pass that rock, we're on Terrasen soil."

Not quite daring to believe she wasn't still asleep, Aelin walked toward that rock, whispering the Song of Thanks to Mala Fire-Bringer for leading her to this place, this moment.

Aelin ran a hand over the rough rock, and the sun-warmed stone tingled as if in greeting.

Then she stepped beyond the stone.

And at long last, Aelin Ashryver Galathynius was home.

~ ACKNOWLEDGMENTS ~

I think it's common knowledge by now that I'd cease to function without my soul-twin, Jaeger copilot, and Threadsister, Susan Dennard.

Sooz, you are my light in dark places. You inspire and challenge me to not only be a better writer, but to also be a better *person*. Your friendship gives me strength and courage and hope. No matter what happens, no matter what might be waiting around the next bend in the road, I know I can face it, I can endure and triumph, because I have you at my side. There is no greater magic than that. I can't wait to be majestic tiger-vampires with you for the rest of eternity.

To my fellow lady-in-arms and appreciator of all things feral/shape-shifting, Alex Bracken: How can I ever thank you enough for reading this book (and all my others) so many times? And how can I ever thank you enough for the years of e-mails, the countless lunches/drinks/dinners, and for always having my back? I don't think I would have enjoyed this wild journey half as much without you—and I don't think I would have survived this long without your wisdom, kindness, and generosity.

ACKNOWLEDGMENTS

Here's to writing many more scenes with flimsy excuses for having shirtless dudes.

These books would not exist (*I* would not exist!) without my hardworking, supremely badass teams at the Laura Dail Literary Agency, CAA, and Bloomsbury worldwide. So my eternal love and gratitude go to Tamar Rydzinski, Cat Onder, Margaret Miller, Jon Cassir, Cindy Loh, Cristina Gilbert, Cassie Homer, Rebecca McNally, Natalie Hamilton, Laura Dail, Kathleen Farrar, Emma Hopkin, Ian Lamb, Emma Bradshaw, Lizzy Mason, Sonia Palmisano, Erica Barmash, Emily Ritter, Grace Whooley, Charli Haynes, Courtney Griffin, Nick Thomas, Alice Grigg, Elise Burns, Jenny Collins, Linette Kim, Beth Eller, Kerry Johnson, and the tireless, wonderful foreign rights team.

To my husband, Josh: Every day with you is a gift and a joy. I'm so lucky to have such a loving, fun, and spectacular friend to go on adventures with around the world. Here's to many, many more.

To Annie, aka the greatest dog of all time: Sorry for accidentally eating all your turkey jerky that one time. Let's never mention it again. (Also, I love you forever and ever. Let's go cuddle.)

To my marvelous parents: Thank you for reading me all those fairy-tales—and for never telling me I was too old to believe in magic. These books exist because of that.

To my family: thank you, as always, for the endless and unconditional love and support.

To the Maas Thirteen: You guys are beyond amazing. Thank you so much for all your support and enthusiasm and for shouting about this series from rooftops all over the world. To Louisse Ang, Elena Yip, Jamie Miller, Alexa Santiago, Kim Podlesnik, Damaris Cardinali, and Nicola Wilkinson: you are all so generous and lovely—thank you for all that you do!

To Erin Bowman, Dan Krokos, Jennifer L. Armentrout, Christina Hobbs, and Lauren Billings: You guys are the best. I mean it. The ultimate best. I thank the Universe every day that I'm blessed to have such talented, funny, loyal, and wonderful friends in my life.

ACKNOWLEDGMENTS

And to all my *Throne of Glass* readers: There aren't enough words in the English language to properly convey the depth of my gratitude. It has been such an honor to meet you at events across the globe, and interact with so many of you online. Your words, artwork, and music keep me going. Thank you, thank you, thank you for everything.

Lastly, thanks so much to the incredible readers who submitted content to be part of the *Heir of Fire* trailer:

Abigail Isaac, Aisha Morsy, Amanda Clarity, Amanda Riddagh, Amy Kersey, Analise Jensen, Andrea Isabel Munguía Sánchez, Anna Vogl, Becca Fowler, Béres Judit, Brannon Tison, Bronwen Fraser, Claire Walsh, Crissie Wood, Elena Mieszczanski, Elena NyBlom, Emma Richardson, Gerakou Yiota, Isabel Coyne, Isabella Guzy-Kirkden, Jasmine Chau, Kristen Williams, Laura Pohl, Linnea Gear, Natalia Jagielska, Paige Firth, Rebecca Andrade, Rebecca Heath, Suzanah Thompson, Taryn Cameron, and Vera Roelofs.

Watch the trailer now: